W9-BTT-519

THE BLAST ROARED THROUGH THE NARROW DRAW, echoing off the ridge above them, bouncing back at Scratch from the trees he had wanted to reach. He watched the old mule pitch forward, throwing Josiah over her neck and into the open just below the small white cloud above them on the hill.

Scratch shifted the rein to his right hand, clutching it tightly alongside the rifle. He jerked back on the pony's head as he passed above the young man, wheeling the animal around in a tight circle so that he would be between Josiah and the next shot.

"C'mon, boy!" he brought the pony up on the struggling trapper so that Josiah stood on Scratch's left. He put his empty hand down and grabbed for Josiah's left wrist. Pulling up, he swung the younger man behind him as well as he could while the pony dashed through the snow toward the trees.

Josiah struggled to get his right leg over the pony's rump but the hides strapped behind the saddle prevented it. The right leg was useless, repeatedly being kicked out of the way as the pony clawed across the flying powder, the animal's flared nostrils snorted blossoms of white mist . . .

CARRY THE WIND

"IMPRESSIVE . . . SUPERBLY DETAILED . . . VIVIDLY CONVEYS THE DAY-TO-DAY LIFE OF A GRIZZLED MOUNTAIN MAN. [INCLUDES] A TERRIFYING BATTLE WITH THE BLACKFEET. . . . THE EFFECT IS ONE OF RICHNESS."
—*Publishers Weekly*

"THIS IS THE MOST AUTHENTIC MOUNTAIN MAN NOVEL WE HAVE."
—Winfred Blevins, *Give Your Heart to the Hawks*

Carry
the
Wind

Terry C. Johnston

BANTAM BOOKS
TORONTO • NEW YORK • LONDON • SYDNEY • AUCKLAND

For what he means to his old man
this book is lovingly dedicated to my son:
Joshua Seth-Matthew

*This low-priced Bantam Book
has been completely reset in a type face
designed for easy reading, and was printed
from new plates. It contains the complete
text of the original hard-cover edition.*
NOT ONE WORD HAS BEEN OMITTED.

CARRY THE WIND

*A Bantam Book / published by arrangement with
Jameson Books*

PRINTING HISTORY
Jameson edition published September 1982
Bantam edition / March 1986

ISBN 0–553–25572–X

Published simultaneously in the United States and Canada

PRINTED IN THE UNITED STATES OF AMERICA

H   0 9 8 7 6 5 4 3 2 1

The old man sang his death song then;
His voice rang clear and high:
O Sun, thou endureth forever,
But we who are warriors must die!

Stanley Vestal
Fandango, Ballads of the
*   Old West*

Carry
the
Wind

1

It was already swelling up, aching with the dull throb that's always by your side. But he hadn't known he was hurt until he put his weight on the foot to get out of the old mule's way.

Hobbling a few steps over to plop down beneath a tree with his old rifle used as a crutch in place of the injured foot, Scratch tried to pull the moccasin off.

"You sure did a good 'nough job on my hoof," he grumbled at the mule. He pulled a knife from its sheath at his side and began slicing the leather moccasin off the foot. He would try to cut the sinew stitching of the moccasin "so's some squaw can fix it, maybe." All this time, the mule kept up her buck and jump dance, with the load he had been trying to cinch down on her swaying from side to side.

The skin on the foot was like stretched leather, white to be sure, rarely seeing the light of the sun, maybe only once a year, but it had the feel of leather, nonetheless, from repeated dunkings in those mountain streams, followed by the same natural drying out of the moccasin.

Scratch stumbled and hopped over to the mule, grabbing onto one of the ropes that held some pelts to her back, and began the buck and jump dance with her, half riding, the good foot sometimes bouncing off the ground, working at the knots that held the packs to her back. Those bundles finally flew off as the final knots came free, and Scratch landed among them back up near the trees.

"Thar now, you cussed animule, let's jest simmer down some," he coaxed her as the mule slowed her wild jig. She stayed close, her picket pin had held her nose into the center of a wild circle while she had bucked. He began to pull apart some of the baggage she had thrown off. From it he pulled a pair of his winter mocs, those moccasins of buffalo hide sewn with the hair turned in and big enough to fit over another pair of everyday moccasins. It still hurt to pull that big moccasin over his lame foot, the tight skin starting to discolor from the broken blood vessels.

"You're ol' bag of bones, you are, gal. An' you could sure put a man in a fine fix up here. If'n I only knowed what made you so froshus this'r mornin', but then, I figger you're jest gettin' on in your years, cranky an' such, like'n me," he muttered, more to himself than to the mule, which stood nearby watching the old man with one eye while munching on some of the green shoots that grew up in tufts here and there in patches near the trees.

"If'n I weren't such a good soul, I'd more'n likely raise your hair an' trade your hide to some naked 'Rapaho, an' leave your carcass behind awaitin' for them coyotes what's been staying' on our heels." He rose again, wrapped one arm around the rifle and hobbled over to where the mule stood a few steps away.

"Theys had 'em a hard winter's knock too, don' you reckon, Hannah?" Scratch stroked her muzzle, and eased down on her side, to find the open gash along the spine near her hindquarters. It wasn't a clean incision, nor pretty. Looked like someone had worked a knife back and forth to get that crazy, wandering slice in the mule's hide. That's when it hit him. Scratch stumbled over to the packs again and tore them apart. "Damned sure," he grumbled, mad at himself as he found it. He hadn't packed that bundle too well days back, and the knife he had taken off that Blackfoot brave had worked down through the baggage until it started to ride into old Hannah's hide.

"Glor-r-r-ree! This'r Blackfeet sticker rode down on you an' run in an' outta you ever' time you bucked!" he mumbled, looking over at the mule. He slipped the knife into his scabbardless belt, pushed himself up on one leg, and hopped over to her side once more.

"Here I thought you was jest gettin' ol't an' touchy, lady," he soothed, stroking her around the bleeding gash to get her used to the feel of his hands around the tender wound. Scratch balled up his cheeks to collect all the saliva he could. He removed the chaw of tobacco with two fingers, some of the brown, syrupy juice running down his lower lip and onto his gray-flecked whiskers. Tenderly, lovingly, the old man worked it into the open wound, chattering all the time to the old mule, coaxing her into letting him probe and push around in the torn flesh. She raised her head, cocking it back toward where he stood, looking over her shoulder at him, as if inspecting the surgery.

"Ain't a soul as can say you ain't got some more miles in you, Hannah," he cooed at her, keeping one hand on the wound, while the other reached up to take the beaver-pelt hat from his head, underneath which was a faded-blue bandanna tied tightly at the base of his skull. His long hair, here and there showing patches of gray, fluttered easily in the early-morning breeze.

Scratch put the beaver fur over the wound and held it in place for a moment before both hands began cutting the fur bandage down to size. Hannah looked away from his doctoring and went back to chewing. "I'll take care of you. Ain't gonna be me as gets rid of you, yet anyhows. We got a few more tracks to go, we does," he added, plopping back down on the ground right beside her. Scratch cradled his rifle across his lap, looked up at his mule, and felt suddenly very old, looking back across all those years, all those faces, all the fights, and all the lonesome a man could want.

"It's been a golden kind-a lonesome, ol' Hannah." He pulled the moccasin from the swollen foot, tugging and yanking to free it over the swollen instep. "Hope it ain't broke, gal. We'd be Injun bait for sure then. That'd be damp powder, it would, an' no ways to dry it for this coon."

The man was only around thirty-eight years old, he didn't remember exactly, but he knew he had been in the mountains close to eight years. Up in the high country a man was judged to be old if he had passed that many winters by and kept his scalp, or his sanity. Up here a man's age was figured by how much he had seen or done rather than by the passage of years. Scratch pulled what was left of the beaver fur over to him and wrapped it around the foot. Pulling the big Blackfoot knife from his belt, he looked momentarily at the blade neatly engraved with the initials "H.B.Co.," enclosed between two small antlered deer, and went to work cutting fringe off his leggings. Tying the cut fringe end to end, he soon had a long lace which he used to wrap around and around the fur, holding it securely in place, and finally tied it up around the ankle in a knot.

"First time I see'd that foot in close t' a year. Ugly,

ain't it, lady?" He stuck it up in the air and wiggled his toes toward the mule, which paid him no mind. Maybe it's not broke, maybe not, he thought.

It was still early morning and the sun was just beginning to creep down off the tops of the trees to warm the ground, and his tired body. He hadn't slept well for the past couple of nights, dozing fitfully, half awake, with his eyes closed but his ears perked up to every sound the night breeze brought to him. Scratch had been a few days out of Park Kyack and was now closing in on Crow country. The Crow prided themselves in never having taken a white man's scalp, but, "Them Crow can sure strip a man naked of pony an' possibles faster'n I care to blink," Scratch had told a man once. So he didn't sleep well while alone in their country. He listened for the animals through the night when he lay down for a few hours' rest. And during the day he stayed up close to the tree line in the valleys, eyes moving back and forth along the skyline, watching the movement of shadows, getting information every second and instantly calculating each one of those bits and pieces. A man had to figure fast in the mountains, but this was not the arithmetic he used to chalk down on a slate board back in Kentucky as a youngster. This kind of calculating meant a future of staying alive up in the high country. The man who survived in the mountains had to understand everything those hills told him. They were the teacher now. Some men were lucky, but most couldn't stand to fail more than once in this school.

The sun caressed his tired body, lulling him into dozing easily, head down. Scratch slipped back over the years, his eyes barely open, but focused on a young boy, tall and gangly, barefoot, slipping away from the road that led to school, down the slope and into the cool forest with the squirrel gun he had secreted away from over the fireplace at home. He was sixteen and not spending much time in school now, preferring to reach out into the forests on a Kentucky hillside, blasting away at a squirrel now and then, but mostly dreaming of the day he would carve out his own future in the wildness around him. Into his picture slipped a young, pretty girl, already eighteen, the one waiting for that young boy to finish his schooling, get a job, and marry her.

She kept after him about leaving school, just as his

4

folks nagged him. But his father didn't beat him any more for cutting classes, for the boy was getting too big for that now. The young man finally left all that behind, and the girl too, knowing in his own way that he couldn't be a farmer like his pa.

He finally slipped away before morning light, gathering up a new shirt and a few biscuits from the meal the night before, along with some spare flints for that squirrel gun his pa had said was his now. The boy was quiet, and careful, not making a sound. He wasn't going to be caught now, having made his decision to leave after the violent argument with his pa the night before. They had argued and spit angrily at each other that last night, over school, over his never being around to help with the planting, over the boy not wanting to be a farmer, until his pa had finally said that was the way it was going to be and went off to bed. His mother hadn't said a thing, sitting there by the fire in that stiff-backed chair, sewing up a new shirt for her son. Even then she knew what her son would do.

His dark form slipped out of the cabin, bare feet moving through the damp grass around to the back of the place and quickly into the edge of the forest. He paused there, turning to look one last time at the little cabin, where his brothers and sister lay sleeping, the chimney encircling a whisper of thready smoke from last night's fire. He breathed deeply the cool air, then cut into the darkness of the predawn shadows of the forest.

He didn't know, nor would he ever know, that a pair of eyes watched him leave. While her husband snored soundly, his mother made her way quietly to the back window, pushed the gingham curtains aside, and watched her son leave home. She had whispered a prayer for him that morning, before the new day's light awoke her husband and started that terrible day of searching for the boy, she having to lie about seeing him leave. It was a prayer of simple words, more a wish for someone to watch over the boy, watch after him until he found what he needed, found what he was looking for in the forest.

The boy had nearly starved to death at first, then found work loading the boats that plied the river. The wages held him for a while before he drifted down the

Ohio to its junction with the Mississippi. From there his path led further south. He stayed as close to the river as possible, using it as his highway.

He happened upon a new settler's farm one night and slipped inside the shed that served to house the farmer's stock animals. The next morning he was awakened by someone kicking the sole of his boot, opening his eyes to stare up the muzzle of the farmer's rifle. The older man put him to work straightaway, and taught him something of blacksmithing too. That way, he paid for his keep and slept in the new barn at night, taking his meals with the farmer's family. He stayed with the settler for some time, learning the blacksmith trade, hunting some for the table, enjoying the sleep on the hay, with the stock animals' heavy snoring lulling him to sleep each night.

He awoke one morning, shivering under the one blanket he owned, and snuggled down deeper into the hay. Then he suddenly snapped awake and stuck his head outside the blanket, blinking his eyes into focus in the early light. It took him a moment to realize the fog around him was his own breath, the chill of the early autumn making everything crisp and well defined. He had the feeling again, knew this was another morning to be moving on, moving upriver to the town growing into quite a city. The town the farmer told him about, St. Louie.

He scratched a note out on the back of a bill of sale he found, forming the letters as best as he could remember and hoping his words would say to the farmer and his family what they had meant to him. He then stepped his horse out into the dull, gray light sneaking down from the overcast sky. The blades of grass crunched and crackled underfoot as he walked the horse down to the bank of the river, thinking to himself that winter would not be far behind this frost. He turned to look at the farmer's cabin, knowing there would be pain in his leaving. There had been a pain that he would never know of, for new life was beginning to stir deep within the body of the farmer's oldest daughter. She had loved him deeply, stealing away late at night to nestle down beside him in the sweet hay, rising to return to the cabin before dawn. She had only been something to take his mind off the whores the men spoke of when they were out of earshot of the womenfolk

6

and talking of the glittering village of St. Louie. For her, he had been the dream that had stepped out of the forest one day, and made her finally feel at home in the wilderness.

And now he would never know of the pain he was leaving behind, nor of the daughter she would have, the baby girl who would have his eyes and nose.

Upriver in St. Louis he found work with a blacksmith busy with the labors of outfitting the expeditions into the mountains somewhere out there beyond the Missouri and the plains. He worked hard, saving all he could, sleeping in the livery, and watching the comings and goings of the strange melting pot that was St. Louis. Along the muddy streets rode the rich businessmen, most of them French, their women daintily hugging their parasols on their shoulders. He blinked in amazement at the sight of his first mountain trapper, long hair flowing, tied back from his face by a red bandanna, showing a left ear pierced to hold a big silver earring.

The trapper spent long nights with the man in the livery, the younger man lapping up the stories of the mountains, the trapper lapping up the cheap liquor, until he would finally fall into a drunken sleep alongside his horse. The young man would then slowly crawl away to his bedroll and drift off into sleep, to dream of the willing dark-skinned women, the battles with the painted and feathered dark-skinned men, the hand-to-hand combat with the grizzly. Tall stories, sure, he told himself, but they were what he fed on for several weeks, until one night the trapper didn't stumble into the livery as usual, and the man went to look for him.

In every tavern and grog shop he searched, down the streets bunched close together near the river, until the light of dawn exposed the body lying half in and half out of the water lapping against the shore by the wharves. He pulled the old man into his lap and slapped the trapper's cheeks, but no life glowed in the dripping body. He looked for a sign of a struggle, but there hadn't been one. The man had drunk himself to death, there by the river, cursing and staring at the water rolling out of the north, finally plopping down into the shallow current, never to move again.

He went back to the livery to fetch the trapper's horse and then returned to the body. He struggled to put the big man's corpse on the animal's back, and led the horse downriver a few miles, away from people, into a lush wooded area, where he scratched out a hole big enough for the man. He covered the body with dirt and leaves, and finally finished by strewing the grave with wildflowers growing in that stand of trees. Then he led the horse back to town, to force himself through the months of numbness and loneliness until the following spring.

He was finally able to talk a shopowner out of a .54-caliber flintlock, not the best Pennsylvanian he had put his hands on, but it would do. All the rifle shops were busy these days, trying to supply the fur companies heading upriver or setting out overland to the Shining Mountains. The rifle was not pretty, but it was as true as the finest rifle that ever went west to the mountains. A heavy Deringer with a slightly Roman-nosed stock, heavy flintlock with a flat, gooseneked hammer, and a cast brass patchbox with the top finial in the shape of an eagle's head. The young man worked long and hard to hold it steady on target. By day he labored, but in the evening he returned to that quiet grove of trees upriver to practice with the big rifle, there within earshot of the trapper he had laid to rest.

He kept that horse brushed and fed, rode it on his day off, leaving before sunup, returning to the livery after dark, dropping from the animal's back the old saddle he had repaired and falling into the sleep and those dreams of the Shining Mountains. He spent those days waiting, waiting for a chance to move west. He knew the time would come when he would awaken one morning and push past the sleeping shanties lining the river, past the taverns that would be finally closed with the first light, past the whorehouses where the tenants were at last going back to their beds, this time for sleep.

He moved west across the plains alone, not knowing the dangers of solitary travel. Maybe it had been his type of good fortune, or maybe just something silently answering his courage, but he hadn't seen an Indian during those weeks of pushing from water hole to water hole across the sea of buffalo grass until he hit that river the trapper had told him of, the Platte. He wove through the days, winding along the river, following its every twist and turn, until the late part of one afternoon when he aroused himself out of the dozing sleep the sway of the horse rocked him into, looked across the smoked-glass horizon, through the haze of heat rising off the land, and barely made out the change of scenery. He whooped and hollered, kicking the startled horse into a wild headlong gallop toward the mountains until he finally realized it would take a few more days before he reached the foothills. But he could see them now, those mountains the trapper had spoken of, each day the snow touching their peaks becoming more vivid. Then one day he crossed the north fork of the Little Laramie and let himself melt into the blue belt of mountains that stretched from the Mexican provinces to the south, all the way to what was English country up north.

There was a slight crack in his remembering, followed by the cry of a magpie as it took to sudden flight. Scratch didn't move a muscle, but just sat there listening to the forest. His eyes rolled from side to side as far as he could see without moving his head, as his fingers inched their way up the stock toward the trigger guard. Someplace in his mind he counted the brass tacks stuck in the rifle stock, knowing by the count of each one how far he was away from that trigger. The breeze shifted the hair hanging down his face around him eyes, so he could see a little better to the left now. The wisp of breeze brought all kinds of news to his senses.

Scratch knew it was a horse that made that snort down in the valley a bit, and the breeze faintly brought to his nostrils the smell of a man, not an Injun, but a white man. Hannah caught it too, and raised her muzzle into the wind to suck more of the smell. Her nose and his could tell the smell of a white man from the smell of an Injun, and the next breezed drifting up to him confirmed it. He shifted his legs slowly to be more balanced when he made his move as the fingers finally reached the end of their journey to the trigger.

"Careful now, you ol' buzzard," he said softly to himself, being careful not to squeeze down on the trigger in his anticipation, "leastways, not jest yet." Another crack, another limb broken underfoot, and Scratch was even more sure that it was a white man: no Injun would make such a mistake. "Stiff boots," he mused, thinking what hell it would have been to get a boot off his swollen foot. That's when the shadow moved on his left, there among the trees, then crouched down to make itself less of a target. The old man squinted and could barely make

9

out the felt hat, sitting still now behind some brush. A bundle of pelts lay between him and the shadow at the tree line where all was quiet now. Pulling his good leg up next to him, he gave one good shove and slid behind the bundle.

"I heerd you, you nigger," he hollered around the pelts. "Ain't no use keepin' yourself secret in them trees." He pulled the hammer back until it clicked to comfort something inside him.

"You might'n come on out now—got a ball for your paunch if'n you choose not to." The felt hat began to move a little. Scratch took his skinning knife from its place at his belt, having left the Blackfoot rib-sticker back on the ground where he began his push to the bundle. "Cain't waste no ball on no white nigger," he muttered under his breath, shifting his weight slightly.

The felt hat rose, with the face of a young man beneath it, eyes as big as the quilled rosettes on Scratch's leather shirt. The rifle he carried seemed heavy for the young man and Scratch remembered when he had trouble handling his. A couple of tentative steps brought the young man into full view. Scratch took his chin off the ground, rifle muzzle pointed all the time at the intruder's chest.

"Point that squirrel gun somewhars else, an' we'll palaver 'bout this." The felt hat's rifle slowly dropped, until the butt clunked against the ground.

Scratch quickly sized up the rifle felt hat was carrying. "C'mon over here. Lemme take a lookee at you," Scratch commanded, pointing his own rifle away from the stranger.

With the squeaks, moans, and groans of stiff leather, the boots came over. It was a sight, the young man standing over Scratch, looking down at the old man, and Scratch propped up on one elbow peering out from between strings of hair, his eyes working up and down the intruder's frame. Storebought woolen clothes, dirty to be sure, and torn here and there. And, oh, that felt hat, sorry looking it was, all crushed and pushed out of shape. The stranger had started sprouting a good growth of facial hair and his store-bought leather belt was notched up tight around the skinny waist.

"How long's been since you et last?" Scratch asked, looking into the stranger's eyes, as the young man sat down on the bundle next to him.

"Couple days, maybe."

"Maybe, hell, young'un!" he snorted and let out with a good laugh.

"I been doin' all right," felt hat said quietly.

"Wagh! More'n likely you ain't et in some time." Scratch poked the young man once in the stomach lightly with the muzzle of his rifle. "Prob'ly skeert more game off with them boots an' that white-man smell 'bout you than you ever see'd, prob'ly smelt you comin' a mile off, they did!" The stranger dropped his eyes from the old one's gaze.

"I took you for an Injun, sittin' there," said the stranger, making a motion alongside his head, and moving his hand up and down several times to show he was referring to the old man's long hair, braided on the right.

Scratch snorted again with a quick chuckle. "Why, thankee, stranger. I 'preciate bein' took for an Injun, I do!" He sat up and cradled his rifle across his lap once more.

"Best fetch your animal afore some red nigger makes off with him." The young man rose and moved off into the trees that dropped away from the clearing, hurriedly heading down into the valley. Scratch put his knife away, got up, and hopped over to pick up the big Blackfoot sticker, placing it in his belt. He set to work retying the bundles Hannah had flung to the ground, and was finishing the last when the young man and his horse came crashing through the brush into the clearing. Hannah made known her objections as the horse came close, so the stranger tied his animal away from Scratch's pony and mule.

"We been ridin' these here mountains together for a time, we have," he said to the stranger while looking at Hannah, who was quieting down some now. "She's like me, she is: gettin' ol't an' set in her ways, that mule is."

Scratching his right temple, the old man asked, "Where you movin' to, son?" The young man moved back over to him.

"I was told there were good beaver in these parts. Fixin' to bring some in."

"You trapped any yet?" Scratch squinted one eye and cocked his head to the side.

"Well, no—not as I can rightly say I have," confessed the young stranger.

"Jest as I figgered. You wander into these hills, with them squeaky boots, all starvin' an' cain't bring no beaver to bait," he snorted. "Hungry, young'un?" The stranger looked away from Scratch. "Course you are." He turned away to untie one of the bundles and brought out some jerked meat. "It's tough but tasty, an' likewise, it'll fill an empty meatbag that noways see'd a bite of food for over a week, I'd care to set."

The stranger bit off a chunk and began chewing the stringy meat into a pulp that could easily be swallowed. "Don' swaller too fast now, boy!" Scratch chided. "Give it time to get softened up a bit!"

Greedily the young man began swallowing and went to take another bite, choking on the first that wasn't ready to be swallowed. He rose, gasping, choking, banging away on his back as Scratch hobbled up and started banging away on the young man's chest too. Finally, the big chunk of jerky plopped out onto the ground. Wheezing, the stranger sought to catch his breath.

"Tol't you to take it slow an' easylike, I did." Scratch poked at his young visitor and chuckled some more to himself.

The stranger finished his meal, coming close to destroying what store of jerky Scratch had saved, and sat down against the bundle behind him. Scratch was busy loading his pipe bowl from the small quilled pouch that hung around his neck. He then took some cloth tinder from a possibles sack hanging over his shoulder and got a spark started in it by striking flint with steel over the wad of tinder. Carefully, he moved the tinder up and over the pipe bowl, then inhaled looking over at the stranger who just barely licked his lips.

"You wanna smoke?" Scratch queried between puffs to get the pipe going. The stranger answered with his eyes and moved up closer to the old man. "I ain't got much 'baccy left, but'll shares with you, seein' as how I be headin' toward ronnyvoo."

"What's that—ronnyvoo?" he asked watching the old man carefully.

"Fellers from all over these here mountains come on down to a spot what's already picked out for the gatherin' up," said Scratch, pulling a plug of tobacco from the pouch. "Place where a trapper gives him his beaver away an' gets a y'ar worth of fixin's for what beaver he took in." He tore a small hunk from the twist. As the young man cradled his pipe, eagerly poked the tobacco into the bowl, then took the still glowing tinder from Scratch with his other hand, Scratch concluded, "You drink, find you squar or two, fight some, too. Ronnyvoo—purty near what a man works for all y'ar long."

The two sat in silence, the young man drawing the smoke into his lungs deeply for the first puff. He coughed and sputtered as it went down, for the tobacco seemed to grow stronger with age in the mountains.

"Been almost a y'ar since I bought me that 'baccy," Scratch said quietly as the visitor finished his coughing spell. Sitting quietly too, his guest made a real ceremony of drawing the smoke from the pipe stem, then lifting his chin to exhale. Scratch emptied the charred remains onto the ground, breaking it up and tamping it out fully with the bottom of the pipe bowl. "Soon's you finish your smoke, like to have you help me load Hannah," he said, motioning at the baggage with the stem of the pipe. Scratch looked down into his lap, and only then released the hammer on the rifle.

The young man finished his pipe and tucked it away carefully into the front of his shirt. Scratch rose from the ground, leaning on his rifle as the young man pulled a bundle onto his shoulder with a struggle.

"Yessirree, we gonna have to get some meat on you, boy." Scratch led him over to Hannah, stroking the mule's neck as the young man put the bundle on her back, cinching it down with a rope wrapped around her elk-antler pack saddle.

"If I weren't right here, ol' Hannah wouldn't let you come so close t' her. Ol' gal'd nip an' kick at you—jest like a damned demon she can be at times!"

The young man returned with another pack of furs. "You had a good y'ar, ol' man," he said like a question, but really commenting on the size of the packs of beaver pelts Scratch had taken out of the streams in the high country.

Scratch quickly grew irritated and snapped back, "I ain't so ol't I cain't pin your ears back to your ass, if'n I

13

takes a likin' to, you lil' calf!'' He didn't glare at the intruder, but went back to scratching Hannah's neck. The stranger walked off to fetch the last of the bundles.

"Looks likin' you gotta l'arn some manners, 'sides l'arnin' 'bout the mountains." The old man looked into the old mule's eyes. "We gonna get this young willer branch ready to stay alive in these hills. 'Twouldn't be right for us to go off an' leave this'r lad to have his scalp lifted an' awavin' from some red nigger's lodgepole, now would it, Hannah?" The mule snorted back to him and the visitor looked over at Scratch, eyes big.

"That's right, lad. You're more'n jest lucky to still be wearin' your purty ha'r. Must be you says your prayers each night afore you close your eyes to sleep!" Only Scratch laughed at what he thought was funny.

The visitor tied off the last knots, then spoke. "You think you're so smart, don't you, ol' man? Why, I'll bet you cain't even write your own name!"

Calm and deliberate, Scratch chewed on that for a few long moments feeling the young eyes boring into him, then spoke. "Maybe you can write your name an' cipher real good, but so can I with some lil' work at it. But, you young pilgrim pup, let's see you stay alive up here in these'r hills for much longer. Why, boy, it's outta the goodness of me heart that you're gonna get to tag along'st with me to ronnyvoo, jest to make sure that purty ha'r o' your'n stays right there on your topknot. Wouldn' wanna have to have it both'rin me, seein' the like of you lyin' in your own blood, gut-shot with a red nigger's arrer, him a standin' over you, ready to raise your ha'r whilst you're still suckin' air."

"I'll tag along with you, but don't go thinkin' you gotta watch out for me, stranger. I'll do all right by myself, anyways," the young man came back testily.

"It's a wonder you still got clothes on your back, pilgrim. How long's been since you left the settlements?"

"Been some time—don't really matter much to you . . ."

"Not been long, stranger, else'n them clothes don't last long up here. Leastways, get your horse an' let's be makin' tracks. Sun's been up too long an' we got a ways to go afore we lay eyes on Seedskedee."

The young man moved off to his animal, as Scratch struggled briefly to hoist himself up onto his pony's back with the bad foot. He shifted his weight when finally up,

14

adjusting his rear to sit comfortably on the Spanish saddle. It was only a form of a saddle, with large leather horn and broad, flat stirrups comfortable to moccasined feet, with a small buffalo robe thrown over it. Scratch rode over to Hannah, took up her freed picket rope, adjusted the flintlock across his thighs, and headed down toward the valley along the edge of trees, singing a song of his own making, as he'd often sung to the animals, this one about the Indian women, the watered-down whiskey, and the free-for-all life he was heading for at rendezvous:

> Shinin' times I'm sure there'll be, for Ol' Scratch
> Is a friendly coon, that's me!
> Whiskey, womens, a hug or two—
> Goin' where the sky's always blue.
> No red niggers to devil you thar—
> Only other trappers ready for b'ar!
> I'll spin 'em yarns they loves to hear—
> Heerd 'em least once or twice ever' y'ar.
> Shinin' times I'm sure there'll be, for Ol' Scratch
> Is snortin' for ronnyvoo, yessirree!

2

Hannah snorted, in her own way happy to be moving out once more. Scratch twisted himself around in the saddle to look back at her when she broke into his song, cutting it off midsentence. Back up there, where he had left him, the young stranger was having a hard time mounting the horse and handling the long rifle at the same time.

"'Hoa! 'Hoa, girls!'" the old trapper called out to the horse and mule, pulling on the horse's reins to give the command meaning and yelling out to Hannah at the rear. "Our friend is havin' a lil' trouble gettin' started."

Scratch sat there a moment, twisted around on his saddle, watching the stranger's horse slowly dance around in a small circle, with the man at the middle of that circle, left foot in a stirrup, bouncing up and down off the right foot trying to push himself up onto the animal's back.

"You comin', lad?"

The young man's head popped once more over the back of the horse as he responded, "Wha-ha-ha-hat?" Then the head bounced back out of sight, and all that could be seen was the right hand that held that long rifle.

"I said, I mean—I asked you if you was comin' today, son!" as he chuckled more to himself. "Course, if'n you want me to wait whilst you works out your problem...."

"Naw, I'm comin'," he blurted, squirting over onto the back of the horse, behind the saddle. He then pulled himself with his left hand on the horn up into position, kicking his legs at the same time to push himself off the animal's large flanks. "Said I'm comin'. Damned animal gets scary every now an' then." The dapple carried him down toward the old man some forty feet away.

"Yeah, I can see that both of you don' know the same steps." His visitor looked sheepish once more as he rode up alongside, not really looking at Scratch, but moving his eyes around here and there to avoid the old man's piercing gaze. "Harg! All this'r child's got to do is get you better truck, is all. We gonna talk some coon outta a better smokepole for you, or I ain't the tradin' nigger I thinks I am!"

The sun was high and hot by the time they stopped for a noon rest beside a little nameless creek. Scratch was feeling good, warmed by the sun that flowed over him like thick, sweet molasses. He leaned back against a tree, facing the sun and began to feel the looseness slowly coming over him again, that casual bright happiness at being free and headed to rendezvous. He squinted and turned in the high light to look at the young man.

He was sitting by the creek, watching the water with his back to Scratch, preferring to stay near the animals that were lazily chewing their lunch of new grasses along the bank.

"Where'd you say you come from—your home, that is?" Scratch slid down noiselessly beside the stranger.

"Didn't say."

To the answer, the old man just nodded his head and pursed his lips a bit. The two sat silent for some time, the old man watching the young one gaze at the stream, trying to figure him out, measure him, this spunky little loner beside him. Scratch rose slowly and hobbled over to Hannah, nuzzling her muzzle, then let his fingers wander up to scratch between her ears. The mule's eyes closed halfway, enjoying the vigorous rubbing.

"You're a might touchy 'bout comp'ny. I jest wanted to know somethin' 'bout the man I'm ridin' with."

"I got my reasons."

"Laddee, up here in the high lonesome, a man as says he's wantin' to be your friend, you should take it for jest that," said Scratch, turning to face the young man; "a man as is openin' his hand an' willin' to teach you what he knows..."

"Didn't ask you to teach me nothin'. Didn't say nothin' 'bout that," the stranger interrupted.

"Specially a man as can prob'ly get as lonely as you are," Scratch continued as he came back over to sit on the creek bank beside the stranger. "Son, this'r coon ain't see'd a white man in, goin' on nigh seven, eight moons now, most likely. Hannah thar, she's a good lis'ner, but I gets tired ever' now an' then of hearin' the sound of me own voice. Not meanin' to push you, nothin' like that." He squirmed to lean back on his elbows, stretching out both legs and wiggling the toes on the bruised foot that was beginning to feel much better already.

"Name's Scratch." He lifted his eyes slowly up from the other side of the stream to float over the hillside opposite them. "Been up here more'n seven seasons, yepper, seven seasons now. Come outta Ohier by way of Missoura." Scratch was talking more to himself and the hills than to the man beside him, the way he had done all during those long years of lonely.

"Run 'ways from home, I did, from a pappy as wanted this'r child to be a farmer jest like him." He balled up a cheek and spat toward the creek, his tongue licking the juice at the corner of his mouth, then nestling the quid of tobacco back neatly between his gum and cheek.

"Them was times, they was. I spent some y'ars on that river, l'arnin' to be a business man, properlike. Got the hang of it, quick too, but it weren't for me. Naw, I wandered on down to the Big Muddy an' headed north lookin' for somethin' as I didn't know what. Spent 'bout a y'ar with a settler an' his fam'ly, hired-hand-like. 'Tweren't so bad workin' like that, knowin' you could pick up an' move if'n you wanted, not like what'd been back home with my pap callin' the tune.''

Out of the corner of his eye, Scratch saw the younger man picking through the grass for small stones he began to toss aimlessly toward the other side of the creek. "Left me a gal back there, settler's daughter, she were, an' purty as a speckle't pup. Dizzied my eyes right off. Had long brown-gold ha'r she'd tie back into two braids. Made her face jump right out at you that way. Ah, she was some now. Good to me, too, the way the good Lord knows a woman outta be to a man." Scratch craned his neck around to look fully at the young man, "You leave a woman behind too, son?"

"Why you gotta be flappin' your jaw so much, ol' man?" he snipped back at Scratch, eyes suddenly alight with fire, then got up to move off toward the horses. "We cain't be sittin' here all day, yappin' 'bout your past." He jumped up on his dapple, more easily this time, cradled the long rifle across his lap, and looked down at the old man.

Scratch slowly rose and made it over to his horse, pushing off the ground to plop into the saddle. "S'pose you're right, son. Lots a pilgrims as come to these'r mountains, wantin' to run 'ways from somethin', 'spectin' the mountains to take care of 'em. Wolves has et many a time on greenhorns as thort they knew these'r hills. Thems the kind as have theys bones scattered all over by such scavengers as wait for others to do they killin' for 'em. This child ain't one to be lollygaggin' when thar's trail to put behin't us." He turned the horse and led Hannah off the creek bank into the fast water, the horse lifting each leg, then putting it back down on the rocky bottom very precisely, Scratch feeling the shifting of her muscles between his legs with each practiced step. With a quick push, he kicked her up and onto the opposite bank, continuing to follow the sun in its westward journey.

The pair traveled in silence for most of the afternoon. No words were spoken, the only noises coming from an occasional limb broken underfoot and the constant creaking of saddle leather under numbing buttocks. Then Scratch stopped dead in his tracks. He threw up his left arm to tell the other man to stop too. He cocked his head from side to side slowly, straining to hear. Easily turning himself sideways in the saddle to look at the man behind him, he put one finger against his lips and motioned the young man to come alongside him.

"Thar's game about. If'n you want supper, we best be afoot to make meat for our kettle," he whispered, then slid off the pony quietly, to pad silently about on the ground, tying both the horse and Hannah up to a bush. He pulled the soft quilled cover from his rifle, holding the stock with one hand while the other yanked the cover free with a quick jerk on the muzzle fringe.

The other man walked over to tie his animal up, then moved off behind the old man. It was while following Scratch up the low rise that he could closely observe the trapper's queer walk, which looked more pronounced to the greenhorn than it really was. The old man walked with a back as straight as a wiping stick, not crouched over as if stalking prey, but moving about atop bent knees, with a somewhat bowlegged gait, accented all the more as he winced from the weight put on the swollen foot. Silently the young one moved along behind Scratch, hypnotized by the way the older man moved, each step set down as if ready to spring, then moving onto the other foot. It reminded the young man of the squat prairie hen, skittering here and there, waddling from place to place. He let out a little snort of laughter.

Scratch stopped in his tracks, wrenching around violently. "What's so damned funny, boy?" he whispered hoarsely. The young man stifled his laugh, and Scratch was off again without another word, only his dark eyes telling the man behind him to keep his mouth shut.

They moved up through a part in the aspens that were coming to full-leafed glory following a long mountain winter, over a little rise, until Scratch motioned the man behind him to follow him into the edge of a stand of trees. As the young one came up beside him, he pointed across and down the edge of trees lining the little bowl that was sheltered from the winds. Patches of snow remained in the shadows where they stood, here and there dotted with the huge cloven prints of a large animal. Scratch motioned the other man's attention to the prints in the melting patches of southern snow, then stretched his arm for the other man's attentive gaze to follow, pointing out a few dark forms along the edge of the shadowed aspens.

He alone moved off cautiously through the trees, staying up in the shadows, now and then sticking his nose up higher in the wind, measuring each swirl the breezes took in the bowl. A few hundred yards off from the animals the younger man was watching the first of those dark forms venture slightly out from the cover of the trees, putting its nose into the air too. It took a few steps more into the clearing until the young man saw the rack above its head, a rack so immense that even at the distance across the bowl it seemed as if the animal had a tree strapped to the top of its head.

"Elk!" he cried out in a hoarse whisper. He quickly stifled it in his joy as Scratch turned on him from a few yards away and growled, "Shush, goddammit!"

The old man moved quickly now, hopping over downed timber, dodging in and out between the shadows, moving around in a skipping hobble to the right side of the bowl, staying hidden as he finally skittered to a stop across from the bull elk. Here he set himself behind a tree, easing his rifle up to his shoulder. Carefully, Scratch drew back the hammer with a gnarled thumb until he felt the lock click, then let his breath out slowly in bits and pieces.

Followed by three cows and a young spike bull, the majestic male animal moved on out of the trees into the grassy bowl, with his nose still up in the wind. Halfway across the green floor, he stopped suddenly, turned his head from side to side slowly. The old man's heart jumped in his chest. "Snake shit!" he thought. "Critter moves off now, ain't got a whore's chance to lay a ball in him!" He held his breath and nestled the side of his face down firmer onto the cheek piece. Nervously, Scratch waited long, quiet seconds for the bull to bolt off, sure the elk would hear his heart pounding up against his ribs. His ears roared with every pulse. Then, as suddenly as he had stopped, the bull lowered his head to gather some grass, moving his snout from side to side, grazing as if without a care in the world. The wait seemed endless to the old man, trying to measure what the elk would do next. Finally, the bull lifted his head, sniffed at the wind again, and headed toward the hidden man once more. Plodding along some ten yards behind him followed the cows and the lone spike bull, all heading toward the shadows of the trees lining the bowl where Scratch stood waiting.

He sucked in his breath, telling himself, "Hol't it, you

ol' coon; hol't it," as the bull kept coming—coming in almost a straight line for him. Then, without the slightest warning, the elk moved off to the hunter's right. Scratch had to step around the tree some to keep a bead on the animal, waited for a moment, letting the air ease out of his lungs, then pulled back on the trigger slowly. Flint struck fire and the powder in the pan shot through the touch-hole with a sudden phitt. Then the explosion from the muzzle. Scratch could see nothing ahead for a moment while the gray film of smoke hung close in the trees where he had hidden.

Not waiting, though, he pulled the horn around to the front of his body, cradled the rifle against him, and measured some powder out into his right palm until it reached just the right crease on the leathery skin. He placed the side of his hand over the muzzle and began pouring powder down the barrel while he looked up from his work into the bowl. Scratch smiled as he saw the large bull had gone down in his tracks, the cows and spike bull having stopped where they were when the shot rang out, confused that the leader had chosen this spot for a nap. He chuckled to himself that he might be able to drop another.

From his possibles sack he picked out patch and ball, set them on the muzzle, and began to drive them home when another shot cracked the still air. He stepped back behind the tree, drove the ball home and pulled the stick clear of the thimbles beneath the barrel. Quickly priming the pan, he peered cautiously around the tree. Back up in the stand he had come from, another gray film of smoke hung in close to the trees. "Must be the boy," he assured himself, then turned to look back at the small herd. The spike bull was down on his stomach, snorting blood, frothing at the mouth, and struggling to find strength in his legs to rise. The cows now turned to sniff at him, then bolted across the bowl to the north, noisily crashing through the trees until they could neither be heard nor seen by him.

"Damn! Why, of all the stupid. . . ," Scratch muttered under his breath.

The young man was already jogging down from the line of trees into the bowl when Scratch stepped out to await him. Cutting through the high meadow grass, the older man cut across the younger's path and stood gesturing violently with his right arm. When the young man was finally within a few yards of him, Scratch sputtered, "You . . . you stupid . . . pilgrim! Poor bull an' no cow. Winterin' in the mountains, have you? Ain't you l'arned nothin'?"

He was sputtering and spitting to get the angry flow of words past his taut lips and tangled tongue.

"Wh-a-a . . ."

"Goddammit! Why didn't you pick you one a them cows to drop?"

"Why the hell you gone so crazy?" the young man shot back, somewhat dumfounded at this greeting from the older man. "You shot you a bull yourself!"

"Been plannin' on it for some time, too! Ain't for meat, pilgrim!" Scratch abruptly turned on his heel to move off toward the downed animals.

"Why you all over me for droppin' the other one?" the young man asked as he followed on Scratch's heels.

"Poor bull. Fat cow." he stopped and spat the words out, then turned once more to drop beside the larger of the bulls. The animal was dead, sure enough. "Ain't for the meat!" he snarled once more without turning his head. "Need me the robe," he added, as his fingers plunged down into the animal's fur. "You shoulda took a cow for meat. That be knowin' your poor bull from fat cow."

Scratch rose from the animal and walked over to where the young spike lay. He had rolled over on his side, his one wide eye staring wildly up at the two hunters, his chest still heaving and laboring to pull in air.

"Dammit!" was all the young hunter said, mostly under his breath, as he pulled a fancy pistol from his belt and knelt beside the young bull. As he put the muzzle beside the animal's ear, Scratch reached down to put his hand over the hammer.

"No, son. What's done is. . . . Up here, you don't throw 'way a good G'lena pill on a job as a knife can do as good when a critter's snortin' with funk."

He pulled the Blackfoot knife from his belt and knelt at the head of the animal, cradling the lower jaw in his left hand to pull the bull's neck up taut, and slit the flesh long and deep with one swift motion. There was a gush of blood and frothy fluid as he dropped the head back to the ground, then rose to move over to stand beside the young

22

man. With the muzzle of his rifle, Scratch pointed out the hole in the flesh down low on the chest, a small hole just faintly ringed with a small ooze of blood, a hole that bubbled and spit out the pinkish fluid.

"An' 'sides you pickin' poor meat, you didn't hit the vitals; jest went through his windbags. He'd been long time dyin', he would. Elk's big critter—gotta put your ball up higher, behin't his shoulder, 'bout here," moving the muzzle of the rifle up across the fur, "or way up here, on his neck," pointing out where to place a neck shot.

The air was still except for some birds calling out back up in the trees on the side of the bowl. Scratch shook his head once when he looked down at the rifle the young man was holding—long, small-caliber Pennsylvanian it was. Shaking his head once more, "You did make you a fine shot, leastways, laddee, with that squirrel gun," he mused, turning his head to measure the distance covered by the young hunter's shot from the trees. " 'Tweren't bad 't'all... 'tweren't bad shot." He made a small clucking sound. "Now you go fetch them ponies an' get 'em here straightways, else'n some wandrin', thievin' red nigger'll have me skins an' Hannah too, whilst I get on the skinnin' an' dressin' first whack."

The young man turned without a word and started off. "Say, son, you gotta ball ahuggin' that breech, don' you?" The stranger stopped, then turned to look back at Scratch. "Best you always load up soon's after shootin' your rifle as you can. Never know what s'prise be waitin' for you up an' over that rise." He spit once, ground it into the grass with his toe, then kneeling down beside the elk began a long slice through the flesh from neck to tail.

With a small roasting fire going against the ledge on the north end of the bowl, Scratch showed the young man about graining a hide, then set him to work fleshing the skins. While the young hunter was humped over his work, Scratch set out cutting chunks of meat as big as his fist to hang over the coals on sharpened sticks driven into the ground around the embers. Silently the young man went about his business until the roasting meat sent slivers of delicious smells carried on the evening breeze to his nostrils. He raised his head to look over at the fire hungrily as Scratch pulled the last of the packs to the ground from the hobbled animals.

"Grease hungry, ain't you, son?" He turned back to

his work on the skins, pulling the sharpened stone toward him stroke after stroke, peeling fat and excess flesh from the hide. "Tell you the truth, I'm suff'rin' from an empty paunch meself. Ain't had a good elk steak for some time, it's been."

He kicked a stone over to the edge of the coals and turned to the packs on the ground. From one he pulled a battered kettle and lid, from another a waxy pouch, then set them by the fire. Scratch retrieved the bloody knife from the fire where he had stuck it beneath some coals, carefully wiping it quickly back and forth over his leg until it shone once more, cleansed of blood and hair by the glowing embers.

Returning from a little stream gurgling with mountain runoff, he placed the water-filled kettle on the stone over the fire. Into the water he threw coarse grounds of coffee from the pouch, stirring the water with his fingers until most of the grounds were sodden. After wiping his hand off on his shirt, Scratch moved around the fire to turn the pieces of meat roasting on the stick.

"Appolaz. These here sticks are. Leastways, that's what the greasers call 'em. Good idea too for roastin' hump ribs an' all." He went on chattering about this and that, fussing with the fire or the meat, cussing at the water, which was taking a long time to boil, until it finally began to bubble and spit into brewing action.

When the young man had finished fleshing the skins, Scratch moved over to fold them up after salting. All four sides were folded in, with the two longest sides touching; then he rolled them up into a tight bundle. From a pack he pulled a coil of stout cord which he used to bind the skins, flesh side in, hair side out, pushing down with his foot while he pulled up on the cord to make the bundle as compact as he could. After tossing the two hides over with the rest of the packs, Scratch knelt by one of the hunks of meat, drawing his knife across it to produce a thin slice of meat. Eyes wide with anticipation, the young hunter watched him put the meat into his mouth, a strip of flesh well done on the outside and pink in the middle. He licked his lips unconsciously as the old man ran a long tongue across his mustache and over his chin to catch every savory drop of grease. From where he sat, Scratch stirred the coffee brewing in the small kettle with a green limb.

24

All was quiet in the lengthening shadows of early evening. Sitting on his haunches, the young one watched Scratch from behind, for the first time now really seeing the older man. He could see the long, dark mustache standing out boldly against the premature gray of the thick, uncombed beard wrapping Scratch's face. And for the first time he looked at the old man's hair carefully; it too was flecked and streaked with gray, one single thick braid on the right side of his head, encircled with a piece of red cloth. The hair that hung down from the back of the head, however, was not like the hair on the sides. Instead of the streaks of gray, it was coal black and hung straight down past his shoulders, unlike the long gray hair that was curly and wavy except for the one, tight, red-wrapped braid. It struck him as funny that the old trapper should have such different, peculiar hair pouring out from beneath the blue bandanna tied down on his head. A loud growling rumble in his stomach, however, returned his thoughts to supper.

"Get your knife busy, boy, an' fill that paunch. It's talkin' louder'n your mouth ever could!" He motioned for the young man to begin eating while he rose to fetch two pint-sized cups from a parfleche. By the time he had poured them both a cup of hot, thick coffee, the younger was busy ripping strips of flesh from one of the small roasts, holding a piece in his mouth outstretched with one hand, while the knife in the other hand neatly whacked off chunk after mouth-filling chunk. He handled the knife well, index finger along the top of the blade, expertly using the knife against his lips as if it were but an extension of the finger, sharpened to do a job.

"You handle that sticker right slick, son. Shoulda let you do the skinnin' on them critters," he said, as he pulled a chunk of meat off for himself. They sat in silence once more, each filling a gnawing hunger with the rich meat and washing it down with the heady coffee Scratch had brewed.

Supper over, the young man leaned back against his saddle and bedroll, feet close to the coals, and sighed contentedly. Scratch messed around, poking the embers some, then said, "You been needin' that for some time, ain't you?" There was no answer. Scratch turned his head to look at the deepening purple of the evening drift into the bowl as the sun dropped quickly behind the ridge to

25

the west. The silence was heavy on him once more, weighing as it had few times before. He looked now and then over at the youngster, then looked back on his early days with a secret craving to recapture them once more, to move through the newness of the mountains again, to share the newfound joys of being free and alive in these hills for just one more time—all through this young man.

"Name's Bass. Titus Bass." He paused for a moment. "But most call me now by a name I got hung with some y'ars back. Ol' Scratch, it is."

He chewed on his thoughts awhile, then continued. "Give me that name when I was comin' to my first ronnyvoo, '26 it were. That was a time. Had met me three fellers outta the Bayer Salade, down toward Wah-Too-Yar in them southern Rockies, an' they had felt sorry for this coon."

He had been cocky in those days, cocky and starving. Now, in looking back, Bass could see he was lucky then to be still wearing his hair. That was when the three trappers happened on the scene. "These'r fellers wake me up one mornin', tappin' on the bottom of my hoof. They'd been Injuns, I'd been wolf bait for sure that day. Lordee! How they laughed at this here child, whoopin' an' hollerin' like they was Injuns."

And you could have fooled Titus Bass then. "They looked the Injun, they did: decked out'n skins, theys ha'r long an' flappin', yahooin' an' cloppin' theys mouths like'n it were a scalp dance. They made fun of this here nigger, sure 'nough." He could see the trio had been somewhat justified in giving him the fright they had, seeing as how he had not been very careful up to that time.

"Yessirree! Bud, Billy, an' Silas felt sorry for me an' teached me what I would need to keep my ha'r. My clothes was store-bought'n, linsey-woolsey they was, an' in a bad fittle by the time I met up with them crazy niggers, holes an' all wored in 'em, you see. 'Sides, the seams was full of lil' graybacks by then." He looked over at the young man, squinting. "You're not carryin' graybacks, is you? Them lil' critters'll devil you for all time if'n they ever get a foot in your door."

Titus smiled slightly and sighed. "Don't figger why the good Lord ever put them lil' grayback nits in the mountains for. Guess'n the same reason He give us Blackfoot too," he clucked. Otherwise, he thought, we'd get messy and wouldn't pay any heed if we didn't have them Bug's Boys around. "Well, I'm gettin' 'way from my story." He pulled tobacco from his pouch, stuffed it into the bowl of his pipe. Looking again at the young man, he tossed the rest of the plug across the fire to the stranger.

Lifting a coal from the embers between two green twigs, puffing rapidly on the pipe stem until he finally drew in a long breath, the older man continued, "Least-ways, I was carryin' a whole passel of them lil' critters 'long in my clothes an' ha'r."

To recall it now, the vivid memory drawn up painted a picture of the young trapper tagging along after the trio of experienced mountain men, heading for rendezvous, young Bass scratching and scratching. "Had the graybacks bad, I did. Well, those boys come to callin' me 'Scratch,' on account of all that itchin' I was doin' alla time." The name had been given him, and there it would stay.

"Fin'ly got me decked out'n set of Yuta skins. Good Injun woman as you'd ever wanna meet made them skins for me that winter we hole't up with them Yutas, up in Park Kyack as I rec'llect. Didn't scratch no more after that, but that damned name was stuck to me so hard that I couldn't shake it. Scratch it was—an' Scratch it be today."

That winter finally passed, his first spent in an Indian village, and then the spring trapping season. "By the time I left them three coons, they was callin' me Ol' Scratch, on account of me gettin' the green wored off so's to be a reg'lar mountain man. You see, son, when a man's friends think a lot of him they call him Ol' this or Ol' that. It's a badge of honor, it is, an' I felt myself right pert to have them three call me Ol' Scratch." The momentary glow from the warm memory was washed away as a colder reverie replaced it.

"Last time I see'd them boys was up near the Three Forks, fixin' they was to head down for tradin' plews for whiskey an' womens to the first post they come to on the river. Give 'em my plews too, I did. An' asked 'em to have a swaller or two for me afore headin' back." Scratch now grew pensive for a few moments, knocking the burnt tobacco out of the pipe bowl, then relighting it.

"Never see'd 'em since. Others would tell me as them three made off to St. Louie with my catch an' quit the mountains. Naw, I tells 'em." He shook his head, "Billy an' ol' Silas wouldn't do anythin' of the sort to Ol' Scratch. Now that Bud, he was a wild one, he were. But, I cain't bring myself to calc'late of them coons makin' off with this'r child's skins. They musta lost ha'r down the Missoura or somethin' such."

He sucked in a long breath and glanced over at the motionless youngster before continuing his story. Bass had been alone for the most part ever since, except for one squat white-headed ex-preacher who had thrown in his lot with him some years before. In most ways, Scratch was quite accustomed to being alone for he had rarely found a man with whom he would want to set down traps. His brow wrinkled up sternly as he thought of the big trapping brigades plying the mountain streams. "Fellers this far north an' up is hooked an' tied to some stuffed-shirt board of deerectors back to the Missoura, catchin' skins an' 'sendin' up theys ha'r for thems as sits back in some parlor back east, sippin' fine whiskey, beddin' down 'tween soft sheets each night with some white-skinned gal." He shook his head, "Such is not for this'r child. Not for me, it ain't! Titus Bass has a stick as floats differ'nt'n most."

He turned his head and gazed down the valley, "Fellers south of here work outta Taos wint'rin' ground, keepin' mostly to the mountains south of here an' some west, too. Titus Bass likes to stomp round from time to time on the Seedskedee, maybe the Snake, workin' up to Yallerstone country once't-while. Them's good streams, they is, with as big a beavers as you'd care to bring up to bait," he mused, nodding to himself.

Scratch looked up between the trees at the gathering darkness, picking at the side of his beard. "Leastways, it was good country." He spit into the fire that was slowly dying. "Till them coons as come up the Missoura 'gan to trap all that country clean. That kind's trappin' up every'thin' outta the streams that has a flat tail on it. Streams ain't what they use to be, they ain't."

So, he kept mostly to himself, keeping out of the way of the large fur-trapping brigades, which he always described as "a whole shitteree of fellers what traps alla beaver up, an' them flat tails they don't trap they scare away." The only time he could cotton to being around so many people was rendezvous time. That was the fat season for Ol' Scratch to be shining.

"Ronnyvoo," he mused. "I can set my truck down ongside other skin trappers. I can sell my plews to one of hem big comp'nies—now, that's where Titus Bass gets calped proper ever' y'ar—then get me some geegaws for squar or two, but mos'ly sittin' round with them fellers to arn an' tip a cup or two of Billy Sublette's liquor through he day. Thens when I can stomach so much comp'ny ound me without it turnin' my milk sour. What that clerk lon't steal from me on my plews, I'll have to give 'im back on foofaraw an' whiskey, so's I guesses I'm fotched est 'bout as good as them skin trappers, anyways you ays your sights. Leastways, Ol' Scratch can move off ome end of ronnyvoo where he pleases—ain't no booshway o tell this'r coon where he's gonna set traps down."

"What's a booshway?" the young man asked, finally urning his head to make eye contact with Bass across the ire.

"Him's the one what leads them big fur brigades: t's . . . it's . . . booshway, you know." He stretched his legs oward the fire. "An' I can winter outta robe season where wants to. Mos'ly take me cold bones up to the Absor'kees. Real partial to them Crow, I am. Thieves that they be, heys still the warmest lodges I've laid my robes down in. An', whooooeee!" He let out a low whistling sound. "They ikes the white man, that they do. White man has horse-lesh, you see, an' them Crow is squampshus over horse-lesh. Jehoshaphat! That's winter doin's, that is, with hem Crows. They *bah-park*, big medeecin, for this ol' coot. Many's a man as gots a squar stuck way up thar in Crow country. If'n you can find where them red critters be come full winter, split up in small bands as they do. Arapooesh, that's my wint'rin band." He finally looked over once more at the young man, nodding in agreement with himself as he turned his head.

Scratch emptied his pipe bowl into the glowing coals, hen stood up, stretching the muscles tired from a day on horseback, kinky from the butchering, and tight from being still at last by the fire. he kicked out his robes so that his feet would be by the fire, then wrestled down into the hides, finally letting out a contented, satisfied sigh.

"Best you get some sleep now, friend. Be movin' afore first light, we will," he murmured, rolling over on his side away from the young man.

The younger one sat mutely by the fire for some time,

staring into the embers that every now and then sent up a small flame to dance briefly here and there. Later, he moved his saddle up a way, and stretched out beneath his blankets. Lying on his back, the young man's eyes were fixed on the darkening canopy overhead, studded with the dim yellow-gold stars of early nighttime darkness. He lay there a long time, watching the sky through the tops of the trees, watching the stars as numerous as the miles he felt he had come to get away, miles he had put between himself and what had been left behind.

From north to south, a shooting star blazed overhead for an instant, then died from view.

"Most of 'em come out here to get somethin'. I've come out to get away. Ain't nothin' left behind now, faded like that star, all burnt up." He rolled onto his side, facing the old man, noticing once more the braided strip of hair out from the one side of the man's head and the straight black hair spreading out over his shoulders, the blue bandanna snugged down over his ears. He studied Scratch some more, buried within his buffalo robe, until he heard the old man breathing more slowly, more deeply.

"Scratch," the young man said softly, almost whispering. "Scratch, the name's Josiah, Josiah Paddock." Then he let the air rush out of his lungs, as if a weight too long carried had suddenly been taken from his shoulders. "Josiah Paddock, Scratch."

Long, still moments passed. Then the young man pulled the blanket up close to his face. He closed his eyes, feeling his body ease off from its long tenseness.

"Thank you, Josiah. Thank you."

3

Stepping out into the edge of the muddy street, Paddock took in a long, pleasant breath of air filled with the fresh perfume that followed the rain. He turned and waved a good-evening farewell to his employer standing at the window of Smith's Store. It had been a good day, a busy day, in the store where Josiah clerked, waiting on the variety of people who came to Smith's to be outfitted, or to buy a rich velvet for a ball gown. Here a customer could pore over crockery, hardware, and dry goods brought in from faraway Philadelphia and Baltimore, or purchase the simple woolen garments made of linsey-woolsey. He enjoyed his work there, the day-long bustling, but mostly his getting to talk with those who came in from the distant reaches to the west. His ear was becoming tuned to the musical speech of the buckskinned men from upriver who would stride right up to the counter, not content to waste their time shopping, and ask the young man for beaver traps; $20.00 a half dozen they were at Smith's. Josiah would stir one of those rare characters into conversation from time to time, but mostly they bought what was needed, then went on their way, with better things to do, with better places to be than in St. Louis, spending their few fleeting moments jawing with some young store clerk.

As he stopped, waiting for a carriage to churn past through the puddles dotting the thoroughfare, he looked around him at the streets of the Mound City, his place of birth. Setting out up Third Street, the LaRue des Granges of bygone St. Louis days, Josiah's mind slipped back once more to catch the wonders seen by a child's eyes in the growing city. For the young boy, St. Louis was a view of wagon wheels twirling past him at eye level, the tired, ploding feet of the oxen pulling the carts and wagons of the new settlers, moving off to one side defensively as a French lady swooshed by in her gay-laced gown that pushed against the young child holding his mother's hand. For the boy, always standing obediently beside his American mother as she shopped, it was not a world of faces, but one of feet and legs: watching intently with the wide eyes of awed innocence the moving sea of beaded moccasins and leather work boots, sturdy-buttoned high-top shoes, or silken slippers mostly hidden beneath a swirl of ruffled cloth. What sounds delighted his young ears, not only a daily diet of English, but conversation around him spiced with French and Spanish tongues, not to mention the rhythm of trapper talk, the singsong of the river's voyageurs, and the strange and varied languages of the western natives who wrapped themselves in blan-

31

kets to wander in and out of the city's shops when they came to St. Louis. It was a child's adventure land. And he was this evening once again filled with awe of this place, once again filled with the joy of constant discovery. The sky held long its light gray of early evening, the moment suspended after the gentle spring shower.

Crossing Elm Street, Josiah jumped a large puddle to hurry out of the way of an oncoming carriage, then stopped to watch the Frenchwoman ride by. Her driver stoically looked neither left nor right as the young man tipped his hat to the lady before moving down Elm toward First Street. At the corner of First, he held the door open for an old man leaving the Robidoux bakery, and entered. Josiah was bombarded with smells and fragrances that he had come to love over the years, the heavy yeast perfume wafting gently among the delicate aromas of breads just pulled from the huge stone ovens. Pausing by the door, as he had done every evening for several years, he slowly closed his eyes and drew in a deep breath, savoring the atmosphere of the bakery.

"Ah! Monsieur Paddock. The same for you this evening?" asked old Joseph behind the counter.

"Nothing else but." Josiah walked over to the aging man who wore a flour-dusted apron tucked around his waist.

"Oui!" He pulled out two still warm sugar-crusted pastries from beneath a protective oilcloth towel.

"No, Joseph. Just one."

"Thees one is on me," replied Joseph, dusting them with a final coating of spun sugar before wrapping the pastries up lightly in newsprint and handing them to Josiah.

"Here, then. Let me pay for one of 'em, Joseph." Josiah reached across the counter to present the old man with two coins.

"Non, non!" Robidoux put his hand up to Josiah as he stepped back, then wound his hands in his dusty apron. "Monsieur Paddock has been a good customer, non? Oui! And I have come to look forward very much to seeing you each evening when you come in. Non! I will not think of you paying for the breads tonight! Now, go! Take them and go!" He waved his arm to motion Josiah out, with the comical stern look he tried to use when often he would good-naturedly throw the young man out of his shop. "Take one to Angelique when you see her tonight. Go now, and have you a good evening. I have work to attend to."

Josiah backed from the counter, his smiling eyes winking at the old man as he tucked the package under his arm. Back on the street, he stopped once more to feel the cool breeze caress his face. It was damp, the air heavy with moisture after the rain. He turned up his collar against the breeze, heading back down Elm toward the building that housed the offices and printshop of the *St. Louis Beacon*, over which he had held a small room for the past several years following his mother's death in 1827. Stuffing the package inside his worn coat, he buttoned it while crossing Second Street.

Josiah could sense the old city growing younger and younger all the time. In recent years he felt the pulse of the town, sitting, as it did, at the crossroads of a country straining for room, beginning to stretch north and south along the mated Missouri and Mississippi rivers. Here was the lifeblood of a continent, running thick and strong, flowing with the heartbeat of the individual, that man who moved toward the setting sun so that he might stretch wide his arms without striking a neighbor. The wide verandahs of the French traders entertained the silver buckle and brocade slipper at numerous parties and balls, while the backyards of the struggling American settlers stretched into a wilderness many spoke of but few had seen.

Along these muddy streets moved every sort of man and woman in America, each a part of the soul of a growing country that was St. Louis. In her taverns and grog shops, one man's money was as good as his neighbor's. Here lilac-perfumed, lace-ruffled Frenchmen brushed against upriver men who wore only animal skins and smelled as bad. One could look about these rooms and see vermilion-daubed Osage chiefs drinking alongside the best of St. Louis society, and bending elbows with lice-infested interpreter-traders from posts of the North. Here too was a social structure in which the beauty of French maidenhood had to compete with the charms of black-eyed, copper-skinned squaws immersed in the constant struggle for a man's attention in a world where passion and a lack of inhibition were those qualities much sought after.

At the corner, Josiah paused briefly to melt into the

small crowd gathered around a man preaching an impromptu sermon, waving a worn Bible at the end of his outstretched arm, warning all listeners of the evils awaiting them within the streets of St. Louis on this Saturday night. Josiah smiled faintly to himself, then pushed on down the street, skirting occasional puddles along the way. Everybody's got something to sell, he mused silently as he left the preacher. Indeed, in this town a palmful of bright beads bought a beaver pelt, and a small cup of raw, diluted alcohol acquired by barter a buffalo robe from the Indian trader.

It was a city changing, growing as much by the people coming through as by the business they brought. Three newspapers and a bookstore St. Louis had in this year of 1831, along with more than four plays each month, in addition to enough social parties and balls to keep several professional hairdressers occupied full time. In the billiard halls, men moved at their leisure, while women swept through their parlors entertaining French gentry and the noble classes. Past Josiah went the men pulling behind them the threads of a growing American fabric, men who had that day been settlers registering claims at the land office, or dreamers who had just purchased an outfit for each man they would lead beyond the river to the mountains lying against the horizons of the mind.

He headed over to Main Street, LaRue Royal of years now faded and gone, deciding not to go directly back to his room, but to wander along the levee as the light began to fade. A score of steamboats lay tied up at the wharf, their daylight hours filled with bustling activity, being loaded and unloaded with the commerce brought from the East, bar lead and bolts of fancy cloth, then to be jammed with the commerce of the West, a wealth of furs piled high upon their quarter-decks. Along the street Josiah stopped to look sadly at the dead body of a dog, lying partly in a muddy puddle. He started to go, but stopped again to ask of some children floating toy boats in nearby puddles, "Do you know whose dog this is?"

"Ours, sir. A good dog he was, too. Kilt this afternoon by a Frenchman in his fancy carriage." They went back to playing with their boats, pulling up at the side of the puddle to load and unload tiny blocks of simulated cargo. Josiah pursed his lips, and went on his way. He passed the Chouteau-Berthold Store, being locked up for the night by clerks working late, in a two-story building at 11 North Main. This was the street that for years was St. Louis, occupying the first terrace up from the river. Americans would refer to this part of town as "under the hill," looking up from the bank as the terrain climbed sharply away in places, ending abruptly at the limestone bluffs, above which St. Louis was extending her arms.

He crossed Walnut, looking to his left up the narrow street snaking its way upward toward the hill where the old fort and tower of Spanish days had stood; that intersection of Walnut and Fourth Street was now crowded with small shops and homes. Above this levee, surrounded by thick stands of oak and maple, stood the homes of wealthy French fur merchants, overlooking the river that was their gateway to fortunes awaiting. Turning up Washington, he climbed the hill past old brick and wood homes until he stopped in front of Number 37. Through the window, he could barely make out the dark wood and browned metal of the sturdy, short rifles on the walls of the Hawken shop. Here he paused to squint up close to the windowpane in the dim light, feasting his eyes on the produce of the Hawken brothers' craft. Long had he wanted to own one of those rifles. Many a day he had come down on his brief lunch time to fondle and hold this weapon or that. Each time he would sigh, as he did now, knowing full well he had not enough money to buy such a rifle, what with his weekly rent, food, and the presents he frequently bought to surprise Angelique. Besides, he consoled himself as he walked on, there was a fine full-stocked Pennsylvanian back in a corner of his room. Around here, he had no need of anything better.

Pushed up along the river, the city's population had fluctuated between six and nine thousand in the past few years. St. Louis, evolving from its Spanish and French heritage, was now welcoming a new Protestant population as well as American business and architecture. Brick warehouses stood quiet now, their wooden doors shut until Monday to allow a day of rest for those who worked filling the pockets of men grown wealthy in the fur trade or new industry.

"Josiah! Where ye been?" a dark form called out to him, as it rose from the wooden steps leading up to his room. "Been waitin' for ye some time." As the form moved toward him, Josiah could see the beaming face of his good friend Mordecai Thayer. Slapping Josiah on the shoulder, he whispered hoarsely in his way, "Got paid today, an' I feel like a spree. Can I buy ye supper an' drinks at the Green Tree?"

"I s'pose. Goin' to see Angelique tonight, but that's not till later. Yes, I'll take you up on your offer! Jest let me change my shirt, so's I can be off straightways from the tavern to her house later on." He led Mordecai up the wooden planks to unlock the outside door to his room. Putting on a freshly laundered shirt, Josiah tucked in the tail, cinched up the wide leather belt, then dropped the pastries inside the front of his shirt. He pulled on the coat again, locked the door at the landing, and they were off to dinner.

Turning up Church Street, the pair passed businesses and homes that still displayed addresses bearing the street's old name, LaRue de l'Eglise, so named for the Roman Catholic cathedral and its church buildings lining the avenue. In this era of transition for St. Louis, one was often asked where this narrow city lane was, one visitor using the French name, the next asking for Church Street, yet another asking directions to Second Street. Each man would end up along this winding, busy thoroughfare. Past the cathedral, the men turned into a small yard, walking past a large sign swinging in the evening breeze, painted to show a large, green oak tree shading the weary traveler.

Ex-trapper Thomas Eddie had purchased the tavern in November 1827, a man more than capable of handling the thirsty, noisy army of sorts that gathered there anytime day or night. Here Eddie wandered from table to table, talking with the trappers and traders who conducted much of their business over the mugs of alcohol. Here too, flocked the U.S. Army officers and farmers, store clerks and blacksmiths, along with an occasional party of Frenchmen. From group to group, Eddie flitted about this place, nervously awaiting the customary brawl that would break out sooner or later every night. Wanderers pushing through St. Louis often took a small room above the tavern from Eddie, at the rate of $3.50 a week, which included board, meals served hot and hearty by some buxom, fair-skinned lass with an ample smile for every man.

Mordecai and Josiah wove through the maze of tables, sitting down at the end of one long table by the large stone fireplace. A happy lass came over to take their order, and Josiah was not able to take his eyes off the soft charms that strained against the white chemise above her tightly laced bodice. When she returned with two mugs, she smiled down at him with her eyes, not just with her fresh, unpainted lips. The two men sat quietly for a while, watching and listening to the mountaineers down the table from them.

This was his favorite tavern, for he loved to come to the Green Tree for its own very personal atmosphere. The brawls and fights here were not as serious as in many of the city's grog shops, for most were good-natured bouts between friends who merely wished to settle an argument about a river, or a tribe, or a squaw with some fun that would liven the whole place up. For the most part, the thieves, thugs, and gamesters stayed away from the taverns where mountain men congregated. What foolish few showed up, in hopes of some easy money, more often than not were thrown out the rear door into the wagon yard after having their heads pounded on by a mountaineer, full of the cheap but potent alcohol and ready for a St. Louie spree. More often they would be gamesters, trying to ease away a few coins from the trapper's purse with a game of chance; the thieves that hung around the levee taverns did not come to the Green Tree, not willing to risk the certain drubbing they would suffer if they tried to take the whole purse from the buckskinners back from the mountains.

These were the men the two friends listened to that evening, men recently from the icy streams of the high country, having made it to St. Louis with a few seasons' catch that put coins into their purses, anxious for women and whiskey, a spree, and a song or two. Most meant no man harm—but if trouble ever came their way at the Green Tree, they were not ones to back off.

"Three foofaraw Frenchies jest rode up," one of the trappers told his comrades at the table as he put refilled mugs down before them. Mordecai looked over at the door, seeing the Frenchmen tying their horses up outside, illuminated in the pale glow of the tarred torches hung from brackets out front. He watched them over Josiah's shoulder as they entered the milling tavern, then stood looking over the room. Now and then a customer would look up from his drink or card game to give the recent arrivals a once-over, then return to his dinner, drink, or yarning. Mordecai could see through the room's smoky atmosphere that these were well-bred Frenchmen, dressed as they were. He knew instinctively that these men had not come to the tavern to drink. He knew they had come on business.

They did not go to the counter to order, but continued to stand by the door, looking over the crowded room, looking at all in the place without moving. One of them tapped another on the shoulder, pointing Josiah out, and the three moved through the tables toward the two men seated near the fireplace. Mordecai watched the trio approach, feeling a strange lump growing steadily in the pit of his stomach.

They stopped at the end of the long table where Josiah sat looking into the fire, one man in front, his two companions flanking behind, all disdaining to be too close to the men in greasy buckskins around them, each of the trio bold and haughty as he looked down at Josiah.

"Monsieur Paddock," one finally addressed Josiah, who looked up at the men around him only then, "I am Henri LeClerc. We were told we might find you here," he said, lifting his head to scan the room with a thin look of contempt.

Josiah eased back on his stool, relaxed as he stared briefly at each of the two behind LeClerc, then took another drink from his mug. Setting it down, he looked back at the Frenchman. "What can I do for you?"

LeClerc pulled some fine, soft riding gloves from his hands. "Is not what you can do for me. Is what I can do for you, Monsieur Paddock. We are both acquainted with Mademoiselle Angelique Saucier." He paused to roll the gloves up in his left hand. "Is about her I wish to speak with you."

Josiah took in a short breath of air, pushed himself back a little further from the table so that he could sit flatfooted, not locked under the edge of the table.

"What 'bout Angelique? You related to her some way?" Josiah cradled the large pewter mug between his two hands as it sat on the table.

"Non, not as yet, Monsieur. Mais—but I will be within the space of a few weeks. We are to be married, in la cathedrale, next month."

Paddock felt his heart suddenly starting to pound more loudly now. He readjusted himself on the short stool. The room seemed to be closing in around him. He was beginning to feel too warm, too close to the huge fireplace.

"I spoke with Angelique myself 'bout marryin'. She never told me yes—but she never said no. There must be some mistake, monsur," he spoke, knowing his reply was far from the truth. "Think you must have the wrong girl . . ."

"Non, there is no meestake. Only a simpleton could have believed the girl." He seemed to muse for a fleeting moment. "Ah, she plays with hearts, my young friend—and she has toyed with yours. Angelique was the one who told I might find you here," he paused, "among the rats of the river swamp."

"Now wait jest a minute, ye fancy ruffled. . . ." Mordecai retorted, rising to answer LeClerc's condemnation, but Josiah firmly pushed his friend down onto the stool again.

"Hold it! Mordecai, hold it!" Josiah sat back down himself, looking across the table at his friend. "The man came here to talk with me." Then looking back at LeClerc, said, "Angelique sent you to talk with me, right? To tell me this?"

"Oui. And to say that you are not to see her again . . ." He droned on, but most of it Josiah did not hear. The pounding was loud at his temples now. He began to shake his head slowly from side to side in gnawing disbelief. As LeClerc was continuing his speech, listing ultimatums, Paddock suddenly pushed up from the stool, knocking it back across the hearth toward the fire, throwing the contents of his mug into the Frenchman's face.

Around them the room got quiet, as if someone had stopped the world and all were straining to hear what was taking place between the two men. The moment that Henri raised his hand to wipe his face, Mordecai stood up to try to catch Josiah, who lunged at the startled Frenchman. LeClerc's two friends roughly pushed Paddock away, as some buckskinned mountaineers who had been within earshot of it all pulled Josiah back.

"Easy, easy, frien'. The Frenchies got ye outnumbered this go-round." Paddock regained his balance, standing between two trappers who slowly released his arms. He glared at Henri, so overwhelmed with hate that he was imprisoned on the spot, unable to move.

LeClerc removed from his sleeve a handkerchief, with which he mopped his face and the front of his short-waisted riding coat. Very calmly, deliberately, he began to speak, still looking at his dripping coat.

"You are an animal, Monsieur. I will not be dirtied by fighting you with my hands." Josiah shook with tremors of rage that rumbled low in his bowels. "But, I will meet you tomorrow, as the sun rises, on the island in the river. There will we fight like gentlemen, with the peestols, if the Amereecan is one who is ready to die like a man." He turned to leave, followed by the two companions who occasionally looked about them at the men in the room.

Josiah froze almost motionless, fingering the handle on the small knife stuck in his belt, watching the doorway even after the three men had ridden away.

"Pay 'em no mind, son. Them Frenchies still thinkin' they own the river, St. Louie, an' alla women an' whiskeys ter boot. Give 'em no heed—French as made this'r town, but Amer'cans as made 'er what she be today," advised one of the mountaineers at his side.

"Pay ye Pheneas no mind, boy!" injected the other man in buckskin. "Been me, I'd raised ha'r, I would, right hyar an' now! Woulda used my knife ter peel them buttons off'n that fancy ruffl't shirt that Frenchie was sportin'. Get yerself over to that island early, boy, afore sunup, an' give the bastard what'n he deserves," he counseled, as he lifted his cup to his lips, took a drink, then swiped at his dripping mustache with the back of a greasy sleeve. "'Sides, that way ye got him out'n yer ha'r, an' ye got the French gal fer yer own ter boot!"

"C'mon, now. Let me buy ye a swaller of Eddie's likker," Pheneas said quietly as he wrapped an arm around Josiah's shoulders.

But the young man shook his head from side to side slowly. "No. No thank you. Got somethin' to see to..."

"Course, son." The mountain man patted Josiah's shoulders a few times firmly, almost fatherly, then removed his hand to pull his drinking companion back to the fireplace.

Paddock's eyes would squint a little, then release and squint again, staring into the fire, yet not really seeing it.

Josiah started slowly to walk away, then stopped to turn around, looking back at Mordecai. "Got somethin' to see to, somethin' I gotta be doin' now." He then made his way through the milling tavern customers. The room was noisy once more, with a group of men playing Old Sledge, laughing and cursing loudly as they slammed their cards to the table, often upsetting their never empty mugs. At the door, Josiah didn't stop as he brushed by two men coming in, knocking one of them aside as he pushed himself into the cool, damp spring-night air.

He climbed up the long slope following the lane that reached out into the countryside on the outskirts of St. Louis, tracing the bluffs overlooking the river. On past several old French homes, surrounded by thick gardens, with their wide verandahs encircling the entire house, their old upright timbered walls dark in the mist-shrouded moonless night. Josiah entered through a heavy iron gate, crossing the dew-wet lawn to the porch of a limestone house. Furiously he banged on the door with both his fist and the iron knocker. A young maid answered the door.

"Monsieur Paddock..."

"I wanna see Angelique," he interrupted, looking over her shoulder down the hall. Eyes wide and startled, she let him in and directed him to one of the parlors off the hall. He waited several long minutes in the high-ceilinged room with rich mahogany furniture, a black walnut floor, couches of velvet, tables with coverlets of lace, and a delicate crystal chandelier overhead.

She came in without a word, standing at the door she closed behind her. From the middle of the room, he turned at the sound of its closing, seeing her in the faint light dressed in a white gown. This was the woman he loved deeply, her raven hair curled atop her head, hanging ringlets framing the pale skin that blushed over the cheeks. Her lips were dark red, like blood, he had often thought to himself. She did not move as he came over to her.

"Angelique?"

"You must go." She stepped away from him, moving gracefully behind one of the couches by the double door leading to the wide verandah.

"I won't go without you." He moved closer to her,

41

tentatively. "We'll go downriver. New Orleans, you'd like." He tried to hold her shoulders in his hands, but she pulled away. Her mood suddenly changed.

She laughed, throwing her head back, and turned to look into his face. "For what? To run off with a poor man? A man who will always live like some wild animal?" She laughed again, circling the couch, putting it between the two of them. "He will find you in New Orleans. He will find you wherever you will run!"

It was coming all too fast at him. He was trying to make sense out of what this beautiful coquette was telling him.

"What will you do? Be a pirate on the river? Or take to the seas to kill and steal?" Angelique folded her hands in front of her, arms hanging at her sides. "Non, Monsieur Paddock, I cannot go with you. Non. I *will* not go with you! You have nothing to offer me now, while Henri offers his family, his tradition, his money. Life with you would be the peasant for me. I do not want to become one of your Amereecan women, following her husband to the wilderness, dirty, and dressed in her homespun. Is that what you want for me, Monsieur Paddock?"

Angelique worked herself into a fit of hysterical laughter, mocking laughter. He came around the end of the couch, fires boiling deep within. "To think I...I ever felt...something for you!" Josiah grabbed her shoulders, trying to shake some sense into her, to shake the laughter out of her, or both. Frantically he clawed to hold the tops of her arms, to shut her up, to end that crazy, mocking laughter from her suddenly ugly contorted lips. She reached out to slap him, but he caught her wrist, squeezed it hard, then let go. Josiah wheeled around as the door opened. Monsieur Saucier, framed in a shaft of bright light, shot into the room from the hall.

"Get out! Get out of my house!" he bellowed at the young man.

Josiah fingered the handle of his knife tentatively, then decided against anything so direct. Through the French doors he was gone, into the night.

Outside the gate he stopped to hear again her hideous laughter, which only slowly began to fade from his ears when someone called out.

"Josiah, it's me." Mordecai emerged from the darkness of the trees bordering the wall. "Ye feel like finishin'

42

our spree now?" Josiah did not answer for a while, looking back at the house, deep in his own thoughts. "C'mon. I'll buy ye a few cups." He put his hand alongside Josiah's neck to pull him off the spot where it seemed his friend had taken root.

It was dark along the narrow streets of the city when they dropped into town. Josiah was lost in his own world on the way back, but Mordecai was on the lookout for the thugs and riffraff that plagued the dark byways after sundown. There was still no regular police force in the city. The streets were up for grabs, contested only by the strong of will against the roving bands of brigands. Those who spoke of the St. Louis nights laughed over their mugs, saying that "God would never cross the river!"

Back at the Green Tree Inn, Pheneas and his younger companion had left. The place was still noisy. They sat again by the fireplace, served by the girl with the smiling eyes. After a few silent moments of drawing on their mugs, Josiah raised his into the air, signaling the girl for another round. She refilled his mug, smiling more warmly this time with those fresh, smoky-green eyes. Josiah sat and drank, speechless, draining the mug quickly. Mordecai could see his friend was intent upon a stupor.

"After ye left, I heerd that a Captain Gantt is headin' toward the mountains in two days, on the twenty-fourth. They's sayin' he's got close ta seventy men; gonna head 'cross the wide open to reach the Rockies." Mordecai drew long on his mug, then continued "That's what we oughter do, Josiah. Let's put this town behind us, leave it far behind, an' head to them Rockies!"

Josiah didn't speak, staring into his mug.

"Ye been tellin' me often how ye liked it so up ta Fort Atkinson with Mr. Dougherty. Now we could go an' see them things ye heerd tell of for ourse'fs. What ye say, Josiah? Ye fer it?"

Paddock lifted his mug once more into the air. As the young woman was refilling it, she slipped her fingers around Josiah's to hold the mug. He looked again into her eyes, seeing something warm there now, something private. When she had left to serve other tables, Josiah looked back to Mordecai. "I'll have to sleep on it. Besides, I've somethin' to take care of tomorrow at daylight."

"Ah-h-h, you don' haf ta go out there. Cain't think of a man as would blame ye fer not goin'. Ye knows yer rifle

43

and knife well 'nough, but them pistols is 'nother thing again. Ye ever shot one of them fancy pistols, Josiah?"

"No sir, not as I can say..."

"They's somethin' differ'nt with 'em, an' thar's not a man as would blame ye fer not going out in the mornin'. Anyways, we could be gone with Gantt an' his men in two days, Monday we will, leavin' all this behind. C'mon, man! Say ye'll go an' we'll make it to the Rockies afore fall!"

"Mordecai," he spoke firmly, "you knowin' me as your best friend an' all, should know I ain't gonna back out on this'un. That son of a whore picked a fight with a Paddock, an' this man ain't gonna back away, tail tucked 'tween his legs."

Josiah emptied his cup and the girl was back again to refill it without his having to raise it. He watched her walk away, back to the counter to pick up some plates heaped with food, ordered by another table. Mordecai kept after him, "Ye cain't be doin' it fer Angelique, then..."

"Naw, ain't doin' it on her 'count. That bitch as strung me along good, then throws me out. 'Mademoiselle Saucier,' it was all the time'; highfalutin French she is. That whore played me such a fool for so long these months, me pantin' after her like some bitch in heat! Blind I was, not to see after all that time, ever' time I saw her, suckin' up to me the way she did, makin' a big show of her Amer'can caller round town an' all. I jest played the fool for her, I did, bein' blind to what she really had in mind. Ain't gonna be blind again." He raised his mug into the air. "Naw, Mordecai, ain't gonna do it on her 'count. Tomorrow mornin' is for Josiah."

The buxom maid came up to the end of the table beside Josiah, filling his mug from her pitcher. "That's not all I want, pretty lady." She looked up at him as she finished pouring. "But right now I want somethin' from the kitchen." He winked at her. "Bring me what's best of whatever's left in the pots. I got a hunger to fill." As she turned to go, Josiah remembered the pastries tucked in his shirt. Unbuttoning it most of the way down, he pulled the package out to lay it on the table before him.

When the young woman returned with a plate heaped with steaming beans and meat, a large chunk of bread stuffed on the side of the tin platter, Josiah handed her the package. "These are for us, but for later. Save 'em for when you get off work tonight. I'll wait for you out back in the wagon yard." The smile in her eyes and at the corners of her mouth grew gentle now, not hard or plastered on as it seemed to be for other customers. She can talk with them eyes, she can, he thought to himself as she went back to waiting on the thinning crowd. Josiah dove into the hot food, filling his happy grin with each dripping spoonful, his eyes chuckling along with Mordecai.

4

She led him up the narrow wooden steps to the second story balcony and entered a door that led down a short hall, only then turning to him, placing one finger lightly against his lips, asking him to be quiet. Closing the door behind him, Josiah suddenly felt himself getting warmer in the stuffy hallway that led past a few doors until she stopped to unlock hers. He felt light, as if, were he thrown from the roof, he would float softly to the ground. Until now the alcohol had yet to go to his head. Mordecai had marveled that Josiah was not a raving lunatic by the time they parted at the tavern, as many times as Josiah had his mug refilled during the late evening. Before he went his way, Mordecai had instructed him where they should meet on the levee in the morning, where his employer had a skiff they would use tied up along the river.

Josiah felt the first licks of hazy numbness creeping across his forehead, the first sign of drunkenness he always got after a bout with the cups. Beads of sweat began to break out over his brows. Standing in the hall beside the woman, the only thing he wanted right then was to get the door open—just lie down on her bed for a few moments to settle the dust in his mind. The food helped absorb some of the alcohol; he was thankful for that as he leaned back against the wall next to her door, easing his head back and slowly dropping his eyelids.

She called to him in a whisper that seemed to float up to Josiah from out there, somewhere. Then she touched his arm lightly. He opened his eyes, saw the door was open, and slipped past her into the room. It was small, much like his own. He looked around, letting his eyes grow accustomed to the darkness. On the opposite side of the room away from the bed, the one, lonely window stood partly open, the light cotton curtains lifting gently with each new breeze. Josiah felt cooler, better here in the darkness as he went over to the window to look out on the levee and the river. Up to his nose came the musky fragrance of the waters flowing by to the sea. Its damp coolness drifted past him to fill the whole room as he turned around to move back toward the bed. He sat on it first, feeling its welcome softness swallowing him up as he lay back.

Some of the light fuzzy cobwebs seemed to disappear from his forehead as he loosed some more muscles. She pulled off his boots, then slid up beside him, sitting on the edge of the bed, unbuttoning his shirt. Her fingers wandered across his chest, like little padding feet moving through the thick, curly hair. She pulled the shirt all the way off. He opened his eyes as she bent over him to brush her lips against his only briefly. Josiah began to reach for her as she pulled away from the bed, crossing the room to a small wooden chest. He closed his eyes once more. The girl lighted a large candle atop the chest, its glow warm and feathery, like a veil touching only the corner of the room where he lay. Eyes closed, he did not notice, his mind gradually emptying of everything past, present, and future, feeling only the softness beneath him, the musky breeze brushing against his cheek and bare chest.

Just at the edge of his mind, he could hear her padding across the room like a cat. He was beginning to deepen into sleep as he heard her come to the other side of the bed. She slowly pulled the blankets and quilt back to the foot of the bed where she stuffed them under his legs. Then he felt her weight as she crawled onto the bed, sliding over to lie against him. On one side of his chest, he began to feel the heaviness of one of her breasts. He lay there, coming back to full consciousness with his eyes still closed, absorbing the coolness of the small room about him. Josiah concentrated, for a moment letting his mind and body focus on his skin where her breast lay. He moved his left arm to cradle her head. She snuggled closer to him.

With his left hand, he began softly to run his fingers over the smooth skin on her back. She took in a deep breath, then let it out slowly. Her fingers sought out the muscles across his chest and shoulders, kneading them with slow, tiny movements as if feeling the texture of a piece of cloth, then smoothing the area she had rubbed with fingers flat and outstretched. He lay for a long time, enjoying the feathery massage as her fingers wandered ever so gently lower and lower until she was playing across the tight muscles of his upper abdomen. Each time she brought her touch across the skin, he could feel it quiver and jump. Josiah knew she could feel it too. She traced nonsense patterns around his navel, twisting the little hairs between her fingers, then returned to running the tips of fingers across his belly.

The stirring submerged in his loins began. It started off softly, slowly rumbling. Josiah lay there unmoving as she pushed against him even more tightly, his eyes still closed. Part of his body was all so alive, feeling her move over the skin stretched and taut across his flat belly, while the other half of his body and mind now studied each little movement his penis made as it began to throb and harden between his legs. For long, delicious moments he savored the approach of oncoming pleasure, enjoying each second privately with himself as his penis grew. Then he rolled away from her to rise off the bed, looking down at her in the thin veil of yellow candlelight. He kept his eyes on her, scanning the woman's body as he unbuckled his belt, released the buttons on his fly, and slid the trousers over his feet. Undoing two buttons on his underwear, Josiah slipped out of the last of his clothes, leaving them in a heap on the floor by the bed as he lay back beside her.

He rolled onto his left side, gathering her head and shoulders into his left arm, pulling her close to him once more. She answered him, rolling on her side to face him, her left hand wandering down his chest, across his stomach that jumped eagerly with her touch, then her fingers encircled his penis delicately. He sucked in a quick breath with a sudden tingling rush of sensation, feeling that his body was growing warmer with every pounding of his heart. He could look down in the dim light to see one of her breasts fully. Josiah cupped his hand around it and kneaded the flesh gently, working up to the nipple. The breast, large, but not flabby, excited him as he put his hand in the crevice between the two soft mounds. She was big-boned, and carried the breasts well now, but he mused how they might look in ten years. He recalled an Osage woman in her middle years, with pendulous breasts, his mind picturing also how older St. Louis women bound themselves with tight girdles laced just below their breasts to push them up and out after they had lost their youthful tone. But now he was feeling hers, breasts firm in their softness, nipples erect beneath his touch.

Josiah moved his hand down the shoulder and top of the arm that held him lightly between his thighs. Across her small, round buttocks he rubbed and kneaded, gently at first, then with more urgency as she began to stroke slowly and evenly on his member. He brought his hand suddenly around her hip and into the hair at the top of her mound. From her mouth crept a low cry, as if it were caught deep within her throat, straining to break free. He parted the skin that lay over her treasure, moving a finger gently up and down within the parted folds.

"Please," she raised her head a little so that she could look into his face. "Please now," as her head dropped back onto his shoulder. Her whispered purring came more evenly but deeper now as he began to rub more quickly. She squirmed over him as his lips sought hers. He found them soft, thick, and moist. When she turned her face away to run her lips across his shoulder, he could smell the damp muskiness of her hair. She had released the one braid she wore, her long hair spreading over the side of his face. He could see across her forehead and around the sides of her face the hair stuck wet and damp. She bit lightly where his shoulder and neck met.

"I don't even know your name," he thought he said, rolling her over onto her back, looking down into her face for a moment before mounting. Her thighs opened a little more as she pushed her hips up to meet him.

She was sleeping now. He lay there on his back, the woman cradled up against him like a young child, trying to figure out what time it must be. Josiah rolled his head slightly to the right, looking at the window, through the dancing curtains, out into a starless, overcast night. His breathing was slow and deep as he stared at the window overlooking the river. The candle was burning low, casting only a dancing circle of light against the wall at the middle of the room. He watched the flame flicker, its glow fluttering in the soft breeze, until it died slowly and the room was filled with a heavy gray once more.

She turned away from him in her sleep, rolling onto her side. He waited while her breathing became more relaxed again, gently removing his arm from beneath her neck. Josiah rose slowly from the edge of the bed and dressed, finally buttoning the shirt she had draped over the back of the room's only chair. He returned to the side of the bed to pull the blankets up over her folded arms, looking down one last time at the flesh that sloped smoothly from her shoulders to the tops of her breasts peeking out from beneath the arm she had curled against her.

He moved across the room quietly to the door, stopping suddenly as he caught his smoky reflection in the faded mirror over the wooden chest. Josiah stood looking at himself in the dim light, measuring the image reflected there, as one would size up an opponent. He looked away, his eyes moving down to the top of the chest. Raising his hand, he reached out to touch the newsprint-wrapped bundle lying there, opening it and spreading the paper out to look at the two small pastry loaves. Josiah looked up again at the mirror, then turned to glance back at the young woman, her hair spread across the pillow where he had been. By the opened package, she had put the long red ribbon she braided in her hair. He picked it up, weaving it briefly between his fingers before putting it inside his shirt, and opened the door.

Stepping out into the night air, he moved down the steps, stopping at the street to turn his collar against the damp chill. He started to his left, walking down the narrow street toward the oldest part of the city. From a few blocks away came the twanging notes of someone attempting to play a banjo. He continued closer to the sound as he heard someone bellowing out an Indian chant that started low, then grew high-pitched, "Ho-o-o-yi-yi-yi-yi-yi! Ho-o-o-yi-yi-yi-yi-yi!" Josiah turned the corner as a harmonica joined in with the banjo and singer.

At the door of the Rocky Mountain House, he stopped outside a moment, listening to the mountain man roar his

Indian song with the fullness of his lungs, while the banjo picker and harmonica man attempted to follow along. Josiah opened the door and went to the bar. This tavern was another favorite of the mountaineers, he thought to himself after ordering a mug.

Leaning back against the counter, he watched two buckskinned trappers dancing amid tables pushed against the walls. While they were attempting to simulate the pattern of some Indian dance in their stupor, one of the men would grab the other to spin around and around as his partner. It was quite a scene, the banjo picker stomping his foot on the wooden floor in time with his own rhythm, the harmonica player dancing here and there around the fringes of the men watching the two dancers, everyone clapping and adding their own blood-lust Indian war whoops from time to time.

Josiah finished his mug and set it back on the bar. The tavernkeeper tapped the side of his arm, "Wanna 'nother?"

"Naw." Then he thought a moment. "But get me a bottle of that stuff, will you?" He paid for it, pausing at the door to watch the dancers for a moment, then plunged into the narrow backstreets of the city. He stuffed the bottle into the waistband of his pants and pulled his coat tighter around him, heading down to the levee.

Josiah wandered along the street that ran parallel to the levee, stopping short by the body of the dead dog. It still lay where he had last seen it. He had not been sure in the dark just what it was, but knelt down to touch the body, feeling the rigor in the dead animal's muscles. Josiah scratched between its ears a couple of times, then rose to his feet. Pulling the bottle from inside his coat, he yanked the cork from its neck, holding the bottle out at arm's length.

"Here's to you, friend. You deserve better'n this. Hope they do better for me when I'm gone, ol' boy. Ain't no way to treat a friend. Ain't . . . Well, here's hopin' they don't treat me like they done you, leavin' you out for the rats to gnaw on. Take my best with you wherevers you gone." He brought the bottle to his lips and poured the diluted alcohol down his throat. He felt it warm his stomach, taking another slug from the bottle as he walked a few steps away to sit and hang his legs over the levee, the river running persistently beneath his boots on its trip south.

He twisted around, holding the bottle aloft as if to present another toast to the dog, then turned back to watch the river flow by. Josiah stuffed one hand into his coat after readjusting the collar up around his ears, the hand with the bottle pulled tight against his belly. The waves lapped and rolled against the levee where he sat. It made him dizzy to watch each muddy crest that went by below his boots. He took another drink, then looked out over the expanse of the river.

In the early-summer warmth of June 1809 Josiah's father, Ezra Paddock, pulled away from St. Louis, headed upriver with Manuel Lisa's 350 men, half of whom were Americans, the rest a mixture of French-Canadians and Creoles. Paddock signed on in the hope of making a good killing quickly on the upper river, then to return home to his young wife, Sarah, who waved goodbye to her husband from the levee, and who was beginning to show signs of new life in her womb.

During the ordeal of pulling the barges upriver, Ezra kept reminding himself that he was doing this for Sarah and the child: by day wading through the thick brush along the banks of the river, soft mud sucking at his boots with every step as he hunched forward pulling on the rope strung out behind the men, each one struggling to haul the barges north against the river's current. At night he lay restless, unable to sleep many times, thinking of the child that would be born before his return to St. Louis. But he would return rich, he kept telling himself, not to be a farmer scratching at the soil any longer. Perhaps he could buy into a small shop, he dreamed. Then, yes, then he could do all he wanted to do for Sarah, for Sarah and their child.

The Americans pulling the barges north for Lisa were to be on their own hook once they arrived at the trapping grounds near the mountains. It was the promise of hope Ezra had been waiting for, the Company agreeing to subsist him and the other trappers-to-be on the trip upriver. In turn, the men would work cordelling the boats against the Missouri's muddy current. With each step closer to the mountains, his face swollen with the bites of mosquitoes and flies, his arms and shoulders sunburned through the rips in the worn fabric of his shirt, Ezra Paddock kept telling himself what one season in the mountains could mean to his family. At the headwaters Lisa would furnish them each with a rifle, lead, powder and, six good beaver traps, along with the service of four of the hired French hands for every American, to be under that one man's command for a period of three years. What would his child look like when he finally made it home, he mused that day, forming pictures in his mind to numb the taut, tortured muscles. Sarah wanted a girl, but he wanted their first to be a boy. Extra pushed himself through each day of agony, every step bringing him closer to the mountains, closer to his fortune, closer once again to his little family.

By the time the men had reached the Mandan villages, most of the Americans had turned around, hoping to make it back to St. Louis on foot. They had for many weeks been living on boiled corn, Lisa not allowing the Americans to eat even the boiled pork kept in small, wooden kegs. Pulling the barges twelve to fourteen hours a day, on a diet of nothing more than the corn and what little game the inexperienced hunters would bring in now and then, didn't put meat and muscle on a man's bones. Each morning's roll call would find more men gone, deserting in the night. Ezra would bow his head, telling himself to go on, to keep going as the ranks thinned. He had come this far, and he would go all the way. He was working on a dream, he told himself, a dream he was making come true.

Things would be better when they started trapping, he told the others each night around a small fire on the sandy beach, things would be a lot better when they started pulling beaver out of the streams. Paddock rallied many a man's hopes during the trip west from the Mandans. His optimism was contagious, and he had a way of smiling when his name was called out each morning in the roll call before the sun rose, the Spanish trader, Lisa, giving each man his assigned position for the day on the cordell. On he would push day after day that summer and into the fall, the briny sweat from his brow dripping into his eyes with a stinging blaze that made it hard to see. He could not take his hands from the rope to wipe his forehead and eyes, but it did not matter. Ezra's feet were his eyes, with each step feeling their way along through the mud, sometimes stumbling over a hidden snag moored up against the brush along the bank. But he would rise again and again, cooled by the water that gave him temporary relief from the insects, to smile at the men behind him as the mud ran off his head and shoulders, and to join his muscles with theirs in their grueling task.

On to Manuel's Fort at the mouth of the Bighorn, built in November 1807, they pulled. One of Lisa's men, Andrew Henry, would lead the detachment of Americans farther into the mountains, west to the Three Forks of the Missouri in the spring. But now, by the fall of November snows, the men lay snugly back in Lisa's Fort, thinking of the one they were to build in the months to come, a fort near the spot where the three rivers join, tumbling together to begin the Missouri's race to the sea. Ezra counted the days and weeks and months in his head each night, listening to the wind howl and pound outside the walls. It will be soon, he thought, his mind's eye once again beholding his wife standing on the levee.

Sarah had a long and difficult labor that November of 1809. Her older sister, Ruth, helped with the delivery after twenty-eight hours of ordeal, able to do nothing more during it all than keep cool cloths on Sarah's forehead, soothing her with soft words, letting her sister grip her hand white-knuckle tight with each painful contraction. Ruth had taken in the young mother-to-be when Ezra headed upriver, and now she delivered the child grown from his seed, brought forth from Sarah's womb.

In a delirium, following the long ordeal, Sarah asked her sister weakly, "Is, is it a girl?" when she heard the child cry.

"It's a boy, Sarah, a boy."

"Thank you, Lord," she said repeating it several times, softer and softer each time, until she fell into a deep sleep for many hours. The baby slept by his mother for a long time too.

By the end of March, Henry's men were heading closer to the mountains, and by early April they had built their tiny fort between the Madison and Jefferson rivers.

On April 12, 1810, Sarah Paddock marked her son's five-month birthday with her sister's family.

Far away from the young mother and child, up near the Three Forks of the Missouri on a nameless little stream, a group of five Americans began to stretch out along the banks to set their traps.

Sarah had named the child Josiah, a name she had long favored out of the Bible verses read to her as a child.

The Americans never saw them coming, never heard a sound until the Blackfoot war party was on top of them.

Everyone agreed that the boy favored his mother more than Ezra. Sarah thought about what her husband would say when he saw his son for the first time.

Five bodies lay in the early-morning sun, their white, bare flesh turning red throughout the day as the sun beat down on them. Ants collected quickly to crawl over and into the bloody, gaping wounds on the back of each man's head where flesh had been torn from skull.

After the little party with Ruth and her children, Sarah put the baby to bed for his afternoon nap in her room, then lay down on the bed to rest through the quiet of the middle of the day.

A hawk descended to roost briefly in a tree overlooking the scene of the skirmish, then fluttered away in search of a meal, and all was quiet once more along the stream.

The next day Sarah felt like helping her sister with the planting of the family garden, both women struggling with hoes and rakes at the rich, dark soil, turning it over and over before dropping the seeds beneath the folds of earth.

That day, too, sod was turned by the men who had found the stripped and mutilated bodies of their companions, hastily burying the stinking remains as best they could, each knowing the wolves would have the bodies back up within the week.

It brought tears to Sarah's eyes when she watched her son crawl through the garden along after her as she tilled the soil.

John Dougherty pushed stinging tears back as quickly as they came, watching a friend wrapped in a heavy blanket lowered into a shallow grave.

That night, Sarah read to herself and the sleeping baby, alone in their room in the cabin, able to find some comfort from her loneliness in the words of the New Testament.

Near the Three Forks, men had decided to head downriver, abandoning their new fort.

By August 1810, Dougherty had arrived back in St.

Louis, his first task being to visit Sarah Paddock. All the way from the upper Missouri, the man had gone over and over what he would say to her, forming the sentences carefully, rehearsing the lines every day until he felt he had it right. Day and night blended together in a hot, sticky blur: each day he would repeat his lines to himself as he would to Sarah, each night he tried to picture how she and the child would look from Ezra's constant chatter about his growing family.

He knocked on the door of the settler's cabin, hoping this would be the end of the search begun in St. Louis. It opened, framing a full-bodied woman he guessed to be in her early thirties.

"Sarah, Sarah Paddock?" he pulled his hat from his head.

"No," the full-faced woman said to him, then turned to call into the room, "Sarah, a man's at the door to see you." She left Dougherty standing outside as another woman approached out of the dim light of the cabin. He felt the worms squirming around inside his guts once more, the worms he had first felt when they had begun hurriedly to throw clods of dirt into Ezra's shallow earthen tomb.

The woman squinted up at Dougherty in the bright light of early afternoon. He felt hot, suddenly, without his hat to cover the back of his neck. The worms twisted around some more.

"Yes?"

"Are you Sarah Paddock, ma'am?" he started, as he had rehearsed so many times before. He watched her young, bright eyes fall and rise over him one time before she answered.

"Yes. I am that." Her eyes met his only for an instant, then looked down at the hat he held in front of him with both hands, running his fingers back and forth over the edge of the brim. "Why is it that you have sought me out?" she asked in a tongue thick with some heritage he tried to put his finger on as she spoke her few words. He had to begin.

"Ma'am, my name's Dougherty. John Dougherty, ma'am..." As he dropped his eyes from the questions in hers, he saw the child. The baby had crawled after his mother, now coming around the edge of Sarah's dress as it dragged the floor. The little boy stopped at the edge of

55

the door, looking up at the tall stranger, then put a tiny hand out to slap playfully at the toe of Dougherty's dusty boot. The worms tumbled and gnawed, in a fitful rage now. He forgot what he had practiced to say for so long, his mind burning hot in the sun.

"Josiah, you lil' piglet, now you know better'n that." She picked the little boy up, placing him at her side in her arms, his little legs straddling her hip. "Yes, Mr. Dougherty?"

"Ma'am . . ." The worms bit and chewed around inside him. "C-could I get a drink of water from ye, right off?" He mopped his brow with the back of his hand.

"Why, yessir. Jes' a minute." Sarah took the child with her as she dropped back into the darkness of the cabin interior. He stood outside the door, staring after her, thinking how unlike what he had pictured her she really was. He tried to pull forward the words he had rehearsed, but they would not come. She was not as pretty as he had thought her to be all those past months, as pretty as Ezra had led him and the others to believe. Why couldn't he remember his speech, he asked himself. She wasn't homely, just plain, looking drawn and tired in the shadow of the cabin door, strands of brown hair plastered wetly to her forehead and the sides of her cheeks. Where were the words?

Sarah returned to the door with a large tin cup, alone, without the child. He drank the cool water slowly, buying the seconds while he could. Finished, he handed the cup back to her and tried once more.

"Mrs. Paddock, I knew your husband on the upper river. We was good friends all the way up." Her eyes stayed on his, little wrinkles appearing between her brows. He cleared his throat, looking down at the toes of his boots, then back up into her eyes to continue. "Ezra was as good a man as I ever knowed, Mrs. Paddock." It was coming hard, so hard, but he pushed forward, as he had learned to keep pushing forward behind Ezra Paddock on the trip north. "He was the kind of man, that, wal', he kept a lot of us goin' when things seemed the worst, ye know? Ezra could pound his way through that river brush all day long, that big rope cutting into the top of his shoulder an' all, an' he could pull up at night to make camp, wearin' the bigges' smile ye ever saw. Ezra was some man, he was." He stopped, his mouth frozen, for the last had rolled out too quickly. Her eyes darted back and forth at his, not steady as they had been before, but searching out more of what lay behind his.

"Mrs. Paddock, your husband was kilt by Injuns, Blackfeets, last April, up the river," he got out, then watched her face. The expression was unchanged except that below her eyes the skin sagged almost imperceptibly. "We buried him an' t'others up thar where they was kilt. A man as even knowed a little verse from the Bible said it over the graves." Dougherty looked down to see her hands gently wringing one of the folds of her dress near her waist, twisting it into a roll then releasing it, over and over.

"Didn' bring none of his things back with us. The Injuns, they took ever'thin' off the bodies." He fought the feeling high in his throat, the gagging lump that told him he would cry, and struggled to swallow it back down for a while. "So s-sorry, Mrs. Paddock." John dropped his head finally to stare at his boots again for a moment: then, "If'n thar's ever a thing," he looked back up at her face, "anythin' at t'all, I wanna help, ma'am. Ezra Paddock was one of the best men I will ever know in this life, an' the next. I jest wanted ye to know how I felt."

"Thank you, Mr. Do . . ."

"Dougherty, ma'am. John Dougherty."

"Thank you, Mr. Dougherty. You have been very kind to come out of your way to seek me out, to tell me this. Thank you."

He started to go, but turned around to face her again, "Please, ma'am. Jest want ye to remember if'n thar's anythin' John Dougherty can do for Ezra Paddock's fam'ly, you holler, hear?" She nodded her head up and down silently. He turned from her then and got aboard his horse. John twisted to the side in the saddle as he started down the road, looking back to see her still standing in the doorway, leaning against the door frame now, looking off into the miles of forested wilderness that yawned away from the cabin.

He had long been gone down the road that wound its way south through the trees toward St. Louis when she finally moved from where he last saw her. Sarah had been unable to move, her body seeming to be some heavy machine that simply refused to heed her commands. She stood by the door, watching the afternoon sun play its changing intensity of light on the trees surrounding the cabin, undisturbed and alone as the time crawled by, for the family was in the garden out back, unaware that the woman still stood in the doorway, eyes fixed on some distant spirit that lay hidden beyond the shimmering horizon.

Finally, the young woman turned around in the open doorway. Slowly, she took small, inching steps, as if struggling with a heavy anchor that held her bound to the spot, an anchor tied to every muscle on her thin frame. Sarah reached behind her to close the door once inside the cabin, to shut out the softening glow of late-afternoon sunlight, to close out that world beyond the door that was unforgiving of a dreamer's innocence. Leaning back against the heavy wooden planks, she welcomed the cool and dark, thinking how like herself Lazarus would have felt in his own cool and dark, until commanded to rise and walk again. Her legs sagged, fatigued to the breaking point by the weight of the anchor she had pulled this far. As her knees began to buckle, Sarah felt as if she were becoming smaller, hopelessly smaller. She fought against the persistent weight of the cool and dark that pushed her down, the back of one shoulder against the door as she crumpled to the floor. Tiny, tiny, she felt, drawing her legs close up to her body, measuring the great burden that surrounded her in the cool and dark. She drew her legs up tighter to her chest as the dry, parched agony began to crack and fester within her core, spreading slowly its destruction through her body until she could fight the clawing fingers of despair no longer.

Ruth found her sister sometime later, Sarah's body racked with volcanic sobbing long after there were no tears left. Her body still shook with tremors of cold deep within as Ruth carried the young woman to bed. She lay on her side, legs drawn up fetally as Ruth pulled the quilts over her shoulders, still quaking with the shock waves from her battle with that last, bright, small light within her soul that refused to go out, like a tiny candle that kept lighted the way back should she choose to follow.

John Dougherty could not deny the spirit. He led a fur brigade north from St. Louis for Lisa the next spring, not returning until August 1812. From time to time that winter, the man battled the icy tongues of wind-driven sleet to visit Sarah and the young boy. Back again and again he would plunge into the mountains each trading season, always returning to make good his pilgrimage to the little family during the next few years.

By 1818 Sarah had moved into the growing city, seeking not only a job for herself but schooling for her son. She found employment as a clerk in a small shop, the owner a widower who let Sarah and the child use a small room above the store as their own. The boy grew quickly, and as the months flew by his face resembled more and more his mother's, soft and plain. Ezra's face had been handsome in a rugged way, its lines sharp and chiseled as if out of stone. But the boy's was not a handsome face, plain yet softened to accent the fires smoldering behind the eyes. He played with others close to the levee, learning rapidly that his companions respected his friendship. Often were the times when another group of older, bigger boys would bully Josiah's small circle of friends. Into the melee Sarah's son would descend, having learned that the power in his legs which gave thunder to his kicks was becoming a strength with which foes would have to reckon. His young playmates invented games for the boy to play, sport that Josiah would practice as the others held pieces of lumber over their heads for him to reach with the leaping explosion of his legs.

In 1819 Dougherty became deputy Indian agent and the primary interpreter under Benjamin O'Fallon, and was based at Fort Atkinson, which sat atop Council Bluffs, overlooking the river north of St. Louis. The following spring he returned to the city, responding to a letter sent to him by Sarah. The shopowner had proposed marriage. Josiah chose to keep Paddock as his name, rather than assume his stepfather's. John Dougherty took the boy north with him on his return to Council Bluffs, so that Sarah and her new husband could enjoy a summer of honeymoon alone in her new home among the rooms at the rear of the store.

During the next five years, Josiah would accompany Dougherty north to the fort in the spring, returning to St. Louis in the early fall as the man brought in the summer's trade in furs, always anxious with the impatience of youth as the winter crept by so that he might once again renew the cycle. Those summers were bright, fleeting moments for the boy: mornings filled with hunting alongside Dougherty and learning to handle well the long rifle, afternoons of practice in knife throwing taught by the colorful voyageurs and hired men who lounged about the post, evenings spent in rapt attention to the bawdy, bloody yarns spun by those in from the streams to the west. Three days after his arrival at the fort in the spring of 1824, Josiah witnessed a loud, profane argument between the U.S. Army commander at the post and a scarred, grizzly bearded older man who appeared at the gates. Josiah joined in the knot of spectators surrounding the two men that evening, asking Dougherty who the old trapper was.

"Graybeard, Ol' Graybeard they calls 'im on the up-river," he replied, only half intent on the dispatch he was writing for O'Fallon. "That's a man as was hugged and fotched horrible by a she-bear grizzly with cubs up to the Grand River last y'ar. He was dyin', but not dead yet, while his friends left 'im for the buzzards. Glass." John looked up from his papers to stare past Josiah to the door. "Glass. That's a man as lived on hate for long months, he did, crawlin' down to Fort Kioway, feedin' mos'ly on the thought of drawin' blood from them that left 'im for dead. He swore he'd wear the skelps of the bastards that pulled out on 'im." He now looked over at the young man. "One of 'em's here at this fort, Josiah; joint the army, he did."

"Were it the colonel, the one the ol' man were argeein' with?"

"Naw, naw. The colonel was jest the one as had to tell the man as Graybeard wanted was now on the army payroll, an' if the ol' man kilt a army employee, he'd be hung within a day. Naw, the one as the ol' man wants is Fitzgerald, that quiet one as keeps to himse'f mos'ly. Made the ol' man mad, sure 'nough, didn't it?"

"For 'while, thought he was 'bout to take the whole post on one by one jest so's he could end up with who he wanted!" Josiah turned to leave.

"Boy, get ye that ol' man to tell his story. A big yarn it be, bigger sure than thems ye heerd afore, but his'n is a tale as ye could lay your pack an' plunder to, for true it be."

Josiah found that the old man had pulled out before sunrise the next morning, leaving nothing behind but the questions in a young man's heart, questions that hung on him like some strange itch needing to be scratched.

The following summer Josiah finished his formal schooling at the age of fifteen. He took employment with the *St.*

Louis Enquirer, running errands and doing odd jobs for the paper's owner-editor, Charles Keemle, who had recently bought out Thomas Hart Benton. Keemle admired the youth's fire and ambition, hoping to see to it that Josiah was nurtured and brought along to become a newspaperman.

The winter of 1826–27 roared in cold and damp. Sarah was taken that year with pneumonia, Josiah having helplessly to watch as his mother's thin frame wasted away through the weeks. He wrote to Dougherty, telling in simple words of Sarah's passing from this life, of her clutching the frazzled, worn Bible to her breast through the last few days. John made the trip south to the city, through the icy blasts that drove up and down, in and around, tearing at the clothing Dougherty fought to wrap warmly about him. Josiah's stepfather had the woman buried in the finest funeral he and Dougherty could provide.

The young man grew restless in his stepfather's home, uneasy and filled with a sense of incompleteness. They argued often and loudly through the next long months, until Josiah finally moved out. He took a room at Charles Keemle's new *St. Louis Beacon* at the editor's suggestion, as the young man had become more and more despondent as the weeks went by.

Benjamin O'Fallon had felt the icy hand of pneumonia that cold, damp winter too. Yet he survived, eventually having to admit that his health would not permit his continuing as agent. With O'Fallon's retirement, Dougherty was selected to continue the work at Council Bluffs, moving onto Fort Leavenworth when the army abandoned the cantonment at Fort Atkinson. In November 1823 John had married Mary Hertzog, who steadfastly refused to join her husband in the north until Dougherty moved to Leavenworth to become upper Missouri agent.

The gray, creeping illness tapped many shoulders around Josiah through the years, Charles Keemle himself becoming bedridden with the disease in the late fall of 1829 following the approach of another brutally icy, wet winter. In his absence, a managing editor assumed leadership of the daily business of running the newspaper.

He and Josiah clashed almost from the start, for it seemed to young Paddock that the man had long harbored ill feelings and distrust for him, and now he was free to wash Josiah out in Keemle's absence. It tried every fiber in his patience to wait out Keemle's illness under the man he came to hate, until Josiah finally could take it no longer and resigned. The paper's editor was saddened, disappointed that Josiah had left the staff, yet he convinced the young man to maintain his room above the offices, in a glimmer of hope that one day he would talk Josiah into returning to the *Beacon*. Keemle even helped to locate another position for the young man with a friend, the owner of a general-goods store, arranging the job secretly so that Josiah would not seek out a position with one of the other newspapers. In this way, Keemle hoped that the young man would be available to return to the world of newsprint and sticky ink once his own health improved and he was no longer bedridden, away from the reins of the *Beacon*.

Young Paddock was touchy when he first came to work at the store, still rankled about the man who cost him the job at the newspaper. Josiah had become ultrasensitive about those who thought less of him for his youth, or those whose years of experience placed them before him for one reason or another. He was out to prove he was as good a man as any other while perhaps not as wealthy or as handsome. He softened as the weeks rolled by at the store.

One bright afternoon a beautiful young woman came into the store while Paddock was on a short ladder stocking shelves. Mr. Smith waited on the woman while she shopped, every now and then the young clerk stealing a look at the beauty. Later he ask his employer who the woman was. "Mademoiselle Saucier. Her father's made his purse in the fur trade. Why, son?"

"Aw-w-w, don' matter, I s'pose. Never see her again anyways."

"I don't figure it that way at all, Josiah. You see, she asked who you were."

"Mornin', Josiah."

He looked over and saw that it was Mordecai. He had come up quietly and sat down beside Paddock on the levee, remaining beside his friend a long time before saying a word, and looking out across the awakening horizon on the river's eastern shore.

"Didn' wanna disturb ye at first. Looked like ye was

thinkin' hard on somethin'." Mordecai got up as Josiah rose shakily to his feet, rubbing his cramped thighs. "Been figgerin' on forgettin' this fight, have ye?"

"Naw. Lookin' forward, I am, to gettin' this thing settled, one way or t'other."

"You're sure 'bout that, Josiah? I mean, we still got time . . ."

"I says I'm ready." He moved off down the levee, followed closely by Mordecai, who caught up with him. "One of us, that son of a whore or me, is gonna come back here later on, able to put this whole shebang behind 'im." Mordecai stopped him at the skiff. "Asides, I'm figgerin' it'll be me as comes rowin' back from the island."

They pushed off into the muddy waters, both men taking an oar to slice away at the river, cutting at the rolling waters as they sat in silence for a while. Now and then one of the two men would look over his shoulder to chart their course across the acres of brown soup, just beginning to catch the first faint outline of the island as the fog was gradually lifting off the pen-and-ink colors of its shore in the thin, gray hints of impending dawn.

"Lookin' like you didn't get much sleep last night, Mord," he asked like a question, then turned his head forward again, snuggling back down into the upturned collar of his coat.

"Didn'. Fitful, too. Figgerin' way to talk ye outta this."

At that Josiah laughed heartily, the sound carried away over the water, then softened against the thick, absorbent layer of the cottonlike fogbank.

"Don't see much for ye to be laughin' at, Josiah."

"Mordecai, you are some now. Here you was all night figgerin' way to talk me outta this lil' scuffle, an' I'm figgerin' this here's 'bout the best way to give them folks 'bout to be married a weddin' present them French won't forget! That's some now, ain't it! An' all you got for your trouble was some lost sleep! Ain't that reason 'nough for a man to be laughin'?" Mordecai sat silently, without response, suddenly sullen as he pulled at the oar. "Lookee, if'n you cain't laugh at that, Mordecai, have you ever heard of anythin' as funny as a man rowin' out to his own funeral? Now that's some funny, ain't it?"

Mordecai grunted grudgingly in agreement, and chuckled along with Josiah poking fun at himself, shaking his head up and down in acknowledgment.

"'Sides, Mord, I'm still figgerin' that LeClerc bastard's the one as is rowin' out to his."

The men sat in silence, straining at the current, continuing to look back once in a while over their shoulders as the island started looming ahead out of the thick, wet mist that drenched and chilled their clothing from the outside, perspiration soaking their shirts on the inside.

"If'n ye do kill LeClerc," he looked over at Josiah for a moment, "what then? I mean, them French is close, dog ye, they will, till they get ye. Cain't go back to St. Louie. Won' be healthy fer ye. Josiah," he looked back over at the man rowing beside him, "what ye gonna do then?"

"Ain't thought that far 'head yet, Mordecai. Jest one thing a' time, I say."

"Thought 'bout headin' west, Josiah? The captain's group is headin' out tomorrer mornin'. Ye could go with 'em, if'n ye get outta this blamed-fool stunt of yours."

"Ain't thought much 'bout it..."

"Ye damned well start thinkin' 'bout it, ye stupid son of a bitch!" There was an edge to his voice, a sharpness that caught Josiah by surprise. He twisted his head around to look into Mordecai's eyes. "Yeah, now's the time to start thinkin', Josiah."

The two men pulled the skiff in among the debris left by the river current along the island shore, Josiah wading through the mud as he struggled with the bobbing craft, tugging at the bow to get it beached. They headed inland, up from the beach, into a thinly wooded area, the trees still topped with low-hanging fog.

"Josiah," Mordecai stopped, reaching out to pull on Josiah's arm to stop him too, "I'm thinkin' ye could head north up to St. Charlie..." Josiah yanked away and walked off. Mordecai stopped him again, "Ye could lay low up theres, an' Monday head outta town, 'long the trail north. Ye'll find us." Josiah began walking slowly this time, Mordecai at his side. "I'll see that we get signed up, down to the Hawken shop, with Gantt's men. Ye'll find us on the road. Jest lay 'long the trail. What ye say? Josiah?"

"One thing a' time, Mord. One thing a' time."

They broke out of the edge of the wooded area, looking across a small open spot that lay near the center of the island. Bloody Island—Josiah rolled the words over in his mind, picturing the duels that had brought infamous notoriety to this spot, words that began to clear the stringy webs from his head. Here the genteel society of St. Louis redressed its differences. The gallant duels had been courtly affairs of honor, with one of the antagonists issuing a challenge. To this island in the Mississippi would row the two principals and their seconds, here to this last vestige of a field of honor, the concept of honorable combat between honorable men remained one of the final threads still clinging to the decaying fabric that once was a noble French colonial society. Antagonists would pace off to their positions, turn, then coolly fire at their adversary: one to live, one to die.

They waited in the cool damp, Josiah shivering slightly, more from the first flush of adrenalin than from the mist that hung heavy overhead. Turning at the sound of muffled footsteps, the Americans watched the Frenchmen approach, the wet grasses allowing only a whisper of sound among the trees. Henri LeClerc was followed by his two companions of the previous night. As the men walked toward Josiah, Mordecai looked down at the small, wooden chest held under one man's arm.

"Monsieur Paddock, I had not really expected you to appear aujourd'hui." He clicked his heels together and bowed his head forward smartly. "Je le regrette, umm, I am sorry that I misjudged you, Monsieur." Looking back up at Josiah, he spread an arm out toward the opening within the ring of trees. "Shall we begin without delay?"

"Yes."

LeClerc started off, with Josiah at his side, their companions following across the grasses that here and there sent thick tufts of scrawny weeds up through the flat carpet of new, green growth. Henri stopped, turning to look at the American as he untied the cloak from his neck. Josiah unbuttoned his coat as LeClerc gave the cloak to the companion behind him who did not hold the chest. He watched the Frenchman, feeling the blood thickening with adrenalin and venom pounding hotly around inside his head, straining at the temples with each pulsation of his heart. He handed the coat back to Mordecai, who stepped up alongside him. The Frenchman who carried the chest now stepped forward between the combatants, the small case cradled upon his left forearm as he opened the lid, to exhibit the two matched pistols laid deep within

65

soft velvet. Flintlocks, inlaid with crusted gold that flashed even now in the gray light.

"They have been in my family for many, many years, Monsieur," LeClerc explained as Josiah stared down at the weapons. "You have your choice of them," he trailed the sentence off expectantly, waiting for Josiah to decide. They were beautiful pieces, the American poring over them as they lay in their box. Silent and beautiful, nestled within their velvet blanket, yet untouched by hands that would pull them once again from their rich womb to explode one against the other.

"Monsieur, which do you choose?"

Spurred into action, Josiah chose the pistol closest to him, his fingertips pulling the weapon gently out of the chest, to hold it cradled in his hands, admiring it more and more, as the French second presented the case to LeClerc so that he might take his weapon from it. Paddock felt the heat that had once been only in his brain now reach to his hands as he held the pistol in front of him. LeClerc's companion now presented the American with a small metal pouch, inlaid also with the same rich, crusted gold. Josiah poured a charge of tiny, black granules across the pan after pulling the hammer back, then handed the pouch over to Henri.

"Merci," LeClerc responded with another slight tip of his head.

Josiah used a fingertip to push the powder close to the touch hole. "These things ready to go?"

"Oui, Monsieur, they are." LeClerc handed the pouch back to his second, who placed it in the chest, then closed the lid. "We are ready, too." The two Frenchmen backed off from Henri, as Mordecai slapped Josiah once on the back before stepping a few yards away from the two men. "We shall stand back to back, here, then Maurice shall count off our ten paces. When we have reached our tenth pace, we will turn, take our aim, and then fire, at your will. Is that satisfactory with you, Monsieur?"

"S'pose that's the way it's done with you folks," Josiah said thinly as he stepped up to Henri, both men turning to place their backs one against the other.

"Monsieur Paddock, if it is of any consolation, Henri Duchesne Dubois LeClerc admires your courage, for as I have said, I had not thought you would appear . . ."

66

"Let's jest get on with it," Josiah snapped, the tidal wave of feelings inside of him beginning to crest.

"Oui." LeClerc motioned to one of his companions with a nod of his head, and the count began.

"Un . . . deux . . . trois . . ." The two men paced off slowly, following the cadence of the count as they walked off, each man alone, across the field. "Cinq . . ."

Josiah felt the pounding in his chest, the hot surge with each beat of his heart forcing his breathing into shallow, quick, gulping gasps.

"Neuf . . ."

Mordecai turned his head back and forth between the two men as they paced away from each other. Josiah burned deep within his own private eternity. He stared at the edge of the trees before him yet saw them not, as a vision of Angelique appeared before him, laughing and mocking him once more, her face contorted by that hideous, sneering laughter. The vision loomed closer and closer, threatening to smother him . . .

"Dix." The count was finished.

Paddock stopped, and turned slowly around. LeClerc was turned and waiting for him, waiting for the American to raise his pistol before he would raise his. Josiah brought the weapon up from his side slowly, his arm at full length. Across the field, LeClerc raised his pistol.

Angelique's face was gone now, but her crazy laughter remained behind to haunt his ears as he looked across the wide open, and down the muzzle of the Frenchman's pistol. On and on the laughter rang in his ears, echoing inside his tortured head. It ended only when LeClerc's pistol spat fire at him. The round ball struck Josiah along the left side of his head, knocking him off his feet. He lay on his back in the wet grass, feeling its welcome coolness against his burning body.

Things seemed black to him, then shafts of light pierced sharply across his vision. He wondered if he was blind, wondered if his eyes were closed. The laughter was still there, coming back to him as the echo of Henri's shot began to fade. He could hear someone running over to him. Mordecai, he thought. Then he raised a hand up gradually to run fingertips along the deep furrow that had been cut through his scalp just above the left ear, taking

67

flesh and hair along with the bullet, leaving a warm, sticky wound behind. He held the fingers out in front of his face as his eyes strained to focus.

"Sweet Jesus!" It was Mordecai's voice above him. Josiah held the fingers in front of his face. "Sweet, sweet Jesus! He's done it to you!" Josiah blinked his eyes, straining to see, and squinting them as the mist clouding them began to clear. He looked up from the bloody fingers to see Mordecai standing above him, peering down into his face. He smiled at his friend's ashen face. "Sweet Jesus, Josiah."

There was a new pounding in his head as he sat up. He tried to shake it off, but it clung there with claws that tore around his head, refusing to let go. He turned slowly over onto his hands and knees, the pistol still clutched tightly in his right hand. There on the ground, he knelt, looking down at the pistol. He eased the hammer forward until it sat silently against the frizzen. Josiah brought his legs up under him, attempting to stand. Mordecai reached out to put a hand under his arm to help him up, but Josiah pushed the arm away. "No . . . no," he said quietly.

Paddock rose slowly, turning around to look across the field to see LeClerc standing alone, the two others a few paces away. The Frenchman stood motionless, as white as Mordecai, looking back at Josiah in disbelief. Paddock touched the side of his head once more and brought the bloody fingertips around in front of his face. Fuzzy-headed, he looked again at LeClerc, who brought his arms up from his sides and dropped the pistol. Henri stood frozen, anchored to the spot.

"Monsieur Paddock, I am at your disposal," he said in a quiet way, with a thin brush stroke of courage around the edges.

Josiah looked at him across the grass for long moments, before stuffing the pistol in his belt. "He will find you . . . he will find you wherever you run," came the words of Angelique again. Josiah started across the field toward the Frenchman, tightening the pistol down inside the waist of his pants, as LeClerc and his companions got a strange, pinched look on their faces.

"Non, Monsieur! From where you are!" LeClerc yelled at him, the words forced, their pitch strained and cracking. "From where you stand!"

Josiah kept coming, closing the gap between himself

and the Frenchman. Closer, he could make out the sharp terror that tugged at LeClerc's face. Then he was directly in front of the man who had shot him, insulted him, and taken Angelique from him. He enjoyed seeing the terror of Henri's ashen face.

Josiah smiled, "Monsur LeClerc..." With a powerful thrust Josiah's leg crashed into LeClerc's groin, doubling the man over in pain as the air rushed from his body. The Frenchman collapsed to the ground, hands covering himself as he groaned in agony. Paddock's summers with the voyageurs learning foot fighting, coupled with his native strength, now served him well, savagely.

Paddock stood over the man lying at his feet, looking down at the ruffled cuffs tucked between LeClerc's legs. "Monsur an' Madam LeClerc." He drove home the last syllable with the toe of his boot crashing into the Frenchman's chin, lifting it from where it lay against Henri's chest with a dull, sickening thud. Blood first spurted explosively, then began to trickle from the corner of LeClerc's mouth on the thick-laced collar as he lay crumpled like a ragdoll on the ground, senseless. "Monsur an' Madam LeClerc." As he started to kick the man again, the two Frenchmen came at him. Josiah grabbed the first by his coat along one arm and shoulder, pulling the man forward across his leg, and sending him sprawling into the grass. He then leaped into the air, curled his right leg up, and popped it into the second man's broad chest, knocking him backward over LeClerc's body.

Mordecai jumped onto the first attacker, spreading Josiah's coat over the man's head, beating the Frenchman's covered face wildly with his huge, gnarled knuckles. "Take 'im, Josiah, I got this 'un!"

Paddock kicked LeClerc's head furiously, again and again, driving the toe of his boot into the man's face, crushing it into a bloody mass. Then the man he had kicked in the chest rose to leap onto Josiah's back. They struggled to the ground, the large Frenchman on top, strong in his hold around Paddock's arms, pinning him face down in the wet, musky grass. The weight seemed to push the breath right out of his body as he struggled to free an arm. Reaching around behind him and finding an ear, Josiah dug his fingers savagely into it. The man on top brought his knee up into Josiah's groin over and over, between legs Paddock fought to close. Josiah strained to move his arm. He pulled his hand around to the man's face, clawing up the cheek. He heard Mordecai yelling somewhere in the background.

Josiah felt where the top of the cheekbone ended in the orbit and plunged his clawing fingertips into his opponent's eye. The Frenchman gave a grunt of pain as the fingers tore brutally at his flesh. The knee kicking at Josiah's groin stopped and he rolled the huge man off his back. Josiah quickly rolled the man over, then knocked him unconscious with a clublike fist. Paddock looked up to see Mordecai standing over the still form locked under the coat.

"This'un's out. How 'bout yours?"

"Yep," Josiah replied weakly, his body still shaking with the last flushes of combat. Mordecai walked over to LeClerc's body, looked down at it, then knelt beside the Frenchman. He put an ear over the man's face, then on Henri's chest. Slowly, Mordecai brought his head back up to look at Josiah.

"Sweet Jesus, Paddock! He's dead! He's dead!"

"That's what we come for, man! Didn't we?" Josiah rose to his feet, touching the bitter sting at the side of his head, a dull ache welling up from his groin. "Well, didn't we?"

"Sweet, sweet . . . ye kilt 'im with yer feet!" Mordecai mumbled, following Josiah as he took off across the grass. They ran quickly toward the trees until Paddock abruptly stopped. Mordecai slid to a stop across the wet grass a few yards past his friend.

Josiah turned slowly, deliberately now. He looked back at Mordecai, as if to answer some unspoken question that masked that man's face, then nodded once, his own face expressionless. Only then did he begin to walk quickly, finally trotting, back across the grass to the spot where lay the rich-grained wood chest that had held the two pistols.

He stopped. Staring down a long moment, Paddock finally knelt as he glanced back over his shoulder at his friend still standing at the edge of the trees. Once again turning to look at the case, Josiah slowly reached down and opened the lid. Nestled within the deep folds of velvet were the keys he would need to unlock the majestic power of the French flintlock in the days, weeks, years to come.

A chill trickle at the back of his neck suddenly brought the world back around him like a cold grip. Josiah slammed the chest shut and swept it up into his arms with one motion, his legs answering quickly as he raced back toward the trees that rimmed the meadow.

With a swift flick of his right arm he motioned to Mordecai to precede him, then dropped the arm back down to help the left clutch the wooden chest against his body. The two men ran quickly through the stands of trees back to the beach where the two boats lay tied close to each other. Only then did Josiah stop and turn to face Mordecai.

"You take your'n, an' I'll take the Frenchies'. Get back to St. Louie an' get us our fixin's we'll be needin'. I'll get a horse somewhere 'long the way. If'n what you say is true 'bout that cap'in headin' for the mountains, I'll be lookin' for 'im tomorrow, up outta St. Charlies a ways. I'll see you then." He untied the Frenchmen's boat. "Now, be off with you, Mordecai. You got work to do afore I see you next!" He pushed off into the current and leaped into the boat. He allowed the slowly churning waters of burnt umber to carry him south a short way before putting his back into the struggle with the oars. Off to his side he watched Mordecai's skiff disappear into a thick mist still hanging close over the water.

Once the other boat was only a misty shadow, Josiah drew the oars out of the water to lie along the gunwales. From its place near his wet boots he retrieved the wooden chest and sat it upon his thighs. Bringing up the lid with both thumbs, Paddock hunched over the velvet interior. While his left hand opened the folds of his shirt, the right selected the worm, ball screw, and mold from the case and dropped them inside his shirt. The next move was to the two small powder flasks, which he tucked within his wide belt on either side of the large buckle.

Closing the chest for the last time, he held it within his hands a long moment before flinging it overboard where it was quickly lost to the churning, muddy current and flotsam. Josiah leaned forward and took up the oars once more, pulling with his whole body now. The splash of Mordecai's oars had faded completely, leaving Josiah alone with his own sounds and his own thoughts. He whispering to himself, "One thing a' time, Mordecai. One thing a' time."

5

He banged on the door with the side of his fist, then looked up and down the street, banging away again. Josiah heard a voice yelling at him from inside, telling him to stop, that someone was coming. He brought his hand away from the door, standing nervously still in the cold early-morning drizzle, his hair stringy and dripping down his face, his clothing soaked and clinging to his skin.

The door cracked open; behind it a black face squinting from interrupted sleep peered out at him.

"I need to see Mr. Keemle, now."

"He's not 'wake yet. Don' wanna wake 'im. Needs his rest, sir. Mister was up mos' night coughin', sick he was . . ."

"Boy, you jest tell 'im its Josiah Paddock who's wantin' to see 'im. You jest go do that." The black face disappeared as the door opened for Josiah. He stepped inside and the servant closed the door behind him. The black man looked him over and then spoke, "Ya wait right hyar, sir. Check wid' the mister fust." He moved off up the stairs.

Josiah stood waiting in the entry, shivering now as he had not done before, feeling the warmth returning slowly to his damp, chilled body. He had not been here for some time, and looked around from the entry to see if things had changed. The black man came to the head of the stairs, motioning him to come up without saying a word. He led Josiah to Keemle's room and opened the door for the young man.

"That'll be all, Lucius. Thank you," the man in bed told his servant, who closed the door and disappeared down the hall. Josiah felt bold yet sheepish at the same time. He stood by the door, looking across the room at the man who sat propped up against the headboard, a heavy brown shawl pulled around his shoulders, clutched about him with both hands. In the dim light, Keemle looked to be much older than his thirty-one years, his skin a flat gray. He looked very tired, face drawn and sallow, with dark canyons under the eyes that still shone brightly at his young visitor. His dark hair flowing to the collar of his nightshirt was mussed, and he had grown his sideburns long, down to the end of his jaw, since Josiah had seen him last. The man needed a shave, Josiah thought, looking from Keemle's chin up to the thin aquiline nose.

"It's a goddamn bloody hour for you to be gettin' this body up from its sleep, young man." Keemle chuckled lightly to help loosen the uneasiness he felt coming across the room from Josiah. "What brings you here at such a witchin' hour?"

"I need to ask you for some money, Mr. Keemle. I'm goin' west, today." He took a couple of steps forward, then stopped again.

"What you plan to do west, Josiah?" Keemle adjusted himself once more on the pillows against the headboard.

"Don't know as yet. Find somethin' to do. They can always use 'nother man out there, I s'pose," he replied, looking at the small rug beneath his feet.

"Josiah, pull you up that chair, next to me over here, an' sit yourself down." Josiah pushed the chair to the side of the bed and sat down to face Keemle. "I want to tell you 'bout this man as is laid up now with the pleur'sy, jest a lil' story 'bout that man before you met 'im." He leaned over on an elbow to bring himself close to the young man.

"I gotta be off soon."

"You'll be gone soon 'nough—so sit still an' get your ear up close. I wasn't always a newspaperman, you know. Started off in that business early in my life, but it took a toll on me soon. By the time I was twenty. How old are you, Josiah?"

"Twenty-two, sir."

"Well, by the time I was twenty I had my fill for awhile an' headed north. That fall of 1820 I was sent as a clerk for the Missoura Fur Comp'ny up to their post on the Kansas. It were differ'nt. An' the next spring, Pilcher sent this Charles Keemle on north to the mountains with Jones an' Immell, where we put up a post on the south bank of the Yallerstone River. Yes, friend, I knew 'em all: Pilcher, Drips, Vanderburg, an' Font'nelle. Man gets him an education fast clerkin' on the upriver. Would you pour me a glass of water from that pitcher, Josiah?"

Paddock poured the water, handed the glass to Keemle, and took his seat once more, not quite as edgy now. "Never knew you was in the west, the mountains."

"Lotsa things you don't know 'bout me, son. Anyways, we did real good 'long till spring of '23, round 'bout the end of May as I recall. Up near the gateways to them mountains, strung out 'long a narrow buffalo trail the party was ridin' single file, you know, next to the river. An' then there was all this yellin' an' screamin', made my blood cold then, an' lookin' back on it now, it do make it cold again. Hundreds of 'em—Blackfoot they were—hundreds of 'em. Rode down on us, killin' our leader right off, who carried out a white flag too. When it seemed to the rest of us to be the time to be gettin' 'cross the river, we left five behind an' four others as was wounded. Most of us crossed that river an' made it to a Crow camp where we holed up awhile. Billy Gordon made it in the latter part of the day, comin' round'bout way on foot, his horse shot from under him. That man covered territory that day." He finally took a drink of the water he had been holding.

"We talked 'bout the mess we was in, an' 'cided to head down river. So's we made some skin boats an' raised our cache of goods an' pelts, beatin' it back to the Mandans. When the news of what happened to us reached Pilcher, he 'cided to get downriver some more. Leavin' the Mandans, we headed south an' got inter the fracas with the Rees. You see, them Rees had torn a good hole in Gen'l Ashley's men an' plans. An' now Leavenworth was headin' north to even the score. Well, Pilcher was itchin' to do some wound to some Injun or other, hurtin' he was from losin' men an' plunder to them Blackfoot the way we did, so we tagged 'long with the campaign back upriver. That were a goddamn mess too, as Leavenworth didn' even want to he'p the traders even up the score very bad. Pilcher was boilin' mad by that time, he were red with anger, but not much could be done as them Rees slipped 'way at night, headin' north leavin' their villages." He took another drink, then wiped his lower lip where a drop clung with a nightshirt sleeve.

"Pilcher wanted them Ree towns burned, so we burned 'em. But we was still downriver with no way to get back up to the mountains, till Pilcher heard Ashley was sendin' a man named Smith overland on horseback. That was all Pilcher needed to know. He sent me an' Billy Gordon to lead the men overland, follerin' this Smith an' Ashley's men. It were a chase that y'ar, but we fin'ly caught up to 'em, Smith an' all, at a Cheyenne village west of the Black Hills. We talked with this Smith, then traveled with his group till we reached the Bighorn, where we wintered with the Crow. An' after a spring hunt, our group headed back east, deviled by a Crow war party that took a real likin' to our horses, trailin' us for quite some ways. Well, Charles Keemle ended back in St. Louie in the middle summer of '24, an' come to buy the *Enquirer* from Benton the next y'ar." He drained the glass, handed it to Josiah, who rose to fill it again.

"The rest you know already, 'bout me sellin' the paper out from under you in '26, an' buyin' it back again in '27 to change it to the *Beacon*, as you was there then." He sat up straighter now, slowly moving as the pain in his chest made him wince. "Thought a time or two of marryin'. Need someone round 'sides Lucius from time to time." He pursed his thin lips, licking them with the tip of his tongue. "S'pose I'd really like to go back again, up there— but that were 'nother life—seems so far 'way from this room now, talkin' 'bout it."

"I've got to go, Mr. Keemle." He rose a little out of the chair, facing the man in bed more squarely, "I've got to . . ."

"What you done to yourself, Josiah?" Keemle was looking at the left side of Paddock's scalp, hair matted with blood, the edges of the wound dark, almost black, with the coagulation.

"Cain't tell it now—but no matter what they say 'bout me, want you to know none of it's true, Mr. Keemle," Josiah said, touching the side of his head once again with his fingertips.

"Son, you run like this, never come back here."

"Don' think I really want to, anyways—but I'll get the money back to you somehow." He pushed the chair back away from him.

"I know you will, Josiah, I know you will—I ain't worried 'bout that." Keemle leaned over, opened the door of a small chest that stood beside the bed, from which he drew a cloth purse. Digging in it, he began to pull out coins, placing them one at a time in Josiah's palm, as if counting them in his head. "Go now, over to Tharp's liv'ry. That man should be 'round by now. Get yourself a fine horse an' all the rest you'll need. Tell that Tharp that Charles Keemle sent you—he should outfit you right. If he don't give you what you think is the best, tell 'im I said I'd see 'im skinned an' hung out to dry!" Keemle chuckled lightly as he closed the purse, returning it to the wooden chest. Josiah turned to leave. "You got a coat for your trip, Josiah?"

"Did have, till this mornin'."

"Get in that wardrobe, friend, an' get you that red an' black one . . . yep, that's the one, a heavy blanket coat as will ward off the chill in them hills."

Josiah had turned to look back at Keemle holding the shoulders of the coat. "You've already done 'nough for me . . ."

"Shut your mouth an' take the coat with you." Josiah pulled it on over his shirt, Keemle seeing for the first time the outline of the big pistol butt stuck inside his belt, the shirttail draped over it. "Now, before you go, come over here so's I can say my fare-thee-well to a friend as I'm gonna miss." Josiah moved back over to the side of the bed, Keemle taking Paddock's right hand between his two, gripping it firmly. "Johnny Dougherty an' I both remember a young Paddock—that was y'ars back, Josiah. We've both talked 'bout the man we wanted you to be, but—guess you're gonna have to find your own way now, son. You growed some in the last year since I seen you . . . an' if'n you're headin' for where the sun sleeps each night, you got some more growin' in store—just like Charles . . ." Keemle coughed, a heavy, wet cough, and gripped Josiah's hand tighter.

"Josiah, if'n you make it through to '34 or '35, come back . . . or send word then," he answered Paddock's negative gesture, "an' we'll consider this debt paid in full. If you don', then I'll know I've lost more'n jest the money an' the coat; I've lost a good friend." He fatherly patted the back of Josiah's hand. "Keep your eye 'long the skyline, but don't you ever look behind you. What you're runnin' from might be gainin' on you. Them ghosts'll haunt you only if you let 'em." He took his left hand away, leaned forward and patted the side of Josiah's shoulder, then let go to sink back down into the pillows.

"Now, friend, be off with you, to wherevers you goin', an' pay heed to them as will teach you what you'll need to know."

Josiah turned from the bed, then stopped facing the door, afraid to turn around to show Keemle the moisture in his eyes. Damn you—a man ain't s'posed to cry. What you cryin' for? he thought. The tears stung bitterly as he fought to push them back. "Thank you, Charles, friend.

76

But, don't you worry 'bout Josiah Paddock. Never seen a ghost, but common sense tells me"—he swallowed hard, fighting the lump in his throat that cracked as he spoke— "common sense tells me a man as believes in ghosts deserves to be deviled by 'em." He opened the door without turning around, and left the house quickly.

At the livery over on Barn Street Josiah found Tharp opening for the day. He told the blacksmith what he had come for, and was shown a few horses that did not impress him.

"Charles Keemle sent me," he said, looking at Tharp as the older man squinted one eye at him. "He said you would do right by me, Mr. Tharp."

"He did, did he, that..."

"Said he'd hang your hide out to dry if you..."

"That man's bound never to change is he, son? Well, if Keemle sent ye to get the best that Amos Tharp has to offer, then the best I'll sell ye." The blacksmith brought out a large horse, then stood waiting while the younger man walked slowly around the animal, inspecting, touching, appraising.

"How much this'un be?"

"Sell this'un to you for Keemle's price o' forty dollar— be fifty for any'un else."

"Ain't got near that much." He watched the other man's head drop before he continued, "Got you anythin' else I can take a look at?"

"Needin' ye somethin' strong, are ye?" He spat into the dry dirt mixed with scattered grass and hay. "Goin' out there?" he nodded his head toward the west.

"He'll need be lastin' me some, yep..." He did not get to finish this thought as Tharp took the first horse back to a stall and closed the stall door before heading farther back into the stable where the shafts of gray light were only beginning to penetrate. Within a moment he appeared with a large dappled mare that appeared to need some fattening up.

"Ain't full-blood—this'un ain't—like the other," Tharp began as Josiah walked around the animal slowly. "Just horse, this'un be. But all the horse he'll be needin' whar you're goin'." Tharp now peered knowingly at Paddock so that the younger man had to drop his eyes once more to look over the animal. "Good bottom, this'un'll have; some sixteen hands as I see it." He slapped the animal on the rump. "With a lil' fattenin', this'un'll take ye where you're headin' for."

"Keemle give me only twenty-six dollar. Thought it would be 'nough for your best."

"Ain't 'nough for my best."

"Saddle, fixin's, too."

"Price ain't never no object with that man. Cuz he never pays my price," Amos snorted derisively.

"It be a deal?"

Tharp drew up his lips, spit to the side, then remarked, "S'pose I been taken again by that son of a bitch! Pick yourself out some horse trappin's—over there." Tharp gestured with his arm.

When Paddock had selected the saddle and tack, then readied his new animal, he walked over to where the old blacksmith stood by the door. "Twenty-six ye got of Keemle's money, twenty-six it be. Ye got some fine flesh an' fixin's there for twenty-six, boy. Go on an' I'll take this up with that scurvy coon myself."

Paddock led the horse out of the darkness of the stables into the muddy street where the clouds seemed to be breaking up, the drizzle having ceased while he was bartering with the livery owner. He mounted and started north from town as the sun began to break through the thinning curtain overhead, splashing the road here and there with bright bursts of warmth and color.

As he was leaving the old city, Josiah thought of stopping to turn around, to look one last time at St. Louis before he left, but something nagged him to keep going without delaying even a moment. He felt sad as he rode the trail toward St. Charles, feeling like something big in his life had just been torn away, had just ended. He choked again on the lump in his throat, wondering if it were the tears threatening to return, or only fear. He decided that it was the fear, that new fear of the unknown mingled with the fear of knowing he could never return to the familiar people and places of his past. He justified the knots wadding up in the pit of his stomach as being not his sadness at leaving it all behind, but his excitement in what lay before him. Josiah tried to remember the trail north from St. Louis, attempting to reach back into his memory to recall those travels of the past with John Dougherty—but things looked much different to him now.

The countryside he passed through on this early

Sunday morning was dotted with small settlers' homes, in addition to several handsome French houses owned by the more wealthy, each supporting its own large garden and an ample orchard. The trail he rode had by now become part of the famous Boone's Lick Trail, every year crowded by more and more of those seeking out more and more room for their families. The Florissant Valley was the sweet honey drawing them to this land, a valley of rich and fertile blacklands. "Yessir. Can see why the man as would be a settler might become attached to this place," he said aloud. The land about him was heavily covered with hazel bushes, prairie plum, and those crab-apple trees. He remembered a young boy roaming the woodlands around a settler's cabin, climbing the trees, eating his fill of apples until his belly ached, then returning home to a disapproving mother and aunt. Josiah kicked the dappled mare into a gallop, pushing things behind him with the speed of the horse, the wind pooling tears at the corners of his eyes. He finally reined in the animal, bringing her to a walk once more. Paddock liked the way she had responded under the touch of his heels, bolting off without hesitation, carrying him smoothly along the road to ease him away from the ragged edges of his emotions. "Yep, girl. We'll be gettin' on jest fine, I bet you." He leaned forward a little to pat the side of her neck, then stroked her mane. "Friends like you an' me gonna do all right together, ain't we, girl?"

He passed the church and convent, and little communities comprising a few homes clustered around a common grove, following the trail that ran parallel to the endless stream of limestone bluffs that charted the course of the river. The sun was finally burning off the thin curtain of cloud cover, brightening the fields and those newly whitewashed homes in a palette of color. The houses became more and more frequent, telling him they were coming closer to St. Charles.

"Hey, girl, lookin' like its 'bout to fair off today!" he observed as he rode into the town nearly as old as St. Louis itself, sitting near the confluence of the Missouri and Mississippi rivers.

Across the river from the town sat the squat Fort Bellafontaine to the north. As he rode along the east-west main street, Josiah was enveloped in a growing community that was filling with residents who shoved up against one another along either side of this main thoroughfare that lay wedged between the Missouri and the river bluffs or "Mamelles." Around him the little town was coming to life, beginning to bustle once more with activity that belied the fact that it was Sunday morning. As he looked down at the people he passed, Josiah recalled Keemle once remarking that St. Charlie was the dumping ground for the refuse of Kentucky. Then he heard the church bells pealing out their invocation. His ears echoed. He remembered the little boy, tiny hand clutched tightly in his mother's, being led through the woods to church in St. Charles each Sunday morning, come rain, snow, or shine. He remembered the Bible his mother always carried to those church meetings, held under one arm against her breast, his little legs scurrying to keep up with her pace as they hurried to town, walking closer and closer to the sound of the church bells. He remembered, this Sunday morning, as he rode farther away from those church bells, leaving St. Charles behind. Pushing the memories away, Josiah suddenly thought he should have purchased something to eat back there, but—no, he really didn't feel hungry. That could wait until later, maybe till tomorrow, if he had to wait that long.

A few miles west of town and into a more sparsely populated area, Paddock reined his horse off the trail and led her into the thick woodlands toward the river. They took it slowly, weaving through the stands of trees, Josiah having to duck low from time to time beneath their heavy branches. He twisted around in the saddle, and could not see the trail, figuring he had come over a half mile since leaving it. Ahead was a small glade, shaded by a few oak, where he thought he might find a comfortable dry patch of grass nestled against the trees.

Josiah slid from the horse, tied her near the spot he had chosen, then pulled the saddle from her back. She rippled the muscles down along her spine from shoulders to rump, feeling it free, without burden.

"Feels good, don' it, girl? Not havin' someone back there ridin' you, heavy on your back, tellin' you what to do, which way to go? Right, girl?" He stroked her muzzle a few times, then patted it. "Right."

Removing his coat, he folded it over one arm, then dropped to his hands and knees, crawling around under the oak near its trunk, looking for grass that might be less damp from the rains than the grass without the cover of the tree's branches. He found a spot and spread the heavy blanket coat out, rolling the collar up a little to serve as a pillow. Josiah had just sat down when the urge overcame him. He stood up and started to unbutton his fly, then stopped, looking around him in a circle. Josiah caught himself and laughed, "Hell! Ain't no one round here gonna see me takin' a pee." He unbuttoned the fly all the way and relieved himself, splashing a nearby bush.

Sitting back down on the coat, he looked at the dapple and felt happy that he had ended up with this strong animal. Josiah smiled, then lay back on the coat, curling his arms under him, and let out a long, slow sigh.

He slept for a long time before waking. The sun was going down. Already it had lengthened shadows to the east, giving the sky a deepening orange-to-purple glow. He felt a chill and wiped his eyes. Yawning, he looked around at what he could use for firewood, then rose. Gathering twigs and branches he would need, Josiah brought them back to his tree when it struck him.

"Damn!" he said aloud. He didn't have a striker or flint, no way to start a fire. He kicked the pile of wood several times, scattering it across the glade in his anger with himself. Plopping back down, Paddock drew the coat around him without putting his arms in the sleeves, thinking on what to do. His forearms crossed over the fancy pistol in his belt, not realizing he had ready flint and steel in the weapon's lock to make a warm camp.

Rising, he put the saddle back on the horse, mounted, and directed her toward the river. Josiah rode up and down the bluffs overlooking the river for hours in the moonlight, something to do, something to occupy his mind. When he finally returned to the glade, he was surprised that he had been able to locate it. He knotted the reins to a thick bush, pulled the saddle from the horse, and dragged it over where he could use it for a back rest. Josiah threw down the saddle blanket over his patch of grass, adjusted the saddle so that it stood upright, then leaned back into it.

Digging through his coat pockets, he found a small hunk of tobacco leaves pressed together as the tail end of a twist would be. He wished he had his pipe with him, hoping Mordecai would remember to pick it up with the rest of his things in the room. A lot can be left behind, he thought, but a pipe could not. Paddock toyed with the tobacco hunk between his fingers for a few moments, then placed it between his teeth. It was dry, absorbing all the moisture there was in his mouth as he slowly bit down on it. He chewed, gagging a little, more from the dryness than from the taste, although he had never chewed tobacco before. Finally the hunk loosened up, then became moist and syrupy, a little of the thick juice being swallowed as he gulped without thinking. It made his empty stomach jump. He gagged a little. Gotta remember to spit, Paddock! he thought, telling himself this was not the time to be getting a bellyache. His head swam a little and he tried to spit. It wasn't working. Josiah spit the hunk out and grabbed a handful of grass to chew on. It was laden with dew and helped kill some of the scratchy fire at the back of his throat.

Josiah sighed and leaned back again into the saddle, stuffing his hands deeply into the coat pockets, and looked at the stars coming out in the deepening black. He freed the bottom button on the coat, slipping his hand inside around the pistol butt. Josiah felt comforted, not quite so alone. He started to withdraw his hand from within the coat when his fingers brushed by the fabric strip protruding from the front of his shirt.

He rubbed it thoughtfully for a moment between thumb and forefinger, suddenly numb with not knowing what it was that had worked its way out of the front of his shirt. Then, with the peace that comes from finally knowing, Josiah smiled to himself. The strip of cloth now completely free of his coat, he looked at it briefly, then wrapped it around his hand, remembering the woman. Remembering the night before.

The smile now moved from his lips to catch and hold on to a place inside him. Yes, the woman. She had comforted when it was the deep, searing pain of loss he had felt. She had given to him when it was he who was driven to do the taking. She had opened up to him when he felt anger and bitterness closing him off. And she had kept him open through their moments together. Those moments were with him now. And, now, he was not alone.

"Sleep. Jest go to sleep, Paddock," he told himself aloud, then snuggled deep into the collar. The ribbon lay curled in his hand.

Birds were singing above him in the branches as he blinked his eyes open. The sun was coming up. He bolted upright into a sitting position, hoping he wasn't too late. A cramp in his neck roared out at him where he had slept on it wrong through the night. The aching cramp inched him alive until he became fully aware of the dull pounding in his head. Suddenly he was awake and the searing tenderness of the furrowed wound along the side of his head screamed at him for attention. He touched it with hesitant fingertips. Splinters of light crossed in front of his eyes. He would not touch it again.

The mare snorted as he rose to his feet and went over to her. He nuzzled the animal, then unbuttoned his fly to relieve himself. Hands free of his penis as he urinated, he flung his arms wide, stretching both back and chest muscles out of their stiffness after a night on the cold ground.

Josiah gathered up the blanket, threw it on the horse's back, then cinched the saddle down along her belly. He shook each of his legs for a moment, then climbed into the saddle.

"Let's go, girl. I ain't gonna be late for this meetin'," he barked, kicking her sides. She too seemed expectant this morning. They wove away from the river until coming to a little rise that sloped down toward the trail. From here he could look south along the road through the trees for some way down its dusty ribbon. He dropped to the ground and sat, holding the reins lightly in one hand as the horse began to eat her breakfast. The sun became warm, making him uncomfortable in the coat. Josiah took it off and tied it behind the saddle after rolling it up. Then he briefly touched the ribbon within his shirt and the comfort it gave him was slowly becoming more familiar now.

He walked around to the dappled mare's head, scratching her under the chin. "What we gonna name you, girl?" Josiah patted her between the eyes, "Got any ideas?" She deserved a good name, a title, he thought, as good a title as any of them French ladies. "That's it! We'll name you Lady—Lady Missoura! How's that sound, girl? Lady Missoura!" He stepped around the dappled mare and was patting her rump when he heard something down on the road. Josiah ran down the slope a few yards, looking through the trees back south as far as he could see. Around a bend in the road, through the border of the overhanging oaks, he saw them coming, a large group of mounted men, leading a greater number of horses laden with packs.

"Whoooeee! That's them, Lady Missoura! That's them! Here they come!" he hollered at her, running back up the hill. Paddock jumped into the saddle and kicked her down the slope onto the flat alongside the road. He brought her into an easy trot as he bore down on the head of the column.

"Need to see the cap'in!" he called out, reining the horse up by the side of the road as he met them.

"That's me, mister. What can I do for you?"

"Name's Paddock, sir. Josiah Paddock." He turned the horse to ride beside the man who led the column. "Mordecai Thayer signed both us up with you, didn' he?"

"Paddock... Paddock. Yep. Remember that name from roll call this mornin', son. You wasn't there."

"Told Mordecai I'd meet up with you 'long the road outta St. Charlie."

"All right, then, boy. Get yourself in line an' we'll get you squared away when we camp for the night." He motioned Josiah back along the string of men and animals with a nod of his head.

Josiah turned the horse around and urged her into a trot as he raced along the line of men, each looking him over as he passed by. "Mordecai!"

"Josiah Paddock!" His head jerked up when Josiah had called out his name. "Ye made it, didn' ye." He tossed the long Pennsylvanian rifle over to his friend.

He pulled his horse around so that he rode alongside Mordecai. "You got to my room. Good!" He stroked the wood of the rifle, feeling it suddenly strange and new again for him. "What else'n you pull from my truck?"

Mordecai began to empty pockets until Josiah had no place else to put things. "Hol' it! Hol' it! You can give me the rest tonight! An' did you get that ol' pipe?"

"Yep. Back on your pack animal, Josiah." He motioned with a thumb at the two animals he had strung out behind his horse.

"We on our way, Mordecai! We really on our way!"

"Bet you're happy, huh, Josiah? Are you happy now? Happy leavin' it behind you, Josiah?"

"B'lieve I'm gonna be, Mordecai. B'lieve I'm gonna be."

6

From St. Charles the party moved west across country, following the Missouri along its banks, the river's course leading the men west and some north until they reached Fort Osage, sitting on the south bank of the Missouri. Here the Gantt and Blackwell men stayed over for two days, picking up food supplies and resting the animals after the first long leg of the journey west. Each of the men was glad for a chance to rest, to acquaint his feet with the ground once more, to shake the numbness out of buttocks new to riding constantly through the daylight hours with only a short stop for a noon break. The men traded with the Kan-Saw Indians through two days, trading beads and shiny pretties for the meager corn the tribe raised and stored in their small dirt huts. Josiah alone was anxious and nervous, wanting to push west to the mountains and trapping, tiring at the slow pace of the caravan of men coaxing the plodding animals along. He was fidgety through those two days, and nothing Mordecai could say would alleviate Josiah's short temper at the long hours of waiting.

When the party finally pulled out of Fort Osage, it took them a little more than a day to make it to the mouth of the Kansas River. They spent the night camped where the water from the Kansas, flowing from the west, dumped into the Missouri River, as it came from the north to begin its eastward journey. Josiah seemed happier that night, not quite so anxious and more relaxed.

"Now we're getting somewhere, Mordecai," Josiah said, slapping his friend on the back when they dismounted to make camp for the night.

"You're puttin' it behind ye, ain't ye?"

They had come some twenty-five miles after leaving Fort Osage, and Gantt gathered the men for some instruction that evening following supper. He was going to run the brigade with military firmness and resolve, he told them. Discipline would be swift and sure for those who broke the rules. From here on out, he would be doubling the horse guard at each night's camp, every man having to take a turn at watch every night. And, there would be no room for dissension, he told them. Each man was to keep his complaints to himself for the good of the rest. Josiah listened, burning inside as the orders were handed down by the man. He chafed under such a leader, who demanded unswerving loyalty without question. Most of his happiness at reaching the Kansas disappeared. Josiah slept restlessly that night.

Within two weeks, the party had reached the Republican River, camping where it joined the Kansas, and crossing the river at first light the next morning to begin their march northwest. The shimmering bleakness of the flat landscape was matched only by the hardship of staying in the saddle through the endless hours under the relentless sun. Food became scarce; game was scattered far from their path of travel. For days now they had repeatedly come upon signs of a brigade that had gone this way better than two weeks before. Hunters began to return each night with little or nothing. They had killed the last of the beef Gantt had brought along, and most of what they now had to live on were some wild turnips and sweet corn, traded from a band of Otoes they had met. There was quiet, hushed talk of turning around.

The heat poured down over every man, hot and sticky, and always the empty bellies groaned. Josiah's neck grew red and raw under the wool shirt where it chafed and scratched his hot flesh. He began to have doubts, not of himself, but of the leadership of the group. Each night around small campfires he heard others grumbling and complaining out of earshot of the commander. But Gantt felt the hunger along with his men, and finally ordered that two pack animals be sacrificed. One was Mordecai's. He had to load his gear onto Josiah's packhorse. The meat was tough, stringy, without taste; Gantt had chosen the two weakest animals to be slaughtered. At least it was food, something to fill an empty belly. It relieved the problem of hunger for a few days, but over seventy men quickly went through the two scrawny horses. Josiah chewed on his thoughts through the next few days, wondering each night if there would be a tomorrow as he lay down in his bedroll to sleep—each morning awaking to find no cheer in the rising sun, only more doubts that this might be the last day.

No game found for many days by the hunters began

taking its toll in squabbles and short tempers among the men each day. And still they continued along the Republican until Gantt finally decided to strike north, away from the river, and head overland to find the Platte. On their way, all that the hunters could drag in for the supper kettles were a few wolves from time to time. And then the wood supply began to run out. Each night it was a struggle to find enough firewood to burn for the many smoky little fires the men huddled around. The grumbling increased. Many were beginning to talk of turning back, abandoning the trip as hopeless dream-turned-nightmare. The men fed on their growing anxiety, their growing anger. There was no firewood. There was nothing to cook over a fire even if there was wood to burn.

One evening the men began to unload the animals, the same ritual they had practiced many a night before, when a hunter came riding toward camp shouting. Many of the men grabbed their rifles as the man rode down on them, thinking it might mean he was being chased by a wandering war party. The hunter reined up in a cloud of dust to announce that he had killed two elk up ahead a few miles, that he needed help in loading the meat aboard more horses. Men volunteered eagerly, and that night the air was a little happier around the small fires others had started, using the dry midsummer grasses for fuel. They had reached the Platte, Gantt told them that evening, the river lying just beyond the next rise, having been located by another hunter. Gantt said things had taken a turn for the better.

But to Josiah it seemed ordained that things would get bad again. And they did. Game scattered wide from the path of the marching column, and bellies pinched again with hunger. Firewood was always a scarce luxury and what substitutes they tried only smoldered brief moments before going out. Again the talk of abandoning the journey and heading back east to the settlements was on each man's lips. Josiah had tired of the slow pace, tired of the lack of game and wood, and was sick to death of the blunders of the group's leader.

Josiah and Mordecai were chosen for the first watch, their assignment to protect the herd of animals hobbled some thirty yards away from where the rest of the men had begun to bed down for the night. They were to awaken the next watch in two hours before turning in for the night. Paddock picked up his rifle by the barrel and walked over to the horses. As Josiah was rebuttoning his fly after urinating, Mordecai walked up, his rifle slung carelessly over his shoulder.

"You're awful quiet tonight, Josiah."

"Ain't got much to be chatterin' 'bout, what with an' empty belly an' itchy feet, Mord." He moved over to sit down at the edge of the herd at the bottom of a little rise.

"Gettin' to me, it is, too."

The two men sat quietly, each in his own thoughts for some time, watching the horses eating what little edible grasses there were.

"You still wantin' to get into them mountains?" Josiah asked, turning his head to look over at his friend.

"S'pose. Why?"

"You see, I been figgerin' on what'd take for us to jest take off, leave this slow group behind."

"Ye meanin' desert? Jest desert?"

"Yep. Figgerin' you an' me could make much better time by ourselves, takin' jest that one packhorse of our'n and slippin' 'way tonight."

"Aw-w-w, shit! They'd find us for sure. Send some men out to catch us, Josiah."

"Been figgerin' on that too. See, what with all them others talkin' 'bout headin' back east, why, if they send some jackasses after us, they send 'em east lookin' for us. An' we'll be headin' west from here, won't we, Mordecai?"

"Hadn' thort 'bout it like that."

"Well, you with me then?" Josiah scooted over closer to squat in front of his friend.

"Don' know, Josiah. Soundin' pretty risky, desertin' on the group like that. An' we wouldn' be able to eat any better by ourse'fs than we eatin' now, right?"

Josiah shook his head, "Naw, don' figger it that way. Mordecai, the game's bein' scared off by this whole big passel a greenhorns an' horses, while you an' me move 'bout quieter by ourselves, see. We'll do jest fine on that 'count!" He looked over his shoulder to check on the possibility of their being heard, but all was very quiet back in camp as the forms of the sleeping men lay as motionless as logs. Mordecai sat without saying a word. "Will you trust in me, Mord? I come 'long with you this far— will you go 'long with me from here on?"

"You're makin' it sound mighty temptin'."

"Hell, yes! We'll do lot better without these fellers,

jest you an' me, an' we can figger them traps out by ourse'fs. 'Sides, Mordecai, this way we won't have to give our catch back to the cap'in. What beaver as we take will belong to only us, now won't they?"

"That's right! You an' me workin' only fer ourse'fs!"

"Now you got it. We've had our fill of the cap'in an' empty bellies long 'nough. You comin' with me or not. Will I be countin' you in or out, Mordecai?"

Mordecai looked over at the sleeping forms, then back to Josiah, and back to the forms once more. "Guessin' ye talked me inter this'n, Josiah. I'm with ye!"

"Now we'll be waitin' for a good while, let them others get good an' asleep, then you slip back into camp an' get our truck an' such. Bring it round to the other side of the animals. That way, them fellers over on the other side of camp as is watchin' for Injuns won't hear us leavin'." He put his hand on Mordecai's shoulder and gripped it hard for a moment. "You're not gonna freeze on this, are you?"

"Naw. I'm with ye, Josiah!"

"Good. Now, we'll jest sit here quiet as church mice while they get into some good, deep sleep," he whispered, leaning back on his elbows, his rifle laid between his legs.

Mordecai squirmed a little inside, but shook it off as if it were only the chill in the night air. Josiah got a head on his shoulders, he thought, an' he's figgerin' what's bes' fer the both of us.

Rarely did they move in the next two hours, restlessly watching the horses, coming to their feet whenever an animal would snort and blow, then sitting back down. They saw the next watch change on the other side of camp, and sat some more as the night overhead became black with few stars dusting the heavens.

"Now, go get our truck an' bring it round the rise," he said hoarsely to Mordecai. The man moved away, handing his rifle to Josiah, waddling back to camp in a crouch. Josiah watched him move slowly, carefully through the sleeping men until he could no longer discern Mordecai's form, it blending with the night. He counted the long minutes since his friend had left, then gathered the rifles up and crawled off around the herd. Josiah found their horses and stood among them until Mordecai came up, struggling with the packs. Swiftly they loaded the one pack animal, cinched the saddles down on their horses, then Mordecai stuck his left foot in a stirrup.

"No! Don't! We gonna walk 'em out!" He motioned with his head as he took the mare's reins in hand and started west toward the river. Mordecai took up the rope halter on the pack animal and the reins of his horse in one hand and followed Josiah. They crept along as quietly as they could, moving through the herd. Both turned to look back from time to time, checking to see if they had been seen or not. By the time they had walked over a mile, the men struck the Platte. Here they went into the saddle and prodded the animals through the water to the other bank, crossing the river quietly in the still night. On the north side of the river, Josiah turned and stopped, waiting for Mordecai to come up with the pack animal.

"We gonna do it, Josiah!" he whispered deeply as he came up beside the other man.

"You damned bet we are!" Josiah exclaimed, slapping Mordecai on the back. He then turned the dapple and headed west, following the north bank in the silver moon-light.

The Platte led them west. Josiah found the river strange compared to the Missouri and Mississippi, the rivers of his youth flowing deep and strong. The Platte's somethin' else again, he thought. It did not flow with the lusty force he had expected of western rivers. Instead, the Platte was wide and slow, and it surprised him that it was less than two feet deep in most places. The tales he had heard of the mighty western rivers did not match what he saw of the Platte in the next few weeks. Paddock tried to square it in his mind through each day, but came back again and again to the same nagging doubt—that maybe things in the West were not exactly as they had been described by those men dressed in animal skins who filled the Green Tree Inn and the Rocky Mountain House. Maybe the West was not at all as he had expected to find it. But, he would just wait and see, he told himself. His life had always been a struggle with complications, face-to-face wrestling with twists of fate. Deep inside, unknown to any man, Josiah Paddock fought with the self-doubts, the edginess that always persisted in telling him that one day, things were going to drop from his grasp, fly from his control.

They had been able to find a little game, enough to sustain them as they roamed westward through the roll-ing hills of the wandering river.

"Jest like ye said, Josiah. Ye said we'd be eatin' better by ourse'fs," Mordecai chattered one night over their little fire. His friend just nodded, taking small comfort in the fact that they had been able to find subsistence in their journey thus far following the desertion. He took little comfort and waited, continuing the struggle waged within him. Then one afternoon, the doubts began to take root.

"Hol' it!" Josiah shouted back to Mordecai, pulling up on the mare's reins.

"Do ye see what I see, Josiah?"

They sat on the north bank of the river, looking across the wide junction where the Platte became two rivers. One north and one south.

"Sweet Jesus! Whar we goin' now?" Mordecai looked over at his friend.

"Didn' know nothin' 'bout this. You hear tell of two rivers, Mord?"

"Naw, not as I can say." The uneasiness grew within him.

Josiah attempted to spit, but really didn't have anything in his mouth to blow away. "Tell you, we ain't headin' south if'n that's where that river goes. We ain't headin' south. We gotta be gettin' north, so I'm layin' my money on stayin' with this here bank." He tried again to spit, but his mouth was full of dry cobwebs. Sliding from the saddle, he handed the reins to Mordecai and stepped over to the edge of the river. He knelt and quenched his thirst. Josiah rose and stared out over the junction before returning to take the reins from his friend. He stood between their horses, then looked up from under the brim of his hat into Mordecai's face.

"Maybe it's only 'nother big sandbar, like them as we seen this far 'long the Platte. Maybe the river's jest flowin' round it, an' up ahead this here river pulls itself back together. Anyways 'bout it, it's the north bank we gotta be followin', Mordecai," he said, pointing with an outstretched arm the way across the horizon. "Them might only be clouds layin' out there. An' then, they might be the mountains we lookin' for." He circled the horse and leaped into the saddle. He put his hand on Mordecai's shoulder and looked into his face once more, "What you say? You with me still?"

"Guessin' you're figgerin' is 'bout as good as any man's. Yep! I'll lay my wager with your'n on this'un, Josiah."

"All right, then. Let's go find out if them are clouds or mountains." He nudged his horse away with taps from the heels of his leather boots.

The late-summer heat daily parched man and animal alike, requiring frequent stops to water their bellies and hides. Often they would dip their felt hats into the river to fill the crowns, pouring the cooling water over their heads and necks, soaking the shoulders of their shirts. Past the landmarks on the Platte River Road of the fur traders the men led their trio of plodding animals, past Courthouse Rock and on to Chimney Rock, which would one day become the guiding trailmarkers for a country stretching its arms west into the wide open. Through stretches of dusty, treeless land they pushed, clinging desperately to the river. At times only the Platte fed them. For days at a time no meat was brought in, and they were forced to fish with improvised hooks tied to the ends of short stretches of twine. It filled the stomach while both men ate on their doubts between the few meals.

Up through the late-summer horizon the mountains finally forced their peaks. "Them are the mountains," Mordecai thought out loud.

Josiah did not answer, trying to plot just where those mountains stood in relation to the direction the sun took each night as it went to its sleep beyond the horizon. He figured they were going in the right direction, staying with the river as it was heading on a northwesterly path, but each day Paddock kept looking to his left at the peaks rising to the south. They camped for the night at the mouth of a river flowing into the Platte, laying their bedrolls at the river's edge in a grove of cottonwoods.

The men had finished supper and were sucking on pipe bowls of tobacco, the still summer-night air filled only with the crack and pop of the burning embers in concert with the merging waters. Unknown to either of them, Mordecai and Josiah had reached the Laramie, where the captain's men would camp in a little more than a week before breaking up into smaller trapping parties to plunge into the mountains.

"What month ye figger it to be?" Mordecai asked, breaking the quiet spell Josiah had been in all evening. He didn't answer right away, pulling on the smoke through his pipe stem.

"Maybe...maybe first week in August, maybe second week." He drew again on the pipe, then turned his head to the side to look over at Mordecai swatting at an insect that kept buzzing around his face. "Warm this time a y'ar, ain't it?" Mordecai did not answer this time, trying to catch the pesky insect. "Not as warm as she'd be back to St. Louie, that sticky heat back there."

"Got 'im!" Mordecai leaned over to Josiah, then slowly opened his palm so both of them could examine his catch. Gradually he released one finger at a time to lay the palm open. "Damn!" The palm was empty and he looked around to see if the pestering insect was still about.

"Mordecai, what say you an' me try them hills sittin' off thar"—Josiah pointed his pipe stem almost due west—"other'n tryin' them as we been seein' off to our right?"

"Ye seein' it that we'd do all right by them to the west, huh?"

"Trappin's trappin', an' them beaver'll be up there, waitin' for us now, they are." He took the pistol from the belt of his pants and laid it beside him on the bedroll as he leaned back to cradle his head on a curled arm. "Think we jest 'bout there, my friend. Won't take us no time 'tall an' then you'll be outta this heat an' up in the cool. You'll feel much better when we get up there where it's cooler, Mordecai. We jest 'bout there now." He closed his eyes and thought of sleep.

At the foot of the mountain range they had made camp in the middle of the afternoon, Mordecai bringing in a small buck for the kettle. They sat close to the fire, pulling meat off the bone without conversation in a red glow at the end of the day.

"Halloo!" a voice called out to them, a voice without a body attached.

Both men jerked up, grabbing their rifles and scrambling behind cover. Josiah skidded behind the packs and Mordecai took to the bushes. They looked at each other, then all around, trying to see where the voice had come from but there was nobody to be seen.

"Thet veneeson them coons is cookin', Micah?" another voice cracked the air. Josiah and Mordecai strained their eyes to see where the second voice was.

"Shor look like it, Elisha. Don't it ter ye?" the first voice asked. Mordecai lay in the bushes, trying to finish the bite he had just taken when the first voice had hollered out at them.

"S'pose them niggers'd share thar victuals with'n the likes a us?" Mordecai gulped the piece of half-chewed meat down at once.

"Them look like good boys, they does, ter me least-ways, Elisha. S'pose we ask 'em real p'litelike an' see . . ."

"You fellers ain't fixin' to try an' rob us, are ye, now?" Mordecai called out, turning his head as he spoke to direct the question around him, to wherever the surprise visitors might be hiding.

"Naw, nothin' like thet, son. We kin see ye fit an' ready fer b'ar, pilgrims. We wantin' no truck with ye. Jest show us poor wayfarin' souls lil' kindness an' we behave ourse'fs, we really do."

"Show yerselves then," Josiah hollered out in the direction he figured the voice had come from. "Come on out an' show yer faces."

From above Mordecai on a little knoll pebbles came clattering down the side of the hill on him. He turned around to see a man standing atop the knoll, a man dressed in buckskins who scrambled down the side toward him. The stranger pulled the stunned Mordecai to his feet. "Yer backsides'd made a fine target if'n I'd been fixin' ter raise ha'r, son." He then walked on over to the fire. "Come on in, Micah. Don' be cussed now," he called out to the second man who had not yet appeared. Then turning to Josiah, who still squatted behind the packs, he said, "He's some shy a' times, that'un is." He then turned to yell at the trees once more. "Get yer goddamn ass in hyar afore I get ter meas'rin' yer topknot, nigger!" The bushes rattled as the second stranger emerged from his protective cover. He was big, as big a man as Josiah had ever seen, bigger than some of the Cajuns who worked the steamers back on the St. Louis levee.

"Kick my arse, ye say, Elisha," he laughed as he approached the three men, "Ye ain't growed 'nough ter pick a hug with me gran'mammy!" When the two strangers stood side by side, Micah loomed large over Elisha, who was short but of a stout frame rippling with muscle.

"Gonna kick his ass one these days, I am. On'ry jackass, he is," Elisha said to Josiah and Mordecai. "But

94

he got this'r child outta more'n one scrape'r two a' times. Smells like he sleep with a buffalo cow, don' he?" He slapped the large man in the stomach with the muzzle of his rifle. "But ye boys jest stay upwind a 'im, ye see, an' he won' be no bother to ye."

"Ye gonna get our horses ain't ye, Elisha?"

"Figgerin' ye'd be the one ter do thet!" said Elisha, sitting down by the fire.

"Sold yer hide ter Hudson Bay long 'go, if'n it were worth a thing," laughed Micah, then turned to move back into the trees after their horses.

"Ye pilgrims fixin' ter trap, it's lookin' like?" Elisha asked.

Josiah sat down beside him, "Looks that way."

"Whar 'bouts ye headin' fer yer beaver? What's yer price?"

"We figgerin' to climb into these here hills, tomorrow. See what we can pull out."

"Price too low, son. Beaver ain't got good hide yet, what as one worth the skinnin', leastways. Weather gotta get colder yet, afore them critters get back a pelt as'll be fer the tradin'.''

Josiah handed the visitor a piece of the venison stuck on the end of his knife. "Well, where you fellas headin', if not trappin' beaver?" Josiah asked as Elisha pulled the hunk of meat from the knife with his hands.

"Micah an' me, we been o'er ter ronnyvoo, ter the Cache Valley. Left them doin's early, good spree too it was, as we was figgerin' on takin' round'bout way through them mountains south a hyar. Never seen 'em, we haven't.'' He took a bite and chewed on it, then spoke once more around the lump of meat in his mouth, "Takin' our time gettin' back ter the Green, whar we fixin' ter winter-up after a fall hunt." He chewed some more and swallowed the bite, "Jest never seen thet country on south, an' allays wanted to, what with all them coons workin' outta Touse sayin' what a big belt she be down thar." He pulled more of the flesh into his mouth. "Yer veneeson ain't bad, son, not bad 't all."

"What ye know 'bout this belt?" Mordecai asked. "Ever been in these hills?" He made a jabbing motion with his head to indicate the mountains he and Josiah were planning to enter.

Elisha swallowed and looked up at his hosts, "Ye got any coffee with ye?"

"No. Run outta it back 'long the Platte a ways." He offered the visitor a cup of water from the small kettle they had filled with creek water.

The visitor wiped his right hand free of grease on his blackened buckskins, then took the cup from Mordecai. "Thankee, son." He emptied it and handed it back, then wiped his mustache and beard. "Most steers 'way from this place, trappers an' Injuns alike. Ye won' have no Injun trouble up thar, or no white-man comp'ny either."

Mordecai scooted up closer to the man. "Ye meanin' thar ain't no good beaver?"

"Didn' say thet now. Beavers gotta be good up thar' as damned cold as she gits." He finished another mouthful. "Jest thet gits so damned cold up thar in winter, it do. Better places for this'r child to be come first snow of winter'n up thar. Wouldn' calc'late as fellers like ye two would find them hills very homey."

"What makes 'em any differ'nt than others?" Josiah asked, doubtful that he was hearing anything close to the truth from the visitor.

Elisha picked up on the doubting tone in Josiah's voice, turning to him and looking at Paddock real hard before answering. "Son, ye ain't got much west a hyar 'ceptin' some flatlands. Winter winds bein' what they is, they roar inter them hills with no slowin' down. Makes fer a rougher winter knock'n most other places." He took another bite and looked away from Josiah. "Givin' 'er to ye straight, boys. Thet's rough doin's up thar. But, if'n ye pilgrims is fixin' on gettin' yer pizzer froze off, nothin' I kin say as will change yer minds."

Micah came back through the trees and tied their five animals, three of which were carrying light loads only of possibles, the two strangers having sold their beaver at rendezvous. Micah approached the fire and tested the still warm kettle water with his fingers, before reaching in to pull a large piece of meat from the pot.

"Game's good up thar, boys. Leastways, I cain't figger on the two of ye starvin'. What meat ye bring in won' spoil up thar, thet's fer shore. Damned cold she be up in thet country." Elisha shuddered a little as he thought of it.

The four men talked into the night, Elisha and Micah anxious to drop their yarns on new ears. Mordecai was the one who listened eagerly, Josiah being very doubtful of that man Elisha. The visitors spoke of their plans to move around the base of the mountains before taking off west to head for the Green before winter. Mordecai asked if he and Josiah could tag along with the two of them until they struck away from the mountains.

"Don' make me no mind, boys," Elisha answered, "if'n ye kin stand the smellin' of this mangy dog." He pointed a thumb at Micah.

The group wound their way slowly around the foothills for the next few days, each night sharing what the kettle had to offer and swapping stories between the old trappers and Mordecai. Josiah kept to himself and quiet for the most part, touchy that the two men he was trailing would come to know too much about him. But he listened intently around each night's fire as they spoke of places he longed to see, of things he longed to do, absorbing as much as he could in the short time they would be together. Mordecai chattered, and Josiah listened, both of them learning from these old men of the hills.

"Hyar tell Bridger's men'll be up north thar, not too far a piece, up ter the Powder this fall," Elisha said, stuffing tobacco in his pipe bowl, then handing some to Mordecai.

"No tellin' really whar they coon'll be. He kin tell one thing an' do 'nother, jest ter keep ye off'n his backsides," Micah answered. "Crow'll be lookin' to ease some horseflesh' 'way from 'em, they will, up ter the Powder if'n Bridger really goin' thar."

"Like me them Snakes, I do," Elisha remarked, then lit his pipe. "They likes the horses too, fer shor, but them Snakes leastways knows not to devil a trapper fer his'n."

"Most time, anyways," Micah interjected.

"Right," Elisha agreed, smoke pouring from his mouth. "Most time."

Before the two trappers pulled out the next morning, Micah gave Mordecai a small leather pouch of coffee. "Wantin' ye boys ter have this. Ain't much, but seein' as how ye don' have no coffee, an' how good comp'ny ye been fer Elisha an' me, I wanted ye ter take this with my best to ye, wishin' the best a luck wharevers ye settin' yer tracks." He jumped into the saddle, his long legs bent up at the knees in stirrups that were too short for his great height. He answered Mordecai's grin. "Them greasers

97

allays make thar saddles ter fit a man as is small like they is. Ye pilgrims take yer keer now, an' sniff the wind ever now an' then."

"Yepper," Elisha interrupted. "Bad smell in the air means one a three things: meat's arottin', a redskin's close-'bouts, or this'r coon I call my companyero." He laughed with a wide grin, showing a missing tooth.

"Get yer arse in front of me then, ye scurvy-nigger-jackass-son-of-a-whore, an' we'll be amakin' beaver fer the Green! Mebbe see ye fellers come ronnyvoo nex'," Micah said, throwing up an arm to wave a fare-thee-well as they rode off.

Josiah and Mordecai watched the men disappear to the west, heading for the Sweetwater, before loading up the one pack animal and taking to the saddle themselves. They climbed gradually into the mountains, following the run of the little creek that seemed to offer them a path to guide their melting into the high country. Game was plentiful and the water seemed as heady as wine when it poured down their throats. They stopped boiling their meat and began to broil it over the fire. But each day as they climbed higher, the signs of game were fewer.

In the middle of the afternoon on the fifth day up from the flatlands, it began to snow. The drops were big and wet, clinging to their clothing, soaking their coats and the tops of their exposed pant legs. It snowed most of the next three days. Josiah finally admitted that they would be wise to hole up and wait out the storm rather than beat the animals to complete exhaustion by forcing them through the drifts of blinding white. Finding a tall, old pine with its long branches indicating a dry refuge out of the weather, the two men slid from the saddles and pulled their gear onto the bare ground under the tree, secure from the falling snow. They set their rifles against the trunk and turned to find a place for the animals.

Taking up the reins on the dapple and the packhorse, Josiah told Mordecai, "You get us a fire started an' I'll see to the animals."

"Naw, I'll give ye a hand. Won' take but a minute," he replied taking the reins of his own horse and walking behind Josiah. They found a closely grouped stand of trees a few yards from their own shelter and tied the animals to the low-hanging branches. They started back through the snow, when Josiah wanted to turn back and brush the dapple a little, wiping her down with the saddle blanket. Mordecai stood alongside while he worked and said, "I feel like I could do with a cup of hot coffee. We'll break it out for the first time. How 'bout you?"

Josiah did not have time to answer the question as the grizzly rushed them. The horses had sounded no alarm, only now snorting and pawing at the ground as the bear lumbered down on the men, roaring with blood-chilling displeasure at Josiah and Mordecai for separating her from her cubs. At the first sound from her lungs, Mordecai had been the only one to turn around. His eyes doubled in size instantly. His mouth flew open to utter the alarm to Josiah, but no sound passed his lips. His throat was frozen in fear, seized with a lump as big as his heart, choking any sound before it could free itself past his tongue. All he could do was flap his arm uselessly behind him, trying to get his friend to turn around in those long snail-like seconds until Josiah heard the second explosion of sound from the grizzly's throat. Both men shot away from where they stood, running through the snow, both of them falling a few times as their legs attempted to carry them through the snow drifts. They floundered, fell, and rose again each time, trying to make it back to the rifles before the bear made it to them.

Mordecai dove under the sheltering branches of the tree first, grabbing a rifle and cocking it while he turned back on the grizzly. Josiah was right behind him as he brought the other rifle up and cocked it. The grizzly stopped in her tracks and stood, pawing the air and growling at the men for a moment, then dropped to all fours once more and lumbered at them. Both men stepped out from under the branches of the tree for a clear, unobstructed shot, both secure that there was no danger with two rifle balls between them. Josiah pulled the trigger, but nothing happened. Frantically he pulled and pulled on the trigger, but the hammer would not release.

"Shoot it, Mordecai! Shoot! Shoot!"

Mordecai went to set the trigger on his rifle, but the set trigger wasn't there. He held the rifle up to look at it, pulling on the only trigger there was, the ball exploding into the trees overhead. Josiah pulled back on the hammer, thinking he had not brought it back into a full-cock position, then struggled with the trigger once more while he sought to hold a bead on the grizzly.

"That's mine, that's mine!" Mordecai was yelling at him, but Josiah couldn't figure out what it meant. He fought the impulse to run, pulling back on the trigger with all his might. "That's my rifle, goddammit! Use the other trigger! You're pullin' on the set trigger!"

Paddock didn't take time to calculate what was happening, that they had picked up each other's rifles. Mordecai's had the set trigger, which allowed the front trigger to go off with a light touch. It was with this trigger that Josiah was struggling. He finally gripped the barrel stock in both hands and ran toward the grizzly, swinging the rifle over his head. She stopped, then stood to look at the advancing madman, pawing the air as he came at her, seeking to rip him apart. Mordecai wasn't frozen to the spot for long, leaping into the fracas and yelling, "Your pistol, Josiah! The pistol!" as he ran toward the wrestling match.

Paddock swung again and again, clubbing the bear's body high and low, a deep growl coming from the grizzly each time he struck her with all his might.

"Your pistol, dammit!"

Josiah clubbed her several times over the head, as if he meant to pound her into the ground before backing away. He threw the rifle toward Mordecai behind him as he reached for the pistol in his belt, but the rifle fell short, going off as it struck the ground. The animal was stunned from the beating, dropping to her front legs, then shakily rising again. Much of the bellow was gone from her roar as Josiah pulled the trigger and fired at one of her eyes from less than two arm-lengths away. The striking power of the .54-caliber ball drove her head back as she fell into the snow. Paddock stepped back as Mordecai came up to pick up the useless rifle, running his hand along the wood behind the lock, feeling the crack that ran all the way from the wrist below the tang to the butt plate.

Rolling from side to side in the powdery snow, the grizzly pawed the air with all four legs for a minute, then let out one final snorting roar before she died. The men stood motionless in the slowly falling snow, the scene about them deathly quiet now. Both shook, their blood gorged with adrenalin, staring at the dead animal while their clothing became wet with the fat snowflakes and the sweat dripping down their backs.

"Lemme have your knife, Josiah."

"I'll do it." He pushed Mordecai's outstretched hand away. "This one's my b'ar." He walked up to the side of the huge blonde creature and stood over her for a few moments before starting his first cut to pull the hide off. "Ye jest get that coffee of your'n ready, an' we gonna have grizzly steaks tonight."

Mordecai didn't take to the bear meat, but it soon became all they had to eat. Game had become hard to find by the time they finally ventured out after nine days of continuous snowfall. It was heavy on the branches overhead and had collapsed into their pine-tree shelter a few times each day, soaking the men or putting out the fire they sought to keep burning day and night.

"Winter comes early this high," Josiah muttered one evening from between the folds in a blanket he had pulled about him.

"Too much, too fast," Mordecai replied. "Ye remember what that ol' trapper tol' us, Josiah—'bout this bein' no place to set for the winter? Well, the winter's here, an' we settin'."

"That ol' jackass only wanted to scare us a lil' bit, dammit. That's all. Jest a mite peculiar. We set it out an' it'll blow over, then we get to trappin'. Beaver livin' up here gotta stay warm too, an' that means good skins for us."

The wind drifted the snow all around the tree, but they had beaten a path through the drifts out to the stand of pines where the horses had been tied through the days and nights of snow. Mordecai saw the packhorse first, lying on its side by a snowbank that had blown against the body over the long period of the blinding storm. As they approached, the dapple snorted at the men, as if to tell them what she thought of having been abandoned for so long, of having to remain tied next to the body of the dead animal. Mordecai knelt down and stroked its ear, stiffly frozen into rigor beneath his touch, one eye open wide and blank in its stare up at him.

"She didn' have no chance, Josiah. Wored out. We wore her out fightin' to get this high. Didn' have 'nough left in 'er. Didn' have no chance 't all . . ."

"C'mon. We'll move our horses an' then try some huntin'. C'mon, Mordecai," he said, lifting his friend to his feet by an arm. "Cain't do nothin' 'bout it now, can we?"

"No, no. Guess not."

They moved the two remaining horses to another sheltered stand of trees, beating their way through the snow for the animals to follow, then pushed through the drifts to stumble back to their own tree. By the time they reached their pine shelter, both were too exhausted to think about venturing out to hunt, with only enough strength left in reserve to break up some few remaining pieces of firewood to add to the dying coals. They huddled there through each day in their own misery while their horses pawed at the frozen windswept forage beneath the pines' canopies.

The wind finally died on the eleventh day, and they decided to break their way out, to follow the stream down through the mountains a way and try some trapping. Fingers numbed from the bitter cold in the early-morning air, they began to rearrange the packs so that the remaining two horses could carry the supplies and the men. Woolen gloves had not lasted long, tearing and fraying as they had struggled with wood for the fire during their snow-bound days. Now there were holes in every finger, and the cold tore through to turn the hands to ice. They sat to rest after loading the animals and before they set out.

Belly-deep in snow, the horses balked and fought them at first, until the men dismounted to walk in front of the animals, breaking through the snow for them. Each man took a turn at being in the lead, followed then by his horse, then the other man and his horse, as each could only take the lead for just so long. Back and forth they traded, resting every few hundred yards when they switched positions. Like this they fought through the next four days, the going slow and painful for man and animal.

They came upon the east side of a ridge that dropped them into a little valley, the snow not having drifted much at all, and what snow there was had been blown over by the icy wind until it had become hard-packed.

"We'll set up here," Josiah announced, "an' try trappin' them ponds over there 'long that stream." He pointed out a series of dams and lodges the industrious beaver in the valley had constructed.

Near the ridge there was not much snow at all. The wind had blown the flakes of white against the rocks then swooped them back onto the valley floor. They believed they had found a good place to winter, protected from the deep snow this time, and with a valley brimming with beaver only steps away.

Early the next morning the men set out on foot to the ponds, the air brutally cold and quiet, the moon still overhead and refusing to disappear. Josiah chipped away some ice at the edge of the bank, breaking it with a small ax so that he could drop the trap into the water. He reached around behind him and selected one of the float sticks he had cut the night before, learning from Elisha at least that you couldn't set a beaver trap without a float stick. He did not know what to do with it, only knowing to put the stick through the ring at the end of the chain attached to the trap spring. Now he opened the canvas sack that held their dozen traps, pulled one from it, and threw it to Mordecai.

"Get your arse to work, pilgrim, less'n you want that ol' trapper to devil you." He grinned at Mordecai from where he knelt on the frozen bank.

"Ye mean you're makin' me work for my skins, too?" he asked, then laughed along with Josiah. As he began to set the trap down and started to chip some ice off the pond, Josiah looked up and interrupted his work. "Goddammit, Mordecai. Go on down a ways. You're too close for us both to catch beaver. Go on down an' find your own set. Ain't no beaver gonna come to bait if we got this whole pond rounded with traps."

He picked up his ax, float stick, and trap, then cradled the rifle in his arm, trying to handle the cracked stock carefully. Shuffling through the willows, weaving back and forth along the bank, Mordecai disappeared from view by the time Josiah looked up from his work once more.

"That's one," he said to himself softly, then rose to scan the bank for another trap set. Paddock bent over to pick up the sack when he heard Mordecai yell. He froze, with his hand on the canvas trap sack, instantly trying to calculate what kind of sound it was. Did it mean Mordecai was in trouble, was he hurt, or had he just fallen into the pond and cried out as he broke through the thin ice, the startling cold forcing the sound from his lungs? Josiah straightened up and listened, then bent back down, picked up the heavy sack, and moved off slowly, looking for his next trap set. He had taken only a few steps when he heard Mordecai yell again.

"Paddock! Paddock! Paddock!"

He knew. There was nothing really concrete in his mind. But Josiah knew, nevertheless. He dropped the sack and turned, bolting off through the willows, pushing the branches out of his way with flaying arms as he dodged around the growth along the bank. His lungs burned with the cold, high-mountain air in his sprint toward the sound, branches whipping at his clothing and tearing at his face.

"Paddock! Paddock!"

Josiah skidded to a stop in the snow, sliding down on his knees a few feet away from Mordecai and stopped.

"Sweet Jesus, Josiah!"

All Paddock could do was stare for a moment, unmoving as he looked first to his friend's face, contorted in pain, then let his eyes drop from Mordecai's slowly down to the end of his arm. He had caught his hand between the large steel jaws of the trap.

"Sweet Jesus, Mordecai!"

"I done somethin' wrong, Josiah, don' know—but I done somethin' wrong." He winced again with the pain as he held the wrist of the injured hand with his left gripped deathly tight around it. "It's my shootin' hand, man, it's my shootin' hand!"

Josiah, finally shaken free, went into action and moved over to kneel in front of Mordecai, "Jest take 'er easy, take 'er easy now. We'll get you outta here real quick." He placed the sole of each boot on each of the two springs to free the jaws enough so that his friend could pull the hand out. It was crushed all the way across, bleeding only a little, but swelling around the deep, crushed fissure across the back of his right hand. Mordecai cradled it in his lap, moving slowly with the pain, the hand hanging limp and useless. What little blood was flowing from the wound was freezing quickly.

"Sweet, sweet Jesus! I didn' mean to do this to us . . ."

"C'mon, let's go get you back to camp now." Josiah helped Mordecai hold the arm across his chest as they plowed their way through the snow back toward the ridge.

"Damn, that hurts, Josiah!"

"I know, I know it do. C'mon now, jest take 'er easy an' we'll fix 'er right up," Josiah said, trying to find something to say that would comfort the man, but no words were to be found. Paddock chattered away at Mordecai all the way back, fighting his fear and apprehension for he really didn't know what to do about the hand, what to do about Mordecai's pain, what to do about the trust that filled Mordecai's tearing eyes as he sat the man down by the fire.

"I'm gonna boil some water. You jest sit tight." He gathered some limbs for the fire and placed the kettle full of cold water over the flames. Josiah then turned to the packs and found an old shirt before returning to Mordecai's side by the fire. He began to tear the shirt into strips, "Never much liked this thing anyways," he muttered on at his friend.

"I'm, I'm sorry I done this to ye . . ."

"C'mon now, don' go talkin' like that."

"Feel like I'm gonna get sick, Josiah. My stomach wants to move." He heaved a little on the snow.

"You go right 'head." He pulled a saddle over for Mordecai to lean back against, then grabbed a blanket to throw around him.

When the water finally began to warm, he noticed Mordecai had passed out. Josiah leaned over him and slapped his friend across the cheeks a few times. "C'mon, Mordecai! C'mon, wake up! Wake up!" He came to gradually and groaned in pain. "C'mon now, we gonna soak your hand." He picked up the kettle by its handle and set it down beside the other man. "Put it in there." Mordecai lifted the crushed hand with his left from under the blanket. "Easy now, easy will do it fine," said Josiah.

"Goddamn! That hurts!" he pulled his hand back out of the water.

"Jest easylike, Mordecai. C'mon now, you can do it." Josiah pushed the hand back into the water until Mordecai held it there without Josiah forcing him to. He let the hand soak for quite a while, as he finished tearing the shirt into long strips. Paddock looked up finally and saw that Mordecai had passed out again. He bathed the hand in the kettle as best he could, washing the wound with a piece of the shirt, feeling the crushed and splintered bones yield under his touch, crackling and grating with the slightest movement. It was worse than either of them had thought at first. Mordecai slept through the rest of the day and into the night, waking once every few hours weakly to ask Josiah for some water. By the next day the wound was horribly swollen and Mordecai had begun to sweat even in the frigid temperatures.

Josiah kept the hand wrapped with the strips of cloth, soaked in hot water, alternating this treatment with applications of snow directly on the blackening, wounded hand. Mordecai was restless, but at least he was sleeping through most of it. Paddock had to get away for a while; he had to escape from staying by his friend's side, constantly watching Mordecai breathing shallow and raspy. He rose quietly in the late afternoon and walked back to the ponds, thinking of retrieving the traps left the day before. Josiah went first to the trap that had crushed Mordecai's hand. He stood by the pond, fingering the cold, frosted steel. Then he walked back to where he had dropped the trap sack and put the one in with the rest. Paddock started to turn back to camp when he remembered the one trap he had set and put the sack down. At the bank he knelt by the hole that was refreezing, with a thin crust over the area he had broken. The stick on the end of the chain was wedged against the edge of the thickening ice. He broke it loose and pulled the trap up from the water, a large beaver caught in the jaws by one paw.

Unmoving, he stood on the bank looking down at the beaver dangling lifeless by its paw in the trap, the water on its pelt slowly freezing into ice, exposed to the cold air. Josiah stared at it, looking at the paw, then at the creature's eyes, and back to the paw. He set it down on the ground and opened the jaws, picking the beaver up by the wounded back leg. Josiah looked at it once more, then threw the body across the pond with tremendous force, the beaver landing on the other side among the willows. He dropped the trap in his sack and walked back to camp, fighting his angry tears as the snow began to fall again.

By that evening, the wind was howling, swirling the flakes into a blur beyond their fire. Josiah pulled the bear hide from the packs and threw it down on the ground close to the warmth of the burning logs, then gently lifted the unconscious Mordecai onto the hide. Over his friend he placed several blankets, keeping two for himself as he sat huddled near the embers. His stomach growled hungrily and he remembered he had not eaten in two days. But though his stomach complained, Paddock had no appetite, so he let the pangs pass without feeding. He listened for a long time to the howling wind, accompanied by Mordecai's labored breathing, before falling asleep himself.

Josiah awoke early the next morning and attempted to wake Mordecai, but it was useless. He was now beginning to sweat more, and Paddock began to bathe his face with snow as he kept the hand buried in a small pile of white ice hour after hour. His friend no longer awoke throughout the days and nights asking for water, but began to answer the howling, ice-driving wind with an eerie, delirious, rambling mumble-talk that made no sense to Josiah at all. From time to time Josiah would kneel by Mordecai while he was talking in his delirium, eyes wide open, staring right through Paddock into the swirling snow about them.

"Mordecai, it's me. It's Josiah! Mordecai? Mordecai?" But there was no answer from his eyes; no answer from his lips. Paddock kept up the ritual night after day, in and out of the cycle of bathing his friend's wounded hand and burning face. By the fifth day after the accident, the snow had not let up, not dropping in its intensity or viciousness. He didn't care. He wasn't going anywhere. Forcing himself to eat to keep up his strength, Josiah chewed on small bits of half-cooked bear, choking it down after grinding it between his teeth only a few times.

By the seventh day, Mordecai was becoming ghostly. When Josiah pulled the blanket back to lift the hand out for the ritual snow packing, he could see Mordecai's hand and lower arm had turned gray, the skin bloated and swollen. He stared at it for only a moment before he felt his stomach lurch. He turned his head just in time to vomit what little remained in it. He gagged again and again with the dry heaves. His throat and mouth burned with stomach acid, all that was left to come up with the muscular action of each violent contraction. Finally, all that remained were the tremors that shook through his whole body. Josiah scraped a hand across the snow and clumsily brought some of it to his mouth, most of the flakes smearing across his beard and chin. Over and over he ate snow to drown the taste of the stomach acid etching his throat. The snow coated the inside of his cheeks until they were numbed with cold, melting wetness. He covered Mordecai's hand with the blanket without looking at it, and returned to his own blankets.

The blowing snow lasted through the hours of the next three days and into the fourth. Somewhere in his mind he tried to recall the past eleven days, trying to remember how he had passed them. He couldn't. He only knew it had been a long time, crouched within his blankets through most of it, enclosed within this white cage of swirling, icy snow that bit at his skin like razors. Each day's biggest project was forcing himself to break away from the camp and cross the few yards to where the horses stood, each day scraping the snow clear from more and more ground in hopes the animals could paw up enough to stay alive eating what little undergrowth there was. They too were growing weak and gaunt with the hunger and the cold. Then Josiah noticed they had been chewing on the willow sticks he and Mordecai had cut for their trap sets. They had even been nibbling on each other's tails and manes.

It was then that his brain finally demanded that he feed his stomach, to give something back to his body for all he was demanding of it. Paddock clawed through the snow in search of more wood for the fire before he struggled back to camp.

Josiah searched through all the packs, but the meat had been eaten except for a small roast the size of his outstretched hand. Over the fire he roasted it only enough to sizzle the outside flesh before ripping strips of meat off between his teeth, chewing the raw flesh between teeth set in aching gums while forcing it down. Then there was no more. Mordecai rambled on without ceasing, mumbling incoherently about things Josiah had given up trying to understand. He was delirious, suffering under a fever, his mind and body in a state of severe, traumatic shock. New metabolic processes were taking over now, and Josiah had simply given up. More days passed as Mordecai talked less and less in his fiery delirium. He grew hotter and hotter, sweating more each day, often kicking the blankets off in his sleep as he twisted and thrashed about. The white cage twisted and turned about the two men while Josiah's stomach groaned for food, his brain demanding that he feed it once more. "But, I ain't got nothin' to feed you," he told his stomach out loud, his eyes drooping as he had become worn and frail through the long ordeal.

"Thar's flesh about, boy."

Josiah lifted his head at the sound of the voice, opening his eyes fully, in wonder at where the voice had come to him from.

"Under them blankets, Paddock."

He looked at Mordecai a few feet away, sweating, and as pale as the snow surrounding the heavy blankets. Josiah shook his head violently a couple of times as if to clear his ears.

"C'mon, son. No use in ye goin' under too. That's meat that'll keep ye alive!"

The voice rang in his ears. He couldn't stop it. Josiah decided to answer.

"You . . . you mean, eat on Mordecai?"

"That's the trick, boy."

"Naw, I couldn't. I couldn't!" he hollered back at the wind. "Ain't no way I bring myself to feed on Mordecai."

"No one'll ever know. No one knows the two of ye up hyar now, do they? No one'll ever know, now will they?"

Josiah rose to his knees, looking around him into the blinding white air. "But—I'll know," he cried out.

"Son, he's holdin' ye back, yer waitin' fer 'im to die. Man's gonna die anyway!"

"Mord's my friend!"

"I know that as well as ye do, son, but he'll be gone soon 'nough as 'tis—an' when he's gone that'll he'p his frien'."

"How you figgerin' he's gonna help me then? I mean, I don't understand."

"Stupid jackass—he'll he'p ye keep goin', livin' on his flesh!"

Josiah felt his mind slipping. He fought to rise to his feet, but the legs were shaky and he fell back to the ground. "You meanin'? You meanin' really chew on a man's meat?"

"That's flesh, boy; wither it be coon or elk—or man—flesh is flesh. An' your'n needs his flesh right now!"

The voice pressed stronger, louder in his ears. "Flesh is flesh . . ."

Josiah turned his head to look at Mordecai's body quiet beneath the blankets, his shallow breaths widely spaced, each one sending a slight tremor through his body. He watched his friend breathe in and out slowly for a long time, not really thinking about the man he watched as a person, as a man. Slowly Josiah drew the pistol from his belt and cocked the hammer back, looking around for the voice once more, to give him strength, but all was quiet now through the valley. Josiah rose to his knees and crawled over to Mordecai through the snow. The pistol shook with the trembling of both hands as he pressed the muzzle against Mordecai's temple.

Across the valley the silence lay heavy as a cow elk stumbled along, lost in the snowstorm. All was so quiet that the only sounds one could hear were the thick, wet flakes falling on the white-draped pines. And it was so cold that every sound seemed to splinter in the still, dry air, breaking into a million tiny fragments. The cow bolted off blindly, crashing through the willows at the blast of the pistol somewhere through the white curtain. The blast was followed instantly by the cry of a man's voice, which loudly pierced the mountain air as it echoed from the ridge, "Aw-w-w-w-g-g-g-gh-gh-gh!"

Josiah lay crumpled beside Mordecai after he had fired the shot into the trees in anger and frustration, and then cried out to the peaks above him. As he had put the muzzle to Mordecai's temple, Josiah noticed that his friend had stopped breathing. He was dead. To feel pain no more, to feel bone-numbing cold no more, to ramble on in his delirium no more. Mordecai was dead. He lay beside the body in a heap across the snow, sobbing to sleep, his shoulders quaking violently at the emptiness that overwhelmed him, overpowering him physically as nothing else ever had.

The months had passed quickly, looking back on them as he did now. He tried to calculate what month it might be, for the winds no longer blew violently, the snows were not so deep, and the sun hung longer in the sky. Following his friend's death, Josiah had neglected the animals for some time, but finally remembered that he must attend to them. He remembered now for some reason how fitting it was that he had found Mordecai's horse dead in the snow. It had been the flesh he fed on through the rest of that winter, refusing as he did to leave the valley just yet.

But now the sun came out almost every day, dressing the brilliant, white carpet across the valley in a burst of blinding light. Paddock decided it was time at last to be moving out, to force his way down out of these mountains and wander in search of other valleys. He brought the dapple over to camp and tied the saddle aboard her, placing one bulky pack of supplies and his gear behind it across her rump.

Josiah picked up Mordecai's rifle and held it a moment, fingering the cracked wrist along the stock and remembering the struggle with the grizzly. He then stood it back against the tree. Climbing into the saddle, he looked one last time at the cairn he had built for Mordecai's body after wrapping it in the bearskin. Over his friend, Paddock had placed a pile of neatly stacked timber, wedged together tightly so that no predator would disturb the remains. He had worked for weeks to cut and carve the lumber so that each piece fit around the body exactly. As a final touch, he had put thick pine boughs to drape over the wood cairn, to give Mordecai as decent a burial as he could in this high country. Beside this mountain tomb Paddock had slept each night and eaten each day, refusing to leave until now.

Pulling the reins to the left, Josiah kicked the dapple into movement across the flat white of the valley floor. As he began to climb the other side of the valley, he pulled the horse up and stopped, turning to look back in the direction he had come from, back toward the cairn.

"Don't you ever look behind you. What you're runnin' from might be gainin' on you. Them ghosts'll haunt you only if you let 'em..."

He kicked the mare into motion and climbed out of the valley.

Getting out of the mountains, his dapple had floundered often. She was not strong as she had once been. The winter had taken its toll on her too. The man and animal crawled at a snail's pace through the days of fighting deep snow with a high, bright sun overhead. The warming weather made the going rougher as it softened the icy snow and allowed both of them to break through the crust on the top of the snow, always stumbling along as they pushed on slowly down through the mountains. The streams were beginning to break up, running faster and faster as they became swollen with the spring runoff. Now and then he would camp near some beaver ponds on his way out of those hills. But he never trapped.

Game was scarce at times, but he managed to kill a

buck or doe when food was really needed, enough to feed himself. Through every muscle of his body he could feel his strength slowly returning. Lady Missoura grew sleeker as she fed on the new grasses breaking through the cold earth. They were making it from one meal to the next, from one day to the next. And that was all Josiah expected, satisfied again to take one day as it came to him.

He finally reached the foothills on a bright day around the middle of the morning. Dismounting to let the mare feed for a few moments before continuing the journey, Josiah turned back, his mind once again picturing a high mountain valley filled with the echoing, rambling chatter of a man in a delirium, a man dying. He listened awhile, then shook the sounds out of his head, telling himself there were no such things as ghosts. He leaped into the saddle and raced the dapple down out of the foothills onto the flatlands. Something inside Josiah Paddock had died up there.

Each night found Josiah further west. He crossed some rugged, brutally carved land looking for the Sweetwater the two trappers had spoken of, a river they told him would carry him west to the divide. That was his passion for the next long weeks, to put the wall of a continent between him and what lay behind. He felt that the spine of ragged, shining mountains would protect him from all that had been, showing him all that was to be on the other side of those peaks. He struck the Sweetwater and began to follow its course to the west, its waters flowing past him on their journey to the Gulf of Mexico. Along the river he passed the huge, lonely, turtle-shaped rock in the middle of the plains, a rock on which many had already carved their names and bits of news from the settlements in the east. He then had to detour around a steep canyon through which the river plunged. He met the river once more on the other side of the narrow gate to pass by a landmark standing among the hills, a rock formation that seemed to be cut in two. Josiah smiled as he remembered the cleavage of the tavern maid's breasts and didn't feel so alone.

He pulled up on the dapple's reins slowly, bringing the animal to a halt. Reaching inside his filthy, worn shirt, Paddock located the ribbon that connected him with St. Louis, the ribbon that remained to tie him to the woman who comforted him back there. Throughout the whole winter he had gone without the warmth of remembering while he stayed beside the remains of his friend. Now he could allow himself the freedom of letting the memory wash over him in a flood. The sense of loss that struggled to overwhelm him in St. Louis was strangely akin to the loss that had overcome him when Mordecai's suffering finally ended. He tried to remember the smell of the damp hair he had brushed away from her neck, and sniffed the air. It was too dry here. He could not remember the warm, dusky smell of her, but he thought he remembered her touch. And he didn't feel so alone.

The flat land continued, rising gradually across the many miles of table that stretched toward the horizon. Off to his right, mountains rose through the low, spring rain clouds, their heads pointing toward the blue heavens, beckoning to him. Paddock stayed on the Sweetwater only shortly as it curved to the north. He then struck out to the west to skirt the southern end of the mountains in search of food. He was tiring of what little antelope he had scared up and sought some venison for a change of diet. On the western slope of the range, he found deer hard to find. Josiah had to climb higher and higher through the foothills in search of game.

In the early morning he decided he would leave Lady Missoura in a stand of trees where she could eat while he went out to hunt on foot. He had been unsuccessful for many days hunting from horseback. Josiah slipped from the saddle and tied the horse off, then pulled his drooping felt hat down tighter on his head. Leaning the rifle against a tree, he unbuttoned the fly of his pants and urinated. The dappled mare pawed the ground as she picked through the grasses. He rebuttoned his pants, then threw back his shoulders to readjust the shirt that draped loosely now over his frame before cinching the belt up. There was a lot of leather left when he had it tight around his waist. Paddock scratched at the growing bank of whiskers down the side of his face and under the chin, then picked up the rifle and started up the side of the hill. It looked as if there was a small open spot up a way and there, he thought, he might stand a chance of lying back in the trees and waiting for a nice, fat buck.

Creeping carefully through the aspens and into the pines, he came to the edge of the clearing and halted suddenly, then ducked back behind a tree. Poking his head around the edge of the pine, he looked again. Yep. Two animals. Looked like horses. And down below them a short distance sat the figure of a man. Josiah squinted, trying to make the man out. His back was turned to Paddock. He had long, straight black hair with what looked to be a piece of bright blue cloth tied about his head. Josiah knelt down beside the tree to get a better look at the man. He figured him to be an Indian from the way he was dressed, and from his hair. His palms began to sweat and his throat went dry. To come all this way, in all this time, an' now run into a goddamn Injun here, he thought. He wiped the palms of his hands one at a time across his thighs. The Indian's clothing was buckskin, fringed and quilled, and he had a knife stuck in a belt at his back. That straight black hair was greased and shining in the early-morning sun. A warrior! The thought made his stomach roll.

On the ground around the sitting figure lay scattered packs and bundles. Musta killed some trapper jest lately, he thought and squinted again to see if he could pick out the body of a dead man on the ground, but could not see what he thought he must.

Then Josiah discerned the shape of a rifle butt sticking out from under the Indian's right arm, lying cradled across the redskin's lap. He was calculating what his chances would be of shooting the man here and now in the back, weighing that against quietly slipping away before being discovered. Paddock looked about him nervously, expecting that the warrior might not be alone, only left to guard the plunder until the others in the war party returned. Prob'ly chasin' that poor devil's partner right now, he thought, his mind picturing the story as he felt it must have happened. Then his leg cramped in agony as he knelt by the tree, looking at the back of the Indian's left shoulder, measuring the odds. He had to move that leg to release the cramp, and as he did the heel of his boot snapped a twig.

Its crack sounded like thunder to him. His heart began to race as he looked down and swore at the offending leg, then looked back up to see if he had been heard by the Indian. A magpie took to flight over him, crying out loudly as its wings clawed for altitude. The bird disappeared down the slope toward Lady Missoura, who let out a gentle snort when it dove past her. He figured that was it. He figured this was the time to be going, and began to move, cracking another dry limb underfoot. Josiah froze behind the limbs of a tree, watching the man suddenly push himself behind one of the bundles.

"I heerd you, you nigger," the man yelled at him from around the pack. "Ain't no use keepin' yourself secret in them trees!"

That's a white man! his mind told him, but it just did not fit.

"You might'n come on out now—got a ball for your paunch if'n you choose not to."

Josiah squirmed a little beside the tree. The cramp was no longer in his leg but in his stomach; it pinched him not only in hunger but in surprise and fear that the figure was a white man. He looked back down the hill nervously, but dismissed the thought of making a run for it. The man would be able to get a shot off before he could make it to the dapple. His rifle suddenly weighed heavy in his hand. And Josiah suddenly felt very small. If this was it, so be it.

He took a couple of anxious steps forward around the pine branches so that he came into full view. The man raised his chin off the ground, but kept the rifle pointed at Josiah all the time.

"Point that squirrel gun somewhars else, an' we'll palaver 'bout this," the man called out to him. Paddock looked down at the rifle hanging at the end of his right arm, the rifle that weighed a hundred pounds to him now, then looked back at the man as he brought the muzzle up and the butt clunked to the ground.

"C'mon over here. Lemme take a lookee at you," he told Josiah, then pointed his muzzle away from the stranger.

7

His mind slowly cleared of the haze of sleep, but he did not open his eyes. Lying there quietly for a moment savoring the warmth of the blankets where he kept his chin nuzzled against his chest, head buried deep beneath the blankets, he was unwilling to move just yet. Finally rolling over onto his other side, he snuggled down within his bedroll, then curled his legs up, thinking only of this rich luxury called sleep. How warm and safe he felt here.

The air split with a scream near his ear, piercing through the blankets he had pulled over his head in the night. His body arched instinctively, as he struggled with one hand to pull the pistol from his belt while the other pulled the knife from the top of his boot. Both feet were furiously kicking at the blankets wrapped over his body, binding him.

"Easy, Josiah! Easy!" Scratch hollered as he stepped away from the man he had just awakened with a guttural war whoop. Josiah blinked, rubbed his eyes with the hand that had been trying to pull the pistol from his belt, then looked up at the older man. Paddock sat among the heaps of his bedroll where the blankets had landed as he had kicked at them following the scream in his ear. His heart was still hung high in his throat as he sought to speak.

"Don't you ever do that again, you ol' buzzard!" he choked on the words.

"Didn' know you'd take such a mind to it, Josiah. Best you be sleepin' now with one ear open all time, for the sake of both us." He gestured toward the animals, "C'mon now, we movin' out soon's you wrap them blankets up."

Josiah looked over at the animals as Scratch spoke, seeing that they were loaded and waiting, merely shadowy forms in the predawn darkness. Paddock blinked, looking around at their camp, and found everything as if they had never been there. Rising slowly, he pulled the blankets together, spread them carelessly on the ground and rolled them up. Josiah walked over to his horse and slung the roll over the animal's back behind the saddle, cinching the roll down with the long leather whangs that would keep it in place.

"Good name, it is, friend," Scratch remarked as he crawled onto the piece of buffalo robe over his saddle.

"What's that?"

"Josiah. Good name, Josiah."

"Oh. Guessin' I like it." He put his foot in the stirrup and climbed onto the dapple's back. "Guessin' I gotta like it, seein' as how it's the one's been given me." He pulled the rifle across the tops of his thighs, nestling it down against him comfortably.

"You'll earn yourself one of your own up here, Josiah. Get yourself a name as will be your own, an' no other coon's," Scratch said wrapping the rope that strung back to Hannah around his left hand, then dropping it over the pommel in a knotted loop. "It'll be your'n for better or worse, 'pendin' on the man you make of yourself. Kinda like gettin' hitched up to a white squar—for better or worse it'll be." He nudged his pony forward out of the trees down into the bowl, "Wanna be outta these foothills afore sunup, down into that greasewood afore any pesky varmints are up an' abouts."

As they dropped out of the bowl north by northwest, the young man contented himself with the sights around him. Through the dark shadows of the early morning they rode without a word. Now and then Josiah turned to look back over his right shoulder at the broad, flat plateau they were leaving behind, that tableland at the south end of the mountains that rose through the gray shrouds of mist. Their blue peaks were now barely lighted against the awakening eastern sky on the other side of the divide, and the clouds hung like heavy shawls draped carelessly around the peaks' shoulders. The clouds blotted out almost everything of the mountains except those peaks. The men and animals moved slowly away from the foothills. Paddock shivered in the early chill and pulled the heavy blanket coat collar around his neck. The sky to the east turned gray, then purple, and finally a bright pink over the first few hours of travel. Josiah preferred busying himself with the changing sky behind him to staring at Hannah's swaying rump before him. Gradually every sharp, hoary peak stood out boldly against the sky above the thinning mist. As he rolled from side to side in the saddle, it seemed to Josiah that the mountains moved along with him, like granite giants awaking from their slumber, stirring from their soft, cottony beds.

"They seem alive, don' they," he said to himself, looking over his shoulder at the growing definition of their outline.

"What's that, son?" Scratch had turned around when he heard Paddock speak.

"Said them mountains seem alive, don' they?"

"More 'live 'n mos' think, Josiah." He pulled on the reins of the pony to slow her while Paddock came up to ride beside him. "'Sides Injuns an' critters as like man meat, there's hoodoos an' spirits up there."

"Hoodoos?"

"Them's the spirit medeecin in the high country. An' tha's no baldface neither. Up north toward Hudson's Bay country, the Frenchies got their own names for the hoodoos, half man, half wolf they be."

"You mean ghosts?"

"Not rightly. No. Not ghosts. Back up there," he said quietly, cocking his head back toward the mountains they were leaving behind, "in the mountains is lots of strange you cain't rightly figger out. Ever' now an' then some sound come to my ol' ears, an' Scratch cain't figger out jest what it might be. Injuns say theys spirits makin' them noises."

Josiah laughed, "An' you're no better'n them Injuns neither." But he saw that the old man was not laughing with him. "Aw, c'mon, Scratch! You don't really believe any of that 'bout them ghosts an' spirits up there, now do you?"

He didn't answer for a few moments, then looked back over his shoulder at the mountains, before finally turning to face Josiah. "Don' know as I do. Don' know as I don' believe it all. Only thing this here coon knows is there's lots of y'ars atop my saddle, an' there's been times as Ol' Scratch's been a might skeery. Cain't rightly tell it, in a way as you'd understand, but I get a feelin' ever' now an' then that somethin's over my shoulder, watchin' me. Or, I hear somethin' that jest don' fit right with what I oughtta be hearin' up there . . . you know? You got any idear what I'm talkin' 'bout?" he asked, squinting his eyes into slits with an odd pinched look on his face as he turned once more to look back at the peaks. Behind them the sky was brightening. Soon this western slope would be painted with the splash of morning light.

"I'm thinkin' you been up here too long already, Scratch. You gottin' as crazy as them Injuns talkin' 'bout their spirits an' ghosts an' hobgoblins!"

"Naw. May sound loony to you now, Josiah. Cain't

rightly tell you 'bout it, but, mark these tracks I make with me tongue as they're as clear as any sign you'll ever read. Ol' Scratch knows what he feels. An' what Ol' Scratch feels keeps his ha'r!" He raised his left arm as if by instinct and pulled the blue bandanna down more tightly on his head.

Scratch remembered the nights alone in the mountains, those nights of dark and fear when he could not sleep, waiting out the long hours of blackness many times without a fire, listening to the sounds drift up to his ears from the shadows around him. Memories of those nights spent in gnawing mystery chewed at his stomach now, but he told himself not to let his imagination run away from him. There were nights when a sudden rain had dropped on him, lasted only brief minutes, then was gone just as suddenly as it had come leaving him wet and chilled, leaving him spooked and sleepless. There were nights camped by frozen streams when he heard sounds of some one or some thing as if walking on the ice with crackling, careful footsteps. There were nights of sitting huddled within his robes, staring into the ink-black shadows close about him, straining to figure out what had caused those rocks to slip loose and tumble down some canyon not far away, their dying echo drifting to his ears through the moonless dark with a sound that seemed to bounce around his mind from peak to peak before it was finally stilled.

There were the great sandstone monuments left standing alone in valley floors and deep within canyon depths, solitary sentinels that stood like giants waiting for night and new life, waiting for the unwary and the disrespectful to tread upon their domain. He had seen them from time to time during his daylight travels, and he had always hurried to be gone before the sun fled the sky at the end of the day. He had passed by them in silent, wide-eyed awe, looking up at the huge monoliths, studying them, wondering if the legends about these petrified giants were true—deciding each time not to take the chance, deciding to take an old medicine man's admonition never to sleep in such a place as he would never wake, struggling through an eternity of hell and torture. He had once tried to shake it from his mind as superstitious fear by a superstitious people, but his guts had told him differently. So he hurried the animals away from such places. At night he would listen carefully, hearing the sounds of rocks crashing, magnified over and over as their deathly cries echoed about him, remembering all the while those legends of the giants warring in those valleys and canyons. The sighs of the wind through the tree branches and the quivering of moonless shadows only made more real the fears hidden deep within his bowels. At first light following those sleepless nights, Scratch watched the mists about him swirl uneasily in the early-dawn breezes, watched them closely as they seemed to take ghostly form, then dissipate—that sequence continuing until the mists were finally burned off by the rising sun. The rifle he always pulled more closely to him across his arms never eased the queer feeling he carried inside while he remembered the stories and legends told by the old Crow men around winter lodge fires, stories told by faces deeply carved with the lines of age and experience, legends told by eyes widened with fear and awe at their mystery.

"Two, maybe three days get us to the Seedskedee, Josiah . . ."

"Seedskedee?"

"Prerra hen. In Crow. River as we'll follow north a ways till she turns east an' we make beaver west from there."

The sun was climbing to the middle of the sky when Scratch pulled on the pony's reins. Josiah stopped too and looked over at the old man. "Sandy, friend. We makin' good time." He pushed his heels into the pony's flanks and moved the animals down the bank toward the stream without saying another word, then climbed the other side and continued northwest, keeping the belt of blue, windy mountains off to his right as they plodded through the sage and greasewood, accompanied only by the sun and wind. The animals' hoofs kicked up small clouds of alkali dust that bit and stung a man's lips and nostrils.

The land looked to Josiah as if it had been cut up with a knife, carved out of the rolling hills with some mad scheme in mind. Here and there were small bunches of wildflowers struggling in the sun-baked alkaline soil to break the monotony of the stunted bushes, whipped by the winds. Here and there they would cross some nameless little stream, its banks crowded with small stands of cottonwood that stood out starkly against the bleak surrounding countryside.

"Bad water," Scratch would mutter between cracking

ips when Josiah asked to stop for a drink, "that's bad water."

"Aw-w-w! How can water be bad?" he snapped, as he slipped from the saddle and walked into the stream, dipping cupped hands into the water and pouring it over his head. Scratch did not move, but sat quietly on his pony watching Paddock dip handful after handful from the stream and bring it to his mouth. "Tastes bad, but it's wet! Don't you want any of this?"

"Nope."

"Your tongue a might touchy 'bout the taste, ol' man?" he gibed, throwing some of the cool water at the man on horseback.

"Nope. L'arnt long time ago that it don' pay to drink what water as my animals won' touch."

Josiah stopped his play suddenly as the words hit him. It did seem strange that the animals stood in the creek of cool flowing water but were not drinking. "Why they ain't drinkin'?" Josiah prodded.

"Bad water," he said cryptically as he dug his heels into the pony's sides and pulled Hannah across the stream after him.

Josiah stood dumfounded in the water, looking from the dappled mare that had refused to take a drink, then to stare at the old man's back as he rode away. "Scratch! Hey! Scratch! Why they ain't drinkin'?"

The older man did not turn around to answer the question, just yelling back loudly, "Tol' you. Bad water."

Josiah splashed through the stream running toward the dapple, falling once, then jumped aboard. "Hey, you ol' bastard! Wait up! Wait up, will you!" he hollered, kicking his horse into movement. "Why they ain't drinkin' none of this water! Scratch, goddammit!" He brought the horse to a gallop to catch up with the older man, reining up finally in a small whirlwind of alkali dust. "Goddammit! Now, Scratch, tell me!"

"Jest l'arnt long time ago not to drink no water as my animals won' drink. Make you sick, it will."

"Shit! You're crazy! Water cain't make you sick." He had not really been worried until now.

"You jest wait, Josiah. You jest wait an' l'arn yourself a lesson. You'll find out not to drink such water. Sometimes things ain't what they 'pear to be." He chuckled quietly for a few moments before adding, "That water'll make it so's you can shit through the eye of a needle without hittin' either side of that eye!" He chuckled softly then grew silent.

Josiah stared off into the shimmering distance that lay before them, chewing on his thoughts for a moment. "Still figgerin' you got a lot to teach me, Scratch?"

The old man didn't look over at him when he spoke, "Lookin' much that way, young'un'."

"Maybe so. Then maybe not. We'll get along jest fine if you don't try to jam nothin' down on me. I knows more'n you're givin' me charge for."

Bass turned to look at the young man on the dapple for the first time since they had left the creek. "Maybe so. An' then, maybe no. Pups is always ready to say they's outgrowed the litter afore they's really ready to go fotchin' on their own. Pups is always ready for a scrape or two, till they smartins up an' finds it's sometimes wiser to pick their scrapes, 'stead of roarin' in with the ha'r 'long their backbone standin' up, snortin' in a funk all the time."

The inside of Paddock's mouth was growing caked with a thin alkaline film. He ran his tongue around the inner cheeks and gums to relieve the crusty dryness. "You're thinkin' you're figgerin' me all out, ain't you, ol' man?"

Scratch finally turned away and looked across the milky horizon, "You're the child as is forgettin' that Titus Bass is a man as once a time had that wild feather ticklin' his ass, a pup as come to the mountains brave as a buffler in spring with his nose high in the air. Jest don' black your face to me, Josiah, an' we gonna be two as'll shine in any crowd. You could a done worse than happenin' on to me, by a long chalk. There's niggers as would a ripped your plunder an' nary felt squampshus 'bout it. Niggers an' devils come in any color, an' a man bein' white up here don' claim no special 'count for him. I been down that trail, I have, an' I knows the sign, hard rock or no. Son, I knows the sign, an' I'm fixin' to get through them water scrapes till we get the green wored off'n you."

He looked back over at Josiah momentarily out of the corner of his eye, then turned to face him once more, "Scratch is one as figgers there's some fine man cached up under all that foofaraw you're hole't up behind. But if'n that man Paddock don' wanna freeze into the grainin' as is got to be done to flesh the green off, then we can part when we drop rein to ronnyvoo. Cain't say as I want no truck with you, but I don' want no part of a pup as'll be gettin' Scratch's ha'r parted by some red nigger 'long with his own. If'n you don' care a cuss, then you take your stick somewhar's else come ronnyvoo. Ain't got no itch to go under jest yet 'count of some pup as is a might heavy in horn first time out on the ruttin' ground. You got the makin's of a reg'lar hivernant, you do, Josiah. Jest measure your powder first, then Paddock an' Bass'll shine." He was silent some moments, then tugged on the mule's rope gently a couple of times. "C'mon up here, Hannah, c'mon." He then went back to scanning the country about them from side to side.

Paddock knelt on the bank of the Green River, working at slicing some meat from the quarters of the elk they had brought along with them for the journey. The flesh had dried more than half an inch deep during their march across the arid land, proving its own protection for the soft and tender meat that lay beneath the crust. The animals were restless this evening, swishing their tails and moving around as much as they could in the stand of willows where they were hobbled and tied. From time to time Josiah looked at them, wondering what was making them so skittish this evening. Then he knew.

Paddock slapped at the side of his face, stinging his cheek in an attempt to kill the mosquito. Now they had found a juicy target and began coming in numbers. He fought them as he kept cutting the meat, then decided he would just have to ignore them if supper was going to be put before the fire. Josiah rolled down the sleeves of his shirt and tried to pull each one down over his hands after he had turned the collar up around his ears and cheeks. But they liked his forehead, buzzing around his eyes as he blinked to keep them from landing. He fought them for several minutes, then threw down the knife in disgust and frustration, and sat down folding his arms over his knees to hide his face within them.

"Skeeters bad this here time of y'ar round the Seed-skedee," said Scratch, pulling dried buffalo chips from a huge trap sack which for many years had been given over to carrying such firewood. It had become his insurance policy to carry a supply of such animal dung to guard against not having a fire in those times when greasewood and sage, willow, or cottonwood was not available down here on the flats. Josiah looked up momentarily to see him pulling the round, flat chips from the sack. They looked much like the pastries he once bought each evening from old Joseph Robidoux, then he grunted once before returning his face to the protective womb formed by his arms.

"Drag out such as this here buffler wood an' them skeeters be gone soon. Stuff makes some smoke, it does, an' them skeeters cain't stand that kinda smoke. Here, Josiah." The old man pulled the greasy leather pouch he had slung over his shoulder around to his front and began to dig through it until he pulled out a little vial made of elk antler. "This here'll keep them skeeters off'n you till we gets us a cookin' fire goin' with the buffler wood." He tossed the vial over to Paddock. The younger man opened it, pulling the antler stopper out, and the nauseating odor of the castoreum hit him square in the face. He wrinkled up mouth, nose, and the corners of his eyes as he turned his head to escape the smell.

"Smells jest 'bout as bad to skeeters, too," said Scratch. "Put that on your face, rub it in good, you hear? Any place them skeeter critters is devilin' you—they 'll be gone straightway."

Josiah held the vial at arm's length, but still could not escape the rancid, musky odor of the milky castoreum he poured into his left palm.

"Go 'head, boy," Scratch prodded. "Sooner's the better for you." Such repellent came from two glands that lay just beneath the skin near the hind quarters of the beaver, and was often valued by the trappers as highly as the beaver pelt itself. It was this castoreum that served as the smelly bait that brought a curious, jealous, or territorial-guarding beaver to the trap. Besides, the mountain trappers had learned that such "milk"—"goober," some trappers called it—could be used for many other things in his wilderness life. "Smear it round on you good now. Keeps you from gettin' et up."

"If I don't choke to death from the smellin' of it first!" He began finally to smear it on the back of his neck, already swollen with little red bumps the mosquitoes had left behind.

"Jest gotta l'arn to live with yourself all over, Josiah," said Scratch, striking fire steel against a piece of flint about the size of his open palm, and sending sparks down onto some charred cloth tinder. When it had caught, he brought the tinder to his lips and blew gently on it until a small glow emerged within it. Scratch set the burning cloth down within a pile of small pieces he had torn from the animal fodder and soon had a growing, smoky fire going. "L'arn lots 'bout yourself out here, my friend. Many come the times as you'll do things you wouldn' catch yourself doin' back toward the settlements. We'll pull that man outta you up here, Josiah, pull out a man as'll surprise you, mos' likely."

Paddock finished smearing the repellent over his face and neck, then wiped it across the backs of his hands and around the wrists where they were exposed. Hannah snorted in anger because her tail wasn't keeping the pesky insects away from her eyes; she tried vainly to keep her ears twitching as the mosquitoes attempted to land on her head.

From the Green, they moved on a course north by northwest, heading for the range of mountains through which they would push on to the rendezvous in Pierre's Hole. Scratch set the trail they followed, which lay between ranges of mountains that rose abruptly to their left and right. He pulled Hannah along behind him as he hurried to get through the tablelands and foothills, hurried to get up higher into the forests. Most of the day he had nervously watched the dark bank of clouds rolling east as they pushed west, anxious over what those clouds might hold for early-summer travelers here beyond the divide. The dark sky boiled and foamed until he could make out the thick curtain of rain that was falling heavily from those low-hanging clouds.

Scratch marveled at the speed with which the storm raced toward them. He pushed the little party quickly, hoping they could be within cover by the time it moved over them, cussing at himself out loud from time to time for not having made the right decisions, not having judged that such early-summer storms move more quickly than others, swearing at himself with growing passion for not having calculated that such storms are highly unpredictable as to what they might drop on the unwary.

The high clouds that raced along before the storm turned gray, then began to drop a gentle rain on the men and animals struggling for higher ground. Higher and higher across the tableland they rode as the storm thrust itself at them, darkening the sky and loosing on them heavy drops that snapped and popped against their clothing. The dry earth beneath the animals' feet soaked up the moisture at first, then could hold no more after several hours of the race. The soil turned to gumbo, a thick sticky mud more like moist clay. Scratch struggled with Hannah, cussing at her, pulling continually at her lead rope to keep her moving through the mud, kicking all the while at his small Indian pony's flanks to urge her on through the sticky footing. The men rode in the rain for hours through the afternoon, pleading with the animals to move faster, but the farther west they traveled, the rougher the footing became. The horses and mule began to bog down in the pastelike gumbo, each foot being brought out of the sticky mire slowly, one at a time. Their pace had slowed to a crawl, an agonizing ordeal of driving rain, accompanied by the sounds of Scratch's incessant swearing in tune with each hoof pulled from the mire with a loud sucking sound.

The old man struggled with the animals until finally deciding to stop and wait the weather out. There were no trees where he reined up. Scratch dropped wearily to the ground; his moccasins sank quickly up to his ankles. They were short of a stand of cottonwoods he had been heading toward for the past hour.

"We'll jest have to settle in here, Josiah. Wait it out, short of our mark." Scratch pulled the horse and mule over to a small ledge where he tied them. He then tore his buffalo robes loose from Hannah's back and spread one over the bales of beaver fur, putting the tanned robe fleshside up to turn the rain.

Scratch looked around them as he finished, trying to judge just how long the storm might last. As Josiah dropped from the fatigued dapple and started to untie his supply of pouches, the older man said, "Jest get your blankets out, son. Leave the rest right there." Scratch then walked over toward the dapple carrying a second heavy buffalo robe. "We'll just put this here over your pony's back to keep things dry. Set your truck down in this mud an' it'll get ruin't for sure then." He threw the robe over the dapple's back and straightened it out with Josiah's help, then went around the animal to stand before the young man, "You got a spare blanket there, son, one as you can lend a friend?"

"Here." Josiah pulled a blanket loose from the bedroll and handed it over to Scratch, keeping two for himself as he followed the old man to the foot of the small ledge.

"Set yourse'f down, Josiah. Fold the blanket up under your ass, like this." He demonstrated to Paddock, then pulled the edges up over his shoulders and then his head. The men sat huddled side by side for a while within blankets pulled closely about them until Josiah spoke.

"Cain't we get a fire goin'?"

Scratch snorted, the sound muffled from within the folds of the blanket about his face. "Ain't no use in this downpour, friend. With no cover, she's like a bull pissin' on a flat rock. No way a man could get a fire started, no way he could keep it goin'." He looked out at the greasewood and stunted willow where the horses were tied. "Rain like this here, man's jest gotta wait out," he said, answering Josiah's sigh.

The dry blankets turned the water for awhile, then slowly began to collect rain in pockets formed by the folds of cloth. Soon they were no longer much protection and Paddock squirmed nervously, trying to find a dry place for his numbing buttocks.

"Sit still, boy!"

"I'm gettin' wet!"

"Sure, you'll get wet. Leastways, keep what water you're sittin' in warm. You keep movin' round like that, the water an' mud you're sittin' in will never get warm. Sit still. You'll be wet, but you can stay warmer that way." Josiah moved again, shifting his position. The cold water that had pooled around his buttocks now flowed into the depression in the mud where he sat, sending chills throughout his body once more. He finally decided to make the best of it and to remain cramped and wet in an attempt to stay warm.

Huddled, Scratch was silent a long time. Occasionally he stuck his face out from beneath the folds of the blanket to fight the rain back from his eyes by blinking, looking to the west through the dark sky to measure how long this storm might last. It soon grew increasingly dark about them as the rain continued and he could calculate the storm's course no more.

127

"You 'sleep, son?"

"Shit! You think I can sleep like this! My legs an' ass went 'sleep long ago! But, not me! Hell, no! I ain't sleepin'!"

The older man chewed on his tongue, then asked, "What was your track makin' it to where you picked me up, Josiah?" He thought if he could get Paddock's mind off the wet, off the cramping muscles, things might seem brighter.

"Come 'long the Platte. Why you all-fired hot to know so much 'bout me?"

"Jest thought a lil' talkin' might make the time pass quicklike. That's all, friend." He stuck his head out once more and looked over at the young man huddled beside him, Josiah's face hidden beneath the folds of his blankets. "Headed up North Platte then, huh?"

"S'pose. Didn' know the river split up like it did. At the time thought I'd come to 'nother river. Didn' know which one to take, rightly. Jest knew that I had to keep headin' north. An' the one I took headed that way."

"Come out with any other pilgrims, son?" The old man put his head back within the protection of the bedroll blanket.

"Why!" Josiah snapped back. "You thinkin' I couldn't make it on my own, ol' man?"

"Didn' mean nothin' of the kind, Josiah. Jest that I come out alone 'long the same way." He sighed. "Lookin' back on it, too—this here child's some lucky to get to the mountains without some red nigger liftin' ha'r off'n him. That way's crawlin' with Injuns most of the time. Sioux, Pawnee, too. They give no truck to a lonely white man travelin' through that land. Man as travels 'lone out there jest get hisse'f used for target practice, maybe get hisse'f broiled over a hot fire like a stuck pig by them niggers. I was one as didn' know no better. Do now, howsomever. Lucky, I was, gettin' west of the forks of that river. Where you strike out west then after you left the Platte?"

"Come on 'nother river runnin' into the Platte. Headed into the mountains from there." Josiah let the last few words trail off slowly.

"That'd be the LaRamee, Josiah. Spring fill-up, she flows strong an' deep—strong 'nough she's touchy to ford." He looked out to the horizon. "That spot, where the Platte an' LaRamee join up, be the crossroads east of the mountains. See you any Injuns?"

"Nope, didn't a one."

"You was lucky, as tribes round that country follerin' buffler. 'Rapaho, Crow, sometimes Snake, Cheyenne, too. That north-south trail east of them mountains runs south to the country of the 'Rapaho an' Wolf's band of Cheyenne, almost all way down toward Taos an' Santy Fee. Up north, trail take a man almost to Crow an' Blackfoot land. No country to be come summer—crawlin' ever' ridge an' draw. Pick me my time of y'ar to be in that country."

They sat without talking, listening to the howls of two coyotes calling out to one another to the east. "Ain't no good when them critters is out an' howlin' in the rain," Scratch said, breaking the spell.

"More hoodoos?"

"Might say. Heerd tell a coyote what comes out to howl in the rain is really a Injun as was taken whilst his medeecin was still strong—taken by the gods an' changed into the critter to revenge some wrong done to them gods."

"Shit, ol' man! Ain't no way I'm gonna believe in your witchy stuff!"

Scratch poked his head outside the blanket. "Know a man as you need to talk to. Name's McAfferty—Asa McAfferty. Scotsman by birth. Short, lil' bundle of fire, too." He put his face back in the blanket and began to tell the story of how this McAfferty's hair turned completely white. "As a sign the Lord was pissed at him for killin' a Ree medeecin man, back to '26. Asa got his truck together an' left that country straightways, bein' told by the Lord where to go an' what to do when he got there."

McAfferty had been a preacher back in the settlements, had heard the calling of the Lord back there, and had heard it once more when his hair turned white, calling him into the high and lonesome places. "I trapped me a season—hmmm, no two—afore he jest picked up one day an' fixed to take off, sayin' Lord wanted him somewhars else. Last see'd him two y'ars back. Been out to the big salt in the west they say. Now, that be a man you should talk with 'bout your superstitions!"

"What a preacher doin' out here?" Josiah laughed with some disdain.

"Not rightly a preacher. Jest a man of the Lord. All kinds out here. Each of us touched in some way or other, I s'pose. But all comes to be changed by the mountains, but

129

these here mountains don' give nothin'. They jest 'spect you to l'arn by 'em. Man like ol' McAfferty has come through lotta l'arnin'." His body shook slightly with the damp chill of his soaked clothing. "Ain't really l'arnin' at all, s'pose. You jest feel it in your body, up an' down. Know what I mean?"

"I 'spect you'll tell me anyways," the younger man grumbled.

"Man as 'spects to keep his ha'r, or fill his belly, he's gotta calc'late things alla time. This here child didn' figger too good this day—got us caught in the wet weather, you see. Gotta keep your eye on the country round you, the way he's gonna make 'cross it, an' allays keep eye on the sky. Put all what you know together an' you'll fill your belly, some for your critters, too. Man's gotta take as good care of his animals as he does of hisself. Bein' afoot can spell the end for most men out here. But a man can travel anywhere, even in bad country, if'n he's l'arnt his lessons well 'nough." Bass went on to tell Josiah how to move into and out of new country by using the ridges, using the topography for safety, and urged him to learn all the canyons, passes, creeks, river and peaks, committing them to memory through the slow travel. "Man's gotta l'arn a lot soon to keep him his ha'r."

"Lotta figgerin' on Injuns, huh?"

"Huh?" Scratch said, stuffing a wad of tobacco into his mouth from the pouch he hung about his neck. "Oh, yup. That you do. You see a willer branch floatin' down the stream. Now, I says to myself, is that willer branch there nat'ral? Can it be the work of some critters upstream? An' is them critters four-legged or two-legged? Gotta calc'late it fast, then figger on what to do. Travel through country where a rock be outta place, maybe a branch is broke an' jest hangin' there—gotta figger it all out."

He stuck his head out of the blanket to spit. "Where we'll be come mornin' fair off, up there where them ridges meet the sky, keep your eyes movin'. Maybe jest a snap of a minute to catch somethin' movin' up there. Be it a critter, or a man? If it be a critter—why's he headin' that way, or why's he standin' so strangelike? Such a thing, like why them buffler movin' downwind? Some herd of elk down in the valley standin' still in a strange spot for 'em to be grazin', an' them magpies is makin' strange, funny noises. Gotta figger on what all it means." He let the tobacco leaf sit against his cheek. "You wanna chew?"

"Naw. Not right now."

"Gotta figger you on the Injuns in the country where you be trappin'. Have they had 'em a set-to with some white men lately, an' squampshus for blood. Or, are they peaceful critters, only hopin' to steal you blind. You can read sign from the trail on the red niggers—like, what tribe they be, how many's been 'long the trail, what they was movin' for, all such. How many horses they travelin' with, an' was them ponies loaded or no. Lotta light tracks, they been raidin' for ponies, you see. Sign tells you if'n there be women an' pups 'long—movin' camp they might'n be doin'." He spit again, propelling the brown syrup out through the folds in the blanket wrapped around his face.

"Cain't figger if you like livin' with Injuns, or killin' 'em."

"Jest like livin', son. An' to do that, you gotta l'arn from the Injuns. That be where you start. Injun lived up here afore any man give any mind to crossin' the Missoura." He licked at a drop of juice on his lower lip before continuing. "But a mountain man gotta go on past what the Injun teaches him. Try somethin' new—be ready to gamble. Injun ain't ready to gamble, so we got some edge on him there. So, what you l'arnt back cross the Big Muddy ain't gonna hold you in good stead here, Josiah— ain't gonna do you a goddamn now . . ." He let the sentence trail off and paid attention to the quiet. It was finally quiet. No longer did the rain beat against the wet blankets or splash noisily into the puddles around them.

Scratch pulled the blanket off his head carefully, holding onto the blue bandanna. "Lookin' like the sky's passed over. Pull them robes off the critters an' we'll be makin' for sleep."

As Josiah pulled the hides from the backs of the dapple and mule, Scratch shook the blankets, splattering water as he snapped the soaked cloth. "Lay 'em up here, on the high ground." He pointed to the spot where they had sat out the storm.

They laid down the robes, warmed with the animals heat, then rolled the edges up over their bodies. Scratch let out a contented sigh. It had been a long, hard day and he was tired from just carrying on the way he had in the past few hours, keeping Josiah's mind off the rain and cold.

"Scratch?"

"Yup?"

"What's Crow word for me?"

"Ain't no word for Josiah, son."

"Naw. I mean what's the word for *man* in Crow?"

The old man thought a moment. "'I' tse batse'."

"Ehtt-see, bat-see?"

"No, no. Try it again. It-say botsa. It-say botsa," he drawled.

"It-say botsa. It-say botsa." Josiah repeated to the man beside him in the mud. "That means "man" in Crow, huh?"

"Means 'good an' brave man' in Crow, a 'brave man', Josiah."

"An' that's what I wanna be, Titus. Josiah's gonna be i' tse batse."

After two more days of travel, Scratch led them down into a wide, twisting canyon, urging his pony on through the forested ridges within the canyon's recesses. Here there was better vegetation for the animals, so they decided to stop awhile at midday. Bass dropped to the ground and tied the pony and mule off, then went sniffing around in the nearby bushes. He soon returned with his hands full of rich, red strawberries, plump and still wet from the last night's dew.

"Well I'll be damned!" Josiah's eyes popped at the sight of the delicious fruit.

"You will be, too, if'n you don' go get your own!" Scratch laughed heartily. "Take the kittle an' go yonder to fetch us some more of these here berries."

Josiah headed into the brush, then soon returned with the kettle brimful. They sat on the ground, with the midday treat between them, eating the strawberries slowly, savoring the enjoyment of the unexpected taste in their mouths. In feeding on the new grasses, Paddock's mare moved too close to Hannah. The mule snorted at the horse, then halfheartedly kicked at the other animal. The dapple backed away and went on eating elsewhere.

"Why you carryin' that no 'count, cussed mule 'long with you, Scratch? She's the one lamed your foot up for days, ain't she? She's on'ry with everybody an' everythin'. Why you keep her around?"

"Hannah an' me, we're the pair, we are. That critter's saved me life a time or two." He finished chewing on a mouthful of the berries then wiped his lips and the whiskers over his chin with the back of his sleeve. "Horse critters that get to know the smell of white man don' like the smell of Injuns. Them red niggers smell differ'nt than we, you see. Don' ask me why. They jest do. Maybe its the grease they use alla time, slickin' they ha'r back an' such. Don' know rightly, but them horse critters smell a Injun an' they go to snortin' an' gettin' squampshus. Good idear to have a good horse like that in all kinds of Injun country," he said, plopping some more of the fruit between his lips.

"That's horses. I asked you why you drag that mule along."

"'Sides what I owes that critter for the last good y'ars, bein' comp'ny an' friend to this here lonesome coon, Hannah's better'n horse for smellin' somethin' that ain't right. Mules better'n horse for smellin' for that 'count. They hates the smell of Injuns more'n any horse I knows of." He snatched up the last of the berries and pushed the kettle over to Josiah. "Fetch us some more. Makin' a good nooner treat, they are."

Paddock lifted the kettle by its handle and headed back into the bushes, while the older man lay back and closed his eyes. It was some time before he heard the other man's footsteps coming toward him.

"Scratch?"

"Yup?" he replied, not opening his eyes; he knew Josiah was now standing over him.

"Few days back, you said I'd learn why the animals wouldn't drink that water?"

"Yup." A smile came slowly over the old man's gray-bearded face.

"Said I'd find out why, didn't you?"

"Yup." He finally opened one eye to squint up at Josiah as the younger man stood over him. "You find out why, son?"

"Think I have." He sat down heavily where he had stood, looking pale and ashen.

"Your bowels givin' you hell, are they?" Scratch sat up on one elbow beside Josiah.

"Feel like I'm empty of everythin' inside me. Never shat so much in all my days as what I did while ago."

"Tried to tell you in a nice way," Bass cooed. "Animals tried to tell you, too. Gotta l'arn this way to trust what they say to you, jest like what we was talkin' 'bout with smellin' Injuns."

Josiah hung his head between his knees for a moment, then spoke without raising his face: "Anythin' you can do for it?"

"Ain't much, son. Jest gotta ride the shit out." Then he laughed as he thought of the joke he had told quite by accident. "Yup! Jest gotta ride the shit out!"

"You ain't much help to a man's dyin', are you?"

"Sorry. Felt the way you do a time or two, I have. Critters eat or drink somethin' don' agree with 'em, they stuff down lotta green grass. Watch a critter when he's ailin'. They eat the fresh green stuff. Makes 'em feel lil' more pert it seems. Try it an' see, boy. Works for me. Works for other mountain critters too. Try it."

Paddock crawled a few feet away and began tearing up handfuls of grass; he stuffed the grass into his mouth, chewed, then swallowed it with a gulp.

"That's it, son. Eat as much as you can for now, then we be movin' on." Josiah just looked at him with sagging eyes then nodded his head up and down without saying a word. "Reminds me of a man as took the easy way out when I was a boy, Josiah. Our lil' settlement needin' a teacher got a man come in to hire for the job. Them days, 'bout all they teached was a lil' of the alph'bet an' some cipherin'. Didn' get paid much, so a teacher had to do hirin' out for odd jobs an' chores on the men's farms. 'Sides, such a teacher got paid only a lil' for each head he tried to cram with a lil' smarts. Well, this here young'un come out to hire for the teachin' job, 'bout your age he'd been at the time, so the menfolk of the settlement got together to ask him some questions, seein' if he was the man for the job, if'n he be the man they wanted to teach they young'uns." He looked away now from Josiah and the sight of the younger man chewing slowly on the grass. "One man asked him if he would be teachin' if the world was flat 'r round, you see, feelin' the young teacher out kinda like. Well, he thought for a lil' bit, then he says that he could teach it either way the fathers wanted him to teach it. Now that caught them farmers off a whack, so

134

they went into 'nother room to palaver 'bout his answer. When they come back, one of 'em told the teacher he had the new teacher's job, but they'd just as soon he'd teach the world was flat, bein' that the other was such a new idear an' all." Scratch looked back at Josiah, laughing at his own story. "You see, he took a easy way round a lil' problem. Don' think he l'arnt a thing from it, neither. Man didn' have no backbone, no faith in hisse'f, no faith in his own mind. An' you, Josiah, you're jest the other way. Gotta loosen up an' listen up ever' now an' then." He rose to his feet and helped Josiah up, standing for a moment beside him. "You feelin' like ridin'? We bes' be on our way, son."

"Yep," he answered slowly, with a hollow sound, "in a, in a minute." He then raced for the bushes once more, pulling at his belt and tearing at the buttons on his longhandles. He squatted once more and let it flow through him like a giant flushing of everything within him. A slight faintness overtook him and he reached out to grasp a thick branch in the willows about him. Within seconds he was brought back to painful reality. The beaver castoreum had been smeared on all previously exposed skin, but now a new, juicy, and tender target invited the hungry mosquitoes. It was an awkwardly funny scene he created for himself. Squatting on the balls of his feet, his bowels a gusher, he swatted and waved and slapped at his buttocks to ward off if not kill the invading insects that dove at and bit his tender flesh. Finally the rumble within subsided. When he emerged at last from the brush, Josiah had a somewhat better color to his face.

"You look a lil' lighter, friend." Scratch moved toward the animals.

"Yep. Feel lighter too," he said, putting one foot into a stirrup. "What with that crap an' the juices all them skeeters sucked outta me!"

"Found 'em somethin' new to chew on, did they?" He chuckled heartily.

"Wouldn't been so goddamn funny, your ass they was eatin on while you be takin' a crap!"

"Le's go, young'un."

Josiah swung up into the saddle. "I sure feel lighter—an' sorer," he winced, as he adjusted himself finally on the hard leather.

The rest of the day and into the next they rode

through the winding canyon until they came out onto a ridge overlooking a river.

"That's the Snake, Josiah. Ain't far whar we goin' now."

Paddock slid from his saddle slowly and walked off toward the bushes. "I'll give my best to the Snake, ol' man!"

Bass led them down the ridge into the canyon formed by the river, then began to follow the river's course northward. It twisted and turned, until they came around a knoll to look out upon the expanse of a huge mountain valley. "There it be, Davey Jackson's Hole. We be on the south end of it." He turned to look at Josiah, who sat slumped and saggy-eyed in the saddle. "Look at it, boy," he spoke loudly. Paddock then looked up across the valley, "That's God's country ever there was one, Josiah. That'd be the place God lay claim to if'n He had to settle down. Ain't nowhar's else like it in the whole world. Pilot Knobs, what them parley-voo Frenchies call the three breasts up there to your left, them's the Tetons. Damn! What a sight for Ol' Scratch's eyes this is! You lookin', son?" The younger man slid down from the saddle and made his way stumbling into the cover of some brush. "You'll be rid of it soon," Scratch yelled after him. "Damn! But this is some country for a mountain man!" He turned to look back up the valley.

When Paddock came from the brush, Scratch began talking once more, "That's God's country—only mos' think God stays on t'other side of the Missoura. Some say He's got no place out here. Titus Bass don' feel that way. No sir. God made this here country for Hisse'f an' the like of us, He did. Sure, there ain't no churches pushin' steeples an' bell towers toward the sky down that valley or any other out here. Damn! Look at them mountains! Them are the house of God He made with His own hand for the like of us. Who-o-o-e-e-e! If this ain't the place an' time to be livin', Josiah! If I ain't 'bout the happiest man you ever knowed at bein' alive an' bein' here right now, then I'll be et for a tater by a toothless nigger! C'mon, now. We'll get your ass movin' an' your mind off it."

They followed the bank of the Snake as it grew wider through the southernmost end of the valley, then began to narrow. It was here that Scratch chose to cross the river to the west. On the other side, he began again to speak to

Josiah, to speak of many things on his mind and in his heart. "Ain't no white-skinned, prissy, gussied-up gals out here neither; kinda woman as'll look mean an' hard at you when you're only doin' what you feel like doin'. Same with law an' constables. Ain't none of that foofaraw out here. Only one law for us, takin' care of yourself an' your companyeros. You do that an' ain't nothin' else needed. Man can 'spect to be treated square by mos', an' he can treat mos' coons the same way back. It's them few low, snaky bastards who make things bad for the rest of us. I'm goodhearted by nature, Josiah, but don' take to a man as squeezes his presents out between his fingers, same kind is allays ready with a open hand when the handin' out is good. Them's the niggers as I stay 'way from if I can. Don' want nothin' to do with 'em. They's lot like laws an' lawyers, pushin' you round. An' if they cain't push you round, they fancy you, fool you with all the foofaraw palaver. Them gov'ment coons take what ain't theirs to begin with, an' live off'n a honest man's earnin's. Rattles my ass, it does, to see a man as cain't pay his goddamn taxes get slapped in the calaboose. Goddamn shame, by a long chalk, a goddamn shame to treat a man thataway. Consarn it! I quit them settlements an' want no more talk of 'em! Here's whar we be an' here's whar we stayin', till the Lord's ready to call the name of Titus Bass up yonder into the big belt. God's purtiest sculpturin's to lay sign in, to live out your days, an' them nights full of blazin' sky. Damn! We is mountain men an' we should be more'n proud that we live in this here time, we do."

"What 'bout the Injuns, makin' the livin' jest a might dangerous, like you say?"

"Jehoshaphat! What if the good Lord put the red niggers here, too? What of it? Only adds a lil' fun—only adds to a man's fun, don' it?"

"You're a rich man, ain't you, Scratch? I mean, I see you got all kinds of money for all your y'ars up here," Josiah grumbled. He felt drained, tired, and sore from the ordeal of the past two days. His cynicism now boiled over and he snapped back at Scratch, angered at the old man's bright joy.

"You cain't line your grave with beaver, boy! Ain't no 'count anyways! So what if the truck Billy Sublette brings out here, jammed full of gee-gaws an' pretty foofaraw cost four, maybe five time what it do back in St. Louie? What do it count? Tell me, Josiah? What do it count anyways?"

"Don' know..."

"Damn! I know, Josiah Paddock! I know! It don' count a shit! None of it! None of it don' count a shit if'n you're allays worryin' 'bout where you're gonna spend your money. Only money we got, boy, is ridin' on Hannah's back. Don' you forget it, neither! Them beaver dollars buys us good times an' 'nother y'ar till ronnyvoo. Then we gonna bust our asses earnin' that other ronnyvoo, bust our asses tryin' to save our ha'r. If a man come away from ronnyvoo, headin' out for season, leavin' with a headache from the cups an' the clap to boot, if'n a man come away from ronnyvoo broke, what's it all count, son?"

Scratch paused and softened his voice now, having realized he was arguing with his own past, with his own youthful dreams more than he was arguing with Josiah. "If'n you spend a few seasons up here, an' go back to the settlements broke, what differ'nce it make to you? I'm carin' to bet that you never make it back to them settlements anyways. If'n you don' make a mountain man I'll see you buried up here. An' if you do make the mountain man, get to be the reg'lar hivernant—feller what's spent him a winter in these'r mountains—what I'm figgerin' you to be, Josiah Paddock ain't gonna be one to wanna go back then anyways. Your money's somethin' for those settlement fellers—ain't no good out here. We carryin' the money of the mountains back there on that cussed mule, son. That'll buy whiskey an' womens. It's gonna get you a set of skins an' a mountain rifle too, with some cups thrown in for Ol' Scratch. You'll pay me back come next ronnyvoo, an' work the devil outta you for the debt, I will. You'll l'arn real quick why you come to the Stoney Mountains, Josiah. 'Tweren't for money! 'Tweren't for beaver, neither!"

Up from the valley floor, the men and animals began the twisting climb toward the pass by which Scratch chose to lead them over the mountains. Off to their right the Teton range rose as the Pilot Knobs themselves disappeared. Above them, the snow came into view as the air began to chill. It now relieved Josiah's fever, and soon he had put the heavy blanket coat on once more, buttoning the long-handles up his chest. Into the thick timber they rode, the going slowed by the slippery snow, dropped here by the storm that had dumped the rain on them below. Scratch picked his way as best he could, following the shoulders of the snow-draped slopes. The footing grew precarious for the animals as they minced their way across the wet and melting ice. The climb into thinner air coupled with the rougher footing tired the horses and Hannah all too quickly. The old man finally admitted that here too they would have to stop for the night.

"Sun's west of the pass. We can lay over here tonight. Go on in to ronnyvoo tomorrer." He led them up a slight slope, away from the pass, and into a thick stand of pine where the snow had not penetrated. Josiah was worn, hanging onto the pommel of his saddle as if in fear of falling. Scratch slid to his feet and helped Paddock down. He walked him over into the trees and steadied the young man as he sat on the ground. Josiah hung his head, chin against the neck, and then Scratch saw it. He pulled Josiah's collar down and peered closely.

"Goddamn! You got the ticks!"

Paddock raised his head slowly. "That's what's been itchin' at me."

Scratch pushed his head back down. The older man plopped to the ground and began looking through Josiah's growing hair. "We gonna have some work to do on you, son. 'Sides them graybacks, you got a load of ticks to boot!"

He rose and quickly built a small fire near them, then brought Josiah a large handful of wet snow to eat. The combination of alkaline water drying the body's tissues and the diarrhea robbing the body of needed moisture had sapped the younger man of much of his youthful strength. When there were some small licks of flame flying freely out of the fire, Scratch put the tip of his knife blade down among the embers, then set about pulling gear from the animals. He soon had them a cozy camp put together and meat roasting over the glowing coals as the sun began to fade in the west.

"Gonna help you get over to your bedroll, son, but you're gonna have to help me get your clothes off. That way we check you over real good. Tomorrer, we'll check you over again down below, jest to be sure we got 'em all, when I stop to take a bath."

"A bath? You're kiddin', ain't you, Scratch?" The

word had brought some life back into Josiah as he stumbled over to the bedroll.

"Dammit boy! Man's gotta smell decent to go courtin' squars, don' he?"

"If you say so, ol' man. If you say so."

Between the two of them, they struggled to pull Josiah's clothes off, down to the birthday suit. As the sun went down, so did the temperature. The young man scooted closer to the warmth of the fire, sitting naked on his blankets, his ribs poking at the skin on his chest. Scratch pulled the knife from the fire, the tip of its blade heated for the job at hand, then knelt beside Josiah to begin burning the ticks off the young pilgrim.

"Yeooww! Goddammit!" Paddock pulled away as the blade tip burned skin.

"Settle in, boy. We got a job to do." He put the tip back to work. "Quit your movin', quit it!" He worked more carefully this time, paying more attention so as not to touch the skin with the knife. "Jest gotta touch them lil' devils on the ass with somethin' hot, they back right on out on you. Then I can pick' em off an' throw 'em in the fire...like that," he explained as he tossed one into the nearby flames.

"Why cain't you jest pick 'em off an' be done with it?"

"Ticks don' work that way. Man I knew once't died of fever from 'em. He pulled the ticks off, for sure, but the critters' heads stayed in the skin. That's the baddest part of the lil' devils, Josiah. Heads got all the poison...thar's 'nother. Gotta get the critter to back off by hisse'f or the head stays in to make you sick. Goddamn! Have you got a crop of 'em! Get yourse'f busy too, son! Lookee over your clothes, turnin' 'em insides an' out. Lookee down 'long each seam real close. Thems are critters as like the tight places...an' 'nother to the fire! Ain't got yourself 'nother change of longhandles, do you?"

"Nope."

"Didn' think so. Jest keep workin' an' we'll make your clothes fit to wear again, leastways till we get some skins. Crow skins be the best for you, but them niggers won' be comin' to ronnyvoo. Snake skins'll do for now. We'll get you fixed for Crow skins come robe season when we winter up with Arapooesh an' his folks. Snakes'll be to ronnyvoo—they wouldn' miss the whiskey an' foofaraw for nothin' this side of spring buffler huntin'. If'n they had 'em a good hunt this y'ar, they'll be comin' with the hawkbells roarin'." As he chattered on, Scratch kept pulling ticks from Josiah's body, throwing them into the fire.

"They don' call themselves, 'Snakes.' That's jest the word as was give 'em. Come from the way they move their hand when they use the sign for the tribe name, like this," he demonstrated, waving his hand through the air, fingers outstretched and together in a serpentine movement, wiggling in front of Josiah's face. "They's Shoshones, proper, an' a kind an' thankful group they is. Welcome a white man, mos' time, they do. Them niggers can get mad when you do 'em wrong, howsomever, but they don' steal the way them Crow love to. They believes in a big god, too. Lives in the sun, he does, but with other lil' gods livin' in the moon an' stars, some on earth down here—but they all answer to the big'un in the sun. Snakes tell that spirits of their dead warriors keep a close eye on what the livin' do in ever'thin'. Tell that each livin' brave has some angel watchin' over him, guardin' him from death an' pain—but only so long as that nigger obeys the wishes of the gods. Them warriors got 'em lotsa wives too. But they ain't as hot to screw 'nother man's woman as the Crow be. Them Crow can be downright nasty when it comes to the womens, they can. Not the Snakes. Man'll jest sell you his daughter or his wife for a few hours to ronnyvoo, should you tickle his eye with somethin' fancy an' pretty." He sat back, turned aside, and spat juice at the fire.

"Roll over, boy, an' spread your legs. Go on, I don' like it any better'n you do, but them ticks like to hug upon the ha'rs of your ass bes' of all . . . that's it. We'll get you cleaned up an' then you're gonna get some laydown sleep. Tomorrer's to ronnyvoo an' shinin' times for you . . . back offa there you damned varmint!"

They loaded the animals quickly the next morning before the sun had broken over the divide to the east, mounted up, and continued the hard climb to the pass. Once there, Scratch picked his way along carefully as they began their descent down the western slope. By midmorning they could see the valley floor below them. For Josiah the itching was gone, the cramps and diarrhea seemed to have eased off. The only thing bothering him was the closeness of the rendezvous, with the excitement of the newness they had anticipated these past weeks.

Suddenly the air carried to them a roar that made Paddock's blood chill. The lump in his gut climbed up into his throat, forcing him to remember old fears. More throaty growls answered the first as Scratch stopped the animals in their tracks. He listened for a moment at the air-splitting roars, then jumped quickly to the ground. He checked the priming on his rifle as he pulled the flintlock from its leather scabbard, "Bring your pistol, son. Scratch is curious what's shakin' out there in that forest." He started off into the trees, followed closely by the younger man.

After darting quietly through the pines for about a hundred yards, Scratch stopped them as they rounded a large boulder about the size of a settler's cabin. There before them was a sight few had seen in the mountains. The old man put his finger to his lips, then led Josiah around the boulder and found them a way to the top so that they finally had a grandstand seat for the action below.

In a small clearing at the foot of the boulder lay a wounded elk cow. Scratch figured that some hunter by here recently must have put a bad shot into her, and she had then taken off into the forest to die, losing blood all the way. But, that wasn't all they had perched on the boulder to witness. Around the elk, but ignoring the weakened, prostrated animal, were three of the monsters of the forests. A trio of big, blond animals, grizzly bears full of spit and fire, fought one another for the prize. They had each smelled the blood and tracked the elk, only to find two others after the same meal. Their fierce pride would not let them share the feast. They would fight it out, free-for-all, and the one left standing when it was done, the one not wounded or run off, would have for himself a feast fit for a king of the mountain forests. The ground shook as one would bat another against a tree with a savage swipe of a paw exposing long claws. It was the rut all over again for these bachelors, but this time they would not win some brief companionship from a female, only a full belly. The tide of battle changed again and again, with the odd male jumping on the back of one of the others engaged in a boxing and hugging match, tearing flesh loose with his teeth and talons.

Josiah and Scratch lay atop their boulder watching the battle for close to an hour until one of the males finally killed another and ran the third away. The monstrous victor rose to his feet, turned around and around, snorting

142

and roaring all the time to tell the whole forest who was the rightful ruler here, then dropped to all fours to ramble slowly over to his hard-won prize. Grasping the cow's neck between his dripping jaws, he clamped shut and shook his head from side to side violently, lifting the heavy elk carcass off the ground several times, shaking the remaining life from the dying animal. Scratch tapped Josiah on the shoulder and silently motioned with his hand that they should be going. Both men slipped from the boulder and made their way quietly back to the horses and mule.

"Wounded grizz is bad grizz," Scratch said, pushing into the saddle and cradling his rifle across his thighs. "Don' wanna be round here much longer when that other feller fixes to come back there later on after lickin' his wounds to see if there's anythin' left fer him to eat." He pulled his pony's neck to the side and started away. "C'mon, Josiah! We got ronnyvoo fer us! Damn the boosh-way! Whiskey's watered down with the Green! Traps of English steel for thirty dollar, but none better'n that Man-chester! An' you be careful of that DuPont powder! She's not worth the spit in a dry man's mouth! Many are the one's as'll spout off 'bout theys Dupont, but it's only English or French for this here child! Likker an' lovin' for a man as comes to ronnyvoo, Josiah Paddock! Likker an' lovin' for these here two coons as come a long way to shine in any man's crowd! Wagh! Say it 'gain. Wagh! By damned I are one of the baddest mother's sons as ever'll be come ronnyvoo, an' there's some bad mother's sons down there a'ready, I'm carin' to set, young'un. They's waitin' for the likker an' lovin'. C'mon, young'un! We'll take a horn for the whole shiteree, an' have 'nother for the y'ar to come! Lookee out, Billy Sublette! Titus Bass has a dry on you'll not soon forget!"

8

"I'm thinkin' this be the Pierre," Scratch said, stopping at the bank of a stream and looking down the direction it was flowing. "Drains this side of the pass. Lots of lil' pittle-ass criks as come into her up here. Pierre's a fine one, she is. Take a drink there, son. Some sweet water it be." He turned to look over at Josiah, who wrinkled up his nose a little and did not move from his horse as the old man slid from his saddle. "Don' trust my word on it, eh?" Scratch knelt and dipped cupped hands into the cold rushing water being fed by the snows they had crossed in coming over the pass. "Shoulda trusted my word back to the alk'li crik." He drank for a moment, then wiped his hands across the front of the greasy buckskin of his shirt. Scratch let go a deep sigh and sat on his haunches for a few minutes, looking downstream.

When he spoke again, it was without moving his head to look at Josiah. "S'pose you l'arnin' to trust your own feelin's, eh? That's good. Don' jest take 'nother man's word on nothin', Josiah. Find out for yourself. Sometimes your body tells you better'n your head ever does—you gotta listen to what your body's got to say. Yours tellin' you to be shy right now of water. But, you come through somethin' as many a man whats come through—ain't nothin' more'n too many green apples back home would give you, son." He was pensive a moment, unmoving until he heard Paddock slide from the saddle and touch the earth. Scratch turned to the young man as Josiah came to kneel alongside the stream.

"I wanna trust you, ol' man." He looked briefly into Scratch's eyes, then looked down into the water. "Aw-w-w shit! I'm jest bein' a pup 'bout this, ain't I? Ol' man like Titus Bass cain't be coddlin' a kid, now can he?" He dipped one hand into the cold water to catch some of the liquid ice, then brought it slowly up to his lips and sipped it.

"Taste all right, don' it?"

"Yup. It do." Josiah now put both hands into the water and brought drink after drink to his dry mouth and throat.

"I want you to trust me too, friend. Trust don' come easy, though. I'm willin' to wait you out on that count. There's times, howsomever, Josiah, when all a man's got to lay a bet with is 'nother man, a friend as come through water scrapes an' cold camps with him. Few things you can put your beaver down on out here, 'ceptin' 'nother man what is trampin' the same trail as yourself. What I done for you in the past suns, 'long with what I'm a-gonna do down there to ronnyvoo—that's all a small beaver to pay for your trust, an' respect. Ain't askin' no more'n that from you, if'n you'll be ridin' 'way from ronnyvoo with Scratch. Then . . . if'n you ain't with me for the fall huntin', want you to know I don' blame you none. If'n that's what you really want . . ."

"Whatever got the notion in your head that I was goin' anywhars else but with you, Scratch?" Josiah lifted his head and turned to look at the older man, water dripping from his lower lip onto the front of his shirt where the blanket coat was unbuttoned.

"Moon or two back, this child tol't you plain that if'n you weren't ready to l'arn a lick from Scratch, then you'd have to take your hide somewhars else come ronnyvoo. Didn' want no man as might . . ."

". . . cause you to lose your ha'r." Josiah interrupted, then snorted a brief chuckle. He rose and took up the reins of the dapple. "Jest take it simple that I'm with you come breakup of ronnyvoo, unless you sneak out on me with one of your early-mornin' gettin'-ups. Simple; ol' man: I'm with you, an' I'll run you into the ground someday." He smiled down at Scratch when he had lifted into the saddle.

"Give you a hard time, ain't I?" Bass rose to his feet.

"Not near as bad a time as I'm gonna give you back," he put heels to the horse and started off through the trees downstream.

Scratch leapt onto the pony's back without use of the broad stirrup, leaned forward to grab the reins, then set the animal in motion. "Whoooeeee!" he hollered as he jerked lightly on Hannah's rope to bring her along. Adjusting the rifle across his lap, he spoke quietly now, leaning low alongside the pony's ear: "Think I got me a pardner." He sat back, straightened his spine like a ramrod, and spoke to himself, "Yessirree! Ol' Scratch's got him a pardner!"

Into the valley they fell, the Tetons rising to the east, their peaks towering above mantles of soft clouds, while to their left rose the less lofty Snake River Mountains.

Before them yawned the hole along the spine of the west, a valley floor covered with low, scrawny sage. Through the hole ran the streams that rushed down from the Teton range, streams whose courses could easily be traced by the bordering hemlines of cottonwood and willow. This valley stretched northward from them some thirty miles, and with its bordering frame of mountains varied in width from five to fifteen miles as it ran from southeast to northwest.

Scratch searched along the stream they followed until he spotted a break in the dense underbrush of willow and creeping vines that matted the bank.

"'Hoa!'" he shouted ahead to Josiah. "Hey, boy! We gonna take a short one for the ol' man here!" Bass hit the ground and tied the pony and Hannah up to the willows, then turned to the mule where he pulled free a painted rawhide parfleche. Scratch ran the fingertips of his right hand over the leather's grainy surface as Josiah rode up.

"What's doin'?" he asked with a touch of impatience in his voice.

"Titus Bass gonna scrub a y'ar off'n his hide," he said, taking his eyes from the parfleche to look up at Josiah.

"You're really gonna take a bath, ain't you! If that don't beat the stick!" Josiah laughed as he dropped to the ground.

"Man can live with hisse'f, but them squars got a touchy nose. Injuns take a bath 'most ever' day, if'n they can. Sweat one if ther's nothin' better. Seen 'em crack the ice on a stream in robe season, winterin' with the Crow." He sat the parfleche down near the bank as Josiah followed close behind him. "Them Injuns clean people." He began untying the whangs on the leather case. "Sometimes wonder jest who's the savage, young'un—us, or them." He spoke as if in afterthought. From the parfleche he drew a bright yellow printed shirt, folded neatly, and held it before him a few moments before setting it on the grass. Then he pulled out a folded pair of pants, laying them beside the shirt.

"Thought you was sayin' clothes such as them catch graybacks?" Paddock found a soft spot in the grass to his liking, lay down on his side, and propped an arm under his head.

"These somethin' special." He pulled a pair of fully

146

quilled moccasins out and set them in a row alongside the shirt and pants. "These here breeches an' shirt come out to shine once't y'ar, " he said, as he extracted the last treasure of the parfleche, a pair of leather suspenders with the deep glow of a well-oiled harness, and laid them atop the pants. "Ronnyvoo doin's special time. An' these'r clothes are special for the spree."

Scratch stood and pulled his pouch and horn off his shoulder, undid the ties on the belt around his waist to let it drop to the grass, then yanked the leather shirt off and laid it on the ground next to the clothing. Slipping the antler-tine buttons free from their holes at the fly of his leather pants, he pulled them off one leg at a time, hopping clumsily as he got the pants over each moccasin. Titus Bass stood for a moment by the stream, naked except for those greasy, dirty moccasins and his blue bandanna, looking eastward at the sun rising in the sky over the Tetons. He closed his eyes for a moment, feeling the warmth pouring over him, then let out a slow sigh. As he opened his eyes, he heard movement coming behind him and only caught a fleeting glimpse of the blur moving toward him. It was too late.

Josiah ran headlong into him, pushing the older man off his feet and into the water with a loud splash, followed by an even louder howl as Bass hit the numbing water. He drew up his arms and legs tensely, numbed and shivering, then slowly stood, his hair and beard dripping around a mouth that chattered like the rapid click of a steam locomotive racing over the rails.

"Gog-gog-god-d-d-d-damn you! J-J-J-Josiah!" He eased his way toward the bank, arms clutched around his chest. "You mother's son of a she-whore! Your pups'll eat buffler dung with magpie shit on the side!" Josiah was standing as best he could, doubled over in laughter, one arm around a belly that was already aching from the mirth, his other arm pointed at Scratch. "You scurvy bastard! Said you'd pay me back, did you?" said Scratch, advancing on Paddock as he came out of the stream onto the grassy bank, the blue bandanna about his head dripping over the eyebrows.

"Stay your ground, ol' man! Don' wanna have to hurt you none!" Josiah backed off from the advancing man.

"Tryin' to be the young bull, are you? You lil' calf!"

Josiah started circling around now, dodging back and

forth in the small opening among the willows and vines caught in dense undergrowth. He was seeing the old man's body for the first time, and it surprised him that it was not old. Scratch was not heavy-boned and muscular, as Paddock was, but slim. Josiah looked over the man's frame quickly, having first thought his would be an easy task to fend off the angry man. But now he saw the muscle stretched like taut sinew over the older man's lithe body. He moved like a practiced cat, answering each of Josiah's moves with ones just as quick in the game. There was not a superfluous line in Bass's form; each muscle had been honed to a fine tuning. Slowly, with feints to draw him off every now and then, Scratch put Josiah's back against a thick wall of willow and made his move.

The younger man began to move to the side quickly, but Scratch was all the quicker as Paddock turned. Catching Josiah by the belt with one hand, he drove his other under Paddock's left arm, then grabbed tightly onto the back of the coat collar. Frantically the young man squirmed to pull away from Bass until his feet were no longer touching the ground.

"Got you, you lil' varmint!" Scratch started back toward the bank.

"Put me, put me down, goddammit!" Josiah hollered, then began laughing uncontrollably.

"I'll put you down! I'll put you down all right! But I'll be puttin' you down where I want you down." With a short swing he sent Paddock sailing into the icy creek. "Right there!"

With the momentum of the older man's swing, Josiah had gone in head first with a belly buster, flailing his arms to try to land on his feet. But the only foot that had touched ground before he crashed in the stream had slipped on the mossy rocks, propelling him into the water all the harder. Paddock rose sputtering, pulling his hat from his head and coughing his throat clear, to see Scratch down on his knees in laughter on the bank. As he started out of the stream, the older man stood up.

"You're real goddamn funny, ain't you?" Josiah had a false scowl within his brows but the lines at the corners of the mouth told that he wanted to laugh.

"L'arn you, boy. Don' start nothin' you ain't ready 'nough to finish!" He pushed Josiah back into the stream, the young man plopping down on his ass once again in the cold water. "Gotta see it through, Josiah!" Scratch waded into the water to help Paddock up.

"Naw! Leave me be. You're wantin' me to take a bath so all-fired bad—I'm gonna take a bath," Josiah said, making scrubbing motions under his arms and around his neck.

"I could spit on you an' get more dirt off than you're doin' thataway." Scratch scraped his hand along the sandy bank, gathering a hand full of the grit to rub over his own neck and shoulders, then down his arms.

"Sand? What you cleanin' with sand for?" Josiah stopped his mock bathing.

"Only thing there be to cut this grease an' scum I'm carryin' since last to ronnyvoo."

"Well, I'll be damned if that don't take it!" He rose and started for the bank, twisting the soft felt hat to wring it out as he went. "Man's usin' sand to clean the dirt off!" Josiah plopped down on the bank with a squish and pulled his boots off, then poured water from them onto the bank. Sinking slowly back into the grass, he watched Scratch bathing for a moment more, then closed his eyes and drifted off into slumber.

When he awoke, Scratch was out of the water, standing beside him and slipping the print shirt over his shoulders. The older man was white. He was deeply tanned only from his wrists down over his hands, and from his forehead down his face and neck; a little V-shaped patch of dark skin on the upper part of his chest showed where the leather shirt was kept open. Bass buttoned the shirt up as Josiah stirred into a sitting position and put his boots on.

"How'd you come by that scar 'longside your head, Josiah?" Scratch asked, tucking the long shirttails into the loose waist of his pants.

"How'd you know 'bout that?"

"Seen it last night, workin' to pull them tick critters outta your skelp, son." He bent over to pick up the suspenders and began to button them to the back of his britches. "Couldn' miss that furrow runnin' 'longside your brains like that." He buttoned the suspenders to the front. "Took you a good lick there, you did. Heal't up nice . . . but you'll never have a lick a ha'r there now on, you know."

Paddock rose and patted the side of his head, smoothing his hair down over the scar self-consciously, pulling the hair over the tops of the ears with his fingertips.

Scratch picked up his buckskins, stuffed them in the parfleche, and carried it over to the mule, where he worked to stuff it into a secure pack. "Ain't got no reason to cut ha'r up here noways, son. You can let it grow down to your ass, if you likes. Time was what Ashley didn' want no man with a beard an' long ha'r comin' upriver. You see, the Injuns don' take real kindly to a man with ha'r on his face—so it wouldn' do to wear no beard with Ashley's bunch. The gen'l jest had a thing, too, 'bout not wearin' long ha'r, him bein' citified an' all." Scratch climbed into the saddle. "You ready to see what rippin' an' snortin' they's doin' to ronnyvoo?"

"Yep." Josiah rose onto the dapple's back and they moved off.

"Jest let it grow, son—your ha'r, I mean. All the better up here anyways. Keeps the sun off the back of a man's neck. Keeps his ears warm like some furrysome muffler when them winds get to growlin'. It's dec'ration too! Jest like them red nigger bucks dec'rate theys ha'r, for lovin' or for warrin'. 'Sides, man's got better things to do than be cuttin' ha'r back alla time." He looked over at Paddock for a moment, "So, don' you go worryin' 'bout that thing clear 'longside your head. It's gettin' covered up purty nice, it is."

"Left me a chunk of my skelp back to St. Louie . . . 'long with a lot else," Josiah said softly, just loud enough for Scratch to make out the words as they were riding close beside each other. "This stiff skin 'longside my head gonna long time keep me rememberin' why I cain't go back there now, noway." He turned to look at the older man leaning over at him, intent on what was being said, with his head cocked to one side. "Wounds back there ain't never gonna heal up like this scar," Josiah said, touching the side of his head as he looked away from Scratch.

"You wanna talk 'bout it, son? Not pushin' you now. Jest wond'rin'."

"Yep. Guessin' I do wanna tell you 'bout it . . . now." Josiah stared into the pure emptiness of the mountain air of the valley, struck by its fresh, laundered look that gave him a very real sense of his own finiteness thrust up against those infinite hills. The air about him caused the light of midday to seem detached from the sun overhead, for it felt as if the light were radiating all about him. With it pouring over him like a thick syrup, Josiah felt at ease now, comfortable to tell Bass about how a man could be wronged by a woman, how a man could be driven to kill a man over that woman, and how he had left St. Louis to put that ghost behind him. Paddock felt that much, just that much would be enough to tell Titus Bass.

"I do wanna tell you a lil' 'bout it..."

"You left a gal back there after all, you say. Wagh! Dad-blamed, Ol' Scratch knew it. Jest had that look 'bout you, Josiah—jest looked like'n you'd be the man to have your troubles with the womens. An' you kilt a man over her too! I'll say it again—Wagh! My new partner's no stranger to killin', an' that's some good out here, 'cause these here mountains full a the livin', an' full a the dyin'. Both. Man as has lived full his y'ars out here ain't really 'fraid of the dyin'—only seems nat'ral part of things, only seems a fittin' part of the livin'." He grew silent, listening now to more than the sounds of the stream and the padding of the dappled mare's hoofs over the stones. Scratch listened to his bowels, to the uneasiness that had been growing there over the past several months. He tried to think it away, tried to talk it away with the words he gave now to Josiah. But he could not escape the thought, Titus Bass, you're gettin' ol't now—you're gettin' skairt now, skairt a dyin'.

"Them's what we calls the Big Holes, over there." Scratch directed Josiah's eyes to the low range of less-than-lofty mountains to the west. "They circles on round behind us to the southwest," he said, swinging his arm around in that direction. "Then you can always find this here place again jest by keepin' your eye shaved for them three breasts up there." He brought their eyes back to the east, to look once more at the majesty of those powder-blue peaks. "Most anywhars you be out here in ronnyvoo country, you can spot them breasts a ways off. They'll sign you where you're wantin' to go. You can lay your set to that mark, Josiah. Many's a man what's been lost, maybe wand'rin' lookin' for a place to feel to home, when the coon comes over a rise an' there set them three bee-yu-tee-full breasts to show him home again. Whoooeee! They some, ain't they?"

"An' what is that up there, ol' man?" Josiah nodded forward with his head, ahead of them to the north. They had just come around a twist in the stream to see for the first time the first tribal lodges of Indians who had come to rendezvous. Closer still, Scratch could begin to discern the thrown together lean-tos and temporary shelters of white trappers, nestled through the valley along the cottonwood groves bordering the stream that flowed north the length of the hole.

"Son, that's what a mountain man lives for . . . that's what he'll work his ever-livin' ass off for a y'ar to see. Josiah, we come to ronnyvoo!" He leaned over, standing in the stirrups to slap Paddock a good one on the back. "Jumpin' Jehoshaphat! Now we shine!"

Far up the valley, much farther than Josiah's excited, wide eyes could see, lay the dotting of larger groupings of Indian lodges. Around each camp lay a buffer zone of prairie, empty save for a small ring of a few lodges thrown up and the horses that seemed to blanket the open ground. It was the job of a small number of Indians from each tribe, usually the boys too old to play games any longer but too young to become warriors, to watch over and care for the tribe's herd of horseflesh. Around the herd sat the sentinels alone on horseback or sitting gathered in knots on the ground, guarding their tribal wealth. Here and there an Indian warrior moved about on horseback, moving slowly and proudly as he made his pony cavort smartly, followed by his squaw atop her pony that pulled a travois laden with the personal plunder.

"Things be awful quiet," Scratch broke into Josiah's spell. "Too quiet for snortin' times." He kept his eyes busy as they worked their way past a small village of skin lodges. "Bannocks," was all he said. Scratch squinted into the trees from side to side to make out various small camps of free trappers, while up ahead were larger groupings of white-man camps.

"Ho! Bass! Ye mangy she-wolf!" a graveled voice called out up ahead to their right along the stream. A tall man dressed in leggings with a long, beaded leather breechclout stepped out from the shadows of the overhanging cottonwoods. He was naked to the waist, wearing only a large trophy of hair hung around his neck. As he pulled a small pipe from his mouth, the tall man lifted his arm over his head as a signal to the new arrivals.

"Mad Jack?" Scratch hollered out as he reined his pony in the tall man's direction. "That you, Mad Jack Hatcher? Baddest liar west of the Muddy?"

"Ain't none the other!" came the answer. "Get your ass an' whatevers else over hyar for huggin', ya bald-face, likker-lovin' coon!"

Josiah rode beside Scratch into the knot of improvised lean-tos and bowers. There were several blankets hung low in the tree branches for shade, and beneath them lay or sat other buckskinned white men. For the most part, their faces were in the shade, but a few stuck their heads out to get a clear look at the two men on horseback. Scratch kicked his left leg to the right over the pommel of the saddle and plopped to the ground on a dead run toward the tall man, who stuffed his pipe in the belt tied about his waist. He stood for a moment more only, then headed straight for the bellowing Bass. Josiah feared this was a fight and leaped to the ground, reins held in one hand, the long rifle gripped in the other. He stood watching as the men raced toward each other, then crashed together. But instead of swinging, kicking, and throwing the other to the ground, each man put his arms around the other's chest tightly and began to squeeze, shaking the other and lifting him off the ground frequently. Each was grunting and growling, dancing around and around the other, the tall man towering over Scratch by as much as half a foot. Both men finally dropped to the ground, puffing and panting.

The tall man leaned over and swatted Scratch on the shoulder, "Still got it in ya, ol' coon!"

"Gotta!" Scratch wheezed a little in his answer, "see you once't a y'ar, an' you grow uglier an' bigger ever' one!"

The tall man swung a fist halfheartedly at Scratch, who ducked out of its way. "On'ry ol' shit, ain't ya, Bass?"

"Scratch cain't teach you a thing 'bout bein' on'ry, Mad Jack." He puffed a moment more. "What's price of beaver?"

"Traders not in yet, Titus. Rocky Mountain hyar early on with more'n a hunnert men." He motioned up the valley toward the larger camps. "Vand'burgh's on up aways from thar with eighty-some. American come in a few days back to find Rocky Mountain already hyar. But theys ain't no traders in from the Louis side yet. Vand'burgh's waitin' on Provo comin' in with goods, an' Bridger an' Fitz's worryin' 'bout Sublette makin' 'er hyar in time to beat Provo's train. Fitz went out sometime back to tell Sublette to hurry 'er up."

"No likker?" Scratch blew the words out in disappointment.

"Nary a drop yet. Got a thirst on, eh?" He punched at Scratch's shoulder.

"Might say I do, that." Bass looked up and noticed Josiah still standing with the animals. "Ho! Josiah! C'mon, boy!" he waved his arm widely in the air to signal Paddock over. "Bring 'long the animals an' plunder." Then he turned to Hatcher and spoke softly. "Boy's gonna make a fine one, Jack. Pick't him up west of the Wind River. Good size he is for the mountains—give you a good huggin', he would, too. That boy's my pardner for the season. Yessir, he'll make a fine one!"

"Less'n he catches yer bad habits! Ain't likely thar be a more flea-bit, skin-chewin', squar-screwin', likker-lovin' man hyar 'bouts!"

"Why, thankee, Mad Jack! Didn' know you thought so highly of me. Comin' from you, them kind words is real somethin' special, they is ... Here, Josiah, want you meetin' Mad Jack Hatcher, man as you couldn' trust any less as your friend!"

The tall man got to his feet slowly and stuck out his right hand, squinting one eye as he looked down slightly at the younger man. "Didn' catch yer last name, Josiah," Hatcher said, tightly gripping Josiah's hand.

"Paddock, Mad Jack. Last name's Paddock." He squeezed the tall man's hand back.

"Warn't thar a man with Henry back to aught-nine, name of Paddock?" He let go of Josiah's hand, turning around to look down at Scratch momentarily. Bass wrinkled his brow without saying a word. "'Lijah, no ..."

"Ezra. Kilt upriver just after I was borned," Josiah said, staring back into the tall man's green eyes until Hatcher dropped his gaze.

"Wal', now—ya coons' goin' be beddin' down with us, ain't ya? Ain't gonna hear of ya doin' nothin' else such!" He put a hand under Scratch's armpit and helped him to his feet. "Now ya pick ya a likely spot up hyar in the trees an' we'll make ya to home," Hatch said, starting back to the lean-tos and canopies. "Hey, ya niggers! Want

154

ya meet frien' of mine, ya heerd me tell of him a time or two round my winter fire, ya have—this'r ol' child's Titus Bass, but ya best call him Scratch." Several of the men came forward out into the light from the shadows, standing in a semicircle around the two new arrivals. "An' this'r's Mr. Josiah Paddock, recent of the settlements." One of the smaller men started to step toward Josiah at that time. "Ya can wait awhile, Solomon. Jest wait a bit to ask him yer questions."

Hatcher turned to the side to speak out of the corner of his mouth to Paddock, "Niggers'll wanna know ever'thin' as is goin' on back east, they will," then turned back to introduce the gathering trappers. "Solomon Fish this'un' be," pointing out the man who had wanted to talk with Josiah, then Hatcher began to sweep to the left with his arm, "Elbridge Gray, Caleb Wood, then Isaac Simms an' Rufus Graham. A meaner bunch of dogs no bad-ass Blackfoot'd nary wanna see!" Some of the men grunted in greeting as each stepped up to Scratch and Josiah to shake hands and make a close appraisal of the newcomers.

"Where'd you be spring fur gettin'?" Bass asked of Hatcher as they led the animals through the shelters to a spot not taken by others.

"Down to Brown's Lil' Hole, up through the b'ar kentry. Sipped the wine at the sody springs, we did, afore headin' up hyar. Roll't in early, it's lookin', as we been hyar close onto two weeks now. Jest Injuns an' us, till few days back when Bridger's boys come roarin' in, then Vand'burgh, Font'nelle an' that crew. All of 'em pissed as a struck hornet's nest that they's no traders in yet." He stopped. "Hyar'd be the spot for ya two gents. Got me a chore to bring some firewood to bait now, so I'll be to seein' ya later. Hopin' yer stay is pleasant in our lil' settlement!" Hatcher touched Scratch lightly on the shoulder in parting, then turned away.

"Break down the plunder, Josiah. We gonna let the animules take a dust roll as they been wantin' for some time." Bass began to untie the bundles of possibles and plews from Hannah's back as Josiah took the saddle off the dapple and carried it to the base of a tree where they would be bedding down. "Keep her tied jest 'nother minute an' I'll get the pins." He struggled with the packs as Josiah came up to help, and gradually each one was set on the ground near their tree. From one satchel that held

155

a camp kettle, Bass pulled four picket pins and a small axe.

"Grab them reins, an' Hannah's rope an' you foller me," Scratch said, taking off out onto the prairie a short distance to where the other free trapper's animals were herded. There he drove the long iron picket pins into the crusty soil, then tied each animal to a pin with a long section of rawhide rope. "We'll be to hobblin' them come moon time, Josiah." He finished the last knot and looked up and down the valley. "Good thing most of these red niggers be too proud to steal a hobble't horse from a trapper. Some as would pay no never-mind to steal a drunk trapper's horse, howsomever."

They started back to their cottonwood and willow shelter. "Jest wanna be sure an' certain that we got somethin' to trade for the new ponies we'll be needin'."

As the men were returning across the open land, the noise of snorting horses and squeaking leather came from the south. Into the cloud of dust kicked up by many hoofs Scratch stared when he stopped to look over the advancing tangle of men on horseback. The group came slowly toward them until one could make out the weary faces, the haggard look around the corners of each man's eyes, the dour sag around the edges of each one's mouth, and the crust of filmy dust powdered over every man.

"Halloo!" Scratch sang out to the men at the head of the group. "Who be you, an' where you be comin' from?"

"Sinclair, stranger," shouted back one of the fifteen men, "to ronnyvoo from the Colorady!" He took off his dusty hat to wave at the free trappers coming up behind Scratch. "Who be you?" he asked looking down at Bass as he passed.

"Titus Bass, recent of the Colorady, meself!"

"Pleased I am to make you 'quaintance, Titus Bass!" Sinclair turned back around in the saddle and passed on. The men following him looked anything but enthusiastic about a joyous greeting. No one spoke, and few even grunted as Scratch stood his ground in their dust giving each one a "How do?"

Josiah and Titus had spread their robes and blankets out, stuffed the bundles of pelts back into the willows, and placed a heavy Mackinaw blanket over their heads and anchored it when from a distance some shooting could be heard. Hatcher came running back, hollering at them.

"Nez Percy comin' in, an' ye should see the show! C'mon!"

"Boy! You ain't never see'd the likes of this now! C'mon, an' we'll run up to watch them Nepercy comin' to ronnyvoo," Scratch said. He led Josiah out and they started trotting along behind Hatcher and several other free trappers across the open prairie. Soon they reached a spot near the Rocky Mountain Fur Company's camp where white men were gathering to watch the parade of Nez Perce coming down into the valley. The men stood silent for a long time in the northern part of the hole, watching the spectacle unfolding before their eyes, a spectacle put on for their amusement.

"Might say them niggers is doin' up the openin' to ronnyvoo right nice, Josiah." Scratch smacked his lips, "Look at them ponies! My!"

Down toward the spectators came nearly two hundred and fifty braves mounted on their finest buffalo runners, ponies selected not only for beauty, but for speed, agility, and endurance. Each animal was decked out in the finest its owner could find in the way of ornamentation: long trains of eagle plumes streaming down the sides of the pony, hawkbells tinkling incessantly, strips of scarlet and bright blue trade cloth woven into the pony's mane, perhaps some trade mirrors attached along the animal's tail.

Atop the ponies painted with symbols of successful horse raids and their owners' coups sat the proud braves, most with their long hair stacked above their foreheads in a gaudy pompadour from which hung the symbols of their warrior status. Some were naked except for the breechclout and moccasins, to free them from heavy clothing while they put the ponies through their paces, prancing and dancing from side to side, around and around, up and down along the head of the march. Others sat more stately, they the older warriors, wrapped in buffalo and elk robes daubed and smeared with earth paints in a brilliant display of color and personal pride. In the lead rode the older chiefs, men of age and wisdom who looked neither left nor right as they rode, cradling their trade fusils across folded arms. In their midst rode a white man the trappers strained to see more closely.

Behind the chiefs and to their side rode the medicine men; some were juggling for all to see, others chanting and waving buffalo bladder rattles or beating small drums, as they came down the hill. One old man held small cymbals in his mouth, one attached to his upper teeth and one to his lower, with which he kept up a constant jingling as he chanted to the heavens.

The throaty chants mingled with high-pitched wails as the procession advanced toward the white men, when suddenly the warriors cried out almost in unison with shrill war whoops and set their ponies to gallop. They darted in and out through the procession wildly, racing about back and forth between it and the assembled trappers, yelling in joy and merriment, sending arrows bouncing and skidding across the valley floor. They would lean off to one side of their ponies as they advanced on the white men, one foot up on the animals' rumps and one hand in a loop tied to the ponies' manes, shooting arrows at the trappers' feet. One came close to Josiah and he began to jump aside.

"Don' you let 'em see you movin', boy," Scratch admonished gruffly out the corner of his mouth. "Stand your ground. They's jest showin' you they can put tha' arrer wherevers they wants to!"

Around and around the trappers the warriors raced, while the white men answered back with chants and war whoops of their own. They became more animated now, jumping up and down, slapping others on the back, crying out to friends, "Did ye see that! Did ye ever see such a goddamned thing! That do beat the trick!" as they marveled at the feats of horsemanship and daring.

Suddenly one of the braves came racing headlong for the trappers, then stopped short, bringing his pony to a halt in a skidding, head-reared cloud of dust as he leaped to the ground. From there he ran a few paces and pounced on an imaginary foe, motioning with his knife to show that he cut the enemy's throat, then whizzed the tip of the blade around the topknot, placed a foot on the back of the dead man's neck, and yanked the scalp free. Proudly the warrior stood there for a few seconds, holding aloft his imaginary scalp, then made for his pony, still pretending to hold the bloody trophy in the air, yelling and chanting his own personal medicine and the Nez Perce scalp song.

Without warning, a single shot was fired from the chief's trade fusil, and the young warriors turned their ponies around and raced back to the procession, where they formed orderly columns behind the various clan war chiefs as the whole tribe neared camp. Lances, bows, rifles, and painted rawhide shields were brought smartly to attention as each brave sat rigid in the saddle to pass by the gathering of gaping, admiring trappers, some of whom were applauding and whistling in approval and appreciation for the spectacle they had just been given.

"Why, I'll be et for a country tater!" Scratch hollered out; he leaned forward to squint his eyes at the grouping of chiefs. "If that ain't Asa McAfferty, ridin' the high an' handsome with them ol' fellers!" He waved his arm energetically at the man as the Indians rode by, pointing out the white man with snowy hair and beard to Josiah. Atop the man's head sat a fur hat that glistened in the high sunlight. "That Asa McAfferty do beat all, don' he! Ridin' in to ronnyvoo with them big chief coons!"

Josiah spotted him now, catching glimpses of Asa McAfferty through the throbbing mass of mounted Indians. The old man was dressed in the finest of white buckskins that had not been smoked. From his moccasins trailed ermine skins, and down the seam of his tight leggings ran a broad strip of porcupine quillwork to offset a few scalp locks. Over the low pommel of his saddle poured his breechclout, fashioned of the McAfferty family tartan, a long, thick wool covering of red, black, and green. The man's shirt was without beading or quillwork, but carried a richly ornamented assortment of brass trade beads and strips of scarlet ribbon. Down from his chin hung the white beard topped by a long, pristine mustache Asa curled at the ends with bear grease to point back toward eyes that sparkled with his own sense of importance. Across the knees of his leggings was carried a large-bore mountain rifle, from the muzzle of which was tied a full scalp that included the tops of the victim's ears. McAfferty's pony was decked out in style, but in no way had he let the pony detract from his personal display. He passed on in the bright parade without acknowledging the presence of the white trappers in the slightest. Both Josiah and Scratch watched as McAfferty and the chiefs rode on to the south.

Behind them now advanced the rest of the Nez Perce tribe, strung out down the slopes into the northern part of the valley for better than a mile and a half, winding its serpentine path toward the trappers. Dust rose from the thousands of unshod hoofs as the young boys given the weighty responsibility of caring for the horse herd circled back and forth to keep the ponies gathered up. A pair of continuous clouds drifted back from the two travois poles dragging along behind the squaws' ponies, some carrying a family's possessions, others carrying old men and women too feeble to walk or ride horseback. They sat, wrapped in their buffalo robe cocoons, passing by the white men, smiling with eyes now wrinkled with many winters. Young children sat atop the travois-bearing ponies, tied to the saddles and hemmed in by brightly painted or beaded parfleches. Babies with wide, brown eyes stared out at the noise and movement from their cradle-board prisons slung from the pommel of a saddle or hung from their mother's back. Those squaws yelled and cussed in their tongue at the children, at the dogs racing in and out between the horses' legs, at the sagging strength of the ponies. Their voices rose shrill and loud now as the music of the warriors began to fade down the valley. Ponies snorted and dogs howled and nipped at one another. The pageant of rendezvous at its finest.

The head chief had selected a spot to the south for the village, and there the orderly columns became knots and tangles of mad activity. Travois of lodgepoles were taken from ponies' backs and lashed together before they were raised with the help of a long, sturdy rawhide rope. More and more of the poles were raised here and there across the plain in feverish exercise. A forest was being grown in the hole as the final skinned poles were put in place around the lodge site and the lodgeskins were brought out on the ground. Here the smoked buffalo hides that had been sewn together were tied to the lifting pole, which dropped into place. Women busily pulled the cover around the poles, laced it up, then staked it down before pushing the lodgepoles outward to stretch the cover taut.

The massive herd of ponies with spotted rumps, the

pride of the Nez Perce, was put out to pasture under watchful eyes. They did not really trust the Bannocks. As the lodges were trimmed and filled with family possessions, the women and children boiled across the sagebrush like ants, streaming toward the cottonwood and willow along the banks of the streams to gather firewood and bring in water.

Scratch had headed Josiah back to their camp. "Them Nepercy be up to visitin' soon—be ready for some lovin' an' gamblin'. Tryin' to talk you outta your knife or talk you into the bushes!" He put his hand on Paddock's neck and squeezed it. "You've come to ronnyvoo!"

When the traders would finally arrive with their pack mules of shiny things, the warriors, then children, and finally the squaws would wander from their lodges into the tents of the eastern businessmen. Snake, Flathead, Bannock, and Nez Perce alike would pore over the goods, touching what they were allowed, eyes wide at the gaudy but cheap trinkets. Calculating on what they would buy and what they thought they could steal was a part of the rendezvous game. And there would always be time for a tin or two of alcohol, most of it provided free, "on the prairie," by the businessmen to stimulate trade.

"Nepercy don' like the taste of raw likker, so Billy Sublette sees that they keeps drinkin' by puttin' black 'lasses in the kegs. Makes it go down easy an' faster that way. Use to Hudson Bay's fine rum them niggers is!"

In just a few short hours, the valley had doubled in population. Added to the eighty lodges of Flathead, seventy-four of the Snake tribe, and a much smaller number of those of the Bannocks, were the one hundred twenty lodges of Nez Perce reaching for the sky.

"That village is some now, Josiah. You can count you seven or eight of them Nepercy Injuns to a lodge," Scratch commented as they made it back to their grove. "That herd of ponies is some, too!"

The sun drooped lazily in the western sky as the air turned colder. The summer of 1832 would be remembered for its unusually cool weather west of the divide. In the space of a few weeks, the air would begin to show the rapid advance of autumn, a melancholy time for the trapper as he began to notice the shorter periods of daylight, the cold bite of the early-morning getup, while hurrying through his labor of the fall hunt. In so many ways, autumn was a sad time for the trapper, pushing himself through each day on the short-lived memories of the summer's rendezvous, readying himself for the long, lonely, and idle winter until spring freed the streams for hard work once more in the high country.

"What's the kittle tonight, Mad Jack?" Scratch cried out as he approached a wide, circular fire around which many of the free trappers he had met that afternoon were gathering.

"Poor bull! So be it, less an' less of that!" Hatcher cried back. "But ye come an' sit yerse'f anyways." He motioned with an arm to have the two men sit next to him on the ground. "Bull were slight an' stringy, but it be the best we got to offer at our table."

"You boys take a belly for some elk?" Bass asked the others.

"Ye ain't whistlin' out yer ass, is ye?" Rufus Graham asked, looking at Scratch from his seat on a five-gallon oak keg near the fire where he was whetting a knife across a thick leather strop.

"Ain't never lied to you boys afore, have I?" Scratch put up a hand to stroke and comb his beard with his fingers.

"Never knowed ye afore this!" Solomon came back with the answer Titus had been expecting and wanting.

"Then chances are I ain't never lied to you afore!" he said, and turned away from the fire chuckling as the others laughed, followed by Josiah. They hurried back to their bower where they retrieved a hind quarter of the bull elk and returned to the fire.

"Hear ye now! Fine victuals for you fellers of the uplands!" He plopped the quarter down on a skin next to Hatcher. "Get you busy, Josiah! We need steaks thick as they is true!" Scratch turned to Hatcher, "Got you any of them rabbit droppin's you call coffee beans, Mad Jack?"

"Caleb's up to the crik now, fetchin' water for kittle an' coffee." The tall man turned his head around to look into the timber. "Hurry ya up now, Caleb!" The trapper returned carrying two heavy iron camp kettles.

Paddock bent over the quarter to stare at it a moment as if in contemplation or confusion, then sunk a knife into the meat and began to make a long slice.

"Arrrrgh! Stop right thar!" Hatcher put out a hand and gripped tight to Josiah's hand that held the knife.

"Stop right thar, boy!" Paddock attempted to pull the hand away but could not. "Cain't have ya cuttin' cross't the grain like that! Hyar, let me show ya." Mad Jack took the knife as Josiah opened his palm reluctantly. "Ain't ya showed young Josiah Paddock to cut yer meat, Scratch?"

"Been doin' all the cookin' meself, coon. Child's ain't had the whore's chance to Sunday meetin' to get hisse'f near a piece of meat 'cept to stuff it in his mouth!" Scratch knelt down on the skin near the quarter and chuckled along with Hatcher.

"Yer schoolin' been missin' a lick then, Josiah." He began to cut into the meat with the tip of the blade, using his right hand to pull strips of meat away from the knife held in his left. "But Mad Jack Hatcher soon to find a cure for that'un."

The sun was being lost to the sky and the shadows had darkened outside the ring of firelight that splashed a dancing glow of yellow light across each man's face. As the steaks browned over the hot coals pulled by Solomon's poker to the edge of the fire away from the flames, the hungry trappers carved off slices of meat done to their liking, then turned the meat over, leaving the flesh beneath red and dripping with a thick juice to broil some more. Pint tin cups were filled with Hatcher's thick coffee, then brought potent and steaming to each man's lips to be blown cool enough to swallow in washing down the elk meat.

"Tomorrer, I'll be to lookin' for wild onions again 'long the bottoms," Elbridge commented as he stuffed his mouth with another string of steak, some juice dripping down his chin. The others around the fire grunted in anticipated appraisal of what Gray could add to the next night's meal. As each man filled, he sat back and pulled from his tobacco pouch a small pipe and what tobacco he had left. He lighted the bowl to glowing, blew a column of smoke to the darkening canopy overhead, and stretched his legs in reclining.

"The man I remember ya to be," Hatcher began, leaning over toward Bass, "be one as is out for the funnin' most off."

"Most time." Bass chewed on the end of his pipe stem. "No argument with that neither, most time." He now looked over at Hatcher, "Jest what you speakin' of?"

"How'd the boy come by havin' wet clothes when ya come in?"

"He throwed me in the crik," Josiah butted in.

"Now, boy." Scratch got that philosophical tone in his voice. "I don' take me no argeement with that. I did the throwin', sure 'nough. But it were Josiah Paddock what got his clothes wet."

"Wal', ol' coon." Mad Jack leaned over a little closer toward Scratch but spoke loud enough for all to hear. "I see'd young Paddock in wet clothes when ya rode up to mornin', an' I heerd tell of greenhorns bein' wet behind the ears—but the boy'd been wet all over!"

Paddock shook his head and stared into the fire in silence, certain that he must take the good-natured ribbing as harmless.

"Whar ye be recent of the settlements, Josiah Paddock?" Solomon asked, and made a spot to stay next to Josiah.

"St. Lou."

"Yer gonna have to feed hungry ears hyar, young'un." Hatcher had pulled the pipe stem from his mouth to speak.

"Last green-up?" Caleb leaned forward across the low flames at Josiah.

"No." Josiah thought a moment. "'T 'weren't spring at all when I come out."

"Don' be a miser with your words, Josiah," Scratch said, and knocked burnt tobacco out into his palm and threw it into the embers before leaning back on his elbows.

"What's the new back thar? That's what these niggers is wantin' to l'arn." Mad Jack picked his knife up and plunged it into the ground up to the handle several times, then wiped it off across the top of his leggings.

"Jest what is it you want to know?" With that Paddock opened a flood gate. Questions were fired at him much faster than any Indian warrior could string and fire arrows from a bow. There were questions as to knowing families in St. Louis, St. Charles and the surrounding countryside, questions as to knowing how things had grown and changed in the city, questions about how the country was stretching its arms across the Mississippi, being carried west by settlers, questions about the economy of life back east. On and on through the hours of that night the men fed timber to the fire to keep it merry and popping, while Josiah fed those men about him as best he could the information, the news, the taste of what was left behind beyond the river, all to satisfy starving minds and hearts, hungry for any bit of real information to match their fast-fading memories.

It was around this kind of man, the free trapper, that rendezvous would whirl with life. The rival Rocky Mountain and American Fur companies would count on their own trappers to bring in only enough pelts to remain competitive. It was, therefore, the free trapper who soloed center stage: it was for the free trapper's trade that both firms would compete; it was the free trapper who kept prices down each year, despite the already exorbitant sum asked for trade goods at rendezvous. It was to be these free trappers throwing their hungry questions at Josiah, and the unnumbered others gathering in Pierre's Hole, who would swing the pendulum of success to one company or the other. Knowing the fact of economic life and survival in the mountains, each firm was racing a supply train to rendezvous. Conditions dictated suspense as to what train would reach the valley first, and therefore end up with the lion's share of the free trapper's trade.

"Moon's on the full-up, boys," Scratch finally remarked after hours of uncommon silence during which he had let the attention center on Paddock. "Looks like'n we got a cold night for this time a y'ar, so we best be warmin' robes now." Bass rose and shook both legs, then put open palms over the embers. "You don' wanna wring the boy dry of news jest yet, do you now?"

The others rose from the circle about the fire and began to filter off into the shadows beyond the warm, yellow glow thrown against the cottonwood and willow backdrop. Josiah stared into the fire as the men left for bed until only Hatcher remained. Paddock finally got to his feet and turned into the darkness, waiting a moment for his eyes to become accustomed to the change in light before moving away.

"Thank ya, Josiah Paddock," Hatcher spoke softly without looking away from the glowing goals.

"Huh?" Josiah looked back. "Huh . . . oh, the news. Yeah, you're welcome. You're welcome, Mad Jack."

Behind Scratch, Paddock crept back into the stand of

trees through the gathering of lean-tos where dark forms lay across the ground, hidden from recognition by heavy buffalo robes.

Josiah felt the pressure in his groin before he stopped near their canopy. He unbuttoned his fly and found relief in a long splash on the creepers that ran underfoot in a tangled mat. Scratch was already beneath his robe when Josiah came up.

"You done 'em good, Josiah."

He pulled one boot off and rubbed the stiff foot. "Didn' feel like I did much good. Didn' know really what they wanted to hear." He pulled the other boot free.

"Don' you worry you none 'bout that. They ask you what they want to know—won' ask anythin' to spoil their dreams of what's left back there. What they ask you, don' hurt 'em none to know."

Josiah slipped between his blankets then laid his head down to feel the curly fur of the buffalo robe beneath him. "You give me one a your robes to sleep on, Scratch. Thank you."

"In the rain, you give me one a your blankets. 'Sides, that ain't my robe no more, son. That's your'n, now. Man cain't freeze his pizzer off on a frosty night like this'n." Scratch turned over on his side. "Night, Josiah."

"Night, friend."

Paddock rose earlier than the others, pulled his boots and blanket coat on, then moved quietly south on foot along the edge of the trees. The sun had not yet come up over the Tetons, but the gray in the sky was slowly brightening to a pale blue, the color of cornflowers. He found a private spot with a small downed cottonwood to his liking and undid the belt and fly of his pants. Slipping them down to his knees, he hobbled into position over the log and sat down on it, hanging his buttocks free of obstruction to loosen his bowels.

It was a relief for him to feel what he was leaving behind was firmer now, and not the diarrhea of recent days. Josiah sat contented on his log, gazing up now and then to the patchwork of pink clouds gathered about the peaks until his legs began to numb and he finally felt empty. He leaned forward and swept up a handful of grass touched with frost on every blade that would not turn to dew until the air had warmed. Briskly Josiah rubbed the grass over the side of his pants before cleansing himself, then repeated the process.

He rose and buttoned the fly to his pants, then turned and headed south through the trees. He approached the Nez Perce village and saw much early-morning activity around the encampment. Dogs barked and scurried, yelled at now and then by the women who moved slowly between the skin lodges and the line of trees along the stream, bringing back water and wood. Several children scampered here and there, chasing one another in a zig-zagging movement through the maze of lodges. One little boy ran toward Paddock chasing a large, ugly dog with a stick, attempting to swing the stick at the animal and laughing all the time at the merry chase. He galloped by without even looking up at the stranger.

Once into the tangle of lodges, Josiah approached a squaw bent over a skin she had just unrolled on the ground. He stood a moment, waiting for her to look up, but she did not lift her eyes from her work.

"Mornin'."

Now she looked up at the man standing above her, and straightened to gaze into his face. "Nuoma-watchee?" she questioned, a slight inflection in her voice.

"McAfferty," he said, then decided to ask it with a question, "Asa McAfferty?"

"Num-cocca suish?"

"Asa McAfferty, white man . . . you know, white man McAfferty?" He grew exasperated with himself more than the nonunderstanding squaw, frustrated that he could not communicate with her. He repeated, "McAfferty," and used his hands along the side of his face and under his chin to pantomime a long beard and curled mustache. "A-sa Mc-Af-fer-ty," he repeated several times, along with the gestures.

"Waa yo-yote!" Her eyes brightened and she took a grip on Josiah's wrist to pull him along as she moved through the maze of the Nez Perce village. Near the center of the camp, she stopped before a lodge.

"Batish-ma, waa yo-yote!" She pointed at the hole in the lodge cover, a hole black without light.

He stood motionless, wondering what to do. She let go of his wrist.

"Waa yo-yote!" There was an edge to her voice. "Batish-ma! Batish-ma!" She finally gave Josiah a little shove toward the opening, but he failed to move much from his spot. Now she threw up her hands as if in disgust, then mumbled something as she moved toward the hole herself. Into the doorway she stuck the upper part of her body, but kept her feet outside the lodge and spoke to the tenants inside. He could hear other voices, mostly another woman's singsong tongue and then a deep growl, before the old squaw who had brought him here backed away and left. Josiah watched her disappear among other lodges.

"What slave-of-the-devil white man's out at this hour wantin' McAfferty?"

Paddock jerked his head around at the sound of the growl to see a white head sticking out of the hole.

"Ah...ah, mornin', Asa McAfferty," Josiah stammered, in search for words. "Name's Paddock, friend of Titus Bass." Josiah now wondered what to say next. "Umm... come to meet you...Scratch told me much 'bout you..."

"An' lies they probably be too, boy," Asa interrupted. "Ye wait on your spot whilst I get dressed an' I'll be out to ye." The bearded head disappeared back into the darkness of the lodge.

In a few minutes, the man crouched out through the opening and stood up to full height. At that, he stood a few inches shorter than Josiah, but was wide across the chest and shoulders. There was not much of a neck to the man, as big and muscular as it was. It looked much as if the white head had been plopped down on the shoulders of his brass-beaded shirt without a neck to support it. In one hand he held his head-covering that was a turban-wrap of three beautifully pale marten pelts, the color a blend of faint grays that looked almost blue in the early light. At the front of the hat were sewn the head, breast, and outspread wings of a large bluejay as ornament. The man's other hand combed the long, white hair hanging over the back of the shirt collar, while he eyed Josiah closely.

"Titus Bass, hmm," he finally said, breaking the silence between them. "So Scratch made it through 'nother year." With both hands he spread apart the bottom of the marten turban and pulled it down over his head. "Aye. Man's lucky, that one is, with the way he plays the devil!" He was silent for a moment, smoothing his hair out beneath the fur hat, when Josiah saw it.

Where once a right hand had emerged from the end of his sleeve was now stuck a crude iron hook he was using as a comb. Josiah could not take his wide eyes off it. He stared, hypnotized by the dark, curved hook that appeared brutally sharp at its end. As if held by a magnet, his eyes never left the hook while McAfferty stroked his tangled hair. All the while, Asa watched Paddock looking at the handless arm.

"Scratch want to see me, he does?"

"Not rightly." Josiah finally looked down into the man's eyes. "I come on my own."

"Oh?"

"When you come in with the Injuns yesterday, Scratch, he pointed you out—said that was some, you ridin' in with the chiefs an' all."

"Where else ye expect a man that has married into Nez Perce royalty to ride to ronnyvoo?"

"Scratch didn' say nothin' 'bout that..."

"How could he, boy? Ain't seen his hide in two, three winters. My squaw's new, just recent married up, little more'n two moons back." He reached inside and pulled a blanket out that he wrapped about his shoulders, as Josiah once again looked closely at the hook. "Bass up to the day, yet?"

"Nope. Not when I left there, anyways."

"Boy, what 'bout ye taken' me to see the coon, now?" Asa moved off with Josiah at his side trying to restrain himself from looking at the hook, weaving through the village and out onto the plain toward the horse herd. The ponies were fine looking and spirited in the early-morning air as the sun crept clear of the peaks to throw bright light down into the valley.

"Over here... these are mine," Asa directed. Josiah followed him toward a group of some thirty head. From his belt, McAfferty drew a rawhide halter and slipped it around the neck of a pony, then pulled a second halter from his belt to throw to Josiah. "Pick ye one ye want to ride, as I see ye come on foot."

Paddock chose a docile pony, attached the halter, and leaped aboard bareback while McAfferty laid the blanket over his pony's back and climbed aboard. He was still spry for looking to be so old with that white mane and beard. The men rode side by side north through the valley until back at the free trappers' camp where they dismounted and tied the ponies off to a willow. Asa put the blanket over his shoulders once more and Paddock led him back through the lean-tos housing men stirring for the day, back to the blanket canopy over the long lump sleeping beneath warm robes.

McAfferty stood silent for a moment, beside Josiah over the sleeping man, then spoke in a loud, bass voice, *"Upon the wicked He shall rain snares, fire and brimstone, and a horrible tempest!"*

Scratch jerked up into a sitting position, blinking his eyes rapidly into wakefulness.

"A bright an' good mornin' to ye, Titus Bass!" Asa's voice rang now with cheerfulness.

"A goddamned way to bring a man up," Scratch growled.

"You're the fine one to be speakin' of the things God would damn, ye are, Titus Bass!" He sat down in front of Scratch beneath the canopy. Josiah sat to complete the triangle. "The boy here brought me to ye, Scratch. What be your name again, son?"

"Josiah Paddock."

"Young Josiah sought me an' woke me himself, so I thought I would be the one to return the favor to ye, Titus Bass."

Scratch rubbed his eyes with both hands as Asa spoke again, "Where'd ye meet this devil's son, young Josiah?"

Paddock drew his legs up, "Happened on to him while out huntin' for meat..."

"Lord does work in strange ways sometimes, don' He?" McAfferty interjected and the three men fell silent.

Asa let the blanket loose from his shoulders. As it fell, he pushed it aside with his right arm. Scratch's head jerked down to stare at the crude fork hook at the end of McAfferty's right arm.

"What the...goddamn," Bass began, stammering. "What you...of all the goddamn things, Asa McAfferty!" He scratched at the side of his head nervously, staring at the hook. "Your goddamn hand's gone! What'd you do to your hand?" Scratch reached out tentatively to touch the hook with one index finger.

"Like that, eh?" McAfferty smiled, always happy at the shock it gave to others.

"Well, now—it's some differ'nt, ain't it?"

McAfferty looked down at the hook he laid across his left palm in his lap.

"How'd you come by it? Havin' the hook? How'd you get the hook?"

"Put me an ol't iron fork I use to feed with in the fire an' let it set whilst I searched me out a flat rock. Heated that iron devil up hotter'n the gates of hell, then I beat these two hooks round for the hook with me small ax on the rock." Asa looked back up from his lap, first to Josiah, then slowly moved his eyes to look at Scratch.

"Well?" Bass prodded once more.

"Aye. Carved me a chunk of wood to be 'bout like the end of me arm, then pounded the fork into it." He pulled his sleeve up to show a half-round piece of pine the diameter of the lower arm near the wrist, in which the hook was embedded. It was held to the arm with leather straps tacked to it that wrapped and tied tightly around the arm almost to the elbow. He pointed the tacks out with his left index finger. "Pulled me these tacks from the handle of me knife. Hyar." Asa brought out a big butcher knife from a sheath at his belt. "Lookee there," he said, pointing out the holes in the handle to Josiah. "Still got me that knife. See, pulled me the tacks out of them holes."

Paddock looked from the knife to the brass tacks that held the leather straps to the carved-wood wrist piece. McAfferty's insides glowed each time he showed his new right hand to someone for the first time, glowed with the sense of his own ingenuity, his own resourcefulness.

"You're keepin' two coons starvin' for your words, Asa McAfferty!" Scratch tried once more to pull the story out of the whiteheaded man.

"Well, the knave as shot me 'tweren't much a shot. Got me through the wrist—busted me rifle at that time too. Put that ball through me wrist, an' through the rifle's, too—right behind the tang after it come through me arm. Well, boys, that right arm, it was of no earthly good, but that rifle still had a ball ready. Pick't her up an' I shoots her with the left hand. I was with the Crow then ... did I tell ye that?"

Both Josiah and Scratch shook their heads.

"Didn' tell ye that. Well, some. With the Crow, in that tribe's country—an' in a fix for this boy, I'm to tell ye. Had to cut off me arm here." He raised the sleeve once more to

171

show them the site of the amputation. "Did that medicine with an ol't Injun trick. One of them Crow niggers took him a long buckskin whang, ran it over an' over the blood at the place where the ball smashed them two bones there. Got that whang all bloody, see, then he went to rubbin' it in the sand on the bank of the stream we camped by. I was some out of me mind by that time, hurt the devil it did—an' I did me more swearin' then as I've done all me young life. But the Lord He was patient with this sinner; He could see the trouble I was in, an' He forgive me. One of them Crow set to an' finished cuttin' on me meat with his knife, then set to the bone with that bloody whang. By that time, the blood had dried the sand to the whang an' it made one devil of a saw! He jest cut through them bones like'n ye'd bite into boudins—critter's guts—real slick. One of them Crow sewed best he could, as I was in 'nother mind by that time, jest like ye'd sew the moccasin as needs some fixin'. Them warriors was needin' to get back to home, an' I tol't 'em to leave me be where I lay. They give me one of them trade fusils an' a good bow with some fine cottonwood arrers. Laid me on a robe there, snugglin' up under a big tree. Laid there for days, don' really know if I could tell ye how many days it was, mendin' meself, I mean."

"Ye was alone out there?" Josiah asked, astonishment in his voice.

"Aye. That I was, boy. Laid there for some time, doin' my prayin' for help, for the Lord to show me the way once again. All the time, figgerin' on what to do next, all the time I was layin' there, thinkin' of the fix I was in, an' askin' for what help the Lord'd give me. Could go to the Crow, I thought. But, no, I said to meself. Ain't gonna be no special help down there. Could go on down to Taos, then. But, no, I says again. That's some travel, too. St. Lou was jest as far a piece, an' Taos seemed none the closer to me tree then. Got meself to thinkin' then, figgerin' on feelin' me what the Lord wanted of me to do. Never been west to them posts as are out by that big salt ocean. So I laid me beaver for that way an' made me tramp out thar. Pulled it through, with the grace of the Lord for this sinner—it were Him as showed me sign. Worked south of there a ways, then up an' over the Snake to the big salt, where I made me new outfit at a post." He finally put the knife away. "Got me good with that bow, an' can use this sticker handsome now with me left hand—better'n I was one to use it with me right!"

"How you now with the rifle?" Scratch questioned.

"Ain't been starvin', have I? Nawww. I use this lil' flat part on the hook as ye'd be usin' your trigger finger. Works fine. Aye, she does." Asa looked down at the hook, then straightened out the sleeve over most of it.

"Well, some. Tol't the lad I 'spected you to be to ronnyvoo—an' it was some to see the way you come in to ronnyvoo, McAfferty, ridin' with all them Nepercy chiefs like you did." Bass pulled the buffalo robe around his legs. "It has been some moons, it has, Asa. Three winters it's been?"

"Two. Two of 'em, '30 an' '31. Ain't laid eyes on ye since after the fall of '30 when Bridger an' Fitzpatrick we was ridin' with took them Hudson's Bay freemen away from that fella name of Work. Recall it—jest afore the time as I packed her up an' left ye?"

"Yep. Nary a thing you said, 'cept that you was headin' north of the Three Forks. Thought to myself as you was ridin' off, there ain't nothin' for a preacher's hide up there, that were Blackfoot land."

"Blackfoot kingdom ain't no room for a man of the kingdom of God," Asa mused.

Scratch pulled his pipe out and filled Asa's bowl and his own with the last of the tobacco he had to call his own. "Good to look at your hoary head, it is, once 'gain."

"How ye do the last fur gettin'? Comin' to ronnyvoo a rich man for the tradin', are ye?" Asa queried.

"Rich as I'll ever to be, s'pose. Done fine the past season, an' there's a beaver bank to be stolen by the like a Sublette's clerks this y'ar!"

"Aye! This man is some now, young Josiah!" Asa clucked. "Does better trappin' alone, but he's always one to tie up with a man."

"For all your Bible-totin', parson-preachin' ways, we made the pair in our day, McAfferty." Scratch created a silent moment before Asa spoke.

"Aye. Them days of preacher an' sinner be gone now, Titus."

"You're trappin' this season, or stayin' hitched to the Nepercy?" Scratch lighted his bowl.

"Fixin' to do me trappin'. Been almost two seasons since I laid trap under water. Nawww! Ain't gonna stay with the Nez Perce—just wintered up with the people. They're a fine lot, too, them is. Wintered with them people an' found me a lady to me likin'."

"Ye married up, then, huh?" Scratch asked.

"Aye! That I am! A fine lady an' a beauty for the boot, she be. Princess of them people, as her pappy be one of the war chiefs."

"Cain't see you bein' one that's hitched up, Asa."

"Lotsa things is changed now, Scratch. But there's fire in this boiler yet, me friend, an' a man gets lonesome for the sweet music of a woman's voice after long seasons of hearin' nothin' but other coons round an evenin' fire." McAfferty combed at his beard with his fingers once more.

"Your squar, she make good skins?" Scratch asked, puffing on his pipe.

"Does the grizz shit up to the woods?" Asa snorted. "Good that woman be with the awl an' sinew." He spread his arms wide to expose more of the shirt he wore. Scratch nodded approvingly and turned to Josiah.

"We might be workin' on McAfferty to see what he wants as to have his squar sew you up some skins, young'un."

"The boy be needin' some mountain clothes, does he? What ye wantin' in the way of skins?" Asa asked of Paddock, who looked over at Scratch with a questioning look on his face without speaking.

"Awww," Bass stroked his nose lightly for a minute, thinking. "Needin' one warm shirt, he is, but with none the frills on it . . . maybe two, no three set of leggin's. Then, least half-dozen pair mokersons, none the frills or fancy on 'em, neither. Jest good workin' clothes."

"Ye was sayin' ye had ye a good y'ar, eh?" Asa cocked his head a little to the side.

"That I did," Scratch replied, "but you're not for the takin' on this ol' coon, McAfferty. You do that screwin' on this child, well, there's others as'll do the work for Josiah should your price be a skinnin'."

"All right! All right! Lord Jesus, the man's in a fume! I'll see that young Josiah gets what he needs in mountain clothes as a shot for the ol' days that were—an' asks of ye only what ye be feelin' your own conscience says is fair to pay." He looked from Bass to Paddock, then back to

174

Scratch; they nodded their heads in agreement to the contract terms.

"Ye come round by the noon hour," Asa said, pulling the blanket up about his shoulders, "an' the wife will size the lad up." McAfferty rose and straightened the marten hat down on his head.

"That sets with me, Asa. We'll be there."

The white head left through the cottonwoods and Scratch threw the robe back off his legs to stand. "That hook's some, ain't it?"

"Didn' say who shot him, did he?" Josiah got to his feet.

"Well, now. I'm thinkin' he didn', did he? Coon didn' say who it were who caused him to lose the hand."

"Why the hell didn't you ask him?" Josiah returned, thinking it a reasonable question to ask.

He let a loud sigh escape from his lips as he looked through the trees in the direction McAfferty had taken. "Son, you'll l'arn soon 'nough, but you don' go pryin' into a man. No sir. You don' go pryin' into what a man won' tell you on his own. Don' pry without no need..." His voice trailed off slowly, then he finally turned to look once more at Paddock. "Well, some. We got you skins, son. Skins as'll do the whack till we winter up to the Absor'kees."

Bass had been showing the younger man the grading of plews for over two hours, separating, as a few of the other free trappers were also, the various grades of their beaver pelts. The bundles were broken open and skins were strewn on the ground all about the canopy in the midmorning light, when loud voices were heard coming from near the other trappers' lean-tos. Hatcher came running back with the news.

"Train's in! Trader's come, Scratch!" he repeated several times as he came jogging up to the pair. "Clouds from the prerra to the south tell it! Trader's come to ronnyvoo!" He turned to scamper away.

Scratch hurriedly pushed the stacks of pelts together, "C'mon, son! You'll not want to miss this'un. C'mon now, an' don' you be dallyin'." He smacked his lips, "I can taste the likker now." He picked up his rifle and starting off, then stopped to turn around. "Dammit, Josiah! Be quick 'bout it!"

Paddock stood for only a moment more, trying to sense what was expected of him, then picked his long rifle up and started to run off with Bass. As they broke out of the edge of the cottonwoods to stand with the knot of trappers, Scratch could see to the south a cloud of dust billowing up from the valley floor as an unmistakable sign that it was true.

"Gotta be them, son! Nothin' that size movin' in here from the south 'cept a train!" He lifted his face to the sky. "Ho! Dear Lordee! Make it Billy Sublette an' his likker! Do you hear now? Bless your name an' them kegs as Billy's bringin' to ronnyvoo!"

Josiah had not long kept his eyes on the cloud of dust to the south, for noise and motion were coming from the north, beyond where the men stood. Riders came roaring from their right, headed south down the hole. They blew past in small groups and individually: men standing in their stirrups, one hand on the reins and the other holding aloft their rifles, singing out at the top of their lungs as they flew by at full gallop. Ponies' nostrils flared and snorted, their tails held straight back in the run, as if sensing the importance of the moment as they carried their dust-laden passengers across the sage. Still more men came boiling across the prairie from the north, kicking wildly at their ponies' flanks, spurring them into frantic speed.

Wide-eyed, Josiah watched the trappers burn past, back and forth. Up and down the valley he looked, seeing the racing parade disappearing. He them moved his attention once more up the hole to where more and more riders came pouring in haste, noise, and excitement.

Scratch and several others stood their ground, drunk already in anticipation, a few of the men dancing around in a wild jig with abandon. As if possessed, Isaac Simms moved round and round, chanting his high-pitched scalp song while beating on his stomach as if it were a drum. Josiah could not help but sense the electricity in the air, as goosebumps ran down his arms and a series of cold waves shot up his spine.

Suddenly a roar of rifle blasts was heard to the south, answered by more and more weapons firing. Wild shouting and cursing were heard over the sound of a thousand hoofs; the merry jingling of harness made ready for a grand entrance to rendezvous, mules brayed in protest of the rifle fire, and horses whinnied and snorted in protest of it all. More rifles cracked the air, then others answered in kind.

The pack train became clear beneath the umbrella of dust stirred up as it began to crawl past. Old friends greeted one another and cussed together once more. Tired, saddle-weary greenhorns, suddenly refreshed, joined in the excitement and yelled with the best. Others were engaged with reloading their rifles to fire another martial salute.

"Scratch!" Hatcher ran over to grab the side of Bass's shoulder. "Thar's Bridger! It's Bridger!"

Josiah looked where Mad Jack was pointing to see the man approaching slowly with two others from the north, headed to meet the train. A man in the lead of the pack train pulled to the side near the free trappers and stopped his horse, motioning the mule herders with a wave of his arm to keep going on past him. There he sat to await the approach of the three horsemen from the north.

"Billy Sublette! By damned, I'm gettin' dry now!" Scratch hollered as he grabbed Paddock by the shoulders to dance around and around the younger man.

The three riders pulled up and came to a stop with Sublette, each exchanging a greeting, a handshake, and hearty slaps on the back.

"Gabe! You son of a bitch!" Sublette called out. "Merry Joe! How you goin', Meek? You shoulda been lizard bait long time afore this. L'arn a new tongue yet, Frapp? Good to look at your furry mugs!"

The train continued on past, with others crying out a greeting to Meek, Bridger, and Frapp. Then Sublette looked around to the north and spoke once more, "Where's Broken Hand?"

The smiles faded from the others' faces and Meek hung his head from Sublette's questioning eyes. The trader asked of the men again, "Where's Fitz?"

Bridger finally spoke up. "Sent him out after ye, tell ye to hurry the train."

"Yep, he found me, give me the word, then turned a tail to make it back," Sublette replied, a mystified tone in his voice.

"Ain't showed yet, Billy." There was an ominous note in Bridger's words. "Gone under, I reckon."

"What in the devil happened?" Sublette demanded of

177

anyone who could answer his question. "He left us back there to the Sweetwater to get back here with the news we was comin' in. Left with two fine animals for the race . . . Naw! Fitzpatrick ain't one to go under yet! He ain't!"

"Tom is one what can take care of hisself, he can," Bridger broke in. "Less'n somethin' strange happen't. I'm thinkin', here with Joe an' Frapp, that Vand'burgh's men most likely set some red niggers to Fitz!"

"We don' know that yet, Gabe," Sublette's voice rang out in protest. "Cain't be sure of it. But—if it were to happen that way, American Fur seen their day in the mountains! Gabe, send some scouts out to look. I jest won' feel right till I know what come of him." There was a bittersweet tone in his voice now, full of hate for the competition, yet dressed over with the love of another man of the mountains. "Fitz wintered up with the Nez Percy afore spring trappin'. C'mon. Let's get us to ronny-voo!"

Sublette broke away, followed closely by the others as they galloped past the plodding pack mules. Before his eyes, Josiah watched some eighty-six men move by: William Sublette's forces, Yankee Nathaniel Wyeth's twenty-three green recruits and some remnants of the Gantt-Blackwell venture under a man named Stevens, all pushing along nearly three hundred head of mules laden with plunder for the trade in pelts.

Some of the free trappers were throwing blankets on their ponies' backs and pulling away to follow the caravan north. Hatcher yelled over to Solomon Fish, "Pay me now or pay me later, but make it soon, Solomon. Ya lost our bet on what train'd be first in to ronnyvoo. It don' make me no mind, Solomon. Yer money'll go jest as fast as mine!" Hatcher rode away up the valley.

"Be 'while afore they get the likker out. I'm thinkin' this be the time to get up to McAfferty's diggin's to set that squar of his'n to makin' skins for you," Scratch said, motioning Josiah to follow him to the animals they had picketed. "Likker be ready by time we wrapped up down there. Them kegs come off the mules, men be thicker'n wolves round a downed buffler calf!"

Inside Asa's lodge, Josiah's eyes slowly grew accustomed to the dim light until he could see clearly once more. The white-headed man showed the visitors where to sit, then lighted a pipe and passed it to Scratch.

As Josiah inhaled with his turn at the stem, a woman crouched through the hole in the lodgecover and stood for a moment framed by the light from outside. He could not see her features clearly from across the lodge, only that she must be young by her shape. Man cain't tell 'bout a woman's body in them dresses, he thought as he pulled on the smoke and handed the pipe back to Scratch.

The woman went to the other side of the lodge away from the men after Asa spoke to her, where she bent over something on the floor and gathered some articles in her arms before rising to approach Paddock. Scratch looked over to Josiah to see the younger man staring transfixed at the pretty squaw. He clucked and turned toward Asa to comment for both himself and Paddock, "Your taste in the womens got better, McAfferty. She's some punkins, ol' man!"

While she pulled Josiah's boot off, the woman never let her eyes rise to meet Paddock's. His eyes never left the squaw, poring over her as she knelt in front of him on the floor. She spoke to Asa in a clipped tongue.

"Want's ye to stand up, young Josiah," McAfferty explained. "Put your foot on that piece of rawhide there."

Paddock stood and placed his left foot down on the piece of stiff rawhide that the woman slid beneath him. She turned and drew a burnt stick from the fire at the center of the lodge and used it to trace carefully around Paddock's foot on the rawhide. Her thin fingers then ran over and around his foot as Josiah stared down at her. The woman had learned from Asa that white men had bigger insteps than her own people, the shorter Indian instep coming from a life spent barefoot in moccasins. From her exploring fingers, the squaw came to know just how to cut the soft leather for the uppers on the new footwear in brief seconds of feeling the foot as the young man stood on the thick leather. She tried to push his foot back off the rawhide. The woman pushed a second time, then spoke to Asa without raising her head.

"Says she wants ye to move your foot now," McAfferty interpreted. "Ye get off the rawhide."

Embarrassed, Paddock slid his foot back as the woman freed the leather. His face burned as he turned away to

179

look out the door until he felt that heat of the self-conscious blush drain away from him. The three men watched the Nez Perce squaw retrace the charcoal line with a small, sharp knife as she cut out the first rawhide sole. Turning it over, the woman laid it down on the rawhide and traced two more soles.

She and Asa shared a few chopped words in her people's tongue before she rose again to find a parfleche that contained her sewing kit, then produced a roll of soft-tanned white skins.

"Wants to know if that's what he want for the tops," McAfferty remarked as the woman held one of the soft skins up to Josiah.

He took the skin from her and touched its chamoislike softness before putting it to his face to feel its sensual caress. "Yep. That'll do fine." He gave the skin back to the squaw.

"Sorry, boy, but you don' want them skins." Scratch said. He then turned to McAfferty, "Ask your squar if'n she's got lodgeskin. We be wantin' mocs from the top, the smoked skin—ask her to make the mocs from last y'ars lodgeskin."

Asa and the squaw talked briefly before she rose and went to the other side of the lodge to rummage through more of her plunder. She produced a large roll of browned leather lodgeskin and gave it to Bass this time to inspect. He pulled the hide apart and stuck his face to it, pulling in a deep breath, then another. "Yup. Them'll do the whack, Asa." Scratch gave the skin back to the woman and nodded up and down for her information.

"Such lodgeskin, smoked as it be, won' shrink up on your feet, Josiah, won' pinch or draw up when you soak 'em in a stream." Scratch reclined back on a robe.

With her knowledge of Josiah's foot, the squaw put the knife to work once more and soon had a pair of uppers for the rawhide soles. Then she cut a thong from the lodgeskin that would be long enough to serve to tie the moccasin around the foot, and a short tongue to shield the ankle. From her sewing parfleche was brought out a bundle of tough sinew from which she pulled thin fibers for thread, and set to work attaching the thick soles to the soft-tanned, smoked uppers. With an awl she punched small holes around the sole and uppers and began to sew the footwear together.

His eyes never left the squaw, trying to catch a glimpse of her eyes and face. In less than half an hour, Josiah held his first pair of moccasins in hand. But the woman was not done with him.

She now used a long piece of light blue trade ribbon to measure the outside seam of his pants, then encircled her fingers around his thighs to measure their circumference. Finally, she inspected his chest and shoulders with her wandering fingertips, had him put one of his arms out to his side level with the shoulder to measure its length, and she was done. The woman had never looked into his face through the whole fitting. Only now did she look up for an instant at Josiah. But there was no smile, just a meeting of their eyes before she went over to Asa, spoke for a moment to him, then retreated to another part of the lodge.

"She says three, maybe four days she'll have 'em ready for ye," McAfferty rose to his feet. Scratch stood up and smoothed his pants with the palms of his hands.

"We be back for 'em come that time. Be seein' you then, less'n we see you cozy in the trader's tent, snugglin' up to a cup, McAfferty," Scratch said and headed for the door.

"Ain't much chance of me bein' in the trader's tent, least not Rocky Mountain Fur Company's tent." Asa looked over at Josiah near the door.

"Thank you, McAfferty... an' thank your wife for me, too, uh," Josiah stammered for a minute, then made his way to the door.

"Young Josiah."

"Uh... what?"

"You're welcome, but Scratch'll be payin' for them skins. So, he's the one as ye should be thankin'."

"Yep... s'pose you're right," Paddock said, then ducked and stepped from the lodge.

They rode back to their camp in silence. Scratch finally spoke as they tied the horses up near their canopy.

"McAfferty's got a handsome squar there."

"She's... she's nice-lookin' woman," Josiah said, feeling the heat from embarrassment returning once more. He turned quickly to face Bass. "What you 'spect of me, ol' man? Jest stand there an' let that purty, young thing run her hands all over my body an' legs without it both'rin' me one nit? Is that what you wanted?" The edge to his voice was razor-sharp.

"Not faultin' you a bit, son."

"Jest sounds like you're tryin' to make fun of me."

"Wanted to make some fun of you, I woulda done her back there—we'd all had us a good laugh. Naw, boy! That ain't my stick with you. Ain't gonna poke you out in front of others." Scratch moved under the canopy and sat down. "She was a looker—not a man as could be denyin' that. She had her some fine breasts held under that dress . . ."

"Ain't a gonna touch her!" Josiah exploded as he approached the canopy.

"Didn' have no idear you was, frien'."

"Much as I might like to think 'bout it, ain't gonna have nothin' to do with that squaw," he said, and he sat down beside Bass.

"Smart there, you are. Messin' with 'nother man's squar's nothin' but a lotta trouble. There be some of them red niggers as'll want you beddin' down with theys squars, for the right price, somethin' that makes the screwin' seem all right. But, white man feel some squampshus 'bout them women's doin's. White man out here ain't ready to let you do that."

"Why you keep talkin' 'bout it?" He started to rise, but Scratch caught Josiah and held him down.

"Simmer yourself down some, frien'. We gonna forget it now, all right? We jest gonna forget it. You're both my frien's, you an' McAfferty are, an' Ol' Scratch wants no truck 'tween you two." He finally let go of Paddock's arm, and said, "Pull your boots off an' try them mokersons on now, son."

Josiah pulled the leather boots off and Scratch helped him put the new footwear on.

"Be sure that you pull the toe of the things up to your toes afore you pull the rest of the mokerson up over your heel. Like this . . . stuff your toes in all the way to the front . . . that's good, now you can pull it over your heel. See? That'll keep them things from stretchin' out from all the yankin' you'd do the otherwise gettin' 'em on. Keeps 'em havin' a good, tight fit to your hoofs." Scratch picked up the other moccasin and inspected it. "Put that leather whang round the hoof, wrappin' both ends criss an' cross,

182

back an' forth . . . that's right. Now put this 'un on jest like that." He handed him the second moccasin.

Josiah had them both wrapped on and stood up, looking down with a proud feeling at his feet, "Look good, don' they?"

"That they do, Josiah. Now, let's show you how to walk in them things, as they ain't got a heel to 'em like them boots of your'n. Here, watch me." He took a few steps away from Paddock with his prairie-hen walk exaggerated for the lesson. "You cain't come straight from your heel to the toes, as you does with boots on. See— you gotta come from the heel by rollin' on the outside of your hoof up to the toes, then come off them toes for your next step. Try it . . . yup, jest a lil' more on the outside of your hoof . . . that's good, that's good! Yep! Think you'll do fine! That's the way an Injun walks in mokersons."

The younger man came back to the canopy slowly, getting accustomed to the new sensation of having the earth beneath his feet, almost as if barefoot. Without the leather boots, Josiah felt as if he were caressing the earth as he walked, rather than stomping across it. They felt good. Josiah was pleased and picked up the boots.

"What you doin' with them?" Bass asked.

"Fixin' to throw 'em away to the crik."

"No such a thing! You keep 'em few days anyway— some Injun might jest think them are jest the thing he wants in trade. Come in handy, they will, for us." He bent over and went back to sorting pelts quickly.

When he and Josiah had finished rebundling the plews, Scratch stretched his tired back, "You go fetch Hannah now an' bring that animule here. We take these plews to Sublette's tent an' do us some tradin' for possibles now, so's Scratch can get rid hisse'f a dry soon as he can."

Up the valley, William Sublette had set up his tent and several canopies for shade in the heart of the Rocky Mountain Fur Company's camp, the firm he had contracted to supply. As Bass and Paddock approached, the scene was one of subdued celebration as the atmosphere was much restrained and hushed rather than frantic and loud. Sublette sat at the edge of one of the canopies along with Jim Bridger and Henry Fraeb, heads bent forward in quiet conversation.

Each crude counter that had been thrown up was

surrounded by trappers, selling their furs to company clerks, dickering with those clerks over the grade and price of each pelt. Yet, the beaver was going over to Sublette's side of the counter much faster than it had been pulled from the bone-aching cold of icy mountain streams. He had won the race. And the prize was the free trappers' trade. Hour after hour, day after day, the bartering would continue until Sublette would have over one hundred sixty-eight heavy bales of beaver fur to load up for the return trip overland to St. Louis.

The trading was slow this first day, as many a man gave a measure of respect to the memory of the missing Fitzpatrick, believed to have been killed. Few were they who had the years and experience of Broken Hand, and fewer still were they who had this deepest level of respect shown them by fellow mountain men. Fitzpatrick's fate hung like a gray cloud over the trader's canopies as Scratch led Hannah to a willow thicket and tied her off beside other mules and ponies.

"Get them packs down, Josiah, an' we'll be gettin' over to the tent." He pointed to Paddock where he wanted the bundles to be carried. Each man slung a pack onto a shoulder and approached one of the canopies crowded with trappers and Indians. They set their loads down.

"You wait here, young'un. I'll be gettin' the last'un."

In front of one of the tents Sublette's clerks had thrown up was the largest knot of activity. Josiah watched four clerks handling the trade for alcohol poured from the curved tin kegs, designed and hammered out especially for the mountain trade, to be carried the long miles of the journey west strapped to troublesome mules. They were constructed of a curved design to fit easily onto the animals' backs, and hammered of tin for as little weight as possible. From them, the clerks poured pint-sized drinks along with camp-kettle portions of the alcohol.

Sublette would do his briskest trade with his trader's whiskey. With the markup nearly two thousand percent over St. Louis price on raw grain alcohol, it was still what the trappers desired most of all at rendezvous. As the men of the high mountains became drunker, they would trade more quickly to quench a growing thirst; while the hours wore on, the alcohol would be watered down all the more to stretch its supply. It was commonly known that the trader diluted his supply constantly, but this never seemed to affect the whiskey trade. As a trapper's senses dulled from indulgence, he would soon be unable to tell just what strength of alcohol he was being sold.

That same morning far to the south in the hole, Sublette had stopped the pack train to dilute the alcohol with water from the Pierre. It was then that the extra tin kegs that had been carried west empty were put into service. The grain alcohol was watered down to suit the trader, then a twist or two of tobacco had been thrown into each keg to give the drink a light brown, whiskey color. To smooth the ragged edges of the raw grain, some black molasses had been added. The final touch was then dropped into the containers—a few handfuls of red peppers to put some mouth-stinging bite back into the diluted drink.

The trader then gave the order to resume the march into rendezvous, confident that the rocking motion of the mules bearing the tin kegs would mix the concoction to satisfaction before reaching the trading site The mountain trader had his whiskey ready. The trappers were waiting with their year-long thirsts.

There was noise coming from the south, shouting and some bustling activity headed toward the canopies. Sublette, Bridger, and Fraeb rose and stepped into the light to see what was causing the commotion. In a matter of seconds, every man's attention was on three men riding up on two horses. The two men in the saddles were Iroquois hunters, attached to Bridger's brigade. Behind one of the dark-skinned men clung a white man, holding on for his life as best he could to the cantle of Antoine Godin's saddle. The riders approached slowly and Bridger stepped forward a few feet.

"I'll be goddamned an' sent to hell right h'yar! If that do look like Fitzpatrick!" Bridger announced to Sublette.

Behind Godin rode a man almost unrecognizable. He sat hunched over against the Iroquois in fatigue and starvation, thin as an eastern fence rail, his eyes sunken, red and dull, mere sockets in their skull. The frail body was a mass of cuts and bruises that were easily seen through the remains of the man's tattered clothing. Here and there through the gaping rips and tears of his garments were patches of glowing red that told of a horrible sunburn. He seemed almost out of his mind, bouncing along behind the Indian, staring wildly out at the silent men who parted as Godin moved his pony slowly through the crowd. Empty-handed, weaponless, the scarecrow clutched tightly to the Iroquois' saddle.

"That cain't be Broken Hand! Nawww! He's got white ha'r, that man does!" Sublette stepped forward with Fraeb to stand beside Bridger as Godin brought his pony up to the trio and stopped.

"Looks like Got give him a goot scare, Sublette," the German-born Fraeb commented about the new arrival.

"It is Fitz! My god! Man's had the shit skeert outta him!" Bridger went forward to help Godin ease Fitzpatrick to the ground, "Been through somethin' as turn't his ha'r white, he has!"

"Godin say he find Fitz. Godin find Fitz for Bridger," the Iroquois said as he looked down on the man he had just brought in.

As the haggard, gaunt scarecrow was taken to the shade of Sublette's tent, the trappers began to trickle slowly back to the trader's canopies where they resumed their hearty dickering with the trader's clerks.

"What's doin'?" Scratch came up behind Josiah, putting a hand on the young man's arm.

Josiah twitched at the sudden surprise of the touch and jerked around to look into Scratch's face. "That Fitzpatrick feller jest been brought in, lookin' like he'd been meat for the buzzards in 'nother day."

Scratch craned his neck to look over the crowd of men about him, standing on his toes in straining to catch a glimpse of the man brought in to rendezvous. "It were Broken Hand, eh? That might jest be a tall one, son. Fitz don' have white ha'r!"

"One of them fellers with Sublette said God musta give him a good scare, to turn his ha'r white." He paused, "You cain't trust my word on this'un, eh, ol' man? I took for the true what you said 'bout how McAfferty got his white ha'r, didn' I? Didn' give you no trouble on that, did I?" Scratch turned back around to face him as Josiah continued. "The man jest come in got the same scare as ol' McAfferty, that's all. Maybe both of 'em seen your ghosts an' hoodoos out there!"

"Now you're laughin' at me 'gain, young'un. Thinkin' you knows the ways of them mountains awready. Man as comes in with white ha'r, comes in from out there." He motioned to the mountains with a nod of his head.

"Others don' laugh at that man, they don't. He's been through medeecin, Josiah—an' a smart man'll keep his laughin' to hisse'f 'bout ghosts an' hoodoos. 'Specially the Great Spirit. You don' want to let anyone hear you laughin' 'bout them doin's, 'specially the Great Spirit."

Scratch pulled two bundles along on the ground toward one of the counters that had the shortest line of waiting trappers. Josiah brought up the third bundle and stood beside Bass as they waited on two other trappers busy with the clerk beneath the canopy. Within a short time, there was only one trapper ahead of them, a trapper who had brought only a few pelts to exchange for a kettle of the trader's whiskey.

The older man leaned around to Josiah and spoke out of the corner of his mouth, "I'd like to be one as could do such a thing. But, Lordee! The likker gets in my blood an' there ain't no stoppin' till the beaver runs out. We best get our credit done up now with this clerk feller, so's we can get you possibles afore this child starts to drinkin'."

The trapper in front of them moved away, heading for the canopy next door where the trader's whiskey was being poured freely for those with credit. Scratch pulled the bundles up to the wooden-plank counter, lifted each one up and set it down heavily beside the clerk's ledger book. As the bookkeeper cut open the bundles, Scratch eyed him over carefully, measuring the man he would be arguing with over the grade and price his plews would bring. This one would have to be new to the mountains, still clean-shaven, with only a hint of a new tan on his face. He wore the linsey-woolsey of a store clerk back east, but did not wear a hat beneath the shade of the canopy. He asked for a name.

"Titus Bass, it be, son."

In a cramped hand, the clerk scrawled the name on one of the blank ledger sheets near the top of the page, where he also wrote the date of this first transaction.

"Skin trapper, Bass?"

"Yup. That's right." Scratch kept his eyes on the man while the bookkeeper began to pull plews off one at a time, running his fingers through the pelt after he had unfolded it to full size, turning each one over to inspect it closely. Bass figured the man to be nothing more than a greenhorn, on his first journey west, hired by Sublette for the round trip. But he also knew that Sublette would be one to tutor his clerks all the way out, teaching them the grades of beaver pelts, teaching them how to wring every last cent out of each transaction with the thirsty trappers. Scratch had a feeling this one just might be testy, as so many clerks before him had been.

"You pulled these pelts out better'n most I've seen today, Mister," the clerk said without looking up at Bass.

"If you're meanin' the way I stretches them plews, you're prob'ly right, son." Scratch had been ready to be testy right back, but the compliment threw him off a bit. Then he thought to himself that this tactic just might be another of Sublette's tricks he taught his clerks, to draw the trapper off his guard, to win him over right from the start with a glowing compliment. Bass kept his eyes on the top of the bookkeeper's head as it bent over the piles of beaver he was separating.

"Already I done that, son. Already I graded 'em myself."

"Does look like you have, Mister." He finally looked up at Scratch, then over briefly to Josiah before looking back down to continue his work. "Just wanna see for myself, that's all. You wouldn't want me not doin' my job, would you, Mister? After all, I work for Mr. Sublette, not you trappers. If you find some fault with me an' my ways, I can call Mr. Sublette over here an' let you talk with him."

Bass chewed on that quickly, knowing that he did not want any argument with William Sublette, knowing that the trader would invariably win such a dispute or just tell Bass to take his plews to someone else. But there wasn't another trader in Pierre's Hole. It had to be Sublette or his clerk, and Scratch decided on taking his chances with the clerk as Sublette was a wily fox of a businessman.

"Well?" the clerk looked up again at Scratch.

"You jest keep yourself workin' on my plews, son. We'll see what you got for the bottom line when you're done with 'em."

The clerk and trapper argued only a few times, over the quality of some of Bass's less-than-prime plews, Scratch himself winning a few of the dollars, but the clerk ending up victorious in the long run on more disputed pelts. Sublette's man stood behind each final stack of beaver, counting them when another clerk yelled out to him from the whiskey counter.

"Henry! What's this man's credit?" the whiskey clerk

asked, nodding to the trapper who had stood right in front of Scratch and Josiah and who was now standing at the whiskey kegs with a camp kettle to fill.

Henry examined the trapper, then recognized him without a name and leafed back through the ledger book to find the trapper's page.

"He's good for now. Sold me 'nough for two kettles' worth."

The whiskey clerk took the iron camp kettle from the trapper and poured in diluted alcohol as Henry went back to his counting. At the completion of the count for each stack, the clerk entered a number and grade on Scratch's page. He then took portions of the stacks back to the rear of the canopy where a crude scale was standing. There he began to weigh the various grades and added more numbers to the page. Back and forth he moved under the canopy, carrying the pelts to the scales to weigh them carefully, then coming back to the counter where he would enter a new number to the ledger.

"You been a store clerk, Josiah," Scratch whispered in the young man's ear. "Take you a look at that page an' tell me what it say."

Josiah looked up and down the counter, then whispered back, "You mean you don' know how to read?"

"I l'arnt once a time, boy. But I forgot now. Was a bus'nessman myself, on a time back, real properlike. But I always had the others as could do the readin' an' writin' for me." Scratch pointed out the book. "Tell me what it say, boy!"

Paddock leaned forward over the counter, cocking his head around to read the upside-down page in a whisper to Bass. "You want me to read the numbers across or down?"

"Dammit, boy! You're the clerk! You're the one as can read—so read it!"

The young man began to recite, reading across the page, not really knowing what the clerk's cryptic numbers meant. Scratch stood watching the Sublette clerk while Josiah recited slowly in a whisper to him, head low over the ledger. The bookkeeper turned and saw him.

"Get away from there!" he came up to the counter as Josiah straightened up and attempted to look as innocent as he could, having been caught in the act. "You ain't supposed to be lookin' at that!"

"I...I..." Josiah stammered.

"Ain't this man's fault," Scratch protested to the clerk. "I was the one as set him to the readin'."

"An' you should be one to know better," the bookkeeper said, eyeing Scratch now.

"Jest wantin' to know how bad the screwin's to be with my plews, son. That's all. Jest wantin' to know..." He stopped talking when the clerk slammed the leatherbound ledger book closed and went back to his scales.

"You made him mad at me, ol' man!" Josiah was back to a hoarse whisper.

"You're not the one sellin' your y'ar's plews, is you? You ain't got nothin' to be frettin' 'bout, do you? Ain't no trouble you can get yourself in. I'm the one as pulled that beaver out up there. An' I'm the one as is seein' it slip quick through my fingers now. I've got me a right to know what that lad's takin' me for." Titus began to kick lightly at the wooden supports that held the counter up, tapping it with his foot. "The one as got that beaver out to begin with got a right to know what screwin' he's to take from the trader. He has that right, don' he? He does! Man works his ass off in the upcountry all y'ar, tryin' to get the beaver out, tryin' to keep from goin' under, that man's got a right, don' he? Well, don' he?"

"I ain't the one as you're arguin' with. I ain't the one as told you that you couldn' be lookin' at the book," Josiah protested to Scratch. He felt caught in the middle: jumped on by the clerk, and now feeling the frustration and anger of the older man beside him, a man he had recently thrown in with, a man who gambled his life on what the mountains could give to him, and a man who once again had to settle for dealing with a clerk from back east. This touch of the older man's past came each summer to ridicule the strong sense of his own freedom. The clerk approached the counter and opened the book to Bass's page.

Scratch looked down at the top of the man's head once more as the clerk dipped the quill pen into an ink bottle repeatedly to bring the figures scratching down on the page. The bookkeeper looked up, "That be all you're going to sell this year?"

"Yup," Scratch said sullenly, nodding his head up

and down a bit as the clerk drew lines under some numbers and wrote out the totals at the bottom of each column.

"What's it come to?" Josiah asked, surprising both the clerk and Bass, who looked over at him. The bookkeeper glanced up, eyed him briefly, then went back to his page.

"The man's got one hundred eighty-three pelts. Of them, he's got near two hundred eighty pounds. That makes forty-six pelts at fifty-eight pounds of poor quality..."

"Forty-six plews are poor!" Scratch bellowed. Josiah put a hand on the older man's arm as he leaned forward in an attempt to read what was written on the page.

"Forty-six at poor quality. Then you have seventy-two that are good, at one hundred nine pounds. Your prime comes to sixty-five pelts, weighing one hundred thirteen pounds." He wrote something more near the bottom of the page. "Your total will be $840.00, Mister. That'll be to your credit over to the drygoods counters." Josiah whistled lowly at the total dollar amount.

"Only $840 . . . $840! You're stealin' me! You're stealin' me!" Scratch fired at the clerk.

"Hey, hey! Jest simmer down. Scratch, jest simmer down, simmer yourself down some." Josiah pulled at the older man's arm, seeing its fingers gripped white-knuckled on the edge of the counter. "The $840 is fine," Paddock said to the clerk. "It's fine, ain't it, Scratch?"

Bass leaned over the counter unrestrained by Josiah, who tried to hold onto him, "Jest give me my paper, boy!" Others gathered around the canopy were staring, closed-mouthed, at the scene between the trapper and the trader's clerk. "Jest give me my paper what says that $840 on it an' I'll be goin'."

The bookkeeper took a small sheaf of paper from a pocket in his vest and wrote down a number on it with the quill pen.

"That say $840?" Scratch stuffed it toward Josiah without taking his eyes off the Sublette clerk.

"It says '$840.00, credit to Titus Bass,'" Josiah responded.

"Then we be goin' now. We through here, we are." He turned to take a step away, then leaned back in close to the clerk. "You was through with me, weren't you? Through with your screwin' me, son?" He then turned on his heel to storm off. Josiah trotted after him a few yards before he caught up to the older man.

"Don' do you no good, no good 'tall," Scratch was muttering to himself.

"What?"

"Don' do you no good, bustin' your ass in the up-country all y'ar long for that pittle-ass $840."

"Them's good wages back there, Scratch."

"Back where?" he asked, looking at the young man's face as they walked.

"Back to where you an' me come from, $840 would be the damned fine in wages." Josiah eased back as Scratch slowed his pace. "I know a man as once told me it weren't for the beaver he was up here. Told me it weren't the money, neither." Scratch looked over to Paddock again. "Man didn' never tell me what he was upcountry for, but it weren't the money, he said."

"Young Josiah." Scratch stopped and put a hand on Paddock's shoulder, gripping it near the neck. "You're growin' ol't on me already, you are." He pulled the younger man to follow him, walking on again. "We're to tradin' now. Let's go to see what they'll be stealin' from us two ol' coons!"

They stepped up to a counter beside two other men in buckskins who were looking over trade goods. A clerk rose from a blanket on the ground to approach the counter.

"Afternoon, gents. What can I be doin' for ya today?" The clerk was older than the bookkeeper who had graded the plews, had a slight paunch from middle-age, and square-rimmed spectacles hung low on the bridge of his nose.

"Let me an' the young'un be seein' what you got in the way of medeecin irons—rifles, I mean to say," Scratch addressed the clerk.

The man on the other side of the counter went to a stack of folded blankets, atop which were several long rolled blankets that he brought over to set down on the wooden shelf. As he unrolled each from its blanket, the clerk took the rifle out and laid it carefully on the counter. Bass peered briefly at each one as it came out of its protective cover, until there were seven lying before him.

"Ain't you got any others?"

"All we got, Mister. Bridger bought him up most of 'em earlier on in the day. Got a fine one for Mr. Fitzpatrick, he did. But them's all we got now as Bridger took his own pick for his men."

"Hmm." Scratch stroked the side of his beard, looking closely at the rifles atop the counter, then addressed the clerk once more, "See that most of 'em be them newfangled precussion ignition, eh?"

"Yep," the clerk replied as Bass picked a rifle up. "It's gettin' to be the thing back east. Ever'body's buyin' such a lock, or havin' they rifle made over to it."

Scratch pulled the hammer back several times, easing it back down over the nipple on the percussion rifle. He studied it for several minutes in silence, then handed it over to Josiah.

"What you think 'bout that?"

"Ya buyin' it for the young man?" asked the clerk.

"That I am." Then he addressed Paddock, "You like that'un?"

"Looks a lot like one I had my eye on in the Hawken shop back to St. Lou. Think I could live with it..." Scratch took it from Paddock's hands.

"You couldn' live with it, young'un," Bass set the rifle back on the counter. "Such a rifle jest might get you kilt." He looked over at other rifles once more.

"What ya mean?" demanded the clerk, as Josiah had stood unspeaking when the rifle was taken from his grip.

"Heered 'bout them precussion things, I did. Gotta buy them little nipple huggers, don' you?" He squinted down at the clerk.

"That's right. We got the caps for that rifle."

Bass turned to Josiah: "What you gonna do when you run outta them lil' nipple huggers, Josiah?"

Paddock didn't answer. He didn't have an answer.

"That's right. You said nothin', an' that's what you'd do if'n you'd run dry on them nipple huggers—nothin'. Gun ain't no good, even if you got powder an' all the G'lena lead you can carry. Still ain't no good." He picked up a flintlock, looked at it for a moment, then flung it over to Josiah. "That's what you're needin'."

"That's an ol't one," the clerk remarked.

"Been used, ye mean?" Bass wanted to know.

"Nope." The clerk leaned forward over the counter to point out the lock. "Ya look there, ya can see to the frizzen it ain't been used." He wiped his finger across the lock. "Still oiled up good."

Scratch put his finger to the lock and then took the

rifle from Josiah. "You coulda oil't her up, man. Why you say it's an ol't one then?"

"I'm told this'un been to ronnyvoo a few times before. No one's bought her, yet. But she's a fine piece of work, ain't she?" The clerk measured his words carefully to make the sale.

Titus played with the hammer and frizzen, looked over the inletting around the lock and tang on the full-stock rifle. "What's the balls number to the pound?"

"Thirty-six to the pound."

"It be .50 caliber then?"

"That'un is." The clerk leaned forward on the counter, supported on his elbows.

"An' that'un?" Scratch pointed to the only other flintlock left among the seven rifles on the counter.

"That be fifty-two to the pound."

"A .45 caliber?"

"Yep."

"Don't want it then." He went back to looking at the heavy rifle in his hands, a rifle weighing over ten pounds. "Looks to be Lancaster," he commented as his eyes momentarily lifted to glance at the clerk who nodded in agreement. The weapon was indeed a version of the Pennsylvania-Kentucky style of craftsmanship, with its full maple stock, a checkered wrist, a big six-inch flint-ignition lock with a single trigger, a forty-two-inch barrel, a plain iron patchbox and a steel Kentucky-style trigger guard.

Scratch hefted it a few times in his own hands, then brought it gently to his shoulder, nuzzled his cheek down on the stock, and squinted along the barrel. Slowly he swung the rifle in an arc away from the trading canopy, causing Josiah to duck out of the way as the barrel passed over his head. Bass took it from his shoulder, looked it over again briefly, then handed it back to Paddock. "You be likin' that, young'un?"

"It's heavy."

"An' well it should be for the upcountry."

"Heavier'n my rifle."

"Wagh! Will you listen to that!" He grinned at the clerk. "Squallin' jest like a badger kit what got its tail burnt with powder! Shee-it!" He shook his head a moment. "An' you ain't no puny nigger neither!" He tapped the top barrel flat with a finger. "This'un look to be the only one a them guns you oughtta be calc'latin' on."

"Why you don' like precussion?" Josiah questioned about the lighter half-stock rifle.

"Like I said, what you gonna do when you run outta them nipple huggers? Huh? Your life ain't gonna be worth a grizzly shit then, son. You run outta spare flints with that rifle, well—most men can find themselves somethin' work 'bout as good. Simple as that, Josiah. This precussion here will sell your life for you. That flinter, well— you'll find it'll be buyin' your life back for you time an' again." He turned the rifle on its side as Paddock held it in his outstretched palms. "What you cipher it say there, boy?" He pointed to the engraved letters near the bottom of the lock plate.

"Henry..." Josiah turtle-necked his head forward a little to look more closely at the name. "J. J. Henry."

"Who that be?" Scratch turned after he spoke to direct the question toward the clerk.

"Builds guns back east..."

"I awready figger't that," Bass snorted. "Ain't no nigger buildin' 'em out here!" He suddenly peered closely at the clerk, leaning part way across the crude counter. "I wanna know 'bout the nigger."

"And I'll tell ya if you give a man half the chance." He paused to let Bass lean back away from his face. "I hear tell it only be guns for the trade out here. Started early on, more'n fifteen year ago, makin' 'em for American Fur, far back as..."

"Jest how Sublette come on such a rifle then—ain't it no good?" He nodded his head in the gun's direction while keeping the measuring eyes on the clerk.

"My first trip out with Sublette—goin' back two year now—he'd made him some deal with Vanderburgh for a few rifles. Fella was needin' somethin' from Sublette in a bad way, so Sublette stuck him for some rifles." He gestured quickly in Josiah's direction. "That be the last of 'em he got from American Fur in the bargain."

"Then it jest be an ol' Injun rifle..."

"Naw. No such. They made for American Fur's men." He watched Titus raise an eyebrow at that. "Builds 'em better'n Injun guns."

Scratch looked down at the lock. "A damned-sight big

hammer on it—like Injun guns." He felt a little testy in his cautiousness.

"That be true," the clerk replied quickly, "but sturdy and built to take whatever ya hand it to be doin'."

"I s'pose," he countered slowly.

"She ain't pretty—nothin' like that."

"Don' care me nothin' 'bout it bein' purty—jest so's it bring him meat an' save his ha'r for a while," Scratch said, nodding his head in the direction of the young man standing beside him.

Scratch mulled and weighed it all in his mind while turning the rifle over and over in Paddock's hands. Finally he brought the hammer back slowly to listen to the crisp engaging click of the lock as it snapped first to half, then on to full cock.

"You made your mind up?" Paddock finally asked, having tired of the weight of the rifle during the long and careful examination by the older trapper.

"You're the one as is doin' the pickin' out. I'm jes gonna lay down money for it. Jest want you to know that if'n you buy that precussion thing, we might both be buyin' us a lot of mis'ry, son. Jest that me, I'd feel a whole consarn better if you'd take this'r flinter." He tapped the Henry rifle once more, then let his hand drop to the counter.

"Then, let's do it." Josiah started to hand the rifle back over to the clerk.

"Naw, you keep it. It's your'n now, lad." Scratch pushed the full-stock rifle back toward Josiah. "An' I'l wager you'll never be sorry for buyin' that rifle from Billy Sublette. He knows him the mountains—been out here some time hisse'f—an' knows him what it takes." Scratch turned to the clerk. "How much you be askin' for it?"

"If ya won't be tellin', I'll sell it to ya for Bridger's price, sell it to ya for $110."

"For $110!" Scratch hollered, the words caught in his throat. "Shit if that be Bridger's price—$110! You're askin' a lot that!"

"Sh-sh-h-h! Sh-sh-h-h! She's every inch worth it," the clerk whispered. "That's bottom."

"Bottom's $110, you say. Things is gettin mighty low for a man as needs a good rifle, has to buy it in the mountains, needin' it for the mountains. Hmmm...consarn, $110 is some. Whooo!" He leaned a little closer to stare directly into the clerk's eyes only inches away. "Boy, you throw you in for us a mold, two jags, couple a screws an' worms apiece, an' you sol't yourself that gun for Bridger's price!" he leaned back and chuckled lightly, never taking his eyes from the clerk's.

Slowly the man's eyes left Scratch's and wandered to the right where other clerks were busy selling goods. Finally he brought his eyes back to bear on the two men across the counter from him. "Ya got yer gun..."

"An' fixin's," it was stated matter-of-factly.

He drew in a breath, "An' yer fixin's."

Bass then craned his neck down the counter, "Where's your powder an' lead?" The clerk moved them down to the kegs of powder and the blocks of lead. Bass looked over the kegs. "What's powder goin'?"

"Two-fifty the pound."

"American?"

"That's right."

"Got you any English?"

"That I do—for four, even, the pound."

Scratch calculated for a moment, "Gonna have to do with fifty pound. Gimme forty pound of the shootin' stuff, an' ten pound of the primin' powder, all of the English then. What's you lead?"

"One-fifty, Galena."

"Hmmm. Gimme hundert-sixty pounds of that." He looked over the supplies at the back of the canopy shelter as the clerk was putting powder and lead on the counter. "What's honeydew goin'?"

"Tobaccy's two dollar the pound."

"Get us twenty pound of that. An' twenty pound of your coffee, too. Two pound of that pepper. What's your flints?" he asked, squinting to focus in the dim, shadowed light of the canopy.

"Fifty cents to the dozen."

"Awright. We take a even gross off your hands." He watched the clerk turn to dip a hand into a five-gallon wooden keg that brimmed with the charcoal-colored stones.

Dropping the brimming handful onto the counter, the clerk quickly began to scoop the flints back into an empty hand, counting up to six before a rough hand clamped itself onto his wrist.

"Naw! None of these'r Englisher flints! Them." He removed his grip from the startled clerk's wrist and pointed to another small keg behind the brimming one. "Them's the ones Titus Bass is gonna take me—for fifty cents to the dozen, I might add—them purty amber ones. I want me them Frenchies."

Obediently the clerk swept up all the gray stones and dumped them unceremoniously back into their keg. He then drew two large handfuls of the French flints and dropped them on the counter.

"You count with 'im, son," Scratch prodded Paddock with an elbow, and watched as the younger man bent his head over the counter to keep tally with the clerk.

"That be better," Bass complimented as the man behind the counter was finally dumping the last of the rich-colored stones into a small burlap sack. "Got you wipin' sticks around? Straight-grained—hick-ry, that is."

"I do."

"Lemme pick me out half dozen or so. They be?"

"Dollar a stick."

"If'n the grain be straight an' they be cured proper, I take 'em." He watched the clerk rotate on his heel to retrieve a large bundle of the round wiping sticks. "Fire steels?"

"By the dozen."

"Gimme one. Dozen o' them awls there, too. Yeah, one of your square axes, too. What you takin' for them butcher knives?"

"Seventy-five cents apiece."

"Four of 'em. An' the lookin' glasses?"

"They be fifty cents."

"Ten o' them'll do. How much is the askin' on them iron kittles?"

"Have me differ'nt sizes. They come two-twenty-five a pound."

"Take me a small one—what's it?"

"Eight pound. Be..." the clerk bent over a piece of paper, "be eighteen dollar." He raised his head, "Yep, eighteen dollar. Ya be needin' blankets?"

"What'r they goin'?"

"Three point for fifteen dollar. Comes to five dollar a point."

"Five dollar a point? Man cain't even keep hisse'f warm for cheap anymores. We can do without. Lemme take a look at your gee-gaws, at them shinies over there."

The clerk brought forward small wooden trays holding beads, bracelets, finger rings, necklaces, trade ribbon, vermilion paint, brass tacks, and more.

"What's the paint goin'?"

"She's six dollars to the pound. Chinee."

"Jehoshaphat! Burn me better'n that powder. Gimme a pound of this paint, then. These beads be to my likin'. Mix me 'bout four pound of them, good, shiny colors I want, too. Then gimme some of them brass nails. What'r they?"

"Fifty cents to the dozen."

"'Bout ten dozen'll do. Got any flour now?"

"That I do." He motioned with a thumb over his shoulder. "Two dollar a pound."

"It been dry all the way?"

"Aye. It has."

"Four pound of flour, then." Titus looked over the stacks of trade goods, inspecting them from afar. "Now, for my tooth that likes some sweet, what's your sugar?"

"That be two dollar for the pint."

"Got a buyer there. Gimme five, five pints. What's them, there?" pointing out some unmarked boxes.

"Raisins. They one-fifty for a pound. Ya want some?" The clerk leaned over to pick up one of the tin containers and brought it to the counter.

"Ain't never had me no raisin afore." Scratch peeked into the container as it was opened. The clerk stuck his hand in and pulled a good-sized palm out filled with the fruit.

"Try 'em. Might be the thing for your sweetsome tooth."

Scratch chewed, and thought, then chewed some more until he finished all that the clerk had given him. "Them I like. One-fifty to the pound, you say?" The clerk nodded in the affirmative. "I'll take me . . . ten pound of 'em."

"Ten pounds!" Josiah blurted. He had been silent for so long during the trading, but now his words surprised even him.

"Ten pound, Mister Clerk," Scratch repeated, a flat sound in his voice to let Paddock know to shut up. He played with the end of a small bolt of bright red calico, then toyed with some hawkbells in the wooden trays while Paddock and the clerk waited. Finally, Titus drew his hands away from the trinkets. "What that come to, my charge?"

The clerk bent over a piece of paper again, scratching at it furiously with a quill he dipped repeatedly into a small inkwell. "Your coffee comes to forty dollar. Pepper is twelve dollar. Beads be twenty dollar, an' the fire steels is two dollar. Them awls will be two dollar, too, an' the ax is two-fifty." He went back to figuring some more, adding up and down the column of numbers several times.

When he finally lifted his head to look the older man in the face, the clerk pushed the square spectacles further up on his nose. "Come to seven hundred forty-four dollars an' fifty cents."

"Ooooh!" slapping a hand to his stomach. "Took me a ball in the meat bag there," Scratch replied, then handed the clerk his slip of paper giving him $840 credit from Sublette for the beaver traded. "Gimme 'nother paper as says what I got left in credit from you."

"That I'll do," he said, as he scribbled down another amount on a sheet of paper then gave it to Scratch. The clerk went to pulling together the goods Bass had just purchased. When his back was turned, Scratch handed the paper over to Josiah.

"How much I got left after that screwin'?" he whispered.

Paddock looked down at the paper. "Ninety-five dollar an' fifty cent," he read in a low whisper.

Bass took the paper back and stuffed it in the front of his calico shirt. "Ain't much for a child as is got the dry on I got. But will have to do. They got me by my shortest ha'rs." He turned, "I'll have you get the ponies an' ol' Hannah. Bring 'em here, an' we'll load up for back to camp."

Josiah took off and returned in a few minutes with the animals. They wrapped the loose trade goods in a blanket, bundled the heavy lead, powder, and edibles aboard Hannah, cinched the load down, and began to plod back to their campsite.

"Scratch took a skinnin', he did. Slick as shootin'."

"We didn' have to buy that rifle," Josiah protested.

"Boy, that rifle was a mountain gun. Plain as she might be, she'll be center-shootin' for you."

"I looked to buy me a rifle like that back to St. Lou, an' forty dollar it were." Paddock kept the dappled mare close to Scratch's pony.

"That were back to St. Louie. They make you pay 'em for mules bringin' the rifle out to you."

"I coulda done with my own..."

"Shit! Boy, you ain't even been deviled by Injuns yet! That rifle you got back to camp ain't one as neither of us can care to set with. This'un," he leaned over and tapped the new Henry, "this'un be somethin' we'll lay both our sights to. That squirrel gun you have jest won' wash when the bet's down! I'm happy with that Henry gun, an' you damned well better be happy with it too!"

"You done me nice, Scratch. I ain't givin' the notion that I don' 'preciate it neither. Jest... jest that its a lot of your money, an' you don't have much to be spendin' now on my skins, with much left over for your likker."

"Shit, boy!" Scratch howled. "I can get rid of my dry with this ticket." He patted the front of his shirt. "An', 'sides, there's other coons as'll be happy to buy ol' Bass a drink of the trader's John Barleycorn, willin' to get a drunk on with me. We done fine, son. Yep, we done fine back there. They happy to get my plews. I'm happy to have me 'nother y'ar to live in the upcountry. It comes out even in the end. Way I look at it, always does."

9

"We'll be to tryin' your eye here, Josiah." Scratch reined the pony to a stop along the creek bank. He dropped to the ground and pulled the brightly quilled cover from his rifle. It was hung with long fringes from end to end, those at the muzzle longer than the fringe near the opening just past the lock on the rifle. It was a soft, smoked skin, made of cheverel—the fine, delicate leather made of the skin taken from an unborn antelope calf.

Josiah hitched the dapple to a willow and untied a small possibles pouch from the rear of his saddle. In it were the balls made when they had arrived back at their camp.

In a small pot set over the bright coals of the camp's fire, Scratch had placed two small pigs of lead soft enough so that one could scratch the surface of the bars with a fingernail. As these melted down under Josiah's watchful eyes, Bass had gone to find a man among the free trappers still in camp who would have another bullet mold to fit the new .50-caliber rifle. Rufus had one he had continued to pack along although his rifle had grown from a .50 to its present .52 caliber under the skillful hands of a St. Louis riflesmith. Scratch traded a pig of lead for the mold Graham no longer needed and returned to the fire feeling better that Paddock now had two molds for his new rifle. Each would be carried in a separate pouch so that the chances of being without a mold for the rifle would be cut down to acceptable odds.

As the lead was melting, the old man cut small pieces of thick buffalo hide to wrap around the metal handles of the mold so one's hands would not be burned in the bullet-forming process. With the consistency of the lead to his satisfaction, Scratch put Josiah to work with a small iron dipper he used to ladle from the pot the molten lead, which was then poured into the single-cavity mold. Each ball took only a short time to set up within the cavity, but Josiah found it hot, boring work over the fire and pot. All the while, Bass added small pieces of lead to the molten mass until he felt Paddock had enough balls to serve him for the near future.

Now Titus laid the skin cover out on the ground, set his own rifle down on it, then turned to Josiah.

"Lemme see your rifle, boy. I'll be first as to shoot 'er. See jest what she does." He took the rifle handed to him, "A ball, boy?"

Josiah dug into the pouch and pulled out one of the lead bullets which Scratch popped between his jaws. Into his mouth then went the cap of the powder horn from which he poured the black granules up to just the right line across his palm and dropped the charge down the muzzle. From his own pouch, Bass pulled a square linen patch, which he placed over the muzzle, then popped the ball back into his right hand to put it in the center of the patch. Pulling the ramrod free of the thimbles beneath the barrel, he slowly started the ball on its way down. When all the patching had disappeared within the muzzle, Titus rammed the ball home to the powder against the breech.

"Some are the times as you might be usin' a leather patch, son. It'll work," he said, pulling the hickory wiping stick from the barrel, "in a pinch, if'n you ain't got nothin' else but."

From the small antler horn slung from his pouch strap he poured a small charge of powder into the pan. "Lookee here—see 'bout how much I'm a puttin' in there, so mind you how I done it." He then brought the hammer back full cock and returned the frizzen to its place over the powder in the pan. "She's got a half-cock settin' on this here hammer, Josiah, so when you go to settin' it, make sure you pull the hammer all way back, else'n you ain't gonna have the fire you need goin' into the pan. 'Stead, you'll have yourself goin' off half cocked."

Titus looked out over the stream some forty yards across until he spotted a likely target against the opposite bank that rose sharply upward about twelve feet. Protruding from the face of the bank was a light-colored rock that appeared, from where they stood across the stream, to be some two feet in diameter.

"Lookee there at that white rock, Josiah. Keep your eyes on it now." He brought the rifle to his shoulder.

He had a peculiar manner in aiming a rifle, as he found it difficult to hold the heavy barrel steady on a target. It had not taken him long to develop a method of permitting the rifle muzzle to wobble from side to side over his target. As it would weave back and forth, Scratch had learned to squeeze slowly, taking as much of the wobble out of the movement as possible, then he would pull the trigger as the dancing muzzle crossed his mark.

The hammer flew forward and the burning powder raced through the touch hole with a a spitting sound, followed quickly by the muzzle blast. In an instant, a cloud of white dust spewed free from the bank to the right of the rock.

"Dammit! She don' shoot the way me own does." He handed the rifle to Josiah. "You try 'er, boy. She's your'n." As Paddock took the rifle from him, a man appeared atop the bank just above the target rock.

He jumped up and down, from side to side, in an angry dance, yelling and cussing at them to stop the shooting. All he wore was a bright red woolen shirt that ended at his navel and a pair of moccasins tied around the ankles. Naked from the waist down, the fuming trapper's penis bounced and jumped against his belly as it stood erect. Bass looked over at Paddock, then back to the trapper cussing them out for interrupting him.

The half-naked man then yelled into the trees to his right where a naked squaw emerged and slid down the bank to run into the shallow stream. Her young breasts danced as she fought her way across the rocky bottom, holding her dress clutched tightly beneath one arm. Both men watched her approach them as the angry, bottomless trapper ran back and forth across the opposite bank yelling in his most profane tongue for her to return to him, then for Bass and Paddock to catch her and turn the squaw around.

The woman leaped out of the water to Josiah's left and stood on the shore to step into her dress while the man across the stream implored her to return. As she pulled the dress on, the squaw faced the man, pulled the bottom of the dress back up to expose herself, and ran a finger within the hair between her legs. Then she turned and ran past the two men laughing.

"Seems we broke into the man's fun, didn' we, Scratch!"

"That it do, son." He looked away from the squaw, retreating into the trees back toward the rendezvous site, to see the lonely trapper turn sullenly away into the brush above their target.

"Hope he can do somethin' with that frozen cock of his," Josiah snorted as he leaned forward with folded arms on the muzzle of his rifle.

"Kinda feel myself sorry for the ol' boy, I do." Scratch mused a moment as he looked across the stream, "Squar got what gee-gaw she wanted from him afore he got the forkin' he wanted. Real shame, 'tis. Two coons like us breakin' into a man's fun!" He turned to Paddock, "You gonna stand there gettin' your own cock harder'n that Henry barrel thinkin' 'bout it? Or you gonna load that rifle an' practice till you're shootin' center?"

While Scratch sat on the grass and took his own rifle in his arms, Josiah loaded the new Henry. Bass let drop the pouch and horn off his shoulder. Along the wide strap he had sewn a small pouch to carry an awl with an elkhorn handle that was kept in a carved cherrywood sheath. Titus drew this out and began to pick under his fingernails, scraping dirt onto the awl point, then flicking it off with another fingertip.

"You'll have to name your own rifle, too, son—if'n you wanna." He put a hand down temporarily on his cradled across his lap. "This tool be called Ol' Make 'em Come, onna count of that's what she does best—makes 'em come—be they red nigger or fat cow. Ain't a critter as stands no chance in front of this here tool, they don'. Mind you them brass nails we traded the clerk free of?" He looked up at Josiah. "Well, we be addin' them to your rifle when you start makin' coup. These here"—his fingertips ran over the rounded brass tacks stuck along the forearm and butt of his rifle—"each lil' nail count for a coup Ol' Scratch struck on a troublesome brownskin. Keeps me count that way. You ready?" Josiah was plunging the wiping stick back through the thimbles. "Shoot 'er center, son."

He missed the first several times in trying to hit the rock, and grew more and more frustrated as the small puffs of dust rose from the left and right of the white stone.

"Shit! I cain't shoot this goddamned thing!" He slammed the butt down against the earth.

"Consarn it! That ol' boy we skeert off whilst ago ain't gonna give up, is he? Ain't he gonna go get him 'nother squar? That's the puddin'! He ain't gonna give up till he gets some squar stuck center, ain't he, Josiah? Now, shut your mouth an' keep tryin'. L'arnin' a rifle like that take you some time, so you simmer yourself down an' don' make it any rougher on yourself."

"She's wobblin' on me!" Josiah squeaked.

"Make 'em Come do the same to me, but you jest let 'er wobble to an' fro whilst squeezin' on that trigger."

Josiah poured charge after charge down the barrel until he was hitting the rock with some regularity, dancing a little jig from his offhand stance each time the sandy rock spit out a small cloud of dust to announce he was on target.

"Now, let's try you one more." Scratch looked back over at the opposite bank until he spotted what he wanted. Off to their right stood a cottonwood atop the sharp bank. Facing the men was a small white patch that stood out boldly against the dark cottonwood bark.

"See you that cottonwood, one what has had a limb

broke off over there?" Bass pointed as Josiah tried to follow the directions. "Want you to hit it once an' we'll take 'er in for the day."

It looked as if Josiah missed offhand. He set about reloading. "How far you figger that patch to be from here?" he asked of Bass.

"Not more'n . . . hmmm, looks to me like it cain't be more'n twice't the distance from here to that rock you been hittin'—but I'm figgerin' that spot be only 'bout this big." He circled the index fingers and thumbs of both hands to estimate for Paddock that the white patch was only six inches in diameter. "We'll try you on a rest. Lay down on your belly an' get cozy—lemme have your hick'ry." Scratch took the wiping stick. "Put this here in the ground under the muzzle a ways for a rest, then get yourself set so you can hol't that front blade on the spot."

Josiah drove the end of the ramrod into the soft earth and lifted the muzzle onto it. He squirmed from time to time, inching across the ground until he could lie comfortably with the rifle against his shoulder, his cheek along the stock and the rifle held steady on the target. Paddock eased the hammer back, let out a full breath, and held only an instant before he squeezed the trigger. Even before the muzzle blast was gone from his ears, Scratch was down the slope into the stream.

"C'mon, Josiah! We'll be seein' how you did!" He turned to scamper across the rocky creek. Paddock followed closely on his heels as both men splashed wildly across the cold, rushing water, soaking moccasins and their pants below the knees. They climbed the bank and approached the tree.

"Damn!" Scratch squinted up at the white patch. "You shoot 'er center, almost plumb center there, boy. Two holes." He pointed to the black marks in the white bark with an arm outstretched above his head.

Josiah smiled as he looked up at the tree target, rubbing his hand softly over the wood rifle stock. He sat down and laid the rifle across the tops of his thighs, then started to untie the leather whangs wrapping the moccasins around his ankles.

"What you doin'?" Scratch's voice made him stop.

Josiah looked up at Bass. "Wanna get these off before they pinch my feet—that's what I'm doin'." He went back to work on the whangs.

"You'll be sorry, son. I'll be sorry seein' you ruin good mokersons like that." He sat down beside Josiah on the bank. "They fits good now, don' they?"

"Yup."

"An' you oughtta be wantin' to keep 'em that way. Take 'em off to dry an' them mokersons most likely'll never be fittin' you again, Josiah. Take 'em off wet an' them things'll shrink up bad 'nough you'll never get 'em on 'nother time."

"Ol' man, they gonna dry an' pinch my feet!"

"So if they do. So if they do. You jest go soaks 'em again an' again. Come a time when they won' be pinchin' anymores, not no matter how bad you get 'em wet."

Josiah looked disgusted, "Tellin' me I might be havin' to sleep with cold an' wet feet?"

"Yup. For 'while, it do. You'll get use't it." He slapped Paddock lightly on the thigh "Tie 'er up an' we be gettin' back for a pony ride."

Josiah reluctantly began to wrap the moccasins back around his ankles. Scratch continued, "Get up to the Absor'kees, we'll be gettin' you couple sets of some cold doin's mokersons. Them as you got there'll fit you good in weather like this," motioning to the pair Josiah was retying, "but we get some Crow like I gots. Really three pair of mokersons. You got the inside pair that fit you snug. We now have to get you 'nother few pair that'll go over them mokersons, ones as'll turn out the cold an' wet. Then we lay us down a fat cow what is got 'er a winter robe for the outside set, mokersons as'll be done up of tough, strong buffler hide. That's what you're needin' for winter doin's." He rose to his feet. "Man out here travels on his feet as well as his ass. Gotta take care of both. You've already l'arnt what not to do 'bout your ass, ain't you? Jest tryin' to tell you what not to do 'bout your hoofs."

It was late afternoon with the sun threatening to disappear behind the ridges to the west when they mounted up to ride north. The two men moved past the circles of fire being fed by trappers preparing evening meals until they arrived at the outskirts of the Snake village. Both men dismounted and led the horses into camp.

"Hackgunn," Bass halted near an old squaw skinning out a puppy in front of her lodge. She looked up at the two visitors.

"Mi-yah, ka cunni hanche how-yi, Hugga-pa?" He asked her for the lodge of a friend of his. The woman gave them directions and the two men led their animals slowly through the lodges. Bass drew to a stop in front of the one to which he had been directed.

"Yup. Be the one. That's his medeecin." Scratch pointed out for Josiah the tripod of carved and painted pine in front of the lodge entrance. Suspended from the tripod hung a small buffalo-hide shield with crudely painted figures dancing across its surface. Draped above it was the whole hide of a large badger, from head to tail. It had been sewn up after skinning, then beaded around the four legs with large glass beads traded from white men.

"Hugga-pa! Ma boni! Ka cunni hanche how-yi!" Bass spoke the words clearly with his slight drawl as he addressed the open door of the lodge.

"Huh?" Paddock asked the older man. "What you sayin'?"

"Tellin' him a ol't frien' is greetin' his lodge, son." A man stuck his head out of the doorway, silhouetted from the rear by the fire burning at the center of the lodge. He came out to stand before Scratch, slapped his chest over the heart with a clenched fist, then opened the hand to present it to Bass. They shook hands as Josiah looked the warrior over.

From his neck hung the supreme token of bravery and courage, a ring of bear claws with interspersing hunks of the animal's hair, taken in ritual combat with only a knife for a weapon. The warrior's hair was braided in a long queue down his back, a braid that almost touched the belt about his waist that held leggings and breech-clout in place. Intertwined within the queue were numerous brass rings that fell the full length of the braid. Down his forehead the brave's hair was combed straight and had been cut off square across the eyebrows.

"Pa mi yah," the warrior said, gripping Scratch's hand. He patted the trapper on the shoulder, then motioned Scratch and Josiah to enter the lodge.

"C'mon, Josiah," Scratch said. "He be askin' us to come in."

Inside the Indian brought out a pipe and filled the bowl with his own curious mixture of tobacco, willow, and herbs. With the pipe lighted, he blew smoke to the sky, then the earth, followed by smoke blown to the four winds. The silent brave handed the pipe to Scratch who sat at his right hand on the robes laid out for the guests. Each of the white men took his turn at the pipe before it was returned to the Snake warrior to be held across his arms.

"Tchant!" he smiled over at Bass.

"Tchant bia dumaya," Scratch answered, then looked past the Indian to remark to Paddock, "It always be good to see old friends again."

"Tai quan?" the Snake asked with his dark, smiling eyes.

"Mabonie, peup na ry-ant, naro naotoks?" Scratch asked, then leaned over to Josiah to whisper, "Askin' for his squar's trail food. Whooo! My Snake's needin' practice, bad—'cause my Snake's bad."

The warrior spoke over his shoulder to a squaw sitting on robes out of the light thrown off by the small fire. She put aside the work she was involved with and picked up a large parfleche in the shape of a box, which she set beside the brave before returning to her domestic chores. Slowly the brave opened the ancient parfleche and drew out two small pieces of something dark. Taking them in each hand, he leaned forward to give one to each of his visitors. Josiah stared at his while Scratch took a bite and chewed with a faint crunching sound.

He looked over at Josiah while chewing. "Eat, boy. Be sociable! Won' hurt you. It be what we come here for to buy," pushing all the words around a full mouth.

"Hi-hi, teicuhbi?" the warrior asked as Scratch finished his portion.

"Wils, wils." Bass stuck an open palm into the air to show three fingers. 'Now, we gonna start tradin' talk with the nigger. Tietskoah, ra-antoshomi naro namp pieati." From a pouch at his side, the old man pulled out various articles that he placed neatly in front of the Indian: a small pile of brass tacks, a handful of beads in mixed colors, four small mirrors, and two awls. The Indian looked down at the goods before him for a few minutes in silence, then patted the top of the parfleche by his side.

"Peup sharet?" he asked.

"Namp peup sharet," Bass replied. "Ain't 'nough plunder for him, Josiah." He clucked his tongue inside his mouth.

The Indian shook his head slowly from side to side,

smiling at Scratch. The white man put his hand inside his pouch once more, then leaned aside to Josiah and whispered, "He be stingy with his trail food, this'un." Bass pulled two of the butcher knives he had purchased that day out of the pouch and set them before the Indian, then stared into the bronze face. Again the warrior shook his head slowly from side to side. Bass sighed and pulled out a small bunched roll of bright gold trade ribbon. He put it on the robe alongside the other plunder.

The Snake remained quiet for a moment, then began to finger the articles set before him. "E-weet mish weet. Bishey tai-kup boun-a-cie tonie."

"Ka nee wa-ton. Sho ship," Bass replied to the brave. "Thinkin' me we got 'im now, boy."

"Shin-bun-ha-nah. Ma boni," he said nodding his head in the affirmative this time and slapping his thighs with both hands for emphasis.

"Shin-bun-ha-nah!" Scratch took the parfleche handed to him by the warrior and said, "We got us our deal," as he rose to his feet. "Kah-key, wah-hintz wipe mish." He motioned to Josiah to stand with him.

The three men left the lodge and stood outside in the evening air before Bass spoke once more to the Snake.

"Bou-na yo-ye makish sela, monno-alle so-watsumme." Bass then bowed to the warrior. "Sayin' it been good tradin' with him, sayin' he allays gets the better of me. They like to hears that, son." He stuck out his hand to the Snake and both held each other for a long moment until Titus turned and climbed aboard his pony, adjusting the parfleche in front of him atop the pommel. "Tieks toah, mi-minie-lo. Se-ah watchee go-gumla su."

"Se-ah watchee go-gumla su," the warrior answered in return and raised his hand as the two white men moved away.

Josiah was silent as they moved away from the village. Turning around, he saw that they had finally come far enough away from the lodges. To the side he spit out a mouthful of the food he had refused to swallow. Scratch looked over at the noisy blowing and snorting Paddock made, spitting food to the ground as they rode.

"What in the goddamn hell was that?" he sputtered as he finished emptying his mouth, picking free some stubborn bits caught between his teeth.

"Pemmeekin, boy! Trail food. Didn' take to it, eh?" he

snorted, giggling a bit as he watched Josiah ridding the last of it in his mouth with a finger.

"Never eat it again, less I have to!"

"Trail food's for the starvin' times, times as we'll come on now an' then. We made us a good bargain in that trade, Josiah. Got us whole parfleche of pemmeekin for a few lil' gee-gaws. 'Twere them butchers as caught the boy's eyes. He's a good'un, that Snake be—name of Slays in the Night. Hunted me many a time with that nigger. Was the time this coon even thort me 'bout takin' the squar he has for his own now, thort 'bout it till she made it plain she had her eyes set on Slays in the Night..."

"What was the damn stuff made of?" Paddock interrupted, painfully.

"Taste like the squar put some chopped meat bits in it. That be why this here child goes to them to get his trail food each y'ar. 'Long with that, she puts some pounded roots an' cherries she let dry afore she pounds 'em up fine, jest like flour. Then that gal'll stir it all up an' pour in the fat off'n some fleecy buffler cow. That lard hol'ts it all together. She done that up last fall jest afore the first heavy snow, then put it up in small skin pouches, lettin' it age an' ripen through the winter. Slays in the Night knows this child comes round once't y'ar for his squar's pemmeekin—so he had 'er make some up special for me."

"It were ripe, ol' man."

"All the better, too. Keep you from bein' a starvin' pilgrim come the lean times when this nose of mine cain't find us no more game. Jest keep that under your hat an' mind you of it when our belly gets to pinchin'—hollerin' for somethin' to eat. Time is, you'll be ready to dinner on this nigger's trail food."

Bass was the last to finish supper, kneeling in close to the remains of the roasting elk while the other men leaned back away from the fire one by one as bellies were satisfied.

"When ya finish up stuffin' your meat bag, I got a s'prise for ya, Bass," Hatcher drew on a bowl of fresh tobacco.

"Got a s'prise for me?" Scratch sat back and stabbed the earth several times with his butcher knife, driving it deep into the ground to clean grease and fat off the blade. As he turned to watch Mad Jack rise slowly with a wobble and stumble off to his lean-to, Titus rubbed greasy fingers on the ends of his gray-flecked hair to wipe them free of tallow.

Caleb sat with an all-knowing smile on his face, rubbing the blade of his knife over a flat piece of obsidian he carried as a whetstone. Hatcher approached the fire carrying a large iron kettle that sloshed from side to side as he wobbled back to the circle of light thrown out by the fire.

"Mad Jack, do be keerful with that now," Issac chided the trapper.

"Don' spill none of that bee-yu-tee-ful mountain nectar," Solomon chimed in. "Scratch ain't even had the chance to see what his s'prise be yet!"

The tall man set the kettle down in front of Bass. The old trapper looked at it, then put a finger into the liquid and brought it to his lips.

"My, my . . . my!" Titus smacked his lips with a popping sound and plunged a finger back into the kettle.

"Eeegod, coon! There's better ways as to be drinkin' that stuff!" Hatcher protested.

Scratch looked up at Mad Jack, then over to Josiah, "Niggers here 'bouts don' take to a man as is tryin' to be gen-teel whilst drinkin' his likker." He put his two hands around the sides of the kettle, "So, when a man's in the comp'ny of niggers such as these mangy varmints, you drink as they does." With that he brought the kettle to his lips and started gulping as much as he could while sloshing it down the front of his calico shirt before he finally pulled the trader's whiskey away from his mouth, gasping and sputtering.

"Man ain't got no manners at *all* in our dinin' parlor!" Hatcher knelt down between Bass and Paddock, then dipped his pint tin cup into the kettle. "Tonight, we palaver for young Josiah Paddock!" He raised his cup high in the air. "An' palaverin's dry work for this brigade of motherless childs—so let's likker!"

At that there was a rush on the kettle by all, each man dipping his cup in and pulling it out to spill some of the whiskey on the other reaching arms. Josiah was kept away from the kettle in the rush.

"Best you get started, boy!" Scratch prodded him with an elbow, then took a dip with his own cup into the whiskey. "These here old coons ain't 'bout to serve you tonight."

"Hey, ol' man," Hatcher asked, pushing forward for another cup, "ya still got your wood-holler mouth bow?"

"Yup. That I do. Still packin' her 'long with me," Bass answered.

"Why don' we get on the hoedown trail? Ya fetch your mouth bow." Mad Jack rose and steadied himself. "I'll be to gettin' me fiddle. Hey, Elbridge! Fetch your squeeze box. We be doin' some music for dancin', singin', an' cause to wet the whistle!"

Hatcher went back into the dark, followed by Scratch and Elbridge Gray. Josiah sipped at his cup of whiskey, pulling in the first drink slowly. The liquid hit his tongue and the back of his throat as if he had swallowed burning embers. Paddock coughed and spit, sputtering some to clear his throat before he caught his breath.

"Whoooo . . . yeeee!" was all he could get out, beating himself on the chest with a clenched fist.

"Ain't that some?" Rufus asked of him.

"That's . . . that's some . . . burns . . ."

"Make you break to a sweat, boy," Bass said, entering the circle. "Take 'er easylike for start. Stuff'll kick you in the balls less'n you take care right off."

Hatcher and Gray came back into the light. From a beaded rawhide pouch, Elbridge pulled a small mariner's accordion that looked like a small octagonal box until he popped loose the leather strap holding the end pieces against each other. He pumped it a few times tentatively, then watched as Mad Jack opened a worn, battered, light-brown violin case.

"Get your tune, man." The tall man looked around the group of trappers. "What ya boys wanna hear tonight— somethin' as Gray an' me can play for ya?"

" 'Cumberland Gap,' " Issac Simms responded. "That ditty do remind me to home."

" 'Cumberland Gap' takes me back 'ways." Hatcher pushed the bow across the fiddle's strings slowly a few times, then moved it gradually into a snappy beat, followed by the other trappers clapping their hands or slapping their thighs along with the lusty tempo. The fiddle player held his instrument low under his right breast as he caressed the strings with the bow of his left hand. He moved the song into a snappy instrumental introduction

213

while tapping his left foot, weaving around in place from side to side from the waist. Gray caught the tune on the accordion, picking up the harmony to play a background for the crying fiddle. Scratch stuck the mouth bow between his lips, braced it, and started plucking a three-note range of rhythm.

When all were involved in adding their own music to the song, Hatcher led into the words:

Me an' my wife an' my old grandpap,
Goin' to raise hell in Cumberland Gap.

Cumberland Gap is a famous place,
With no clean water to wash you face.

C'mon boys, an' take a nap;
It's seventeen miles to Cumberland Gap.

No place like it on the map;
We'll all raise hell in Cumberland Gap.

The small band sang it over several times, until Josiah finally caught most of the words and could mumble along with the rest of the trappers. At the finish, Hatcher knelt down by the kettle in front of Bass and dipped his cup into the whiskey. He nearly lost his balance upon rising, stumbling into the edge of the fire and splashing those close around him with alcohol.

"Oooooee! Lord ready to send me to fire an' burn me already!" he exclaimed, kicking a small cloud of ashes from his moccasins.

"Lord ain't gonna take you, Mad Jack," Bass commented. "An' you know damned well, devil ain't gonna want the competishun none when you goes under! Ain't gonna be no place for a nigger as yourself to go when you dies— we'll jest have to skin you out an' leave your meat an' marrow for the buzzards!" He lifted his cup as if in toast to Hatcher, then swilled the liquid down.

"How 'bout 'Ol' Buckeye Jim'?" Mad Jack set his cup down after taking a long drink. "Ya knows that'un, don' ye, Gray?"

Elbridge dove into the tune, this time taking the instrumental lead with the wailing strains of his small squeeze box.

Way up yonder above the sky,
A bluebird lived in a jaybird's eye.

Buckeye Jim, you can't go.
Go weave an' spin,
You can't go, Buckeye Jim.

Way up yonder above the moon,
A bluebird nest in a silver spoon.

Way down yonder in a wooden trough,
An old woman died of the whooping cough.

Way down yonder on a hollow log,
A red bird danced with a green bullfrog.

Buckeye Jim, you can't go.
Go weave an' spin,
You can't go, Buckeye Jim.

The Appalachian lullabye had a haunting melody, made even more so by the scattered wail of the accordion and the high-pitched scratchy notes of Hatcher's fiddle-playing. Rufus Graham wanted it sung again when they had finished.

"Minds me of the time when I was a pup, an'...an' my mam singed to simmer me down each night—them long, hot nights back to the Virginny hills, hearin' her purty notes..."

"Cain't b'lieve ya was ever a pup!" Hatcher replied. "Cain't ever b'lieve ya had ya a mam as would own up to havin' a pup such as ya'd been." He put his bow back to work across the fiddle strings to play 'Buckeye Jim' a second time.

"There's a ol't one, boys," Scratch began after the lullabye was finished, "name of 'Springfield Mountain,' it be. Know it, Hatcher?"

"Cain't say as I do," Hatcher said, finishing another draw from his cup. "But if'n Gray hyar can lead off, I'll be to catchin' up with the tune. Got that tune in your head, Elbridge?"

Gray put a few notes together, then began with more certainty to play the eastern mountain melody that dated back to 1761. The tune carried visions of smoky hills and wooded hollows, of a lover's lament and a wise man's warning to star-struck young men.

On Springfield Mountain there did dwell
With a ring-ting a-tim, ring-a tid-en-nah-den-nay.

On Springfield Mountain there did dwell.
Timarrow!
On Springfield Mountain there did dwell
A lovely youth I knew well.
With a ring-ting a-tim, ring-a tid-en-nah-den-nay.

This lovely youth one day did go
Down to the meadow for to mow.

He mowed awhile an' then did feel
A pizenous sarpent bite his heel.

He turned around an' with a blow
He laid that pesky sarpent low.

They carried him to his Sally dear
Which made her feel so very queer.

"Oh, Johnny dear, why did you go
Down in your father's field to mow?"

"Why, Sally dear, I supposed you knowed
When the grass gets ripe it must be mowed!"

Now Sally had two ruby lips
With which the pizen she did sip.

Dear Sally had a hollow tooth
An' the pizen killed them both.

So Johnny died, gave up the ghost,
An' off to heaven he did post.

Come all young girls an' shed one tear
For this young man that died right here.

Come all young men an' warning take,

An' don't get bit by a rattlesnake.

Scratch dipped his cup into the kettle once more and held it aloft, "I do 'preciate that, boys. Ain't never heered it played what it don' grab at my heart. Thank you, thank you both."

"How 'bout playin' one for Ol' Scratch—tune as was writ for the likes of such a likker-lovin' mountain man," Mad Jack chirped to bring the others out of their reverie. "Gray an' me do a good thing with 'Blessin' on Brandy an' Beer.'" The fiddle and squeeze box jumped in together with the merry and rollicking strains of the old drinking song:

When one's drunk, not a gal looks but pretty,
The country's as gay as the city,
An' all that one says is so witty.
A blessing on brandy an' beer!

Bring the cup!
Fill it up!
Take a sup!
An', let not the flincher come near.

Oh, give me but plenty of the liquor,
I'd laugh at the squire and the vicar.
An' if I'd a wife, why I'd kick her,
If' e'er she pretended to sneer.

Though I know it's a heavy disaster,
Yet I mind not the rage of my master.
He bullies, an' I drink the faster,
A blessin' on brandy an' beer!

With a cherry-cheeked maid I've an eye on,
I'd do many things they'd cry fie on.
Ee-god! I'm as bold as a lion!
A blessing on brandy an' beer!

A blessing,
A blessing,
A blessing on brandy an' beer!

On into the night Hatcher kept his fiddle strings

warm with activity as Gray pushed air through the small accordion. Between songs, Bass gulped at his tin cup, then picked his mouth bow up once more to join in the musical accompaniment. Paddock was enjoying his first Rocky Mountain rendezvous concert, lying on his right side, then on his left to watch first one musician then another.

"There's one as would be for young Josiah Paddock, recent of the settlements, I'm thinkin'." Hatcher looked down at the young man after hours of music. "Elbridge, let's play that tune 'Wayfarin' Stranger' for the lad."

Gray's accordion caught hold of the light, delicate notes pulled together to create a bittersweet song of the melancholy man on the move, backed up by the gentle sliding of Hatcher's bow across the fiddle strings.

> I'm just a poor, wayfaring stranger,
> Traveling through this world of woe.
> Yet, there's no sickness, toil, no danger
> In that bright land to which I go.
> I'm going there to see my father,
> I'm going there no more to roam.
> I'm just going over Jordan.
> I'm only going over home.
>
> I know dark clouds will gather round me,
> I know my way is rough an' steep.
> Yet beautiful fields lie just before me,
> Where God's redeemed their vigils keep.
> I'm going there to see my mother,
> She said she'd meet me when I come.
> I'm just going over Jordan.
> I'm only going over home.
>
> I'll soon be free of every trial,
> My body will sleep in the churchyard.
> I'll drop the cross of self-denial,
> An' enter on my great reward.
> I'm going there to see my brothers,
> Who've gone before me one by one.
> I'm just going over Jordan.
> I'm only going over home.

On the second time through the song, Hatcher seemed

to let Gray sing alone for a moment, then came in to repeat each line right behind Elbridge to create the feeling of a mournful echo over the song. When they finished, the group fell silent, each man in his own thoughts until Mad Jack sat down and placed the fiddle and bow across his lap.

"That's the evenin' music for ye niggers, now. Let's be tellin' young Josiah 'bout what we seen an' done to the Stoney Mountains," Hatcher said as his cup was taken and filled by Bass. "Ye all gots a story to tell—be good time to let the young'un in on the magic in these'r mountains. Solomon," he turned his head toward Fish, "ye got ye a tale 'bout sneakin' a peek to a Blackfoot camp."

"I heerd that'un afore, an' could count the ha'rs atop my pizzer for the times he's tol't us that'un," Caleb growled.

"Shut your mouth, nigger," Mad Jack pounced back. "Let the man tell the young'un 'bout his story. Go 'head, Fish, tell it again. Tale do get better each time with the tellin'."

The trapper began his yarn, embellishing it more this time than he had done before, changing a thought here or there to reweave a tale of his own bravery into a new fabric still mostly of truth, but not without a thread of falsehood here and there. They were stories of a man's exaggerated sense of his own courage. Stories told and retold over winter-night fires as exercise for the mountain trapper who felt dwarfed by the towering peaks and the great expanse of country through which only a handful of white men had traveled before. The tales were begun with a germ of truth, nurtured by fertile imaginations, and watered with loving care from the whiskey kettle each retelling.

Fish told of a spring hunt three years before when one evening the small band of trappers he was traveling with discovered a sizable raiding party of Blackfoot warriors. The white men backed off silently, undiscovered from the Indian camp, to argue as to what was to be done. Bragging led to daring, and soon Solomon had to put up or shut up.

His story was one of smearing his face with vermilion, pulling a buffalo robe over his shoulders, and walking into the small Indian encampment. All the braves were gathered about the fire, engrossed in their own tales of coups counted and ponies stolen, as Fish approached them knowing his fellow trappers were behind him on the ridge, watching for his success or failure.

Out of the inky darkness the disguised trapper stepped slowly up to the fire to stand behind the warriors as the Indians sat huddled around the glowing embers. Fish stood quietly, listening to the pounding of his own heart and the strange Indian tongue, all the time waiting to be discovered. But the Blackfoot warriors paid no heed to the disguised white visitor, more absorbed in their own stories than in the dark form standing among them. Solomon told of kneeling within the group and stealthily sliding one of the warrior's knives under his robe. He rose quietly and slipped back into the darkness of the surrounding trees to make good his escape up the ridge.

The trapper returned to his friends in their hiding place to collect their wagers and exhibit his prize, a Blackfoot dagger manufactured in England and bearing the Hudson's Bay seal on the blade. He passed it around each rendezvous fire for inspection.

"Solomon's up to the bung with shit!" Caleb protested at the end of the story.

"Tell your own, Wood! Ye got a story to top it?" Elbridge injected.

"Aye! That I do." Whereupon Caleb began to tell his own whopper of traveling to a Crow village to escape pursuing Blackfoot. One of the war chiefs took him in as his guest for a few days and grew to like the trapper.

Consequently, the old Indian one evening offered Caleb his choice of five daughters, all of whom were in their teenage years, yet of marrying age within Crow custom. The trapper could not decide quickly enough to satisfy the old boy, so the Indian announced that Caleb would have all night to make his choice. Father left the lodge with his squaw, leaving behind the bewildered white man with the five giggling young women. The oldest put the cover over the doorway, then each of the five undressed before the shocked man. They approached Caleb and undressed him without too much resistance on his part, then began their playful lovemaking.

"Them Crow gals l'arn tricks hidden 'way up thar in Absor'kee country, tricks to make yer cock stay hard all night if'n that's what they wanted. Damn! Them wimmens is some! I did wanna get it over with after 'while—my cock was throbbin' an' 'bout ready to go off like some hot-fired steamboat stack—but them squaws wouldn' let me explode. They jest kept playin' with me while I laid on my back snuggled in them buffler robes, each one takin' her turn: over an' over feelin' me, puttin' her mouth 'round my pizzer an' nibblin' at it with little bites, then sittin' on me to bounce up an' down with my cock inside 'em till I thought I was 'bout to go crazy right then. Wal, them wimmens kept me goin' for 'bout all night it was..."

"You're as full of shit now as ye was of love juice then!" Solomon interrupted.

"...nigh onto sunup next mornin'," Caleb continued, ignoring the comment on his veracity. "They kept playin' with me an' I hadn' blown the whistle yet, when the oldest, she said somethin' to the rest of 'em in Crow an' they crawls off to theys robes to sleep. Whoooeee! Big sister climbed in with me an' started playin' her tricks with me again, but this time havin' me all to herself—an' both of us knowin' the others is watchin' the fun. That gal did things to me as would make a man's eyes bug out—I thought I'd scream, wishin' I could go under right thar', just that way with that squaw rubbin' my tired ol' cock up an' down, then puttin' it in her mouth to sing Injun to me! Woman kept me like I was a wipin' stick till the sun hit the lodge afore she let me whistle in her. An' when I did, 'twarn't like nothin' I never done afore, an' likely ain't never to do such again!"

"Five squaws on ye all night an' ye didn' toot her whistle?" Hatcher asked.

"Five of 'em, doin' ever'thin' no whore back to St. Louie wouldn' begin to think of doin' with a man—an' it was all free! I made sleep an' stayed in the robes that whole day. Got me hitched to that big sister with all the tricks that night."

"What come of it, Caleb? The squaw, I mean?" Rufus found the question riding high in every man's mind.

"Bitch was good for 'while, some punkins ever' night. L'arnt a few off that slut, I did. But she run me like a ragged woolen after 'while. Got to screamin' an' bellerin' for foofaraw alla time—couldn' keep her happy no more in the robes 'cause I couldn' keep her happy with gee-gaws an' shinies. Had to lodgepole that bitch up to the Bighorn, close to her own people. Sent her packin' home.

Eased the mis'ry, howsomever, with a pouch of plunder for her ol' man. Squaw was somethin', boys—while it was good—but this child never wants to run into that bunch of fork-lovin' sisters again!"

"Shoulda had ya this bunch 'long with ya!" Mad Jack remarked, dipping his cup into the dwindling second kettle they had brought to the fire after the first was emptied. "Boys hyar know how to handle theyselves in such a fix, don' ya?" The others whooped and hollered with the thought of running into such a situation, wishing it had been they in the story although most of the men passed it off as one of the biggest whoppers they had ever heard tell of when asked. Each man now warmed to the yarnin' and gave his own version of feats done or seen.

"Bass?" Hatcher finally looked over at the older man after many stories. "Young Josiah heerd tell of yer ha'r, ain't he?"

"Nawww, he ain't. I ain't tol't him 'bout that yet." Titus's words were somewhat slurred by a tongue thickened with alcohol.

"Most boys hyar heerd me tell of it round a winter fire a time or two, but they ain't heerd tell of it from *your* mouth. Go 'head an' tell it—we'll keep your cup full an' your jaws from dryin'. Go 'head," Mad Jack prodded, while pulling on Scratch's shoulder to help him into a sitting position.

All eyes were on Bass as he set his cup down in front of him. He snugged the blue bandanna down on his head with both hands and took another drink.

"C'mon, ol' man. Tell your tale." Josiah spoke for the first time in hours.

"I'm a gonna." He blew his nose, snorting the mucous on the ground, and wiped his nostrils with fingertips that he then dried on his beard. "Ever' story's gotta have a startin', an' I'm collectin' on jest where I'm to be startin' mine. Well, now . . . You boys knows that Ol' Scratch'd sooner spit face on to the wind than tell no lie, so pin your ears back an' give a lis'en-up to my tale."

Those around him squirmed a little to make themselves more comfortable. Josiah lay down alongside the old trapper, resting his head against the palm of his hand while he leaned on an elbow.

"Been up to the Three Forks with the coons as took this'r child to his first ronnyvoo. Come the green-up after winterin' on the Yallerstone, jest north of the place as those who track it call Colter's Hell, them three coons up an' decide they's gonna head down the Missoura for whiskey an' womens early on—cain't wait for these here times, they cain't. Had us a good fall, an' even better spring fur gettin' that y'ar—had us a passel of that beaver plunder in our packs. Well, them boys all says I'm to be the child as gots to stay behin't with the horses an' other truck, so I wishes 'em my best an' watches them three head down the river in them two dugouts we'd made for 'em. I yell out to 'em to have a drink or two on Titus Bass."

The first few days out after leaving his three partners at the river, Scratch had gotten lonely—and he did not mind telling the others of that fact. Each man around that fire had fought loneliness and conquered it to one degree or another. Every man around that fire could identify with Bass. Despite the feelings, Scratch knew he had work to do and places to go himself, so he turned his face south as he was to be meeting his three trapping partners along the front range of the mountains to the south in some three to four months. They had arranged their own rendezvous point, Bass told the men circling the firelight, so Bass went to work pushing his horse and pulling beaver all the way to Park Kyack.

"My, my, what a fine place that be! Snuggles up a might close to the Bayou Salade in runnin' for a piece of heaven, that valley does. Elk there be bigger'n I see'd afore, an' the deer—why, them bucks stand almost as big as my lil' Crow pony. Beaver come to bait, jest as sure as you'd lay down your money on a whore's featherbed for a forkin'. Slick it were!"

In time he moved out for the planned meeting with Bud, Silas, and Billy. Bass wrinkled his brow contemplatively. "Scratch waited on them coons, an' I waited some mores." It got past time for their rendezvous, then it was past time for the traders' rendezvous, too. Nevertheless, Bass explained how he decided to head for rendezvous country anyway, moving out of Park Kyack over the divide, dwelling all the time on how certain he was his three friends must have lost their hair. "The Big Muddy's allays been fair boilin' with red niggers, an' Ol' Scratch jest calc'lates as how they bought more'n they could barter for on that river's track."

On the west side of the divide, Bass came upon a little river he had since been told was the Yampa, Ute land it was. He made camp along the waters for two nights, trapping as he may, slipping along easy and carefree in new country. Then he suddenly read signs that there were brownskins about. "Now, there I were, 'lone an' such, an' had me 'leven other ponies 'sides the one 'twixt my own legs. Got to figgerin' I looked a might invitin' to them niggers." Scratch paused and picked up his cup. "This yarnin' be dry work, an' a desert I'm makin' of my tongue." He drained his cup and handed it to Hatcher for a refill.

He started heading out quietly back to the east along the river, east toward more friendly country in Park Kyack. Then Hannah started snorting softly—her signal to Bass that she smelled Indians. "I laid into the bank, stayin' 'gainst them trees an' come round a bend—an' Lordee! There stand four of them red niggers jest waitin' for me. I comes to a cold stop an' figgered on what this body was to be doin'. I reach 'round an' set that string of ponies loose an' kicked my own in the ass. Ol' Hannah stayed with me as best as the gal could, tied to my saddle tree, she were. Well, Ol' Bass is runnin' an' kickin' that pony, yellin' for Hannah to be on the make, too—all time hearin' them niggers comin' after me."

His quick thinking seemed to pay off to a degree. He turned momentarily to see three of the braves attempting to round up the loosed ponies, but one warrior seemed to have more of a desire to count coup than collect horse-flesh. He turned tail and kept on. "That was some race that day—don' know me how much ground I covered, what with bein' skairt an' all, in a piece of strange country."

Soon he looked behind him to see his pursuer there no more. He brought the pony to a halt and began to think, think about those ponies entrusted to him by his three partners. He figured he could make a good show of it, so looking to the priming in his two pistols and his rifle, Bass headed back toward the action. It was not long before Hannah snorted again as the one lone warrior broke from the trees on the opposite bank and made for the white man. "I put heels to my pony jest as I hears the nigger's gun pop an' somethin' pounds me good on my back." Scratch reached around with his left arm to point out the general area of his upper right shoulder.

He pitched forward on the bank, "out colder'n a preacher's wife on her weddin' night," and came to again in hearing a pony stepping over the riverbed rocks. "I laid there hearin' that pony comin' closer, but not thinkin' good—jest keepin' my eyes closed to play the possum. Then I felt the lights go out again."

When he came to, his head was hurting something awful, along with the arm. He opened his eyes slowly, trying to shake the clouds away, "an' what I be lookin' at were that nigger sittin' with his back toward me, scrapin' off my topknot!"

At the last few words, Josiah's eyes got bigger. Bass let the words hang heavy in the air as he took another gulp of the gut-wrenching alcohol. "'Bout all I could see of the nigger were his mokersons an' leggin's," so he studied the quillwork design until he passed out again.

Later that day he came to once more to see that the Indians had left the scene. "Consarn the damned! At best, dyin' be a one-man job." He drank some water slowly, then took wet moss off the rocks, scraping it off with his fingertips and plastering it on his aching, bare, exposed skull. That done, he heard an animal snort behind him. He turned quickly, believing the Indians had returned for him—but it was only Hannah. The warriors had not found the mule. "Mule's got a head 'bout her an' she laid low waitin' for the country to clear of brownskins. When she saw me movin', she made her way back to me."

"Yeah? What happened then?" Josiah now sat up close to Scratch, enthralled with the story.

Bass continued, telling of his trip north into Snake country where he was put on the mend and reoutfitted. He had no need of a rifle, however, for he had found his weapon on the Yampa's bank. "When I come pitchin' off the pony, I gone one way an' the ol' medeecin iron gone 'nother—right into the willers." After a period of convalescence with the Snakes, the trapper headed south toward the Bayou Salade once more, trapping two seasons, all the time wearing beaver fur over his bare skull.

"One evenin', Ol' Scratch was out trappin' a lil' crik in that valley when two niggers come ridin' up slow on me." He made ready his rifle, and the pistol at his belt. The visitors stopped some distance off and made a sign that they wanted no truck with Bass. With that, the two warriors rode on up and began to talk sign with the trapper. It was not long before Scratch looked down at one of the brave's moccasins.

"An' what does this coon see? Whooooeeee! The Lord was good to Ol' Scratch that day, He were—sendin' me that nigger. His hoofs said there sat the nigger that stole't my topknot. Well, theys lookin' me over real good, figgerin' on my plunder, when Scratch up an' pulls ol' Make 'em Come for the work at hand! Blows that one nigger's jaw off—hit him with my .54 here—an' he goes a sailin' back as his friend yells an' kicks his pony my way."

The trapper dropped his rifle and pulled out the pistol just as the second warrior jumped off his mount onto Bass. The Indian received a ball in the top of his arm for his trouble. "We lay on the ground huggin' an' scufflin' till he's out cold."

Bass drew in a long breath, then drained his cup once more. He began his narrative again by telling how he made his way slowly to the first warrior. "'Tweren't much left of that boy's face—lookin' like you'd beat it all day with a rock, it did. Nigger were only 'bout fifteen foot from me when I blew the cocksucker's lights out. Jest pulled my knife out an' set it to the tune. Whizzed his skelp off, down to the top of the ears—'bout all that was left of his noodle. Scraped it clean a bit, whirled it round in the air to blow off the blood, an' walked over to his friend."

The second warrior was still breathing so Bass slapped him. He came to with a start and stared up at the trapper as if he were some big medicine. Scratch dragged him by the hair over close to the body of his dead companion so he could watch the white man work on the body. "Split the skelp-stealin' nigger wide open with my knife like this," describing the grisly incision made from the groin up to the base of the neck with his finger, "then I put my hand inside an' started pullin' it all out, jest like you was dressin' out a critter." The second warrior never took his eyes off the trapper.

"I wrapped it up by pullin' the nigger's heart out an' took it over to the other fella. Stood right in his face an' tore me a bite outta it—lettin' him see me eat a hunk of that other forker's heart. The I cut the skelper's balls off an' stuffed 'em in what was left of his mouth."

All were hushed, so quiet they could hear Josiah gulp. Bass said none of it had been embellished in the least, that Arapahos would still be after his hide for what he had done to one of their warriors. Then, "I made sign for the breathin' nigger to go back an' tell his people what'd happened afore I left him to go back to settin' my traps, easy as you please."

The next morning, Bass pulled out, going past the scene of the previous evening's skirmish. He found the wounded warrior had crawled off some distance. He watched Bass dismount, walk over to him, and sit down with his weight on the Indian's arms before beginning to sing his death song. "I squats down an' carves a big *T* on his right tit, an' a big *B* on his left'un. Figgered them 'Rapahos'd really get big medeecin outta that—the nigger comin' in with his story, carryin' my letters the way he was!" He threw his cup toward Hatcher. "Fill me up!"

"You . . . you still carryin' the Injun's skelp, now?" Josiah asked. 'Is that the one you're carryin' on your belt, there?"

"Nawww! That were Blackfoot, some moons back, boy." He raised his hands to his head and for the first time since he had met Paddock, the older man untied the knot holding the faded blue bandanna on his head. "I traded ha'r with the nigger . . . took his'n for myself." Bass pulled the bandanna off with one hand as the other wrenched around to Josiah's face, shaking a long scalp he ripped from the crown of his head.

Paddock jerked back, lost his balance, and fell into the edge of the fire. The other trappers howled with laughter as Josiah scrambled to his feet. Scratch stood up, still shaking the long black trophy in Paddock's face.

"I'm wearin' the nigger's ha'r as my own, boy!" He advanced on the young man as Paddock moved slowly away. "Few knows I be bald back here," he said, twisting his neck so that Josiah could see the neat white circle of exposed cranium bone. "You fillin' that cup, Mad Jack?" he asked, though his eyes were fixed on Josiah's.

"Gettin' to it right now, Scratch."

"Son, gotta keep my noodle covered up most time, 'specially to the day. Sun'll do a mean, nasty thing to a man's skull. So's I wear the nigger's ha'r as my own, over my lil' spot." Hatcher handed him the cup. Titus lifted the whiskey in a toast: "Here's to red niggers as knows who Titus Bass be!" Bass drained the cup, then said more softly, "I do b'lieve I gotta drip." He stumbled out into the darkness away from the fire's light.

Josiah stayed by the fire as the others drifted off to their bedrolls. So he was alone with his thoughts. Here was the man who was outfitting him with such kindness, such friendship Paddock had known only twice before. But suddenly, another side was exposed: that of a man living in a wilderness that required of him at times to be just as wild and unforgiving as the worst savage. He chewed on the thoughts for a long time. Finally he picked up an elk robe from the ground where the men had been sitting and put it about his shoulders.

As he stepped away from the dying fire, the young man felt the chill of the cool night air envelope him. He drew the robe closer around his body and melted into the blackness in the direction Scratch had gone. Staring into the inky night, he stumbled over something.

Paddock knelt down and saw it was Bass. The old man was snoring loudly, dead to the world. Titus had not even buttoned up his fly after urinating on the ground where he lay.

He watched the older man snoring peacefully for another moment, then slowly took the elk robe from his shoulders and laid it over the body of Titus Bass. The young man rose to walk back to his bed and sleep.

The sun first touched his face with a gentle, warming caress. He stirred, turned over, and nestled deeper into his robes. Josiah dozed awhile longer, until the sunlight pouring over him made the robe unbearably hot. He kicked at the robe, freeing his legs to lie a few minutes more until the shaft of light broke through the branches to aggravate his comfort. He sat up, his head spinning. His stomach wanted to come up. He fought it back down with gulps of air until he felt things were under control. Shivering slightly, he put his coat on and rose to his feet.

Moving deeper into the willows, Paddock relieved himself, then knelt by the creek. The water danced over the rocky bottom, gurgling past the stones that lay in the water's midst only as temporary detours to its progress. He put both hands into the water and brought a cold splash to his face. The icy liquid dripped slowly from his growing beard and mustache. He bent over and slowly sipped the refreshing water, then combed his hair back with wet fingers. Things looked brighter now. Then he remembered Scratch.

Josiah found the older man where he had left him the night before, tucked among the sage, snuggled under the elk robe. The side of his face lay in a small pool of drying vomit he had upchucked in his sleep. Standing over the snoring man, Josiah smiled faintly, almost warmly, before moving away on foot up the valley. He figured he would just spend the day by himself and it felt good to him to have the whole day free with nothing to do but be Josiah Paddock.

Almost without sound, he whistled happily to himself as he walked through the border of one of the large trappers' camps, recalling as best he could some of the melodies of the night before.

"Hey! Boy!" A voice called out to his right. "Ov' hyar, boy!"

Josiah looked around at the sound of the voice, then saw the squat man coming toward him. Paddock stopped, watching the stranger approach. The short heavy-set man wore a yellow woolen undershirt, and leather breeches held up by suspenders adorned with worn and patchy quillwork.

"Boy? Ya read, cain't ya?" He pushed a bundle of small paper toward Josiah.

Paddock looked from the man's face down to the paper, then up to the face once more. "Yep. I can, that."

"Hyar, now." The man stood alongside Josiah now and held the papers close to Paddock's face, his gnarled finger moving across the writing. "I cain't, ya see, boy...will ya read them words to me? Will ya, boy?"

Josiah looked back at the man's face again as he pushed the papers further away from his eyes. The man wore the look of an excited child anticipating a gift.

"I got me liquor...give ya drink of liquor, cup a liquor for readin' them words to me," he said pulling slightly on Josiah's arm to start the young man toward one of the bowers made of willow. "C'mon, boy. Get ya cup a liquor an' ya'll read the writin' for me."

"Don't want me no liquor." Josiah pulled his arm free.

"Get ya somethin' ya want then. C'mon, boy, jest read them words for me." His eyes implored Josiah to come with him. Paddock nodded his head faintly in affirmation that he would read to the man and followed the squat trapper to the bower. Handing the papers to Paddock, he set about dipping his cup into a kettle of alcohol and motioned for Josiah to sit on the robes beside him. Three others came up to the crude lean-to, followed by a handful more.

"Can we hear yer letter with ye, Stinkfoot?" one of those who approached asked quietly, almost shy in his politeness.

"Yep. Yep. C'mon now, boy. Read me them marks," the short man's words dripped with impatience. The other trappers, now numbering eleven, sat in front of the short trapper and Josiah, each crossing his legs and leaning forward as Paddock looked once more at the papers he held.

It was indeed a letter. He turned it over to look at the back of the last page, reading the address:

Ruben Lusk. in keer of Rocky.mntn.Fur.Comp.
Misstur. W. Sublett.
Ste. Luis. Mos.

Josiah turned it back over to the first page and glanced at the date in the upper righthand corner, "23 March."

"Dammit, boy. Now, start yer readin'," Stinkfoot chopped his words with great impatience and anticipation. Paddock looked up at him briefly, then began to read:

Deer brother Ruben.
Mama's hart gos out to yu & mine to with this post. we ar all fine & well & hope the same be with yu, deer brother. we cum thru the last yeer with sum bad news fer yu Ruben. i am sorry to be the 1 as to rite it but yur father dyed last novm. Took sick to hiz bed & never got up then. It wuz teribul winter wat with the plursee goin round. Mama hed a tech of the gray & she pullet thru alrite, not a famlee in the holler cleer up to flechers corner not bin teched with it. father cryed when yu went Ruben but he got better when he went back to werkin in the feelds with Sam & Mikel.
Yur brothers is werkin in the feelds now & they tell me to rite they miss the hand yu wood be with them if yu did not go west from heer. it haz bin moren three yeers now sinz we seen yu & ever body missez yu badlee ruben. Mama cryed many time cuz yu never rote the famlee wat yu waz doin or wear yu wuz. I got sum uther news fer yu. Sally got marreet to Jacop Deetz up to skunk-run holler & sally is big with chilt now. she

wantd to wate on yu Ruben but yu never cum back &
she cum to me to ax me wat I wood do with my man
gone fer 1 yeer & no werd & Jacop Deetz cum ax me to
marree him. i tol her the truuth Ruben & I wood marree
Jacop strate off & yu wuz not cumin Back Heer most
like. Mikel is marreet to Sara yu no & they have now
a nuther baby. sam is gettin biger all time jest turnt
sixteen & werkin in the feelds with Mikel he is gettin
stron as a hurs like yu waz. wether been good to Us &
the crop is gettin stron to. ever day we see Suttlers go
bye in the waggins headin war yu wint three yeers agoe.
three YEERS Is Long enuff Ruben? when yu cumin
home? Ruben? heerd yu wint west cross the rifer to the
mtnz & I don heer if yu will ever be home to see Mama
afor she passes on. preecher Sims sez Miz Lusk yu take
yur hopes to the Lord & Ruben be home afor yu go to
meet the Lord & maker. he sez yu be ther in the mntz
with all kind theefs & killers & tells Us on the injens yu
live with Ruben. Mama cry to heer yu livin with injen
wimen & all. Mama cry to hev yu a way from Us deer
Brother. Kin yu cum home now? we want ur brother
Back Ruben & yu far a way now. i don even see if this
leter get to yu in the mntnz but I pray to the Lord he will
see it to yur hands. at nite ech nite Ruben we pray a prayur
fer yu speshull. Lord wach over Ruben Lusk & carree him
home to hiz famlee. Wach over him & holt him in yur
hand Lord. give him the strenth & mind to cum back to
Us. give him strenth to find hiz way back to kentckee.
We love him Lord & want him to be a good man to. Lord
talk to Ruben & bring him home with yur werds.
Deer brother Ruben i hev sed all in my mind & post this
leter to yu. i hope it cums to YU in good hands & noin
the LORD haz YU in HIZ hart & in HIZ hands.

yur Sister
Lucy

Josiah looked up from the browned, folded paper after a
moment, first at Ruben, then the others sitting before him on
the ground. Lusk was staring into his cup, motionless as
Paddock stood and handed the letter back to the man.

"Thank ya." The trapper looked up at the young man, "I
thank ya, son." He rolled the pages of the letter
together neatly and put them down the front of his yellow
undershirt. "Hyar." He put a hand to his belt and pulled
out a long, curved butcher knife. "Want ya to have this."
Josiah hesitated. "Go 'head, boy. It's your'n, for the readin'

of my letter. I'm sayin' thank ya best way I knows how. Take it." He pushed it up at Paddock, who finally took the knife and stuffed it into the belt of his pants. A few of the men got to their feet and stood around Josiah.

"Trader's got some newspapers. Will ye read us the newspapers, too, son?" one of them pressed forward. "I'll get one from Bridger if ye'll read it to us."

"Maybe some other time." Josiah started to move off. "Some other time. Lotta news in that letter there. Read your newspapers to you some other time." The knot of men parted for Paddock as he stepped away.

"Thank ya 'gain, son!" Ruben called out. Josiah turned and waved to him.

Not far away a small group of trappers sat cross-legged on the ground around a skin they were using as a table for a card game. He approached them and sat down. Each of the men was drinking heavily for early in the day, dipping his cup repeatedly into an oak keg with an open top. They sloshed and dripped the alcohol over the dog-eared, greasy deck of cards, wiping them off across leather-covered thighs. The deck was a curious mixture of worn and dirtied paper playing cards stacked along with others made of animal hide. As a card became too worn to be useful any longer, or was lost in a drunken game, the trappers would fashion a replacement from stiff buffalo hide, then paint its own distinctive markings on the substitute, using blood for red symbols and a burnt charcoal stick from the fire for black.

"What you playin'?" Josiah asked after watching for several minutes, unable to recognize the game.

"Euker," said one of the four men, looking over at Paddock. "Wanna deal in?"

"Nawww. Jest watchin'."

"Jest as well. Don' know if any of these'r coons wanna deal out, anyways," the dealer remarked. He was referring to the fact that usually only four people played euchre, in teams of two, each member of a team sitting opposite his partner. The dealer's face was one of hard lines, as if chiseled with some labor out of the same expressionless granite of the mountains. He straightened the thirty-two cards, a deck with its sixes, fives, fours, threes, and twos removed for the game. Stone face had won the deal in the four-man draw, his being the lowest card selected from the deck. Before each player he now set three cards face down in one stack, with the same for himself. Then followed two more cards also dealt face down, but in a second stack in front of each player. When

232

this was finished, the expressionless trapper slowly pulled out one card for each man and set it before the two stacks. This card was dealt face up to indicate the trumps each man would bid on to play the hand.

The player to the dealer's left studied his trump for a moment, then said, "I order it up!" He accepted the trump card given him by the dealer.

A graying man sitting across from the dealer, stone face's partner, in turn accepted his trump with "I assist ye!" and the hand as dealt was to be played.

Josiah watched the dealer, expecting him now to speak. He did not. Instead, he signified his acceptance of the trump card by discarding one of the face-down cards in front of him, then placed his face-up card in his hand. He then turned to the man at his left, who had designated the trumps to be played, "You're 'the maker,' Thomas. Play it."

The four men began to bid and bet on the power of their hidden cards, hoping to win the tricks or at least keep their opponents from winning enough. Paddock watched the players scoop cards toward them as each trick was won or lost. As the hand ended, the dealer and his partner had won two points due to the other team's inability to score at least three tricks.

"You're eukered, Thomas!" stone face cried out happily from behind the unmoving face. From a small pile of rifle balls in the center of their hide card table, the dealer drew out a pair of balls that served as markers to keep score in the game. "That be two fer the dealer." He sat them in front of his folded legs on the edge of the skin.

They continued play until Thomas's team had won with five points, although many players set the winning number at seven or even ten. Paddock watched the fast bidding, the easy winning and losing in the shade of the trappers' lean-to. Euchre was fast becoming the country's most popular national game, played with two, four, or six players. But he soon became bored with it and left without being missed.

Josiah strolled aimlessly for a while until he noticed a noisy knot of men gathered around an Indian and his pony. Stepping up to the edge of the circle, Josiah found the trappers and warrior busily discussing business by means of what little common tongue could be understood by all, but mostly with the use of flying hands that told of words unspoken in sign language. The buck-skinned men were presenting trinkets to the Indian, who showed his approval by putting them within his pouch, or signified his displeasure by handing them back to a trapper and shaking his head rapidly from side to side.

"What's doin'?" Josiah whispered as he stuck his face up close to a trapper near the back of the group. The man turned his head around to move his eyes down, then back up Josiah's body.

"This nigger wants to show us some pony tricks. Gotta pay fer 'em, howsomever," he whispered back, then turned around as he caught a glimpse of the Indian mounting his pony out of the corner of his eye. "Musta got 'nough plunder fer the showin'."

Paddock stepped back as the other trappers began to fan out so that each man had an unobstructed view of the brave's performance. "Injuns does theys tricks fer us, if we pays 'em," the trapper explained, stepping back beside Josiah. "Jamie hyar says this Snake nigger's s'posed to be some on a pony."

The Indian had ridden off some distance from the assembled men, then dismounted. He slapped his pony on its rear and they both bolted off toward the trappers. With one hand held tightly to a leather loop around the pony's neck, the warrior bounced aboard the animal's back, sat only momentarily, then slipped off the pony's right side to bounce once more off the ground and onto the pony in full stride. As the animal raced toward the white men, the Indian straightened his leggings and brought his right leg up on the animal's back. There it was tucked into the loop near the pony's shoulders. He turned sideways on the animal and brought the left leg up, putting it shakily across the widest part of the animal's rear flanks. Carefully, unsteadily, but matching each move the animal made in its gallop, the Snake warrior rose to his feet. His legs were straightened most of the way as he came riding up to the trappers, but with his knees flexing often to absorb the shocks of the animal's gait. Just as he neared the men, who began to scatter a little before the animal's approach, the warrior pulled some on his right foot in the loop, causing the pony to veer smoothly to its right just before colliding with the white men. He circled the animal in front of the awed trappers several times, standing on the pony's back with his long hair flying loosely with the speed, the short fringes along the outer seam of his buckskin leggings fluttering and snapping against his legs.

The white men hollered and cheered their approval of the performance, most feeling they had gotten their money's worth. But the warrior was not finished. As the pony slowed its gait gradually into a tighter and tighter circle, the Snake carefully pulled his bow from his back. After he had it over his head, the Indian pulled an arrow from the wolfskin quiver at his belt. He strung the arrow and brought the animal out of its tight, slow circle to gallop in a wide loop back toward the trappers. When he was close, the arrow was set free, flying through the air until it struck the ground at a sharp angle between one trapper's feet. The others howled and laughed as the startled man jumped back.

"Nigger didn' like ya squeezin' your presents out, Jason," the man next to Josiah called out. "Must feel you're bein' stingy a might with your givin'!"

The brave approached the group and dropped to a sitting position on the pony's back. He brought the animal to a halt in their midst and slipped to the ground.

"Ya much a runner, friend?" the trapper asked Josiah as he turned away from the group and began walking off.

"Nawww. Not really. Why you ask?" Josiah questioned of the man walking at his side.

"Thort ya might'n be willin' to be racin' me on foot, is all." He motioned to a long line of men more than a hundred yards away, "Havin' 'em runnin' races, they is. If ya ain't for racin' 'gainst me, care to wager an' set a lil' on me then? I can hoof it with the best of 'em, I can. C'mon."

Paddock later wandered away from the large number of trappers and Indians gathered to compete against one another in foot sprints and pony races. The victors of each event were given their prize, a cup of whiskey, which was swilled down quickly, then each man returned to the competition to build another thirst. Often trappers would throw up, emptying their stomachs, and turn right around to drink some more.

In the shade of the cottonwoods behind Sublette's tent and canopies was a large gathering of Indians and trappers. Josiah stood with the many others watching those sitting on the ground playing a game native to the mountains but foreign to the young man from St. Louis. On robes spread in the cool shade were various clusters of activity and interested spectators standing about to watch the players in each group. It was the Indian's game of hand, a game of chance loved by the white trapper as well. Josiah knelt behind a trapper playing with one of the brownskinned dealers. He swatted at a pesky squadron of gnats buzzing around his eyes.

The Indian waited until the white man had placed something of value to both of them on the robe between himself and the Indian. The bronze dealer then did likewise. When the stakes were agreed upon by both, the

235

Indian opened his right hand to show a small piece of animal bone held in his palm. It bore the peculiar painted medicine of its owner at the ends and had been carved delicately in its middle. The trapper nodded his dark head once and the Indian closed his hand slowly to conceal the bone within the clenched fist. He brought his two hands together as he leaned his head back and closed his eyes to begin chanting, then pulled the fists apart. At this signal, the young Indian brave who sat beside the dealer began to beat on a short section of hollowed log with a stout club in a rhythmic cadence to accompany the wailing chant. As the dealer seemed to go into a trance, not really looking at his hands as they moved, the trapper kept his attention on the one hand he believed held the piece of bone, trying to concentrate against the forces of the screeching chant and the loud, ringing tones of the hollowed log. The Indian brought his hands together once more, then moved them apart just as suddenly, his arms outstretched and shaking violently with each crescendo of the chant. He placed the fists together again, one hand over the other this time, then reversed their order before pulling them apart with his arms outstretched. Over and over the movements were repeated but became more slight as the game went on. Finally the Indian ceased his chant and his partner no longer beat on the log.

The dealer opened his eyes and stared at the trapper's face, presenting the white man with two clenched fists. The trapper made his choice. The hand was empty. He cussed some under his breath and dug deep into his pouch once more for another trinket to bet in the game. Over and over he played until exhausted with his inability to catch a glimpse of an idea just where the bone was hidden.

The trapper rose and turned away from the group. Josiah sat down in front of the dealer. The Indian stared back at him a moment, then placed a string of bright glass beads on the skin between them, a wager he had not lost all morning long. Josiah then understood that he too must wager something in the game. Patting the pockets of his pants, the young man's hand tapped the handle of the knife given him by Ruben Lusk that morning. He brought it out from his belt and laid it down beside the string of beads. The dealer nodded approvingly. A young squaw stepped up behind the Indian and stood looking over his shoulder at the hands that opened to show the location of the bone for the last time. Paddock looked up at her only briefly, then back down to the dealer's hands as they closed to hide the bone.

The chanting trance began, accompanied by the loud pounding on the log, as the dealer sought the power of his medicine in this game of chance. The hollow ring of the log was disconcerting to Josiah, as was the screeching wail of the Indian's chant. But he convinced himself not to listen, that it was a diversion, used to detract the player from his concentration on the placement of the bone. He shut out the noise, putting it in the background of his consciousness, and stared at every movement of the dealer's fingers. Having concentrated on shutting the chant away from his mind, he eventually no longer heard it. His eyes watched the hands pull apart, shake rapidly, then crash back together, his mind thinking only of this practiced ability to center his attention on one thing at a time while closing the door on perceiving other activity about him. As he watched and concentrated, Josiah felt something within him saying he was going to win this Indian's beads.

The hands slowly separated before him and were held motionless. In a moment there was a crack in his concentration and he realized that the chanting and beating had ceased. He realized that he must choose a hand. Josiah looked into the smiling eyes of the dealer. With his right hand he tapped the Indian's left without looking away from the dealer's eyes. Even before he looked down into the opening palm, Paddock knew he had won as the laughter drained instantly from the dark eyes. There in the left hand was the piece of painted bone. He had won.

Josiah pulled the knife and string of thick glass beads into his hands and rose as the Indian quickly set down another wager between them. The warrior looked distressed at not having another try at the young trapper. Paddock shook his head and backed off without saying a word. His place was filled by the young squaw who had been standing over the dealer's shoulder during Josiah's game. She placed several brass finger rings in front of her to match the wager of the dealer. Paddock decided to watch this young plain-faced woman play. She lost and the young trapper stayed on as she placed a handful of lead balls down as her second wager. Again she lost to the dealer.

Repeatedly the young woman put down a trinket, and each time it was pulled to the dealer's side of the robe. Eventually the squaw sat before the Indian with nothing but her long doeskin skirt. She had wagered and lost moccasins, her belt, knife, a small pouch emptied of its trinkets, the ribbons in her hair, and the loose skin blouse she had worn. Naked to the waist, Josiah looked over her small, firm breasts that shook ever so slightly with her stifled sobs of anger, disbelief, and sadness. His eyes moved up, past her plain round face to the part in her hair that was colored with red earth paint.

Paddock glanced down at the beads in his hand, then back at the squaw. He felt sorry for her, having been lucky himself and watching her lose everything she had wagered. He thought that if he gave her the beads it would ease the pain of loss and the squaw would become happy once more, able to return to her people with something to show for her gamble.

Josiah threw the beads down before her. She lifted her face to look up at him and their eyes touched for only a fleeting moment before she picked the beads up. The squaw looked up at him intensely once more, to study the young trapper's face as she fondled the beads between her fingers, then held them against her breasts, spreading the strand out wide so that the bright red glass caressed her nipples. She stroked her breasts and the beads at the same time, the nipples becoming harder, then threw the strand down suddenly in front of her to wager them in another game.

Josiah jerked a little, involuntarily, as he saw her place his gift down for another gamble. In anger and disappointment, the young man turned away from the group of gamblers and spectators so as not to see her lose again. The ghostly forms of two women emerged in his consciousness. A French lady to whom he had given himself—and she had thrown his love in his face. And then the woman in the small room. She had had nothing more but herself to give to him, and he had taken that gladly, giving her only his anger at the Frenchwoman in return. But, that still made him warm, in this place, at this time. The nameless tavern maid pushed away the ghost of Angelique, and it made him warm to remember her giving to him. Now he had given of himself once more, to this Indian girl, and she had thrown his gift away. He sighed and touched the ribbon within his shirt. It still tied him to a good place and a good time, when he had not been rejected. He would be able to forget the young Indian squaw now.

Nearby stood a gathering of trappers and Indians, spread in a halfmoon about a trapper and his squaw. Josiah stepped up to watch the show.

". . . baddest bullwhipper, bullshitter, squaw-stripper north a the Colorady, me friends. An' I'm aimin' to show ya it ain't none of the secon't that I'm the baddest with the first," the trapper barked. Josiah moved closer to look the man over, having first mistaken him for a warrior alongside his Indian wife. The boaster had clearly adopted the clothing, mannerisms, and look of the Indian. His hair floated past his shoulders, ending almost near the middle of his back. One side was braided with a bright red ribbon and over the other ear hung hair gathered in ermine skins. His deep golden-brown hunting shirt carried sleeve fringes that trailed the ground and quillwork across the shoulders, down the chest and sleeves. From the belt that held leggings in place hung a dark blue velvet breechclout that displayed more bright quillwork. His leggings were colorfully painted with horizontal yellow and blue stripes that began at the knee and continued to the ankle. From the heels of the quilled moccasins trailed fringes longer than a foot and wider than a man's hand. Around his waist the trapper had tied a wide, colorful voyageur's sash of red, green, yellow, and blue in which he had placed his pistol, a tomahawk, and a long-stemmed stone pipe. In his right hand he held a Spanish whip, a riata, made of tightly plaited hair from a horse's tail so that it was less than half an inch in diameter. As the trapper unfurled the riata slowly with a casual snap, the long eighteen-foot snake glowed with the luxurious black sheen of precious French silk trade ribbon.

Josiah looked back at the trapper's vermilioned face, then glanced over at the squaw, whose face was likewise painted with the reddish color. She stepped some distance away from the trapper, then placed a white bone between her teeth and stood motionless. The trapper brought the riata back, then forward with a faint snap. As he popped the end of the whip, the bone was pulled from the squaw's mouth and came flying back to land at his feet.

The trappers gathered to watch the riata tricks clapped and whistled approvingly. Next the woman pulled a dagger from her belt and held it on the top of her head, the tip of the blade within the part in her hair and the handle pointed skyward. Again the riata flew through the air and bit the handle of the knife to snap it away from the grasp of the squaw. It came sailing back to land in the dust near the trapper's feet, just as the piece of bone had. Again more cheers and whistles. Josiah turned away to head back to camp, following the growth of cottonwood, willow, and tangled creepers lining the stream.

Here and there near the trees were small clusters consisting of an Indian warrior and a trapper in animated discussion, while the women gathered beside the brave stood silent throughout the dickering. The warrior had spent hours that morning preparing himself for his role as rendezvous pander, a supplier of flesh to sex-hungry white men. First had come the sweat bath, which had cleansed him of the soil and odors of the long, dusty journey to the valley. Next his squaw dressed him in his finest of ceremonial skins, then brushed his long hair until it gleamed with the shine of a freshly oiled rifle barrel. A favorite headdress was shaken out so the feathers and plumes spread to full glory. Body paint was then painstakingly applied. He was then ready to drag the women of his family out to the trappers' camps.

With wives, daughters, and even unmarried sisters strung out behind him, the Indian Beau Brummell strode through the gathered white men like a carnival barker singing out in broken English or with lewd sign language the praises of each woman's sexual abilities and excellence. A trapper might stop him and the dickering would begin. The white man would choose a woman. A price would be agreed upon and paid on the spot to the warrior. Then the trapper would lead the squaw of his choice into the willows for privacy or lay her down where they stood to get his money's worth of sexual pleasure and relief with dispatch. Josiah tried to hide his shock as he walked past such a scene: the Indian buck and two other squaws watching a white trapper open his fly, roughly pull up the fringed dress on the woman spread below him, and push his penis deep within her.

Paddock hurried on, passing by another white man who stood animatedly arguing with an Indian on the price asked for a moment's right to the warrior's sexual property. The white man protested that the Indian should be paying him to service his squaws, stating that he was the largest bull, the longest-lasting and most notorious mountain lover loose at rendezvous.

If you picked any man gathered in Pierre's Hole, you would find the greatest whatever-you-could-name, in addition to a man ready to prove just that at the drop of a doubtful word. A wide-eyed greenhorn, awe-struck at every turn, was all it would take to set that mountain man to proving he was exactly as advertised to be. At the very least, a greenhorn could stimulate a lie about one's abilities or prowess.

In addition to the public fornication and unashamed bartering of those pleasures the trapper had long done without, many squaws wandered by individually on foot or atop a gaily painted and adorned pony. These were the solitary Indian women seeking only one thing. They were in the market for marriage to a trapper. They advertised their wares with the softest of white doeskin dresses and gleaming jewelry as they strutted to and fro through the white man's camps, letting all who approached know that they were not to be taken into the willows without first something more permanent and lasting that a furtive sexual liaison. Such a squaw sought after what was regarded as the highest estate she could enter upon: marriage to a white trapper.

As the man of the mountains got drunker, the alcohol became weaker, as did his resistance to the unstated charms of marriage to an Indian woman. If she remained among her people to marry a man of the tribe, she would be consigned to a life no better than a slave's. Her husband would hunt and go to war, but every other chore would be hers: cooking, cleaning, tanning, sewing, tending children, collecting firewood, and every labor connected with erecting and dismantling the family lodge. It was a dismal life that aged her early. To be sure, she would do the same for a white husband, but her efforts would likely be more appreciated. And although there was a slim chance she might hitch herself to a trapper who would with joy and frequency beat her, there was almost no chance that she would not suffer such brutality at the hands of an Indian husband. The white trapper was well known among the squaws of mountain tribes for his gentler approach to women, be they white or brownskinned helpmates in the wilderness. And what if her white husband occasionally came home in the evenings drunk and beat her? Was she still not better off in the long run with a man who would spend his all each summer at rendezvous to purchase the finest of assorted trinkets, ribbons, and bright baubles to make her eyes shine? An Indian husband would do no such thing for her, she would tell herself as she primped and preened for the hunt.

The noise and laughter from a group of nearly two dozen men caught his attention. As he melted into the crowd, Josiah found a shady spot where he stood to watch several trappers throwing tomahawks at an immense cottonwood. The tree had been neatly stripped of its bark to expose a large white circle the competitors were using as their mark. They were involved in a match of five throws, with the trapper coming the closest to the center of the white circle each of the five attempts winning the match.

One at a time, each man walked up to the tree, turned around to put his back to it, then paced his step back to the right distance for his throw where he would scratch the ground with his tomahawk. At the lines scraped across the soil, several of the competitors had also driven long stakes into the ground. Each individual's stake was identified by a strand of beads or a long piece of trade ribbon in a particular color hung to differentiate it from the other stakes. Each trapper knew the exact distance from which he could attain just the right number of turns through the air that would allow his weapon to cling to the white bark after hitting the tree. Behind the throwing line moved others who were partial to one competitor or another, snaking in and out through the crowd of spectators and laying bets and taking odds. After each throw there was a hurried and profane reshuffling of wagers between the onlookers. A tall man finally emerged the victor in the match.

As the tall man came back toward the crowd to claim his prize from a blanket thrown on the ground, Issac Simms rushed up to him.

"Mad Jack! Ye won it! Ye won it!" bubbled Simms, his voice high-pitched with the excitement.

"Coon, don' tell me now thar' was any doubt in yer head 'bout it," he said, bending over the blanket to select his prize.

"No doubt 'bout it! Got me papers hyar sayin' we be

on the wagon for some free drinkin' over to Bridger's camp tomorrer after supper! Boys bet me likker, an' they lost." He spread a piece of paper out that made good the promise of free whiskey to show to Hatcher.

"Now jest whose likker was ya bettin' with, nigger?" he said, standing to look into Issac's face. "Ya ain't got no more notes what say ya got whiskey come from the trader, so . . . jest whose whiskey was ya wagerin'?"

"Wal', wal' . . . ye see . . . seein' how ye was gonna win anyways . . . I figgered, wal' . . . I thort it wouldn' hurt none to lay me set on the match," Issac explained, stammering.

"An' what if it was that I lost?" Hatcher raised the tomahawk into the air over his head menacingly. "Been *my* likker *I'd* lose, wouldn' it? Eh? Eh?" He advanced on Simms, who backed off slowly.

"No harm down, Mad Jack!" putting one arm out in an attempt to wave Hatcher back. "Ain't no harm done . . ."

"No harm done! Bettin' with my likker ya was, an' the man says 'tweren't no harm done by it!" Hatcher stopped his advance and bellowed his proclamation to the crowd of onlookers who laughed at Issac's predicament. "Nigger's bettin' 'nother man's likker an' don' even tell him of it! No harm done by it! Wagh! No harm done!" He shook the tomahawk in the air. "I got me notion to part yer ha'r with me 'hawk, ya scroungy coyote!" He let his arm fall slowly to his side. "If'n ya weren't so god-danged ugly already."

A washed look of relief flooded over Issac's face. While the onlookers laughed along with Hatcher, one of the spectators stepped forward to announce his challenge.

"What man 'mong ye be good to throwin' a knife?" He stepped up to the competitors' line. "I'm carin' to set there ain't a man 'mong ye what can snuff my candle come to throwin' a sticker. An', here's my wager to the blanket!" He threw a sleek otter hat to the ground among the other prizes. "What man 'mong ye make your sticker sing 'gainst the mark? Eh?" He turned in a slow semicircle, making eye contact with everyone gathered about him.

First one, then two more, and finally another came forward, each to throw his wager on the blanket. Josiah stepped out from the fringe of the crowd and walked up to lay the new butcher knife down among the other articles placed on the blanket as an entry fee. The braggart who had started it all stood looking down at the knife, then picked it up to examine it more closely. He was naked to the waist, with thick, curly hair growing over his shoulders and midway down his back. Paddock's eyes ran off him quickly as the man inspected the knife, thinking the trapper looked more animal than human. The bear of a man tossed the knife to Paddock.

"Ain't 'nough, boy! Ye play with me an' ye gotta wager somethin' what's worth my winnin'!" He looked about him at the spectators for approval.

Josiah looked from his face down to the knife in his hands, then felt the touch of a hand upon his shoulder. He looked up to stare into Hatcher's eyes.

"Josiah Paddock. Ya be willin' to wager on yer sticker-throwin', eh?" He turned to look back into the crowd. "Issac! Issac! Get yer ha'ry ass over hyar!" When Mad Jack's eyes moved back to Paddock's, the tall man whispered, "Ya any good with a knife, son? Meanin', do ya think ya stan't a chance in this here?" He leaned close to Josiah.

Paddock's eyes never blinked as Hatcher's bore into his. "I b'lieve I can win, that I do. L'arned me throwin' a knife from Frenchies up at Council Bluffs. Voyageurs, they was. Taught me some summers at Fort Atkinson."

"Harg! When was ya ever to the Council Bluffs, young'un?" Hatcher pulled his face back behind a voice thickened with doubt.

"Man as was with my father on the upriver took me there each summer for a stay with him. Four summers it was..."

"An', jest who be that man?" he interrupted with another doubting question.

"John Dougherty, he was, that man. Workin' for O'Fallon on the river." Josiah never let his eyes flinch during the examination into this piece of his past. Hatcher's eyes burned into the young man's for a long moment, then softened. Issac Simms came up to the two men.

"Issac," Mad Jack turned to the trapper, "gimmee that note what says we got likker comin' to Bridger's camp." He stuck his hand out to Simms.

"Mad Jack! Ye ain't a gonna set this down on Paddock is ye?" He pulled the paper close to his chest.

"That I am." He reached for the note and pulled it from the other man's grasp. "Playin' with me own likker, ya was, Issac Simms. An' now, I'm fixin' to play it." He handed it to the grizzly bear trapper. "Hyar, now, McLeod, ya big nigger. Is that prize a one worth the settin' or be it not?"

The big man looked over the scratchy marks on the paper, then into Hatcher's face. "Ye won this throwin' your 'hawk, coon." His words were edged with some hardness. "You're fixin' to set it down for my winnin', heh? You're fixin' to bet this whiskey on the boy, here?"

"Aye, nigger. That I am." He turned his head to glance at Paddock, "Bettin' on Josiah Paddock an' what he's l'arnt from them parley-voo pork eaters. Them's the coons as can give ya shave with a sticker from ten paces. Be a joy to me to see the lad take a puff or two outta yer fat sails!"

The big man chuckled from deep within and knelt over the blanket to put the note inside the otter hat. "Jest so it won't blow 'way before I win it."

"Lookin' to be yer the only wind blowin' hyar 'bouts, nigger!" Hatcher replied to the big man, who then walked away to the tree and counted off his paces back to the throwing line. Mad Jack leaned over to Paddock to whisper, "Go be doin' it, lad."

Josiah had stood quietly through the betting, stunned that Hatcher was wagering on him. Finally he found words, "Hatcher, I don't want you backin' me none . . . I don't need your help . . ."

"Nigger wasn' gonna take yer wager, son! Ya was needin' somethin' more'n that big butcher," Hatcher remarked. "'Sides, I ain't doin' it for ya—ain't a doin' it for Josiah Paddock at all. I'm layin' my set for Ezra Paddock . . . had me older brother as was kil't upriver with yer pa. Now, go skin that nigger, boy!" He pushed Josiah slightly on the shoulder toward the throwing line as he stepped back to the edge of the spectators.

Issac was still fuming as he stayed close to Hatcher, whispering loudly to the tall man that they should not have laid such a heavy bet down on a boy of whom they had little knowledge. Mad Jack told Issac he knew enough, and to keep his mouth shut.

Josiah stepped up to the line with the others. The big man threw first, hitting the white mark easily. Two of the following four trappers failed to strike the target and dropped out. Paddock moved over to face the target directly, drew his arm back and let the knife go. The four men approached the target to retrieve their weapons. From the edge of onlookers, Hatcher could see that Josiah's blade had stuck just within the white mark. Good enough to stay within competition, but not nearly as good as the big man's throw.

"Mark yer pace, Josiah!" Hatcher sang out as the young man pulled his knife from the tree and headed back to the line. "Step it off, boy!"

Josiah whispered low as he passed by Mad Jack, "Ain't never l'arned that way, Hatcher. Jest feel my throw." As Paddock came back up to the line with the other two men, the hairy trapper called out loudly.

"Pup here's gonna lose his friend's whiskey!" He laughed with a roar while some of the others chuckled along with him.

With the second throw, one of the other trappers failed to hit the white mark, but the big man came once again close to the center with his toss. Paddock took his stance, drew back and let his knife fly. It struck the tree well within the mark, just above the braggart's knife. Hatcher whooped and danced a little where he stood, hollering his approval.

After two more tries, the only competitors left were the big man and Josiah. The fifth time, both men again hit the mark easily. A sixth, seventh . . . By the twelfth time, neither man had failed to hit the target. Some of the spectators had gone to gather more fellow trappers to watch the competition and the crowd began to swell. Issac Simms stepped back into the onlookers to move about taking wagers on Josiah as Mad Jack grew drunker on the excitement. The two men flung their knives at the target another dozen times and both struck their mark. At last, the big man stepped up close to Paddock, some of the smile gone out of his eyes.

"Care to make it more int'restin', boy?"

"What you got in mind?" Paddock asked.

"We put a playin' card, one for euker or game of Ol' Sledge, an' toss to it." He signaled a friend of his who came up with the remains of an old deck of playing cards and handed one to the braggart. "We be seein' what man be the better now." He went to the tree, put some of the slimy tobacco from his mouth onto the back of the card, and stuck it in the middle of the white mark. He came back to the line after the tobacco had dried and threw his knife. It struck the corner of the card, cutting it off.

Josiah's throw struck the side of the card, but no closer than the big man's attempt. They pulled their knives free, repositioned the card, and walked back to the line.

"Got ye any special prayers, boy? Best ye be sayin' 'em now," the man said while pulling something from his possibles pouch. "I'm doin' my medeecin now, an' no man stan'ts a chance 'gainst my medeecin." He opened his palm to expose to Josiah two thumbs cut off a white man's hands which were strung together on a thick piece of sinew between glass beads. He stroked them up and down, "Coon as gimme these here was the last coon what thought he was better'n me with a knife, boy!" Without another word, he continued to stroke the dried, mortified thumbs while looking into Josiah's eyes staring at the crusty digits. After a few moments of medicine-making, the big man put the thumbs back into his pouch and took his stance once more.

His knife struck the card, cutting it in half. The half below the knife dropped from the tree. The other half hung precariously, held in its place by the knife blade stuck in the bark. Some of the men in the crowd cheered, seeing that Josiah had less than half the card to aim for now and with the big man's knife in the way.

"Ye wanna try it, boy?" the man asked, turning to Josiah. "Or ye wanna jest gimme the match right here?"

Josiah stood silent for a moment, looking at what was left of the target. "Man's got a right to try round here, don't he?" The crowd was quieting when he stepped up to the line. Hatcher was silent. Paddock spoke once more to the big man: "That be what it's all 'bout up here, ain't it? Every man's got a right to try an' win the big'un for himself. Ain't that right?" He drew his arm over his head and brought the wrist forward with a snap. The knife seemed to move in slow motion, as if hung in the air for an agonizingly long moment. When it struck the tree, the two men left the throwing line and ran to the cottonwood, having to push through the onlookers who pressed around the target.

"I'll be god—" Hatcher never got the words out as the men about him pushed and jostled him out of the way when the two contestants came up. The big man stood staring at the target for a moment, then looked over at Josiah. The crowd was silent as he turned once more to look at the position of the two knives. What remained of half the card sat atop the braggart's knife, so that his weapon did not actually penetrate the target. But it was no longer needed to hold the card to the tree. Just above his knife was Josiah's. The young man's blade pinned the remains of the queen of spades to the cottonwood now. His knife was caught squarely in the middle of her regal face.

"Ya say ya win?" Hatcher asked. He had fought his way back up to the big man in front of the tree.

The big man did not answer immediately. His eyes were glued to the target. Moments later he raised his eyes, searched the faces of the onlookers for support, and asked, "Well, does the boy here win or no?" No one was quite sure what the man was getting at. "Well, dammit! Ye all struck dumb? I says the boy beat me! An' slick as an otter slides, too! Be there a man 'mong ye coons as would say I'm wrong 'bout givin' him me hat an' his note to boot? Well?"

Finally a few of the men who had backed the big man began to turn to Josiah to congratulate him verbally and the big man gripped Josiah around the shoulders with one strong arm squeezing him tightly. The onlookers cheered both for Josiah and the unexpected graciousness of the loser.

"C'mon, boys." The big man began to push men out of the way as he pulled Josiah along to the blanket. "There's a hat to be tryin' on ye." He took his grip from around Paddock's shoulder and bent over to pick up the otter hat. Taking the note from inside the hat, he sat the fur cap atop Paddock's head. "Aye! Will take ye some more ha'r to fit ye rightly, lad—but I'm thinkin' with ye throwin' the knife like ye does, won' take ye long to be gettin' the big head like I gots!" He pulled the cap down fully over Josiah ears so that it came to rest just above the eyebrows. The sleek otter fur hat was a beautiful sight, with a long, flat tail of the pelt not used in covering the head flowing down his shoulders and back. Josiah pushed it up on his head a little as the big man put his arm around the young man's shoulders once more.

"Ye might be needin this, too, young'un." He handed

Paddock the whiskey note. "But, right now, yer drinkin's on me—an' Alexander McLeod's to be buyin' the likker for the winner!" He took his arm away and slapped Josiah heartily on the back as Hatcher came up with the two knives from the tree.

"Thought ya niggers might'n be needin' these." Hatcher gave the big man his knife and handed Paddock's back to the young man. Josiah stuck it in the sheath at his belt next to the butcher knife he had sought to wager in the contest. "I'd soon be in yer mokersons, Josiah Paddock, drinkin' McLeod's whiskey." He stuck a hand out to shake Josiah's, then looked over at the big man. "Ya ridin' out with Fitz come breakup?"

"Not this season, McLeod ain't," came the answer from the shirtless man. 'I aim to be headin' out with Milt Sublette an' them as is goin' to Snake country till next ronnyvoo." He looked down at Josiah, "Well, let's be movin', boy. Throwin's a thirst maker if ever there was one, an' I got me one made!"

"See you to camp, Mad Jack," Paddock said, moving off with McLeod.

"Yep. See ya to camp, Josiah," Hatcher replied as Issac came up.

It was dark when he moved south out of the Rocky Mountain Fur Company's camp. The air was chilly, carrying with it more of those first hints of an early autumn that year. But Josiah walked along loosely, warmed by the whiskey and feeling light in the early evening. Above him the darkening canopy was being glittered with tiny lights and the moon was pushing its full face over the mountains to the east. He left sounds of laughter and music behind him as he set out toward the free trappers' camp, slowly melting into a world of dim background noises.

As he stepped to the edge of the willows and unbuttoned his fly to urinate, Paddock felt the light fuzziness across his forehead and upper lip. He finished sprinkling the leaves and stepped out of the blackness toward the large fire around which were gathered shadows of dancing men he figured to be his camp. There was one man who was having a hard time keeping his balance in the whirling jigs the others were leading him in, stumbling and scuffling around the flames in drunken glee. Josiah was close enough to recognize Scratch's voice as the other dancers came to halt their wild whirling.

"... an' this here coon as come to ronnyvoo this day been one to trap the likes of Colorady waters, too, Ol' Pete is." The shadow Paddock took to be the source of Bass's voice was patting another shadow on the shoulder. "An'... an' I'm for doin' the preacher's work in the up-country, I am, if it needs be done. Niggers, let Ol' Scratch tell you there ain't 'nother dog alive this side a hell what needs the Lord's baptizin' the way Ol' Pete here does." With that Josiah watched Titus lift a camp kettle from the ground by its handle, juggle it in his hands a moment, then pour the contents over the top of Pete's bare head before the unsuspecting drunk could move away from the soaking. A roar of cheering and laughter rose from the others around the fire at the baptismal. Paddock shook his head and moved closer to the unholy congregation. Many of the shadows pressed toward the drenched trapper to offer their congratulations in profane comments on his saintly qualities and uprightness. One of the shadows knelt by the fire, picked up a burning timber, and rose with it in hand to stumble toward Pete. The shadow faced Ol' Pete, then brought the fiery torch up to set the alcohol-soaked trapper on fire. Bass and the others jumped back as the flames caught hold and grew to envelop Pete's head and the upper half of his body. They whooped and hollered with shrill laughter as the human torch darted here and there in wild, panic-stricken fear. He finally turned to run off into the night, lighting his own way through the darkness. Josiah broke into a dead run.

Pushing other drunks out of his way, Paddock bolted headlong toward Pete and caught the trapper with a flying tackle as the burning man set off across the sage. Josiah began to beat the flames out as best he could with flattened palms and the soles of his moccasins while others, finally brought to some of their senses, came stumbling up with robes and blankets to use in extinguishing the flames. One of the drunk trappers had even taken up a heavy Spanish saddle to use in beating the smoldering remnants of the unconscious man's clothing.

Paddock tried to push them away from Pete, but the men were as energetic in helping put the flames out as they had been in getting them started. Over and over the drunken men beat the prostrated body with sticks, fists, and feet. In addition, the man with the saddle, recognized now as Rufus Graham, continued to use it brutally in his attempts to help. They all yelled for one another to fetch water from the creek. Josiah pushed and pulled the men away again, but it seemed in vain. Someone hit him on the back of the shoulders with a savage blow. Paddock stumbled to the ground, landing on his hands and knees, dazed. He shook his head to clear it, then shook it again, and rose to turn on the drunk trappers.

"Next man that touches me gets his heart cut out!" he yelled out above the laughter and swearing of the drunks. "You hear me! I'm meanin' it, you goddamn stupid assholes!" The men moved slowly away from the body of Ol' Pete as the young man pulled his knife from its sheath. "You killed this man!" Paddock pushed the words out breathlessly. A stranger, a man Josiah had never seen before, stepped forward.

"I was the one as knocked ye down!" the stranger stood before Josiah. "An' I'm a fixin' to wade into yer liver, pup!" He pulled a long butcher knife from his belt. As he turned the blade slowly in his hand, a glint of reflected firelight bounced off it. One of the shadows moved out of the darkness and jerked the stranger around.

"If there's a nigger as to do any cuttin', I'm the one you're wantin', you yaller squar!" bellowed Bass's voice as he faced the stranger and pulled his own knife. "Young'un here gets what's left of your worm-eatin' carcass when I'm through bonin' you."

The stranger backed away a few steps and began to circle Titus as Josiah stepped up to grab Scratch's arm. He pulled the older man backward to the ground roughly.

"Ain't no one takin' my fights for me, ol' man," Josiah said, stepping over Bass to advance on the stranger.

They circled and feinted a few times, each man sizing up the other. The stranger made a stab at the air and Josiah pulled to the side. The young man's opponent had counted on Paddock doing just that and brought the knife flashing to the side through the air, the flat of the blade parallel to the ground. The tip caught Josiah clear across the stomach. He slapped his hand and forearm over the wound, then brought the arm slowly away to look down at the blood beginning to come through his cloth shirt. The knife had not cut through the skin into the muscle across his gut, but the slice ran from side to side the full width of his abdomen. He raised his eyes to the stranger, eyes that clouded over for a moment. When Josiah blinked them clear again, standing before him was Henri LeClerc, knife in hand. He blinked again, but could not loose the apparition from his mind.

"You're wantin' to die again, are you, LeClerc?" Josiah's words poured out full of rage mingled with fear. "One time's not 'nough for the likes of you, eh?" He tried to control the fear. Josiah advanced on the stranger, backing him toward the fire.

The man looked back at Paddock's face strangely now, not quite sure what madness had come over his young opponent. The other trappers moved out of the way as the stranger danced back and forth in front of the advancing Paddock, wondering too what it all meant.

"We make it two this time, LeClerc. Here an' now. St. Louie dyin' wasn't 'nough for you. Make your dyin' last this time, Monsur!" He moved toward the frightened and retreating man, a stranger who had only wanted a good-natured contest with the blades, a brief struggle until his opponent would give in when cut. But this young man had not given up. And he was calling the stranger by a French name.

"Ain't you gonna shoot me again, LeClerc?" he pulled his hair aside to expose the scar running along his head. "Ain't you gonna try to blow my head off, Monsur?" Josiah stopped to laugh. "But you cain't! I got your pistol, parley-voo! I got your pistol!"

By stopping in his tracks, Paddock had drawn the stranger off guard. Josiah now flexed his left leg after taking two running steps and lifted into the air. Lying almost horizontal, Josiah struck the stranger in the chest with a powerful left leg while the right knocked the left arm out of the way and sent the knife spinning backward out of the man's grasp. Paddock put his left arm out to break his own fall before the stranger hit the earth. The man had been sent tumbling backward some twelve feet through the air. Getting to his feet quickly, Paddock rushed the prostrate man and started to deliver a sharp kick to the rib cage when he stopped. He reached down and picked the stranger up by the front of his shirt. Josiah held the man in front of him a moment, staring into his face, drew back his right hand and sent the stranger sailing back once more with a loud crack as the fist crunched against the cheekbone below the left eye.

"That's 'nough now!" It was Scratch's voice. Josiah felt hands and arms grab hold of him. He fought to free himself to go after the stranger. More and more hands laid their grips on him as Paddock struggled and yelled to the faceless stranger. The man sat up, holding the left side of his jaw in his right hand.

"Goddammit! You're gonna stay dead now! I'm...I'm gonna see you stay dead this time!" Paddock was screeching, trying to loosen himself from the grasp of the other trappers who had gathered around the young man to help Scratch hold onto his new partner. The stranger got to his feet, backed off a few steps, then stumbled into the darkness, heading north across the prairie.

"Easy, goddammit!" Scratch's fingers bit into Josiah's shoulders. "Easy now, boy! It's done, it's done! Coon won' be messin' with you none now!" Josiah's body seemed to go limp, no longer struggling to free itself. "Simmer your kittle some, Josiah; jest simmer it some!"

Paddock closed his eyes tightly and lowered his head, shaking it slowly from side to side. He looked up into the faces of those gathered around him, then remembered where he was. "What? What the hell...?"

Titus was the last to let go of the young man. "What the hell is right! What the hell we niggers done?" The others were fast sobering up as Scratch turned away to take a few steps toward Pete who lay on the ground moaning. "Lordee! What's it all track? We set a man on fire...an' a coon pulls a knife on the boy here an' cuts him...an' Josiah's near outta his head...what's it all track?" Bass knelt beside Pete as Josiah bent over the burned man with him. "Pete? Hey, Pete? You hear me, coon?" The body groaned some more in painful reply.

"Let's get him over to the fire now—get to fixin' him up," Josiah said, taking charge. He directed the others to help carry the wounded man into the light. There they could see the extent of his wounds and the loss of most of his red hair from the torching. They bathed his wounds with water, then daubed them with bear grease Hatcher pulled from his packs. After more than an hour of hushed attention, the trapper's eyes fluttered and opened halfway into dark slits.

"Aye. You're back to the world, is you, Pete?" Scratch

253

cooed in mellow, mothering tones. He lifted the wounded man's shoulders and pushed a cup toward Pete's lips, but the man turned his head painfully from it. Scratch pushed the cup forward again, "Ain't likker, man! It's water, jest water." He got the cup to the burned lips, "Now drink it. Slow! Drink it slow." Bass looked up from Pete and turned to Hatcher, "You got my medeecin?"

"Aye." The tall man gave a skin pouch to Titus.

"Here, Mad Jack, you be watchin' Ol' Pete here. I'll take a lookee at young Josiah's guttin'." He rose and his place at Pete's head was taken by Hatcher. Bass scooted over to sit beside Paddock. "Lemme have a look-see there." He reached for the wound.

"Nawww. Ain't nothin'." Josiah kept his arm guarding the abdomen.

"Move your hand, boy," Scratch commanded. He put a grip on the young man's wrist and pulled the arm away. Carefully he unbuttoned the shirt and pulled it down over Paddock's shoulders so that it hung by the belt around his waist. "Awww, now. That don' look too bad—you're right there. But it do need some tendin' to." He opened the drawstring at the top of the pouch and brought out a small antler vial. Bass pulled the stopper and poured some of the thick liquid into his left palm. Dipping the fingers of his right hand into the liquid, he moved to smear it over Josiah's wound. But the young man pushed the old one's arm away.

"God! Whoooo! What's in that stuff?" He turned his head to the side to escape the odor of the strange salve.

"Jest lil' beaver milk, son. Mix it with me own roots an' such is all." He began to smear the thick substance over the full length of the open wound. Josiah flinched, his muscles twitching. "Heal you up nice, it will. Don' look like we gotta be doin' any sewin' on it, but you're needin' somethin' as to tie it up for 'while." Bass took the shirttails from Josiah's belt and pulled his own knife out to begin cutting the garment into a long dressing. "Hatch, get Josiah his blanket coat . . . yonder, to our lean-to."

With the wound covered with a thick layer of the salve, Titus wrapped the shirt fully around Josiah's abdomen and tied it tightly, telling the young man to suck his gut in as he wound the ends together. Hatcher came up with the coat and put it over Paddock's shoulders.

"I tol't 'em how ya won the sticker-throwin' 'gainst

McLeod, Josiah. Ain't many a man as can say he done that!" Hatcher looked over to Issac Simms, who had taken his place in tending to Pete. "How be the man?"

"I'm...long...yer trail...Hatcher," came Pete's voice softly and raspy through the night air, as if it were forced up through gravel from the bottom of a stream.

"Boy be good to throwin' a sticker, but he's gonna be needin' work on l'arnin' to use a knife come fightin' a man," Scratch said, then scooted back toward the burned trapper.

Not far away came two shadows approaching the fire. One of them sang out with Solomon Fish's voice.

"Josiah! Josiah Paddock, recent of the settlements!" He came closer. "Got me s'prise for ye, lad! Ye be the one as gets the s'prise this night!" Fish stepped into the light at the edge of the fire and moved around toward Josiah, who was intent upon his wound. Fish was accompanied by a young squaw each of the men examined through their glazed eyes. He stepped around to stand in front of the young man and tugged on the woman's arm to bring her to his side. "Squaw was up to Rocky Mountain's camp, she was, askin' for a man. I was thar with some coons, havin' me meat, an' this squaw comes up askin' to find this one coon. One a the niggers with me knows the Flathead, he does. He tried to get her come into the bushes with him—but she'd have no of that. Pushed him 'way an' give him a cussin' he said he'd never heerd the likes of afore. So, he asks her jest what nigger was the one she was lookin' for. Tol't her he didn' know such a man, then sent her on her way. We went back to drinkin' an' 'nother nigger asks what man she look't for. Wal', Lordee delight! If'n what that nigger said the squaw spoke of didn' sound like Josiah hyar!"

Paddock finally looked up from the dressing around his middle at the mention of his name and moved his eyes from Solomon over to the squaw. He looked closely for a moment, then recognized her as the young woman who was concentrating on losing everything in the hand game that afternoon. His eyes dropped down her frame. She now wore another loose skin blouse and moccasins with leggings that were tied around her calves. Solomon stepped out of the way so the firelight could strike Josiah's face.

"Ye know each other?" he asked.

"Yep." Josiah looked back at the squaw's face. "She

255

was losin' jest 'bout everythin' she owned to a red nigger. Game of hand, it was. Give her string of beads I won in the game, an' she gone an' wagered them, too."

The squaw knelt down in front of Josiah and began to touch the dressing over his wound lightly, then moved her eyes slowly up his chest to touch his eyes with their dark light.

"Seems like she knows you, too, Josiah," Scratch commented.

With her fingertips she started to move the arm Paddock held protectively guarding the front of his abdomen. He pushed her hand away gently, but firmly. Then she saw it. Hanging from the waistband was the wide, wrinkled, and worn strip of cloth. The woman reached out to touch it but Paddock caught her wrist. No one would take the St. Louis ribbon from him.

They studied each other's eyes for a long moment before he finally released his firm grip on her wrist. Only then did she drop her eyes from his, again to try to move the arm he held protectively in front of the wound. This time he did not resist. She took his hand and stood, pulling on his arm as she came to her feet and looked down into his eyes once more.

"Seems to be the squar's wantin' now to thank you for the present, son." Bass said, rising to his feet and pulling Josiah up with a hand under the young man's armpit. "She can be doin' more for your mendin' than any of us niggers," Bass's words responded to the questioning look Titus saw there. "Squar'll fix you up, son. Go on, now. She'll be mendin' you places you didn' know was hurtin'." He pushed Josiah slightly off in the direction the woman was now pulling him.

Paddock grabbed at the front of the blanket coat over his shoulders to hold it about him. He turned around to look at the smiling men gathered round the fire as the young woman pulled him away from the firelight and into the fringe of dark shadows at the edge of the trees.

"Best we go back here." Josiah pulled her in another direction, indicating they were to move back through the lean-tos. The women hesitated at first, unsure now that Paddock was taking the directing hand. "This way," he whispered, then took her hand gently in his to lead her among the willows and cottonwoods to the blanket canopy he and Scratch had set up.

Releasing his grasp on her small hand, Josiah took the otter hat off and sat down among the robes, pulling Titus's bedding back so they could slip beneath it. For a moment his thoughts flew back to St. Louis as his capote slipped from his shoulders and he dropped his eyes to stare at the worn strip of ribbon hanging at his waist. Josiah slipped it loose and held it across his palm before raising his eyes to look at the young Indian standing before him. When his thoughts had once more returned west to him, the trapper set the ribbon aside, draping it over the Damascus steel of the French dueling pistol. He then set about untying the moccasins.

When he had them off his feet, Paddock looked up at the young woman standing just outside the canopy and watching him. He let the blanket fall from his waist as he stood up to move closer to her.

"You ain't 'fraid now, are you?" he asked quietly, pushing her long dark hair back over her shoulders. For a fleeting glimpse of time he saw once more the gentle blend of neck and shoulder lines where he had brushed back blonde hair. Paddock dipped his head into this curve, smelling not the sweet animal musk of a St. Louis woman, but now the fragrant perfume of sage and wildflower.

He savored the natural cologne that filled his nostrils, then drew his face back from the curve of her neck. Josiah ran his hands down off her shoulders, the fingertips lightly touching the firm mounds beneath the soft buckskin blouse. His hand went on down to find the bottom of the garment. He slowly raised the blouse over her head as the squaw brought her arms up to assist him in removing it from her body. As it was freed from her, the young woman shook her hair loose, letting it settle, flowing draped over the backs of her shoulders and arms, a small fold of the black tresses falling over her right breast. Paddock brushed it aside with his lips as he stooped to kiss around the breast, then let his tongue seek out and discover the nipple. A slight shudder ran through her body. He felt his penis begin to stir from more than a year of dormancy. Its last awakening was across the river.

She took a half step toward him to press against his body, then moved away slightly, reaching down in search of his belt within the hanging shirt. He gently pushed her hand away and looked into her face.

"You been havin' it like that too long," he whispered, then gazed upon the small but round and firm breasts. He reached up with both hands to run tickling fingers over the responsive nipples that grew hard and erect under his caress. "Been broken in you've been by men as would jest as soon take an' run." His fingers kneaded the firm flesh stretched over the two mounds. "It oughtta been different your first time—no animal hot an' breathin' hard for the ruttin' over you. It oughtta been different." He went to his knees and untied her moccasins. One at a time he loosed the whangs from her ankles and gently pulled the moccasin from her foot, then tossed it under the canopy among the robes and blankets along with her skin blouse.

As she stepped out of the second moccasin, he tossed it to join the other and rose to look into her face once more. The young woman untied her belt and let it fall to the ground, then slipped her thumbs into the waist of the long doeskin skirt and pushed it down over her hips. One leg at a time, the squaw stepped out of the skirt, then tossed it beneath the canopy. She now stood completely naked before him. The woman pulled Josiah to her.

He ran his hands over the dome of her shoulders and held her close to him, feeling the slight, trembling quiver of emotion pass through her. Only then did he realize he too was trembling. Yes, Scratch had been right. He had been burying a deep pain within him. Not allowing a release. A painful piece of him remained across the river. It had been buried deep within him, festering, never healing. He turned to look down at the tattered ribbon lying across the pistol. Perhaps that deep wound would now begin to ooze its poison and he could begin the slow process of healing.

He held the young woman, feeling her quaking lightly against him, the side of her face pressed against his bare chest. Josiah grew more conscious of the stirrings within his own body that commanded his penis to enlarge and grow erect.

"We'll make it like it was the first time for you," he whispered, grasping the back of her neck gently to bring her head away so that he could peer down into her round face. The first time for a woman. He had always hoped it would be his quiet gift from Angelique. But he pushed that ghost further away with every growing pulsation of his heart now. The Indian woman was regarding him with wonder, studying the young white man who stood before her only talking while she stood before him naked, willing and ready.

Paddock thought he recognized something in the face, so he turned away to look at the dark forms rising from the plains to the west. The large soft breasts that had smelled of animal musk for him that last night across the river. So much space. So much time. Yet he still marveled at the warmth her memory brought to him. He had not been her first, but she had been there for him, when he had needed her. And now, this Indian woman came to fill a void deep within him. He would not be her first. But no matter. A release of the poison was needed.

"We'll wash all the others away tonight, an' make it a first time for both of us." Josiah cupped her chin in his hand and bent forward to touch her lips with his. She maintained contact only a brief moment, then pulled away. The woman stared back at him strangely.

"Man never kissed you, eh?" he chuckled through a whisper. Funny the things you can take for granted. The softness of those musky, damp breasts. The taste of whiskey on those warm wet, St Louis lips. "Man told me you Injuns don't go in for such things." But I need, too.

The squaw stepped away from him and moved toward the robes beneath the canopy, then reached back and took his hand in her two, pulling him down to the buffalo bed.

"Most white men prob'ly never took time to kiss you neither, have they? Eh? Jest wantin' to spread your legs an' get it over like a pony race, I bet." He followed her to the edge of the robes as she lay down. Josiah stood for a few minutes, content to gaze at her in the increasing moonlight that had climbed over the mountains to the east. The silver rays played over her body, showing contour and shadow delicately in the soft, pale light. She finally grew impatient once more and stretched her arms up toward him. He was gladdened that once again arms were opened to admit him within. But when he did not come immediately to her side, the young woman sat up in front of him and reached for his belt.

This time he did not stop her. The squaw unbuckled his belt with some difficulty, marveling at the metal apparatus on the end of the leather strap. Her interest and fascination ended, the woman sought the secret of freeing the buttons on his fly from their holes. She pulled and tugged to open his pants the way she knew the white man's breeches were to open in the front. But she grew frustrated after a few clumsy and ineffective attempts to move the buttons from their prisons. Desperate, the squaw put her fingers into the waistband of the trousers and attempted to pull them down over his hips. It failed.

Josiah chuckled again, gently. "Here. Let me show you." He took the index finger of her right hand into one of his and the thumb of her right hand into his other. He showed the young woman how to twist the button to the side to slip it through the narrow button hole. The top button at the waist was free. She looked up into his face and smiled, her eyes sparkling with childish wonder. She giggled softly at the new discovery. Looking down at the fly, the woman loosened the next button, then looked up at Josiah's face once more to smile. This was something he enjoyed—being undressed by a woman. He beamed back at her, enjoying her amusement with such a simple thing he had long taken for granted. She freed the last three buttons and slipped her fingers inside the flaps at the front of the breeches, spreading them apart so that the pants fell easily off his hips. She stared for a moment at his escaped erection. Tugging now and then, the woman finally pulled the pants off his legs and laid them at the head of the robes. She lay back down and stretched her arms to him once more, moving her eyes from his down to the erect member.

"You're jest a child," he whispered softly as he slipped down beside her, "an' ain't had no chance to grow up yet." Josiah nuzzled down within her embrace as she lay back, surrounded by her dark arms that enveloped him tightly. As he moved his hand over her breast once more, cupping it within his palm, the woman tried to pull Paddock on top of her.

"Is that all you know?" He pushed her arms against the robe. "Jest get on an' get off?"

She resisted as he again brought the hand down to caress her breast, but he pushed her arm away without much of a struggle. He kneaded the breast, then dipped his head to it. Josiah brushed his lips against the full diameter of the firm mound, then moved his lips to its center to nibble lightly upon the nipple he put between his teeth. He continued for a few minutes until he felt the tenseness vanish from her body. As she relaxed, Josiah raised his head and put his lips against hers once more. She tightened the muscles in her jaws and clenched her lips shut. He opened his eyes to look into her wide, staring orbits gazing at him in bewilderment. He drew his face away from hers a short distance. The taste of St. Louis was still with him and he wanted, no, he needed, to replace that taste with another.

"We gonna teach you to kiss a man right, we are." Josiah put two fingers to her tight lips and tried to pull them apart gently. "No, dammit. Don't fight me now. I ain't aimin' to be hurtin' you." His voice was more gruff, a little hoarse with desire. He pulled the lips apart as she loosened them for him. Paddock bent over again and pressed his mouth against hers. She kept it open for him now. His tongue darted out and sought to open her teeth. St Louis had tasted of whiskey.

The squaw resisted for a moment, then slowly parted the teeth in resignation as she had done with her lips. Immediately he tasted the mountains as his tongue wedged through the opening and found the tip of her tongue. She pulled it back at the touch. Josiah sucked a long breath from her lungs and the tongue relaxed. He caressed it with his once more, darting back and forth over it until she responded in kind, to plunge back and forth into his mouth. The taste of the mountains. Broiled meat, red, and filled with the juices of the land. The sweet tang of wild onions mixed with berries. Tastes that did not grow stale. He finally pulled away from her when he had drunk in his fill.

"I'm thinkin' you could l'arn to like that, squaw." He then bent over to kiss her again. As they pressed their lips together, the squaw drew breath from Paddock's mouth. He reached with one hand to pull her left wrist down from its embrace about his shoulders. Josiah took the hand and guided it down his stomach to the groin, then assisted her in wrapping her fingers around his penis. As she touched it, her fingers drew back and he felt her whole body go rigid once more. He left her lips to look into her eyes.

"Won't hurt you. Look." He rolled away from her a little on his side so that she could see his member as it stood erect against his belly. Gently taking her hand, he led it once more to the penis while he watched her eyes staring at his male sexuality. Tentatively, she let him move her fingers over the head of the shaft, then slowly up and down its full length. After a few minutes, he removed his hand from hers. The squaw continued to caress him. Josiah looked into her eyes, smiling with wonder and amazement, knowing that she was experiencing this touch for the first time, although she had probably served many a man before who simply wanted an immediate sexual release. Her eyelids widened almost imperceptibly every time she would feel the penis jerk and twitch with a new surge of swelling and erection.

When he sought to place a finger between the folds at the entrance to her vagina, the squaw resisted. Finally relenting, she let him touch her there. Josiah realized this too must be new to her. Most men had simply spread her thighs and thrust their member into her brutally. He realized that no man before had ever sought to touch the gap between the two folds of soft flesh in which lay the secret to a woman's excitement. Gently he rubbed a fingertip up and down the cleft, kneading the clitoris within. As her pitch of excitement rose, the squaw forgot about moving her hand over his penis, but gripped it tightly between both hands. When she reached her climax she tore her hands away from him and placed them over his hand between her legs, holding him there until she had finished shaking and he heard a faint moan caught in her throat.

He gazed down at her face as his finger began once again to slide up and down within the cleft. Josiah continued to massage as he buried his face against the side of her neck where some of her hair was bunched. Inhaling deeply, he took in the sweet smell of smoked leather and sage from her skin. It smelled so damned good to him. His nostrils filled to replace the pain of remembering. Paddock inhaled deeply once more as he felt her breathing moving more rapidly. His lips trailed down the skin between her breasts and his nostrils caught the faint fragrance of some wildflowers he had missed before while kissing the mounds. Josiah drank in the perfume as the squaw's hand pushed his faster over the spot between her legs where her attention was centered. She rose to a second climax, and a third came quickly on its heels.

"I'm bettin' that be your first of them," he whispered in her ear, knowing she knew no English, knowing she

262

could not understand his words, but knowing the two of them were sharing for the moment a common language among peoples with different tongues. She moved one hand back over to encircle his penis. "You're l'arnin' 'bout a man finally, ain't you, lil' squaw?"

Paddock lifted himself over her and slowly let himself down on the young woman. "It won' be long now. It be my turn. Cain't wait no more." He took the hand that held the penis in his and helped her guide it into her vagina. She gasped as he began to push the member slowly within the soft folds of flesh. He felt resistance as he moved his hips forward a little at a time, enjoying the tightness about the penis against the walls of the vagina. From her throat escaped brief, whimpering cries each time he advanced. Retreating slightly after each thrust, Josiah slowly lubricated the canal until he finally broke through the resistance he felt and plunged within her his full length.

She pushed her buttocks toward him, grasping his within her hands as her breath came short and fast once more. He continued to retreat and advance within her tightening vagina until she climaxed again. Josiah kept up his slow pendulum movement until he felt the blood rushing to his temples and the surge within his groin driving him to push even deeper within her. It overwhelmed him as he climaxed along with her peak, feeling himself explode as never before. Not like the others. Never like this across the river. His mind felt like shouting, but all that crept up from his throat was a low growl of long-awaited relief, a faint cry of the lost when finally discovering a familiar landmark.

He lay atop the young woman for a long time, his head buried against her shoulder, the side of his face caressed by her black hair. He imbibed the fragrances of sagebrush and wildflowers and smoked skins through the long minutes he had no desire to count. No longer was there pain from that poison he had been carrying. Only the gratitude of release.

After what seemed like a delicious eternity, Paddock heard the squaw faintly snoring with the deep breath of slumber. He raised his head slowly and looked down into her face, turned to the side. She was asleep beneath him.

Josiah eased his soft penis from her and slid gently off the young woman's body. He reached to his feet and pulled Scratch's robe over them. Before lying down, Paddock brushed the woman's hair from her shoulders and pored over her body again in the silver light. Then he turned his gaze to glance at the tattered ribbon draped over the pistol near the foot of the buffalo bed. Looking once more at the Indian woman, he now knew she was entwined with him, with the ribbon, with his deepest needs.

He dropped his face to the curly mat of the buffalo robe and sucked in a contented breath of the nippy night air. Josiah closed his eyes. He had needed this. But he hadn't known how much until now.

10

The next five days blurred together, each period of bright daylight interrupted by only a few hours sleep to prepare for the next. Rendezvous for the free trappers was peaking by July 15. Little beaver remained in their packs for trade with Sublette, who had all the business sewn up tightly as Provost's train had not made it to Pierre's Hole on behalf of the American Fur Company. Vanderburgh's men along with Fontenelle's brigade had finally given up in resignation and begun to trade furs to William Sublette for necessities only. The embittered men moved through the Sublette trading canopies in tightlipped, grim-eyed silence, buying only what would outfit them for another year in pursuit of beaver.

Josiah had awakened on the morning of July 10 to find the young squaw massaging his member. In the early light that slowly brushed over the valley before the sun poked its head above the mountains, Paddock made long and gentle love to the squaw beneath him within the buffalo robes. She had finally spoken to him as they cradled together before dressing, teaching him a few Flathead words for those objects he pointed out. He had taught her his name. There was something touched within him each time she rolled the sounds across her tongue, repeating "Joze-ze-awww" until he was satisfied with the inflection she gave to his name. Paddock had walked the young squaw back to her people's village later that morning. But beyond the edge of the lodges she had stopped him from going any farther. There she had turned and taken from her neck the small pouch she had tied at the skin blouse the evening before. The young woman had held it against her breasts, then put the short loop over Josiah's head as he bent forward. Before he could say anything more, before he could touch her, she had turned and run into the village, turning only once to remind him again with a wave of her hand not to follow. Paddock had held the pouch in his palm until he returned to his camp.

Josiah had knelt on the buffalo robes and stared long at the tattered, fading ribbon. At last, he took the strip of cloth into his fingers and stretched it out its full length. Slowly, definitely, the young trapper wrapped it around the thong at the top of the buckskin pouch and secured it with two tight knots. There was a sense of completeness with the entwining.

And now Paddock had not seen her for five days. He had looked among the clusters of squaws gathered near the trader's canopies and searched the faces of the young women who followed the warriors into the trappers' camps to be sold and bartered. In the late moments of each afternoon he had ridden to the edge of the Flathead village to seek a glimpse of the elusive plain-faced young woman. Josiah did not know her father had done everything in his power to prevent her from leaving camp to see the young white man each day.

It was past midmorning when Josiah left the knife-throwing competition near the trader's tent with a trophy won in the contest. He carried a large knife in his right hand, his fingers caressing the handle and guard. Paddock's weapon carried a second edge honed to razor sharpness that ran from the tip more than two inches back along the top of the blade. He looked down at the knife in his hand and thought that he would have to learn how to throw this heavy, deadly weapon when he returned to camp. He made plans to have Scratch show him how to make a sheath so the knife could be worn at his side when he became proficient in throwing the balanced weapon. His mind raced to camp and then brightened in remembrance of the squaw. Josiah looked down at the small skin pouch around his neck, then lifted it with a left hand to his nose. Drinking in the delicate fragrances of sagebrush and the smoked skin of the pouch, his mind went reeling back across the days to the memory of that night he had spent smelling her. Within the soft sack he had found pounded leaves of sage along with the colorful petals of various spring wildflowers. Near the bottom rested a small stone that gleamed with streaks of dark, lustrous blue and a blazing red that rivaled any sunset, dusted over with flecks of a pale yellow. He twisted the rock against the leaves and petals within the pouch to expand the fragrance as he held it beneath his nostrils.

"Hey! Hey, there!"

Josiah looked up from the pouch. A young man walked up as Paddock came to a stop.

"I know I know you from somewhere." The stranger put a finger to his lips and squinted his eyes as he looked Josiah over. "You . . . my god! Ain't you Paddock? You're Paddock, ain't you?" He snapped his fingers in front of his eyes that were cutting into Josiah's.

"Am I s'posed to know you?" Paddock looked back at the young stranger more closely now, the fingers of Josiah's right hand caressing the knife handle. "Where I know you from?"

"God, man!" The stranger's eyes went down, then back up Josiah before him. "Never did I think to see the likes of you to the mountains. Ever'one thought you'd run out!"

Josiah glared back at the man, straining his mind to attach something vaguely familiar with the nagging thought that this stranger's face was from somewhere out of his past. But, just where? "I'm 'fraid you got one on me, friend. You know who I be, but I cain't figger on where I know you from, or who you be."

"If this don' beat all! Wait'll them others hear 'bout this!" He was bubbling now. He then stuck out his right hand toward Paddock. "Oh . . . forgot, forgot me manners. Name's Keane." They shook hands as Josiah continued to stare into the face, something like a gray, filmy curtain in his mind keeping the memory faint, not recognizable but nagging him to step back and remember. "Frank Keane? . . . Name don' do it for you, eh?" the stranger continued. "I was with you with Captain Gantt."

266

Josiah's hand tightened on the knife. "Let's see—you was close to, signed up with, another man, wasn't you?" The stranger put his hand to his chin and stroked the bare skin in contemplation. Josiah's body tensed as he fingered the handle of the large knife. "Oh! Yep. You come west of St. Charles an' joined up with us, didn't you? That friend of your'n signed you up with the captain. We thought the two of you run out back east on us when we come to countin' roll one mornin'. An', here you be to the mountains! Why—where's your friend? He get here with you?"

Something like eagle talons clutched at the pit within Josiah's bowels. "Ah...no. He...mean to say...man didn't come out with me all the way here. Stayed back to the east...back in a belt, back...there."

"That be a shame, it is! Every man oughtta get at least one ronnyvoo." He reached to take Josiah's left arm in his hand. "Well, now. C'mon..." Paddock shook the hand off. The stranger jerked back in surprise. "Sorry...sorry, man. I didn't want nothin' but to talk with you—tell me 'bout how you made it here, is all. Didn't wanna trouble you none. I'm sorry..."

"It's, it's all right." Paddock stared at the ground between the two of them. "Did nothin' wrong. I jest figger there's some as are still touchy by me runnin' out on the bunch like I did, is all."

"Shee-eet! Listen, man. Many were the ones as wanted to do jest what you done," Keane said. He was looking at Josiah when Paddock raised his head. "What with times so bad, they's many as wanted to be movin' out. But we didn't know jest how bad things would get then, we didn't." Keane paused and gazed closely into Paddock's face, seeing much of the color flush out of the flesh beneath his eyes. "You all right, man?"

"Yep," Josiah replied. "Yep, I'm fine."

"Well, c'mon now an' we'll talk 'bout it. Sure you got a tale or two to be tellin' 'bout your..."

"Don't wanna talk 'bout it none," Josiah snapped.

"All right," Keane answered. "All right. Jest want you listen my story, if you want. Don't wanna pry none into your 'fairs, Paddock. You can jest listen my story, all right with you?"

"Hey, don't mind me, Keane." Paddock tried to bring a hint of a smile to the corners of his mouth, "I'm fine. Fine now. Yep. I do wanna hear your story now. If it be worth the tellin', then it be worth the listenin'—an' I'll always be a fella to listen to any big tale."

As the two men walked to a quiet, shady spot along the creek, Keane asked Josiah to help him remember just when Paddock had disappeared. With the correct time frame determined, he plunged into his story of the last nine months.

"Captain heerd the mornin' you left that you an' your friend had gone. He cussed some that mornin', the captain did, but more 'bout the horses you took with you. Well, we had a big council that mornin' afore movin' out, the captain warnin' others as was thinkin' 'bout doin' the same as you did. Said he'd decide later on that day 'bout sendin' a party back to look for the two of you. Never did, an' what a boon that'd been for that big puffed-up captain if'n he'd gone east after you! All the time you headin' west afore us! How'd you do for meat, Paddock?"

"Meat weren't no trouble," he picked up some stones between his legs and tossed them into the creek as Keane continued.

"Not long after you disappeared we come on some buffler, an' then some antelope—ready we was for that meat! Had to cross over the river to the north side in some boats we made up of them buffler skins, stretched out on a frame they was. Moved 'long the north bank, passin' days of seein' nothin' but them big rocks 'long our way . . . did you see that one that stood way up high, standin' right up in the middle of that flat country, like it was a tall chimney, like that?"

"Guessin' I did," Josiah answered, "though I'm not rememberin' it rightly jest now."

Toward August 27, Keane continued his tale, the group ran onto the Laramie River. There they camped for a few days, digging caches in which they buried goods they did not want to carry further west. One afternoon three Indians and a white man came upon their camp from the south. It was Tom Fitzpatrick, having been down to Sante Fe, heading back toward the central mountains.

The group put in a total of nine days at the camp before the captain broke the men into three groups, each of which was to search for its own trapping ground. The plan was laid to have the three groups rendezvous back to the caches the next spring when Blackwell returned with new supplies. Keane himself was assigned to the group headed by a man named Stevens, and it headed up the Laramie River into the mountains. Keane got himself lost.

"I'd been out trappin'. Got myself lost from the rest. Went out lookin' for 'em, but couldn't make where they was camped. Night come on so I figgered to fire me two shots in the air, rifle an' pistol—didn't get no answer from 'em. As it turned out, I happened onto 'em the next day. Asked 'em why they didn't answer my shots. They said they thought it was Injuns, an' they didn't wanna tell them Injuns where they was."

Traveling got rough but they soon ran onto a buffalo trail that looked as if it ran through the mountains. Following it, the party descended into a valley where it started to snow on the men. The snow continued for several days, leading the trappers to decide upon spending the winter right where they were. Buffalo was in good supply so the men were not immediately worried for food. The horses and pack animals would not take to the peeled cottonwood, however. "Damned animals starved rather'n eat that cottonwood. After 'while, only critters we had left was two ol' scrawny mules."

They passed a joyless Christmas and New Year's, then one day Stevens sat the men down to announce he had been to Sante Fe before. He wanted to head south to attempt buying some horses. Keane was one of the eight-man party that attempted to head south, leaving four men behind in the winter camp. The snow got deeper and deeper for the men traveling on foot, and the jerked buffalo meat soon ran into short supply. The eight finally moved back to their winter shelters.

There they fashioned snowshoes from what leather clothing they had and the remainder of fresh hides. Stevens had the eight men select two beaver hides apiece to haul to Sante Fe from those they would trade for horses. The two hides would soon be all there was to eat. They roasted, fried, and boiled the flesh. Then it ran out. They had turned around to return to their winter valley when they ran onto an old buffalo bull. Althought it was lean and stringy, it proved far better fare than the beaver plews.

A third attempt to force their way south was made, this time the party running into Indians and being robbed for all their trouble. The cold, starving men stumbled back into camp, having totally given up on making it to Sante

Fe. They stayed in their winter valley until the weather cleared, then headed out to the caches on the Laramie River. "Close as Stevens an' a man name of Leonard could figger it, we got back there 'round 'bouts the last of May. But there weren't 'nother soul back there waitin' for us."

The other groups never did show up. And Blackwell never did return from the east with new supplies. The Stevens group remained by the caches until Bill Sublette came by, heading for rendezvous. The word was that Blackwell had gone out of business. "That did it! Every man was for stayin' with the captain all the way out, starvin' an' nearly froze to death and that bastard gone outta business! Sublette said he could make things a lil' sweeter for the man as would wanna stay on in the mountains—said he would buy our plews an' we could tag 'long with him to ronnyvoo. We was sure to get work with Rocky Mountain Fur, he said, what with them always needin' men. So, we come in to ronnyvoo back on the eighth."

"Yep," Josiah said throwing the last stone he could find among the grasses on the bank, "saw the trader come in. Didn't know you with the captain come in with Sublette, though."

"Captain Gantt's bunch come in a few days afore we did. An' shee-eet! Jest like Sublette said, this is some doin's, ronnyvoo is. An' ever' man what wants a job with Bridger, Frapp an' ol' Fitzpatrick got one when they head out for trappin.' Sublette's lil' brother be here, too, an' he's takin' a brigade to Snake country this y'ar . . ."

"Met a man the name of McLeod, Alexander McLeod?"

"No, Paddock," Keane answered. "Cain't say as I have."

"Jest wonderin'. He's with Rocky Mountain. Headin' out with Sublette an' them to the Snake country too, come breakup. You'll be meetin' him—friend of mine, big feller he is, that McLeod."

Keane was silent for a minute when Josiah finished, then asked, "You ain't told me 'bout what your doin's was after you split out."

Paddock stared at the stream, not answering Keane's suggestion to talk about his winter's experiences.

"Paddock?" the man finally peered closely at Josiah. "Paddock, you with me?" Keane reached out to touch the man beside him lightly. Josiah jerked, caught by surprise in another place.

"Oh." Paddock looked over at Keane, then went to his feet and stood up. "Tell you 'bout it sometime, I will. Best be goin' off now . . . told 'em I'd be back to camp to . . . help with the noon meal—fix the noon meal for 'em. Gotta shoot with a new rifle of mine, too. Tell you 'bout it 'nother time."

Keane rose and put out his right hand again, "See you on down the trail then." The two men shook hands as Keane continued, "I wish you best of luck, Paddock. You made 'er this far after leavin' us. Lesser man might'n give up an' headed back toward the east—or worse, starved to death afore that. Ye made it here an' that makes me feel some good. If ever you see that feller you split out with again, you tell him I wish him the best of luck, too. You hear?"

Paddock had started to turn away, removing his hand from Keane's, then turned back around for a moment to reply, "Yep. I'll . . . I'll do that." He headed in the direction of camp, repeating the words softly to himself, "I'll do that," and looked into the trees about him to see if his whisper had been overheard.

When he felt he had come far enough, Josiah turned and looked around him through the tangled maze of willows and creepers. For the last few yards he had fought with all his strength against the talons ripping at his guts. Paddock took a few more steps along the bank, trying to fight his way against the power overwhelming him, trying to cuss it away under his breath through clenched teeth. The huge bird clamped its long talons tightly around the prey, spread its wings, and with a great rush of air took to flight. The young man could not see now. Tears clouded his eyes. He tried to blink them away as his jaws began to ache in their strain to swallow back the cry of anguish. Josiah stumbled and fell face forward onto the sandy bank. Trying to rise once, then twice, he gave up. The great bird felt its prey quiver one last time, then life pass from it. Josiah collapsed, sobbing. The tears would no longer be blocked. The wound, tearing apart within, burst and began to bleed once more.

Scratch called out to him as Josiah walked back through the lean-tos toward their canopy. The older man rose to his feet, crawling out from the blanket shelter to watch the young man come up.

"Where you been, friend?" Bass looked at him close-ly. "Didn' finally happen on that squar, did you?"

"Nawww." Josiah brushed by Titus and knelt under the blanket, pulling his shooting pouch and powder horn to him.

"Might'n jest as well forget that for this day, Josiah." Bass crouched under the shelter with the young man. Josiah peered at the older man, a questioning look behind the eyes whose red he had tried to erase away with the cold creek water. "Tol't you last night we was gonna have to be makin' it to the Nepercy village for ponies today. You been gone so long we don' have us time to be shootin' your rifle," Bass said, looking out from under the shelter to the west. "Gettin' on late now. Jest might have us time to get them ponies if 'n we hurry it up." He scooted to the edge of the robes and came out from beneath the Mackinaw blankets. Picking up a large buffalo-hide trade sack, Scratch looked down at Josiah, "Best get you two of them blankets, son. Sure to be, bring that big butcher knife 'long with you, too."

As Paddock gathered and folded the two blankets he owned, the older man asked, "You wantin' to be keepin' that squirrel gun of your'n, Josiah?" The young man turned to look at him. "Jest thought if'n you'd be willin' to part with it—that long rifle'd sure to make some red nigger's eyes shine . . . if'n you're one to trade 'er for pony-flesh." Paddock looked away and pulled the bed-ding back to expose the long rifle. He ran his fingers across the wood of the stock and forearm.

"Yep," he answered after a few minutes of lightly caressing the weapon. "I be for tradin' it." Josiah picked the rifle up and slid backward out of the shelter. He stood using the weapon to help himself up. "Don't be needin' it no more, do I?"

"Don' calc'late as how you'd be usin' it, son," Bass replied.

"Then, I wanna get rid of everythin' what 'minds me of what's left back there," he said, looking into Scratch's eyes and giving a quick nod with his head toward the east. "I'm to be a new man out here, Scratch—then I'm to shake off the old soon as I can. So, I'll be tradin' everythin' what's from back there." He bent under the canopy and picked up the pair of worn boots. "Take these here, too. You said some Injun might be wantin' somethin' such."

272

They headed toward the fringe of prairie sage where the animals were picketed. Josiah pulled loose the knot and brought the halter rope with him as he struggled aboard the dapple with the long rifle in one hand and the pair of boots under his arm. When he was on the horse's back he looked over at Scratch again.

"You understandin' what I'm meanin'?" Paddock asked.

Bass turned to the younger man from where he stood beside his pony, one foot in the stirrup. Slowly he pushed himself up into the saddle. "Think I do, son. Man leaves lot behin't back there. An' if'n he's fixin' to make the stake out here, that man's gotta shake hisse'f free of all of it. You're doin' it. Chip at a time, you're doin' it. When time comes, you can tell me rest of what Josiah Paddock was back there. When you're ready, you tell me 'bout where you been since't you come out with that bunch from St. Louie. In your own time, son. When you're ready to be shakin' it loose from you jest by the tellin'. Ain't so much int'rested in what you was, Scratch ain't. Not now." He nudged the pony away with taps from his heels. Josiah followed and came up alongside Bass. "This ol' man don' care a whack for what was. You an' me gonna make things what they gonna be from now on."

They rode in silence heading south for several minutes before Titus spoke again. "Hatcher ain't to camp no more. Moved north some."

Josiah looked over to him without saying a word. The older man kept his eyes forward for long moments before he used words once more.

"He an' Caleb been trappin' pardners too long, I figger it." Bass continued to put long slices of quiet between his sentences. "Had 'em a squabble to this mornin' what's been brewin' for some time now it looks." Paddock readjusted the rifle, waiting for Scratch to carry on. "Don' rightly know how it started. Guessin' only them two coons know the whole thing." The younger man adjusted the tops of the old boots under his buttocks so that he sat upon them rather than carried them under his arm. "They figgered to be settlin' the hash with a huggin' match—no knives—jest man to man. They wanted it that way." The pieces came slowly. "Both of 'em wore out to a thin frizzen by the time they give up on beatin' t'other's noggin'."

"Hatcher leave then, you say?" Josiah wanted to prod Bass along in the story.

"Yep." Titus was silent for another moment, refusing to be pushed into hurrying the tale. "Pack't up plunder an' possibles right there an' then. Said he was headin' to Rocky Mountain. Gonna work for them. Man said he might'n be willin' to work a trap line with Caleb Wood after y'ar with Rocky Mountain boys. Only time would tell. An' he rode off not long afore you come back to camp."

Paddock was quiet for a few minutes, then asked, "That kinda thing happen 'tween men as been ridin' together for a long time, Scratch?"

"Hell yes, son! Ain't no calc'latin' it—jest happens. Two coons get on the other's wrong side jest once too many. Time tells 'em it be best to split the plunder an' make new tracks."

"Happen to us, can it?" Josiah asked.

Scratch turned to look over at the young man. "Yep. Can happen to us, son." Then his eyes sparkled with a smile at their corners, "If'n we let it." Paddock smiled back at the older man, then looked forward. "Son?" Bass continued.

"Yep?"

"Who be this Lee-clerk feller?"

At the mention of the name, Josiah turned back to Bass. "I ain't told you that name afore, I haven't."

"Jest other night when that nigger cut you." He looked at Paddock's burning eyes. "You called that nigger Lee-clerk after he whizzed you with his sticker. Jest afore you fotched shit outta him."

Josiah turned away from Bass's eyes. "'Twere the man I killed back to St Lou, Scratch."

"The Frenchie parley-voo? What stole't that gal from you?"

"LeClerc didn't rightly steal 'er from me," Josiah replied. "Slut never was mine from the startin'."

"You kil't 'im, though—didn' you, Josiah?"

"Yep. Man was dead when I left 'im." His eyes squinted a little. "Friend of mine told me later that his buryin' was to be some big doin's. Nigger's family was big in the trade upriver. Friend told me they was all swearin' they'd see me dead for the killin'..."

"Weren't it a doo-hell—what you tol't me how you

274

kil't 'im?" Scratch asked, needing to clarify it in his own mind.

"Yep. It were. Didn't kill 'im with the pistol." He paused a moment. "Killed 'im with a beatin'. Made 'em no difference, I'm told—it bein' a proper duel. They was wantin' me dead, one way or t'other."

"All that over a gal!" Scratch clucked his tongue against his teeth. "Them womens do get a man in the fire kittle! Lordee, they can turn your innards to grits an' your meat to rock sometimes!" He paused and looked away from Josiah. "You ever come on that lil' squar as come lookin' for you that night back some?"

"Nawww. Ain't seen 'er or been told of 'er since." It took Paddock's mind back to the night and morning spent with the young woman. The thoughts of it warned him now like an ember that would continue to glow through a cold night. "Squar smelled good, she did."

"Prob'ly had to," Bass chuckled, "havin' to fight your smell." He pinched his nostrils together with a thumb and forefinger and wrinkled up his face. "That beaver milk you smear't over you to fight them skeeters don' set too good on a man's skin after 'while. An' that medeecin I put on you didn' do you no good for the lovin', neither."

Josiah touched his stomach through the buckskin shirt Bass had given him to wear in place of the torn woolen shirt still used as a dressing. "When I won't be needin' to keep it tied up no more, Scratch?"

"We take a lookee this night. Best tell you then. If you're mendin' up good, won' be but 'nother two, maybe three days an' we can take the wrap off'n you. Man mends up fast up here. But we don' wanna hurry it none too fast." He saw the massive herd of Nez Perce ponies gathered beyond the village and turned his animal slightly to the west. "We go round this way, round the lodges."

As they rode slowly toward the herd, one of the Nez Perce sentries spotted them and came up, instructing the two white men to stop. Scratch spoke with the warrior in sign language, telling the man what they had come to trade. Josiah looked over the Indian, who was reaching his prime at an age close to twenty, sitting proudly atop his decorated pony. He answered that yes, he had a good number of ponies of his own, but that he did not want to trade. The warrior began to turn away to leave.

"Lift your rifle up, Josiah," Scratch ordered. Paddock

raised the long rifle into the air above his head and caught the Indian's eye. The brown man stopped to look at it before Bass asked if the Indian had an interest in such a rifle. The brave moved his eyes from the older man to the rifle above Josiah's head, then nudged his pony closer to the white men once more.

Paddock looked to Scratch with a question on his face when the warrior put his hand out to say he wished to look the rifle over. Bass nodded his head once. The Indian took the rifle and stroked it, cocking the hammer back and pulling the trigger a few times to smile at the sparks as flint struck steel. When he looked back up at Bass after a few minutes of inspecting the lock, the warrior slapped his pony's neck lightly and stuck two fingers in the air.

Bass chuckled and shook his head from side to side to tell the Indian that two ponies would not do. "Nigger thinks he's gonna get by cheap for your squirrel gun," Scratch said, leaning forward and taking the rifle from the Indian's grasp. Titus shook his head no again, then patted the rifle and the side of his pony's neck before showing five fingers. The warrior looked down from the fingers to the rifle Bass held with a serious expression over his bronze face. He finally shook his head to tell Scratch that five was too many and held up four fingers this time.

"Tough lil' nigger for his y'ars, this'un is," Titus said, then slipped from the saddle and moved over to Josiah. "Gimme them boots of your'n." The younger man lifted his buttocks and pulled the worn footwear out to hand them to Bass. The older man patted the side of his pony's neck and pointed to the Indian, then tapped the barrel of the rifle and pointed once more to the Indian. He finally held the boots aloft and pointed a last time to the Nez Perce. When he thought the warrior understood, Scratch set the boots and rifle down, then raised six fingers in the air. As the warrior slid from the bareback of his pony, Bass stepped up to Josiah's side again, "Gonna sweeten the honey lil' bit." He pulled one of the blankets from behind Paddock's saddle and laid it on the ground with the rifle and boots.

The Nez Perce knelt before the goods offered and picked up a boot to examine it. He pantomimed putting it on his foot and Bass nodded his head up and down in the affirmative. When the Indian set the boot down again and rose, he went over to Josiah's large horse. The warrior

276

walked around the dapple, feeling and patting the horse, then stroking each of its long legs. He came back up to face Scratch. He patted Bass's pony, the rifle, the boots and blanket, then touched the side of the dapple's neck and pointed to his own chest with a finger before putting seven fingers up.

"That nigger wantin' my horse?" Josiah screeched.

Bass kept looking into the Indian's face while he replied to the young man's question, "Lookin' that way, son."

"Tell 'im he can slide!" Josiah roared back, looking down into the warrior's startled face. "Nigger ain't gonna take Lady Missoura! No way, no way I'm gonna let 'im take this horse!"

"Hush your mouth, Josiah!" Scratch never took his eyes off the Nez Perce as he pushed words out from the corner of his lips to Paddock. "Animal's worth a mess of Nepercy palouse ponies—ain't worth much more to you up here. Trade 'er for some fresh Injun ponies . . ."

"You can slide, ol' man!" Josiah barked. "That nigger an' you can dicker all day but you ain't gettin' Lady Missoura!" Josiah began to pull on the horse's halter rope to guide her to the left in leaving, but Bass was faster and grabbed the rope, jerking the horse's head to stay the young man's attempt to turn away.

"Stay your ground, son. You're the child as said he was one to rid hisse'f of ever'thin' from back there." Titus looked up to Josiah for the first time in several minutes. "If'n you're meanin' it, then the pony's gotta go. Nigger wants 'er—an' we wants us a handful of ponies. Now, you're holdin' up the trade, Josiah. Are you skinnin' yourself of what's back there, or was you funnin' this ol' man here?" Josiah did not answer. "Are you gonna be shakin' free, son?" Still no answer came from the young man. "Eh?"

Paddock looked from the older man to the Nez Perce, who was watching the two white men arguing, then turned away to look to the Tetons in the east. He sat silent for a few minutes more, staring in the direction where the lowering sun was running out long shadows. At last, he turned back to Scratch.

"Dammit." There were hints of moisture in his eyes. "Horse got me out here, Scratch. She brought me this far . . ."

"I know, son..."

"I don't feel right in doin' this."

"Horse done you her part. But you gotta let go of it all, if 'n you want it to let go its hold on you."

Josiah was silent in shaking his head slowly from side to side a few times, then slid gradually from the saddle. He walked around to stand beside Bass.

"Trade 'er." He gave the picket rope to the older man. "Trade 'er an' be done with it."

Bass held eight fingers in front of the Indian now. The warrior stroked the side of the large dapple's neck, looked back at Scratch, and finally nodded his head one time with consent. Into the Nez Perce herd the three men rode to be shown those animals from which Bass could select the eight ponies for which he had bargained. Each animal received a careful inspection for girth and saddle sores, a quick look into the mouth, and finally an inspection of each hoof. From the Nez Perce herd Scratch chose eight strong, young ponies, only three of which had the distinctive spotted rump for which the tribe was noted. One at a time the ponies were selected and a rawhide halter placed around each neck. As he pulled the animals from the herd, Bass tied the halter to a long stretch of rope in which he knotted loops so that the ponies would be strung out in a line to be taken back to the trappers' camp. When the eighth was hitched to the rawhide harness, Scratch and Josiah removed their saddles and put them aboard the animals each man had chosen to ride. Paddock finished tying the two blankets he had not traded to the warrior behind the saddle and stepped over to hand the Nez Perce the halter around the dapple's neck.

The Indian took the rope and beamed at the white man. Josiah took in a long breath and put his arm over the animal's neck. He stroked its forehead with his other hand for a few minutes as the older man and the Nez Perce looked on. Josiah finally spoke when he pulled himself away from the horse and moved to climb aboard a pony with a spotted rump.

"C'mon, ol' man. Let's be leavin' now."

If a mountain man were asked to make a choice between his pony and a full-time night-woman squaw, the choice would be simple. Few men, if any at all, would choose the squaw. The price asked for horses in the mountains was high, often more than twice as much as good horseflesh would cost a man back east. But out here where the horse was the prime object of the Indian's way of life, the central support of the red man's daily life, a white man being acculturated into that Indian lifestyle came to depend upon his animal just as dearly as the red. A good pony made it easier for the trapper to make meat for a pinching belly. A good pony carried him over the rough, barren landscape quickly into the gardens of each Rocky Mountain valley. And most of all, a good pony would serve his master as sentry and transportation when it came down to those times when Indians were wanting to cut the trapper's hair a little too closely. Unlike the earlier fur trade on the upper river when men rarely moved away from the water courses, the scope of the beaver hunter's life had now changed, requiring him to plunge deeper and deeper into the recesses of the mountains, to go where no keelboat and often no canoe or dugout could travel. The horse came to mean life to a trapper, and many a man's success or failure depended in large part upon the animal between his legs.

Bass and Paddock did not talk as they led their ponies through the maze of Nez Perce lodges. When Titus recognized McAfferty's lodge, he pulled up, slowing the easy pace.

"Most times rather have me a good pony under me than a good-forkin' squar," Bass said as he slid to the ground. "Halloo! McAfferty!" Titus sang out.

Asa lay stretched on the ground in front of his lodge, his white head nestled on the Nez Perce squaw's lap. She was slowly working over his head, parting the hair in small creases in search of lice. As she found one, the squaw pulled it off the scalp and put it between her teeth. The woman cracked each vermin and threw it aside, then searched for more. Asa opened his eyes to see Bass standing before him. As he put the hook over the squaw's busy hands at his white head, the short man took his shoulders from the woman's lap. He looked from Scratch up to Josiah and quickly down the string of eight ponies.

"Been tradin', I see." McAfferty pursed his lips as he got to his feet to walk along the line of Indian ponies. He looked closely at each one, then strolled back up to Bass. "How bad he take ye?"

"This child's sayin' the nigger didn' get me 'tall." Bass then nodded to Josiah. "But, the young'un had to trade the big animal he come out on. Brave wanted that horse bad. Josiah might say we didn' make a good trade . . ."

"Young Josiah'll soon be l'arnin' the worth of ever'thin' out here soon 'nough," McAfferty interrupted. "Don' take long for a lad till he's got it all in its place proper up here."

"Your squar wrappin' up on them skins for the boy?" Scratch asked.

Without answering immediately, Asa turned to the Nez Perce woman. They spoke briefly before she went into the darkness of the lodge to continue her work on the garments.

"Says she'll have 'em ready for Josiah the next sun." Asa moved closer to the young man still sitting on horseback. "Ye try to talk the lad outta that fancy saddle, Scratch?"

"No, haven't," Bass answered. "Not as yet, anyways."

"Oughtta get the young'un a good mountain saddle." He looked up to Paddock, "Do ye much better. Lighter, too. Injuns cut the frame outta strong wood, then take a piece of wet buffler hide and stretch it over the frame. Sew it up. When it dries, the hide whitens up as it stretches. Then ye jest throws a blanket over it an' ye got a Injun mountain saddle." He patted the rump of Paddock's pony and stepped back over near Scratch. "Ye might'n even get ye greaser saddle as Bass has." Josiah turned to look at the older man's saddle more closely. The wood frame had been strapped tightly together with wet rawhide thongs that, when dried, cemented each piece of the frame to the others. Over the whole frame then was placed the mochila, a large, square piece of leather thick enough for boot soles. A slit in the rear of the leather drape allowed for the cantle while a hole in the front slipped over the low, saucer-shaped saddlehorn. From the rear of the cantle there dropped to each side a small saddlebag sewn to the mochila along its wide skirt. In one of the bags, Bass carried a long piece of hemp rope he used for picketing the animal in the mountains. Wolves would chew through the leather rawhide halters but refused to touch the hemp. Beneath the large, wooden stirrups with flat bases wide enough to be comfortable to moccasined feet was the single horsehair cinch that held the saddle to the animal's back.

"Where a man come on a saddle like that'un up here?" Josiah asked with a hint of cynicism.

"Man don', up here," Scratch answered. "Gotta take you to Taos to fix you up with such as that."

"Mine'll do till then," Paddock commented wryly. "Ain't made my ass sore."

"But the bitter water did," Bass chuckled.

"Josiah run on some bad water, eh?" Asa chuckled lightly along with Titus and stroked his beard with the crude hook.

"Oh, he live't through it all right," Scratch replied, "an' he's willin' now to be l'arnin' by his wrongs."

"Well, now," McAfferty pursed his lips between the white beard and mustache, "ye laddees are to be comin' to supper with me the next evenin'. Time'll be that Josiah's new clothes are ready an' I'll have the woman pick us a plump lil' pup for the dog-feast celebratin'. What say ye, Scratch?"

"Do sound like some way to do it up right!" Scratch answered, then turned himself to Josiah. "That fit with you, son?"

"Dog?" he swallowed a little. "Ain't never et dog."

"You be in for a treat, then, young'un," Bass said, and looked back at McAfferty. "You see us the next night, then. Comin' on sundown time." Scratch moved off to climb aboard his pony. "Dog is some fine doin's, Asa! We'll be doin' things up right for the boy here, won' we? Proper victuals for puttin' skins over a man's back," he said, winking at McAfferty.

"Said I'd do the skins for the ol' days. Let ye have 'em for Josiah," Asa replied to Bass. "Skins for nothin', Titus." His merry eyes winked once more at his older friend.

"I do b'lieve you're on the track," Scratch replied.

"See ye then, Josiah!" McAfferty slapped the spotted pony's rump with his hand and stepped back to wave the hook in the air at the two men as they pulled out of the Nez Perce village.

It was some time on their journey back to camp before Scratch finally spoke. "Tomorrer, Scratch'll want you to be puttin' least twenty-some balls through that Henry. You ain't shot it this day, like I been havin' you do ever' day. Twenty-some ball tomorrer, Josiah. By that time, this child should be happy with your shootin'. I'm wantin' that ball to be goin' where your eye's lookin' ever' time. You're gonna smell nothin' but burnt powder tomorrer, son. Nothin' but burnt powder."

"Good evenin', gentlemen," the short, white-headed man called out as Bass and Paddock rode up and dismounted. "A fine evenin' it be too."

Josiah and Scratch tied their ponies up to the stakes holding down the McAffertys' lodge cover, and sang out their own greetings in the deepening purple light of sunset. Asa came up to the younger man and put the hand on his shoulder.

"Me son, let me be the one to show you what's in the kettle this night. This be the feast fit for the savage beast, dog." He directed Josiah to go before him into the lodge. Scratch brought up the rear. "To be more rightly, you will sup this night on a pup," standing near the center of the lodge, he smiled at his own little rhyme. "Me squar, the new Mrs. McAfferty, is one what we owe our thanks to. This late afternoon, she made her journey through the camp, catchin' this pup an' that, feelin' an' pinchin' each one she got 'tween her hands—all to check it for bein' plump an' grease-fat for this feast. When she'd found a pup almost too fat to walk, my wife placed a rawhide cord round its neck an' hung the critter from the smoke-flap pole outside. There it hung till all life'd slipped from its young body. Ah, 'For they shall soon be cut down like the grass, an' wither as the green herb,' so the Word says. It was with the cry of the devil that this pup wailed—most pitiful, most pifitul. Whilst the pup was sucking its last breaths, the lil' Injun chil'ren come round an' laughed merrily at its doom. Nary 'nother dog could be found near our lodge whilst all these goin's-on, for it look't to be each one knew jest what was happenin'.

"In less time than it takes the sun to travel far 'cross the sky, me squar took the pup from its deadly noose an' set it here on this fire." Asa now pointed to the fire at their feet near the center of the lodge. "There she kept a constant eye to turn the pup all the time, this done till all the dog's ha'r was burnt off. This poor animal was then cleaned in a kettle of water from the creek an' its head rightly taken from its body. She has dressed it out, cut it up, an' put it back to the kettle over the fire there to boil. It looks now to be close to eatin' ready—been cookin' for some three hours now. I've sent me wife to her pappy's an' she'll not return till I go for her. So, ye see, Mr. Bass an' meself are needin' a likely lad to be servin' this fine meal to us, as I have me no squar hyar to do it. Young Josiah, ye be the lad for the squar this night." Asa directed Scratch with the short arm to sit at his right side upon the robes near the fire. Josiah watched the two men sit and moved to McAfferty's left to take a seat.

"No, young Josiah." Asa moved to prevent him from sitting on the robes. "Ye are to be the squaw this night an' ye'll not be sittin' with the men, Mr. Bass an' me."

Josiah's eyes flashed from Asa to Scratch. "Well, what you want me doin' in your lil' funnin' . . .?"

"Boy!" Scratch interrupted sharply. "This here ain't no funnin'. A squar don' talk to a man less'n he asks her to talk. She don' even raise her eyes to him less'n she has to. McAfferty'll tell you what's to be done."

Josiah thought it best to play along with the older men in their game with him as the butt of the joke. He slowly lowered his eyes and bowed his head slightly.

"I find your words right, me friend," Asa commented, "an' we best be gettin' our supper goin' afore we puts this young'un in a blue fume!" He pointed to the opposite side of the lodge, "Over there, ye'll be findin' two pieces of hard buffler hide, 'bout this big. Fetch 'em an' bring 'em to the fire. They be the plates for Mr. Bass an' me."

"Gettin' fancy an' foofaraw, you be, McAfferty," Scratch responded, "puttin' dog on such as a plate."

"These be Injun plates, me friend." Asa watched the young man find the pieces of stiff buffalo hide, each about the size of a large serving platter. These he brought over to the fire and set them on the ground. Paddock waited to be told what to do next.

"This squar might not be the beauty to drive your savage breast to feelin' the fires of hell, Mr. Bass," he looked sideways at Titus, "but she knows to keep her tongue quiet. Pull ye out some pieces of that dog in the kettle, young'un—put some on each of them hides an' bring 'em over here."

Josiah put his hand into the still warm water, immediately pulling his hand back out. Tentatively he stabbed at the water with his fingertips a few times before being able to plunge his hand in to grab the floating pieces of meat from the kettle. Upon each of the buffalo platters, Paddock placed two pieces of the smooth, mushy dog meat. To his touch it felt almost like handling the stomach or intestines of the game he had gutted. But this revolted him. Josiah swallowed hard as he bent over the kettle at the side of the fire, fighting back his stomach's threats to twist and come up. He felt sickened with his empty stomach, not having eaten all day in preparation for this meal. And now he knelt over the kettle by the fire. The front part of his body and face burned with the heat from the embers. His nose, directly over the odors, occasioned thoughts of vomiting. And his back was chilled and cold from the breeze floating freely in the doorway. He picked up the first platter and stood to take it to the men.

"That don' look like'n 'nough to feed this hungry man, squar," Scratch remarked. "That 'nough to be feedin' you, McAfferty?"

"I'm thinkin' not, Mr. Bass," Asa was quick to answer. "Put more of that dog to each plate, young'un."

Josiah knelt again over the kettle and pulled more pieces of the slimy meat from the warm water. When there were but two small pieces left within the pot, McAfferty spoke. "That be lookin' better, squar. Now bring the feedin' to the men of this lodge."

He took first one platter to McAfferty then the second to Scratch. Each man placed it across his folded legs and began to eat as Josiah sat back by the fire. The young man watched the men tear meat from the bone ravenously, every now and then wiping greasy hands across their clothes or through their long hair. Asa would stroke the hook over his right thigh after every few bites before diving back into his meal. Not a word was spoken while the meal was consumed. As each piece was finished, the diners would throw the stripped bones out the door where they would be snatched up by dogs more fortunate than the plump puppy. On and on the men smacked their lips loudly, licking their fingers frequently, until Josiah's hunger returned in full. He watched them closely when they were intent upon their meal and paying no attention to him. His empty stomach growled, ordering him to feed it. Gradually, each man finished what he had on his platter. All the bones had been thrown out the doorway. McAfferty ran his left index finger over the stiff buffalo-hide platter and licked it, smacking greedily until he had cleaned his own plate. Bass followed suit. Josiah's stomach roared its hungry protests now. He quickly looked away from the two men as they raised their eyes to gaze at him.

"Tol't ye a squar don' say a thing, young Josiah," MacAfferty barked.

"It's talkin' more'n the boy has all day, Asa," Scratch added.

"Be ye full-up, Mr. Bass?"

"B'lieve I've found my set, McAfferty. B'lieve I'm set to that meal," Titus answered. "Dog is some fine doin's, it is. Your wife she makes some fine victuals, she does."

"If'n ye be full-up, then the squar can be eatin' now." McAfferty looked over to Josiah. "Go on, squar. It be your turn to eat. Go ahead now."

Refusing to lift his eyes to look at the white-headed man, Josiah also fought the impulse to let a glimpse of a smile cross his face. Slowly he moved his hand over the kettle and chose between the two small pieces of dog meat left within the pot. The shiny, slimy meat was slippery to hold between his fingers as he brought it to his lips, trying all the time to look as little as possible at the nauseating appearance of his dinner. Conscious that he did not want to appear to be too eager in his appetite, Paddock took a small bite. He chewed slowly, running his tongue back and forth over the meat he was masticating. It was not exactly a foreign taste. Nor was the taste anywhere near as revolting as the appearance of the meat. He pulled as he chewed, attempting to place a mental finger on the peculiar flavor of the boiled canine. It had a certain relish to the taste, and was delicate without being bland. The meat had a slight savor of sweetness—that's when he touched the memory with the finger. It reminded him of squirrel. Yes. The squirrel eaten in his early childhood with his mother and her sister's family. He finished the first piece without letting his mouth enjoy its part of the meal, sending the meal pulled from the bone quickly down to satisfy the yawning pit in his stomach. Josiah put the clean bone on his bare thigh, then reached into the pot to grab the last piece.

"Throw your bones out the lodge, squar. Dogs'll clean up after ye," Asa said.

The young man tossed the bone out the doorway and dove greedily into the second morsel. He ate more slowly, however, wanting it to last; it was to be all the dinner he would get. When he had thrown the bone outside, Josiah licked the slimy grease from his fingers, then brushed them across the growing beard wrapping his face.

"I do feel me the need of some coffee," Asa remarked, then turned his eyes to Bass. "Ye be likin' some to wash your supper down?"

"Yep," Titus replied. "I could do with it."

"Aye." McAfferty looked back to the young man near the fire. "If'n the squar'll look, she'll see the pot 'side the fire. It's been cooked, squar, an' ye'll find us cups over there." He pointed to a group of parfleches and bundles across the lodge. Paddock rose from the fire and went over to kneel among the baggage. He found two pint tin cups quickly but continued to rummage through the leather cases.

"Only got me two cups, squar," Asa commented. "What ye lookin' for there?"

"Lookin' for 'nother cup. There be three of us. Why you only got two cups?" Paddock asked without turning around.

"Ain't got but need of two, squar," McAfferty responded. "Only two be drinkin' coffee this night. Squars don' get coffee."

Josiah rose and turned quickly to return to the fire as Titus chuckled along with McAfferty. He poured the dark liquid from the pot that had been set at the edge of the coals to simmer just near boiling after its brewing was completed before the two guests had arrived. The first cup he presented to Scratch.

"Nawww! Squar, don' you know your propers?" he barked at Paddock. "Host of the lodge gets the first cup!"

Josiah scooted still bent over to hand the cup to McAfferty, then went to the fire for Scratch's. The two older men blew and drank their coffee in silence for a few minutes after Paddock had made himself as comfortable as he could on the dirt close to the glowing embers.

"Mr. Bass an' me needin' more coffee," McAfferty directed.

The light was very dim as he threw some wood onto the coals and picked up the two cups to refill them. Bass leaned back and filled his pipe bowl as McAfferty pulled a flat rock to his side, then lifted it carefully between hand and hook to set the stone between his folded legs. Paddock set the steaming cups of coffee before the two older men. As Titus pulled a small twig from the coals to place it over the pipebowl, Asa took a wide, heavy knife from the quilled sheath at his left side.

"Lemme have a lookee at your sticker there, McAfferty," Scratch requested between puffs to ignite the tobacco. He tossed the twig back to the fire and took the knife that was handed to him. "Got me one as is jest like this'un here. Took it off Blackfoot nigger as was fixin' on countin' coup on me." Titus turned the blade and bent his head over the metal so that he could look more closely at it in the growing light from the rekindled flames. Near the handle was engraving he recognized: the initials "H.B.Co." enclosed within two small, antlered deer. "Mine be Hudson's Bay, too." He handed it back to Asa. "How'd you happen on it?"

McAfferty took the knife from Titus and was silent a brief moment. "Got it west to the big salt ocean." He said no more and fell into silence again. Scratch did not push the subject but went back to drawing on the pipe. Asa drew the edge of the knife across the flat rock slowly in the same direction time after time within the silence surrounding the three men. He always kept the top of this favorite sharpening stone soaked in hot bear grease, which improved the edge he could put on a blade.

"Would like you to tell the boy what man Asa McAfferty be." Scratch's words finally broke the long quiet. "Want you to tell him lil' 'bout your life, Asa—if'n you'd be to it."

"Aye," McAfferty responded slowly. "You're knowin' I'm always one to tell me life, Titus Bass. Boy's needin' to know what man it is he be makin' him the trek north to Three Forks, I s'pose." He lifted his cup to his lips and blew on it before drinking. As he sat it back down by his left leg, Asa looked over to Josiah. "Best ye move that pot closer to the coals now. It's gonna be gettin' col't afore ye know it. Keep it warm."

Paddock scooted the coffee pot into the edge of burning embers, almost knocking the top from it. He caught the top in time and set it in its place on the pot.

"Squar wantin' to know 'bout McAfferty, is she?" He looked back up at Josiah. The young man caught himself nodding his head in answer to the question directed to him as a squaw. "Well, McAfferty was begatted an' born in '94. That makes me an ol't man by some ways to lookin'

287

at it—a young'un by others. I be full-blooded Scot, I am, an' most proud of that—though I was born this side of the east ocean. Me pappy come over in '89, he says it were. Pappy always said he got here when this country got it first president. Brung him his wife an' three boys over here then. Two girls an' me was to come 'long later on. Moved out, right off, to get into the wild to be tradin' axes, blankets an' such as that to Injuns for skins. Simple life it was, but a good one too for him an' me mother.''

Asa went on to describe the moving of his family west from North Carolina to the "Cape" west of the Missouri River at a time when few white men had ventured that far to settle the land. He told Josiah how he had come to learn both reading and writing at his mother's knee, from the Bible, every night after supper. In 1810 his father moved the family on west to the Little White River, St. Louis being a good week's ride east of their little settlement.

"The next y'ar, when I was seventeen—I remember that—that was the y'ar the ground shook under me feet. The shakin' started off early to the mornin', afore the sun even come up. I woked up, me pappy yellin' at me, 'Asa! Asa! Get up, boy! Fetch the dogs. They under the floor after a coon, boy! Fetch 'em out!' Me pappy thought the rumblin' an' roarin' come from the dogs chasin' a coon critter under our cabin. When we all got up, we could haar the dogs outside the place, howlin' an' yowlin'. Pappy knowed right then it weren't the dogs under the floor. The ground was shakin' an' rollin'. We got to our knees an' went to the Lord in prayer. For, 'Thou art my hiding place; thou shalt preserve me from trouble; thou shalt compass me about with songs of deliverance.' Me mother started to sing 'Shall We Gather at the River' an' me pappy's prayin' loud. Trees outside was shakin' an' big limbs was breakin' off. Nigh all day it gone on: the house shakin', me mother singin' with me pappy an' me prayin'. We all was 'fraid the world was comin' to judgment right on that track, that very day. Got tired of it after 'while, I did: ever'body wailin' an' whinin', me sisters cryin' loud. Fin'ly tol't 'em if the world was comin' to judgment an' was to see us all swallowed up, there 'tweren't a thing I could do 'bout it. Close to the sun goin' down, it all come to a stop an' nothin' didn' shake no more. Me pappy an' mother said it was sign of what she'd been thinkin' 'bout me—thinkin' I was to be a preacher. I said there was no such sign to that!

"But come later on that y'ar, we had the big comet star come over, a big burnin' star flyin' 'cross the heavens. To this'r child that was sure sign. Best ye'd ever wanna read. Put up there by the Lord tellin' me he wanted me for his callin'. I set me stick right then an' there on preachin'."

By 1816 Asa McAfferty was out preaching. He put up a small cabin and took in a wife. "That lady was some." Asa sounded a little wistful now. "Rebekka Suell, the oldest of nine children in 'er family. We was livin' off a small garden she'd tend to with me doin' some huntin' from time to time, 'long with what me lil' congregations give us 'long the circuit I'd ride."

He never laid a claim down on his landholding, however. In 1819 two jumpers came in and filed on McAfferty's land; the government backed the interlopers and threw the Scotsman out of his home. That seemed to have done it for Rebekka. She pulled out on Asa about the same time and he set to drifting. He preached where he could, picking up a meal here or there, sleeping in the woods or in some man's animal shed. He forced himself through those times, alone.

Asa grew quiet as he stopped the dagger blade from its track across the flat stone. With his hand he pulled a piece of thick, smooth leather to his lap and put it across the right thigh. McAfferty pulled the blade back and forth across the leather strop in a steady rhythm, feeling it yank slightly in his left hand each time, knowing the strop was doing its job on the large blade.

"By '21 I'd wandered back up close't the Missoura settlements. I weren't of much earthly good by then, when I heerd a man speakin' of a feller named McKnight. This McKnight sounded like a right proper Scotsman to me. He an' a feller name of James fixin' to lay beaver for the greaser country, they was. I was one as no longer had me a home in them settlements, an' I'd wearied of the dishonest an' faithless in men. Asa was one leavin' nothin' behind back there, settin' off to greaser country. I had me no wife, had me no fields. An' me flocks seemed not to take me warnin's of the devil's work to heart, they didn't. Aye. Asa McAfferty was a lad ready for the west: where a man need not to lay down a claim, an' where a man is dependin' only upon the Lord an' mayhaps 'nother man for his salvation from day to day." McAfferty began to work on the other edge of the knife. By 1824 McAfferty joined up with a John Rowland down in Taos. forming a loose-knit group of free trappers. Rowland, being a Welshman, and Asa took to each other right off. The group wandered north from Taos and trapped for over two years before ending up near Aricara country in 1826. "Them critters never took to a white man."

Asa halted the knife and looked up at Josiah to continue his story. "We was layin' set up to that Ree country an' got happened onto a big war party of them critters, comin' back from fightin' them Sioux on down south. They was all fired up from countin' lotta coups an' wantin' to do some tradin' with us, they said. We saw us no way but to trade with 'em. Night come on an' us fellers all gathered up round our fire to the edge of that Ree camp, ever'one of us ready for what be comin', knowin' Rees be good ones for ha'r stealin'. *'Though a host shall camp 'gainst me, me heart shall not fear. An' now shall me head be lifted up 'bove me enemies 'round 'bout me. Deliver me not over unto the will of me enemies.'* I was doin' some bit of prayin' an' readin' from the Book that night. This ol' feller, a Ree medeecin man, come up to me, sayin' he wants to talk with me 'bout me Bible, personal-like. I go off a ways with him an' that feller jest wants me Bible! Says he wants me medeecin. That red devil was not to get me Bible, he weren't. Tol't me then he'd have it by mornin' the anyways—'long with me skelp hangin' to his medeecin bundle. I come down to havin' to part his ribs with me knife when he gone an' struck out at me with his 'hawk. That red devil was dead when I look't to him. That fix was a fine one, it was, for this knave. Shakin' like the tremblin' earth come the judgment day, I creeped back to them other white fellers an' tol't 'em quiet what'd happen't. Tol't 'em what them Rees was gettin' blackened up for. Them fellers jest look't an' look't at me with the queer on their faces. Rowland fin'ly tol't me what they was all seein' at on me. Said me ha'r was white. I'd be damned for the crucifyin' if it weren't the true thing. Lord turn't me ha'r white! Sign it was for this man that I wasn't to be messin' round thar no more—sign 'bout killin' that Ree medeecin man."

His hair was some big medicine for the other trappers, so they all crawled out of that country before first light. It was not long before McAfferty split off from the others. "I liked the lonesome, I did. Been like that for the most part—on me own 'ceptin' when I run on this slave of the devil name of Titus Bass, here. *'The Lord bringeth the counsel of the heathen to nought: He maketh the devices of the people of none effect.'* That be jest 'bout it, young Josiah." McAfferty rose to put the knife back into his belt. As he sat back down, the man stretched out, pulling a bow out of his way with the hook.

"You say you l'arnt to handle that purty good, eh?" Scratch asked, pointing to the bow with the stem of his pipe.

"Aye," McAfferty replied, "that ye might say. Still I carry it 'long with me. Might be need of it from time to time."

"I put a ball out there better'n you put your arrer," Bass remarked as he adjusted himself more comfortably.

"That might be right," the white-headed man contested, "but it be not much better a distance than this here bone bow. An' ye know for the sure an Injun can load an' get five arrers or better in the air afore ye reload, aim, an' touch off that rifle of your'n."

"That be the true," Titus stroked at his beard with the stem of his pipe, looking into the flames. "Best you keep your lil' Injun doin's, Asa." He knocked the ashes from the bowl and began to refill it with fresh tobacco. "Rifle shoot center out some past a hunnert yards, she will— kep' like new, she will. Aimed by a man in no hurry that rifle will shoot center, she will. Up to couple hunnert yards that rifle can kill, maybe more'n that."

"For the matter of it, an Injun good with a bow can kill up to couple hunnert yards, Bass," McAfferty said, still pushing the question.

"Takes me only count of twenty to ram ball home, aim, an' touch 'er off . . ."

"An' in that time ye'll be lookin' like a porky wearin' arrers fired off by an Injun as can shoot five to your one ball," Asa interrupted. *" 'But God shall shoot at them with an arrer; suddenly shall they be wounded . . .' "*

Josiah had gotten to his knees to attempt refilling the tin cups with coffee. As he pulled the heavy pot toward him across the embers, the young man tipped it slightly and the liquid bubbled out the top and spilled onto the

291

coals. At that instant, Asa interrupted his verse, dropped the bow, and grabbed the edge of the buffalo robe to pull it over his head. He bowed his covered head to the ground and was silent for long minutes. Bass was quiet too, looking from McAfferty to Josiah, who was fighting the smoke to refill the cups from the hot coffee pot. The white-headed man finally spoke when he pulled his head out of the robe and glared at Paddock.

"Squar to be more careful now!" his voice had as sharp an edge as the knife he had been whetting.

"Jest a might messy," Josiah answered testily. "Ain't no harm done."

"Ain't no harm done by it, boy?" Asa shot back. "Them ashes raised up by a boilin' kettle or pot cause ye sickness in the eyes. That's Injun. Man gotta set tight till the ash cloud settle back down if'n he don't wanna get sickness in his eyes. *'Lord, how are they increased that trouble me!'* " He raised his eyes to the top of the lodge where the poles were bound together. " *'Many are they that rise up 'gainst me!'* Squar gets a lodgepolin' for such as that, young'un'. Best ye be more careful the next time, keepin' your own eye on what you're doin' when round the fire."

McAfferty shook his white head slowly before looking back at Bass, "Where ye be headin' for plews come breakup, Scratch?"

"Ain't thought 'bout it right jest yet, Asa," Titus answered. "Maybe north an' west some, up toward Snake country. Been 'while since't I was up there."

"Ain't got ye a set then?" McAfferty rose to a sitting position.

"What you got on your mind, Asa?" Bass looked over to the white-headed man. "Spit it out. You been chewin' on it. Spit it out, preacher."

"Jest thinkin', is all," he replied. "Jest thinkin' that if'n ye'd be willin', ye an' the young'un ain't fixed sign on where you're headin', the two of ye be for headin' out with me."

"Where'd you make medeecin for this time round?" Titus asked.

"Medeecin tells me head north an' east some, out'n up toward the Three Forks this y'ar," Asa replied. Scratch whistled with a low, long sound. "Up to Three Forks this y'ar."

McAfferty had his own private medicine he relied upon to tell him where he would set his traps each year. There was often something mystical, even magical, about how the free trapper would select his destination for the next season. Some of the white men would even pay a handsome sum of trade goods to a friendly medicine man, to recommend a destination the red man would see in a vision-for-hire. Such a consultation with such a native visionary was considered private, protected, and inviolate. No other free trappers were to know of the man's destination. But Asa McAfferty relied not on another's medicine, but on his own visions of where to be and when to be there.

"That be up to Blackfoot country, McAfferty," Bass remarked.

"Aye. There best be Blackfeets where I'm layin' beaver for," he replied. "There be Blackfeets up to the Three Forks for sure, an' that's where I'm headin' out."

"You're thinkin' we make the threesome, do you?"

"Aye to that too, Bass," the white head nodded. "Keep our lil' group nice an' small we will. Ain't trapped me in some time now, so I'll lay set with ye for the season. Lay set with the both of ye, if'n you're willin' to be goin' to the Three Forks."

"That's some, it is," Titus looked over now to Paddock. "Willin' to be headin' for some country thick in Bloods, Gros Ventres, an' Piegans, Blackfoot all, young'un?" Josiah couldn't answer with words. He didn't know what to say. Bass did not give him much time, "Good! Then Josiah an' me be with you an' makin' for the Three Forks, McAfferty." He turned toward Asa, "Beaver some rich up there. Pull us some packs outta that country, we will."

"Aye. Like to move 'bout in small numbers when huntin' the beaver," Asa remarked. "That critter is the shy animal. Big brigades such as that Rocky Mountain stompin' through beaver country skeer some off, movin' the critters 'way from their haunts. With all them men an' all that noise they make, beaver won' come to bait."

"Well, now, Asa. You know Rocky Mountain's fixin' to head a shiteree of fellers under Bridger up to the Three Forks come breakup, don't you?" Scratch asked.

"Aye. I know that. We'll jest have to see to it them boys don' get in our way." Asa looked away from Scratch's face and peered into the dying flames. "Rocky Mountain's headin' toward Three Forks. There be Blackfeets to the Three Forks. An', we three is headin' up there with me medeecin settin' the track for us." He turned his head slowly back to look again at Titus. "Lord, time is gettin' on now. What say we be gettin' this young'un dressed proper for the mountains? Cain't be lettin' him get froze up afore we get to cold doin's at the Three Forks country, can we, Mr. Bass?"

"You be the one with them skins you're givin' him on the prairie, Asa. You be the one to dress him out, too." Titus motioned to McAfferty to signify that he should go ahead with his plans.

The white-headed trapper rose from his robes and went to a darkened edge of the lodge where he opened a large, flat parfleche in the dim light thrown out by the dying fire. McAfferty brought the bundle over to the fire. He opened it slowly and pulled first one legging out, then the other and handed them to Josiah hung over the hook on the short arm. "Them to your likin', lad?" he asked.

Paddock ran his hand over the leather and nodded his head up and down without looking into McAfferty's face.

"Grab your belt there an' stand up. I'll be to dressin' you proper."

The young man responded by taking his belt from the three wide loops around the waist of his woolen pants and got to his feet. McAfferty took the belt from Josiah, then buckled it with little difficulty around the young man's waist. He held the top of one legging out between hook and hand. "Step in there, slip your foot through." Paddock put his leg into the leather cylinder and McAfferty tied the long thongs to the belt. The second legging then went on. "Now get your feet covered with them moccasins ye been wearin'." Josiah sat down bare-assed in the dirt, and Asa pulled several pairs of moccasins from the parfleche and tossed them to Scratch. "Them meet your mind for Josiah to be wearin'?" he asked of his old friend.

"They look the set, these here do," Titus nodded.

When Josiah rose to his feet once more, McAfferty pulled out a long rectangular piece of soft cheverel, kid-skin leather smoked to a chamois caress against the skin. The white-headed man knelt in front of Paddock and put the middle of the rectangle between the young man's legs. He then brought the front up over Josiah's genitals and

294

through the belt. The back was brought over the buttocks and tucked through the belt. Both ends now hung down close to his knees. Josiah squirmed slightly to adjust the leather in his crotch, then lifted the front to feel the softness of the breechclout.

"Now your shirt." McAfferty turned to the parfleche and pulled two more pairs of leggings out, which he tossed to Bass. Slowly he brought the long leather shirt out and shook it to full length. "Stick your arms over your head, son." Paddock raised his arms so that the older man could slip the shirt over them and finally pulled the opening over his head. Asa straightened the shirt out over the young man's body, then stepped back to look at Josiah. Scratch got to his feet with a low, approving whistle.

The long, thin stringlike fringes ran down the sides of the leggings and along the full length of his arms. The top of the shirt had been sewn together much like a cape to fall off his shoulders down the tops of his arms to cross him midchest. Long fringes hung from the seam of the cape, fluttering lightly in the night breeze within the lodge. Paddock ran a hand over each sleeve, then smoothed the leather across his chest and abdomen: The tail of the shirt reached halfway to his knees. It would keep his crotch and buttocks warm.

"It is good, no?" McAfferty asked of both of them.

"Your squar does some fine work, Asa," Bass said, stepping close to the young man and reaching out to touch the shirt. "You happy with them skins, Josiah?"

"Yepper," he answered happily. "They's much better'n them store-bought clothes, ain't they? Never knowed somethin' could feel so good 'gainst your skin. You ain't never gonna get me back in them other things now."

Titus turned to McAfferty, "You're not wantin' nothin' for 'em, Asa?"

"No. I ain't," he answered, still looking at Josiah. "Boy here looks good in 'em. Said I'd do 'em up as a whack for the ol't days we had us together, Scratch." He now turned to look at Bass. "Boy looks good in 'em, an' that be pay 'nough for me. 'Member me comin' west as a lad. Wish't I'd had me set of them skins right off back then." He looked to Paddock again. After a moment,

McAfferty stepped to the door. "Be gettin' me squar now. Time for the robes, it be. I'm settin' on pullin' plunder up in four days. Settin' out in four days, Scratch."

"Sets by us," Titus said, and moved along with Josiah to the hole in the lodge cover. The three men knelt through to stand under the night canopy dusted with white flecks like sparkling sugar. "We'll be seein' you that mornin', Asa." The older man moved off with extra moccasins in his shirt and the leggings over his shoulder. He leaped aboard his new pony.

"Don't know jest what I can say, McAfferty," Josiah began.

"Nothin' to be sayin', lad," he answered. "You're headin' with me to Three Forks. Be lots of time for sayin' what's on your mind." He took a few steps away from the young man. "I gotta be gettin' a squar now. Be to seein' ye in four days, Josiah. We settin' for the Three Forks, Scratch. An' ye knowin' if I ever be ready to go on my own, be leavin' ye again, ye'll not be s'prised by it." The old white head turned and disappeared among the lodges before Paddock wheeled about and jumped aboard his Indian pony with the bundle of old clothing tucked beneath one arm.

"These some, ain't they!" He leaned over and slapped the very quiet Bass on the shoulder before smoothing the shirt against his skin once more.

"You'll be needin' good skins up to where McAfferty's medeecin takin' us, son," he replied softly.

"Why the hell we goin' up there?" the younger man asked as they moved off. "Mean, if them Injuns is so bad, why we goin'?"

Bass clucked. "Three guns better'n two, son. We goin' 'cause beaver thicker up there—Blackfoots run off the big bunches. We got us a better chance. Jest the three of us. Smaller punch. Harder to find, or catch."

"Nawww," Josiah responded, after a little thought. "I wanna know why you is goin'—seems to be somethin' else."

Bass looked up and studied the sky for a few long moments before forming his answer. "Somethin' brung me an' the white head together again, son." He slowly looked back down at Josiah. "My bones tell me to be follerin' McAfferty—somethin's pullin' me north with him."

"Your hoodoos again?"

"Might be sayin' that, Josiah," he answered. "There be reason for ol' Asa showin' up now. Reason for him to be wantin' me to go to Three Forks with him. My medeecin tells me to foller his medeecin—see which nigger got him the stronger. My bones jest itch, plain itch, to be seein' what's pullin' him up there."

11

"You 'wake, son?" Scratch asked quietly of the robe-covered form at his feet. The lump under the buffalo hide stirred a little, then rolled over. "Playin' 'possum, ain't you?" He pulled the robe off his legs and kicked Josiah's buttocks.

"Goddammit!" Paddock barked back at the older man, then pulled the robe back from his face to peer over the edge of the fur at the man who had kicked him. "Never do wanna let a man get his sleep, do you?"

Bass didn't answer. His eyes moved from Josiah's face up the mountains across the creek. After he yawned and stretched, Titus put both hands under the torn calico shirt and scratched through the hair across his chest. All the time he looked at the peaks through blood-daubed eyes that burned a little in his attempts to keep them open. It irritated him to feel this way. Titus thought back to the time when as a young man he never greeted a morning with this heaviness in his mind and body. He sighed.

"Got you them graybacks now, eh?" Paddock mumbled sleepily as he watched Scratch raking through the hair on his chest with dirty fingernails.

"Shit! Ain't got no nits, Josiah. If ever you was 'wake when I got up, you'd be knowin' I'm one to itch when I get up," Bass responded. "Ain't no graybacks."

"Jest thinkin' you might gotten some out to McAfferty's last night."

"I dare to set that McAfferty's got him one the cleanest lodges goin' this side of the big muddy. Ain't never

297

knowed that man to be troubled by them lil' critters. He's one to be real partic'lar 'bout such things." Scratch slowly straightened out his shaky legs and stood. "I'd swear to that on my own hook, I would, Josiah. Asa can be some queersome at times, but he ain't one to be livin' with no pesky varmints such as them lil' devilsome critters." He put an index finger inside his mouth and ran it around the inside of his cheeks.

"Got you graybacks in there what need scratchin'?" Josiah snorted.

"Nawww." Scratch pulled his finger out and wiped it on his pants, then repeated the process once again. "Got me some scum in my yapper this mornin'. Feels some like'n I've been drinkin' the hole at a water hole 'stead of the water. Musta been that dog of McAfferty's." He looked down at Josiah now. "Some a that grease caked up in my mouth, I'm guessin'." Bass shook each leg one time, then set off toward the creek when he snapped his fingers and turned around, returning to the canopy. He crawled in across his robe and began tearing at one of the leather bundles. From it he pulled an old, dented coffee pot, blacked over more fires than Scratch dared remember. The older man rose to his feet and headed to the creek once more, tossing the coffee pot into the air and catching it several times. The whistled notes of a song disappeared with him among the willows and creepers along the creek bank.

"What you so goddamned pert 'bout this mornin'?" Josiah hollered after him. But there came no answer from the man down at the water's edge. "What reason he got to be so goddamned pert this mornin'?" Paddock asked himself. He sat up and drew back his shoulders, yawning wearily. Shuddering slightly in the chill air of the overcast morning, Josiah reached behind him where the new leather shirt had been placed the night before to serve as a pillow. Bringing it to his lap, the young man ran his fingers over the leather and played with some of the fringes between his fingers. Then he spread it out and pulled the shirt over his head, tugging at the tailored garment to get it over his large chest. Kicking some at the robe over his legs, Josiah stood up outside their blanket canopy and straightened the breechclout and leggings he had not taken off when he had crawled under the robe to sleep the night before. The air was chilly to him yet.

Josiah looked up at the overcast sky to the west, a thin bank of clouds moving to the east as he watched them for several minutes.

"Gonna have us some wind this day," Scratch's voice broke through the willow clumps as he approached the canopy. Josiah turned his head around from the west to look at the older man come up. "L'arn you to be readin' them clouds, too, son. Take a lookee there an' mind you what you see, Josiah." Scratch put the coffee pot full of creek water on the ground and crawled under the blanket shelter to rummage once again through his packs. When he found the large sack of coffee beans and an old cast-iron skillet, Titus returned.

"What this here sky tell you to read?" Josiah asked as both of them looked to the west.

"That there dark sky," Scratch pointed with his right arm while his left held the sack and skillet, "it tell you we gonna have us some wind this day—kinda dark blue it is, gloomy-lookin' too. But she'll be fair; no rain neither." He now moved one scrawny index finger back and forth horizontally pointing at the base of the clouds. "You see them high, humpied-back clouds there risin' up from the big flat bottom? Well, that be 'nother sign of some wind comin' in." Scratch turned to the east to look over the sky surrounding the peaks above them. "Over here you can be one as to eas'ly see that soft, silkylike red in the sky there. That, young Josiah, be 'nother sign for you to mind of wind comin'. When's sky to the east gets purty red color, 'bout like the color of them silk dresses them St. Louie night womens be wearin', that give you track on what to 'spect for the day. Windy, it'll be."

Josiah continued to look to the eastern sky as Scratch set the sack down and then the skillet alongside the full coffee pot. The older man went into the shelter and began to dig through his shooting pouch. After cussing quietly under his breath for a few minutes, Bass finally dumped the pouch's contents on the buffalo robe and scattered the articles angrily with his hands.

"Ain't here!" he hollered as he looked up at the young man gazing down at him.

"What ain't?" Paddock questioned.

"My paper!" Scratch shook the pouch over the robe a

299

few times, then turned it rightside up and stuck his hand within it. "Some goddamned mother-whore-polecat stole't my paper!"

"What paper you got stole't?"

"What paper I got stole't?" Titus's voice squeaked a little in his anger. "The paper as said I still got me some money comin' from the trader. That be what paper I got stole't from me!" He looked closely at Paddock's grinning face and stopped the hand searching the inside of the shooting pouch. "You be knowin' what happen't to my paper, young'un?"

"You're the one to be knowin' all 'bout the weather an' the sky, 'bout Injuns an' trappin'," Josiah said, kneeling under the blanket canopy, "but you cain't mind you where you put your paper." He had to chuckle at the older man, knowing it irritated Bass to be left in the dark in this manner. Paddock reached for his own shooting pouch and pulled it to him. From the pouch he produced a small envelope of brown waxed paper that he began to unfold. Inside the waxy envelope was Scratch's paper. Bass smiled when he saw it. Josiah passed the receipt over to the older man.

"You be the nigger as stole't it from me, eh?" Titus's eyes twinkled as he smiled at Josiah.

"No such a thing, ol' man," Josiah protested. "You be the nigger what gave it to me to keep from you." He held the pouch up and shook it at Bass. "Told me to hide it from you—place where it wouldn't be very easy to find." Paddock tossed the heavy pouch back on the buffalo robe. "You was wantin' me to keep it from you while you was drunk, Scratch. You thought it be a good idea not to have all that money to one time in wettin' that scummy dog-eatin' mouth of your'n."

"I give it to you for that, eh?"

"You give it to me when you was drunk," Paddock answered, "an' that be why you're one not to be 'memberin' it now, you ol' polecat."

"Titus Bass is a nigger to be forgettin' much track when he's in the cups, he is," Scratch clucked a tongue against his teeth and threw the loose articles on the robe back into his own shooting pouch. "Got you nursin' to me now, have I, young'un?"

"You might be sayin' that," Josiah replied. "I looks to it like I'm jest watchin' over what a friend asks of me to be doin', is all." He crawled out from beneath the canopy with the older man. "What you fixin' to spend your money to this mornin'?"

"Get me some likker, boy." He rubbed his empty hand over his gut, then pointed at his mouth. "Some likker to cut this scum in my mouth, here."

"How much you eyein' on spendin' on likker?"

"Now you're mother-hennin' me, young'un," Scratch bit back with a false tone of hurt pride in his voice, "an' it don' fit you good."

"Jest mind you that be lotta money to be spendin' to likker, Scratch..."

"I knows me my own mind, young'un," Bass interrupted, "an' I ain't gonna be one to be buyin' likker when I be needin' more truck for the next y'ar. I be sober as a constable what would throw me to the cal'boose when I take me a bead on the likker horn." He put the waxed paper inside the waistband of his pants and pulled the long tail of the torn, yellow calico shirt over his belt. "Get you that pot an' foller me, Josiah."

Scratch carried the sack and the skillet through the trappers' camp to the fire where some coals still glowed. From the fire's edge he pulled some branches the men had gathered and broke them into suitably sized pieces. Dusting some of the cold ashes from the embers with a stick, Bass scraped together what coals were still glowing. After he had placed some of the broken wood over the embers, Scratch put his head down and blew long, gentle breaths into the coals. Quickly they grew to a bright-red life and flames began to lick at the dry kindling. The broken branches caught hold and the older man put more wood over the flames.

"Watch me what I do, Josiah." Scratch pulled the sack to his side. "An' mind you to be doin' it with care now." Scratch opened the drawstring at the top of the cloth sack and poured some of the oblong coffee beans into the cast-iron skillet until the bottom was just covered. Setting the sack back down, Bass smoothed out the beans across the bottom of the skillet and removed a handful, which he placed back in the sack.

"What is that?" Paddock asked.

"Coffee beans, boy," Titus answered. "An' mind you not to put too many in the skillet here, jest 'enough to cover the bottom, like this here." He put the skillet over the edge of the growing flames, setting it down on three small rocks. "You're gonna be roastin' our coffee this morning', so don' burn it. Ever' now an' then shake the skillet like this." He demonstrated for Paddock that he wanted the beans shaken slightly as they roasted by agitating the skillet handle. "When you get them roasted, put this here bunch to the side—get you somethin' to put 'em in—an' do likewise with 'nother skilletful. Two of them skillets be 'nough for two pots of Scratch's coffee." He got to his feet. "Now mind you, keep them beans hoppin', son. I'll be back afore you're done, most likely." Titus patted the spot where the waxed paper containing the note was held against his body and turned toward the ponies. He climbed aboard the one he had chosen to ride and headed north toward the trader's tent. Josiah looked after him for a few minutes, then remembered he was to care for the coffee beans.

He was shaking the second batch of the beans when Scratch came riding in from the north. In front of him across the bare back of the Nez Perce pony sat a five-gallon wooden keg he held onto with one hand. Against his crotch rode a leather satchel. Bass moved past the fire and dropped the satchel to the ground. It landed heavily before he took the oak keg in his arms, clutching it against his chest. By bringing his right leg up and over the pony's back, Scratch plopped to the ground. He brought the keg over to the fire with a smile on his face.

"You wait long 'nough, get you good tradin' from Sublette." He set the oak container down on the ground. "Sublette's not one to be takin' nothin' but pelts back to St. Louie." He turned on his heel and moved back to retrieve the leather satchel. This too he dropped to the ground by the fire.

"What be that?" Josiah was interested in the heavy sack, still shaking the skillet as he looked up at the older man.

"G'lena, son." Bass walked away toward the lean-tos and canopies. "Lead."

When he returned he carried two pint tin cups and a small smoked-skin pouch in his hands. After he had set the cups down beside Josiah, Bass began to scoop handfuls of the coffee beans from the piece of chopped wood where the young man had put them after roasting. Into the small pouch he dropped the beans.

"Them ready?" He nodded toward the skillet Paddock was shaking.

"Think they be." He brought the skillet away from the flames and dumped its contents onto the cut timber. Scratch put his hand into the pile of beans, bouncing them against his palm as he put them into the pouch.

"They be plenty ready—hot they are too." When all the beans were in the pouch, Bass drew tight the drawstring at its top, then chose a small, hand-sized stone from the edge of the fire. Placing the skin pouch atop the cut timber, he began to pound the beans with the small rock.

"Smell me coffee makin's," Elbridge Gray said, approaching the fire and rubbing his eyes with both hands.

"That's the doin's," Titus replied. "Sit yourself down when you got your cup in hand. Got you some whiskey whilst the coffee's brewin'."

Gray turned back into the lean-tos while Scratch continued to pound the roasted coffee beans against the cut timber. This crude mortar and pestle soon gave him the consistency of grounds he desired. As he opened the skin pouch and dumped half the coffee into the pot, Elbridge returned with a large cup in hand, followed by three more of the free trappers who had been stirred from their slumber by Gray's announcement that Bass had whiskey for the drinking.

"An' a bright mornin' to you!" Bass nodded to each of the arriving trappers who sat down close to the fire. "Have you coffee ready in a bit." He took the handle of the pot and placed it on the stones over the coals. Bass reached behind him and took the large Blackfoot dagger from his belt. He handed it to Josiah. "When that water in there goes to bubblin', mind you it to start stirrin' with the sticker. Don' want it to bubble over, Josiah." Titus backed off as Paddock scooted closer to the coffee pot. He reached for the wooden keg and rolled it to his side. "Time not be long afore that coffee's brewed, but time 'nough for some likkerin'."

The four trappers gathered around Josiah and Scratch as the older man hefted the keg onto his thighs and put one of his tin cups beneath the wooden spigot. Turning the handle, Bass watched the light-brown alcohol pour into the cup. The others grunted their approval as each of the cups was filled just short of brimming.

"Buy ya that keg this mornin'?" Gray asked after taking his first drink and wiping his mustache across a sleeve.

"Yep," Titus answered as he filled Josiah's cup.

"Cost ye some, it did—what with the trader askin' a dollar a gill for his whiskey," Elbridge commented. "Four dollars a pint, that makes it. An' ye brung ye in a five-gallon keg back. That's some!"

"Trader's lookin' to be packin' up, he is," Bass replied after he had taken another drink and looked at the job Josiah was doing in stirring the water in the coffee pot. "Made me some deal for this jack o' likker, Titus Bass did. 'Tweren't no four-dollar pint, this whiskey weren't. Keg'd cost me some that way. Let's see me...."

"Five-gallon'd cost ye some eighty dollars, it would," Elbridge remarked, quick as he was with figuring such things.

"Eighty dollar, say you," Scratch said quietly as Josiah looked over at him.

"You spent you eighty dollar on likker?" Paddock's voice was a little sharp.

"Boy's like some fat motherin' hen, he is." Bass clucked like a chicken, then took another drink. "Didn' cost me no eighty dollar for this keg." He patted it with his left hand. "Trader real happy to sell me his likker some cheap, he was. Not wantin' to have to be carryin' it back to St. Louie." He kept Josiah in suspense awhile longer by taking a long draw on the whiskey in his cup. "Fifty dollar he took, an' threw in the keg to boot, too."

"Ya ain't slidin' your words, is ya?" Caleb asked over the edge of his mug.

"Nawww. Ain't," Titus responded to the doubt. "Sublette was ready to be sellin' such even to cuttin' prices, he was."

"Spent you fifty dollar for likker, eh, ol' man?" Josiah asked. "What be in this here sack?" He motioned to the heavy satchel Scratch had dropped near the young man. "How much the G'lena cost you?"

"Twenty-five pound took me same in money. Twenty-five dollar."

"G'lena?" Caleb spat out whiskey in surprise.

"Sublette's the tradin' child now. He's not one to be takin' lead back to the settlements." Scratch turned his head to look at Caleb Wood. "Was to one an' fifty a pound, G'lena was few days back." He looked back at the coffee pot Paddock was stirring with the big knife. "Now lead be down to dollar for the pound."

"That leaves you with only round forty-some dollars, Scratch," Josiah remarked.

"Leave me with nothin', son."

"What?" Paddock turned to look into Bass's eyes.

"Watch your coffee, boy." He lifted his chin to nod at the boiling pot. "She's boilin' deep now. Take her from the coals." Bass finished the whiskey in his cup as Josiah pulled the heavy pot to the ground away from the hot embers. Titus poured his cup one-fourth full of whiskey, then turned it over into the coffee pot.

"What's that for?" Josiah questioned again.

"Settle them grounds," answered Scratch. "Let it set for a minute now whilst I have me 'nother whiskey."

"How'd you spend all your note? Shoulda had you some forty dollar left?" Paddock was still confused.

"Give the trader forty dollar for somethin' Elbridge's been wantin'." Bass raised the long tail of the calico shirt and put his hand beneath it to bring out a flintlock pistol he had stuck in the waistband of his pants. Each of the men leaned forward now to look over the pistol as Bass handed it over to Gray.

"You're still wantin' them books, huh?" Elbridge questioned as he took the pistol from Titus.

"Yep," Bass nodded. "You said you'd trade me them if'n I'd get you that pistol," Titus said, pointing to the flintlock Gray held, "the one you had your eye to what the trader had for the sellin'."

Elbridge set his cup down so that he could fondle the pistol with both hands, "Ye must be wantin' them books 'bout as bad as me wantin' this pistol."

"You're still for the trade, ain't you?" asked Scratch, concerned that the trapper would not want to complete the bargain struck days before.

"Yep. Ya can have your books," Gray replied. "But I don' know what you're wantin' 'em for. Hatcher said ya cain't read . . ."

"That's right," Bass shot back. "I cain't." He leaned over the coffee pot, then picked it up to pour himself a cup of the hot black liquid.

"Cain't see as how they are gonna do ya any good,

then. Jest be more to carry with ya," said Gray, looking up from the pistol to Bass.

"Said *I* cain't read, Gray," Titus retorted, then sat back on the ground next to the oak keg. "Didn' say me nothin' 'bout havin' me some coon to read them books to me. Now, did I?"

"Nawww, guess ya didn'."

"Josiah here can read with the best of 'em," Titus replied as Paddock looked over at him, raising his face from the cup of coffee he was pouring for himself. "This here pardner of mine gonna be l'arnin' me to read from them books all over 'gain this here winter with them Absor'kees."

"I am, eh?" Josiah asked.

"That you are, young'un." Bass blew on the coffee and brought it to his lips. "Been l'arnin' you some I have, ain't I? Now it be time you be l'arnin' me to read 'gain." He took another drink, then nodded at Elbridge. "Gray, get them books now, will you?"

"Yessir." He rose to his feet. "Got your trade, Bass." After a few minutes he returned to the fire with two books, which he handed to Scratch before taking his seat once more by the fire to finish his whiskey.

Titus sat his cup of coffee down as the books were handed to him. He placed them in his lap, one atop each thigh. First touching the biggest of the two, a thick volume with a fading dark-blue cover, Titus caressed the collection of Shakespearean tragedies as gently as any man would touch something very special to him, with a reverence for something newly within his grasp. Scratch moved his fingers over to the book entitled *The Pilgrim's Progress* resting on his left thigh. Its white leather cover had become soiled and greasy over several years among Gray's packs. "You're gonna be takin' me to school, Josiah."

"Titus Bass's goin' to the Rocky Mountain college, Paddock," Gray commented. "You're gonna be the teacher in that trappers' lodge lit'rature society." He rounded the last two words off with big syllables of impressive dimension.

"Listen to that nigger talk!" Caleb snorted.

"Man's had some schoolin', that one has," Bass replied. "Ain't none you other niggers got no books, any ways you lays your sights to it. Gray be a man with some smarts up top, more'n you can say, by a long chalk. An' a man as wants to l'arn will be one to listen to him."

The Rocky Mountain college taught men through practical lessons in survival skills, and many of them also enjoyed the learning brought them through literature. Many a trapper, including those who could not read themselves, had others read to them. The few who were better educated than others were the teachers in this open-air institution of higher learning. They were those trappers who often quoted passages from a favorite author. Jedediah Strong Smith had for years packed along some twenty volumes of his favorite literature in addition to his ever-present Bible.

Caleb Wood grunted but was interrupted from saying anything more as some noise broke from the north. The trappers' attention turned to watch the approach of a large group of white men moving slowly in their direction. Bass and Gray got to their feet as the mounted riders leading pack horses began to move past their fire.

"Billy Sublette's lil' brother movin' out," Titus commented.

"Milt's headin' for the Lewis River," Gray remarked, then nodded toward the squaw who rode behind Sublette and to his right side. "Takin' his fam'ily with him, that one is."

Milton Sublette rarely moved through the west now without his young wife. Since his marriage to her back in 1829, the woman always traveled with her husband's brigade during its hunting journeys. For the past few months, the squaw had been nursing Milt back to health. Early in the spring, Sublette had been cut up badly in a knife fight and was now convalescing from the wounds that refused to heal. She had given him two children, one born in 1831 and now old enough to ride in front of Milt on his father's horse, and the other peering out from the cradle board slung from his mother's back.

"Gettin' 'em a late start to the day," said Scratch as he looked overhead at the sun breaking through the clouds. The wind was beginning to gust across the flat prairie. It was now past midday.

Beside Sublette rode the German-born trapper Henry Fraeb, who would help Milt command the brigade of Rocky Mountain Fur Company trappers. Fifteen of the men were directly attached to the company, many of them Canadian half-breeds. With the company men rode Alexander Sinclair with his fourteen men, now hired on with

Rocky Mountain under a loose business arrangement. Bringing up the rear of the group rode Nathaniel Wyeth with his remaining eleven Yankee greenhorns. Wyeth had approached Milt Sublette days back, asking to travel along with the company brigade until they had passed through Blackfoot country. Sublette had agreed, feeling that even if the Yankees were not proven mountain men yet, their mere presence bulked the detachment moving out for the fall hunt. These greenhorns just might help to deter a wandering war party from acting too hastily.

This mountain mixture of irritable, cranky men moved lethargically past the free trappers. For more than a week most had joined in the orgy of rendezvous drinking. They were still somewhat testy at being the first group to leave Pierre's Hole, being the first to push out onto the hot prairie with aching heads. Some moaned and groaned as the rocking and swaying of their horses gave rise to that feeling of nausea. This group would move southeast out of the Hole, cross over the Teton Pass to strike the Snake River, which they would follow west, then north in their search for beaver during the fall season. However, with such a late start because of the sluggishness of the men, Milton Sublette would have to order a halt this evening after a journey of only some seven miles down the valley. At their evening fires they would be joined by a small party of Flatheads, who would request to travel along with the brigade through dangerous country.

The last of the men pulled past, with Alexander McLeod bellowing out his parting words to the free trappers. "Keep your skelp locked tight, Josiah Paddock! Ye niggers watch the skyline! I'll be one to see ye come ronnyvoo next y'ar. This here child'll be lookin' for your ugly faces at them doin's! Keep your powder dry, niggers— till I lay eyes to ye 'gain."

There was always some sadness at the breakup of rendezvous. Men bade farewell as cheerfully as they could to friends they would not see for another year. Despite hearty words and cheerful cussing, each man knew that the next rendezvous would find some old faces missing. Some would go under in the next few months: victims of the ever-present danger of Indians, and also victims of freezing to death because of a miscalculation in the winter weather, or of sudden death because of a misstep by a pony mincing along the edge of a rocky ridge. Week in and week out, year after year, an average of one of these trappers would go under every ten days. And the next rendezvous would be clouded by their absence from the evening fires; toasts would be made to their memory. The hard, cold, brutal men who haunted the recesses of the Rocky Mountains in search of beaver were, more often than not, more sensitive than they would like to have it known. Their friendships were deep and abiding, although each man knew to keep a respectful distance. After all, it deeply hurt these men of freedom and passion when each rendezvous a friend did not ride in to celebrate. Each man kept his distance for it might be he who would not be joining next year's orgy of liquor and loving—and no man wished others to grieve over his death. Judgment was swift at the hands of a grizzly, but just as swift from the kick of a mule. They might drown, starve, or die of thirst. But they were not men to dwell too long on the tragedies of the past. They could not allow themselves the luxury of lingering long on memories of friends taken from them. In the lonely high country there were always enough problems at hand to solve. The weather was an unending demand on the trapper's mental energies, as were the details of his job of pulling beaver from the streams. Not to mention unfriendly Indians. Each trapper knew there was enough in the present to concern himself with, without adding the additional burden of nervous worry. After all, those who had gone under had moved on to the hunting ground where sign marked every stream and where each new morning promised a beautiful day. No man wanted others to grieve over his passing on to this hunting ground beyond the sky.

"Pour me some of your coffee, son," Titus yelled back to Josiah, who had stood to holler out his farewell to McLeod. Bass then turned and came back to sit by the fire. "Niggers ain't gonna make no ground on theys trail this day." He took the cup Josiah offered to him and blew on it before taking a drink. "Ain't hardly worth the gettin' up an' goin' what lil' bit of trail they'll be markin'." He looked overhead at the clouds once more, then looked back at Paddock beside him. "You be hungry now?"

"Not rightly, I ain't," he answered, "not jest yet."

"Ain't hungry myself, neither," Scratch commented

before he took another drink from his coffee. "We'll be two to wait 'til supperin' then; got us some work for this day, what be left of this day, anyways."

Paddock leaned over the coffee pot and rewarmed his cup, "What you thinkin' of us doin'?" He leaned back on his haunches and looked at Bass over the rim of his cup.

"Got us a tree to be choppin' down, Josiah." He looked away from Paddock.

"Got us a tree to be choppin' down?" He sputtered a little as he swallowed the hot, dark liquid. "We got us all kinda wood for the fire here. Don't need us more of that. What you thinkin' of that work jest to be doin' work now?"

"Ain't been thinkin' of work jest to be workin'," Scratch answered. "I ain't the nigger as does such a thing. Sure an' certain we ain't needin' wood for this fire—ain't no track there. But, we got us whole passel of lead to that cottonwood you been plunkin' to past number days. Titus Bass ain't one to be leavin' good passel of lead to a damned tree if'n he can be doin' anythin' 'bout it."

"Fixin' to pull the lead outta the tree, huh?" Gray asked as he made himself more comfortable on the ground with the whiskey keg between him and Scratch.

"Yepper. Ain't got nothin' better to be doin' this day, elsewise," Bass swallowed long on his coffee. "Time be this critter's mendin' up for the fall hunt. Gotta be makin' me balls, too. This here child's not goin' where we's headin' without some passel of balls for Ol' Make-'em-Come, I ain't. Melt me down some G'lena."

"Whar' ye an' Josiah fixin' to be movin' out to?" Solomon Fish asked.

Bass finished his cup of coffee before answering, then snapped the cup downward a few times to shake loose the coffee grounds. "Makin' beaver to the Three Forks, we are, come breakup." He waited for the comments he expected in the still moments that followed his reply.

"That's some," Elbridge shook his head slightly from side to side. "Blackfeet's thicker'n fleas on a coon dog up at that mark."

"Ya niggers goin' up with Bridger's boys then?" Caleb asked.

"I heerd they was headin' that way after trappin' west of there some, I did." Bass looked down into his empty cup. "But, we ain't on the tramp with them fellers

310

this season. Nawww, jest three of us goin' up there straight off, first whack at breakup."

"Who be the other man?" Gray queried, then looked away from Scratch, who continued peering into his cup.

"Child's name be McAfferty," Titus volunteered. "Trapped with him some y'ars back. That white-headed nigger as come in with them Nepercy to ronnyvoo."

"He trap them Columbia waters then?" asked Gray, leaning over to the keg and filling his cup halfway with the diluted alcohol.

"Wintered up with the Nepercy, he did. Injun princess caught the nigger's eye. Hitched hisse'f to her afore that village broke up to move toward ronnyvoo. She's a looker, too—ain't she, Josiah?" He nudged Paddock in the ribs with an elbow but got no answer from the young man except a fleeting look out of red-rimmed eyes. "Young'un here took a shinin' to that squar right off. Says he didn', but this here nigger knows the better on that." He nudged Josiah again.

"You're startin' in on that shit again, ain't you, ol' man!" Paddock snapped back.

"Jest tellin' the true, is all it be, boy!" He chuckled a little as the others looked on. "This here child be one to see it in your eyes when she was fittin' you to them skins . . ."

"Fittin', hell!" Josiah squeaked a little in protest. "Feelin' be more like it! Squar run her hands everywhere you'd care to be havin' a squar run her hands over you, ol' man!"

"An' you liked you ever' bit of it, too. Awww, don' be takin' it all so hard now, young'un." Scratch had that soft tone in his voice suddenly. "Squar jest doin' what needed doin' to fit you, that be all. If'n that squar took a shinin' to you back, she'd let you know. But, she be one to last with one nigger till he lodgepoles her, way I figger that one. I seen me my number of squars, I have. That one be McAfferty's till he up an' decides to kick her outta his robes. Nepercy princess she be, an' that makes that squar one to know somethin' better'n go jumpin' from robe to robe. That one l'arnt better'n that, I reckon. Scratch knows them womens, he does, an' that'un be McAfferty's till McAfferty's tirin' of her—Scratch knows him them womens."

"Josiah don' stand any chance against that ol' white-headed shit, huh?" Gray prodded at Paddock.

"Ain't that way 'tall!" Josiah sought to protest. "You got it all wrong!"

"Ain't none of us heerd how you got it right, Josiah?" Scratch requested as he stabbed Paddock in the ribs with a bony elbow.

"Goddammit! Ain't gonna touch that woman! Don't want me none of them troubles," he quieted his voice somewhat. "Woman troubles make for bad times for a man. Had me 'nough of that. Don't want me no more troubles over a woman."

"Finish that coffee of your'n son," Bass said, rising, "an' we'll be gettin' this workin' your skittish 'bout outta the way."

Paddock drained his cup and Bass tossed his cup to the young man. Titus leaned over to begin to pick the five-gallon keg up, then set it back down before he had brought it to his waist.

"What the hell is this nigger doin', anyways!" he bellowed. "Likker's here for the drinkin', coons! Will be wantin' me some of that barleycorn when the sweatin's over." He turned on his heel and went back into the grouping of shelters carrying his two books and followed by Paddock.

After they had stopped by their canopy to search for an ax Bass remembered having borrowed from Caleb Wood, the two men made their way down to the creek, through the rushing water, and up the other side.

"That white spot be jest 'bout black now, don' it?" queried Bass, patting the trunk of the tree below the target. Titus then reached for the ax held by Josiah. "I'll get 'er goin' down an' you'll be wrappin' the skinnin' on this job."

As Paddock stepped back out of the way, Bass gripped the handle of the ax and swung the blade toward the cottonwood. It bit into the trunk about three feet above the ground and held. Titus had to step forward to yank the ax from the tree's grip. When he stepped back, Scratch leaned the handle against his leg and removed his shirt. He then tucked the sleeves of the torn calico shirt into the waistband and belt of the trousers he wore. Again he gripped the handle and swung widely at the trunk. He chopped at the trunk several more times, then stopped. He leaned the ax against his leg once more, spit into his palms, and rubbed them together.

"You want me to take a crack at it?" Josiah asked.

"Nawwww!" Titus picked the ax up as Paddock reached for it. "Shit! This ain't gonna be no trouble, son. 'Sides you'll be breakin' it up after I get it down anyways." He brought the ax back to the side, then forward against the trunk. The sound of the blade biting into the cottonwood rang through the cluster of trees and willows along the creek as the older man labored away. Eventually the cottonwood fell from its base, the heavy top branches landing in the creek. Bass stood still and let the handle slip through his hands until the blade touched the ground. He puffed a little and wiped his forehead. Taking the bottom of the shirt that now hung well past his knees, Titus mopped his face with the calico. When he had run the shirt over the back of his neck, he let it hang once more from his belt. Scratch only then dropped the ax handle to the ground.

"C'mon." Bass turned to Josiah briefly before moving slowly down the bank toward the fallen tree. "Gotta pull 'er up the bank some."

Paddock came down the bank into the water with the older man and put his large arms around the trunk of the cottonwood as Scratch did likewise above him. The two men lifted the heavy timber off the ground enough to slide it through the stream with short, choppy steps and closer to the sandy shore. With both arms gripped tightly around the trunk, Bass pulled and tugged at the tree with its bark held against his abdomen. Both men grunted with exertion and groaned profanities as they slowly heaved the cottonwood along.

"You sure . . . this be . . . all so goddamned . . . damned . . . worth this trouble?" Josiah puffed. "Lotta work . . . for . . . lil' . . . lead."

They made it to the bank and let it drop on the grass and sand. Then Bass, breathless, answered: "Lead we'll pull outta that trunk . . . might'n be jest . . . the ball . . . as saves your ha'r. Ain't one to carry . . . no more lead'n what . . . I gots powder for. Ain't gonna carry . . . no more powder'n what . . . I gots lead for. One don' do a child no good without the other . . . an' . . . we be needin' . . . this lead, son."

Bass took his shirt from his waistband and introduced his arms into it. When he pulled it down over his head, Titus saw what had happened to the shirt. One sleeve

313

was barely attached to the shoulder and the front of the shirt across the chest was ripped from side to side.

"Awww," was all he could say for a moment. "Goddamn! Lookee here, will you!"

Josiah lifted his head as he straightened up and looked over at the older man. "That be ruined now."

"I can see that!" Bass whined a little. "My ronnyvoo shirt!"

"You tored it some gettin' drunk an' wrasslin' these past days, Scratch."

"But I coulda sewed 'er up with them lil' holes!" He held the shirt out from his body to assess the damage to the bright yellow calico.

Paddock moved up the bank to stand beside the older man. "We'll get you 'nother afore we push out on breakup."

"Cain't get 'nother!" He shook the loose, torn shreds of the shirt. "Cain't get me 'nother, Josiah! Ain't got me no beaver left now! Ain't got me no paper as says I got goods comin' to me from the trader! Shee-eet!"

"Cain't you mend it?" Josiah asked, in desperation to find an answer to Scratch's despair over the tattered rendezvous shirt.

"Patch me it up, I could," he answered, "'ceptin' it would'n' be fittin' for ronnyvoo then. Man's gotta be dressed the fine foofaraw come ronnyvoo, an' no patched-up shirt gonna do. Look worse'n some ol' quilt back to home it would!" Both men's thoughts flew back to home, back to soft beds where a man could climb beneath clean sheets and a patchwork quilt. It strained the mind to fight off the memories.

"Get that ax, son," Bass directed as he pulled the remains of the shirt over his head. "Put yourself to busy choppin' that target outta the trunk." He bent over the tree to indicate to Josiah two imaginary lines on either side of the white patch, then stepped aside as Josiah moved past him to pick up the ax. "I'll be goin' back to get us somethin' for the lead ye'll be diggin' out." He scooted down the bank into the water. As he trotted across the rocky bottom of the stream, Titus heard Paddock setting the ax to work on the cottonwood.

By the time Scratch returned, the young man had finished on one side of the target and set to work on the other. Bass crawled up the bank wearing his own long leather shirt. In his hand he carried the new cast-iron kettle. Scratch moved past Josiah to find a soft spot in the grass above the young man. There he plopped down to look on as Josiah axed the cottonwood, sending large chunks of the tree into the air each time he sank the blade into the wood.

"Bring that hunk up here on the flat," Scratch directed when Josiah had completed separating the target from the rest of the tree. The young man dropped the ax to the ground and puffed momentarily before leaning down to heft the one section. Struggling up the bank, Paddock dug into the sand with his toes through the moccasins. Paddock dropped the section of cottonwood at Scratch's feet and fell to the grass, relieved it was over.

"Catch your breath, boy," Titus said, rising to his feet. He headed down the bank and brought the ax back up, then rolled the section of trunk away from Josiah. When he had it standing flat on its end, Bass brought the ax over his head and swung downward. Over and over he repeated the action, having to set the trunk upright a few times before it lay about him in several pieces.

"Lazy time be over, Josiah! C'mon over here an' get your knife busy." Scratch turned back to the pieces of cottonwood on the ground. "An' bring that kittle with you." He sat down on the grass and took one of the split pieces into his lap across his thighs before pulling the Blackfoot knife from his belt. Josiah came up and sat down near the older man, putting the kettle down between the two of them. "Gotta dig the lead outta the wood now. Wherever's a hole."

"I can see that," Josiah said testily.

"Sure you can, young'un," Titus remarked. "Get touchy with lil' work, eh?" He stuck the tip of the knife blade into the wood and began to work it around in search of the ball that had marked its path through the wood but had not exited the other side of the tree.

"Ain't the work," Paddock replied. "Sorry I bit at you, you mangy ol' man." He looked up to see Bass eye him and smile. "Jest gettin' tired now of all this sittin' round here." He pointed his knife toward the valley of the trappers' rendezvous.

"Wearin' on you, eh?" Bass went back to work with his knife.

"Wanna be movin' out to do what I come to the mountains for."

315

"You'll be gettin' 'nough of that soon now, Josiah. Be this time come next y'ar, you'll be lovin' these here shinin' times—ronnyvoo doin's an' all. You'll be bug-eyed to take a horn of medeecin water come that time, you will. I'll swear to that float stick. Man swallers that fire down here 'cause he won' get it for 'nother y'ar—maybe never 'gain for some coons. Man swallers fire to forget them as'll never be drinkin' with him 'gain. Drinks to forget all he's come through jest to get hisse'f that drink to ronnyvoo. That makes this whole consarn somethin' purty special, don' it?"

"You come up here to trap beaver, didn't you?" Josiah asked without looking up.

"Tol't you afore man don' come up here for the money, not the beaver. 'Sides, plews come summer ain't worth the trappin', howsomever, Josiah." The older man kept working at the wood until he freed another piece of flattened lead, which he dropped into the kettle with a hollow sound. "Beaver ain't got good plews this time a y'ar, an' ever' nigger up here's needin' new fixin's, new outfit maybe. It be good idear for this ronnyvoo time. Man ain't got nothin' better to be doin' than come outta the upcountry to spend some a them beaver dollars he'd froze up to get in this past y'ar."

"We got us our outfit, don't we?" Paddock stopped his knife and looked over to Bass. "We can go talk with McAfferty 'bout movin' out." He set back to work pulling lead from the wood. "Them fellers Sublette an' Frapp moved out already. We could be movin' out come the mornin.' Got us a ways to be goin' from the sounds of it, to hear you tell it."

"Ain't that far a piece from here, young'un," Scratch answered. "Them Blackfoots is close 'nough to us here, them niggers is."

"What makes the all-fired differ'nce when we move out?"

"It don' now, I guess. Jest gotta dig this here lead outta this tree. Then we go back an' spend rest a the day makin' balls for the both us."

"You still figgerin' on wint'rin' with them Crow—what'd you call 'em?"

"Absor'kees?" he asked, then hurried on without allowing Josiah to respond. "Yepper. Ain't no man gonna keep me from Arapooesh's band."

"McAfferty's got him a Nepercy squar 'long with him. How them Absor'kees gonna take to her?"

"Crow ain't got no truck with the Nepercy, far as this here child knows of. Damn, if that would'n' take the circle!" Bass clucked his tongue. "I'm settin' my sights to them Absor'kees, howsomever you lay it."

"That'd have us where our ha'r was short, if'n they didn't take to McAfferty havin' him a Nepercy squar 'long, it would." Josiah threw another piece of lead into the kettle. "Hey, ol' man, you figger you can show me to makin' a sheath for this here sticker?"

"Outta rawhide?" Bass questioned. "Certain we can. You can be doin' it from me showin' you 'bout sewin' with sinew whilst I'm mendin' mokersons."

"You ain't givin' no answer to my question, Scratch." Paddock was a little irritated. "We gonna move out in the mornin', or ain't we?"

Bass stopped his work with the knife to look up at Josiah, "Son, said we had us some things to be doin' this day. An' tonight we'll jest stay by the fire an' drink outta Scratch's jack o' likker."

"An'?" Paddock looked into Scratch's eyes.

"An' tomorrer we'll see what set McAfferty's got to the end of his float stick. See what he thinks of movin' out early."

"All right," Josiah said, a little resigned.

"With that squar an' all her truck, it'll take ol' Asa some time to be packin' plunder an' possibles to the breakup." Scratch set back to work. "Don' really b'lieve you're gonna move that man till he's ready to be moved."

"Jest who in the goddamned hell's gonna be booshway in this here group?" Josiah had not taken his eyes from Scratch. "Is it gonna be McAfferty this an' McAfferty that? Is that man gonna be booshway?"

Titus kept picking at a bullet hole in the piece of wood in his lap, working the knife blade deeper and deeper into the cottonwood for a few minutes before he answered. "By some sign, McAfferty be booshway. Then, by 'nother sign, Ol' Scratch be booshway."

"That ain't tellin' me nothin'."

"Hush up minute, boy! You're wantin' all your damned questions given back to you in nice, purty lil' packages, ain't you? All wrapped up in purty paper with a purty lil' bow tied to the top?" Scratch spoke quietly, but evenly

317

without an edge to his voice, without the sound of malice. "I ain't got them kinda answers for you, son. I ain't got 'em for you." He now looked at Paddock.

Josiah stared back for a flickering moment, then dropped his eyes and went back to work with his knife.

"Me an' that white-headed nigger never work that-away, Josiah." The older man continued looking at Paddock. "He lays some sets, an' this here child calls the tune on others. McAfferty's said he's wantin' to go up yonder to Three Forks, but he's wantin' to tie in with us too. Man cain't take us no place you an' me don' wanna go, now can he? We ain't pups for that, is we? No-o-o-o, we ain't. McAfferty give us chance't to say no to him, didn' he? I like me that man's medeecin, I does. Been good, it has. But I cain't for a skinny bull figger on why he's all fired, primed-in-the-pan ready to be headin' up there to Three Forks. But Ol' Scratch here is one to find out. Might'n be int'restin', it'll be. It be bloody country, up there is, but rich to the beaver too. An' if a man cain't say he tried, then what's it all track? If a man's 'fraid an' skittish 'bout such, so squampshus he ain't 'bout to try, then what's it all track?" He finally lowered his eyes to the timber across his lap. "I'm jest one to say we'll give 'er a try with Asa. Wander on up to that country an' see how the land lays the set for trappin' an' trouble, both. Yessir. Like to see me what McAfferty's medeecin is got wind of up there. I'm wint'rin' to the Absor'kees, ain't no double set to that! An' one way or t'other, you an' me gonna be layin' trap down 'long the Yallerstone come spring breakup. McAfferty can lay to it or no. If'n he don', it won' make me no never mind. I jest got me a itch as needs to be scratched, Josiah." He paused. "That be it, young'un. Ol' Scratch got him a itch as needs some scratchin'." Bass finally put his blade back to work. "Leastways, that Bridger feller ain't moved out yet. Josiah Paddock can sign up with them Rocky Mountain fellers if'n he don' like the way I reads sign. Said you could do that alla time."

"Thought we had us that all settled, ol' man." Josiah lifted his eyes. "Thought we was gonna be pardners come breakup. Now, if you don't want me 'long with you for some reasons—maybe you an McAfferty be better off without me—then you tell me straight out, up to the muzzle, right now."

"My, my, my!" returned Scratch, surprised. "How

318

you do turn the trick on this child here! Alla time I'm one to figger you're thinkin' you don' wanna be my pardner, an'...an' you're really thinkin' I ain't wantin' to be yer companyero! Whoooeee!" he snorted in short laughter. "If that don' take the circle! Dammit, Josiah Paddock, you an' me is thick! I feel me I can count on you—like I ain't be one to count on nary 'nother man since't McAfferty. I feel me like you're figgerin' you can count on me, too. An' that makes this ol' coon feel good some, it does. I jest wanna see what medeecin's callin' McAfferty up there—an' if'n that white head's medeecin don' set with us for spring breakup, why then there'll be two coons makin' beaver 'way from the other nigger, an' them two coons'll be you an' me: Titus Bass an' his pitch-fired companyero Josiah Paddock, a young'un as is gettin' farther an' farther down the tramp from them settlements he's left behin't." He shook the knife blade at the younger man, "You read my sign, boy? Eh? You readin' my sign here?"

"I'm readin' it," he laughed at the corners of his mouth at Bass's smiling eyes. "You're layin' it heavy to the trail, an' I be downwind from you. I'm readin' your sign."

"Then get you back to work there, young'un." He waved the knife blade once more at Josiah, then pushed it back into the cottonwood timber across his thighs. "I got me a dry on 'gain, so's I need me some likker, an'...an' I'm one as can spit more'n that tin cup can hol't, so's Ol' Scratch is gonna mother that whole jack o' likker this night. Less'n them other niggers made it bottom dry. I'll be liftin' ha'r then, son! With me a big dry to pack an' no likker to help it. I'll be liftin' ha'r."

"Bullshit!" Josiah chuckled as he plopped another piece of lead into the camp kettle. He looked up at Scratch, who was chuckling too.

The sun had moved low in the western sky by the time they carried the kettle back to their camp across the valley creek. With supper out of the way, the trappers gathered to whittle down Scratch's keg of trader's whiskey. Bass put the lead on to melt and prepared to mold round balls. He thought of something else crying to be done while waiting on the lead to soften. In the light at the fire's edge, Titus pulled thick, stiff rawhide from a pouch, along with an awl for Josiah and one for himself. He set the young man to measuring the large knife against the rawhide for size. While Paddock was cutting

the leather down to the proper dimensions for a belt
sheath, Titus tore strips of sinew to suit the job at hand
and put them in his mouth to soak while he looked over
the pairs of moccasins he would need to repair. From his
lips protruded about an inch of each of the sinew strips;
these tips of the tendon thread he would keep dry and
stiff to serve as a needle to begin the trip through the
awl-punched holes. With the top of the keg serving as
something flat and solid beneath the rawhide, Paddock
set to work punching holes in the thick leather. Bass
started the lacing with a few stitches and then handed it
over to Josiah to complete, showing him how to stitch
around the long hole at the side of the sheath. There, he
explained, was where Paddock would hang the sheath on
his belt.

With the younger man at work on a double overhand,
locking stitch Bass had learned from the Crows, Titus
settled down to repair his many pairs of worn moccasins.
He blended his sewing, bullet-making labors with drinking and yarn spinning, accompanied by the other free
trappers around the night fire. This day-end celebration,
compared with those of past evenings, was muted, for it
seemed to each man that rendezvous was moving to a
close. A chapter in their brief lives was concluding and
they fought the melancholy of it. Soon they would find
themselves on a hillside overlooking Pierre's Hole, turning in the saddle for a last look at the valley of summer
memories, a look that would have to sustain them through
the coming year. The memories would pull hard at each
man's soul—there would be missing faces around next
summer's campfires.

Milt pushed his squaw away. She had been attempting
to look over his wounds this morning, trying to explain to
him that some of the lacerations might require new poul-
tices of chewed roots. The Thunderbolt of the Rockies
didn't feel spunky greeting this new day. On top of the
nagging headache, thirst, and diarrhea from his general
physical malaise, the young captain was irritated that his
brigade had not covered more ground the previous day.
And now the men were slow in rolling out of their robes,
slow in moving to pack the horses to resume their march.
Sublette's anger gave him some new vitality as he hobbled

around the small encampment kicking at those trappers who were refusing to budge from the warmth of their bedrolls just yet. The rudely awakened men saw from Milt's scarred and slow-healing face that he meant business.

Sublette returned and sat atop some packs beside Henry Fraeb. Old Frapp could afford to be philosophical about such things.

"Take keer, Soblette," he handed Milt a pipe filled with fresh tobacco. "Not goink to move dem 'for dem ready to move dis mornink." He looked into Milt's eyes and could see the pain the younger man was attempting to hide behind them. "We can stant to use some time now, to whip dem into shape. Do not let hit frazzle you, Milt. Dem still 'memberin' renduzvooz." He helped Milt light the pipe from the dying fire at their feet. "We got us goot bunch here. Dem jus' neet some time for dem to be goot workers."

Sublette looked back into Fraeb's eyes as he puffed to get his pipe started. It irritated him that he was irritated. He had a name to uphold out here, he was constantly telling himself. But he had done well in doing just that. When the name of Sublette was mentioned in the Rockies in connection with some outstanding deed, men still asked whether the storyteller was speaking of William or Milton. And now the younger Sublette brother was slowly becoming conscious of his driving ambition, his burning desire to excel where William had. So, Milt was hard—even brutal at times—on himself. Always driving, always pushing, Milton Sublette wanted to be the first there with the best every time. It followed naturally that he would drive his men relentlessly on occasions. But, most of all, Milt Sublette was hardest on himself.

As he drew on the newly ignited tobacco, Milt looked over to see the young squaw puttering around with her possibles while trying to tend to the two young children. The one boy old enough to crawl wore one of his father's old calico shirts, which the woman had cut down to look much like a long nightshirt. Earlier this morning she had taken the younger child down to the edge of one of the beaver ponds nearby. Here she had loosened the straps of the cradle board and pulled the infant from its protective cocoon. The messy task of cleaning the inside of the cradle board and bathing the child then followed. She would have little opportunity to clean the excrement from the baby's cocoon in the next few months, and she wished it to be done this morning before hitting the trail with her relentless young husband.

The squaw looked back at her man as she relaced the ties binding the infant to the cradle board. She smiled at her man, her heart filled with the joy that she had been the one this man had chosen for his wife. Sublette's eyes softened as they turned away from hers to look about the slow-moving men in camp. They were gradually getting the animals loaded with the coming year's supplies. He looked past Fraeb to watch young Wyeth's Yankees finally stirring. "Greenhorns!" he muttered.

"Vat iz dat?" Fraeb heard the man beside him mumble something.

"Yankee greenhorns!" he replied with force yet quietly. "Wonderin' now if I was smart in bringin' 'em along with us."

"Dey help, Soblette," Henry commented. "Give us more men. Dozen more. Help skeer Injuns huway."

Milt did not answer verbally. He only nodded in the affirmative while continuing to stare at Wyeth's eleven stalwart recruits.

"Dey ones who stay on wit' him. Not ones go back wit' yer brot'er," Fraeb continued. "Dey be goot men too, Soblette. Dey make him goot men to stay."

"S'pose you're right, Frapp." Milt turned and tapped the back of Henry's shoulder. "They coulda gone back with Bill, like them others." He rose and stretched the taut, healing muscles across his chest. Milt sighed and looked about him at the camp he had been forced to choose the previous day. Here at the south end of the Hole, with the mountains beginning to close in on three sides, he had finally ordered a halt near the bottom of a small defile. Through it flowed a stream where beavers had industriously been at work damming the water so that much of the area had become a shallow swamp. Bordering the ponds were thick groves of cottonwood and willow, interlaced with the ever-present creepers and vines which lay like a tangled mat here and there about the camp. He sighed and stretched once more, "S'pose you're right. Jest don' wanna lose no time. Got us a long way . . ."

The rest of the words froze in his mouth. His eyes had caught some movement high above the camp along the hills the trappers would be moving through in the

322

hours to come. He first thought the black specks might be a herd of elk gathering up. Milt watched them for brief seconds, squinting his eyes until he had discerned that these could not be elk. There was an order to their march.

"Ya?" Fraeb had heard Milt drop his thought mid-sentence and now rose to stand beside the younger man.

"Don' say nothin' right now." Milt shot a glance at Henry. "Lookee up thar', Frapp. Tell me what it be that you see."

The German, slowly turning his head from Sublette's face where he had read more than fatigue, darted his eyes along the skyline until he saw what he was asked to watch. "Ya," he commented quietly. "Dey not animals."

"I don't think so neither."

"Some coots comin' in late to renduzvooz?"

"Prob'ly all it be. They be mounted and comin' down in two lines. Prob'ly Font'nelle's train," Milt replied, referring to the packtrain headed by the man Drips and Vanderburgh had hoped would be the first trader to arrive in Pierre's Hole. But the American Fur Company train had not yet shown, and was daily expected to come in—late. "That be a good one, Frapp! Font'nelle comin' in with plunder to trade—an' Billy's got all the beaver in his packs!" He laughed hoarsely along with Fraeb.

"Ya! Dat comp'ny hain't got no one to sell goots to now!" Henry chuckled some more.

The black objects along the hillside now formed long, distinct columns as the two men watched from the distance. Joe Meek came up to them.

"Ya seein' what I'm seein', Milt?" Joe asked, watching the faraway objects now drawing more attention from the trappers' camp. "Buffler?"

Milt and Fraeb watched a moment more before Sublette answered, "Not movin' like that, it ain't buffler, Joe." He doubted now that this was the American Fur Company trader and turned to Meek, "Go get Sinclair—an' Wyeth, too." Joe started to step away, "Keep 'er quiet 'bout this, Meek. Don' wanna fret nobody now." It had to be Fontenelle, he told himself. But he couldn't make it fit. The trader coming into the Hole was way off his course. Milt struggled with it in his mind, thinking that there should not be another group that size in these mountains at this time of the year unless it would be the American Fur Company's packtrain finally limping into rendezvous.

"What's up, Captain?" asked the Yankee Wyeth, coming up to the German and Sublette.

"Got us some vis'tors comin' in," he nodded toward the hillsides becoming covered with the two columns. "We're figgerin' 'em to be Font'nelle from American Fur, but we ain't jest sure right now. Get your boys ready, Wyeth, but don't scare 'em none. For right now."

Nathaniel Wyeth stood beside Sublette a moment more, watching the wave of riders coming over the crest of the distant hill. The Yankee was descended from a long line of seafarers along the eastern coast. His eyes strained to discern the intent of the objects coming down into the southern end of the valley as if he were atop the crow's nest at sea, spotting an object against the far horizon.

"I'll get my glass," Wyeth remarked dryly and turned away.

Milt watched after him for a few moments, seeing the Yankee commander moving quietly among his men as he told them of the approach of riders to the south. Sublette saw each man's head look up as he was told. But they held their places quietly, as Wyeth had instructed them to do.

"Ye wantin' to see me, Milt?" Alexander Sinclair had come up to stand beside Sublette.

"Nothin' wrong right now." He looked at the long, thin face of the free trapper who had taken command of a group of men after Gantt & Blackwell had folded. "Think we may have us some comp'ny here, afore long." He pointed to the hillside without stretching his arm out, holding his hand close to his chest to indicate the direction in which Sinclair was to look.

"What ye want me to do?"

"Jest let your men know. Check their loads an' such. Jest get 'em ready is all," Milt replied.

"Ya want them Flatheads to know?" Meek asked.

"Yep," Sublette answered. "We better. Don't want them niggers doin' somethin' crazy. Tell 'em jest to stay where they is now. Don't want 'em gettin' all excited 'cause 'nother trader's comin' in. Tell 'em we don' know what it is right now."

Joe moved off at once to carry Sublette's instructions to the Flatheads, who had come into camp the evening before, requesting the company of the trappers on their northward journey to their homeland.

"We'll see what it be on the horizon." Wyeth had come back up as Meek took off. He snapped out the sections on his long brass spyglass and brought it to his left eye. The right was not so strong, so Nathaniel had become accustomed to putting the mariner's early-warning spyglass to his left eye. He sighed as his eye adjusted to the lens, then moved the spyglass slowly up along the hills until he caught the leaders of the two columns. He took another short breath and let it out as he sought to steady the instrument. The figures snapped clear and sharp before his line of sight. Those about the Yankee were quiet. The camp was silent, eyes and ears on the small group of men who were now waiting for some word from Wyeth. The Yankee took a short gasp of air and uttered the one word others were not expecting.

"Indians!" He brought the spyglass away from his eye and looked at Milt. The color had suddenly drained from Sublette's face.

"Lemme see!" Milt took the glass away from Wyeth.

"Can ya tell what they be?" Meek asked. "Crow mought'n be wand'rin' out this way now."

Sublette had taken the glass, and looked for a fleeting moment at his young wife and two children before putting the instrument to his eye. His wounded leg hurt suddenly. He could not hold the spyglass steady on the approaching Indians and handed it back to Wyeth.

"Count 'em!" he snapped.

All eyes in camp had moved from the small knot of men to the objects pouring from the hillside. No loading of horses, no tying of bundles or bedrolls. All attention was paid to the cavalcade approaching their camp. That one word spread like prairie fire through the nervous trappers: "Indians!" Wyeth's men stirred and moved about. Turning on them, and with a quick downward jerk of his right arm, Nathaniel told the eleven green recruits to sit down and keep their silence. He put the glass to his left eye once more and brought the Indians into view, "Some of 'em on foot..."

"Jest count 'em!" Milt snapped again.

"Looks like they're all off the top of the hill now," Nathaniel remarked, then fell silent as he tabulated the size of the unexpected Indian village.

Fraeb, quiet these past minutes, now moved his head to the side and looked at Sublette's squaw and children.

325

Henry thought back to his own Snake wife he had left at rendezvous. As she was expecting a child soon, Fraeb had told her to stay with her own people for the fall and winter seasons. He now watched Milt's wife busy gathering up the one crawler, who refused to let his mother prevent him from playing. The boy did not understand the look across his mother's face as she looked at Milt, trying to conceal the fear she felt rising within her. Sublette gnashed his teeth, then turned to Meek at his side.

"Send two riders back to ronnyvoo," he directed Meek, who nodded. But Milt was not finished. "Get one to tell Billy an' 'Bridger we got us a lotta comp'ny out here. Tell the other to get word to them free trappers—Nez Percy an' Snakes, too." He looked away from Meek's face but still gripped Joe's arm. Sublette saw some activity at the front of the columns, then noticed a large flag being unfurled for the white men to see.

"Union Jack," Wyeth spat. "British flag."

Milt clutched the side of Meek's arm more tightly as the column came off the hillside onto the flat, the Indians now whooping. The women and children brought up the rear of the party, with the warriors smartly quirting their horses and prancing about as the two files snaked their way onto the prairie. They stopped their march as they came off the hill, but milled about yelling and whooping more loudly than ever at the trappers.

Nathaniel finally took the glass from his eye and looked into Sublette's face for a long moment before speaking. "Little more than hundred fifty of 'em."

"How many warriors?" he asked of Wyeth, then remembered the Yankee was on his first trip to the west. "How many men in the front, there?"

"More than half," he answered tersely. "Maybe eighty—could be a hundred there."

Sublette's stomach churned. He looked from Fraeb to Meek, and once more to his wife and children. He moved his eyes back to the Indians, who had stopped just out of rifle range. Milt felt Joe's hand on his wrist and looked at his friend.

"Want me to get them riders goin'?" Meek asked.

"One of 'em's comin' out!" Sinclair split the air with his words.

An Indian moved slowly away from the front of the stationary throng and started to cross the distance of something less than half a mile that yawned between the two groups.

"We neet us time," Fraeb commented.

"We ain't got time," Sublette remarked as he watched the solitary man approach. "That one's a chief."

The Indians felt the need for time also. For this they had sent their war chief out to parley with the white men. He had instructed his warriors in preparation to greet the white men as friends, for he had been instructed himself by Kenneth (Red Coat) McKenzie, head bourgeois for the American Fur Company at Fort Union, to keep an eye out for his clerk, Fontenelle. McKenzie had told this chief, Baihoh, that the trader's packtrain would be in the vicinity of Pierre's Hole about this time of the year. McKenzie had told Baihoh that he would be greeted warmly by the white men, that he would be welcomed for trade. The chief had ordered his impetuous young men to stay their weapons, to put aside any thoughts of attacking this small cluster of white men they easily outnumbered. These were Fontenelle's white men, he told the braves. They were friends of their good friend, McKenzie.

"They be friendlies?" Sinclair asked. "With that English flag? English give it to 'em?"

"Could be," Milt replied.

"Coot be," Fraeb repeated. "But . . ."

"But them niggers may have raised it," Sublette interrupted, "like you raise ha'r. A trophy for the winner."

Baihoh brought his pony to a halt halfway between his people and the white men, and waited. Across his left arm ran the long, slender stem of a pipe. Baihoh had taken it from its special medicine bundle with the prescribed ritual of chants and ceremony. He had laid objects of reverence and mystery atop the empty bag before boarding his pony to approach the white men. Over these holy objects he had performed his medicine, touching claws, rattles, the special feathers and skulls, bringing religious herbs and tobacco to his nostrils to smell. In this way he would take their power into his own body. Baihoh now sat motionless atop his pony, waiting for the white men to send someone out to greet him. He tugged at the bright blood-red blanket wrapping his old shoulders, shivering once in the chill air.

"Get your men to take them packs off their animals," Milt said to Sinclair. "If the horses go, I don't want no goods goin' with 'em. Frapp, you tell our boys do the same. Want me a breastwork thrown up fast." His mind busy counting the white men he had with him, Sublette felt his stomach jump at the thought of being so outnumbered. His leg ached terribly.

"They gotta be Crow," Sinclair offered as Fraeb moved away. "If'n they'd be somethin' else, them niggers'd be down on us like shit to a privy hole by now."

Milt thought it strange that the overwhelming force of Indians had not moved to attack yet. Everything in him said the unexpected visitors should have rushed the small force of white men. He thought a moment more. "Told you get your men movin' packs," he turned on Sinclair. Alexander looked into the slits that were Milt's eyes and left the knot of commanders.

"Gimme that eyeglass," Meek requested of Wyeth. He brought it to his right eye and peered through it at the tail of the columns as the Indians finally reached the plain. Along the file of women and children he moved his eye. The squaws wore the short skirts of the Crow, but still Meek did not utter a sound. He moved the glass again to look over some of the warriors milling around the head of the columns. The braves had no distinct hairstyle. Some wore the fluffy pompadours and straight bangs of the Crow tribe. Other warriors were adorned with the long, wrapped braids and scalplocks like the Sioux and Arapaho. His mind twitched as he looked at the coarse fringes decorating the shoulder seams and sleeve ends. They looked like Blackfoot hunting shirts. His mind still catching fire, Meek brought the glass up to train on the chief. Joe focused his eyes on Baihoh. Atop the Indian's head was a large buffalo headdress with the horns attached. Feathers fluttered in the breeze from the tips of the black horns. He dropped his gaze from the Indian face smeared with paint and a faint smile. Meek's vision then held along the chief's left arm. There rested the squat, thick bowl of green soapstone ahead of the long, slender, carved wooden stem adorned with colorful trade ribbon, feather drops, and brass tacks. Joe stuck with the pipe a moment more and one word popped to the front of his consciousness—Blackfeet! He was just about to utter it when he saw through the lens that the impatient chief began to speak. Joe took the glass from his eye to listen to what the Indian had to say. As Baihoh began his speech, all doubt in Meek's mind vanished like a spark quickly extinguished in a gust of wind. He knew that tongue.

"Blackfeets!" he yelled. "Them's Blackfeets!"

"Get your men goin' to ronnyvoo now, Joe!" Milt barked at his friend.

Meek tossed the spyglass to Wyeth and took off to set the two men on their way back to the rendezvous encampment some seven or eight miles north up the valley. Milt stared at the chief, then peered behind Baihoh to the plumed and painted warriors milling close to the timber.

Baihoh watched with curiosity the two riders dash away to the north. He was somewhat mystified. This was Fontenelle and the American Fur Company men to whom he was presenting his pipe as a pledge of peace. His warriors did not want to observe a truce with any white man, but Baihoh had stuck his neck out to guarantee that these men would offer trade to the tribe. He had ordered the unfurling of the Union Jack to show the American Fur Company men that he had taken the flag from John Work's Hudson's Bay brigade in battle.

"Bug's boys!" Milt muttered. His mind raced as he thought of buying time until men from rendezvous could come up.

"Blackfeet?" Wyeth asked. "What be so special 'bout Blackfeet Indians?"

Sublette was annoyed at the Yankee's ignorance of mountain realities. "Meanest kinda Injun you'd ever wanna run onto," he replied. "Blackfeets mean war out here." With his words Milt knew the fight to come would be a hard-fought contest, with no quarter given on either side. The white men faced a large village, symbolized by the horse and dog travois in the rear behind the nervous, antsy warriors. "Blackfeets mean war," Milt repeated to himself.

Baihoh's tongue had caused all doubt to vanish as to the tribe across the grassy plain from the white men. The language was Blackfoot, all right. But there was one tribe that had adopted the Blackfoot tongue many years before when it had split from the Arapahos and had become part of the Blackfoot confederation: Gros Ventre—Atsina—the "Big Bellies." Because their own language was difficult to handle and only sparsely known among white men, the Gros Ventre of the prairie usually spoke to strangers in the Blackfoot tongue. They had learned the language from

329

their Peds Noirs cousins through long years of fighting and hunting alongside the Blackfoot tribe. Although the mountain men would occasionally call them Big Bellies to denote the tribe's habit of stuffing themselves, often uninvited, in every lodge they visited, the Atsina were lumped together with the Peds Noirs. To the white trapper, these were Blackfeet. They were beggars of the Rockies. Beggars of the first degree. Even their close cousins, the Arapaho to the south, had given them the appellation "Spongers" to signify the primary trait of the tribe. Their thievery caused the tribe continual fighting with the trappers who haunted the fringes of Blackfoot country.

Only the past winter they had been blamed for burning the American Fur Company post at Fort Piegan. The tribe had been south to visit its distant relatives, the Arapahos of Colorado country. Now after three years of living off the tribe to the south, the Gros Ventre were heading home. This was the tribe that had cut up William Sublette's supply caravan one night while the trader was making his way to rendezvous. This was the tribe that had caught Tom Fitzpatrick alone, out in the open, on the prairie. They had forced Fitzpatrick to abandon his horse to save his life. With the new prizes from the raid on Sublette's packtrain and the famous Fitzpatrick's pony in tow, some of the tribe were anxious to get home to celebrate with the appropriate feasting and dancing. These eager warriors had pushed on ahead of the main body, trailed by their women and children. They had climbed over the mountains to the western side of the divide to steer clear of the Crows.

The tribe had been formerly poor in horseflesh as most of the good ponies could only be found in the Spanish settlements to the south. By the year 1825, the Gros Ventre had traveled south to visit the Arapahos for the first time since the two tribes had split up. They became rich in horses and headed north victorious. On their journey they were robbed of their stolen horses by the Crow tribe. The Gros Ventre were poor once more. The warriors had become bitter from the experience, and also fierce and inveterate combatants, willing to fight to the last man to protect what they owned.

In 1829 the tribe had moved south for another southern visit to the Arkansas River. With the plunder accumulated after the three-year sojourn and with the pride of having successfully attacked the white trader's packtrain, the warriors were anxious for another chance to prove themselves in battle. They were up early to push on to their homeland that morning, and had caught the awakening white camp with its britches down. Baihoh had crested the hill to look down upon the distant white camp still in sluggish preparation for the day's travel. He remembered McKenzie's words and ordered his eager warriors to do nothing to jeopardize the trade with Fontenelle.

The chief had ridden out to meet the white man Fontenelle. If he had suspected he was looking at the encampment of McKenzie's fierce and hated competitors, the Rocky Mountain Fur Company, would the Gros Ventre chief have ridden out alone with the pipe across his arm? He could see his men easily outnumbered the whites. If he had suspected this was a Rocky Mountain Fur Company brigade, why would he not have attacked? If he had suspected this to be McKenzie's competition, why did Baihoh bring the warriors' families, the women and children, down from the hills onto the dangerous prairie? If he had suspected this was anything but Fontenelle's packtrain, would the chief have allowed his young men to whoop and holler as they approached the white men? The Gros Ventre do not attack in such a manner—they would sneak up on their enemies as silently and as deadly as they could. Baihoh came forward with the pipe and called out in Blackfoot his merry greeting to the American Fur Company white men.

That pipe across the chief's arm galled Milt Sublette. He wasn't about to let any Blackfeet get away with that old trick. He looked behind Baihoh to the milling warriors, believing them to be making preparations for war. Sublette thought to himself that they needed time, too. That pipe stuck in his craw. Milt had too many friends who had gone under to the Blackfeet. He wasn't going to fall for the ruse of an offered pipe. Deep within his bowels Sublette knew Baihoh had come forward with the pipe to buy a little time for his warriors, to gain a closer look at the enemy, to count heads and rifles. While a useless parley was going on, the chief would be waiting for reinforcements to come up. Milt only hoped his reinforcements from rendezvous arrived first. He stomped around in a small circle, his head bent forward. Sublette was angered at the arrogance this tribe had exhibited in coming onto the plain with war whoops and yelling, blankets fluttering in the morning breeze. It maddened him that they had boasted in this manner before attempting to wipe out his small, overwhelmed force of trappers. Milt cussed the useless Yankee greenhorns. He raised his head to look at the small group of Flatheads and swore loudly at them in English, knowing they still would not understand the words—only his tone of voice. Milt spat on the ground. The Blackfeet would be all the more arrogant in battle and eager for blood with their enemy, the Flatheads, within the white man's camp.

His wounds bit at him and made him feel faint. He swore at his leg. He was in no condition to lead the coming fight. Wyeth was still so green he smelled of freshly cut grass. Sinclair was in no better shape than Sublette himself. The free-trappers' partisan had lost some toes the previous winter to frostbite. With the loss of those toes, Sinclair could not be counted upon to lead an effective fight on foot across the flat plain. He could go to battle only on horseback or in close quarters in the willows and creepers. Milt would have to count upon Fraeb and Meek to lead the fight. But Sublette was not ready to fire the first shot. He figured they would stand the defensive while hoping, praying, the reinforcements arrived in time. Control of events was soon to drop from his grasp.

"Dat cusset Injun vants to talk," remarked Fraeb, also grown impatient while watching the chief sitting alone atop his pony halfway between the two groups. There came no answer from Sublette or any of the assembling Rocky Mountain fur trappers. "Tink we shoot go talk vit him, Soblette?" Milt did not get a chance to answer.

"I'll go talk with that nigger," came a voice behind Fraeb and Sublette. The words had come from Antoine Godin, an Iroquois hunter and trapper attached to Milt's brigade. Sublette turned to him as Godin continued, "I know enough of his damned tongue to palaver with him." His eyes glared, seemingly on fire. Godin turned to the Flathead chief at his elbow to ask, "Your rifle charged?"

The Indian's eyes flashed into Godin's, and he nodded in the affirmative. "Then you cock it an' foller me!" Godin moved off toward the horses. This Iroquois half-breed was ready enough for the scrap. The Blackfeet had killed his father, Thierry, two years before along a little mountain stream some seventy miles from Pierre's Hole, a stream the trappers had come to call Godin's Creek. The Blackfeet had rejoiced in the man's scalp.

Antoine had chosen his companion for the parley well. He knew that if he were to take one man along with him, it would be the Flathead. The tribe had been continually at war with the Blackfeet for many years, and now the hatred for its enemy was hereditary. Two men who had not only a familial but a very personal burning for revenge against the Blackfeet were the men who rode out that morning to approach the chief waiting on the prairie, a chief who exhibited a posture of peace and goodwill for the white camp.

Across the grassy no man's land the two riders moved their ponies slowly. Antoine, agile and Indian-skinned himself, dressed in his fanciest of leather shirts, turned his head below the wool hat atop his head and spoke to the Indian riding beside him.

"Keep your muzzle low but your finger on the trigger, friend. When I take the nigger's hand to shake it, you be ready. I'll take a Blackfeet's hand for only one thing."

The Flathead did not reply, but signified he understood Godin with a nod of his head. This squat Indian felt the two eagle feathers tied to his long braids fluttering in the breeze. Along his arms danced scalplocks interlaced with fringes. He looked away from Antoine's face to study once more the chief they were riding out to meet. The Flathead's bowels burned with hatred. He was inflamed with tribal memories of fighting the Blackfeet, his people armed only with stone-tipped cottonwood and willow arrows and spears, whereas the enemy fought arrogantly with British Northwest Company trade fusils, smoothbore muskets which made the fight mere sport for the Blackfeet. His heart now gorged with the challenge he had been told months ago was issued by the Blackfeet: that the Blackfeet would exterminate the Flatheads this year.

Baihoh watched the two riders approach. His eyes darted from one to the other. The chief became nervous, seeing both riders to be Indian. One he knew to be an enemy—Flathead. The other was dressed like a white man, but looked to be also an Indian. This was not Fontenelle's packtrain. Baihoh's pony pranced and pawed at the earth at the approach of the two men. He shifted the pipe a little across his left arm and became conscious that he should show no signs of anxiety as the riders came up.

Baihoh threw his shoulders back proudly within the bright scarlet blanket adorned with a broad band of colorful quillwork.

"How ne tucka?" ("How do you fare?") Baihoh called out in Blackfoot as the two men came closer. "Cristecoom, cristecoom nah tose. ('The Great Spirit watches over me.') Yamaa mahtsee, ahecooa nin nah. ('I am a warrior, a great chief of my people.')" The two riders were close. He lifted the pipe across his chest. "Nahto steea, ahquayneman pistacan." ("We will sit to council, with the tobacco pipe for all.")

Godin pulled up on Baihoh's right hand while the Flathead chief stopped on his left. The Gros Ventre's eyes flashed from Antoine to the Flathead, who spoke first.

"Squoishten-weitsthum. ('I have seen Blackfeet this day.') Tapskillto. ('Killers of my people.')" As he peered angrily into the Gros Ventre's eyes, the Flathead could see Baihoh adjust the pipe across his chest. "Quil-kouil, ekoinih star koi so mai noots. ('You have come to talk in your red blanket, holding onto a pipe of peace.') Who it squoissehten sto misto. ('The Blackfeet are squaws when they do not have a gun to shoot.') Quellah kai en tapin sodle-lodle mints. ('I have the rifle this day, my peoples' enemy.')"

Baihoh clenched his lips together tightly and moved his eyes from the Flathead to Godin. He would try to talk sense to this man. The Gros Ventre chief brought his right hand slowly away from the pipe across his chest and presented it to Godin.

Antoine looked down at the hand, smiled, and took it in his right hand before he moved his eyes back up to stare into Baihoh's. He gripped the Gros Ventre hand tightly. Baihoh saw the smile in Godin's eyes just before the Iroquois half-breed spat the one-word command at his Flathead companion. "Fire!"

Baihoh's eyes widened at the order and jerked his head toward the Flathead who brought the muzzle of the cocked rifle up to point at the Gros Ventre chief's heart. The Flathead wore a smirk around his mouth for a brief moment before he pulled the trigger of the leveled rifle at point-blank range, enjoying the twisted grimace of betrayal that painted over Baihoh's face. The force of the lead ball ripping through his body threw the mortally wounded man out of the saddle as his Indian pony reared slightly and jerked back away from the scene. The animal tore away, back to the line of trees where the stunned Gros Ventre warriors stood open-mouthed at the murder of their war chief. Through the white-gray cloud of burnt powder Baihoh fell to the ground as if in slow motion. The pipe he had held across his chest slipped from his grasp and shattered into several pieces, for the ball had passed through it on its way to Baihoh's heart.

The Flathead raised the rifle overhead as he looked down at the fallen enemy for an instant before jerking on his pony's reins to bring it around. Kicking dust up with every step, the animal was set in motion by the Flathead, spurring his pony back to camp. The Gros Ventre warriors howled with a rage mingled with grief at the loss of their war chief. Their cries for revenge filled the air along with the wails of the squaws behind them. Some of the braves stepped forward to fire at the lone rider left on the plain. With the lead balls whistling past and splitting the air about him, Antoine Godin leaned to the right off his pony to grasp the edge of Baihoh's bright scarlet blanket. As he pulled on the corner of the quilled blanket to yank it out from under the dead Indian, Baihoh's body rolled across the ground as if Godin had set a heavy top in motion. The Iroquois half-breed snapped the red cloth into the air, gave a throaty war whoop, and turned his pony to the north. Across the whole of the distance of his ride back to the white camp Godin whooped and waved his bloody trophy. In the blanket was a single hole. He had in hand a prize worth more than any scalp, symbolic of the revenge he had taken for his father's death. The bullets fired from the smoothbores followed after him but Antoine galloped back into the trappers' compound without a scratch. He leaped from his horse before it had come to a full stop.

Wyeth had witnessed his first mountain action; he was stunned and open-mouthed at the brutality in the quick chain of events. The Yankee was near Godin as the Iroquois dismounted. *"This was Joab with a vengeance!"* Wyeth yelled out to Antoine. *"Art thou in health, my brother?"* quoted the Yankee from reverent literature. The Battle of Pierre's Hole was on.

Some of the Gros Ventre women now moved their ponies and children deeper into the grove of cottonwood and willow, beating animal and child alike to spur them into action. The braves continued firing and one by one fell back to reload within the protection of the willow-brush cover. They were stunned. Their ritual for peace parley had failed them. But these were Indians steeped in the mettle of Blackfoot tradition—Gros Ventres eager for the fight, boiling for the spoils they knew would be theirs when they had wiped out this small force of white men. Many of the warriors continued to taunt the whites, running out a short distance across the prairie to yell threats of obscene mutilation, brandishing their personal medicine charms, anointing themselves with paint hastily brought out of sacred bundles, and waving their fusils overhead. Several rushed about to retrieve their medicine shields from which the covers were stripped for action. They believed that the magic of the shields would make the Indian warriors virtually invulnerable to the white man's bullets. Amid the noise of the howling Gros Ventre village, some women were pulling horses and dogs back up the hillside or farther south into the valley, while other squaws emptied their hands and went to work pulling deadfall and brush together within the grove of cottonwood and willow. The Indians would let the white men lead a suicidal attack. No warrior had ventured out on the plain to collect the remains of the Gros Ventre war chief.

As the women scurried about constructing the crude breastwork from natural materials, the warriors continued to rain lead and arrows across the grassy prairie at the trappers. Confident their enclosure within the swamp would give them additional protection, the Indians chorused threats of mutilation and promises of quick death should a white man venture to attack their stronghold. They shouted out that the white men were squaws for not coming forward to the fight. Immediately behind the breastwork, a few of the women broke off to begin digging long trenches within the structure, tearing at the soil with knives, tomahawks, and even bare hands if nothing else was available. Here they would make their stand just outside a loop in the little creek with the hills rising about them.

Milt ordered the men of his Rocky Mountain brigade to close quarters and make a short dash to the left where a small ravine ran obliquely to the Indian fortress on its way to the creek. Singly and in small groups, the while trappers began to dash forward to the ravine while those behind kept up a covering fire. Sublette watched the migration begin, then turned to locate Wyeth.

"Keep your Yankees here, Wyeth," he commanded above the noise of sporadic fire from the muzzleloaders. "Them damned greenhorns ain't worth a spit right now!

Keep 'em down behind the packs. Get 'em movin'! Now!" The Thunderbolt, as Sublette was known among the Rocky Mountain trappers, turned to move his small family behind some thick baggage as the air carried the sounds of the children's cries to his ears.

Wyeth heard the force behind Sublette's words and got his eleven men to scoot behind the assembled tangle of baggage and packs. He told them to keep their heads down, informing them that here they would be out of danger and would not be joining in the fight. They were frightened, every man—but some itched for the battle and chafed under their leader's order to remain hidden and out of the way.

Nathaniel now turned away to direct the actions of several men from Rocky Mountain Fur and Sinclair's trappers, getting them to secure all the animals in camp at a safe distance out of rifle shot. He was determined that even though Sublette had ordered the Yankees to take no part in the fight, Nathanial Wyeth was going to exhibit himself with courage during the conflict.

Sublette's trappers were closing within a good distance for a rifle shot along the ravine. From there they kept up a warm fire, sending lead into the grove where they heard more activity from the Gros Ventres than they could see through the dense brush. Each man knew he and his companions were outnumbered, but took heart in the fact that for the time being they had the Indians digging in and surrounded. Still the Gros Ventres were good shots with their McKenzie rifles and excellent shots with their elkhorn bows. Most of the men knew all too well that a charge or rush upon the breastwork would be suicidal. All they could do for the time being was fire into the tangled grove where they heard The Gros Ventres screaming back at them. The two runners sent back to rendezvous were riding the seven miles at breakneck speed. All Sublette's trappers could do now was to keep from getting shot. And wait.

12

He was dozing lightly in the chill of early morning when he was kicked in the back by Scratch as he rolled over in his sleep. Josiah sat up immediately, blinking his eyes. He was blind for a moment. Then he realized the old man was asleep and had not done it intentionally. Paddock looked out from under the canopy as he scratched at his beard. He let out a sigh. Rolling onto his left side to pull the buffalo robe from his legs, Josiah was stabbed in the back by the wooden handle of the heavy-bladed knife he wore at his waist. Looking at it, he was proud of the somewhat crude workmanship on the rawhide scabbard for the sticker—it was his workmanship.

Standing to fight with a groggy head, the young man thought of making coffee to ward off this dizziness from last night's work on Bass's keg. He thought a moment and remembered that the coffee pot was still by the fire. But he would need to roast and grind some more beans. Slowly crawling across the robes beneath the blanket canopy, Josiah found the old man's bundles and seized the sack of coffee beans. He had everything he would need. Paddock's heart jumped when a hand suddenly gripped his left wrist and the buffalo robe flew off the older man's body. He was staring down the bore of Scratch's .54-caliber flintlock pistol.

"Hear you now, young'un!" the older man rasped. "Don' you be goin' messin' with my possibles like that when I'm 'sleep!"

"Jest gonna make us some coffee, goddammit!" He was still battling the surprise and tried to shake the hand loose from his wrist. Bass lowered the pistol.

"Don' mind you makin' coffee at all, son." Titus released Josiah's arm. "Jest don' want you doin' such as you did again—me 'sleep an' all." He spat over the robe to the grass. "Coulda put a ball through you without even knowin' it was you as was there."

Paddock began to pull the sack of beans from the canopy. "Some damn thanks that be! Man doin' you lil' favor by gettin' coffee makin's out an' roastin'—you say you'll shoot him!"

"Josiah, jest do us both a favor," Bass said, putting the pistol back into his belt. "Don' go messin' 'round like that 'gain on me when I'm sleepin'." Bass pulled the skillet out of the bundles and slid it toward the young man, "Do us both a favor—you'd be the sure an' sorry if I kilt you with a ball, an' I'd be the sorrier 'cause I'd be the one to have to live with it on my mind. No more worry for you then, son." Titus scooted out from under the canopy. "But me—I'd have to carry that on my mind." He smiled with the corners of his crow-footed eyes as he nudged Josiah lightly on the shoulder. "You woke this here child up the worst way a man wants to get up—ready to kill or be kilt. Damn," he spat again, "don' you ever do that again, you lil' polecat!" Scratch winked at Josiah. "Weren't you 'bout to be makin' coffee?"

"Well, now. You don't get you none this mornin' for pullin' that pistol on me," Josiah retorted.

"Awww, don' take it like that, companyero." Bass shook his old legs from the hips. "We headin' where there'll be lil' sleep for a man an' a whole bit passel of chances for gettin' hisse'f a ball to the lights. Jest you be thankeeful that I'm a coon as can come up out'n my bedroll like I did there. Jest you be thankeeful for that." He pawed at the ground with his moccasined toes a moment looking into Paddock's eyes.

"It all be gone now," Josiah replied; "all to forgot now."

"Get you that coffee goin' whilst I'm takin' care of my mornin' pissin' chores." Bass turned away from the young man and headed toward the willow-rimmed stream. Josiah pushed on to the fire.

After he had stirred last night's coals into new life with some fresh kindling, Paddock poured beans into the skillet. With them over the fire it was not long before the aroma of roasting coffee greeted his nostrils on the early-morning breeze.

"Ye do make some mean coffee," Solomon hollered out from his bedroll.

Paddock turned to see the trapper's head raised and looking at him. Some of the others beneath the cover of the lean-to were stirring at the beckoning of the faint, early-morning fragrance of roasting coffee beans. Josiah kept up the careful shaking of the skillet as the beans browned, nodding a greeting to each trapper as he came up to join Paddock by the fire. The sun was nearly breaking over the Tetons to bathe the entire valley in light when the sound of driving hoofs was heard coming from the south. Gray stood and moved out to the edge of the prairie to watch the approach of a solitary rider.

"Man's in a hurry, that'un is," Elbridge remarked loudly to the trappers about the fire. "He's latherin' that animal."

As the lone rider approached he began to yell at the top of his lungs. At this distance, none of the free trappers could understand what he was hollering. Josiah pulled the skillet from the coals and set it on the ground. He rose and went to stand with the others watching the rider come up.

"Who is he?" someone asked.

"Don' know." There could be no answer yet.

"Blackfeet! Blackfeet!" the rider yelled as he whipped his pony, slapping the animal's flanks with the felt hat he held in a free hand. He was riding hard, his buttocks kept out of the saddle by standing in the stirrups.

"That nigger say Blackfeet?" Gray asked of Paddock.

"Sounded like it," Solomon Fish answered.

"Down the valley! Blackfeet down the valley!" The rider was near to the group of attentive trappers. "Get yer guns! Blackfeet—down the valley!"

"Yep," Josiah answered now, "he said Blackfeet."

"Where in tarnation...," Solomon started, but the rider reined up the lathered pony in a small cloud of dust just before he reached the assembled men.

"Goddammit! We got us..." the rider said, breathless, "got us Blackfeet down the valley! Sublette's camp got 'em pinned down for now! Injuns got us outnumbered three to one! Get your gun! Get your gun! I gotta tell Sublette an' Bridger! Jest get your gun! Come a runnin', all ya niggers! Blackfeet down the valley!" He put his heels savagely into the pony's ribs and the animal jumped away.

"Great graybacks!" Caleb shot in. "We got us some Blackfeet to fight!"

"Le's go!" Solomon turned and dashed off to the lean-to.

"Get Bass saddled up!" Gray took off in a trot yelling back to Josiah, who was suddenly left alone. "Tell that nigger he's got some Blackfeet down the valley!"

Paddock was finally stirred loose from his spot by the frantic activity about him. He didn't know what to feel—he was numb. "Blackfeet!" he said to himself quietly. "Blackfeet!" more loudly this time. He felt the surge of adrenalin shoot straight through his body with the excitement of his first Indian fight. It helped to flush away some of the fear he felt rooting him to the ground where he stood. "Blackfeet!"

"Get movin', Paddock!" Wood hollered out as he ran past, the first to get ready. "Get Bass movin', too!" He was headed to the edge of the prairie where the ponies were tethered.

Josiah finally moved from where he had been anchored with excitement and fear. He took off on a dead run through the lean-tos and shelters, finally skidding to a stop by the blanket canopy. Bass was not there.

"Scratch! Scratch!" he yelled out as he turned his head, throwing his voice into the willows ahead of him. He took a step in that direction when the older man appeared.

"What the hell's wrong with you, boy?" Bass stepped out of the tangle of willows buttoning up the fly on his pants. "Get a man off his shit..."

"Blackfeet!"

"Blackfeet!" Scratch's head jerked around from side to side.

"Down the valley!" Paddock blurted out.

"South?"

"Got Sublette pinned down," Josiah said, pointing south with his arm, "down the valley!"

"How you know it?" Titus buckled his belt.

"Rider come in," Josiah took off at a trot beside Scratch. "Says them Blackfeet got Sublette's men downed three to one!"

"I can let that shit go 'nother time!" Scratch dove head first beneath the blanket canopy. "Whoooeee! Josiah, we got us Blackfeet fight!" He threw back the buffalo robes, both hands busy pulling at knife, shooting pouch, rifle, and an old fur hat. Titus slid back out and stood, hurriedly throwing the pouch strap over his right shoulder and pushing the knife between his belt and waistband of the pants. "Get your truck, boy!" he shot at Josiah to put the younger man into motion. Paddock had been somewhat hypnotized by watching Bass complete his speedy preparations. "Ever' man's gotta have him his first Injun fight—an' yours could'n' be better'n if I'd picked it myself. Blackfeet! There's Blackfeet down the valley waitin' for you, Josiah! C'mon!"

Josiah pulled the new rifle and his shooting pouch

heavy with balls to him, then latched onto the powder horn. He saw Scratch's still lying on the robe. "You want this?" He picked up the older man's powder horn.

"Gimme it!" Scratch leaned forward to take the horn from Josiah.

"Figgered you might be needin' it if Ol' Make-'em-Come's to be shootin' any Blackfeet!" Paddock slid out from under the canopy.

"Goddamned smartass, you are, young'un!" He slipped the horn strap over his shoulder where it hung tucked close under the arm. "Let's go!"

Josiah took off a few steps behind the older man, struggling to put the straps of both powder horn and shooting pouch over his shoulders as he trotted out to the ponies. Bass climbed aboard his animal bareback after pulling up the picket rope. "Throw me your rifle!"

Paddock did as he was instructed and tore loose the knot that held his pony to the picket pin. He jumped to the back of his animal smoothly and righted himself ramrod straight.

"Here you go!" Titus threw Josiah the rifle. "Let's be makin' trail sign!" Bass dug his heels into the pony's flanks as he spun the animal around and headed south onto the prairie covered with sage. Paddock was not far behind. Already the valley was filling with riders spurring their ponies down toward the action. White men kicked horses into furious speed beside the Shoshone and Flathead warriors, who had also been told of the Blackfoot village. Like racing ants, hundreds of mounted riders were covering the plain, filling the air with whoops and laughter as they sped southward.

Only minutes before, the dispatch rider had whipped his lathered animal into the Rocky Mountain Fur Company camp to the north. William Sublette had been engaged in directing the work of his packers and clerks, who were busy loading furs into bundles for the trip back to the States. Robert Campbell, Sublette's partner, had been sitting on the ground under the tent with a small manuscript of paper on his lap and an inkwell at his side, writing a letter to his brother back home in the settlements. All activity had come to an abrupt halt when the runner came with the urgent news.

"Blackfeet! Blackfeet!" the man panted. "Blackfeet got Milt pinned down! They got us three to one!" Trappers scurried out of shelters, tents, and from beneath canopies to crowd around the perspiring rider. "Blackfeet down the valley! Get yer arms, boy! Milt needs ye come a runnin'!"

Campbell jogged up to the scene of milling trappers and stood beside Bill Sublette. The trader listened to little more before turning to find Bridger in the crowd.

"Gabe! Milt an' Frapp pinned down! Let's be puttin' our ponies to the run!" He turned away from the rider as most of the trappers scattered back to their shelters to get their weapons, "C'mon, Bob! We got us Blackfeet to take care of!" They dashed back to the trader's tent. "Get us our ponies!" Campbell took off to retrieve an animal for himself and Bill.

Sublette was immediately crowded by his clerks and packers asking if they were to go. "No!" He snapped. "You're to stay here! You ain't gonna go down there an' get cut up!" He knew all too well what might happen to these young American and French helpers, greenhorns all, if they should become involved in a fight with Blackfeet. He continued to impress upon them his orders to stay put and guard the camp as Campbell came riding up, leading Sublette's saddled pony. Bill grabbed Bob's rifle, pouch, and horn along with his own and tossed them up to the mounted man. He pulled the cover from his own rifle and took the reins from Campbell. Bob snapped the fringed buckskin scabbard from his own rifle and pitched it near the side of the tent before sticking his arms through the straps on the powderhorn and pouch.

Bill muttered something and dropped the pony's reins for a minute to yank his coat off his back. He quickly rolled up his sleeves, then dashed back into the tent. He emerged with a pistol stuffed into his belt.

"Let's be findin' what Milt's got himself into down there!" Campbell said as Bill mounted. "If them Blackfeet got Milt pinned down, it'll be a different story when we get there!"

Bridger had his favorite runner, a small buffalo pony, picketed beside the bower where he had been lying and enjoying a bowl of tobacco when the dispatch rider had arrived in camp with the news of the fight. Dropping the pipe onto the robe when he returned from hearing the rider's news, Jim quickly saddled his pony. He always complained how flea-bitten the animal was, but it was a pony a man could count on when the cards were down.

Bridger pulled his coat off and dragged it under the bower with him as he retrieved rifle and supplies for the coming fight. He forked the pony between his legs and turned south with the other trappers scampering across the plain.

The prairie was now crowded. Men were kicking their horses into furious speed. As soon as a man could grab his rifle and possibles, he boarded his horse and moved down the valley. Blistering across the plain were a few hundred riflemen by the time Sublette turned to Campbell to shout out some instructions as they rode beside each other at full tilt.

"Bob!" Sublette had to yell above the clamor. "If I go under, want you to take care of things back east for me!" Sublette went on to make a verbal will to Campbell as they rode, itemizing what he wanted done with his personal possessions should he be killed in the coming battle. Campbell then instructed Bill in what to do should he be the one to go under to the Blackfeet. Amid the noise and dust rising from the valley of Pierre's Hole, Sublette and his friend Campbell appointed each other the executor of their verbal wills. Many a man this day would appoint another to take care of things in the even of his death. This was the soldier's manner of preparing for battle, his mind eased that his last requests would be seen to by a friend.

The word was being passed from camp to camp, through one village after another. It was a word that brought red man and white alike to the common cause. Flathead and Snake joined the white trappers in the rush south across the plain. Every man had a vested interest in this fight. Age-old tribal memories were brought to mind as the warriors slipped aboard their fastest buffalo runners; each trapper knew at least one friend who had gone under to Bug's Boys. Everyone in Pierre's Hole had a score to settle this day.

"Josiah!" Scratch yelled above all the noise of pounding, unshod hoofs and excited, scared men. "Foller me, son!" Bass pulled slightly on his racing pony's reins to bring the animal slowly to the left as they neared the Nez Perce village.

Here was a scene of sheer pandemonium. The younger teenage boys were busy whipping and guiding the horse herd closer to the lodges, working their way in a ring about the animals to spur them in closer for added protection from the Blackfoot threat. The Nez Perce village was the encampment farthest to the south in the valley. They feared the Sublette forces would be overrun and the enemy would push north through the Hole. The Nez Perce knew they would be the first to suffer the onslaught of the Blackfoot charge. From among the lodges dashed riders just mounted and armed, emerging in small groups to burst southward. They yelled back and forth at one another as they sped past Bass and Paddock, shouting exhortations for the coming battle and singing their own medicine songs for the death that might accompany this coming fight.

Into the village Scratch led Josiah, into the howling of dogs and the barking of squaws giving orders to children. Some of the women were beginning to mount their own ponies now to take off on their warriors' heels.

"What them squaws goin' for?" Josiah hollered over to Titus.

"Figger to be some plunder for 'em this day, I reckon," Scratch answered as they pulled up at McAfferty's lodge. "Then too, some of them squars'll go to the fight to be close to their men. If'n he's striked down, she can sing his death song for him." He leaned off to the side toward the opening of the lodge. "McAfferty!"

Asa's young squaw poked her head out of the doorway momentarily before pulling it back inside to announce the arrival of the white riders. Asa brought his face to the doorway, then crouched low to step from the lodge.

"What brings ye?" the white-headed man held a small pipe in his hand and was barechested. Josiah stared down at the right arm bound in leather that held the iron hook to the wrist.

"Jehoshaphat, McAfferty!" Scratch puffed. "There's Blackfoots down the valley! Cain't tell me you ain't heerd of it." He swept his arm about to indicate the frantic activity in the village. Everyone was up and moving: warriors mounting, a few of the squaws leaving with them while other women stayed behind to herd children into lodges, and small boys running about chasing one another with toy bows. Everyone in the Nez Perce village was up and moving—everyone but McAfferty.

"I heerd tell of it." He put the pipe stem to his lips and drew on the smoke as he peered back at Bass and Paddock.

"Well, ain't you comin'?" Josiah asked.

Asa slowly pulled the stem from his mouth and looked down into the pipe bowl before moving his eyes back up to Paddock. "Ain't got me any truck with them Blackfeets. McAfferty don'..."

"Shit!" Bass interrupted with a snort. "Ever' man up here got truck with them devil niggers. Ever' man has see'd what them Injuns does..."

"Ain't never had me a run-to with Blackfeets," Asa interrupted. "Cain't say as I have me any hate for 'em, neither. Blackfeets ain't the ones I carry the black heart for."

"You've changed, Asa McAfferty." Titus let slide the quiet words.

"Don't doubt me that one set, Titus," he answered. "Don't want me them Blackfeets down on me—not now— don't want them Blackfeets down on me."

"You ain't comin' then?" Titus asked.

"Cain't say it any plainer, Scratch," the white head replied. "Don' want them Blackfeets down on me now."

Bass stared at the short man for long moments of silence. The air empty of words at this place would in time begin to write the final chapters in another mountain tale. "C'mon, Josiah," ordered Scratch, continuing to stare into Asa's face. "Titus Bass's got truck with them Blackfoots—an' Titus Bass's gonna kill him McAfferty's share this day. Let's go!" He yanked hard to the right on the reins to twist the pony's neck to the side in leaping away from Asa's lodge. Josiah looked at the short Scotsman for only a moment before digging his heels into his animal's ribs to follow Bass. At the edge of the village, Titus slowed to let Josiah come alongside.

"How you figger it?" Josiah asked the older man.

"I don'," was the answer. "McAfferty not wantin' any truck with them Blackfoots—I don' figger it." With that he put the animal between his legs into a full gallop, not waiting for Josiah to stay by his side. They melted into the frenetic rush of riders scurrying across the prairie.

The Gros Ventre village heard the approach of hundreds of hoofs before espying the arrival of some two hundred trappers besides over five hundred Indians from the Shoshone, Flathead, and Nez Perce villages. Much of the bravado of their boasts and promises of death to the white men quickly disappeared as the Gros Ventres watched the swelling numbers of enemies come across the prairie. Some covered their mouths in sheer astonishment and surprise before moving backward to take final cover within the fortress thrown up by their squaws. Behind the brush and deadfall, within the trenches and foxholes hastily dug, they vowed to continue their fight. Milt's trappers saw the retreat from the ravine where they continued to pour lead toward the Gros Ventre position. The women and children received word from the retreating warriors. None of them had expected anything like this. None of them had expected a rendezvous encampment nearby. But the grassy plain before the Gros Ventre warriors boiled with activity. The warriors commanded their women and children to retreat back up the hillside. Those who could not fight were told to make good their escape. The women would be saved this day so they would live long years of mothering sons who would avenge the deaths to come this day in battle. Farewells were hurriedly made before the squaws were pushed south. Those women who elected to stay now set to work reinforcing the barricades or frantically clawing at the earth to deepen the trenches inside the fortress. With the retreating Indians would go the word of warning and challenge, a challenge to be given the entire village somewhere still to the south across the mountains. The brave ones left behind could only hope to stay the attack by the trappers long enough to allow their families to escape to fight another day.

A Canadian-Indian half-breed attached to Milt's brigade in the ravine looked behind him at the massive arrival of reinforcements. Made bold by the presence of overwhelming numbers or perhaps by a desire to strike the second blow of the battle, the half-breed let loose a war whoop from his throat and dashed from the draw toward the willows. Within the first few steps of his headlong run for fame, he was shot in the chest. The ball spun the half-breed around before throwing him to the ground. At the puff of smoke from the Gros Ventre rifle, several of the trappers aimed their weapons and returned a volley of lead.

But no one now showed any particular interest in rushing the fortress. One trapper snaked out of the ravine to grab onto the collar of the wounded, foolish half-breed. Keeping his belly pressed against the ground, he pulled the casualty back to the cover of the trench where an attempt was made to stop the blood pouring from the unconscious man. The trappers stared down at the half-breed bleeding to death and realized the enemy had a clearer sight of them than they had of the Indians holed up within the brush. It tended to make a man cautious. With the arrival of the allied warriors, many were emboldened at first to make an attack; eager to strike a coup to be recited around lodge fires to come; eager to snatch up the spoils of the battle. But they soon grew reluctant to make that suicidal run toward the enemy fort as word spread of the half-breed's foolhardiness and its price.

William Sublette whipped his horse into the midst of the confusion. Campbell called out for one of the Wyeth men to take their horses away from the battle scene. Young Milt hobbled up to his older brother.

"Good to see you, Billy," he said.

"Bet it be," the older Sublette replied. "Got yourself a lil' Injun trouble, I see. How many you figger?"

"Wyeth counted 'em with his glass," came the partial reply. "Maybe only eighty to hundred warriors. Dug in back there in the willows, back toward the stream."

"You try stormin' it yet?" Bill asked.

"Nawww. Jest got the boys strung out 'long that wash over there." He pointed for William to see. "Cain't see us much of a thing in there; hear a lot goin' on, but cain't see a thing of them niggers holed up in there." He paused a moment and looked back into his brother's eyes. "I ain't much good for this fight, Billy. Cain't move fast—my leg is . . ."

"Get yourself low over there," Bill interjected, pointing to the ravine where Milt had directed the trappers of his small brigade. "Stay put. I don't wanna lose you, Milt." He nudged his younger brother forward toward the others before turning his head from side to side to overview the whole skirmish and the lines being set up by the arriving trappers. As they left their ponies, the men sprinted forward only a short distance to take their places beside the Sublette brigade. Everyone was stationary, firing only a few random shots in the direction of the Gros Ventre fortress.

Bill was angered that more was not being done to

take the fort, angered that the outnumbered Gros Ventres were not being pressured more. He pushed forward to the ravine from which he could catch a glimpse of the brush cover thrown up by the enemy. Sublette was impressed. The fortress was in a good location that provided more than adequate protection, if for no other reason than that it could not be seen by the white men without exposing them to Gros Ventre lead. Still, he told himself, he had never been one to lie back. There was a job to do and he would have to step into this leadership vacuum. Bill scooted back out of the ravine to the main line of gathering trappers where Bob Campbell stood waiting for him.

"Bob," he said, looking hard into his partner's eyes, "I'm goin' in after 'em. We ain't gettin' a thing done thisaway." He pulled the buttons at the front of his shirt from their holes and took it over his head. Tossing it to the side, Sublette then untied the knots that held his leggings to the belt about his waist. After pulling his feet free of the leather tubes, Bill stood naked save for his breechclout and moccasins.

"Hear me good, men—each of you!" Sublette shouted to the hundreds gathered about him. "We ain't gettin' a thing done waitin' out here for them Blackfeet! I'm one to tell you if'n we don't put a ball an' blade to them niggers in there, why—we ain't gonna be able to show our faces in these here Rockies again. Our enemy is here. We couldn't make it any better! Less'n we take that fort, Americans ain't gonna stand a chance west of the Powder an' north of the Yellowstone! You hear me! An' now, boys—here are them Blackfeet niggers. The niggers been prowlin' round us for days jest waitin' for the chance to jump us—jest waitin' for the time when they thought we wasn't ready for 'em. Them's the niggers in there jest darin' the palefaces to come on an' fight like men! But here we sit, buried in our holes. We gonna be squaws? Eh? Are we men to match these here mountains? Shit! There be a good chance some of us'll fall here today, but we'll go under knowing we went to that big belt in the blue fightin' Blackfeet! An' fightin' Blackfeet be a good cause! Will your lives be worth the tinker's dam, will your possibles an' ponies be safe, if'n we don't teach them

Blackfeet they cain't get away with callin' these here men squaws? Will we let them niggers spread the word 'bout us in the mountains?"

The men about him had turned from time to time to look at one another during Sublette's speech. They now raised a cheer and many rose to strip their shirts from their chests.

Bill turned to Campbell, "Bob, you know the Flathead. Go now an' tell 'em of goin' to rub their enemy out." He pressed his palms together to dramatize the word "rub." "Go tell 'em that. An' say to 'em that we need their help. Jest let them Flatheads know we're beside 'em in this—that we white men are goin' in there to rub them Blackfeet out." Campbell nodded to his friend and left without another word. He translated some of Sublette's speech for the Flathead warriors nearby as others gave the gist of Bill's proposal to the Shoshones and Nez Perce.

Sublette motioned for Milt to come to his side. The younger brother came up and Bill gripped his shoulder tightly, "Milt, you stay behind on this'un'. Want you to know Bob's to be in care of my things if I go under today. I've told him what to do. Jest want you to know that Bob'll take care of things back east if this is my day to die." He pursed his lips and looked once more over the assembled trappers. While his brief declaration was being presented to the friendly tribes, Bill turned away from Milt to address the trappers again.

"Back to ronnyvoo, I got your beaver to take back to the States," he shouted. "There ain't no beaver country be open to you if we don't take that fort—now! Nez Perce watchin' us! Flathead an' Snake, too! The Crow an' 'Rapaho gonna hear of this—that we didn't take that fort! They'll say we're squaws, same as the Blackfeets! Then there ain't gonna be *no* beaver country open to us." Campbell came back up to Sublette's side. "I'm goin' in with Bob an' any other coons as wants to rub them niggers out. Who's with me for the fight?"

A few of the trappers stepped forward toward Campbell and Sublette. Bill nodded to each one as the thirty-odd whites gathered about him. When it seemed as if no others were to appear from the hundreds who had listened to his exhortation, Bill hollered, "Let's go!" Both Sublette and Campbell raised their voices into the air with a shrill war whoop to accompany their dash toward the willows.

Behind them followed the white trappers and about as many Indians. Titus Bass had stripped his leather shirt off and stepped forward when Sublette had called for volunteers. Somewhat reluctantly, Josiah had come up to stand beside Scratch. Before either had time really to ponder his decision, both found themselves sprinting headlong into the willows.

"Jesus Kee-rist!" Josiah hollered as the advance slowed and the white men about him slid to a halt behind clumps of willow.

"Sh-sh-sh, boy!" Scratch hoarsely whispered. "I come to fight! I ain't one to be hangin' back on this. That Sublette ain't one to push no man out front. He's gonna lead the way." Joe Meek scooted past Scratch and darted up to the left of Sublette. Bass grew silent as he looked forward through the thick undergrowth, feeling within himself the desperate, teetering balance between the need to show courage before the others and the fear he felt rising up within his bowels knowing the enemy was now like a trapped animal—and all the meaner for it. Slays in the Night, the Snake warrior, came crawling up beside Titus and whispered in broken Shoshone so that Scratch would be able to understand. The Snake warrior told Bass that he was a strong fighter, a Shoshone much accustomed to combat in the brush. But Slays in the Night said he feared the cover about the enemy fortress to be impenetrable. He spoke of the danger of being alone before the fort, subject and helpless before the dangers that awaited the man who stormed the enemy's position. In quieter words, the Snake warrior concluded by saying that he would not shrink from this fight, that although he might die, Slays in the Night smelled Blackfeet this day and there was killing to be done. After all, the Indian then turned to face the dense grove, it was a good day to die. The warrior gripped Scratch's wrists tightly for a brief moment and crawled off to join the Indians who were taking up the north flank about the fort while the trappers with Sublette were moving out to stage themselves along the south flank.

Bill had given the battle what it needed most: a leader. To Josiah's left snaked Alexander Sinclair and his brother, Prewitt, along with a few of the free trappers who had joined Milt's brigade for the fall hunt. Sinclair had grown bold and proud by the actions of Bill Sublette and Robert Campbell. He pushed through the grass and creepers to share their glory along with sharing the danger of sudden death. Wyeth moved past Josiah and stopped near Sublette, who clutched the earth only a few yards away from Paddock.

"Bill," he whispered to get Sublette's attention, "them Indians over there need someone to command them."

"Yep," was all Sublette replied.

"I be the one, Bill," Wyeth volunteered. He'd had it in mind when he had crawled out to the willows. Nathaniel had promised himself that he would not be found wanting in courage this day. "I'll see that the starboard doesn't fall short." With that he slid off to join the few Nez Perce, Flathead, and Snake warriors who lay bunched together. Wyeth spread them out around the fortress on its northern flank. Bill could only smile in watching the young Nathaniel slither off to take charge of the friendlies. A few months before this Yankee had been an ice merchant in Boston. And now he was not only getting the green worn off, but taking a leading role in the fight as well.

Sublette motioned to Meek to come to his side. "Joe, take you some of them men an' go down that way, along the creek. Wanna spread out round 'em a lil' more."

Meek pushed himself away and snaked from man to man, gathering a good-sized force to follow him as the southern flank would be spread toward the creek.

Bill waited for Meek to move his force away, then turned to motion to those left behind to follow him into the thicket. One by one the trappers set off behind Sublette, Campbell, and Sinclair, pushing their way laboriously through the swamp created by the industrious beaver, which had taken refuge when all the commotion had begun. Each man moved slowly and cautiously for no one could see more than ten to fifteen feet in front of him because of the tangled brush of willow and creeper. Carefully a man would move aside a branch here and there to peer ahead, ever mindful that in so doing he might make a handy target of himself. Bill would advance in the lead at times, then Campbell or Sinclair, each one turning on occasions to yell a warning or a come-hither to those behind. In the swamp the trappers crawled and slithered. From their position they could catch a glimpse now and then of Meek's detachment, co-commanded by Tom (White-hair) Fitzpatrick, who had recovered much of his strength through the "medicinal" properties of whiskey and buffalo meat. Everyone believed he would force a show of the enemy, force the Indians into the open for a final, quick, and decisive battle on the plain once they had the warriors on the run.

Josiah moved up beside Campbell, with Scratch coming up on his right hand. Bass put a half-dozen balls from his pouch into his mouth. Bill's brother Andrew, younger than Milton, moved over Paddock's moccasins to nudge his brother's leg. William turned around to see that Andrew had come to join the skirmish. He smiled at the young man, then looked forward once more. Their small group now numbered seven men, the rest having left for the creek with Meek and Fitzpatrick. A few yards off Scratch's right hand lay two Americans Bass did not recognize, both of them looking past Titus to await the next signal from Sublette.

It would prove to be an interesting postscript to this day's famous battle that Antoine Godin and the Flathead chief who had accompanied the Iroquois half-breed onto the plain to kill Baihoh were not among those who plunged into the fight. Instead, these two who had fired the first shot of the skirmish lingered near the trappers' encampment, watching the others go to finish what they had begun.

After much wet and dirty work in struggling through the dense undergrowth, the party found itself at the edge of an opening in the brush. Not far away each man could now see clearly the fortifications of the enemy. The Gros Ventre squaws had prepared well their fort before leaving their warriors. The trappers could see the deadfall and scattered limbs interwoven between the standing cottonwoods and willows. None of this could protect the enemy, each man thought to himself, but it surely did hide them. The squat shelter of brush had been topped with bright blood-red blankets, buffalo robes, and leather lodge covers, all of which enhanced the concealment of the Gros Ventres. The trappers could not see the enemy well enough to aim a shot so Sublette proposed to move across the open to the very wall of the fortification. As the men to his right and left moved from the last fringe of willow, the Gros Ventre warriors opened a brisk fire with their smoothbores. Snuggled down within their foxholes, they could fire beneath the bottom log of the deadfall ramparts. The first explosions from their McKenzie fusils wounded some of Meek's men and forced all to scurry back behind the cover of the willows once more. There each man caught his breath and struggled to keep from rustling the clumps of willows where he lay. Each movement of a branch, each snap of a dry twig, brought a Gros Ventre ball to answer the sound.

Josiah lay shaking in the midst of his cover. He struggled to force down the lump in his throat. Around him among the trappers was only confusion and second thoughts. Many of the men Fitzpatrick and Meek had led down to the creek had been with Milt all morning. They were astounded at the fortress thrown up by the enemy, a fortress constructed without the white men knowing it, even though they had been only two hundred yards from it.

Sublette ordered his men to push deadfall in front of them when they chose to advance a second time. From behind these logs the trappers fired an occasional shot at a target they were sure of throughout the next two hours. Both Scratch and Josiah were soon stuffing their muzzles with unpatched balls for convenience and speed. Each time his mouth was empty, Bass would pull another handful of lead from his pouch and pop the balls inside his cheeks. The sun beat down on the baking men, those with Bill Sublette now wishing they had taken off toward the creek with Fitzpatrick and Meek. Their mouths dried, then cracked from the relentless sun's heat. Some men sucked on leaves for moisture. It was hotter today than it had been throughout the entire rendezvous. Things always had a way of turning out like that. The trappers vied for the precious little shade available while the air laden with burnt powder stung their nostrils.

Alexander Sinclair tired of the slowness of the battle and wearied of the scorching heat. He had chosen to remain behind a clump of willow rather than take refuge behind a downed log as his brother had done somewhere to the rear. He turned to Prewitt to ask for a covering fire while he pressed forward across the open between the trappers and the fortress. Sinclair, ahead of the others, pulled apart some of the willow branches concealing him. In the instant he looked clearly at the fortress of the enemy, Sinclair's companions saw a gray puff of smoke blossom from behind the Indians' crude shelter. A rifle burst hit the air. Alexander jerked back off his hands and knees into the tangled mat of creepers.

His chest burned with the ball that had entered but not left his body in its ricocheting path. Fighting for breath, the partisan felt blood oozing into his mouth from low in his throat. He choked and spat to be rid of the warm fluid. But still it came. Eyes cloudy, Sinclair struggled to see about him through the haze of heat and smoke. He spotted Campbell at his left hand through the willows.

"Campbell," he squeaked. "I am shot—oh, dear God!—I am shot!" He spat more blood, still welling up from the chest wound. There had never been the need to tell the others he had been hit—they had seen the bullet strike Sinclair. "Campbell," he again gasped. "Take me to my brother. I beg of you, man! Take me to my brother!"

From his spot less than a yard from the wounded man, Campbell inched backward around the willow and reached for Sinclair. Not close enough. Bob cursed beneath his breath. He inched forward from the willow cover a little more and strained his arms to reach the dying trapper. Still not far enough. Campbell took a deep breath and moved barely a few inches this last time, then stuck his arm out toward Alexander. He caught hold of Sinclair's ankle, grabbing tightly the top of the moccasin that wrapped about the bottom of the wounded man's leg. Campbell steadied himself and moved the man about a foot. He took a better hold and dragged Sinclair more than two and a half feet the second try. By inching himself along, Campbell gradually got Sinclair behind the willow cover once more. He looked down at the wound Sinclair was clutching.

"Campbell, I may not last," the man sputtered as blood crept from between his dry lips. "Take me to my brother, I pray you, man!" He fainted.

Robert nodded to the unconscious man before he took hold of Sinclair's arm to move his body backward some more. Cautiously, with agonizing slowness, Campbell got the man back to a reinforcing line of trappers behind the main skirmish flank. He instructed them to take Sinclair out of the swamp. As the two men began to drag the casualty from the area, Campbell turned his face again to the fortress and crawled back to the brunt of the action. He was careless in moving through the undergrowth. The dry grass and twigs snapped from Campbell's impatience to return to the skirmish. As he moved past a Rocky Mountain Fur Company trapper named Phelps, a ball whistled through the air. With a dull thud it crashed into the trapper's left thigh. Phelps cried out in pain as he gripped the wounded leg with both hands. Campbell twisted around to look behind him at the injured man. He realized he had caused the trapper to become a target; he had been too noisy. Bob cursed himself as he slid backward toward Phelps. He stuck his head around a clump of willow after reaching the bleeding man and spotted Bass.

"Hey!" he called out in a loud whisper, then ducked his head. "Hey!" He whistled low to attract Scratch's attention. Bass looked behind him from where he lay, not sure if Campbell meant him. "Yep! You!" Campbell said, motioning with his arm "Come over here, will you?"

Titus looked about him once more, then studied the fortress for a moment before sliding toward the wounded trapper and the man who had caused the injury. Across the dry, brittle grass, Titus slid ever so slowly. Still he found himself making noise that sounded like the thundering hoofs of a buffalo herd to his ears. Another piece of lead whistled out of the fort and went spinning through the willow over his head, snapping off a branch that landed on the back of Scratch's neck. He froze for a moment, fighting the impulse to remain where he lay. Eventually he battled back the reluctance to continue his crawl, but still wondered what madness had possessed Campbell to call him over. Titus finally slid belly-flat alongside Phelps and stared over at Campbell with angry, questioning eyes filled with disbelief.

"Take this man out!" Campbell whispered loudly. "Take him back..."

"You son of a bitch!" Scratch shot back. "Take him out yourself! He got your ball for you—least you can do."

"I ain't gonna argue with you, man!" Campbell's whisper was quieter now but still persistent. "I'm askin' for your help."

"An' you booshways can slide! I ain't gonna haul this man outta here."

Phelps groaned, still clutching the wounded thigh with both hands white knuckled. "Please—oh, my God—somebody! One a ye!"

Scratch looked down at the face and studied it for a moment before lifting his eyes once more to peer at

Campbell. "I ain't doin' it for you, booshway—doin' it for him," Bass said. He rolled his rifle off his chest, slid the straps from his horn and pouch off his shoulders, and grabbed Phelps's belt. A foot at a time, Titus began to drag the wounded man from the dangerous willows. Campbell pushed up by Sublette, who had moved more to the left for a better sight of the fort.

Bill had seen what had happened to Sinclair. Most men realized what awaited them if they made a foolish move. Sublette was disgusted that they could not get a good shot at the targets within the fort. The trappers were pinned down. From his new position he watched closely several openings in the brush the Indians had gathered about them. Within a few minutes he spotted what he wanted. Through one of the loopholes the enemy was using to fire their devastating shots, Bill caught a glimpse of a pair of eyes peeping out at the trappers. As quickly as thought could become action, he brought the riflestock to his cheek, aimed, and fired. The eye disappeared, exploded by the penetrating lead ball to the Gros Ventre warrior's head. Bill drew back down to reload as Campbell slid up beside him.

"You see somethin'?" Robert asked in a dry whisper.

"Watch that hole." Sublette grinned and motioned his head for Campbell to look. "You'll soon have you a fair chance for a shot." He struggled to drive home the charge of patched ball within the powder-caked barrel. He could not. Bill looked about him before peeking once more at the fortress. Sliding backward a couple of feet behind some more willow, Sublette rose to his knees to try to force home the ball against the breech. The man in front of him turned at the sound of Sublette's cursing the resistant lead.

At that instant more smoke blossomed from the enemy stronghold and the air shattered with another rifle report. The trapper in front of Sublette who had raised up to look around at Bill now pitched backward, the side of his head chipped away by an Indian bullet. Before the trapper had even fallen backward onto Sublette, Bill felt a crushing blow against his left shoulder. The force of the ball spun him around before he fell prostrate beside a cottonwood, the dead trapper stretched across Bill's naked legs.

Campbell had seen his friend wheeled around with

the force of the bullet. The Gros Ventre warrior who had fired the shot had counted two casualties from one charge. As the bullet had finished its fatal course along the trapper's skull, it had come reeling back to explode against Sublette's shoulder. Bill fought the churning of his stomach in protest against the faint-giving pain. His rifle lay tangled within his legs. The trader struggled out from under the trapper's lifeless body. Bringing his right arm across his chest, Sublette grasped the left arm and moved the wounded shoulder up and down in a few slow rotations. He sighed. It was not broken. The ball hadn't hit a bone. Still clutching the wounded arm, Bill struggled to sit up but grew faint and collapsed again, gasping for air. Bob was beside his friend before a moment more had passed.

"Bob," he begged, "take me back...take me back."

Campbell needed no prodding now. This man he would drag out himself. He yanked on Sublette's belt but could not move the heavy man across the grass. Reaching forward, Campbell put one hand under Sublette's armpit and began to drag his wounded friend out of the swamp. When there was finally enough cover between them and the enemy fortress, Campbell set his rifle down and knelt to pick Bill up into his arms. From there the trader was carried back to Milt's encampment. Flatheads and Nez Perce who had stayed behind came up to take Sublette from Campbell's weary arms. At Bob's direction they carried Bill to a protective stretch of the creek where Campbell bathed the wound. Bob stripped his shirt from his chest to make both dressing and bandage to bind up the bleeding hole. He then directed the Indians to construct a litter so that his friend could be borne back to rendezvous, but Sublette would have none of that. The two white men argued for a few minutes before Campbell finally acceded to letting Bill remain in the trapper's camp where he could direct some of the action though wounded. The Indians propped Sublette beneath a tree as Campbell returned to the fight. From his position against the cottonwood trunk, Bill continued to give orders to the men, spurring more and more trappers into the swamp.

All through the late morning and into the afternoon more riders came down from rendezvous until the only men left behind in the main encampment were greenhorns, clerks, and French Creoles, who knew only rivers and keelboats. They were of no use in an Indian fight anyway. They'd just get in the way.

By the time Bass slid back into the willows for his rifle, horn, and pouch, the Nez Perce, Shoshone, and Flathead warriors under Wyeth's command had fully flanked the north side of the Gros Ventre fortress. Finally stopped from any further advance by the creek, the Yankee set his soldiers to firing into the thicket. Unknown to Nathaniel or the warriors who followed his orders, their bullets were aimed right at Meek's position. Both groups were now caught in a deadly crossfire that did more damage than the Gros Ventres could have ever hoped to inflict. Instead of firing, the men within the crude fort kept their heads low and let the two sides hack away at one another in their ignorance. Through the hours of the middle of the afternoon both sides of the allied forces suffered needless and stupid casualties because of their ignorance of each other. On into the hottest part of the day the trappers battled thirst and the acrid, smoke-filled air. Less and less firing came from the fortress. The Gros Ventre warriors were letting the two flanks battle it out around them; they would save what little powder remained in their shelter, firing only when assured of a target.

A Nez Perce less than a yard away from Wyeth pitched backward. The Yankee stared down at the oozing hole in the Indian's forehead. The bullet had come across the fortress from the trappers beyond. Nathaniel's heart pounded. He could not take his eyes off the hole in the red man's head. It hypnotized him. The words of an old New England hymn drifted faintly into his mind. Wyeth sang it silently, to calm the gut-wrenching fear welling up inside of him. Another rifle report from the opposite side of the fort. Nathaniel jerked his head as he heard another Indian call out in pain and surprise to his right. He knew another man was dead. The Yankee caught himself and ducked his head. The grass beneath his cheek felt cool. He lay still, choking on the mass in his throat. Tears trickled down his cheek. He realized he was crying.

Beyond the fort balls were speeding in the direction of the trappers, fired from the allied Indians' rifles. Campbell rose quietly to one knee to peer out between willow branches to aim a shot. Before he could pull the trigger, a piece of lead came whining between his legs. In fright Campbell pulled the trigger on his rifle as he fell back.

Heart-pounding moments passed before Bob felt over his legs. No wound. He lifted his head to have a look at the legs. No wound. He was lucky today. Campbell was relieved enough to turn to Josiah beside him.

"Dear God!" his dry tongue crackled in a whisper. "I be thankful to the Lord for my skinny legs!" He snorted a quiet chuckle. "With these skinny poles I walk 'bout on, it takes a center shot to get me here!" Josiah nodded at the man's grim humor, all the while ignorant that Campbell's stupidity had caused a trapper to receive a ball in the leg minutes before.

The men attached to Meek and Fitzpatrick were pinned down by the crossfire from the other side of the fort. Occasionally the Gros Ventre warriors would fire a shot from beneath their logs, well hidden within their trenches. Every shot made from inside the fort was meant for a sure target. Every ball had to count this day.

"Frapp!" Fitzpatrick called out in his low, grating voice.

The German-born trapper raised his head slightly in turning to look at Tom. A small cloud of smoke billowed above the brush fortress and Fraeb's head was driven backward. He was dazed. Fitzpatrick was frozen to the spot. Henry lay semiconscious with his head cocked to the side in a clump of dried willow. He swallowed deeply trying to remember where he was. Blinking his eyes several times to clear the haze of faintness from them, Fraeb stared up at the thick limbs of the cottonwoods overhead. The leaves danced in the afternoon breeze. He liked that. It was so hot here. His face felt warm. His head was on fire. With the pain of several minutes behind him, Henry finally brought a finger to the side of his head. It was warm and wet. Without looking, he put the finger to his lips and touched it with his tongue. It was salty and thick. Blood. Fraeb touched the side of his head again, running the finger within the groove left by the bullet's path. A thick lock of hair had been shorn away. "Flesh wount," he mouthed soundlessly. He sighed and slipped into unconsciousness with a thin, crooked smile on his bloody lips.

Through the hot hours at the middle of the day the battle continued. Slow business this was. Only the occasional taunts and harangues from the fort broke the monotony. In battle it was part of the ritual to descend upon your enemy with threats and curses, calling him a boy, a squaw who wears dresses, even a man who goes to the robes each night with another man. You might even be accused of having rabbits or swallows in your family tree—anything timid and fearful. And always came the taunts that you ate the carcasses of long-dead animals or the dung of your enemy if you were fortunate to get that. And so the Gros Ventre warriors needled the allied Indians. If they pushed a Nez Perce or Flathead into blind anger, if they pushed the enemy into rushing the fort in a rage, so much the better. He would be killed—one less warrior to worry about. From their foxholes the Gros Ventres shouted and sang out their taunts. And waited for a charge. But there was no chance of that.

A single Indian might rush the fortress where he thought it weak. He might touch the walls of the fort, perhaps even fire a ball or arrow into the Gros Ventre compound before snatching a buffalo robe or a blanket and dashing back to the safety of the willow. Such a trophy would earn him praise. Such a prize would be as good as a scalp any day. It was sport to the allied tribes. They dared each other to perform the deed repeatedly. It was a test of bravery and courage at its finest, with a little of a gamble thrown in for good measure. Those warriors struck down in the foolish play were not mourned for long, but the victors received whoops of triumph. The curtain around the fortress was disappearing. But the Gros Ventres stuck to their foxholes. The blankets were being taken, but this sport did not accomplish a thing in battle. It killed no one.

Henry Fraeb was found unconscious and brought out of the swamp by two trappers. A Flathead squaw was stationed near him to attend to his wound. The German awakened as water was dripped between his lips by the woman. Within the thick brush, one of Fraeb's neighbors decided that he had had enough of waiting the battle out. He started to push forward the log he had been behind for more than an hour. By the time he had made it within a few feet of the enemy's breastwork, the log had been struck with balls many times. Behind the man rose stout cheers as he inched his way to the foot of the fortress. From this position, the trapper yelled back that it was the trader's whiskey that made him the warrior he was this day. Then suddenly he left the security of the log and dashed to the top of the fortress wall where he stuck his head over the edge. The man's head snapped back as two balls entered the brain just above his eyes. The body crumpled to the earth over the log he had brazenly pushed up to the fort in his drunkenness. From inside the fort several arms came out to drag the trapper's body into the foxholes under the bottom logs of the wall. Whoops and yells arose as the Gros Ventre warriors now had sport to play. Stunned into silence, the trappers could easily imagine what was being done with the trapper's lifeless body.

Zenas Leonard, along with companions Smith and Keane from the defunct Gantt & Blackwell group who had hired on with Milton Sublette, did not want to be found lacking in courage. The trio of trappers pushed into the underbrush with two Flatheads. Slowly they circled the fort until they reached a spot where they supposed they would not be detected. They got no closer than forty yards from the wall when one of the Indians was struck in the head with a lead ball. The four remaining men dropped from their hands and knees to their bellies. Each man was still, holding his breath. But Smith's foot twitched nervously against the dry grass about him. Another shot rang out. Smith's nervousness earned him a ball through the abdomen. Leonard pushed forward for cover behind a clump of willow, but the balls were coming at their position too furiously now. Zenas decided to retreat. He turned to make good his escape only to find that Keane and the Flathead had deserted him. Leonard scooted back to the wounded Smith, who begged to be carried out. That suited Leonard just fine. He now had an excuse to retreat without being accused of cowardice. Reputations burned and tarnished under the sun. Zenas pulled Smith some distance back to safe cover, then put the wounded man on his back. Still on hands and knees, Zenas pushed on. Near the body of the Flathead first shot lay Keane, life oozing from him. Leonard carried Smith out of danger, returned to remove Keane, then set off once more for the skirmish.

By late afternoon, Jim Bridger was irate over the pace of the battle. Resolved to get something done, Gabe pulled away from the skirmish line and crawled back into the trappers' encampment. There he approached Bill Sublette with the proposition he had in mind.

"Damn!" Jim tried to spit, but his mouth was full of dry cotton wads that choked his tongue. "We'll never clean them goddamned niggers out thisaway. How ye set to puttin' fire to their fort an' burnin' the whore suckers out?"

Sublette studied Bridger's flashing eyes. Bill was disgusted too. It aggravated him to have to sit back and watch the battle mope along with no resolution in sight. But Bridger had an idea. Ol' Gabe could always be counted on to come up with something to break a stalemate—one way or the other.

"Yep, we better burn 'em out, Gabe." Sublette twisted his head around to shout at the encampment about him. He felt the breeze stiffen in his face. Bill smiled at the help Mother Nature would give his trappers as he bellowed his orders out to the men. "Burn the niggers out! We'll fix 'em that way! Burn the fort an' pick 'em off as they come out on the run!"

Bridger moved about carrying his command to others to have them gather dry wood. Some of the squaws who had followed their warriors to the battle site spread through the swamp to drag back deadfall and brush for the torching of the enemy stronghold. Most of the trappers were happy to see something being done. Finally. The battle had seen little progress either way, but still the wounded were being brought back to the camp. Now they could push the wood before them to the open and set fire to the dry, crackling grass. The breeze would do the rest. The trappers felt cheered as they were back in control of things.

As the squaws had scurried off at Bridger's direction, the allied warriors still in camp asked what was going on. When the plan was laid out for them, the Nez Perce and Flatheads raised a mournful protest. Shouting their objections to both Bridger and the wounded Sublette, the Indians howled that they did not want the fort destroyed. Although it would bring a speedy conclusion to the battle, the friendlies did not want to see the enemy's possessions destroyed in the fire. They protested that this was a village on the move, a village that had been visiting. They would be laden with plunder and prizes. There would be robes and rich-colored blankets. The victors would be able to fight over the shiny trinkets and rifles. No! They did not want to see the enemy stronghold put to the torch. After all, the enemy was surrounded, was he not? He could not escape, could he? All the spoils of victory were as good as theirs now, and only a fool would destroy his own plunder.

Sublette and Bridger heard them out for long minutes, then vetoed their objections to the plan. The firewood was carried into the willow jungle and the process began of placing the timber where it would ignite the enemy fortress. Bridger crawled about on his hands and knees while the bonfire material was put into position, carrying the word to trappers and Wyeth's Indians alike that soon there would be plenty of targets at which to fire.

Inside the fortress the weary Gros Ventres noticed a change of mood among the attackers. There was now feverish activity taking place among the trappers, whereas before the white men had been content to lie low in the brush and fire a random shot. But now, what were those squaws doing? Those women of the enemy tribes were gathering dry brush and timber—it was being piled as close to the fort as the enemy dared to approach. What could it mean? They were going to set fire to the fortress! They were going to drive the proud Gros Ventre people from their stronghold! Frantically they looked about them at the positions taken up by the enemy without. Whereas before those positions had been the cause of a murderous crossfire in which the enemy wounded one another, now those same positions blocked all escape! The enemy would drive the proud Gros Ventre out of this trap into a deadly snare to shoot them down—like animals! Not like men. Not like warriors. Like animals! Like dogs!

Like a rapid-spreading contagion, the word swept over the occupants of the wooded fortress and licked hungrily at each man's bowels. One by one the Gros Ventre warriors began the dirge of his personal death song. Instead of girding for death and the journey to the ever-after, the death song was the final mantle of medicine a warrior would cloak himself with to stay death a little longer. It was the final ritual used to prolong death's dog soldier from exercising his grim reaper's prerogative as to time and place. The mournful, often off-key dirges filled the air about the fort and drifted through the swamp on the afternoon breeze. The white trappers who knew the meaning took heart at hearing the Gros Ventre warriors setting themselves to song.

"That's death song," Scratch said rolling his head to the side to whisper to Josiah through a hoarse, dry throat. "They're gettin' ready to die. Seein' the fire that's comin'. They put to theys death song. Gettin' ready to die." He turned his face away from Paddock's once more and watched through the willows what he could of the Gros Ventre fortress when for some reason the singing died away by itself. No torch had been put to the gathered bonfire. No shots had been fired recently. The singing died slowly away and all was quiet for a few minutes before a single strong, clear voice rose over the walls of the fort to be carried on the air to the enemy waiting without.

One of the younger war chiefs who had assumed leadership when Baihoh had fallen heard the many warriors begin their death songs when all knew of the impending end by fire. But the war chief had not sung his song. Wounded in the leg, the man struggled about the interior of the fortress dragging the maimed member, now swathed in a blood-darkened legging. He ordered his warriors quiet. With his personal vision this day, they would not need their death songs. If his personal medicine was strong, each man would live to fight another day.

The dirty, powder-grimed warriors about the war chief fell silent as he moved to the edge of the fortress. The Gros Ventre chief took a deep breath and turned his face skyward to look at the falling afternoon sun. He closed his eyes and began to shout aloud his message to the enemy gathered close about him. All day the trappers had listened to the taunts and harangues of the Gros Ventres, but this voice was something else altogether. It was spooky the way the death songs had ended almost as suddenly as they had begun. What had happened? Nervously, the white men and Indians waited. What was going on? What did the enemy know?

The war chief's clear voice rang through the air as the final taunt. He would try one last, desperate attempt. "My enemies!" All became quiet at the southern end of Pierre's Hole. "When we had the powder to explode with thunder and the ball to fly to your hearts, we fought you in the open! We proud warriors of a great people took refuge in this brush shelter only when we had little powder and ball left among us. We are a proud people and our death this day will be carried on the winds throughout the mountains. Grandfather will tell our friends how we were murdered like dogs. But our brothers will not mourn for long. They will not cut themselves and rip their clothes at our death. Our brothers will find you to carry your death into the dark hole of the insides of Mother Earth! Yes, our enemy, you are mighty and strong of arm this day. And we are small and grow weak without powder and ball. We know you can murder us like the flakes of a spring snow before the mighty sun. You will burn us out like the touch of the sun and we will melt away before you.

"But our women and children have gone. The women carry within their stomachs new warriors to take our place. The children grow to hunt you down. They will know of the murder of our warriors this day. We who will soon be gone like the wind blows the seed across the prairie do not care. What does it matter? We proud warriors have already thrown away our bodies to the Grandfather. If you are hungry for our flesh and gnaw after our bones—if you thirst for our blood, then wait here, our enemy. Stay here by the ashes of our burnt bodies. Stay here, our enemy, and wait while our spirits go to carry on the fight. Stay here, our enemy, and you will have a fight worthy of our people. If you hunger after us, you will soon grow fat with a bellyful of our warriors. Stay by our ashes, enemy, and more will come your way.

"Before the sun hides at the end of this day there will be four hundred lodges of our brothers here to see what you have done, our enemy. Already they are close, following the trail marked by our travois poles. Already they smell the powder of this fight in their nostrils. Our women and children have gone to carry the words of this day to our brothers. A day when the strong took the weak to kill like dogs. Stay here, our enemy, and our brothers will take our places in numbers that are like the pebbles of the stream to count. They are strong, as we are weak. They are brave, as we have grown weary. They are many, while we are few. Their hearts grow full at this time, our enemy, full of fight for you. They are coming now, to avenge our fall. Glory from the Grandfather will come to us in your death. Burn us now and wait. Death will be your final step!"

Throughout the speech most men were silent, ears pricked to the Blackfeet tongue being used by the wounded war chief. Those who anxiously asked of companions, "What's that Injun yellin'? What's the nigger sayin'?" were quickly silenced by those straining to catch hold of the Gros Ventre's words. When the chief's speech was finished, every man who knew a smattering of Blackfoot took his turn in attempting a translation. Members of the allied tribes were asked to help. The words of the chief were spoken and re-spoken time after time through Indian after Indian. One message came through all the various translations, a message that spread like the plague through the trappers and Indians gathered around the fortress— "Blackfeet comin'! Heap lotta Blackfeet comin'! Heap big fight! Blackfeet comin' for heap big fight!" It was amazing that they had gotten at least that much out of all the Shoshone, Flathead, Nez Perce, and French Creole translators.

The broken English shot through the ranks to cause panic. Many men began to slide back toward the trappers' encampment and the ponies. The bad translation of bad English and even poorer Blackfoot said to some that the enemy was near at hand to rub them out. Men moved frantically to reach their horses. In the confusion one of those running hell-bent-for-leather sought to explain his action to the others.

"Blackfeet niggers! Blackfeet back to rendezvous already! They cuttin' up our camps now! Blackfeet back to rendezvous!"

Step after mad step the trapper burst past his white companions, infecting most with the paranoid nightmare of Blackfeet rampaging through the defenseless rendezvous encampment. Panic spread like water exploding through a broken beaver dam. The trappers forgot about the Indians holed up in the fortress. They pulled up stakes and dashed off with powderhorn and pouch in one hand and a rifle in the other. There was mad screeching and scrambling among the horse herd as some climbed aboard the first animal they reached. Arguments as to ownership broke out and men were knocked aside by friends in the headlong rush to mount and beat it back across seven miles to that ill-manned scene of summer celebration. Some heads attempted to grasp hold of sanity in the midst of the panic about them. Sublette called out from his tree to be informed as to what was going on with all those men leaving in an insane dash northward. Bridger, Meek, and Fitzpatrick helped Campbell move about through the throbbing crowd to settle the men down. They were pushed aside for their efforts. Sublette called out for help in rising. No one listened to his pleas.

"Man says there's Blackfeet back to ronnyvoo!" Josiah gasped as he turned to Scratch.

"They's stealin' my plunder!" Scratch went to his knees and threw straps of pouch and powderhorn over his shoulder. "Killin' them back to ronnyvoo! Get your lead out! We movin'!" He took off with Josiah catching up within a few yards.

"Blackfeet kill them squaws back there?" Paddock questioned of the older man breathlessly.

"Blackfoot killin' ever'thin'!"

The two men dashed from the edge of the willow and underbrush into the open filled with milling men and dust, shouting and fistfights among brigade companions. Josiah stopped dead in his tracks and his jaw went slack in his surprise at the mass confusion. Someone put a hand tightly on his shoulder. Paddock wheeled about to stare into the dark, blazing eyes set under a shock of thick, snow-white hair.

"You!" Fitzpatrick shouted at Paddock, though he was less than two feet from the young man. "I want you to stay!"

Bass had advanced a few yards away but wheeled around when he no longer found Josiah at his side. He came back to confront Fitzpatrick. "What you want?" Bass growled.

"You, too!" Tom continued, looking now at Titus. "I want you two to stay here!"

"You can slide, you stupid polecat!" Bass shook his head and brought his rifle up in front of his body. "Sun's got your brains cooked! Ain't no booshway gonna tell Titus Bass to do nothin'! You ain't got a thing on this man!"

"I know that, you crazy loon!" Fitzpatrick had suddenly changed his tone from one of command to plea. "I can only ask you. Them others don't know no better.

You're free trapper. I know. You gotta help. Ever'body's goin' back. Ain't a nigger gonna be left in this here place to watch them red skunks in there!" He pointed toward the fortress with an arm that shook as much as the rest of his body. Fitzpatrick was trying to control his anger and frustration, but little succeeding. "We need some of you to stay back here. I'll stay. We'll get some more to do it too. An eye on the fort, that be all we need. Will you do it, man? For the love of God, will you do it?" Tom's eyes darted between Josiah and Bass, pleading with their deep intensity. Meek came running up to the trio.

"Got me 'bout dozen men!" he yelled above the noise of hundreds of voices and many more hoofs. "Them red niggers was with us till they heerd; not a one of 'em stayin' here."

"Jest as well." Tom turned back to look at the two men he had cornered. "An' you two? What be it? You turnin' out? You goin' back?"

It was Titus who twisted his head slowly to look at his young partner. But Josiah kept looking into the eyes of Fitzpatrick. Gradually, Paddock turned to look into Joe Meek's face, then brought his eyes to rest on Bass's.

"We stayin'." Josiah spoke the simple words evenly. "What you wantin' us to do?" Only then did he turn back to face Whitehair.

The hand Fitzpatrick had nailed on Paddock's shoulder loosened from its grip and patted twice before Tom removed it. "You go with Meek, here. He'll be spreadin' the men out round the fort. Don' want none of them niggers in there to get away." Fitzpatrick spun away for another attempt in begging more help to remain behind. Into the mad, shoving uproar the two partners followed Meek.

"Why you stayin'?" Paddock asked of Bass as they walked along.

"I don' know . . . rightly."

"You got lotta plunder back there. Don't stay on my count."

"But you tol't Fitz 'we,' meanin' both us."

"I ain't makin' your mind up for you. You know that, Scratch."

"You ain't, I know that."

"An' your plunder?"

"What 'bout it?"

"You worked whole y'ar for them plews, buy them goods, all such."

"If my cache be raised when we gets back, me an' me pardner jest gotta work that much harder, I s'pose." His eyes twinkled with the first smile Bass had felt within him all day. Josiah winked back at him.

Bridger trotted up. "Joe!" He put a flat palm against Meek's chest. "I gotta go back! Do ye read my sign?" He didn't wait for Meek to answer. "The whole comp'ny's back thar'—I mean ever'thin' we worked for! I gotta go an' hol' it together!"

"I foller ye, Gabe!" Joe nodded and shoved his head toward the horses, restless with all the commotion. "They'll need a man like ye back thar'; get, now! We got some good coons like these to stay! Go on!"

Bridger looked at Scratch and Josiah briefly and nodded to each before wheeling about to enter the horse herd. He finally located his old flea-bitten gray and spun into the saddle. Relentlessly, Bridger kicked the animal's ribs and slapped its flanks with the butt of his rifle from one muzzle-holding hand. The pony shot away across the plain to join the mad dash back to rendezvous. Fraeb was not far behind Jim. His head swam with the stinging pain. But he had to go back. Henry too had a vested interest back at the summer encampment. His wife was heavy with child. Her time was near. In German Fraeb recited a lyrical childhood prayer over and over as the dust of ponies before him stung his cheeks and mixed with the tears staining his flesh. William Sublette was already on his way back to the main camp, slung loosely in a litter that bounced along behind a horse over the stubble and sage.

"Fitz said ye needed us." Four more men came up to Joe as he stopped in front of the eleven men he had already commissioned. Now there would be eighteen in all. Joe looked them over. Most were free trappers. They would be the ones he could count on in a tough fight anyway.

"Bass! Ye ugly dog!" The voice was familiar.

"Hatcher?"

"Ain't none the other!" Mad Jack sang joyfully, "An' young Josiah Paddock, recent of the settlements." He nodded at the younger man. "You're gettin' a paunch fulla Injun fightin' this day, eh, son?"

Neither Scratch nor Josiah could really recognize the

man speaking to them. It was Hatcher's voice, all right. He said he was Hatcher too. But the trapper had almost half his face covered with a blackened, bloody bandanna that was tied over the left ear. Several rivulets of blood had dried down the left side of Hatcher's neck beneath the knot that snuggled close to the ear lobe. What face was not covered with bandanna was smeared over with dirt and blackened with burnt powder, streaked with thick bands of sweat.

Bass knelt in front of the reclining man. "What in the blue-ball blazes happen't to you, Jack?"

"One a them Blackfoot niggers shot good hunk of my ear off," he said, patting the side of his head. " 'Twas a damned fool thing to do—tried to reach the wall of that forkin' fort. Thort my head was blowed 'way at the first. Had to crawl back to the crik by myse'f. Niggers didn' see me doin' my get'way. Damned fool things I always do. Never change will I, ol' man?" Bass shook his head without speaking. He felt the salt sting at his eyes and wondered if it was sweat, or tears. Meek interrupted everything else.

"We gonna go back thar' now," he rasped, motioning with his arm. "I'm wantin' ye to fan out yourselves an' keep low. No man closer'n twenty paces from 'nother, ye hear? No bunchin' up! Stay out by yourselves an' keep your goddamned heads low!" He looked fleetingly to Hatcher. "No man moves in on the fort! No man fires a shot less'n he can see what he's aimin' to! Ye foller me? We sit it out hyar, make them niggers think they's still got the whole valley out thar' with us. We jest sit tight like a treed coon an' wait till we gets some word down from ronnyvoo. Less'n ye got somethin' to say, let's be doin' it. Move on in thar."

With that the men moved out in small groups toward the willows at the edge of the clearing. There the trappers began to spread out around the brush fortress once more. But now, each man was fanned out some twenty to thirty yards from his neighbors on the left and right. Each man was alone. The minutes crawled by and became that hour when the sky decides between day or night. In the snail's pace of time, each man was alone with his thoughts of thirst and hunger. He would push them aside to think of other things—memories of rendezvous. His mind flooded with thoughts of the women and children north, up the valley, thoughts of powder and ball, traps and beaver, ponies and possibles. Each man went through a lonely struggle to fight the impulse to scream. In the distance, a man set to whistling with mellow notes the melody to "Wayfaring Stranger." The other trappers heard a ball from the fort crash into the brush near the whistler. They waited. The tune started again.

"That you, Mad Jack?" Scratch hollered out, no longer afraid of the enemy's bullets.

"An' the tune be a fav'rite of mine, too!" Hatcher answered, then started whistling the song again.

"Ye ain't hit, is ye?" Bass questioned.

"Not bad!" was the answer. "I jest want the rest of ye he'p me with my song." He choked a little on the pain. His next few notes sputtered off-key.

Josiah had crawled up to Scratch and started to move past the older man without saying a word.

"Where you goin', boy!" he demanded.

"Gonna get Mad Jack!"

Bass caught hold of Josiah's leg and held tight. "Get your ass back there where you was, goddammit!"

"Hatcher's been hit 'gain!"

"I know it, but you ain't doin' a shit if you get yourself kilt goin' after him," Titus dropped his words for a minute as the tune was picked up by Hatcher again. Another ball whistled toward the trapper. Everyone held his breath until the notes sailed through the air once more. "You're goddamned crazy fool, Hatcher!" Bass sang out. "An' I loves you for it!" He turned to whisper to Josiah, "Get your ass back there, boy!"

Paddock moved away without another word. As he slid back through the dry grass, Titus Bass set to whistling the tune along with Hatcher as best he could. Scratch never was much of a musician. The only way he could carry a tune was in his possibles pouch. But his off-key help for Hatcher soon brought the other sixteen men alive. One by one, each began to whistle the song with Bass and Mad Jack. With each new set of notes raised by another accompanying trapper surrounding the fortress, a ball whined into the air. But still the song did not end. Josiah looked in the direction of the new notes as each trapper followed along. Nearly every man was whistling along with Hatcher and Scratch now as the grove rang with their song. It startled none but Paddock when Mad

Jack let the others carry the melody with their whistle while he set to singing the words:

I'm just a poor, wayfaring stranger,
Traveling through this world of woe.
Yet, there's no sickness, no toil, no danger
In that bright land to which I go.
I'm going there to see my brother,
Who's gone before me, that good one.
I'm just going over Jordan.
I'm only going over home.

I know dark clouds will gather round me,
I know my way is rough and steep.
Yet, beautiful fields lie just before me,
Where God's redeemed their vigils keep.
I'm going there to see my brother,
Who's gone before me, that good one.
I'm just going over Jordan.
I'm only going over home.

Gradually the McKenzie smoothbores grew silent. This was medicine. The Gros Ventres listend, entranced as Hatcher choked out the words in his pain from the bullet that had torn into his body below the right shoulder. His arm ached at first, then grew cold. His fingers were numb. But still he choked out the serenade, accompanied by the trappers ringing the fort. Theirs was a vigil to keep.

As Mad Jack finished the two slow verses of the song, the trappers whistling accompaniment gradually died. All was quiet in the swamp once more.

"I'm gonna sleep now, coons!" Hatcher called out to the others.

"You ain't goin' under!" Scratch yelled loudly with all the air he held in his lungs. He waited long moments for an answer. A ball from the fort crashed into the willows nearby.

"Nawww," finally came the weak answer from Mad Jack. "Jest gonna sleep some, 'sall."

"Night, Hatcher!" Bass shouted. "Have you good dreams in that land where you goin'." The tears stung his eyes. "Save a set for me there, you hear? Save a set in that good land for Titus Bass!"

"I'll be waitin' for ye, Scratch." The words came weaker now. "I'm so tired." The hand dropped away from the front of his shoulder where the ball had splattered against a rib and sent fragments of bone crashing through the lung. "God... I'm tired." He tried to spit some blood from his mouth. "I'm so tired... Scratch." And then it didn't matter any more.

Into the rendezvous the rescuers sprinted. But no rescuers were needed. Bleary-eyed camp keepers stumbled out from tents where they had been drinking the last drops of the trader's whiskey on the house. Some had been sleeping off the morning's drunk. They appeared to be just as confused as those riders who came tearing up the valley into the large encampment. Angrily the trappers asked if any Indians had been sighted. The answer was no. Slowly the story was given to the camp keepers that a promise by the Blackfeet to attack the rendezvous had been given during the battle. Only then did the greenhorns feel rescued.

Bridger wheeled his pony into the Rocky Mountain Fur Company camp and spun from the saddle. A camp keeper came forward to take the reins of the lathered animal from Jim. Ol' Gabe looked about him for signs of something to make sense. Nothing did. All was as he had left it that morning. Still wary, Bridger gathered a crew of veteran trappers he could count on to remount and keep a constant guard around the perimeter of the rendezvous site. He told them to keep their eyes peeled for fresh signs of Blackfeet while they still had light. Then he sent them on their way. He too would have a look around for himself. Things were confusing to Bridger. It just didn't wash.

Fraeb tore into the Rocky Mountain camp on Bridger's heels but did not dismount. He took a look in all directions, then put his pony into motion once more. Henry finally brought the snorting animal to a halt outside the lodge where he had left his wife with her Shoshone parents. His squaw's brother stopped him from entering with only the show of a hand. Before Fraeb could question why he was not allowed to enter, a baby's first cries were heard from the lodge. The woman's brother smiled at Fraeb and cradled his arms in pantomime of rocking an infant. Henry laughed with bellyful gusto, whooped as loud as he could, and pushed past the young warrior.

374

Fraeb had forgotten about his wound. Inside the lodge a Snake midwife presented the German with his first son.

Gradually the full impact of the Gros Ventre ruse descended upon the mountain men. Slowly they realized they had been tricked. They had always felt the Blackfeet to be wily foxes, but this took top blanket prize. In small groups the trappers resaddled and turned south once again, now determined more than ever to wipe out every enemy warrior in the fortress. The trappers had been tricked, and that soured their milk some. Bridger would stay behind, however, distrustful of everything right now. He would see to it that his guard stayed in the saddle through the night. The Creoles didn't merit even a first chance from Ol' Gabe. He burned with the idea of Jim Bridger bein' fool enough to fall victim to a wild-goose chase. Gabe was not alone. Many a mountain man was feeling damned sheepish in Pierre's Hole that evening.

By the time trappers appeared back at the swamp from the fruitless race to rendezvous, nearly three hours had passed and the sun had disappeared behind the low range of mountains to the west. In small knots the shame-faced men dismounted and stood around in the clearing near the creek where it had all begun that morning. Quiet rage boiled through each arrival back at the battle scene. Every man had a personal stake in the fight of the previous hours, if only because it had robbed him of precious relaxation. Every man had spent the day under the double yoke of exertion and danger, but the words spoken this evening were grim-lipped praise for the enemy's successful trick. It had worked. It had saved their lives—for the time being. Now it was too dark to set fire to the fort. No one could see the targets running from the flames into the inky darkness. It was too late for that now. Besides, there was not a man already not weary of the bone-tiring battle. They were bruised and stiff from the mule kicks of the muzzleloaders. Hungry, thirst-driven trappers smelled nothing but burnt powder in their nostrils. The enemy's blood could wait until the morning light.

The orange glow of sunset descended into the first licks of purple across the eastern sky. Meek went back into the thickets to carry the word that each of the free trappers had secretly suspected deep within all along: the threat of an attack on the rendezvous had been a hoax. Joe moved from man to man around the dark, silent fortress, telling each one to draw back some distance from the enemy, to pull back strategically to the edge of the cottonwood timber that ringed the swamp. Fatigued, the men scooted back through the dark shadows of the willows where they would not be overrun so suddenly if the Indians attempted a night attack. With a wider buffer zone, they could stand a better chance if the enemy decided to break out.

Meek emerged from the wood and plopped down to relax against some of Milt Sublette's baggage. Several older veterans of the mountains gathered around and lighted their pipes. Together this handful of men would attempt to tally the casualties. The dead already numbered the half-breed, Sinclair, Keane, Smith, and the trapper dragged into the fort. That many for sure. The Nez Perce, Snake, and Flathead women would have greater tears to shed. The number of those known dead among the allied tribes was steadily rising. And it was too dark now to go looking for more bodies. There were wounded on both sides of the allied forces, but Sublette, Fraeb, and most others would pull through. Those men gathered with Meek fell silent for long moments thinking of the wounded trappers who would be lucky to make it through the night. Bitterly they all swore vengeance on the enemy come the first rays of the sun.

Paddock shivered slightly in the dimming light. He smacked at the troublesome mosquitoes that flitted about his face in the damp, cool air at the edge of the swamp. He listened to the murmuring voices from the trappers gathered somewhere behind him. They seemed so far away. Josiah strained to hear what they were saying in their low, terse voices; if he could hear them, it would help overcome the loneliness and fear. The trappers seemed as far away as the rising moon.

He wanted a drink of water. By now he had decided he would give his new rifle away for a drink of water. The insides of his mouth felt cracked, they were so dry. He must think of something else, Paddock told himself in a whisper. Straining to listen to voices from within the fortress, Josiah heard none. It too seemed so far away. All was quiet within the black, looming walls of what was left of the enemy's shelter. The shadows had gone already. All was quiet. The reality of this day was like burnt powder to him: it was gone, spent. But something faint remained to nag at all his senses.

He had to have a drink. Madness would surely overtake him if he didn't. Josiah fought off the memories of a winter's hunger that had driven him to put a muzzle to a man's temple. Just a drink, that was all. Nothing more.

His mind skipped to the swamp. There was water out there in the darkness. Water. Cool. Lips, mouth, and throat. Water. Cool. Josiah let his grip on the rifle go slack. It slipped silently to the grass. Over his head he removed the straps of horn and pouch. He would crawl past the curtain of darkness for it. Water.

On his belly Josiah pushed himself through the grass. He used the hand in front of him for eyes, to feel the obstructions of willow and clumps of creeper. Paddock fought his way along blindly until his seeing-eye fingertips touched something wet. He explored cautiously. It was a small pool. Not moving water. Paddock splashed his fingers about in it quietly. Then he brought the wet fingers to his parched lips. In luxury he smeared the cool liquid over the cracked flesh. Again the hand went into the pool, cupped this time to bring a swallow back for his throat. It was gritty as it slid past his tongue. Sand, he thought. But wet all the same. He could spit it out. Or wait for his stomach to expel it. It did not matter. It was wet. Again and again his hand dipped into the murky, tepid pool. Ahhhh, wet. Cool. Water. Josiah heard the whistled notes of the song. His mind reeled as his hand jerked up. The tune was coming out of the darkness somewhere to his left—far away. He was scared.

"Hatcher?" he croaked. "That you, Hatcher?" Josiah's voice sputtered in fear.

The tune stopped and all was silent for a moment that seemed like an eternity to him. "No, son," came a familiar voice. "Only me, Josiah." The voice belonged to Titus. " 'Bout the only decent thing I can do for Mad Jack now, son. Sing his medeecin. 'Bout all any man can do for him now..." The words drifted off into a stifled sob somewhere out there in the darkness. Scratch composed himself by fighting back the numbing hurt he felt inside with another attempt at the song. It would help him to make it through the night.

*   *   *

Paddock awoke with a start. He did not know when he had dozed off. His thoughts were on stretching his aching muscles. Slowly his mind came alive and he looked down at his legs drawn up close to his abdomen, the rifle clutched tightly within the crook of both elbows. Then he was awake. With a jerk he lifted his head from the camp ground. His neck hurt with a cold stiffness. Looking about him, Josiah realized it would be dawn very soon. Already the eastern sky was paling with the rising sun beyond the divide. First one leg, then the other was pushed out to its full length and rubbed to allow the knots in the leg a chance to escape. Escape. His thoughts snapped. Escape! He had fallen asleep on watch.

Rising up cautiously on one elbow in the gray filmy fog that drifted off the swamp, Paddock strained his eyes to see and his ears to hear. Through the thin, slowly waltzing veil of fog he could just barely discern the shape of the fortress out there. Its outline loomed larger than ever, like a yawning, monstrous crypt. He turned his head to look behind him. No one had seen him asleep. Josiah listened intently. No sounds from the fort. Not a word or rustle from the trappers' encampment out beyond the soles of his moccasins. He shuddered. The air smelled of musty death to him. But that was foolish, he told himself. He'd never really seen death that much to know what it smelled like. Another man from the past had not stayed long with the corpse of Henri LeClerc. Why did he feel this way? Josiah struggled with it until the image of Mordecai's gangrenous arm loomed before his eyes. He pushed it away. Another specter took its place. That old man at Dougherty's fort smelled of death—he had risen from the dead, hadn't he? What was his name? Bass . . . Cass . . . Glass . . . Glass! He had this smell about him when he had come into the fort. But just as soon as he had a grip on that specter, another came to take its place in his consciousness. Sarah. Dear mother—my dear mother. Oh, how he watched her shrivel up and die in that small room behind the store. Day after day, week after week, he had watched her wasting into nothing. Wasting into death. The memory of the odor in that room filled his nostrils, seeped into his mind. He wanted to vomit. Josiah fought for breath. One deep gasp. Another. He might have it under control, but his stomach lurched and he threw up. Gagging with the wrenching abdominal muscles, Paddock threw up nothing more than a little of the foul water from the night before. Once again he felt the grit and sand in his mouth. Then the sting of stomach bile. He gagged again, fighting for air. But nothing was left on his stomach. The lightheadedness had passed. The specters were gone. He shuddered and laid his head back on the ground. Sleep was all he needed for his head. Just sleep.

When he awoke again it was to the sound of loud voices behind him. Josiah jerked up as he heard men crawling through the edge of the woods toward him. Someone was telling a herd of others to start spreading out. Then he saw them. Trappers as red-eyed and miserable as he, moving toward him.

"We're goin' back in," one of them conmented as he came close to Paddock, " 'Fore it gets any lighter, we're gonna do what we shoulda done last night." He scooted past Josiah. The woods were alive with white men now. Everywhere men were again cheering each other on in their common effort. The ring about the fortress was closing. To the edge of the swamp the mountain men crept, numbering only a little more than a hundred this time. Paddock looked at the gray sky above the cottonwoods, then followed them into the swamp. A few more of the trappers came up behind him. The had ridden in this morning from rendezvous, feeling as foolish as any man could for the madness of the previous afternoon, each one wishing he had been among those to stay behind to guard the fortress.

Someone fired a shot. There was some shouting to determine who had done it. Only a trapper. The order was given for the men on the north flank to fire a volley into the fort, then reload while the southern flank fired a round. This would allow some men to have a charge in their rifles at all times. The first volley burst through the morning air. The balls crashed through the brush fortress. Everyone waited for some return fire. There was none. A few of the trappers hurled taunts at the enemy, hoping to stimulate some return fire. None. The order for the second volley was given. Lead clunked with a dull sound into trees and whistled through the brush walls of the fort. Again silence.

A few of the trappers were spooked again. An unearthly quiet pervaded the swamp as the rifles' echoes died. No more was the air filled with threats and promises of the Gros Ventre. It was as if the ghosts could not answer in the foggy, damp light of early morning. The stillness was soon broken with a mournful howl. Every man froze to his spot, listening. It was only a dog. Within a moment came a chorus of wails flying to the heavens. It was the only response the trappers had heard from the enemy stronghold.

Bridger grew disgusted once more. This damned thing needed wrapping up. He rose to one knee and slowly parted the willow branches before him with the muzzle of his rifle. He peered at the fort, trying to make some sense out of this. Aggravated with himself, Jim rose to his feet and pushed out of the brush to the open. The enemy did not fire at him! Somewhat frightened, Bridger stood by the willows for a few minutes before he crossed the grassy open to the wall of the stronghold. His mind was smoldering with it all. The Blackfeet had not returned the trappers' fire. The fortress was silent. When he reached the stronghold, one thing remained to do.

Still holding the rifle pointed forward, his finger ready at the trigger, Jim slashed at the dried brush piled atop the cottonwood deadfall the previous day. No one came to resist his destruction. Bridger's worst fears had been answered. He slowly turned on his heels to yell back at the rest of the trappers.

"Only niggers here dead!" He spit out some of the early-morning chaw of tobacco that always helped a thirsty mouth. "Injuns slipped out last night!"

Others began to emerge from the edge of the swamp to enter the fortress with Bridger. Holes had been dug in the earth in a frantic search for water of any kind. Not a few of the men stood gaping at the empty enemy stronghold, some kicking wildly at the walls in frustration and anger. Not one damned brownskin was still alive. Except for the nine dead warriors and the carcasses of dead ponies strewn over the trampled earth, the garrison was empty.

One could not help being impressed with the size and construction of the stronghold. Gradually man after man approached and entered the fort. One trapper counted twenty-four dead horses, and another counted more than thirty-two of the animals killed with trappers' lead during the battle. Masterless dogs skulked backward at the slow advance of the wary white men. A quiet, muted rage filled most of the men—those daring Blackfeet had slipped from their grasp in the night. Meek found a small break in the wall where the escape had been effected during the dark hours before dawn. It led out through the edge of the swamp to a narrow pathway beaten along the creek. Stepping from the fortress a few yards along the path, Joe found fresh blood smeared on the leaves and branches of the willow and creeper lining the creek bank.

"Niggers carried some a theys wounded out!" he shouted back to Bridger. All Jim could do was shake his head up and down slightly. He knew if he attempted speech his anger would boil over.

The dogs continued to scatter with the advance of the white men filling the fort. Campbell found the warrior shot through the eye by William Sublette. Campbell's smile was not that joyful this morning in finding that casualty. A few of the men looked over dead horses. They identified them as having belonged to the trader. These horses had been among those run off by Indians when Sublette was on his way to rendezvous. They were caravan animals. Another odd-fitting piece to the unfinished puzzle. The warriors that had attempted to overrun the supply train were but an advance force of a much larger village. That was certain. The puzzle was confused. Maybe these Indians had been partially right in their boast about their death being avenged by a stronger force.

After the white men had been within the walls for a few minutes and everything remained quiet, there seemed to be no danger. Flathead, Snake, and Nez Perce dashed forward from the willows to collect the plunder, the booty, the spoils of victory. Upon entry they howled over not finding any. No more scarlet blankets. No trade beads. No rifles or shells. No trinkets to bring a shine to a victorious warrior's eyes. Nothing. Their enemy had escaped with everything. Almost.

In their red anger the Indians pounced on the bodies of the dead Gros Ventre warriors. First the scalp was lifted with as much pride as if the victor had taken the trophy in hand-to-hand combat. Then the corpses were pummeled and beaten before they were mutilated.

As Josiah stepped from the brush to join Bass and slowly approach the fort, the dogs set to howling once more. The eerie gray veil over the swamp had yet to lift. The two men entered the walls. A buzzard took to flight, swooping low overhead, its intended meal being disturbed by the men within the stronghold. Both trappers ducked as the bird registered its protests by winging low over them.

Meek came back into the fort leading a strong, light pony. "Jim!" Bridger wheeled about to watch Joe approach. "This'r be Fitz's pony?"

"Looks to be."

"What I'm thinkin' too."

The evidence added another piece to the confusing puzzle. These had been the Indians who raided the supply caravan *and* caught Tom Fitzpatrick out in the open alone. This was one of the two horses he had taken with him when he set out to carry word back to rendezvous that Sublette was east of South Pass. It was all becoming a little spooky.

"Whar ye find it?" Bridger questioned.

"Up in the woods a ways." He threw a thumb backward. "Got some twenty to thirty head out thar in the trees. Seems they cached 'em out thar when things got goin'."

The warriors milled about inside the fort hoping to pick up a clue here or there that would tell them where the dead had been buried. The corpses would have been raised from their hastily dug graves and scalped. But the earth within the brush compound had been trampled down repeatedly by the survivors to cover all traces of the shallow graves. Back over the well-packed soil the friendly Indians scratched as they howled in bitter disappointment.

Paddock halted. Scratch bumped into him in surprise, then looked down at the scene causing Josiah's stomach to pitch and roll. Near one of the foxholes by their feet lay the remains of the liquored-up trapper who had climbed to the top of the wall and had been shot in the forehead for his trouble. The young man looked down at his first view of the brutal butchery of mutilation. He had heard Scratch talk of what he had done to the Arapaho warrior who had stolen his topknot—but seeing it was something else altogether. Not much of a face was left to recognize on the body the Gros Ventres had pulled into the fort. It had been beaten repeatedly until the head was a lumpy mass from which poured the brain material and much blood. The cerebral organ was now drying after many hours of exposure, and flies buzzed about its juicy treat.

The man's arms had been hacked off and stuck upright into the crudely opened abdomen, the crusted upper arms pointing wildly into the air. These wounds too were covered with thick masses of large horseflies. For a final humiliation, the trapper's penis and testicles had been ripped off and stuffed into what remained of his mouth. Paddock turned white, but could not take his eyes off the horrible brutality done the white man's remains. Finally he turned away to suck in a deep breath.

"C'mere, son." Bass's words were fatherly. He led Josiah out of the fortress in the direction some of the other trappers were pouring to retrieve the horses abandoned in the woods on the hillside. Down by the creek Titus found all the evidence he needed to see where the survivors were heading. "Let's foller 'long here a bit," he said tugging at the younger man's sleeve.

It was not long before the two passed by the first bodies of the enemy, corpses recently dead and abandoned after the Indians had begun their escape from death. Each one had been hidden from the trail with as much design as conditions would permit. The device would hopefully keep those who followed from finding the bodies and raising the scalps. In this way, the survivors could return to the victims' squaws and tell them the hair was safe. The women could then dance in victory.

Nor was it long before things began to sink into Flathead, Nez Perce, and Snake skulls—the survivors were heading out with the plunder. With whoops and chants the Indians burst forth from the fortress. Bass and Josiah could hear them coming up somewhere behind them along the creek. Then Titus was the first to spot her.

A proud dark-skinned Gros Ventre squaw sat on the ground a little further up the trail, leaning against the trunk of a cottonwood. Bass stopped dead in his tracks to study the woman. She held no weapon in her hands but he was not sure of what might lie by her side. Behind him he could hear the howling Indian wolves tearing up the creek path followed by white men's voices. Some of the trappers had also joined in the chase. White man and red alike were eager to strike a coup, kill one of the enemy, in some way to avenge the death of a friend. He was planted to the spot for a few seconds more, listening to the approach of the screaming men, his eyes constantly on the squaw. She slowly turned her head down the path toward the direction of the oncoming noise. Her eyes sought out Scratch's. They did not plead or beg. Instead, the woman merely held open palms up to the two white men standing in the middle of the retreat path. Titus started walking to her cautiously. Her dark eyes remained fixed on his. He could see the improvised bandage around her lower right leg. Blood had dried down to the ankle. The leg had a peculiar twist to it. Somehow, he thought, it was broken. Probably a ball. Less than ten feet from her he stopped again. Now he could see the body of a dead warrior stretched out in the bushes at her left side.

He had been surprised to find her sitting motionless near the path. His heart was more touched by the brave spirit that kept her from crying out in fear of dying. Only now with the approach of Indian voices coming down the path did she speak. In words that Bass could not understand, she asked him to kill her before her Indian enemies arrived. She told him that she wished to take her last breath before they came up to mutilate her body. She begged him to save her from the humiliation of seeing her man butchered before her very eyes. Finally the woman drew from her belt a large dagger that had the blade broken off halfway between tip and handle. With this she pantomimed stabbing her own heart. The dark eyes stayed on his. But now they begged in syrupy pools of tears. He took another step but was caught by the arrival of the Indians.

They pushed and shoved past the two white men before coming to a halt around the squaw and her dead warrior. Slays in the Night slapped Bass on the chest and asked him if he wanted this coup. There was no answer. The Snake warrior asked again of the white man if he wanted the honor of this coup. Titus shook his head without taking his eyes off the woman. The Snake said that the white man was a fool because the woman could bear many more children who would grow to become warriors, enemies who would avenge many deaths. The white man was a fool not to want this coup. From his belt the Snake pulled a short-handled tomahawk. He slapped it against his left palm. He repeated that the white man was a fool, but that Slays in the Night was not. Slays in the Night would count this coup among his richest. With that he stepped forward to raise the 'hawk overhead. With both hands gripping the handle, the Snake brought the blade down savagely into the top of the woman's head. With his strength, Slays in the Night buried the 'hawk almost to the woman's neck; it split her head open like an overripe fruit. Blood splattered across the front of his chest and leggings before the squaw's body slumped to the ground over the warrior she had not left behind. Some of the blood had sprayed on the bystanders, trappers and Indians both. Slays in the Night turned slowly to face Bass, his grinning face flecked with blood and splattered with pieces of the squaw's brain. With some struggle he extricated the blade from the body and used the tip to cut neatly around the topknot. He yanked the scalp from the skull. The Snake asked Titus if he wanted the warrior's scalp as he moved over to straddle the dead Gros Ventre brave.

Scratch answered by pushing his way through the knot of onlookers to continue on down the path along the creek. He heard some of the Indians laughing behind him. There would be enough time to settle that score with the Snake, he thought. There would always be time for that. Their grisly work accomplished, the Indians set on the trail once again, rushing past Paddock and Bass. They caught sight of a squaw running for her life. She had stayed with a warrior also, but now she ran from the enemy. In laughter the Indians set out in hot pursuit. It was not long before they had run her down. They made sport of her death, stabbing her many times, cutting the breasts from her body and tossing them between each other as if in a game. While she bled on the ground, wailing in pain and preparation for death, the attackers stabbed eyes and throat, then opened her bowels. For as long as any of the Flathead, Nez Perce or Shoshone warriors could remember, they had been at war with the Blackfeet. The memories were always fresh and vivid in their minds. For this reason they never spared the mothers of their most hated enemy. It had been a long, long time since these warriors had been able to paint themselves with Blackfoot blood in such abandon. It had usually been the other way around. They finished the job by butchering the squaw after she had taken her last agonizing breath, each of the attackers cutting chunks of flesh from her bones to chew on with joy. They would eat the seed that gave birth to Blackfoot warriors. This was big medicine.

On along the retreat trail the Indians pushed in company with many white trappers who were as eager for revenge as any red man. They came upon a broken-down lame pony here or there, an animal abandoned in frantic flight. Occasionally they would whoop with ecstasy as they discovered an abandoned parfleche, loaded with booty and too heavy to carry in the escape. Several more Gros Ventre warriors were discovered. Upon each of these dead braves the Indians counted numerous coups before mutilating the bodies and lifting the scalps. The trophies were held aloft, accompanied by a cheer, before they were slipped under belts to dry. The Indians found seven dead Gros Ventre warriors left behind before they returned to the fortress for fear of running onto the main village. On their return march they collected pelts and robes, lodge utensils, and trinkets left along the beaten path. They knew other bodies of the enemy had been borne away.

Titus led the younger man around the fortress to Milt Sublette's interrupted encampment. Bodies of the allied Indian dead were being gathered from the brush in the swamp. The whites who had been killed were laid beside them, covered temporarily with robes or shirts to hide the faces. Hatcher, too, would be buried along with the others near the swamp behind the enemy fortress. A wounded trapper had been discovered during the survey through the willows. He was insensible with the agony of his wound. Bridger sent him back to rendezvous on a litter slung behind a pony, but the trapper would not make it to the large camp alive. After a few miles of travel north, the man died and was buried Indian-style. They scratched out a shallow grave before wrapping the body in skins and laying it within the ground. The corpse was buried under earth and poles, then the whole site was trampled over many times by men's feet and horses' hoofs to conceal its location.

The air was mostly still as Scratch took Paddock to their ponies. What little breeze stirred already carried with it the stench of rotting corpses. The decay of death assaulted every man's nostrils. The two men passed by the body of an old Nez Perce chief, who wore his gray hair in the elaborate pompadour of the tribe. Two squaws knelt at his side, attending to his needs. The old man had been wounded the day before in the battle. But now his reputation would grow to carry forth the word of his invulnerability. The chief had been struck in the chest with a ball that had first blown through another warrior. The old man had thrown up a lot of blood, but his skin remained unbroken. He now pointed to the bruised depression for Bass and Josiah to see. It had been circled proudly by the old man with his own vomited blood. That was powerful medicine. He had new powers to ward off death by powder and ball. Titus smiled faintly and turned away. He and Josiah rode north toward the large camp. Already trappers were busy in the swamp digging into the trees to recover the precious lead spent in the inconclusive battle. Neither of the two white men moving slowly away turned to look behind him.

The battle was over, but the aftershocks would be felt for some time to come. Burial chores taken care of, the trappers returned to their rendezvous camps and the allied tribes went back to their villages to nurse the wounded and mourn the dead. It had not been a battle they could boast of before evening fires. White men sat about their dancing cook fires that night discussing the battle, drinking to the health of their comrades and friends who had survived, toasting and honoring the departed. Already legends were taking shape from that hot skirmish in the swamp. In their celebration and in their mourning, the encampment still kept a wary, watchful eye about it. Bridger maintained his trapper guard throughout the reaches of Pierre's Hole. Everyone would sleep restlessly for the next few days. Everyone would await the attack that would never come. Everyone would wait until he thought the main enemy camp had passed out of the territory. Horse pens were constructed quickly. There the trappers' animals were corralled to guard against a raid by the enemy. Something between four and six hundred lodges were somewhere on the other side of the mountains, not really that far away. But the Gros Ventre–Blackfeet never showed their faces in the valley.

The two men had been silent all the way northward. Bass slid sore and tired from his pony. After tethering it to the picket pin, he pulled the fur cap down tighter over the bandanna about his head. Josiah plopped to the ground wearily.

"We still goin' to Three Forks with McAfferty day after 'morrow?" he asked the older man as they headed back through the shelters to their canopy.

"Yep," Bass answered.

"After Asa didn't come with us after them Blackfeets?" Josiah asked, a little dumfounded.

"Yep," was the answer again.

"I don't get you sometimes." Paddock shook his head as he dropped his pouch and horn beside the rifle across his buffalo robe.

"I wanna see that man's medeecin, son." Titus's voice seemed far away, distant now. "He's got somethin' up there, an' now, more'n ever, Titus Bass wants to see what it be. More'n ever Ol' Scratch wants to see what's pullin' him up there." He dropped to his knees beneath the canopy finally to look into Josiah's eyes. "This here child wants him to see what's stuck in ol' McAfferty's craw."

13

The damned thing angered him. Scratch never had been one to let flies trouble him. But this one was a devil. Bass was laid out under a tree, eyes closed, half asleep. Every time he wrinkled up his nose and twitched his cheeks the fly took off, only to land on him moments later. The older man rolled over onto his right side and drew up his feet slightly. That jest might help, his foggy mind thought. There it was again, with all its tickling little feet. Raising his arm, Scratch slapped at the fly. Then it was back again. This time it landed on the left side of his nose. He slapped hard against the cheek, waking himself up with the force of his self-inflicted blow.

"Goddamn critters," he mumbled, blinking his eyes to stare into Josiah's laughing face. "Wha-wha-what's so goddamned funny, boy?"

Paddock's laughter sputtered to a halt. "Fly critter gettin' to you, eh?" He continued laughing. He was on his knees right beside the older man's body, rocking back and forth with his lusty mirth.

"Yep. What be it to you?" He sounded a little testy, just aroused from his sleep.

"Had to go hit yourself on your own face, eh?" Paddock went into another fit of laughing.

"What of it, boy?" He pushed himself up on one elbow to watch his young partner laughing at something strange. Bass was confused until Josiah held out the long coarse hairs to show them to the older man.

"Why—you lil' nigger!" He started to get up to grab the young man but Paddock shot away out of reach before Scratch was even ready to move.

"Fly critters, eh?" Josiah prodded.

Scratch crawled to his feet and rose slowly, dusting the sides of his leggings off, "Nawww, jest some young nigger as I got as my pardner's all." He shook loose the leaves and bark that had worked down inside his breechclout and looked up at the young man again, "Horseha'r, you say?"

"Didn't say. But ain't horseha'r, noways. Mule Ha'r, it is," Josiah replied.

"Mule?" Scratch wheezed. He looked from Josiah to Hannah. "You let him lift ha'r off you, Hannah? Ha'r to tickle me own nose? You let that young nigger lift ha'r off you an' let not one lil' snort to warn me?" He walked up beside the old mule and stroked Hannah between the ears. "That's some, it's gotta be." Lifting his eyes to watch Josiah come up beside him, Scratch continued to nuzzle the animal. "Time was, son, when this here lady didn' want nothin' to do with you, she didn'. Right, gal? You come a ways, howsomever, Josiah, an' the ol' gal knows it. She's right smart judge of man flesh. She's watched you come 'long, jest as surely as myself has." His eyes skipped away from Josiah's face to look up the western edge of the valley. "Where's McAfferty an' the squar?"

"Pulled up pins less'n hour ago," Josiah replied, moving slowly away to fetch his ponies. "Said he wasn' gonna be one to be wastin' trail while you was sleepin'."

"Pushed on." Bass mouthed the words quietly as he hitched the extra ponies to a trail rope dragging behind the mule, then climbed atop his chosen pony. "Nigger's in a rush, that ol' white ha'r is." He reined the pony alongside Josiah as they pushed northward up the western side of the mountain valley, "Got him somethin' stuck under his saddle blanket jest won' let him sit for long."

Theirs had been an uneasy truce since the small party had left rendezvous the morning after the battle cleanup.

Scratch had been involved in sorting through Hatcher's possessions in Bridger's camp when Josiah rode up with word that Asa had come to talk. All he had been instructed to say was to tell Scratch they would leave the next morning. McAfferty had turned his pony around and ridden slowly off, leaving Josiah to stand a little confused and bewildered. The short man had come to talk with Bass, but when Asa heard that Scratch was up in Bridger's camp, he just left his message with Josiah and turned back to the Nez Perce village.

What few words were spoken between the two older men during those first few weeks were polite enough. No one could say they were hostile. The days had passed like drifting leaves in their travel north out of Pierre's Hole; not much was said among the four riders. Near sundown every evening each person had his own chores to attend to, so little conversation took place between the two older men.

Asa had led the way north with two pack ponies trailing along behind him. Just to the rear of the pack animals rode McAfferty's squaw, bringing along two more animals behind her. Scratch and Josiah let their burdened ponies plod along some distance to the rear of the married couple, all the while content with keeping eyes moving and searching the country about them as a rear guard. Bass had been quiet during those first weeks, too quiet to suit Josiah. In fact, it was a little spooky to the younger man. It was as if Titus was enduring something he had been forced into doing. He didn't like it, but he was going to see it through to the end. Bass was one to be that way, Paddock kept telling himself. But it didn't seem to ease any of Josiah's discomfort. This was a new man who rode beside him—a man who seemed no longer to take a vital interest in what Josiah did or in anything. This was a new man riding beside Josiah Paddock, or at least a new side to Titus Bass. Something was penned up inside of him, something that was keeping him tied to Asa McAfferty.

Scratch would take Hatcher's fiddle out of its soft case each night after supper and hold it across his lap. He would stare at it while running gnarled fingers over the worn wood. Occasionally he would bring out the fiddle bow and run his fingers across the rosin-slick gut. His eyes were far away at those times, even when Josiah knelt beside him to speak, perhaps to remind him to turn in for the night. His eyes were far away as the old head would shake up and down slightly in answer before slowly putting the fiddle and bow away. Paddock would crawl off to his robe, glancing at Asa and the squaw before snuggling under the warm hide. Then he would turn his head to look back at Bass. The older man slept those nights sitting up with the robe pulled around his shoulders, the fiddle across his lap replaced with a rifle and Hatcher's two horse pistols. Josiah never knew if Bass slept at all; he was always awake when Paddock finally nodded off and always up before first light, puttering around with the fire when the young man finally opened his eyes. It was spooky.

And there was the morning Josiah had opened his eyes quietly without stirring and seen Scratch leaning over the still glowing embers of the fire. The older man was laying branches of sage across the coals while mumbling confusing words into the canopy of the trees overhead. What few words Josiah caught that morning were jumbled and made no sense; just common words—"grandfather," "helper," "beyond"—but they meant nothing to Paddock. It was enough to make him wonder about the older man. So many things had been turning too fast to comprehend anyway—the battle with the Blackfeet, Hatcher choosing to die the way he did, and Bass refusing to change his plans of trapping with McAfferty.

An ill wind was blowing in the mountains that year. Lots of strange feelings were floating through the Stoney Mountains like restless fog. That big village of Blackfeet never had shown up at rendezvous following the battle. Whereas McAfferty, Bass, and Paddock had pushed out early, the company brigades and most of the free trappers elected to sit things out for a spell. Nathaniel Wyeth's brother, an eastern physician, chose to return to the States with Bill Sublette's packtrain. In return for safe homeward passage, Dr. Wyeth patched up Sublette's shoulder wound, which nevertheless kept the trader in the Hole for several days before he was strong enough to ride. On July 30 they finally got under way and headed east with the largest haul of beaver ever brought out of the mountains, some $170,000 in St. Louis prices. East of the divide the homeward-bound train ran into the main body of the Gros Ventre village. Sublette was lucky in bluffing the Indians, still licking their own wounds. He bought off the village leaders with a few presents and went on his way without a fight. Milt pulled out with his brigade, reinforced with some free trappers and what remained of Yankee Wyeth's New Englanders, and the whole party headed west and north for the fall season. The affair seemed settled. Fitzpatrick was pacified. He had been presented with his prize pony after the battle, the same animal the Indians had stolen from him when they had forced Tom to go afoot to save his hair. Although Tom's hair had turned white, getting that pony back made up for much that he had suffered in fighting his way to rendezvous. So the affair seemed settled.

But not for the Gros Ventre. The survivors of the Battle of Pierre's Hole climbed back over the divide and joined up with the main village. After the run-in with Sublette's packtrain, the tribe had to change its plans and keep to the eastern side of the mountains. They surprised both Fontenelle, who was coming in far too late with rendezvous supplies, and the trappers under a man named Bonneville, an army captain on leave from the service. Smack in the middle of the white men they landed, but the Gros Ventre found the enemy too wary, too watchful, and too strong. Besides, the tribe had spent too much powder and ball in the recent battle. They passed on by the Americans, moving north, into the land of the Crows, Absaroka. The Mountain Crows cut the tribe to pieces, taking plunder and prisoners as hard-won spoils to the victor. To the Crow warriors these Gros Ventres were Blackfeet. If a Crow warrior were to say anything kind about Blackfeet, it was that Blackfeet were strong of heart and very brave, but too dumb to fight well. While their ages-old enemy rode back into the mountains to dance in celebration over the scalps taken, the Gros Ventres, decimated, fatigued, wounded, and empty-handed, straggled back to their homeland—Blackfoot country. Smoldering fires were fueled anew. Sacrifices were made to the spirits. The clans were called in for a huge council. When the coups were all counted and the pipe had been smoked, the Blackfeet, Gros Ventre, and Blood tribes were as one. They knew what to do. They needed only to find out where the Americans would be trapping.

The small party of McAfferty had moved into the semiarid region north of the Hole, that lowland basin where only saltbush, sagebrush, hop sage, and the ever-present greasewood stretched out mile upon mile before a man's eyes. What little grass survived there, buffalo and needle grasses, did so because of deep roots and narrow blades. Thereby the grass took in as much water from the ground as possible while giving as little as possible to the hot, dry air. Only along the watercourses could one find the box elder or cottonwood, which survived because of seasonal freshets. A dry land this was.

From streambed to streambed they pushed, occasionally finding a narrow trickle of cool water for man and beast, though more often than not they had to scoop sand out of the watercourses to allow some brown, milky liquid to ooze up from below. For the past two days they had been without water of any description. Through some of the low gaps across the countryside and along some of the dry watercourses they passed small depressions some twelve to fifteen feet across. Bass once drew to a halt by one of the excavations and got down on his knees to smell more closely of what he hoped to find. Josiah kneeled beside the older man.

"What is it?" Paddock asked.

"Buffler waller."

"Huh?"

"Buffler come dig up the ground to shine up theys horns. Dig 'em a hole like this." Scratch spread out his arms as if magically to encircle the depression. "Them critters lay down in 'em an' waller round in the dirt after workin' on theys horns. Jest like it was the finest bath you'd get back to one a them whorehouses in St. Louis. Them big critters like theys wallerin', them buffler does."

Paddock suddenly noticed the ground damp near the deepest part of the depression. In the center stood a small pool of liquid. He rose to stumble over to it.

"Wouldn' drink me none of that, son." Bass knew just what Paddock had in mind.

Josiah slid to his knees in the damp sand before turning to look back at Scratch, "Bad water, eh?" The doubting tone was back in his voice.

"Worse'n any you had afore, Josiah." He came up beside Paddock.

"Cain't be nothin' but rain water," Josiah said, staring at the liquid. "I'll have me a drink afore it dries up like this here." He took a handful of the wet sand and let it trickle through his fingers.

"Buffler waller ain't no place for smart nigger to be

drinkin'; buffler come here to drink if'n they's thirsty after a rain, an' if'n there ain't nothin' else..."

"Then I can drink here, too..."

"Let me finish, boy. Buffler shit an' piss here too." Titus's words caused Josiah to stop his cupped hands just before they reached his lips. "That's right. That whole mess in there jest been bakin' an' cookin' under the sun. No tellin' rightly what lil' varmits be in that water by now." Josiah continued to stare at the putrid fluid in his hands. Slowly he parted the palms and let the warm liquid pour from them. Scratch put a hand on Paddock's shoulder. "C'mon, Josiah. Ain't much a trip from here. Where you find buffler wallers, a child can find him buffler. May take us some days, but them critters is out there. C'mon now, let's be on the tramp." He helped the young man to his feet and they moved slowly back to their ponies.

"Why you don't carry no water?" Josiah was more commenting on what he felt to be stupidity than asking a question.

"Wagh!" Bass snorted, moving away from the younger man to pick his pony's reins up from the ground. "Womens an' pilgrims need be carryin' water, Josiah! Ain't a mountain man worth his licks up here you're gonna catch carryin' water! Wagh! That's some!" He swung into the saddle. "Now down to the southern country, that be where a man'll drop like a fly less'n he carries water 'longst with him. Water scrapes, them is, down there. Man as works outta Taos an' west a Santy Fee, them coons ain't got a lick a sense less'n they's packin' a paunch or gourd full a water." He snorted to clear the dust crusting his nostrils. "But up this here far north, no man got any call to get worrysome 'bout dyin' of thirst. All man needs to do up here for lil' thirst is chew some, maybe smoke that 'baccy. Seems to help, it does. Want some?" Scratch had dug around in his possibles pouch and bitten off some of the dry leaves which he presented to Josiah. Paddock looked down at the parched, brown twist of tobacco and shook his head sullenly. "Heh! You cain't say as I didn' offer you the chance. Leastways, chewin' or smokin' seems to get a nigger's head off the dry he's got. Nawww, now, Josiah. Not a man with wits still 'bout him gonna die of a dry in this here country. He might be hurtin' an' painin' some for while, but he ain't gonna die." Scratch pushed his pony off slowly.

McAfferty's squaw began to complain at first. Josiah didn't blame her for whimpering quietly in her native tongue. She was a woman, softer than they were, he told himself. What he and Scratch were unaware of was that she was getting rounder every day. Even McAfferty was ignorant that her abdomen had finally begun to show the growth of new life within her. For two she had to eat now. For two she had daily to find water.

Crossing the dry crust of a flaky streambed the Nez Perce woman finally began to reel and weave in her saddle. Her pony no longer received direction from the single horsehair rein. The animal stopped. Asa was unaware of what was happening behind him. Plodding on, he led his animals on up the bank leading away from the parched watercourse. Behind him the squaw drooped her head, then raised it vainly in an attempt to call out to him. No words would come. The tongue was swollen in thirst. Her head drooped again in hopelessness of finding water, in hopelessness of calling out for help.

Scratch and Josiah crested the top of the rise that began a slow descent into the streambed. Less than a hundred yards away both men witnessed the drama under midday's bright light.

"What's goin'?" Josiah squeezed words out from between his own dry, crackling cheeks and tongue. "She ain't moving—somethin' wrong..."

"You keep your ground, son!" Scratch bit back as Josiah started to urge his pony into a faster pace. Paddock turned on the older man with a twisted, quizzical look on his face.

"Ain't you gonna help her?" he squeaked.

"Not one of my doin's, Josiah," Bass reached up to take the wide-brimmed hat from the top of his head and used his sleeve in mopping his brow, "She's McAfferty's squar."

"So, you're jest gonna sit there, not knowin' at all what's goin' on—jest gonna let her fall off an' then ride on by." He looked from Scratch down into the creekbed again to see the woman slump more to the side as if in preparation to fall from her pony. "Ain't you got any heart in there with all that other what's eatin' you up?"

At the words Scratch jerked his head to look over to the young man beside him for a few moments, then snorted and shook his head. "Ahhh... McAfferty!" he yelled at the man riding away from the squaw up the other side of the hill. Asa didn't turn around. Bass raised himself in the saddle by standing in the stirrups, "McAfferty!" It hurt to speak, cracking the dry tissues in his mouth and throat. Still Asa did not respond. Titus began to wave the hat overhead and let out a piercing war whoop. Josiah could see the white-haired man stop and wheel his pony about to look behind him. Bass brought the hand that held the felt hat down to point into the streambed when he was certain he had finally got Asa's attention. Neither Scratch nor Paddock could see McAfferty that well. They could not tell if he was looking back at them or down into the dry wash where his squaw had stopped. He just sat there aboard his pony for several minutes while time seemed to stand perfectly still for all of them. No breeze raised any dust nor moved the sage. Only light flecks of white intruded upon the blue canopy overhead that seemed to radiate heat down on the motionless statues below. None of the ponies snorted or pawed at the ground. It was as if they were going to stay there forever—frozen into eternity and alkali salt.

Then the squaw began to slump in her high-pommeled saddle once more and Asa's voice crackled through the silence that had paralyzed them all into timelessness. His words rang clear above the haze of blistering heat that shimmered and blurred over the land. His words were in Nez Perce. The squaw's head moved a little to allow her to look up the side of the wash at her man. She tried to straighten herself when he barked at her again.

"What's he sayin'?" Josiah asked of Bass without looking away from the squaw's back.

"Don' know me no Nepercy."

"You know what he's sayin', though!"

Scratch glanced briefly at Paddock. "He's tellin' her get the pony movin' or he's leavin' her, I 'spect. Said he'd take his pony an' leave her here if'n she don' come on."

The squaw slid painfully back onto the top of her saddle blanket and with a tortured body gave a small kick into the pony's ribs. The animal began to crawl up the slope toward McAfferty, who watched her get into motion. He then turned to disappear over the rise.

"He'd done it?" Josiah questioned as the two men set their ponies into action down the slope.

" 'Spect so. Leastways, that's what I woulda done," Bass began. "He tol't her if'n she was good 'nough to be his squar, she'd better be one to get movin'." Paddock's eyes narrowed as he watched the woman's back throughout her slow climb up the rise before disappearing from view. Bass led him off to the left to crawl around the hill rather than follow in Asa's tracks after crossing the dry bed. Josiah hung his head with the heat and intense thirst, his mind clouded and reeling with what had just happened. He tried to sort it all out, to calculate just what Scratch would have done had Asa left the woman behind out here. He just did not know what had come over the man, he decided. Then Bass grabbed his forearm.

"Wha-a-a?"

"Lookee, boy!" Titus spoke low but his voice dripped with excitement.

Paddock looked about him to see that they had emerged on the other side of the hill. He shifted his eyes a little to the right and saw that McAfferty had come to a halt some distance away. A few yards behind him sat the squaw on her pony. The woman's back was a little straighter; she seemed to have more life in her now.

"Wha . . . what is it?" the younger man asked as he craned his neck slowly to find out what was going on.

"You don' see 'em?" Scratch's tone was one of childish excitement mixed with some disapproval in Josiah's ignorance.

"What I'm supposed to see?" he said finally, looking into Scratch's cracked face.

"Dammit, son—down there!" Bass pointed to the valley below. "Cain't you see 'em?"

Josiah looked into the valley but did not know what he was supposed to be seeing. Sure, the valley looked greener—maybe even some hope of finding water down there. Then his eyes finally focused. The valley seemed to be moving. Slowly, like the waves of the sea, the valley was moving. Looking more closely, Paddock saw that the movement was not the breeze through the grasses and sage below. Animals were down there. Hundreds of them, thousands of them, even millions, slowly moving to the east away from the mountains. When he turned to ask, "Buff'lo?" Scratch was staring into his face.

"Buffler!" Bass nudged his pony into a slow walk toward McAfferty and the squaw, Hannah and the ponies trailing behind him.

"Buff'lo!" Josiah hollered. The only response he got was a stern, disapproving glance from Titus. Paddock put heels into his pony's flanks and followed the older man as he joined Asa. Titus stood in the stirrups and sniffed the air before speaking to the white-haired man in a hoarse whisper.

"Wind's good."

"That be a good run down there, Mr. Bass," Asa began. "I figger we can leave what ain't needed here an' work our way down slow. Well, some—we get us a stand down there, that'll do us earthly good. *'Many sorrows be to the wicked: but he that trust in the Lord, mercy shall compass him about.'*"

"You been prayin', have you, McAfferty?" Bass slid from his pony and removed his hat to hang it on the bundles draped over Hannah's back.

"Aye, Mr. Bass." Asa looked away, staring toward the valley with a smile on his face within the white beard. He leaned forward with his forearms braced atop the pommel of his saddle. "Aye, prayin' to the Lord for some sign to show me why I picked this country to tramp north. *'Then shall ye call upon me, and ye shall go and pray unto me, and I shall harken unto thee.'*"

Scratch was removing the satchels from his pony that held the horse pistols. "An' your God brought us here, did He, Asa McAfferty?"

"Ah, ye be a slave of the devil, Mr. Bass." Asa removed his cap and pulled his sticky leather shirt over his head. Throwing it back to the squaw to catch and hold. McAfferty continued, "Still not one to believe, are ye?"

Scratch checked the load in his rifle, then motioned to Josiah to strip his pony of all unnecessary weight before answering the white hair. "We jest both got us differ'nt Gods, McAfferty. Done me my medeecin, done me my prayin' to mine too, I have. Last few days. Done me my askin' for sign to my God." Scratch dug into his pouch and removed a number of lead balls which he popped into his mouth. Pushing them between his cheek and gums at the side of his mouth, Bass nodded toward the buffalo herd below, "So, we don't rightly know jest whose God it were send

398

them buffler to us, now do we?" With that he pushed his pony away, leaving the rest of them behind as he walked his animal down the slope.

Josiah came up beside the white-haired man and waited while Asa continued to stare at the valley below. Without looking up at the young man, McAfferty spoke again, " 'Lift up thine eyes on high,' Josiah Paddock"—he stopped to take a deep breath—" 'an' behold who hath created these things.' " He put heels into pony ribs and moved off with the young man beside him.

Ever so slightly Josiah's eyes began to widen as the full impact of the sight below him penetrated his fuzzy consciousness. The prairie valley was carpeted with the animals slowly moving along wavelike. Less than a mile from the herd Scratch stopped and slid from his pony's back. He turned to wave a signal to the men following behind. Bass tied a long stretch of rawhide rope around the pony's neck, then slipped rawhide hobbles over the animal's front legs. The long halter rope was then tied to a large clump of sage. He had chosen his spot well; from here he could approach the slow-moving herd within the cover of a short ravine. Along its side he could creep through clumps of bushes without detection if the wind stayed right.

By the time Asa and Josiah reined up by Bass, their ponies' ears were twitching at troublesome insects. They dismounted and anchored their animals to sage. Josiah swatted at the hot sting on his cheek.

"Goddamn skeeters!" he muttered, then caught himself; he looked up to see Asa staring none too kindly at him.

"Ain't skeeters, boy." Scratch jumped in to fill the uneasy silence Josiah felt. He had started to swat and smack at the pests also. The ponies were swishing their tails to find relief from the biting insects. "Buffler gnats." He spit some of the chewed tobacco leaf on the ground. "Lil' devils can make a man nearly blind bitin' the way they does. Land on you with theys lil' red-hot feet an' bellies, bitin' with them poison teeth." Josiah had begun to scratch at the burning blisters each gnat left behind. "Times are when them nigger gnats make a pony run mad, they will. Give him a fever—man too—jest like he had the ague." He took a toe and ground the drying tobacco juice he had spit into the dust. "You boys ready?"

Bass took off in his prairie-hen crouch, skittering and zigzagging between the brush. Near the end of the ravine, where it opened onto the prairie, Titus halted and crouched behind a bush. "Ain't that some?" he asked of the two men who came up to kneel alongside him.

Less than a hundred yards away the herd moved passively by the concealed hunters. From their hiding place the men could watch bulls preparing for battle over a selected cow. Here and there other victorious bulls escorted the cow of their choice away from the main body of the herd to rut. With no distractions worthy of drawing his attention, the bull would mount the cow to mate with bellows and snorts. Paddock's attention was drawn immediately to two bulls that had ceased blowing their traditional warning and had crashed together for the first blow of battle. The crack of skulls and horns rang with a dull note up the ravine where the men lay hidden.

Both adversaries backed off a few yards to measure each other. Shaking their heavy heads with a snort, then raising their noses to bellow for all to take heed, the opponents pawed at the earth. The younger of the two, anxious for his first rut, made a mad dash at the older, more mature bull. The old one jerked his hindquarters around by pivoting on the two front legs as his enemy stumbled past, unable to make an effective charge. Again and again the youngster attempted to catch the old man napping, but the big bull kept an eye on his opponent while feigning no interest in the upstart. Tiring of this youngster, who had picked himself a cagey old man to challenge, and impatient for the cow that stood some yards off coyly looking on, the big bull finally decided it was time to teach the upstart and others a lesson.

"Best time a y'ar for buffler huntin'," Scratch whispered to the young man beside him. "Ruttin' season they's all gettin' pulled up together. This here be the time when a man can see a herd this size, coverin' the whole prairie, black like that. Them ol' bulls don' give a man no mind at all when they's fightin' or when they's ruttin'. Child can walk right up to 'em an' them bulls don' pay him no mind. Got 'em other things to tend to, it seems."

The young bull raced in for another charge. This time he had the old man's actions figured out. When within range the youngster cut sharply to the left as the old bull pivoted. Deep into the chest of the old man went the youngster's horn. What saved the aging animal from being ripped open were two fortunate actions, one on his own behalf and the other taken by the young bull. Not a proven fighter yet, the youngster did not know what to do when he had made contact with his enemy. Instead of ripping to the side with his horn, he left it in the old man's chest while trying to butt him, using the strength in his hind legs. The cagey oldster then merely moved backward with each blow of the opponent's head until the horn was no longer in his chest. He was lucky. The young bull's horn had not yet grown long enough to puncture a lung. The veteran was hurt, but not with a wound that meant death on the prairie.

Startled, the youngster backed up a few paces, as if dumfounded that he had not seriously weakened his adversary. His chest matted with thick hair now showing traces of bright blood, the old man merely snorted back a challenge, as if to say he wanted the youngster to try that again. Made bold by the smell of the blood he had drawn, the young challenger dashed again toward the waiting bull. With speed and agility that amazed Paddock, the old bull leaped to the side and planted his horn beneath the diaphragm of his enemy. With the force of his blow and the speed of the youngster's dash by him, the horn ripped through the thick flesh all the way back to the hind quarter before it was pulled out, dripping with blood and body fluids. The youngster jerked to a stop and twisted his head about to look first at the old man, then at his own side. From the long, gaping wound began dropping the intestines and abdominal organs, which could no longer be contained within his body. He began to stumble about in shock, stepping on his own entrails, which act only yanked more of the organs from the abdomen. He snorted and bellowed as if begging for help in those agonizing moments of weaving and wandering about, his hoofs crushing his own vital organs and stomping his own flesh and blood into the dry earth. Unconcerned, the victor pranced gallantly over to his chosen cow and escorted her to the tail end of the herd. There he clumsily mounted her and began to mate amid a concert of crescendoing thrusts and snorts. The herd passed on by the wounded, dying bull, leaving him to stand shocked and alone. He made one final bellow atop his quaking legs and collapsed thunderously to the prairie floor. Vainly he tried to get back up on his front legs, head straining to pull the rest of his body up with it. Then the head would lift no more. Belly flat on the ground, laid out in his own blood and entrails, the bull clunked his head into the dust, lifeless.

"There be free meat, Josiah!" Scratch started to move toward the dead bull, still in a crouch. He kept his eyes on the slowly retreating herd for signs of discovery. Asa followed him closely with Josiah on their heels.

Scratch let his rifle clunk to the ground before he took the bull's head with both hands grasping a horn. He struggled to get the head turned to the side, then let it collapse into the dust. Kneeling within the curve of the animal's neck and chest as he pulled the knife from his belt, Bass dug the huge blade into the flesh and pushed it downward with both hands. At first the blood oozed from the slash in the neck, then quickly began to pump. Titus dropped the knife and immediately buried his head within the musky, matted, dirty hair he had cut through, into the wound went his face, his nose submerged in the blood while he held his breath to drink in the warm fluid. With mad gulps the old man sucked and sucked on the dark, sticky blood. Asa stood watching, his forearms resting on the muzzle of his rifle. Josiah's mouth had dropped slightly when Scratch had buried his face within the animal's neck, frozen from astonishment. Finally Bass began to back off and his head emerged from the bull's throat. He turned to look at his two companions. The grinning face was covered with the red, syruplike fluid, from his forehead, where his blue bandanna was now stained, down to his whiskers, which dripped onto his bare chest.

"Want you some a this boy?" he grinned, yellowed teeth contrasting against the dark shadows of his beard and mustache, crimson cheeks, eyes, and forehead.

Josiah could not speak. Vainly he tried to answer. He didn't know if he was going to laugh or lose his stomach. Jerking his head from side to side finally in answer to the older man's question, Paddock closed his mouth to gulp back a queer feeling in his stomach.

"Thought you was thirsty, son!" Scratch snorted. "Prime doin's, this here is. Make the boy in you a man real quick. Young bull this'un is. Medeecin water, anyways you lay your sights to it." He smacked his lips. "Sure you don' want no drink here? Make you feel right pert." Paddock gulped involuntarily again and looked away briefly. "Mother Bass didn' raise no such a fool. Not by a long chalk!" Titus reared his head back to laugh lustily, then fixed his eyes on Asa. "You want any a this, McAfferty?"

Asa took his arms from the muzzle of his rifle and stepped toward Titus. "Think I do, Mr. Bass. Me pappy taught me drink when it's offered to me—an' the good Lord's given us this here buffler herd." He dropped to his knees beside Scratch and slid his rifle out of the way before burying his head in the animal's neck to drink of the blood himself.

"Sure you ain't thirsty now, Josiah?" Bass kept prodding, knowing full well how the young man was hurting.

"Nawww...nawww. Not that thirsty." He ran his tongue around inside his parched cheeks. It felt swollen and bloated out of shape.

"Get your sticker singin' then, boy." Scratch rose from the ground. "We'll take us hump ribs an' liver for supper this night."

Asa drew his head out of the throat as Scratch and Josiah began to cut through the hide and up the chest that lay next to the ground. Josiah looked once at the man, looked away, then looked back at him. He shook his head while staring at the blood-stained face, white hair, and beard. McAfferty smiled with satisfaction and relief as he plopped backward to sit on the ground and watch the butchers at work. He then glanced up the side of the hill toward the dark objects just below the skyline and waved. The objects began a slow descent down toward the three men.

By the time the young squaw had made it to the trio with all the pack animals in tow, Scratch was just beginning to reach an arm into the chest cavity. He felt around inside until he had found the prize he sought. He ripped it loose with both hands. From beneath the bottom ribs emerged the slippery heart, cradled carefully in both palms so that it would not skitter from Bass's grasp.

"Squar's thirsty, ain't she, McAfferty?" He rose carefully to present the heart to Asa. "This here be best drinkin'—for the lady."

McAfferty took the heart given to him after he had gotten to his feet. He balanced the heavy organ carefully while stepping over to his wife's pony and stretched out

403

his arms as if he were offering the richest of alms in a sanctuary. "*'He sendeth the spring into the valleys, which run among the hills.'*" He turned to grin at Bass while the Nez Perce woman eagerly took the slimy organ from her husband. She turned it around in her hands, carefully juggling the heart until she had positioned it where she would be able to drink from the aorta. To watch her, it seemed as if she were drinking from a fine china pitcher or crystal goblet. Slowly she finished and looked down on the three men to smile with the satisfaction of quenching a disabling thirst. After licking her moist lips, she held the heart out to Asa and spoke in Nez Perce. McAffery took the organ and turned to Josiah, "Hyar, Mr. Paddock. Yer the only one that's not had a drink." The young man reluctantly took the heart into his hands, feeling the flesh quiver slightly in his grasp. "*'Men do not despise a thief, if he steal to satisfy his soul when he is hungry,'* Master Josiah." Paddock looked at the short man, then back at the heart.

Scratch had stopped his butchering along the bull's hump to watch Josiah turn the heart slowly in his hands. "Go 'head, son. Take a horn. That's medeecin water, buffler blood is. We'll see how your stick floats now."

Gradually Paddock's lips encircled the aortic vessel. He closed his eyes. Little by little he began to drink what blood remained in the heart by squeezing the organ with a pumping action. The liquid was warm and thick, but not revolting, as he had thought it would be. Josiah took the heart away from his face. "Ain't too bad," he commented with a faint smile at the corners of his red lips. "Not too bad." Paddock put the aorta back to his lips and continued drinking until the organ was empty. The fluid had poured past his parched cheeks and tongue, down past the dry, dusty well he had visualized his throat to be. It was warm and thick, he thought again, like syrup poured over johnny cakes—but it was wet. The heart finally empty of fluid, Josiah took it from his mouth and licked his lips.

"Like that, eh?" Scratch chuckled and went back to pulling hide from the hump. "Man be thirsty or hungry 'nough, he'll get himself a taste for lotta things."

The young woman slid to the ground and came over to the carcass to help with the butchering. "She's the one to be doin' that work, more'n likely," Asa commented. Bass straightened and stood up as the Nez Perce squaw set her knife to work. He backed off and watched her begin to slip the hide off the carcass with even, delicate strokes.

"Man does the killin'," Titus remarked, "squar does the cuttin'." He turned his head to look eastward along the valley at the retreating, slow-moving herd. "Wind's still good." He looked at Asa and Josiah. "Care to run 'em? The whole shiteree?"

"Ye take the young'un with ye, Mr. Bass," Asa said, shaking his head in the negative. "I'll stay here an' finish this."

"C'mon, young'un, we's to runnin' meat!" Scratch took off back up the ravine in the direction of the horses.

Josiah picked his rifle up from the dirt and set off on the older man's heels. At the opening of the ravine he came to a dead halt. Without warning, with no suspicion it would happen, blood gushed from his stomach and splattered to the ground. In one quick lurch he had vomited all the fluid taken from the buffalo heart. He was startled, but not sick. Disbelieving, Paddock stared at the puddle before him on the ground, then licked the blood on his lips. No, he didn't feel sick. The warm fluid had done its job. It had relieved his thirst. Now his body could get rid of it. Slowly wiping his chin and bare chest free of red streaking droplets, Josiah glanced up and saw Scratch looking back at him.

"First time you drink of it, critter's blood'll do that to you," he yelled. "Don' let it fret you none. It's gone now. Outta your feedbag. C'mon!" He continued his dash along the ravine. Paddock looked at the drying puddle once more and took off in a trot toward the ponies. Scratch was mounted by the time Josiah came up. "Check your load, son. See to it that she be damned well seated an' let's go!"

Josiah pounded the buttplate of his rifle against the earth's crust and climbed aboard his small Nez Perce pony. "Want you pay some mind to your pony, son. When we get into the herd, let him have his head. He'll know what to do an' what not to do. You jest foller me an' pick yourself a good young cow, you hear? Them bulls spell trouble for you, they will. 'Sides, theys ain't good eatin'. This here time a y'ar be best for meat huntin'. Robes ain't worth the tinker's dam, howsomever. Jest look for a yaller hide as is turnin' brown. Them be the young cows, seal-fat an' sleek. No bulls." He nudged his small pony with his heels then looked back over his shoulder to shout at Paddock. "You take you jest one shot, son. No more. Jest one ball. If'n you don' make meat with it, pull out an' head back here. Don' wait for me. I'll catch up to you later. Jest one ball." Paddock nodded in agreement and followed Bass down the ravine and past the two butchers.

Titus kept to the southern slope of the valley, a few hundred yards above the herd as he approached the buffalo from the rear. Josiah rode up closer to the older man's right as they walked their ponies through the sage and grass that swept down to meet the valley floor. Both of the trained animals were aware of what they would soon be called upon to do. Their heads nodded up and down in anticipation, but Josiah took his pony's excitement as lack of control. He struggled with the rein tied about the animal's lower jaw. Bass looked away from the approaching herd and saw Paddock working his pony too hard.

"Ease up there, boy," he whispered softly. "Jest let the pony have its head. You give him knees when you're ready to get down in that shiteree of critters. Pick you one out, that's all. He'll do the rest for you. Ease up on them reins . . . that's it." He smiled approvingly as Josiah finally resisted what seemed to be his better instincts and let the reins go slack. "Jest you 'member to keep to the outside of the herd. Don' go gettin' yourself in the smack dab of them critters. You fall off or get pitched somehows, the smack dab of all them hoofs ain't no place to be landin'. Jest keep your pony's nose to the outside here, pick you out one, an' make meat of her." Josiah nodded his head and looked past Titus down at the herd. "You'll do fine first time, son. An' mind you, jest one shot. Don' take . . ." He was interrupted by some new snorting from the shaggy animals below in the valley. They began to mill for a few moments and suddenly bolted. The wind had shifted and the poor-sighted animals, unable at first to see the hunters above them, now had a clear scent of the nearby riders. The sea of furry buffalo suddenly pulsated with new life at the recognition of danger and thundered off in a stampde.

"Boy, you're on your own! Whoooeeee!" Scratch jerked hard on the pony's bridle to lead the animal in a slant down the slope toward the racing herd. "Ol' Make-'em-Come gonna make us meat!" He rode away yelling at the top of his lungs, suddenly freed of the necessity of hoarse whispers any longer. "Here's to mountain doin's! Here's to shinin' times! Running' meat for boss ribs an' buffler tongue!'' Yahooing as he approached the side of the mass of thundering beasts, Bass cut his pony a little to the right where he could ride on the outer flank of the herd while picking out his target. "By god, these be the plumb center of times for a man! Ain't no booshway what knows runnin' meat! Jumpin' Jehoshaphat! We is in the meat!''

Josiah had given knees and heels to his pony when Bass had dashed toward the herd. He slowly released a little more of the bridle rein from his hand. Racing down the slope he decided to test the pony before reaching the noise and confusion of the hunt. With a quick jab he pressed against the upper ribs on the right side of his chosen pony, just behind the front leg. Instantly the animal cut to the left. Paddock smiled all over. A couple of short jabs in the left side brought him back to heading straight for the herd again. Ahead of the young man Bass had already chosen his target and was coursing his animal easily into the midst of the herd. Josiah reached the edge of the black flood of fur and hoofs just as he heard the dim report of a rifle over the continuous clap of buffalo thunder. He thought he heard a wild whoop of joy. There was no sighting the older man now. Bass was lost in the clouds of dust swirling and billowing up from the prairie. Already Paddock was close enough to the moving sea to find himself beginning to choke within the walls of dust that streamed back toward him. Clods of dirt bit at his face as he pushed his pony to higher speed to match the momentum the buffalo had attained. Tears began to stream from the corners of his eyes and mix with the dirt across his cheeks. There it was starting to cake into rivulets of wind-dried mud.

Josiah's animal, head low as every muscle strained in the race, was waiting for Josiah to make a choice. Turning his head to the left to blink his eyes clear of dust and water, Josiah spotted a good-sized cow. "Pick yourself a good young cow, you hear?'' Bass's words pursued him. Through the dancing swirls of dust he tried to discern her coloring. "Jest look for a yaller hide as is turnin' brown. Them be the young cows.'' Scratch's voice rasped again in his ears. Paddock quickly decided the one chosen was his meat. She was moving in and out of the edge of the herd. "She see me?'' he asked himself. "She know what I'm after?'' His palm sweated against the wood along the wrist of his rifle. Within the left hand twisted the bridle rein nervously. Consciously he brought his left thigh out from the pony's side and stuffed the rein between the blanket and his leg where he hoped it would stay. "No use to me now," he muttered.

The cow dashed to her right, away from the edge of the herd. "Got her now—she's alone!" In his excitement, Josiah slapped both his knees against the pony's ribs, not knowing as he did so that the rein dropped from its leg hold. The animal beneath him shot away at the command. It too sensed this was the chosen animal. Now the cow was racing alongside the lumbering herd, closing in on the leaders of the mad stampede where the other cows were gathered. He turned to look back into the dust and noise but could not make out the thousands of bulls bringing up the rear of the startled procession. Somewhere from within the cloud-reaching swirl of dust he thought he heard another whoop of joy. "Scratch havin' his day," he mused as he turned his face back around to fix his eyes on the cow some twenty yards ahead of his pony.

Bass had dropped his first cow easily near the fringe of the herd. With a cheer of victory he jabbed at his pony's side to pull the animal out of the herd and continue its race across the prairie. Titus rotated his rifle in both hands to bring the muzzle up to his lips. He blew a gust of breath down the barrel to clear the touch hole. His left hand creeped up the narrow end of the powderhorn and popped loose the cap. Bracing the butt of the rifle against the toe and instep of his right foot as best he could aboard a galloping pony, Bass spilled more powder into the air than he dropped down the barrel. Frantically he tried to find the thong that held the cap to the powderhorn so that he could return it to its hole. Finally he gave up the search and jerked the horn strap across his shoulder so that little if any powder would be jarred out. Back to his mouth went the muzzle. Digging a lead ball from inside his cheek with a dry tongue, the hunter spit it down the barrel. With the barrel clutched tightly in his right hand, Titus leaned off to his pony's right side. The animal began to course away to the right as if following its rider's command. Bass straightened back up in the Spanish-tree saddle.

"Awww, you're gonna be that way 'bout it, eh?" He

tried again, this time leaning forward against the animal's neck as he prepared to jam the rifle butt against the ground. With a long-arm reach, Scratch placed the butt on the ground ahead of him with a clunk, then quickly swung the weapon backward as the pony raced by the spot where he had succeeded in ramming his ball home against the powder. Back into the bend of his left arm the rifle was laid; his right hand began to search for his priming horn. Frustrated in his attempts to find it along his pouch strap, Bass jerked the powderhorn back down into readiness and spilled powder into the air, across his lap; by good fortune some grains fell into the lock's pan. He tugged to put the horn high across his chest once again, then pulled the hammer back and snapped the frizzen down over the pan.

"Now you can pull right!" he commanded as his knees gave direction to the pony beneath his buttocks. The animal veered smoothly out of the edge of the herd, directing itself more by sound than sight within the crush of racing bodies coming up from the rear. Bass let the sea of cows shoot by, then kicked his animal back into the midst of the herd as the bulls began to make their appearance on the cows' tails.

"We make meat outta one a these'r mean critters now." He suddenly realized that as he opened his mouth to yell it was immediately filled with dust. He tried to spit but there wasn't enough moisture left. Out of the cloud emerged a dark form that began to take shape as a lumbering four-year-old bull. Reaching for speed the pony made its way alongside the mammoth animal. Scratch relaxed his knees from the pony's ribs. That was the cue that it was now up to his steed to stay with the chosen target. From the side of his woolly head the bull peered at the horse and rider with one wild red eye. He angled off to the left a few yards away from Bass only to bump against a larger bull that roughly shoved him back into line. He couldn't escape to the left and the rider was to his right. A feint or two with his horned head toward the enemy caused the pony to veer sharply to the right out of danger. Scratch almost lost his hold but maintained as the saddle. As the bull finished his attempts to scare the pony off, the Nez Perce animal went back to racing alongside the large bull.

Titus jammed the butt against his shoulder, found the

front of the trigger guard with his right index finger, and quickly snapped the barrel down so that the muzzle pointed low on the bull's brisket. His finger snapped off the guard and yanked the trigger back. Scratch felt no kick against his shoulder. The puff of smoke from the pan and the gray billowing cloud from the muzzle blowing back in his face stood out starkly against the brown film in the air. He whooped with joy that the ball had not lodged in the middle of the barrel. But the bull continued to run. Titus eased his pony back to the bull's rear flank while he again sought to yank his powderhorn into service. The black grains streamed down the barrel and flew into the air, splattering into his tired, wind-blown eyes. Just as he put the muzzle to his lips to spit a ball down the barrel, Scratch became aware of a change in the bull's pace. The monster was slowing; other animals were racing by him at full tilt. The pony stayed right with the bull while the shaggy beast began to lose strength in the chase. Finally the bull was almost walking beside the pony and rider. Bass leaned forward once again to drop the butt of his rifle against the ground as the pony stumbled in a hole.

He was catapulted over the pony's neck, his grasp of the rifle barrel breaking free in midair. Titus hit the ground on his left shoulder and cartwheeled through the scrub sage, sand eating at his face each time he rolled, and black powder spilling into his eyes, nose, and mouth as it spewed from the horn. He skidded to a stop and jerked his head up to look at the retreating herd. To his left and right he glanced but could not locate Paddock. Quickly he assessed that the young man must still be racing along with the herd. Then something dull and throbbing in the back of his head reminded the old man to look behind him. His rifle had cartwheeled and bounced along the prairie with him, striking him twice in the back of the head while he had tumbled across the dirt. It was back there, somewhere, a piece of his consciousness told him. He wiped sweat, powder, and dirt from around his eyes, feeling the grit collected beneath the lids. His vision cleared. He looked back at the wounded bull lumbering toward the hunter.

Closer and closer came the animal toward the aching bones that refused to move. Spurts of dark red and purple fluid gushed from the bull's nostrils and mouth as he continued toward the fallen rider. From side to side the animal whipped its head, slinging the slimy blood and mucous mixture into the clearing air. He was snorting blood, and bellowing for blood. The bull stopped once, pawed the ground menacingly, then continued jogging toward Bass. That's when Titus saw the pony. Riderless and free now, the animal, having regained its legs, was running to catch up with the bull.

Although fearful of being gored and trampled, Scratch was still astonished that the pony had not broken a leg in the stumble and fall. "I'll be gone to hell right here an' et for the devil's tater!" he exclaimed out loud. He watched the bull coming slowly toward him, then glanced again at the pony, now racing toward the wounded bull. The buffalo horse caught up with the beast, then rushed ahead of the animal, placing itself between bull and rider. The beast stopped and pawed angrily at the earth again. Around and around the wounded animal walked the pony, all the time staying some ten yards from the whipping horns and lunging head.

Scratch rolled his head from side to side and shakily stood up, feeling the pain in his left shoulder and hip. He wiped more dirt from his face and rubbed the aching left leg. Quickly he rotated his left arm. It hurt but, "Ain't nothin' broke." He spotted his rifle and trotted painfully to retrieve it as the bull made another lunge toward the pony as if attempting to clear the way for an attack on the man. Picking the weapon up from beneath the sage brush where it had eventually landed after bouncing over the prairie, Bass looked below the frizzen and remembered he hadn't even primed the weapon yet. He jerked the strap down and poured powder onto the pan most carefully while watching the bull out the corner of his eye. Around and around the wounded animal pranced the buffalo pony. Scratch's heart smiled that he had acquired this animal for his own. An Indian worked long and hard to train such a buffalo runner. Dirt-stung eyes shot a glance at the pony's ears as he snapped the hammer back and pulled the frizzen down. The animal's ears should have been notched to signify a special buffalo runner. His mind thought that strange—that the Nez Perce warrior hadn't marked the animal as being something out of the ordinary, for special this animal was. Strange too that the Indian had sold that horse.

Bringing the butt to his shoulder, Scratch peered

down the barrel and put the front blade just behind the bull's ear. He sucked in a breath of air and let it out slowly. His eyes then caught the shaking in the bull's legs. Trembling and quaking with unsteady knees, the wounded animal began to weave about while attempting to stand his ground against his two adversaries. Gradually Bass let the rifle slide from his shoulder. His one shot had done the killing. "Ain't no use to wastin' 'nother ball." He cradled the rifle at his right hip as the trembling and quaking ceased. The bull became rigid for a moment, then shook once more before its convulsive seizure tore weak legs out from under the heavy carcass. Like thick syrup refusing to pour in the cold of a winter morning, the bull slowly sank to the ground with a low, snorting gasp. The bearded chin crashed against the soil and the flood of purple fluid from mouth and nostrils slowed to a trickle. The pony stood still a moment more, then bent its head to nibble at the dry grass peacefully.

The animal did not shy from Titus as he approached it to pick up the long rein strung out on the ground. With the rope Bass tied the pony to one of the bull's front legs. Then he stood back a moment to survey the job ahead. Once more he glanced eastward at the disappearing cloud of dust, which told of the retreating herd. He turned his head westward along the top of the hills to see if he could find sight of Paddock. "Boy must still be runnin'. Tol't him, goddammit—tol't him jest one shot. Didn' want him to get hurt. I didn' want the boy to get hurt," he muttered to the hills, then turned again to look at his pony. "Awww, young buck's all right. Prob'ly jest runnin' for hell of it."

Dressing the buffalo out was always a frustrating chore for Scratch, a man more accustomed to handling deer or elk. Those carcasses could be rolled about on the ground with relative ease or with some effort hoisted into a tree for skinning and butchering. With the buffalo's immense weight, however, rolling the animal on its back was out of the question, and a sane man would not even consider attempting to hoist such a beast off the ground by himself, even if there were trees across this treeless valley. The bull having landed on his belly in the final collapse of death, Bass had to shift the carcass only slightly in preparing it for the knife. After laying his rifle alongside the bull's head within the curve of one horn, he tugged and struggled with one leg at a time. With some exertion he pulled the legs away from under the body so they would serve as braces during the tugging and pulling that would be required in skinning the animal. Straightening for a moment to wipe his arm across the soaked bandanna and his forehead, Titus pulled his knife free from his belt. The strap on the pouch and horn chafed at the side of his sweating neck so he pulled it over his head and slung it from one of the bull's horns. Bending low over the animal's neck he stuck the knife into the thick fur and began to slice from the throat across the back of the neck and down the other side to the throat once more. The rest of the hide was now separated from that clinging to the skull. By leaning over the bull with his knees and thighs braced against the beast's ribs, his toes dug into the ground, Scratch could begin forcing his knife blade through the hide along the course of the spine. A squaw after lodge hides would not make such a cut from the nape of the neck back to the tail, but Bass was after only selected cuts of meat. He pushed himself away from the rear flank and braced once again near the animal's hump. Only partial skinning required now, just enough to pull the hide away from the hump along the shoulders. He shifted the knife in his hand so that he could run an index finger along the top of the blade. As Scratch began to cut hide from the bull's shoulders, he was interrupted by some shouting coming from the east.

"Yessir, Ol' Scratch havin' him a day of it," Josiah mumbled as he peered back at the cow of his choice after hearing what seemed to be Bass's second shot of the chase. Now it was his turn. Eating up ground some twelve yards at a time the pony continued to gain on the cow. Josiah leaned forward along his pony's neck while it did the work of catching the target for him. From the corner of his eye he peered again and again out at the hills to his right, then to his left. They seemed to be narrowing into a vee ahead in the distance. He raised his eyes to peer over the top of the pony's head but could not determine a thing about the country before him. Everything was noise and dirt, dust clouds and stinging clods filling the air. He leaned forward along the pony's neck to continue his run. His body felt as if it must have been miles since he had heard Scratch's last shot. His mind felt bruised with the days of heat and thirst. And now the chase. He was out there alone—except for the pony. He must remember the pony. Always keep thinking of the pony.

"You just do that. Keep thinkin' of the pony. Ain't gonna let him spill me—not me. Not now."

Paddock had come alongside the animal. Easing back slowly he sat up straight. Josiah brought the weapon into the crook of his shoulder after pulling the hammer back. He found the trigger, then his target just behind the shoulder and a few inches above the bottom of the brisket where the heart was pumping blood furiously. Josiah pulled the trigger but no puff of smoke emerged from the pan. Startled actionless for a moment, he finally looked down into the pan itself. The frizzen looked good, his flint too. Musta just lost my primin' back 'long the way, he thought to himself to keep from cursing his own stupidity. It was a jostle to pour powder into the pan while riding at full tilt, his eyes constantly moving from the job at hand to the cow. Black grains spilled over his arms and lap, but soon he was done and put the powderhorn away to his side. Josiah snapped the frizzen down while pulling the hammer back with a stout snap. "I know how to aim you—just spit fire this time, ol' gal," he mumbled as he brought the butt once more to his shoulder, found his target, and pulled the trigger. This time there was an explosion from the muzzle following the flash of smoke from the pan.

The cow just ahead and to his left pitched forward on her head, bouncing high into the air with the tumbling crash against the ground. As the cow came rolling off the first impact, Paddock's pony was just passing her. The cow rolled in the air, involuntarily splaying her legs wildly with nothing beneath them now to give her support. A flank falling to the ground struck against the pony's side on its way down. The pony stumbled to the right from the collision's force as Josiah frantically grasped at the spot where the reins should have been. But they were dragging the ground. His right hand hugged about the rifle, Paddock stuck his left hand into the pony's mane, then wrapped and rewrapped the horsehair around his fingers.

"Ho! Ho, you now, goddammit!" he was screaming into the pony's ear. Josiah pulled to the right with his clutching fingers and kneed the pony in the right side. It responded immediately. "That's more like it, critter." The animal led him out of the edge of the herd and to the side of the narrowing valley. Brought to a halt, the pony pawed at the earth as if something more were expected, as if something were unfinished. Paddock caught his breath slowly, drinking in air as he found the loose rein. Finally his heart stopped its racing beat and slowed to a canter. The rest of the herd was passing with thunderous hoofs below him. All the while the young man closely eyed the passing sea of bodies to discern if Scratch was among the huge animals. When the last of the older bulls had run by, Josiah looked westward along the rolling hills of the valley. Scratch was not be seen. Paddock figured he had come a long way since last he had heard that second rifle shot and Josiah wondered whether Bass had fallen only to be trampled under thousands of hoofs. His mind conjured a scene of nothing left of Titus Bass except for his greasy leggings and breechclout. Little else would remain after that herd passed over his body.

"Nawww!" he said to himself quietly. "Ol' Scratch ain't one to go under just yet!" Still, he watched to the west nervously, but figured that with the rolling of the plains he could not see the older man and Scratch could not see him.

Then Josiah spotted the cow. She lay on her side in a massive heap of flesh and fur against a large clump of sage where her tumbling had stopped. "Dead of a broke neck, most likely," he said aloud. He rode over to the buffalo carcass, dismounted, and stepped up to the dead animal cautiously. Then a smile warmed his whole body. He felt warmed by what he had done, by what he had accomplished his first time running meat—and with just one shot. "You take you jest one shot, son. No more. Jest one ball," he heard Scratch saying, as if the older man were at his side. Paddock looked around suddenly and was surprised not to see Bass with him. The nervousness returned. To hear the old man's voice just might be Scratch's medicine. Should he start to dress the animal out or go back to find out what had happened to his partner? Josiah's eyes strained to the west. He'd go ahead and try to dress the cow out by himself. "Ain't gonna be no goddamned pilgrim 'bout it, I ain't. This here my meat an' I'll do the cuttin' on it," he mumbled. Paddock started to set his rifle against the cow's side when Scratch's voice came to him again from out of the blue, clear and ringing this time, "Say, son, you gotta ball a huggin' that breech, don' you?" Josiah instinctively grabbed for his rifle and looked about him to see where Bass was hiding.

"Awww, my head's just playin' tricks with me," Josiah snorted.

"Best you always load up soons after shootin' your rifle as you can," came the voice of the older man at him again. Josiah rubbed his wet palms along the length of the stock. "Never know what s'prise be waitin' for you up an' over that rise."

"All right! All right, goddammit! I'll reload right here an' now!" Josiah did not like the voice in his head talking to him in Scratch's own voice. But most of all, he did not like the ill, nervous feeling that gave rise to that voice from within. He pulled his pouch from side to front and was pouring powder from the horn into his palm when he saw the specks along the northern skyline.

His eyes frozen on the figures contrasted against the cornflower blue sky, Josiah was unaware that he was spilling powder on the ground as it poured over his hand. They looked to be shadows out of some distant dream at first, standing motionless and fuzzy along the sun-shimmered horizon. He caught himself losing powder and looked down at the muzzle. Paddock dusted the grains off the end of the barrel and looked back up to find the figures were moving down into the valley from the northern slope. The shadows were descending easily at first and he could count about nine, no ten of the figures on horseback. Josiah jerked his head around to find his pony nearby munching on grass after the chase. He looked once more to the floating black specks against the hillside; they had picked up their pace in descending to the valley floor. Paddock began to ease toward his pony, then looked over his shoulder at the advancing horsemen.

"Injuns!" he cursed. No doubt of that now. Feathers were streaming from the shadows' heads and rifles or bows being held in outstretched arms. With his left hand the young man swooped up the long rein and leaped onto the pony's back. "It's gonna be a race now, ol' gal! Get yer young ass for the west like ye've never been one to do afore!" The animal shot out across the plain up the slow rise on the rolling prairie with furious kicks from the rider's heels.

The wind from the west had now shifted and was

coming at his back. It cooled his neck as he realized his blood was running cold. He admitted he was scared. The pouch slapped angrily at his side as the pony crested the top of another small rise and raced down its westward slope. He looked behind him to see the advancing riders gaining some ground on him by steering in a sharp diagonal off the northern slope. They just might catch up, he began to think. The his mind raced back to the vision of Scratch, now nothing more than greasy buckskins embedded in the valley floor.

"Sweet Jesus! Bass'll be . . . Bass gotta be up here a ways!" A clump of something gripped its claws within his dry throat. "Bass'll be up here." Then he put his thoughts to the race. From minute to minute he looked behind him at the riders yelling for his blood. Over a third small rise and he began to pick out the dark figures on the prairie ahead of him. Closer he rode without looking back, straining his eyes to stay riveted on the figures before him. The forms began to emerge as a huge mass of a single buffalo, a pony off to the side, and a man leaning over the carcass engaged in the labor of butchering.

Josiah began to yell and yahoo fiercely at the top of his lungs. At first his voice squeaked with the dryness clamping down on his throat. He choked and spat, then tried again. Louder was his warning this time. Should he fire his rifle? Then he remembered it wasn't loaded. There was powder down the barrel for noise but no ball to follow it. He slammed the butt against his thigh in frustration and anger. "Best you load up soons after shootin' your rifle as you can," returned the prudent voice. He would shove it out of the way with his own.

"Injuns! Scratch! Injuns comin' in!" The words mingled with the pounding of hoofs. He watched the figure of the man straighten up to full height from his skinning chores. "Injuns! Goddammit, Scratch! Injuns! Just don't stand there!"

For Bass the sounds coming from the rider hung in the air like feathers, refusing to come to earth, refusing to be understood. They were just sounds until he looked past the charging horseman to see the shadows cresting the low rise behind the rider. Then he understood. Quickly he shot a glance behind him but could not see where they had left Asa and the squaw. Again he looked to the rider.

"Injuns! Just don't stand there!" It was the boy's voice now.

No longer sounds, they were words spoken by the boy. He stuffed the knife back into his belt without wiping it clean. Snatching up his pouch strap he dropped it over his shoulder and grabbed for the rifle. Immediately looking to the priming, he snapped the frizzen back over the pan and quickly unwrapped the pony's rein from the bull's foreleg. In a leap he was on the animal's back and yanking its head around so that he could see where Josiah was. Instantly calculating distance and speed, Bass put heels into his pony's ribs for another frantic chase. He figured that the younger man's pony would just pass his before the buffalo runner attained its full speed.

As Paddock came alongside and began to inch away, Titus saw Josiah open his mouth to yell something at him. "Jest shut your yap an' keep runnin'!" Scratch barked. Gradually the older man's pony began to pick up to its maximum speed. He felt the unsureness in his bowels that the animal beneath him would have enough strength left in him to run full tilt all the way back to the McAffertys and the ravine. Pulling alongside Josiah's horse, Bass leaned over and brought the butt of his rifle smacking across the other pony's rump. It shot ahead for a few yards. The younger man jerked his head back at the animal's sudden burst of speed to stare at Bass for an instant with unknowing eyes.

"Jest keep 'er goin' till she drops on you—full out, boy!" he hollered back at the unknowing, questioning eyes.

Paddock felt better now that he was riding alongside Scratch. Come what may of it, his mind hooked on the thought, at least both of them were in it together. Then the figures of ponies and two people jumped before his eyes as he raced over the top of the last of the rolling knolls. They seemed to hear the approach of all those dust-clawing hoofs and looked up from their work. Instantly the one figure began to wave his arms and the squaw responded to pull the ponies toward the yawning mouth of the ravine. The man reached down for his rifle and continued waving toward the squaw, skittering back and forth behind the strings of ponies to hurry them into

418

the seclusion of the wooded draw. By turns he looked at the approaching riders, and yelled and waved the animals on to the side of the hill.

Bass passed Josiah now and yelled something out to the younger man. Paddock could not catch what was said. He could only look into the dark moving hole above Scratch's chin. They were close to cover now, close to the ravine. But the pursuers were coming on quickly, and now they could all hear the yells and taunts from the braves. Bass slowed a little to motion with his left hand for Josiah to cut into the mouth of the draw first, to lead his horse slightly up the side of the knoll before disappearing into the brush. Then Scratch turned back around to see the strings of ponies just being taken from view into the ravine. He didn't see Josiah's pony stumble.

The side of the hill near the mouth of the ravine was cut with slashes and the tears of erosion. Into this maze Paddock steered his pony with what strength the animal had remaining. The weary animal dodged and darted between clumps of sage and saltbush until one quick turn found a hoofthrust deep within an erosion scar. Pitching forward, the pony threw Josiah spinning to the right. Landing on the side of his head Paddock lay still, unmoving.

Scratch turned around in the saddle to look to his rear as he dismounted on the run at the ravine's mouth. Josiah's pony stood riderless in the brush. Bass's eyes darted among the clumps of vegetation, then quickly looked at the rapidly approaching Indians. Slapping the buffalo runner on the rump, he sent his pony trotting into the ravine past Asa and the squaw.

"Where's the boy?" McAfferty inquired.

"Cain't see him."

"That be his pony, ain't it?" Asa asked, his eyes on the incoming riders.

"Yep, an' that's damp powder for sure." Bass was a little disconcerted in answering. His mind and eyes were working feverishly to see what had happened to the young man.

"The heathens shoot him?" McAfferty queried.

"Cain't say!" Titus hollered back as he finally took cover behind a large clump of brush. "Boy was right behin't me, Asa. You shoulda seen it better'n me, dammit! You shoulda seen what happen't to him!"

The gray fog lifted from Paddock's brain and he

blinked his eyes. They felt open but all was black before him. Within an instant shooting sparks of light flashed across the blackness, brilliant little pinholes of blinding color. Then he found himself staring at the line where the top of the dark hill met the pale pastel of blue sky.

"Josiah!" came Scratch's voice beyond him, out there, somewhere. "Where be you, son?"

Paddock put a hand to the side of his head and felt the queer numbness running through the flesh. His fingers touched the long scar hidden within the dirt and sweat-matted hair. He wasn't cut. Slowly he lifted his swimming head as if it were a great weight. "Easy, now," he told himself in response to the weaving scenery before his eyes. One unsteady arm propped him up as he turned to see Scratch gesturing from the mouth of the ravine.

"Goddammit! Get your ass in here!" Bass commanded.

The free hand continued to rub the side of his numbed head as Paddock turned away from Bass to look east into the valley. The shadows were close enough for him to pick out the unpainted faces of the riders and the flaring nostrils of their ponies. Time hung like a pendulum sitting at the apex of its climb and refusing to swing back down. Closer the Indians came toward the solitary trapper sitting dazed on the prairie. The riders were grouped tightly together in their charge toward Paddock. He took his hand away from his forehead and put it on the ground with the other arm to steady himself. The second hand plopped down on his rifle. Fingers slowly gripped the barrel tightly.

"Them niggers is on top of you!" Titus was hollering.

The words rang clearly this time, finally. Josiah's eyes darted once more to the man kneeling behind the brush, then back to the Indians. In an instant the fog had lifted, and his mind calculated a plan of action. It was too late to risk a headlong run to the ravine now. The enemy was but a few strides away and already he could look down the muzzles of their rifles as the ponies crashed toward him. He would let them come just a little closer.

In one sudden lunge, Josiah pushed himself off the shaky, unsteady legs and right into the path of the onrushing ponies. He rolled over the scrub sage, his rifle in hand until his momentum stopped. The clattering, dust-swirling hoofs thundered over him. Each of the Indian ponies swerved sharply or leaped over him to avoid the man on

420

the ground. In an instant the noise of the hoofs colliding with the dirt faded beyond him. Disappearing from his ears were the throaty yells of the riders. He raised his head to see the Indians dashing by the mouth of the ravine where they fired their first shots. A puff of smoke billowed up from the bushes, then the resounding blast of powder. One of the braves spun off his racing animal. His body slid to a dusty halt in the brush.

Josiah waited no longer. Still clutching the rifle barrel in a death grip, he leaped to his feet and put his legs to work before the remaining warriors turned their ponies for another run past the ravine. His legs found speed in their strength as he dodged and vaulted the saltbush dotting his beeline path to safety.

Within the ravine's mouth Titus was feverishly reloading. "You cover the boy, McAfferty! Jest cover the boy!" Asa scooted on his knees and one hand, closer to the opening of the cut between the two hills where he could see the Indians turning for another rush at their position. He jerked his head to see Josiah running toward them. Asa rose to one knee and braced the rifle against his shoulder.

"Here the devils come, Mr. Bass!"

"I hear you!" He placed a ball into the muzzle. "Where's the boy now?" he asked, ramming the lead home against the breech.

"He's comin'," Asa's replied. "Jest be a race to see who gets here the first off!" He turned his head from the Indians for a moment to watch Paddock racing the Indians back to the ravine. "Pray ye, boy! Give the Lord a prayer!"

"Wagh!" Scratch's commented.

" 'The Lord hear thee in the day of trouble; the name of the God Jacob defend thee!' "

"Do your prayin' with that rifle of your'n, McAfferty!" Bass bit back at the white hair. "That be the defendin' the boy's needin' now!" He pulled the wiping stick from the barrel.

It was going to be the warriors who made it to the ravine a little before him, Josiah decided. At the least would be a draw. Again the braves were tightly grouped as their hard-puffing animals carried them closer and closer, but now they began stringing out in a column. I got me one more chance, Josiah thought, his mind racing with his legs. The Indians bore down on the ravine just as Josiah was within a few strides of the covering brush.

Both hands jerked the rifle up and pulled the hammer back. Just as he pulled the trigger Paddock remembered he didn't have a ball against the powder charge. The pan lighted with fire and the muzzle roared just as a brave bore down on him. Josiah felt stupid and defenseless all of a sudden, but watched in astonishment as the warrior's pony slid in the dirt and reared up at the noisy report of the rifle. Unprepared, the Indian fell backward in a tumbling heap to the ground, both his hands having been occupied with holding and aiming the rifle. The brave got to his knees as the pony darted off and looked up just as Paddock swung the butt of his rifle stock full force into the Indian's face. Josiah heard the crunch of bone and cartilage compressed against the wood but kept running until he dove into the brush between Asa and Scratch. The dull clunk of lead plopping into the earth and whistling as it cut through the branches accompanied his slide behind cover.

Bass's rifle spit fire and a brave dropped his rifle to grab at his shoulder. "Damn!" Scratch exclaimed on merely wounding the Indian.

"'For thou hast girded me with strength unto the battle!' You're to it, young Josiah," Asa remarked.

Powder was being poured down the barrel of his rifle as Bass shot a quick, hard look at Josiah struggling with his horn and pouch. "What ever drove you do a damned fool thing like divin' under them niggers' ponies?" he growled. "Sure way certain it'd been get yourself kilt!"

"Ever seen a horse . . . step on a man, Scratch?" Josiah glanced back at Titus, then continued to pour powder down the muzzle.

"Cain't rightly say I . . ."

"Horse won't step on a man . . . they won't . . ."

"Devils be comin' round again!" McAfferty interrupted with a warning.

"So—a goddamned horse won' step on a man . . ." Bass attempted to continue.

"An' a man . . . white or red . . . cain't aim too good . . . while his pony's jumpin' . . . now can he?" Josiah retorted, still breathless.

"S'pose not," Scratch acknowledged.

"Injuns wasn't shootin' to you or me, was they now, ol' man?" Josiah grinned a little over the lesson he had just given, despite the oncoming riders.

Bass leaned back up on one knee and placed the rifle

against his shoulder while looking at Asa, "Boy's l'arnin' us fast, ain't he, McAfferty?" He turned his eyes back down the barrel and fired. The bullet smashed into a warrior's face and he slid from his pony.

Asa fired, then yelled to Josiah, "Ye hold your load, boy! Keep a ball there whilst Mr. Bass an' me load!" He began to pour powder into the barrel. "Ye count how many of the devils is left now!"

Paddock took his itchy finger off the trigger but kept the rifle to his shoulder as his eye peered over the sights to count the remaining warriors. "Looks to be jest six of 'em now!" Then he saw one of the survivors trotting up alongside his own pony to gather up Paddock's long rein. "An' one of them niggers is fixin' to make off with my pony!" Josiah stood up, making a clear target of himself in his heated, unthinking anger. Instantly his rifle roared and the brave clutched his lower ribs and slumped onto Josiah's pony's neck. The others were bearing down on the trappers for another charge.

"Ye consarned fool!" Asa reached up to pull Josiah down, but the young man needed no help in making himself as small as possible again.

"Serve the nigger right," he squeaked.

"Tol't ye keep your load!" the grim-lipped McAfferty barked. " 'A horse be a vain thing for safety,' saith the Lord's word. Ye get yourself killed shootin' that devil . . ."

"Ease back, McAfferty—I got me a load down!" Bass interrupted as he put his rifle to his shoulder. "All that damned palaverin' to the boy—you ain't got your own load down!"

The charging warriors had now slung their rifles from their ponies' sides and had taken bows from the cases worn on their backs. From wolfskin quivers had been drawn arrows that were quickly notched onto bowstrings. Their rifles were empty and to reload would take all too much time from keeping up the pressure on their quarry. They aimed their ponies once again toward the ravine while they dipped low behind their animals.

"Niggers ain't give us a good shot now!" Titus rose slightly from his kneeling position to scoot out to the edge of the brush. He began to holler and yell at the approaching warriors. He fired at one, dropping him from his racing pony. The four other braves swerved off from the ravine.

"Half starved for ha'r, this child is!" Scratch ran in a crouch toward the fallen Indian, "There's way to rout the fleas 'sides killin' the dog! Get this nigger's scalp fresh—them others see us to be big medeecin!"

"I'll be damned if that nigger don' take the circle! Consarned fool, Titus Bass is!" Asa mumbled. "Ye both fools—both ye can slide. Ye'll be gettin' along jest fine whilst ye still got your ha'r, Josiah Paddock!"

Bass knelt over the fallen warrior with a quick glance at the retreating warriors still on horseback. They were yelling threats in their own tongue, threats at Scratch not to raise the hair. With his knife drawn from his belt, now crusted and stained with buffalo blood, Titus raised the weapon in the air and waved it back at the Indians whose prancing ponies stood some eighty yards off from the ravine's mouth.

"You keep your eye to them niggers for me, Josiah!" Bass yelled, his head half turned toward the white men. "One of 'em raises a bow to give me a arrer, shoot to his lights!" Bass turned back around to wave the knife once more to the Indians and cried out with a triumphant war whoop. He brought the blade down while picking up the braided hair with his left hand. Into the warrior's braids were woven gun screws and brass rings for ornamental medicine. Twisting the braids between his fingers to gather up the hair on the topknot he wanted, Scratch pricked the Indian's scalp with the tip of the blade. But the warrior had played possum on the white man.

Over he rolled off his stomach, pulling Titus with him. Scratch went to pull his left hand free from the Indian's hair but now the twisted braids wrapped around his fingers held them imprisoned. He felt the gun screws and sharp brass rings cutting into the flesh of the bound hand.

"Gonna tickle your hump ribs, nigger!" Drawing back the knife to slash out at the warrior, Bass started to drive the knife home, but the Indian brought his leg up and kicked Titus low in the abdomen. With a whoof of pain Scratch drew the free hand across his abdomen to protect it from the second blow planned by the brave. He jerked on the handful of hair he held, pulling the enemy off balance so that the kicking leg went wild. Titus rolled out from under the Indian's ineffective leg and rose to his knees. The warrior rolled to the side away from the knife-holding hand and drew his own sharp weapon from his belt. The twisting only locked Scratch's hand to the topknot all the tighter. His heart climbing high into his throat, Scratch stared into the dark eyes of his adversary, knowing that he was fighting an Indian with two free hands while he himself had only one to use.

The brave made a savage lunge with the knife as Bass pulled the head off balance again, causing the warrior's weapon to slash only a flesh wound at Scratch's side. Bass jerked the head at the sudden pain as his side was opened up and leaned forward to stand. Again he pulled on the hair, then lashed out with a leg to kick at the rising warrior's knee. The Indian collapsed and Bass started to dive toward him with the knife. The warrior braced a leg between them that sent Titus cartwheeling over the Indian's head to land on his back. Rolling to the side the brave made a lunge with his knife but the arm stayed as Scratch pushed his own arm into the air. His knife went all the way through the Indian's arm. There was an immediate splatter of blood onto both of them and the Indian's knife fell alongside the white man's face. The heavy antler handle of the weapon struck Bass's temple, dazing him.

He remembered thinking as the knife struck his opponent's arm, Now we're even, nigger! knowing each now had but one effective hand. With what arm remained to him, the warrior grabbed at Scratch's wrist that still held a knife. He held it there while the trapper struggled to break either hand free. Scratch fought to his knees with the Indian squeezing his wrist. The knife-holding arm felt tired and he wondered how long he could hold onto the weapon with the Indian shutting off the blood, shutting off all feeling below the wrist. They wrestled back and forth on their knees in the dust and sage until Bass cried out.

"Aaaggghhh! Shoot 'im, goddammit!"

That seemed all Josiah needed after reloading while watching the fevered hand-to-hand battle some forty yards away. The hammer clicked back as the rifle was brought to his shoulder. Down the barrel he could see Scratch collapsing backward, weakened now, as if without strength in his body. His hand slowly opened and the knife seemed to float out of his grasp as if it were a feather spinning lightly to the ground. On backward Scratch continued to slump and the Indian's left hand picked the knife up and drew it back slightly in preparation to strike.

Josiah's finger twitched and the Indian was knocked backward. Immediately his companions set up a howl and put their ponies into action once more. They started to make a large loop back toward the solitary white man heaving for breath among the saltbush.

"Load your rifle, Josiah Paddock." Asa's words were almost calm and coolly stated now. "They smell Mr. Bass's ha'r, the devils do."

Josiah set to work spilling powder down the muzzle and across his hand as he kept an eye on Titus. Scratch sucked in air. You're gettin' ol't, Titus Bass, he thought; mayhaps this be your day. Both hands felt numbed, his whole body exhausted from the battle. Moving the fingers of his right hand he found the palm empty. Something twitched inside his stomach. Now the fingers of his left hand were moved. They felt numb, but tingling with the pressure and lacerations of the gun screws and finger rings. He moved the fingers again as he rose to see the warriors approaching.

Sitting up with new strength, Scratch looked down into the dirt to find the knife that had almost slashed life from his own body. A tired, aching right hand closed around the knife handle. If this here be your day, you oughtta go under with the nigger's scalp in your hand, he thought. He rose to one knee and leaned over the warrior. Stretching out the topknot once more and without another glance at the incoming riders. Scratch sliced the flesh around the gathered hair in a ragged circle. He dragged his other knee up and placed it on the back of the brave's neck. With a ripping pop the scalp was freed and he had his hand back. Quickly he jerked his head up to see two riders bearing down on him.

Spurred into action, Bass stumbled to his feet and began to race back toward the brush. His rifle lay up ahead. Scratch, in a crouched run, bent low to attempt picking up the weapon on the run. He missed. Skidding to a stop, he dove back to grab the rifle. Now both hands were full: the right holding an empty flintlock, his left clutching the knife and the scalplock that still remained twisted about his fingers. He turned at the sound of one of the ponies to see the warrior off to the side with what looked to be a club drawn back at the end of an extended arm. Jest have to wrassle that nigger, too, he thought as the warrior rode down on him. Scratch was preparing to duck when he saw the arrow strike the Indian low in the throat. The heavy club dropped from the warrior's grasp and the empty hand flew to clutch at his throat. Blood darkened the brave's fingers as they twined around the arrow shaft. Slowly he tumbled backward from his pony's rump and plopped onto the ground.

Another blast bit the air and the second warrior clutched at his thigh. He jerked hard on his pony's neck and retreated. Another arrow caught the escaping Indian in the back of his calf and he yelped in pain a second time. Scratch turned to continue his race for cover. Before him stood Josiah with a loaded weapon pressed again his shoulder. To his left knelt McAfferty pouring powder down his muzzle after having shot the retreating brave in the thigh. And behind her kneeling husband stood the Nez Perce squaw with a third arrow drawn; she sent it flying after the escaping enemy.

"This'un's for you, McAfferty. This child was tryin' to wade into the niggers's liver—but it was you as had him where his ha'r was short," he puffed as he skidded in next to Paddock.

"Ain't my ha'r—ye lifted it," replied the white-haired trapper. " 'Sides, young Josiah shoot the devil. 'Tweren't me, Mr. Bass. Boy here done it. *For the arms of the wicked shall be broken: but the Lord upholdeth the righteous.'* Boy saved your ha'r, Mr. Bass." He nodded toward Paddock.

"Josiah?" Scratch asked. "It were your G'lena pill?"

"Aye, Mr. Bass," McAfferty replied, turning his attention again toward the Indians remaining on horseback. The warriors had grouped themselves just out of range and appeared to be discussing the situation. "It jest 'bout 'peared to be the prophecy of the Lord's word: *'The wicked have drawn out the sword, and have bent their bow. Their sword shall enter their own heart, and their bows shall be broken.'* Come close to eatin' your own knife, Mr. Bass." He turned to look at Scratch without a smile on his face.

"This here be yours, Josiah." Bass presented the tangled scalp to the younger man, its flesh red-caked with the edges turning dark brown. Paddock looked from Asa to the scalp, then up into Titus's eyes. "Don' you want it? Ain't you gonna take it?" Bass inquired.

"'That thy foot may be dipped in the blood of thine enemies'?" Asa replied before Josiah could answer.

"I don' rightly figger I can wear it." Paddock finally stammered.

"Why not, son? This ha'r's yours. Nigger'd raised my ha'r less'n you'd shot him." Scratch again held the scalp out to Paddock.

"Go ahead, young Josiah." McAfferty turned back to face Paddock briefly. "'Be strong and of good courage; fear not, nor be afraid of them: for the Lord thy God, he it is that doth go with thee; He will not fail thee, nor forsake thee.' That be your prize from the temple of your enemies."

The young man continued to stare at the bloody trophy for another moment, then looked into Scratch's face, "Nawww. The first one I wear—I'll lift it myself. That'un's yours. I'll raise my own, out there." He nodded toward the prairie.

"Nigger you smashed in the face?" Bass questioned.

"Yep."

"Done that nigger in good, you did. Made him come, slick as shootin'." Scratch slipped the hair through his belt and pulled it down so that the red scalp would point up at the top of the belt around his waist. "What them critters doin'? Naybobbin'?" Bass turned his attention to the remaining warriors still on horseback out on the prairie.

"Talkin' things over it looks to be," McAfferty replied.

"Niggers look to be Bannawks, I'll swear by hook," Titus judged. "Ain't likely they was no war party lookin' for us. Bannawks was jest to ronnyvoo." He scooted closer to the mouth of the ravine and began to reload his rifle. "Nawww, ain't no war party—'tweren't wearin' no paint or medeecin on 'em. Them niggers was jest out for buffler, like we was. Unsartin varmints them Bannawks can be."

"Bannocks are thievin' devils," the whitehair commented.

"Thought at first they'd be Blackfeets," Bass continued. "Jest some poor devils as was after some meat, same as us. Figgerin' on runnin' us out, liftin' some plunder maybe. Don' think them niggers out there rightly figgered on nothin' like this here happ'nin' to 'em. Thought we was gonna be easy pickin's, I'll care to set, an' now they's seen the evil of they ways. They ain't said no medeecin an' they ain't painted up for the fight. Them niggers gotta be skeert now." While talking, Scratch had been wiping his barrel with a spit-soaked patch; he followed that by blowing into the muzzle to clear the touch hole. Now powder and ball were sent down the barrel.

"By the devil I b'lieve you're right, Mr. Bass," McAfferty exclaimed quietly. Scratch looked up to see the four remaining horsemen turn their ponies to the northwest.

"Bannawks!" Scratch went through the motion of spitting on the ground although he had nothing wet enough in his mouth to spit. "Next to Diggers them yabberin' yahoos be poor Injuns. Ain't got many horses; ain't got 'em many rifles neither. They be easy pickin's for Blackfoot, them Bannawks is. Ain't much a proud people, neither; don't care a cuss. Them niggers is runnin' off noways waitin' to pick up theys friends' bodies." He stood and yelled at the retreating warriors: "You niggers ain't worth the shit what your friends take out theys ass! Get on back here! Awww! These here niggers stayed to fight— you ain't good 'nough to carry theys bodies back to your village!" He waved his arm in the air with indignation.

" 'Surely thou wilt slay the wicked, O God; depart from me therefore, ye bloody men'," Asa muttered. With her bow and quiver of arrows, the young woman behind Asa moved up the ravine toward the horses. Josiah plopped back to relax for the first time since midday.

Scratch toyed with the crusty edge of the scalp hanging at his belt while watching the Indians disappear. "Squar's some with your bow."

"She s'prised me herself," McAfferty replied. "Didn' know she could shoot like that. The consarned squar comes up to s'prise this here child ever' now an' then." He seemed more relaxed now as he looked up the ravine to watch his wife among the animals. "Kept me that bow from them Crow for good reason, I s'pose. Didn' do me a lick a good afore I got me hook made." He held the right arm out to look it over. "Had me a notion that bow come in handy, jest a might handy some day, for *'he hath bent his bow, and made it ready. He hath also prepared for him the instruments of death; he ordaineth his arrows against his enemies.'* Praise the Lord! Had me idea it'd come in for some good. It payed some, it did—keepin' it, I mean."

"Ain't a white woman back to St. Louie coulda done such, you know. Kill a man like that. Injun squars is some now, Josiah. Cry for foofaraw they will, an' less'n you give 'em what catches they eyes—they jest as likely to gut you." With an empty hand he feigned stabbing Josiah. Paddock drew back as Scratch chuckled. "C'mon, now, let's get your ha'r."

Paddock got to his feet to follow Scratch out of the ravine. They walked past the single scalped warrior without stopping and moved up to the brave Josiah unhorsed and smashed in the face with his rifle. The Indian's body was stretched out on its side with the face plopped down in the dirt. Both men stopped to look down at the body for a moment before Scratch spoke.

"Take your ha'r, son," he reminded.

Josiah knelt over the body and cradled his rifle across his bent legs before pulling the big knife from his belt. He looked up at Bass for an instant, then gathered the hair at the back of the head and pulled it into the air.

"That's good. Jest take you what you want, much as you want, Josiah," Scratch instructed. "Works best usin' jest the tip of your sticker blade."

Paddock ran the sharp, heavy blade around a large piece of the Indian's scalp. "Yep. Now brace the nigger's head down an' yank it off." Josiah replaced the knife in its rawhide sheath, then put the right hand at the base of the Bannock's head. He popped the scalp free easily with a faint sucking sound. "Sling 'er round good, Josiah. Gets rid of what blood an' gore you ain't wantin' on it." With that the young man swung the scalp through the air several times, sending small droplets of excess blood flying in all directions. "Nigger ain't got him nothin' else as is worth the takin'. I'm gonna get me these'r other skelps. Make 'em a present to the Crow when we winter up to Absor'kee," Titus commented before he turned to look back at the squaw already resuming her work on the buffalo. McAfferty was bent over another of the dead bodies, cutting his trophy free. Bass turned back to the young man as Josiah stood up. "That be your first one—on your own hook."

Paddock didn't answer. He took the toe of his moccasin to dig under the Indian's shoulder and turned the body over. The face and forehead were obscured with crushed bone fragments, and much dark, dried blood had crusted on the fine soil. "That nigger ain't gonna haunt you, Josiah. His soul cain't go on to the beyond now. Ain't no way that'un can haunt you."

"Hoodoos ain't gonna bother me none," Paddock replied.

"Well, now," Bass began, clearing his throat. "I feel me thirsty again." He moved away toward the Nez Perce squaw working on the buffalo bull. "That critter's got him a drink left in him yet." He turned to look back at the young man staring down at what was left of the Indian's face. "You comin', son?" he asked quietly.

Josiah nodded his head affirmatively, his eyes still fixed on the body. "I'm comin'." Titus headed for the butchered carcass. Paddock knew he was now on the prairie, many, many miles and untold days from Pierre's Hole. But he was unable to shake the feeling that the body below him was that trapper who had been mutilated by the Blackfeet during the battle weeks before. The same grotesque face stared back up at him. I done this to save my life, he thought. Nevertheless, Josiah looked down at another man dead by his hands. He blinked his eyes and raised his head to follow Scratch toward the butchering. It wasn't Mordecai's body up there, he told himself as he turned once to look back at the Indian's body. Jest keep you a grip on things, Josiah, the voice in his head continued. That ain't Mordecai's body you killed up there.

"Halloo, son! C'mon an' try some cider!" Bass yelled at him. The older man was kneeling on the ground at the edge of the buffalo hide taken from the bull. Onto the skin the squaw was placing the choice cuts of meat she had selected from the animal. "Ever ye see buffler tongue?" Scratch held up the long, thick piece of reddish-pink meat for Josiah to examine. Paddock shook his head negatively. "Didn' figger you'd ever done such," Titus said, laying it back on the hide. "That be a treat for our camp this night." He patted the top of the amputated tongue with his fingertips. "Here now, want you to help me get a horn of cider," he chuckled, scooting on his knees so that he knelt beside the bull's large stomach. "We be some lucky niggers that critter didn' drop his paunch an' walk on it." His fingers patted the stomach. "Get down here, son," he instructed, and Josiah knelt beside him. "Take your hands an' put 'em like this here on that paunch." He showed Paddock how to hold onto either side of the slimy, fluid-filled stomach.

When the young man had the organ braced, Scratch removed the knife from his belt. With it he cut a long slice

431

in the huge stomach which measured almost three feet in diameter. "Critter's had him lots to eat or, if I figger right, he's all swolled up with water," he said, smacking his lips as the stomach opened. "You jest keep your hands there an' none a this cider gonna spill out on us." Titus put the knife back into his belt, then wiped his dusty palms over his greasy, dirty leggings as if to clean them. Both hands dipped into the center of the stomach and swished around in the greenish gelatinous fluids. Josiah gulped as he looked closely into the well from which Bass was going to draw a refreshing draught.

"What's matter, son? Ain't got you no stomach to be drinkin' from a buffler's paunch? Shit! He ain't gonna drink nothin' you would'n' drink—if'n you was thirsty 'nough!" Bass finished swishing the stomach's juices around and brought cupped hands to his lips. Slowly he poured the liquid into his mouth, some of the fluid dripping onto his chin whiskers and down his chest. Josiah stared at his partner as if being entertained, watching Scratch close his eyes and smack his lips, just the way a thirsty man would do in drinking a refreshingly tart cider. After several more handfuls, Bass looked into Josiah's face. "Jest what water the critter had him last is all you drink. Go on an' splash all that thick shit to the side. Get you some a that water he drinked to this mornin'."

Josiah looked at Scratch smacking his lips and licking his chin, then could no longer resist trying it. He stuck his hands into the water tentatively, feeling its warmth from the animal's body heat and the sun's afternoon rays. Then he too splashed the thicker juices aside and cupped both hands to try it. Paddock, head back, let the fluid trickle from between both palms into his mouth. It had a sting, and a taste not unlike that left in his mouth after vomiting. But not quite the same. The buffalo fluid had only a hint of a vinegarlike acid flavor. Finished, he looked at Scatch, pursed his lips, and smiled with some small satisfaction.

"Didn' say you had to like it, now. Jest that it's 'bout the best drink aside the critter's blood you got goin' out here," Bass commented. "Want you 'nother?" Josiah answered only by putting his hands back into the slit-open stomach to take another draught. "Man most times don' need water out here, you see. Man's body can live off bodies of other critters if'n he has to." He looked around for Asa, who was returning with the ponies to the butchering

432

site. "Asa? You want you any of this cider?" He then looked back at Josiah, who was dipping his hands into the stomach for a third time. "Afore the boy drinks it all to hisse'f?"

"Nawww," McAfferty answered, "but ye'll be the devil 'less ye share the liver an' boudins with me, Mr. Bass."

"Ahhh, McAfferty! You 'minded me of the sweetsome joy of raw buffler liver!" He began to look for the liver among the meat Asa's squaw was placing on the hide. He pulled the organ close to his lap and flipped it over. "McAfferty," said Bass, "your liver is ready, it is—an' we have the gall for sauce to boot!"

Asa finished cinching his animals, then came over to sit beside Bass. Josiah looked on while Scratch began slicing off large pieces of the raw, slippery liver after detaching the gallbladder from the dark, red organ. He set the gallbladder among the three of them and pricked its skin with the point of his knife so that it flattened out to resemble a small bowl. Handing pieces of the liver to McAfferty and Paddock, Scratch took a slice for himself and dipped it into the gall. He brought the raw meat dripping with juice to his upturned lips and let it slide into his mouth. "Go 'head, Josiah. Try you some. Jest like John Barleycorn what ain't been aged none," he said chewing the liver. "Like swallerin' fire at first, then you'll l'arn to like it, I'll swear." Paddock allowed Asa to dip his liver into the gall first, less from deference to age or wisdom than from his interest in watching the older men eat before he tried something foreign to his palate.

Taking the long, thin slice of liver and dipping it into the gallbladder bowl Scratch had made, Josiah brought the meat to his mouth and took off a bite instead of ingesting the whole of it as the two other men had done. He chewed and chewed the raw meat while Bass cut off several more pieces of the liver. Josiah worked and worked his jaws attempting to masticate the meat so he could swallow it. The Nez Perce squaw came up to sit beside her husband on the ground and leaned forward to take a piece of meat for herself, after McAfferty had nodded his head to signify that she could join the men. She dipped it into the gall, put it in her mouth, and worked it from side to side to squeeze all of the sauce from the meat, then swallowed the slice whole. Josiah watched her intently and decided that was the way you were supposed to eat the liver—chew until all the gall was gone, then merely swallow the raw meat. He began to eat with more enjoyment, adding his knife to the two busy cutting slices from the rapidly dwindling organ.

"Save yourself some room in that paunch of your'n for boudins, McAfferty," Scratch reminded Asa before rising to cross to the other side of the buffalo-hide platter. There, stacked yard upon yard, were animal's intestines the squaw had salvaged, despite the bull's having stepped on many of his own entrails. Bass put his hands into the mass of slimy snakes and fished around until he had sorted out a piece some twenty feet long. "Here you be," he chirped cheerfully, holding the intestine in both hands out from his chest as a man would hold a large snake.

"Boy wanna set with me?" Asa inquired.

"An' eat that?" Josiah gulped again.

"Jumpin' Jehoshaphat! Ain't no need to be squampshus 'bout this here," Titus said, shaking the buffalo's small intestine in the air. "Man ain't eatin' no shit till he gets down to the critter's big boudin!"

"That be big 'nough for me. No thankee!" Paddock protested.

"Shit! C'mon, Asa. Josiah don' want none a this. Let's you an' me have us a go at the ends. You care to set?" Bass said, hoping to prod McAfferty into an eating race.

"I know ye be the boudin-lovin' devil, Mr. Bass," the white-haired man responded, "but ye've found yourself here a child as loves to eat as well as any. Let's us have a set at it." He slid over to sit on the ground across from Titus.

Between them the two men placed the twenty-foot snake and each man located his end of the intestine. They brought the ends to their mouths and with a nod of the head started their race. With gulps and grunts each man was now engaged in a contest to determine which of them could eat the most of the raw intestine. More and more inches of the slimy snake began to disappear down their throats, the contestants swallowing the intestine and doing very little chewing on the meat. The Nez Perce squaw looked on and giggled with enjoyment at the spectacle. She clapped her hands from time to time in accompaniment with her laughter. Josiah just watched as more and more of the snake disappeared until little less than a yard existed of the intestine strung out between the two mouths. Scratch's head came forward with a gulp before he yanked his head back to pull some of the boudin right out from Asa's throat.

The last stretch of the contest had begun: it was now up to the two men to determine who could pull more of the intestine from the other's mouth as the entire length of snake had not been broken by chewing. McAfferty let the boudin slip from his lips, then waited for Scratch to stop swallowing to suck in a breath of air. He took advantage of the opportunity and pulled the stolen inches back from Bass with additional intestine being swallowed behind it. Back and forth they battled for a few minutes while Josiah looked on and the squaw chirped encouragement to her man. Finally Asa reached down to his belt and pulled out his knife. With it he slashed through the center of what intestine remained between him and Scratch. McAfferty had admitted defeat in the contest; in slashing the boudin he had declared Bass the winner. They both slowly finished what intestine remained hanging from their lips and leaned back to gulp in air. Gradually Scratch crawled off to the open buffalo stomach to dip his hands inside for another drink. Asa got his wind back to follow Titus to the watering hole.

"You two finished up with your funnin'? Maybe we can be thinkin' 'bout clearin' outta here this afternoon." Josiah rose to his feet and peered along the northern ridge of hills framing the valley.

"Don' get yourself in such a froshus fittle, boy," Scratch began.

"Lad's got him a point, Mr. Bass." Asa looked up along the hills from his spot beside the buffalo paunch.

"You figger ain't too safe us stayin' on here much longer, eh?" Bass got to his feet to stand beside Paddock. Josiah merely nodded his head without looking at the man beside him. "You're prob'ly right too, son. Hate me to say it, but you been thinkin' whilst I was havin' me no-thinkin' fun," Titus admitted. He wiped his palms and fingers on his leggings, then went over to a pack animal where he had left his shirt.

Asa spoke to the squaw, who rose and began to draw in the edges of the buffalo robe to form a container for the meat. The two of them bound it up quickly with a length

435

of rope and secured the bundle to the back of an already laden pony. Scratch took the horsehair reins of his pony in hand and led his string of animals back to where Josiah was standing near the discarded paunch.

"This here might be two I'm owin you for this day, Josiah. Them brownskins as took off be takin' word back to the camp 'bout us an' what happen't here. You're right in sayin' we best be gettin' outta here." Bass turned to see McAfferty and the squaw aboard their ponies. "How you set to headin' back up to the ridge?" Titus pointed south to the rim of hills from which they had come when descending into the valley. "We foller that 'long east—don' like the idea goin' east down here in the bottom."

"Valley gets skinnier down there a ways," Josiah commented.

"An' we don' want us gettin' boxed in up there if'n them niggers come lookin' for us after the sun's dropped," Titus went on. "We gotta go east anyways you lay your sights, afore we hit to Henry's Lake an' head north from there, so I take my set to the top a that ridge. Jest ride 'long lil' under the skyline an' make us a cold camp this night. What say, McAfferty?" He looked up at the short man on horseback.

"Had me same notion afore we come on the buff'lo, Mr. Bass." McAfferty turned his animal to the right and began the slow climb up the slope to the rim of the ridge. The squaw followed along at her respectful distance.

"Had him same notion!" Scratch snorted under his breath as he climbed aboard the buffalo runner. "McAfferty was fixin' to head right smack north if'n it suits him—right plumb center to the whole consarn of them niggers."

"Huh? What'd you say?" Paddock asked, unable to understand what Bass had been muttering.

"Nothin'. Nothin'," Bass said, louder now.

"If it ain't worth the sayin' now, it weren't worth the sayin' first off," Josiah lectured, without looking at the older man.

"Got yourself all worked up to a fine blue funk, don' you?" He pulled the frizzen back to inspect the priming.

"An' you'll wished to hell that Injun nigger killed you too, less'n you take care to that slice 'long your ribs," Paddock said evenly as he turned his head to watch the McAffertys ascend the ridge. "Don't like me seein' a man dyin' just 'cause he ain't took care of what wound he's got."

"You're mother-hennin' me now, son," Titus responded. "Makes this here child feel all the bettersome knowin' his pardner's out to care 'bout his painin'."

"Carin's not 'nough," he replied. "Gotta do more'n care 'bout that wound, ol' man. Carin' don't 'mount to much by itself. 'Sides, ain't doin' it all just for you: I owes some plunder, maybe my hide to you. I aim to see you live leastways till I can pay you for it. Not just for you, Scratch. Got me lot I owe to others. You're just the only one I can clear my books with—that's all it is."

Scratch was silent a moment, looking at the side of Josiah's face staring to the north, before he spoke again. "I'll take care of it to camp after sun drops, friend. I swear that to you—an' whatever's ridin' you to square your books up inside you. But don' go keepin' no number on what you owe me, son. Man cain't be right in the head if all time he's gonna be countin'." He paused, shifting the rifle across his lap while he stared down at the young man. "Josiah? You hear me, son?"

"Huh? Oh, yeah," he said, slightly nodding. "You're gonna fix your gut tonight. I heard you."

Scratch cleared his throat and sucked in a deep breath. He did not want a thing to come between him and the boy, but felt as if something had. He did not know if Josiah had really heard all he had said and was not responding to it, or had really missed the point he had struggled to make. Then he suddenly decided it made no difference, not here, not now. Bass gave heels to his pony's ribs and started to make the climb.

Paddock heard the muted shuffling of hoofs and Hannah's low snort to tell of Scratch's parting. He waited, listening to the sounds fade while continuing to look at the northern hills. Paddock finally turned and looked at the others working their way up the hill, then went over to his string of ponies. He stroked the runner between the ears and climbed atop the saddle. "Had you some day, pilgrim," he quietly said to himself. "Throwed your first buff'lo in her tracks. Had you blood to drink an' liver to eat. An' raised your first ha'r, didn't you, pilgrim? You've come a long way this day, Josiah Paddock." He nudged his pony up the slope.

14

The words were unclear, as though they had been pushed past a tongue tangled and tripped up with corn mush. He opened his eyes slowly; perhaps he could listen more intently if his vision aided him. But blackness was all about. The mumbled words wafted through the fog. To Josiah's right the sleeping form stirred restlessly beneath its buffalo robe. The young man turned to look at Bass.

"Scratch!" he whispered. The old man's restless, mumbling chatter ceased. "Scratch!" Josiah whispered again, this time leaning low over the robe-covered form. A gutteral moan from Titus was heard. One gnarled hand emerged from beneath the robe and pulled the edge of the hide away from the deep-lined face. The old man's dark eyes shone dully in the remaining flickers of last night's fire.

"You're talkin' in your sleep, ol' man," Paddock said, kicking the robe free from his legs and getting to his feet. "Mumblin' again like you done last two nights, you was." He straightened his leather clothing. Bass grunted again and put the one free hand behind his head to hold it up while watching Josiah throw fresh kindling on the still glowing embers. Stirred to new life, the small fire danced more brightly against the backdrop of rocks and trees. Paddock rose and disappeared into the shadows created by the flames.

Scratch heard the young man urinating somewhere among the rocks. When the waterfall had ended, Bass expected to see Josiah step back into the light. Instead he heard the younger man's footsteps disappear deeper among the trees. Titus turned his head toward the retreating sound, then looked back into the glowing flames. The fire at his side seemingly intensified too. His right hand went down to touch the poultice over the wound, patting it gently with his fingers. "Been best to have taken care of it a week ago," he mumbled. "Should'n'a waited. Now look what you done to yourself." He felt too warm and blamed it on Paddock for rekindling the fire.

Not for long, however, could he let himself believe that it was the campfire making him warm. Scratch patted the poultice again, feeling the frayed edges of the torn cloth shirt that wrapped around his body to hold the chewed roots and puffball dust in the wound. It was his favorite shirt—his rendezvous shirt—whose tattered remnants were consigned to binding up another wound. He would think of something else. That would take his mind off the fire at his side. Trying to sit up, Scratch winced in some pain as he twisted from side to side to put his elbows behind him for support. He stared off into the darkness beyond the flickering flames at the hint of embers glowing in McAfferty's fire. Bass grunted and shook his head. Asa didn't want to camp with them, didn't want to eat with them. The whitehair had barely acknowledged traveling with the two partners except for that day over a week ago when they had happened onto both buffalo and Bannocks. It was almost as if this were the McAfferty of old. But it did not last for long. Scratch wanted to spit at the thought, but no moisture collected beneath his tongue. He was thirsty. Rising off his elbows with one hand over the pain in his side, Bass sat up to look over his shoulder at the approach of a form out of the darkness.

"You're a fat squaw's ass!" Josiah whispered in a cutting tone as he brought a load of wood into the light near the fire.

"Wha-a-a . . ." came the sound like a bewildered whimper.

"Take damned care of me. Ain't got you no sight to take care of yourself." Josiah set the wood on the ground quietly and began snapping dry twigs from the larger branches.

"Got you drink of water for me, son?" Scratch inquired. "Need take me a horn."

"You thirsty, too, eh?" Josiah turned to look at Bass before scooting over to stare more closely into the older man's face. Paddock reached up to touch Titus's forehead but Scratch pushed the hand away. "I ain't gonna leave you be, ol' man." He put the hand to the forehead just below the blue bandanna, this time without opposition. "Just get yourself set to that . . . you're burnin' up again!"

"Get me drink of water," Bass said, looking back at the fire. "I'll be seal-fat an' sleek soon."

Paddock slid back toward the equipment around the fire to retrieve the small kettle that had boiled meat the evening before. "I'll get you some fresh." He turned to pad away toward the stream.

"Bring me that!" Bass snapped. Josiah stopped in his
439

tracks and turned back to look at the older man. "Bring me that meat water, boy."

"You wanna drink this here grease?"

"Do me lots better'n plain crik water." Scratch grew impatient and waved his arm at Josiah to bring the kettle over. "Grease hungry, I am. Leastways like a broth my mam fixed when I was taken with fever. An' a brath be damned sight better'n crik water." He took the kettle into both hands and tipped it up to his lips. He drank slowly, consciously, his left eye occasionally looking to the side at Paddock while he drew in the thick, greasy broth left from last night's supper. Finished, Scratch ran first his tongue over the edges of his mustache, then his fingers to collect every drop of the messy soup. The fingers were brought to his lips and given a good licking before they were wiped across the front of his shirt. "Damn uncertain varmints Injuns is." Bass set the kettle down, his fingers remaining on its lip. "The most goddamn uncertain varmints in all this here creation. Brownskins—"

"What you mutterin' 'bout now, huh?" Paddock interrupted, kneeling to pick up the empty kettle.

Bass looked up at his young partner. "Here I set, bein' et up with a fever, a poison nibblin' 'way at my innards—an' *I* was the child as walked 'way from the wrassle with that nigger! Cain't calc'late it one. That Injun's dead an' I got me his skelp. But here I lay, my bones rottin' 'way inside with the poison fever. Can you figger it, son?"

"Your hoodoos, ol' man," Paddock chuckled lightly. "You got the nigger's skelp, all right, meanin' he's trapped down here an' cain't go on. The Injun's just devilin' you for all the trouble you been to him." This time Josiah laughed quietly as he rose with the kettle to head for the stream and fresh water.

"Jest might be a hoodoo, boy!" Scratch yelled hoarsely after Paddock as the young man slipped into the inky shadows surrounding their camp. "Cain't say as what that nigger ain't hoodooin' me now. Sometimes, man cain't rightly say what's reason he's bein' et up with somethin'." He shook his head from side to side while muttering to himself. Slowly Scratch pushed his body across the grass to the fire. Taking a piece of wood he began to stir through the coals near the edge of the embers. When he found the large mass he was searching for the old trapper knocked what coals and ash he could from the lump. Setting the stick aside, Titus reached for his knife and with it he speared the mass of cooked meat that had been simmering within the coals. He smacked his lips unconsciously in anticipation of the late-night treat. Gingerly handling the meat rescued from the fire, Scratch now placed it across the top of one thigh where he began carefully to scrape the remaining ash and soot from its surface. The young man's figure slipped back into the light, circling the edge of the fire.

"What the devil you got yourself there?" Paddock peered closely at the mass across the older man's lap.

"Cain't you tell me what it be, son?"

"Don't know if I really want to know all that bad." He wrinkled his nose up and pulled his face away to set the kettle with the fresh, cold mountain stream water down by Scratch's side.

"Your nose touchy 'bout good vittles, eh?" Bass put the knife blade into the meat and cut free a small slice of the rare-cooked delicacy. He offered it up to the younger man on the point of the blade. "Here. Try you some a that, Josiah." Scratch shook the knife slightly in front of Paddock's face. "Go 'head. Take it."

"Nawwww, don' think I want none—"

"Wagh! Ain't never seen me the likes of such a man, not by a long chalk," Bass snorted as he pulled the slice of meat from Paddock's face and brought it to his own lips still on the tip of the knife blade. From around the chunk of flesh he began to chew Scratch continued: "Passin' up some a best vittles the mountains has 'em to offer a man up here. This here be soft, an' sweet—some damned good meat, boy."

"Aw right. Lemme have a small bite then," Josiah replied, resigned. He leaned forward to accept a thin slice from the end of Scratch's blade. He put it in his mouth slowly and chewed tentatively before asking, "You gonna tell this here sucker that's eatin' your meat for you jest what he's eatin'?"

"Tongue."

"Tongue!" The meat came flying from between Paddock's lips to land on the ground. He coughed twice and began to spit, bending low over the grass as if trying to rid himself of an awful taste in his mouth.

"Jumpin' Jehoshaphat! You actin' like'n you'd jest

441

been give some nigger's guts to eat. I'll be goddamned an' go to hell right here!" Scratch chortled. "Jest the thought of it, eh?" He laughed some more. "Buffler tongue, Josiah. Ain't nothin' much to touch it up here. Leastways, you ain't gonna touch it, is you?" Scratch chuckled while stuffing another slice of the tender delicacy into his mouth. With words the young man was barely able to understand coming around the piece of flesh, Scratch instructed, "You'll be gettin' you taste for all such soon, young'un. 'Long with lotta other doin's. I'll swear that by my own hook!" He leaned over and brought the kettle up to his lips with both hands. Finished with a long drink, Scratch set the iron kettle down and wiped his lips with a greasy sleeve. "Had you blood to drink already, ain't you? Kilt you Injun, too. Right? Am I right? You'll be gettin' on with lotta doin's up here soon, young'un. Yepper—you will." Taking another slice of meat into his mouth, Bass gestured with the long blade of his knife. "That spit-out meat of your'n, take an' throw it over there"—he motioned across the flames—"jest outta the light of our fire."

Josiah leaned forward to pick up the slightly masticated flesh and casually tossed it where Bass had indicated. "Want ye clean camp, huh?" he asked.

"You might'n be sayin' that." Titus smiled at the corners of his mouth. "Jest you watch where you throwed the meat." The young man looked once more across the fire for several moments, then turned back to Scratch.

"What I'm s'posed to be seein'?"

"Jest you hush now an' watch. Don' make you a sound yet. Keep your eyes over there."

Josiah turned his attention slowly back to the edge of the firelight. The quiet of the blackness surrounding their little fire seemed to envelope him and he shuddered involuntarily. He thought he heard something, but really wasn't that sure. He strained his eyes to inspect the rim of darkness. Again the sound came to his ears. A sniffing sound it seemed. Then a head appeared. A coyote, head held low and cowering, pushed its nose forward cautiously as it was drawn magnetically by the fragrance of the meat the young trapper had discarded. Josiah reached slowly to his side and place a hand atop a piece of firewood.

"Boy! Don' you make no move like that!" Scratch rasped in a whisper at Paddock's side, "less'n you want me to feed you to 'im!" Josiah turned to look into the older man's face and slowly released the piece of timber as if he had been the child caught with his hand in the honey jar. The coyote moved forward when the human voice had run into silence, slinking gradually toward the light inches at a time until he could snatch the meat into his mouth. With a gulp the flesh was gone, and as quickly the furry intruder disappeared.

"Glad the critter left," Josiah commented.

"Shit!" was Scratch's reply. "He ain't left. You jest cain't see 'im. He's been round for some time. Since't last evenin' when we was layin' into this here camp, son, he's been round." Bass put his knife to work on the buffalo tongue, took another slice from it, and tossed it across the fire, but somewhat closer to the embers than Josiah had thrown his piece of meat. The coyote waited a few moments in the dark, then slipped back to steal another offered tidbit. "Son. Want you move real slow, so's you won' skeer the critter off, an' drag over some a them hump ribs. What's left. Go get 'em for me."

Josiah moved off slowly to retrieve what was left of the buffalo meat from a pack by their bedrolls. As the flesh was drawn from its protective package of hide, the coyote was joined by another, even more scrawny companion. Paddock scooted back toward the older man and placed the mass of ribs between him and Scratch. Silently both men began to slice away chunks of meat from the bones to toss at the two hungry scavengers. With each morsel snatched up, the coyotes would turn away from the humans to disappear beyond the edge of the shadows, whence the men could hear the loud, ravenous sounds as the animals enjoyed their free meal. Again and again they returned to the first limits of firelight, where they awaited another handout thrown to them by the trappers, who laughed and joked quietly to themselves at the slinking coyotes.

Many were the tales of these canines slithering into a trapper's camp, concealed by the cover of darkness, to chew on leather harness, bridles, and saddles. To prevent such scavenger damage, some of the mountain-wise trappers would use only horsehair bridles, harness very unpalatable to these denizens of the high forests. On occasion a starving coyote, cold and hungry, and unable to fill his

443

pinched belly with what small game appeared on the frozen landscape, was even known to nibble at the leather moccasins on a slumbering trapper's feet.

After long minutes of enjoying the fun a low, harsh growl broke forth from the edge of the inky shadows. One of the coyotes was still in the dark. The other snatched up a chunk of fresh meat and turned to disappear into the shadows with his companion. Another low grunt was followed by a series of harsh growls. The scrawnier of the two coyotes reappeared into the light, followed closely by his partner, both moving backward very slowly. The trappers' attention was riveted on the shadowy curtain of darkness where the guttural growling continued. Scratch cut another slice of meat from a rib without looking down, his eyes fixed beyond the coyotes. The meat was thrown into the midst of the two scavengers. The larger of the pair snatched the morsel up and was moving once more toward the shadows when another warning growl was heard. With dubious courage but with a clear presence of instinct for survival in the face of challenge, the coyote dropped the chunk of flesh and backed up to stand with his partner. Both of them lowered their heads and drew their necks into their shoulders while their flea-bitten tails curled between hind legs and hair stood along their spines. A dark form emerged from the trees. The animal, larger than the coyotes, walked more confidently into the light of the glowing flames. Almost hypnotized both men watched the slow advance of the large animal until it stopped and dipped its head to gobble up the offered meat. As it took the flesh into his mouth, the two coyotes uttered low, moaning growls of their own at being robbed again of their free repast. The thief jerked his head up and snarled back at the two scavengers. In the dance of light thrown off by the flames, Scratch fixed his eyes on the sharp teeth exposed as the animal curled back his lips menacingly in warning. The scrawny coyote's growl changed to a pitiful whine.

"Wolf," Bass muttered as his hands returned to the mass of buffalo to cut another chunk free. This piece he threw closer to the fire. The coyotes started for it but were halted by another sharp, guttural growl and a show of teeth. They stepped aside for the large black animal. The dark, glowing eyes glared across the fire at the trappers before the head dropped to pick up the flesh. The wolf swallowed it whole. Another chunk was thrown to the black thief, who snatched it up and swallowed it without taking its eyes off the humans.

"Josiah," Bass whispered so softly that the young man almost could not hear. "Listen me close afore you move. You good to that sticker, Hatcher tol't me. That right?" he asked without taking his eyes from the wolf to address the young man beside him.

"I s'pose—"

"You go an' ease it out your belt then—real easylike, you hear? Careful now, an' slow," Bass instructed. "When's you got it ready for throwin', I'll toss that black devil 'nother chunk. You make your throw count, son. You throw when the meat's still in the air. You make that sonuvabitch come, Josiah." The last words were pushed and forceful, as if strained through clamped teeth. Scratch could see Paddock nod his head up and down in the affirmative from the corner of his eye. As Josiah began to extricate his large knife from the belt at his waist, Titus put his blade to work slicing another hunk of meat from the buffalo ribs. The flesh was freed from the bone and Bass again peered out the corner of his eyes at Paddock to see the glint of steel from the huge blade flash as it caught the glow of firelight. "You set, son?" His question was answered wordlessly with a slow nod of Paddock's head.

Scratch tossed the piece of meat toward the wolf in a high arc over the flames. As it left Bass's hand, the wolf raised his dark head to watch its flight. When the meat was reaching the apex of its climb, the animal turned his head slightly to anticipate where the treat would land. Beside Bass there was a sudden flash of motion as the young man moved his entire upper body to put force and thrust behind the huge knife. The weapon struck the animal before Titus was fully conscious that Josiah had thrown it. Scratch snapped his head to his right and caught a glimpse of Paddock's follow-through, arm stretched forward to point at the black target across the fire. In another instant Bass snapped his head back to the left to see the knife already embedded high in the wolf's neck. Knocked backward a step or two by the force of the weapon's flight, the wolf jerked wildly around and around in a crazy circle, trying to make sense of this sudden catastrophe. From side to side he shook his neck, repeatedly trying to free it of the huge blade buried deep within his flesh. From his nostrils

445

began to pour a small stream of fluid as dark as his furry coat and glistening with the same inky intensity as his eyes. The wolf snorted to clear his nose, then coughed to sputter free more dark liquid. He rasped hoarsely attempting to capture a breath of air, but that was impossible now. The wolf would suffocate slowly as its wild dance began to cancel itself. The body weaved a few times until the severed windpipe took its toll. In less than a minute, all told, the animal dropped to its side. The legs thrashed spastically a few times, then became rigid before they finally relaxed in death.

"Were that good 'nough for you?" Paddock questioned quietly.

"Slick as shootin', young'un." Bass braced his left arm against his side and gradually rose from his robes as the two coyotes scampered into the shadows. He gingerly walked over to the carcass and tapped it with his toe. Putting a hand to the wolf's chest, Bass felt deep within the dark fur. "Critter ain't beatin'." He turned to look up at Josiah as the young man came around the fire. "I'd like you skin this black devil out for me, son." He backed off a few feet to sit once more at the edge of the fire while Josiah silently went to work removing the hide from the animal. For a few minutes he watched the young man labor at the fleshing job, then spat, as if to introduce his comments.

"Don' care me a shit for such critters. Titus Bass don'. Not one consarn." He spat once more to the side. "Black devil let them other poor critters lead 'im to a free meal, then come in an' take it 'way from 'em. Cain't set with that." Josiah turned to look at Scratch for a moment, then returned to his work without a word. "Catches in my craw, it does—thems as'll let others do theys work for 'em, then come in to take what the gettin's got. That black devil there jest much a nigger as some men be. That'un's been lettin' them two li'l fellers dig up what he wants 'em to dig up, lettin' 'em find what he wants for hisse'f alla time—then comes in to jump theys set. Wagh!" he snorted softly and shook his head. "Critter got runned off from a wolf pack for one why or 'nother an' now he's jumpin' them coyotes' set. If'n that don' take the circle, I'll be damned! Got me somethin' 'bout such doin's as sours my milk. You know what I'm meanin'?" He looked up to see Paddock turn to gaze at him.

446

"Yep," came the quiet answer. "S'pose I do—in a way..." His voice dropped off and he turned back to his work.

"I feel me for them fellers out there in the shadders," Scratch remarked. "They been carryin' that big sonuvabitch 'long with 'em for some time from the looks of it. An' each time he steals a meal from 'em, he's knowin' it'll make 'em look all the harder for the next one. They bellies pinchin' an' drawin' up like'n a hide puckerin' up what ain't been smoked. Consarn! The devil he had it comin'!" He finished by puckering up to spit once more on the grass.

"There."

"Done, is you?" he asked, even though he had watched Josiah pull the fresh hide free from the carcass and hold it in the air. Scratch leaned forward to feel the thickness of the coat.

"Gonna have us a winter this y'ar up here," the older man commented. His fingers caressed the dark fur while his eyes searched the shadows beyond the last touches of firelight. "Ma Nature take care of her own, she is. Gettin' 'em ready for what's comin' up here in the time of...maybe three weeks. Man best pay him heed to this too. When the critters get 'em good coats like this'n, us niggers best be ready for some mighty cold doin's." He let the hide slip through his fingers and rose to his feet again. "You take you that hide over by the packs." Bass gestured toward the other side of the dying flames. "Get out some a that salt an' lay it down over the flesh side, son. When you got it covered, roll it up—ha'r side out—real tight, then lash 'er down good. Jest like you did with them elk robes. Go on now." He shooed Paddock away with a few rapid motions of his arm. Scratch leaned down and took hold of one of the wolf's hind legs.

"You ain't fixin' to eat that, is you?" Josiah asked as if casting an opinion on the older man's culinary habits.

"Nawww," Bass shook his head as he stared down at the bare carcass. "Not this time, leastways." He tugged on the body to get it moving toward the shadows, still clutching his side with the left arm. "I got me buffler so's I ain't got me no need of eatin' wolf meat."

"Thought you had better sense'n go eatin' that critter," Paddock chided.

Titus stopped and turned to face the younger man.

"Ain't a matter of sense, son," came the quiet comment. "I don' need this'r meat. Man gets hungry, howsomever, he might jest find hisse'f eatin' most anythin'." He took his eyes away from Josiah's to gaze at the carcass he was dragging beside him, "I've been one to et worse, lots worse. An' I'll set my mark you'll eat worse'n wolf meat too—"

"You said that afore, Scratch."

"An' I'll keep sayin' it, son. We eat good when we have good to eat. An' when we don', well, then we eat what we can. But I ain't noways gonna turn into such a critter as this'r"—he shook the wolf's leg he held—"a nigger what lets others do his scroungin' for 'im, then jumps in to get the meat on the bone. Takin' for his own right out from under the fellers as got it for 'im. No sir. What we get ain't gonna be count a some other nigger workin' for us, settin' us up, boy. Titus Bass made a better fixins than that." He turned slowly and tugged on the carcass once more to get it moving over the thick covering of pine needles and grass. "Better fixins than that," he muttered quietly to himself as he disappeared into the darkness.

Josiah could hear the older man crunching through the dry needles and leaves, and the wolf's body being dragged alongside the slow steps of Bass. Then the noise of motion stopped and all was still. Then, in the darkness, Scratch's voice could be heard drifting back through the trees toward the fire.

"Here you now, boys." His tone was soft and motherly. "You critters ain't had you much vittles for some time, have you? Here—bringed you the black nigger's meat to feed on. That's some, ain't it? Certain sure it be now. You two what been feedin' him gonna feed on him now. Eat on the nigger what's been leadin' you on a merry chase. C'mon now. I know you's out there—I can hear you, Scratch can. You come have your supper. You worked long for this'un an' I loves seein' you enjoy it, too. Here's the nigger for you—from me to you, both you. See, now, Ol' Scratch knows jest how you feel. You can lay your sights to that. Ol' Scratch is one to know jest how you feel."

"Crow call this'r time a y'ar 'When the Ponies Grow Lean,'" Bass chattered in the cold, charcoal gray of pre-

448

dawn labors. Little light remained except from the waning bright moon of the night before. "Cold mother it can be, this time. Colder'n later on, it seems to a man. Guessin' it's 'cause by the middle a robe season this here child's got hisse'f use ta the queersome aches in my bones." Again and again he turned the stout limb in his hands as he shaved it clear of dried bark with his knife. Josiah, sitting beside Scratch on the frozen crust of earth within the midst of their baggage, looked up at Scratch now and then as the older man spoke on, watching the words come forth from Bass's lips accompanied by puffs of pale smoke that muffled the words in the bone-splitting cold. The older man raised his eyes from his work as he set the finished limb beside his leg in a pile of some half-dozen others and looked into the sky. "Take you a lookee there." He gestured for Josiah to gaze beyond his shoulder. "See them halo rings round the moon there?" He paused to watch Josiah's head drop and rise slowly in affirmation. "When such get real thicklike, like the fog risin' off a beaver pond jest afore get-up, means a snow's comin' in, Josiah."

"Cold 'nough for it," Paddock replied as he set back to work on the limb across his lap.

"Sometimes, it can jest be too damned cold for it to be snowin'," Scratch responded. "Then a coon knows there won' be new snow for him to be fightin'." He paused while he leaned over to pick up the last of the limbs to be peeled. "All a man's gotta think 'bout then is keepin' 'live whilst he keeps his wits 'bout him." He set his knife to work peeling the thin bark from the aspen limb. In the ensuing silence every sound seemed magnified in the cold, still air, seemed suspended for detailed inspection before disappearing. "Son, grab you your rifle an' these here sticks." Bass rose from the ground as if his joints had become frozen from sitting. "I'll be takin' the traps. Let's be gettin' us these cold doin's outta the way now." The new skin over his wound was as taut as a stretched beaver plew but he was no longer bothered by pain.

The two men moved out from the edge of the trees onto the bottom of a gummy mire of grass that stretched across the small bowl where they had chosen to camp the day before. Josiah turned to look about him at the mountains rising around this tiny bowl. Against the paling gray blue of the predawn sky were dark outlines of the peaks in bold slashes of contrast, as though painted by an artist's brush. His attention was wrenched back to lifting one leg and putting it front of the other. Into the bottom they moved with their loads. Paddock readjusted the bundle of limbs tucked at his side beneath his arm. Scratch tugged at the heavy buffalo-hide sack that contained their combined treasure of steel traps. Through the frozen grass that stood like icy sentries snapped brutally downward with the weight of the sack, Bass struggled on with the load he was dragging. With each step the men took across the grass came a rhythmic staccato that accompanied the constant drone of the sack across the icy bottom. A few more steps and the ground was no longer merely spongy beneath their weight. The mire in this beaver marsh now became deeper and more yearning of sucking a man's moccasins from his feet. Each man planted a foot, then brought the trailing one up as the one in the lead broke through the thin crust of ice and sank into the muck of mud and grass. Occasionally a foot would stumble on a rock hidden beneath the icy cap glazed over the mire and the man would use it as firm footing for a single step before plunging back into the mud and cold of the freezing water that seeped from the ground with every succeeding step.

Josiah looked over at the older man, wondering if he would stop for a few minutes to rest. Looking nowhere but at the mire immediately before his next step, Bass continued on, unaware that Paddock had turned to look at him momentarily. Titus was intent on moving them to their sets quickly this morning before the sun caught them out. Paddock studied the intensity of the old face a moment more and decided to go on without a word. He sighed, glanced ahead where the dark gray of the stream bank stood out in the distance against the lighter gray of the mire, and sighed again, his lungs burning in the frigid air. He would continue with his own agonizing plodding. At least he was getting warmer now from his exertion. Still the air seemed to seep within the flaps of the capote. The chill bit at his ears as the air snaked into the hood of the blanket coat. He held the limbs tighter to his stomach and tried to pull his hand back farther into the long sleeve of the coat. Paddock's other hand brought the rifle up to his head; he attempted to pull the hood farther down over his brow. His toes struck the trap sack and he stumbled over the obstruction before stopping to turn around.

"Where you goin', young'un?" Scratch inquired crisply.

Josiah now pushed the hood back a little and realized the man had dropped the trap sack on the ground and it was over the sack he had stumbled. He turned his head to the side within the hood and saw they were near the stream bank. Cold and fatigued, Josiah had been heedless of direction and destination. Only of movement was he aware.

"Drop you them sticks now," Scratch commanded, and Paddock let them fall from his grasp. They fell with a faint clatter onto the trap sack and tumbled to the frozen ground. "You say you trapped afore?" he inquired of his young partner as he knelt to untie the drawstring at the top of the sack.

"Catched me one . . . some time ago." He brought the rifle across his chest and cradled it against his body while each hand sought a warm haven up the opposite sleeve.

"One?" Bass looked up at the man standing beside him. "What'd you use for bait, son?"

"Didn't have me no bait . . ."

"Sounds to the likes of it," Scratch interrupted. "If'n you catched only one, you'd have no bait till you catched him. Wagh!" The word was a faint growl in the frozen air and seemed to hang between them for a moment. "This here nigger's been doin' the trappin' for the past moon since't we broke up outta Henry's Lake—time it be for Josiah Paddock to be bringin' beaver to bait. Freeze into it, boy." He brought a trap from the sack and set it on the frozen ground with a sharp clink. Pulling his hand from the metal, Scratch could feel the tug at his skin where flesh had become frozen to the trap.

For the past three weeks or more, since they had been riding north from the small mountain-valley lake where the wolf had been slain, Titus had insisted that only he and Asa go out trapping. Josiah was instructed to remain behind in camp with the plunder, ponies, and McAfferty's squaw. Bass had quietly commented when the younger man had protested being left one morning, "Son, it's a damned sight better to count your ponies' ribs—leavin' 'em in camp—than your ponies' tracks, if'n they get runned off by some red niggers." Their path north from the lake was taking them straight for the Three

451

Forks of the Missouri River. Leaving a man in camp with the worldly possessions seemed a sensible precaution to Scratch. But to Josiah Paddock it was a blow to his young ego. It was as if Bass did not consider him competent to perform the labors of a trapper. He was left behind to perform the duties of a camp keeper and cook.

Day after day the moving camp was filled with the dull-red trophies of the trappers. The beaver hides were stretched on willow hoops until they gave the appearance of large round dollars. Flesh side up to expose the hide to the sun for drying, the beaver currency dotted the small camp each day the group was not moving farther north toward the British holdings. Paddock would watch the men return from their traps carrying the spoils of their labors. The dead animals were then piled unceremoniously for Josiah to skin and flesh before stretching them on the willow hoops he made while the two older men were away from camp. It had increasingly eaten at him not to be included in the hunt, having to sit behind with the squaw, who stayed bundled in her robes by the fire she continually played with during the daylight hours. Every morning when the men left camp she would rise and move into the forest, where he could hear her wretching and gagging as she vomited. He would watch her return and drink a meaty broth she kept warm by the fire before burying herself beneath the buffalo robes once more. It was a ritual painful to watch. Always he wondered why she never vomited those days they moved farther north on the trail of McAfferty's choosing. Only those mornings they set up camp to trap for a few days. Only then.

"Mind you, son," Scratch interrupted Josiah's thoughts, "the leaves ain't dropped yet from the trees. Gettin' late, it is, for 'em to be droppin'. This'll l'arn you, so listen up. When them leaves drop early, your fall'll be a short one. But the winter to foller'll be none too bad. Howsomever, Josiah, when them leaves don' drop till late on, it tells a man of one thing: we gonna have us a rough winter ahead. Cold-ass doin's, for sure." Bass pushed one of the aspen limbs toward Josiah. "Go crack you the ice on the stream up next to the bank an' start makin' that lil' shelf I tol't you 'bout, where you'll set your trap."

Paddock scooted to the edge of the water and broke through the thin crust of ice with the broad point of the limb. He broke more and more of the frozen layer from the side of the stream and then set to carving out a shelf from the soil of the bank about a foot below the water line. His hands grew numb as they dipped beneath the icy liquid. He pulled them back out and pushed up the sleeves on both arms. Again the hands went back into the water to continue building the shelf as he heard the older man settle back on the frozen grass.

"'Member that rabbit you snare't up two nights ago, son?" Bass continued to whisper, referring to the small animals they had been forced to snare in order to eat when game could not be found and when they feared firing their rifles if elk or deer could be tracked. "I pointed you out one a the critter's hind foots—all that fine heavy fur on the bottom of it—didn't tell you all what I wanted you to look at it for, did I?" Scratch did not wait for an answer from the younger man. "Well, I didn'. Snowshoe rabbit like that 'un gets some heavy fur 'long the downside of his foots, 'nother sign for a man that's a cold winter comin' on. Jest 'minded me of that lookin' out to that beaver lodge over there, son." Titus nodded his head in its general direction as Josiah looked up from his numbing work. "Here on the north side a that lodge you see them beavers' been addin' more an' more wood—more'n you see 'long that east or west sides. Man with his wits 'bout him takes that as sure sign from the beaver there's gonna be cold doin's in the mountains this y'ar. Yessir. Ma Nature takes care of her own, Josiah. It's only man what's gotta catch up an' pay heed to help she's given all other critters 'ceptin' him." Bass snuggled close against his rifle and was silent a few moments. He spoke again. "Lookin' back, Ol' Scratch 'members the dark squirrels taken 'em up lotta nuts early to the fall, too. Even seen 'em taken up green nuts. Ma tellin' 'em lil' critters got 'em a long, hard winter comin' on. Cold doin's for certain. More sign to that than there be sign in a squar's heart."

Paddock leaned away from the stream to straighten his cold back. He began to cough a little and put his hand over his mouth. Feeling as if something were in his chest needing to be brought up, he continued to force the cough until there was the feel of thick phlegm at the back of his throat. He turned his head away from Bass.

"Don' you spit, son!" Scratch snapped quietly, rising to a sitting position. "Don' you ever catch yourself spittin' round where a trap is bein' set." Josiah turned to look at

453

him, feeling the mucous in the back of his throat choking him. "Jest swaller it hard now." He finally leaned back and relaxed the tone in his voice. "Less'n you jest gotta spit, then you can spit into the tail of your coat an' rub it in." Paddock swallowed hard once, then twice, grimacing with revulsion at the thick, syrupy mucous sliding down his throat. "Beaver smell that spit round your trap set, why you might well as taken a shit right here. Spit round a trap set an' you ain't gonna bring 'em to bait."

"Aww right," Josiah said, then choked a little on some remaining phlegm. He cleared his throat and swallowed hard a third time. "Aw right," he repeated, "am I ready to set the trap an' lay her down?"

"Look to be." Scratch said. "Lemme see you set the trap here."

Josiah selected one of the traps and stood over it, placing first one foot, then the other over the springs at either side of the jaws. He rocked back off the balls of his feet so that his weight was transferred from his heels to the two springs, which gradually gave way under pressure. Kneeling slowly, Paddock could now open the jaws with no restriction and set the trigger over one jaw before locking it in a notch on the pan arm. Carefully he brought his hands away from within the jaws, saw that the set was good, and rocked back onto the balls of his feet. He smiled within as he stood up.

"Here." Bass threw him a twig little more than a foot long. "Your bait stick. Put it there in your capote belt, grab you one a them stakes, an' you're ready to get in the water."

Josiah stuffed the small twig into his belt as instructed, then tucked one of the six-foot limbs beneath his arm and knelt to pick the readied trap up carefully in one hand. Stepping into the water around the edge of the carved-out shelf he felt the icy water bite first at his feet, then at his ankles and calves. Carefully he brought the trap below the water where he set it down upon the shelf and seated it firmly, the jaws yawning wide and menacingly. Beneath the water his right hand located the trap chain. Bringing it back up above water Josiah slipped the ring at the end of the chain around the long dry limb. Now he backed up slowly until most of the five-foot chain had been played out. Here he sank the sharp end of the limb into the rocky bottom of the slow, dammed-up stream.

Moving cautiously back toward the bank where the trap was set, Paddock looked up at Bass.

"You're ready for the beaver milk, son," Scratch instructed. "That be what the twig's for."

The young man put his right hand into the front of his capote and located the small vial of castoreum hanging from his belt. He brought it out and pulled the antler stopper from the horn container.

"Dip your twig in it," Bass continued.

Into the vial went the peeled end of the twig. When he brought it out the twig was covered with the smelly, brownish cream donated by a previous unfortunate beaver. After returning the antler stopper to the container, Josiah stuffed the vial back into his pouch hanging at his side over the coat. By now the smell of the castoreum was lifting to his nostrils. It nauseated him at first and he wrinkled up his nose. Then the odor recalled a fleeting memory of smearing the musky essence over his flesh to keep troublesome insects from biting. Finally it dawned upon him—this substance gave to the mountain trappers their peculiar smell. These men trapped the beaver and smelled like them too, he thought.

"Stick 'er in the mud . . . there, jest up from your trap, Josiah." Bass interrupted. "That long twig'll mean you should catch the beaver on his back foot. Short one'll get the beaver by a foreleg. Long like that'un'll make the critter stand up to smell your bait. An' when he comes to take a sniff of it, on the end of the twig in the cut of the bank, a hind leg steps on the pan." Paddock sank the bait stick in the edge of the bank so the castoreum-coated end hung a few inches over the top of the water cleared of its thin crust of ice. "Beaver's a critter as gets hisse'f kilt wantin' to know what other beaver's come in on his staked-out country, you see. Smells him a strange critter in the area an' he's jest gotta find out whose settin' up lodge in his neck a the woods. Critter gets squampshus-like, but his wantin' to know gets the best of 'im. So he comes on up to take a sniff of your bait. Snap goes your trap on his leg an' he'll start divin' for the bottom with a big splash. That's when he pulls the chain down your set pole where the ring gets hooked on the notch we carved on the pole."

455

Josiah stepped out of the water and shook his legs free of the water that had not already turned to ice on his leggings in the cold air.

"Critter ain't got him a prayer's chance of gnawin' through your iron chain," Bass continued, "cain't even gnaw through his leg without air for as long as it takes. He cain't come up for air with that ring locked on the bottom of the stream. Yep. Critter drowns then, an' jest waitin' for you is that pelt. Out there in the stream where no critters such as painter cats or coyotes'll get to him. When you come back to pull 'im up, you're hopin' he ain't pulled your set pole an' all, then got hiss'f to some air. Howsomever, he cain't last too long with that trap holdin' him down an' draggin' that pole. Might be you're a child as'll have to trail that beaver downstream for better'n a mile afore you find your stick. An' where you find your stick, you're always prayin' you're gonna find your beaver." Bass paused and pushed one of the traps toward Josiah with his foot. "You don' find your beaver, you don' find your trap. That's the true an' simple of it. An' mind you what them traps cost a nigger up here in the hills. You don't wanna never loose you a trap. Ever' one's worth the trouble it takes you to find it, certain sure that be. Here with these ponds an' lodges all round, you go losin' a trap means we gotta go drain these here critters' dams an' bust into theys lodges to get it back. I don' cotton to them doin's much, I don'. Not sayin' I ain't got the stomach for clubbin' beaver over the head—why, boy, you seen me set to it with that Injun, ain't you? I ain't one to be skeert of the killin', Titus Bass ain't." He tapped momentarily on his rifle while he paused. "Jest, jest that them critters we come up here for—the critter ever'body's wantin' for furs back east—they jest like a lil' pet, they can be. Catch you a lil' one like I done afore, back to havin' to break up a beaver lodge, an' rub his lil' head like you would your own puppy dog. Why, that critter'll turn up his lil head an' cry like a babe for you. Had me one I brung back to my camp once't—put it inside my coat an' carried it 'long with me for a few days whilst I was in that camp. Next to your best huntin' hound, a lil' beaver make you a good pet as any this here child knows of."

Paddock had set the jaws of a second trap and was kneeling to pick up another limb when Bass rose to his feet and tugged his blanket coat more tightly about him, knocking some slivers of ice from where he had lain in the grass.

"I be on the tramp back to camp, Josiah. Want you put down least a dozen of them sets afore you come back in. We'll see what bark you got to you." He began to move off a step, then turned around to whisper once more to the young man. "You got you shot an' powder, don' you, son?" Paddock patted his pouch for the older man to see. "Good," Scratch nodded. "You be quiet settin' your traps now, you hear? String 'em on downstream from here, but do it fast. Don' let the light catch you out. Try your damndest to be back to camp afore the sun creeps up on you. Don' like me the feel of this here country. There'd be brownskins about—no s'prise to me. Mind you we be close to the Three Forks now. Don' know why McAfferty's trappin' up here when he could be a nigger to trap the likes of the Uinty down south. Cold up here—so cold you go to feel your squar's breasties an' they feel like'n you're touchin' the nose on Ol' Man North hisse'f." Bass shook his head while looking at the ground, then raised his eyes to Josiah. "You're on your own, son. We'll be seein' the ha'r of the b'ar in you by sunup—you get through wadin' these'r streams. My bones feelin' rheumy already an' we ain't even halfsome into the season." He moved his hips from side to side. "See you back to camp, son." He left abruptly.

Josiah watched his form slowly disappear into the dim light, hearing the faint crunch and suck of each step through the marsh as he moved out of sight. He sighed with small relief at being alone, then nervously looked over each shoulder before setting off downstream as his partner had instructed. Winding his way around and between the willow hugging the stream bank, Josiah found a place for his second set. As he knelt at the edge of the water to begin chipping ice from the bank he remembered he had left his rifle some fifty yards back at the site of the first set. Paddock straightened up and sucked in a quick gasp of the brutally cold air. His heart racing, the young man began to weigh the odds of going back now to retrieve the weapon or finishing preparing this second trap. The rest of the traps and limbs were back there too, he thought. He would just hurry through this one, get it finished and in place before going back for the rifle, traps, and poles. The dull-gray fear that set his body to trem-

457

bling slightly was passed off to the cold. Nervously he looked over each shoulder again to reassure himself he was not being watched. The second shelf was prepared and he turned to pick up the trap. There was a soft crunch downstream. Josiah froze with his hand on the trap, feeling himself drawing up inside as if to make himself all the smaller, all the less visible. The faint crunch that had drifted to his ears was not followed by another. His heart began to slow.

He turned silently to pick the trap up, and placed it underwater. Reaching for the stout limb, he decided he would not enter the water here. Instead, he would cut short his time spent in this set by reaching out to jam the pole into the stream bottom from the bank. After slipping the ring of the trap chain over the pole, Josiah lay down on the bank with his chest suspended over the icy water and drove the pole into the muddy, rocky bottom with both hands. Now he realized he had suspended himself between the bank and the pole. Still gripping the limb, he tried to squirm backward to put more of his body and its weight on the edge of the bank. Firmly gripping the pole with his right hand, Josiah took the left from the limb and put it into the water. His palm found the bottom of the rocky stream and his shoulder muscles tensed. The right hand unwound from the pole and he pushed himself backward toward the shore with the left arm, squirming and wriggling with his lower body to assist him. Finally back on the bank, Josiah rose to his knees and shook the left arm, then tried to wring the wet blanket coat and his leather shirt of the cold water. It was already frozen.

Knocking his right hand against the wet left arm and rubbing the cold hand, he set off upstream. The distance seemed longer than that which he remembered traveling downstream from where he had left the traps and rifle. Against a clump of willow he could make out the dark mass that was the trap sack. There he stopped and looked around the frozen earth. His rifle was not there. Putting his hand across his mouth to tug at his cheeks in fear and bewilderment, Josiah let out a low moan of despair. He dropped to his knees and nervously looked about him once more. Down on his hands he went to begin crawling along the bank, low sobs catching at the back of his throat.

"My . . . my rifle," he whimpered breathlessly. "Scratch

come got it 'cause I didn' take it with me." He kept crawling back and forth along the bank near the trap sack. "My rifle . . . my rifle!" Sobbing, he finally stopped and felt near collapse. Clutching his face in both hands to muffle the despairing groans coming up from his throat, Josiah fell forward against the earth and felt the pain bite into his forearm. He lifted his head, blinking his eyes clear of the cold-bitten tears. Then numb fingers inadvertently touching the cause of his pain, he felt the familiar form of a rifle. Both hands clutched the weapon and brought it to his chest, where he cradled it tightly, passionately. Now he sobbed in relief. "I found you," he cried with muted words, caressing the rifle full-length with his hands. The flesh seemed warmed, at least not as numb now, being filled with his rifle.

He took one hand away and wiped his eyes, then his nostrils, and rose to his feet. Checking the frizzen, he found it still locked over the pan. The warmth of relief flooded him. Securing the weapon in the crook of his right elbow, Josiah knelt to pick up the remaining limbs and place them alongside the rifle. With his left hand around the top of the heavy trap sack, he rose and marched downstream once more.

By the time he had made eight sets, the young man was feeling fairly sure of himself regarding the trapper's craft. He had been running those things Scratch had told him around in his mind. Usually, the older man had instructed, a mountain trapper would place his traps in the darkening light of dusk and travel to them the following dawn, when he would skin his beaver out, flesh the hides, and await the coming of another dusk to reset the traps. But such a schedule, Bass had said, was not really necessary in country like this, "stinkin' thick with beavers." What with all the ponds and signs of immense beaver activity, a man had only to be careful of his sets and he could clear a whole stretch of some stream of its furry fortune. One word of warning Bass had given, however. There was a reason why the country crawled with beaver—Blackfeet. Trappers rarely came into this, the southern reaches of, Blackfoot country to wrest its treasure out from under the noses of the Peds Noirs. In this neck of the woods, the beaver thrived with secure abandon. A man could make his set in the morning and pull his trophies up at dusk. If he was careful where he made his

459

sets. If he kept his eyes open and his ears on the alert. If he paid attention to what the forest around him told those who would listen.

Another sixty yards downstream Josiah dropped the trap sack, now growing lighter. He laid the remaining limbs beside the sack and pulled a trap from it. After placing his rifle against the bag Paddock pulled the chain to its full length to straighten the links, then rose and took his rifle in hand. The sky was getting lighter now and he felt the clock within his bowels ticking off the valuable seconds. However, he convinced himself he would find a slide where the beaver had excavated a slope into the stream bank where they could slither into the water dragging their chewed construction material behind them. The bank along this stretch of the stream was steep so he felt good about the possibilities of finding a beaver slide. Walking slowly among the willows, Josiah looked from side to side at the nature of the vegetation along the watercourse. Here the beaver could thrive and prosper, feeding on the aspen that was in abundance, in addition to the cottonwood, willow, birch, and box elder. Everywhere were signs of recent activity of the animal: gnawed stumps and unclaimed saplings over which he had to step. He found one. Dropping to his knee, Josiah took a closer look. The slide left the bank thick with aspen and sloped into the stream. The beaver had even kept the ice broken up near the bank.

After he had dragged the baggage back to the slide, he once again set the rifle in readiness against the sack before setting about his trap preparations. The shelf was prepared on the upstream side of where the slide entered the water. Atop it was placed the trap, and the long pole was then put through the chain ring. Carefully he stepped down into the water from the bank and shakily got his footing with the first two steps. Stretching the chain to its full length, Josiah jammed the pointed end of the pole against the soft stream bottom. He felt the pole sink until satisfied with its security. Bending over to put a hand beneath the icy water, Paddock slid the chain down to the bottom of the stream, where it caught beneath the forked notch in the pole. At the snort from shore where he jerked and turned, a startled splash of cold water being thrown into his crotch. His eyes focused on the form standing guard over his rifle on the streambank.

Josiah, blinking, tried to clear the predawn mist from his eyes. Were they playing tricks on him? He snapped his head from side to side in disbelief, then looked once more to the bank of the frozen stream. Only when he took one small step across the rocky bottom of the stream toward the bank did he painfully realize the form on shore was no apparition. The grizzly roared and snorted as she raised up from sniffing the ground around the trap sack and his rifle. Paddock's eyes widened and darted downward to look at the rifle, which had made him feel secure and less lonely. Now the worms bit and crawled once more inside his bowels. The loneliness and solitude of his situation gripped his shoulders as surely as if the grizzly had taken his body into her viselike arms herself. He shuddered slightly, more from fear than from the icy liquid flowing past his legs.

From the corner of his eye Josiah caught a glimpse of the pale yellow glow of the sun creeping over the mountain, hidden behind a filter of dense, heavy clouds. He looked back at the grizzly. Remembering the struggle with one huge bear almost a year before, Josiah felt himself shaking. Still holding onto the pole he had planted in the bottom of the stream, he took his other hand to slide between the flaps of his capote. It was warmer in there, he thought. Then he thought it amusing to be thinking of such things now. With fingertips creeping along the path of his wide belt, Paddock's hand made it to the butt of his pistol. Some of the loneliness loosed its grip from his shoulders. His fingers continued until they felt the handle of the big knife. At the corner of his mouth the first faint hints of a crooked smile showed. Not so bad now, he told himself. Not so bad.

Slowly moving the concealed hand backward from the knife handle, he again touched the butt of the pistol lightly. His fingertips gradually encircled the grip and tightened into readiness. A solitary finger crawled away from the others to sneak within the trigger guard. Now the hand that had been gripping the pole loosened and glided to the front of the capote where the blanket sash held the coat about his waist. There his frozen fingers finally responded to untie the knot from the sash. As it came loose and the flaps at the front of the coat opened slightly, the sash dropped into the freezing water. Josiah was unaware that the bright red piece of cloth floated

461

away from him downstream. With his free hand the young trapper began to spread the flaps of the blanket coat apart so that the hand holding onto the pistol would have little obstruction in pulling the weapon for readiness to use.

As if he were in no real hurry Paddock brought the pistol barrel from his belt and cleared it from the confines of the coat. The right arm slowly began to rise from waist level, an arm that shook as much from the numbing cold as from the excitement of the impending shot. Inch by inch the arm climbed until stopped by another roar of the grizzly. Josiah froze the arm and weapon in place, unmoving. The grizzly shouted again her disapproval of the human's intentions, as if she understood what the pistol meant. She bounced several times up and down on all four legs over the rifle, seemingly goading the human into a combat she felt sure she would win. Josiah watched the muscles over her shoulders and hump ripple with each bounce onto the frozen earth. Something within him shuddered at every ripple of those shoulders. Then she stopped her provocative dance and ambled toward the edge of the water with a lumbering, side-to-side gait. At the bank the bear lowered her head without taking her dark eyes from her captive. She sniffed the water where Josiah had chipped ice free for his trap set.

Paddock again started to raise the pistol to aim at the huge target standing less than twenty feet from him. The grizzly rocked back on her haunches and warningly swiped with one arm at the trapper in the middle of the stream. Josiah froze. Satisfied that she had cowed this human, the bear took the arm she had shaken at him and dipped it slowly into the water to test the temperature. She jerked the giant paw from the stream and shook it free of the freezing water. She wiped the paw against her thick coat. Snorting again, the bear now rose full height and began to place a foot in the stream. The hind leg submerged, she drew it back out and shook her body free of the water. Again the bear put the leg into the water and dragged the other in behind it.

Josiah looked around quickly to determine the distance he would have to travel across the rocky stream bottom and through the frozen water to reach the opposite bank. He snapped around at the sound of another snort and found the grizzly dropping down into the water. Paddock moved quickly to begin his race, knocking over the long pole he had sunk into the bottom of the stream. Stumbling wildly forward, the young trapper fell to his knees on the rocky bottom with a stifled cry of pain and surprise. His head snapped over his shoulder to see if the bear was continuing in her chase. She had no sooner dropped her body into the stream than she stood back up and beat a hasty retreat to the bank. Thence she scrambled back onto the relative warmth of land. By rippling her massive muscular armor, the bear freed herself of much of the water that clung to her coat, water that was too cold, water from a stream that served as a wall between her and Josiah.

Rising shakily to his knees, Josiah shivered and drew the dripping coat about him more tightly. He watched the bear ridding herself of water and did likewise. Beginning with his shoulders, Paddock attempted to imitate the animal's method of drying off, quickly shaking the muscles of his chest, abdomen, and hips. His legs would have to stay wet. He stood in water up to his groin.

Her attention was drawn to the rifle. Leaning over to sniff at it first, the grizzly then reached out with a paw to feel of it. Finally she leaned close to it once more and ran her nose along its full length, perhaps puzzled by the scent of man on this inanimate object, the scent of the man in the water. With a disgusted snort the bear started to scoot the rifle toward the edge of the bank where it seemed she intended to drop the weapon into the water.

"No-o-o-o!" The word leaped from Josiah's lips. He found himself leaning toward the bear as if in warning. The animal looked up, as though surprised, at the human standing crouched in the stream. She stopped shuffling the weapon toward the water and surveyed her quarry carefully. Paddock leaned back a little, feeling somewhat sorry and anxiously guilty that he had once again drawn the grizzly's attention to himself. "No," he uttered once more in a whisper without heart. "You do anythin' but that," Josiah continued as if instructing the monster in the degrees of sin. It was all right to leave him stranded in the stream if she so desired—that served him right, he supposed, for having left his rifle behind earlier. But to dump a man's rifle into the water—that's where all the fun had to stop.

The bear rose from the weapon and again gazed

463

intently at the trapper, new thoughts feeding her mind. She stuck a paw into the water and withdrew it, seemingly reassured that it was still too cold to pursue the man within its icy reaches. Suddenly she gracelessly sat down on the bank beside his rifle and continued to stare at him. Josiah straightened up and peeked into the pan of the dueling pistol. His charge was wet, through and through. Disgusted that he had stumbled and given his only chance of exit a thorough soaking, Paddock stuffed the hand weapon into his belt and again drew the capote about himself tightly. He was suddenly completely unaware that his powderhorn hung by his side! Crossing his arms, he stuck a hand under each armpit. Releasing a slow, shuddering sigh, the young trapper stared back at his adversary. He could now feel the numbness creeping up his legs with its icy fingers of immobilizing cramps. Josiah was sure this would be a long day. The grizzly sat back as if relaxed in her position above the man, as if assured he would have to come forth from the frozen stream soon. All she would have to do was out-wait the human.

Only four months earlier this female had driven her two cubs into the world on their own. A clock buried by the ages deep within her had instructed her to break two years of family ties with the youngsters. She then had spent a long summer eating on various plants of the high country, and only recently had the grizzly tasted flesh, again in response to a biological clock. It was only during October and November, the waning days of wakefulness before hibernation drives overtook it, that a bear partook of meat. And now, during the Indian's "Moon When the Ponies Grow Lean," the grizzly she-bear was also growing acutely conscious of another rhythm within her. Its stirrings made her inexplicably edgy and irritable. It was the season of the rut and nature was preparing her for a liaison with a male of the species. And nature would prompt her behavior when the meeting took place. But today, this female was being goaded by unseen thorns, being urged by wants and needs she could not comprehend. Her armorlike musculature intermittently flushed with excitement, portending the coming rendezvous with a mate. She scratched at her thick hide with the imposing claws that often found relief in pawing at tree trunks.

Between her massive jaws she salivated around a yawning orifice housing pincerlike fangs, which continually reminded her of the pleasing taste of flesh.

Through the morning's growing light Josiah watched the nervous female, by turns marveling at her patience and angry at his own lack of it. It was the cold, he told himself thoughtfully. Paddock could feel it creeping higher, into his bowels. But perhaps it was fear. Fear, he knew, paralyzed the consciousness even as cold numbed the body. That fear, to be sure, was now engulfing him. A fear so real he could almost smell it; probably the grizzly could smell it on him too. But, damn! He could not see it. He wasn't one to be afraid of anything he could see, Josiah said to himself. It was something Scratch would say to him. But fear was an adversary no man could see to strike or grapple with alone. He would attempt to push it backward, away from the deliberate thought process.

"Ol' Ephraim, they call you," he muttered between chattering teeth. "Least, some a these niggers up here does. Give a name to most anythin', a trapper will. Cain't be set with lettin' things be, without givin' everythin' a name. Just like Scratch—now, you take Scratch—he calls you Ol' Caleb. Yep. Most times just calls you 'Cale' for short. That Titus Bass be a spooky ol' nigger, for sure. You can lay your sights on that, my friend. He be the coon to call you most anythin'—so it ain't so special a name. Don't go gettin' that idea. Just that ol' man got him a name for everythin' up here: grizzes, Injuns, even mountain spirits he calls hoodoos. If that don't take the circle! Just like Scratch'd say himself!" The grizzly seemed intent on the muttering human at bay in the icy stream. She cocked her head first to one side, then to the other to make sense of the nonsensical sounds. "That's right, you listen up now," Josiah continued. "That be what the ol' man'd say to you. Why, you'd figger a man gets older up here through the y'ars an'd get him a lot smarter at the same time. Don't seem to've worked well on Bass, it don't. He gets scarier by the day, seems to me. Scarier without no sense, too. Talkin' 'bout his hoodoos an' medeecin—"

Josiah cut short his monologue on seeing the grizzly rise. She stood to all fours, bounced a few times on her front paws, then snorted. With that rude leave-taking the bear turned and ambled off into the willows. He heard her crunch through the underbrush until no more sounds

465

reached his ears. All was still once more except for the muffled gurgling of the stream shrouded with a film of ice around him. Josiah's jaw, having dropped in astonishment, now began to tremble. The trapper waited, concerned that the animal was laying a trap for him, believing that if he approached the bank too quickly the monster would rush from the willows to embrace him with her mighty arms. The minutes that followed were longer than those earlier, when he stood facing his adversary. Uncertainty again gnawed at his bowels. His eyes attempted at once to penetrate the underbrush and to glimpse the rifle lying on the bank.

"Ain't gonna get to move if'n you wait here much more," he mumbled as if to give direction to his numbed legs. Slowly the right one began to respond. It inched forward; the frozen foot within the moccasin skidded across the rocky bottom. "That's good—right there." He let the tired leg stop. Now he put weight upon it while he dragged the left leg past it. "Far 'nough." It seemed to help to talk to himself as he inched toward the stream bank. The growing light drew his eyes to a moving shadow among the willows. Josiah stopped, as if caught from behind, unable to proceed even if he had wanted to go on.

"Don' mean to give the willies, son," came the old man's voice. Shadow became form as Scratch stepped into view at Josiah's left.

"B-b-b-b'ar," Paddock chattered.

"Wha?" Bass drew around and surveyed the bank with quick rotations of his head. "You say b'ar? Whar? Whar it be, Josiah?"

Paddock slid his frozen feet across the last of the stream pebbles and his knees collided with the shelf carved out against the bank with his own hands. "B-b-b'ar g-g-g-gone . . . hope," he stammered, leaning forward to place both arms on the bank. Josiah sank down into the frozen grass on his chest while his legs from the hips down remained in the water. "G-g-gone, s-some . . . t-t-time 'go," he explained.

"That be why you froze up in the water, eh?" Bass bent forward and put a hand beneath Paddock's armpit. "C'mon up here, son." He tugged on the young man's weight without Josiah's help. "Cain't get you unfrozed up down there. Push, boy! Use them legs, you nigger!"

466

"Ain't got any left," the young trapper replied. "Don't feel 'em noways... might j-j-just falled off... y-y-you know."

Scratch knelt over the younger man's body and attempted to grip the wet capote. He struggled to pull Josiah from the water with one arm, but it was no good. Setting his rifle on the ground carefully and glancing around him into the willows once more for good measure, Bass now used both hands to grasp the coat behind the armpits and pull Paddock up the bank. In the growing cold even such slight exertion caused the older man to rest back on his haunches and suck in air while he surveyed Josiah's face.

"Left my rifle," Paddock began, "up here... grizz come 'long... keep me in the water. Sittin' on my rifle—"

"Ol' Cale thought he'd play with you, eh?" He leaned over the young man and pulled on Josiah's capote to roll him over. "Here now. Get you where I can take a lookee-see whilst I'm talkin' to you. My, my! You do look to be froze up, son. Lemme help you stand up, Josiah. We gotta be gettin' back to camp an' a fire soon. Cold's sunk in all I wants it to already, I'd be a nigger to bet." He half rose and struggled to get the young trapper up on shaky legs. "That be the trick, boy—put your arm round Ol' Scratch here," he said, putting Josiah's arm around his own shoulder, then leaning forward to hand Josiah his rifle. "Lean on your stick now, an' lemme have your weight. We'll jest hobble 'long back toward a fire an' some vittles. Had me notion you'd run on some troubles, I did. Gettin' on light a ways an' ain't laid eyes on you back to camp. Had me notion you'd run on some troubles." He led Paddock into the frozen marsh. "Figgered to come lookin' for you—jest in case you might be needin' Ol' Scratch once't 'gain."

"Coulda done it on my own—" Josiah began to protest.

"Hush your mouth now!" Bass interjected. "Jest keep your cold ass movin'."

As the two trappers were nearing their camp Asa stepped from the edge of the trees to watch them approach. Behind him among the aspens stood his wife holding the reins of their horses and the ropes attached to the pack animals. The short man looked squatter than usual this morning, dwarfed against the backdrop of the tall, slender trees. He was motionless at the approach of the two trappers.

"Jest don' stand there, McAfferty!" Bass hollered. "Punch that fire, will you?"

McAfferty turned without a word and pushed aside two of the pack animals to walk back into the trees where the partners' camp was located. Expressionless, the Nez Perce woman looked Bass and Paddock over as they passed by her, Scratch nudging the animals out of their way with a few jabs from the muzzle of his rifle. Asa, bent over the dying fire, was breathing life back into the coals and adding more kindling to the ashes and embers. He turned his head and looked up as he heard the shuffling of four moccasined feet.

"What'd the lad do to hisself?" he asked of Titus.

"Kept his head 'bout, it looks most like," Scratch responded. "Ol' Cale wanted to talk to Josiah, wantin' to wrassle with the boy, but the young'un jest stayed in the water. Real smartlike it was." He set Josiah down beside the growing fire and onto a large buffalo robe, which he pulled up and over Paddock's shoulders. Kneeling down, Bass tucked the robe tightly around his partner, then rose to help McAfferty stoke the fire. Asa now leaned back and let Bass continue the work on the fire he had rekindled.

"Grizz, eh," McAfferty began as he looked around to gaze at Josiah. " 'Thou art me hiding place; thou shalt preserve me from trouble; thou shalt compass 'bout me with songs of deliverance.' First time to meet a grizz an' ye walked 'way from it to tell, young Josiah. 'Twas the Lord's hands in it—"

" 'Tweren't no first time to meet up with a grizz," Josiah injected. He saw Bass turn from his fire-building duties. "Killed me one last winter."

"That be the true, son?" McAfferty asked. Bass snorted a little and wiped his nose with the back of his hand before smearing the mucous on his leggings.

"That be it, simple," the young man responded.

"Then there be a reason for it," Asa replied. "Meanin' ye meetin' up with a grizz. B'ars like that always mean trouble for a man—carryin' bad tidin's for him that crosses trail with Ol' Caleb. Man can walk 'way from a fight with the critter—why, may not even have 'em a tussle—but it carries bad tidin's for the man. Even the Injuns"—he glanced at his wife—"to them the b'ar is some big medicine. Meetin' up with a grizz is the Great Spirit's way of tellin' a man there's some big doin's in the makin' for him. There be somethin' comin' for ye, young Josiah—somethin' what no man as we know him got a hand in. I pray ye be ready for it."

"Clouds look to be bringin' snow our way this day," Bass injected when McAfferty had paused. He felt uncomfortable with Asa's words, knowing they were true. Already the uneasiness of their truce had grown in dimension. Already it was straining at him, tearing him like a grizzly's claws at his guts. And now McAfferty was putting into words those feelings Bass most feared. The uncertainty about their dance together in time was moving Scratch toward the inevitable, toward the moment when they would both know what the appearance of the medicine bear had presaged.

"Clouds, eh?" McAfferty accepted the interruption of his train of thought, as if he too understood some of the meaning of the grizzly's behavior. He shuffled a few steps around the fire after rising and stared off into the morning sky. "'He that observeth the wind shall not sow; an' he that regardeth the clouds shall not reap.' Don' spend all your time watchin' the sky, me friends. Ye be up here where beaver is waitin' for the takin'—"

"An' Injuns for the killin'—us or them," Scratch interrupted, leaning over to test the heat on the kettle warmed for breakfast earlier that morning.

"Ye look round ye now, Josiah. Rememberin' what ye do see ever' day now," Asa continued. "'God hath made the world an' all things therein, seein' that He is Lord of heaven an' earth, dwelleth not in temples made with hands.' This be where the Lord lives, young man." The whitehair swept the hooked arm out wide, dramatically embracing the whole valley. "It be too bad this be where the devil hisself makes a lodge, too." The arm dropped to his side.

Scratch poured some of the thick broth from the stew kettle into a tin cup and handed it to Josiah. "Here you, now, son. Drink of that an' it'll be to warmin' you from the innards out. Fire here to warm your outsides what are froze up, an' this here meat juice to put a fire back in your innards. Drink up, son."

Paddock cradled the cup between his two hands and brought it slowly to his lips. It was hot, and caused him to suck in a breath of cold air as it slid over his tongue and down to his stomach. A few more sips of the liquid fire and he could sense a warm change within. The cold knot that had been his stomach now seemed to be slowly untying. Josiah peered over the edge of his cup at the two older men staring at him drinking the hot broth.

"'Who satisfieth thy mouth with good things; so thy youth is renewed like the eagle's,'" McAfferty said, then turned toward the woman and the readied animals.

"Looks to be your're leavin' me off again, McAfferty," Bass said, standing slowly and moving to stand beside Josiah. Paddock finished another sip of the broth and looked up first to Bass, then to McAfferty.

"Aye, that I be, Mr. Bass," he said. "Tol't ye too I'd be wantin' toff by meself when we got to Three Forks country. Now jest be the time."

"You're reckonin' on your medeecin?" Bass inquired.

"Aye. Medicine. Prayers. What be it. I'll be seein' ye down to winterin' up with the Crows in Absor'kee, on down the Powder, don't ye reckon?" Asa turned finally to face Bass.

"I figger they be close to the Powder, maybe. Where she dumps to the Yallerstone, this winter," Scratch answered. "You'll be all to the alone up here, 'ceptin' the squar there, McAfferty."

Asa looked into the fire for a moment, then replied, "You're to know I don' worry me none 'bout takin' off on me lonesome, Mr. Bass. 'For all me life is spent with grief an' me y'ars with sighin'.' Don' figger it to be time to be worryin' now 'bout such things. Lots more for Asa McAfferty to put his mind to."

"You're headin' north from here?"

"Aye."

"Smack into Blackfoots."

"Aye." Asa put a foot into a stirrup and swung up to settle down on his saddle.

"Your medeecin leadin' you on up toward that way, eh?"

"That be the tale of it, Mr. Bass." McAfferty turned for a moment to motion his squaw aboard her pony. "'They will go up by the mountains; they will go down by the valleys unto the place which thou has founded for them.' The Lord leads an' Asa McAfferty follers."

"Don' be the fool now, you hear?" Bass instructed.

470

"You're takin' care of three now." He nodded at the squaw, who had adjusted her robe about her shoulders after mounting the pony. Asa turned to look at the woman, then looked back at Bass with a quizzical expression. "That's right, McAfferty. She weren't 'bout to be lettin' you know it, like many them Injun gals is. I'd lay set to her been carryin' your papoose for some moons now." Asa glanced once more at the squaw, who looked at him just as quizzically, not understanding the white man's tongue.

"How ye figger?"

"She's been sick some to each mornin'," Titus replied, "an' eatin' like a full-runned-down pony too. I jest figgered it might be, till I saw her one night as she left your robes to head back into the trees for a woman's duty. She's been keepin' that robe round her all this time so's you cain't tell it. But I seen her stomach, McAfferty. She's carryin' your baby." He nodded once again toward the squaw as Asa turned to look back at him. "I reckon it'll be jest after the first of the y'ar, soon, when the winter sets in real hard. You jest take care of the two of 'em till I see you come into Absor'kee."

The whitehair looked north, staring into the mists around the peaks as he spoke. "How fast ye be headin' out, fixin' to be gettin' into Crow country, Mr. Bass?"

Titus looked up at the small man mounted on the Indian pony, thinking what a strange question it was to be directed to him. "Well . . . well, ain't really thought 'bout it, now, Asa. Gotta raise me my cache, I do. Don' know how I might be feelin'. S'pose 'lot figgers on the weather. Might'n be trappin' our way on down; then, if'n she gets col't, really woolly, might jest point us on down that . . ."

"Jest take your time, friend," Asa interrupted. "Use ye your time for trappin'. Be cold 'nough when you find them Crow fires."

Titus squinted a little, a small furrow emerging between his eyebrows. "You . . . you jest take care of the two of them till I see you come into Absor'kee."

"'I will both lay me down in peace an' sleep; for thou, Lord, only makest me dwell in safety.' It be the good Lord's hand leadin' an' protectin' them, Mr. Bass, not mine," he said, nodding to both trappers he was leaving behind. Asa then nudged his pony forward, pulling on the halter ropes to bring his pack animals along. Over the edge of his cup of quickly cooling broth Josiah watched the pair leave. Scratch stood beside him, staring after the trailing pack animals as they wound their way out of the fringe of aspens and into the marsh. Bass clucked his teeth in comment on McAfferty's heading north and west; he was now a little afraid he would neither know what had driven the whitehair to select the Three Forks, nor know what was driving him into Blackfoot country. As the first soft flakes began to fall from the heavy gray sky, Bass turned to the young man on the ground.

"What he meant—us takin' us our time gettin' to Crow country, them fires be cold 'nough?" Josiah asked the older man.

Bass stared again in the direction the whitehair had taken. "I don' know—but we got us a lot to be doin' afore we can turn our bones east to Crow country anyways." He looked back at Paddock. "That must be gettin' cold on you." Scratch knelt to take the cup from Josiah. Over the kettle he paused a moment to watch the man and woman disappear in the snow. Then he slowly dipped the cup into the hot broth and pulled it out, brimful. The juice dripping down the cup he wiped on his capote.

"You ain't skairt none, are you?" Paddock asked. "Bein' up here where we are an' him takin' off like he did?"

"Me?" He leaned forward to hand the cup to Josiah. "Nawww. Not rightly. Ain't one to be skairt of Blackfoots. Them I can see." He slid down beside the younger man and pulled his robe around him. "It be what this here nigger cain't see what makes me some squampshus. Ain't Injuns what Titus Bass be on the lookout for now." He leaned back in his robe. "Was you skairt when that grizz come up to meet you, young'n?"

"Nawww," Paddock began, then thought better of his answer. "Well, maybe I was—jest a lil' some."

"Only natural, Josiah. A man in his proper mind be skairt of such a critter. It be when you cain't move with bein' skairt that a man's et up with buck ager—givin' you the tremblin' willies an' such. You had your head 'bout you, howsomever, stayin' in the water. Now if we can jest unfroze you, why, you'll come back with some pluck."

Josiah drew on the cup of hot broth for a few minutes

as Bass looked into the fire. Finally the young trapper swallowed a steaming gulp and asked, "Ever you run onto a grizz?"

"Shit!" Bass turned to look at his young companion. "Many's the time, son."

"Ever had one to grab you?"

"Huggin', you mean?" He gazed at the fire. "Ol' Cale hugged up to me once't. Had me only a knife. Stuck that devil critter with the knife clean up to green river an' I didn' pull it back out. That way the devil loses all his juices inside bleedin'—dyin' quicker that way."

"B'ar had your rifle, too, eh?" Josiah inquired.

"Nawww. Fired me a ball into the critter. Jest weren't a good shot. See you now, Josiah. There be jest two places where nigger can put his ball into one a them b'ars an' know his lead'll do the trick. One be jest under the ear, an' t'other be back an' down of his front leg. That be where the devil's heart is, lower'n most critters' 'cause of his size, I s'pose. Cain't always count to your ball goin' in an' gettin' through his thick hide, 'special round this time a y'ar when the grizz is gettin' fat for the winter. Jest under the ear is where you can lay your sights to killin' that devil." He looked into the lowering sky that dropped lacy snowflakes around their tree-canopied shelter. "You really kilt you a b'ar once't, you said, eh?" Bass asked without looking back at Josiah.

"Yep."

"That set Ol' McAfferty back on his ass, it did." Bass slapped his knee lightly. He chuckled softly, thinking of something private until Paddock interrupted him.

"What Asa said, 'bout meetin' up with a grizz—that true 'bout it bein' big medicine to meet up with a b'ar; mean, it spell somethin' big for a man meetin' up with one?"

Bass took a moment to answer, perhaps to choose his words. "There be those niggers up here what says that be the true, Josiah. Jest like the Injuns believe it. Yep." He looked at the younger trapper. "What say yourself, young-'un? You tol't McAfferty you faced down a grizz, had you a meet-up with Ol' Cale yourself. Somethin' bad happen to you after meetin' up with him?" His eyes came burning into Paddock's.

Josiah could not long look into Scratch's eyes. He dropped his gaze and stared into the fire, yet still felt the older man's watchful eye upon him. "Well," he cleared his throat falteringly, "I s'pose it did mean bad for me meetin' up with the b'ar I killed." Pausing to pull the buffalo robe closer about the sides of his face in the chilling air, Paddock continued, "There, ah... mean, I lost me a friend shortly after meetin' up with that b'ar."

"The feller you left Blackwell's brigade with?" Scratch asked.

"How'd you know 'bout that, ol' man?" Josiah questioned.

"Titus Bass jest one to be wantin' to know somethin' more 'bout the man he's ridin' with than Mr. Paddock was ready to tell him," Scratch replied. "Found me out jest what a uncertain varmint you be." He smiled broadly at the younger man. "Takin' off for the hills, 'stead of scamperin' back toward the settlements like'n they was thinkin' you did. That do 'most beat all!"

"How long you knowed 'bout it?"

"Day afore we got in that lil' scuffle with them Blackfoots down to ronnyvoo," he replied.

"You knowed all this time?"

"Knowed from then on I had me a partner what did some thinkin'." Bass looked out past the fire to the snow surrounding their camp shelter. "That's why I didn't put up much of a fuss when you wanted to stay an' watch them Injuns that night when all them other niggers was runnin' back up the valley to ronnyvoo camp. When you said you was stayin', I weren't 'bout to leave an' not see what t'other stuff you was made up of."

"Thought you up an' decided mighty quicklike—"

"I think me like that, boy," Bass interrupted. "Man gotta make his mind up mighty fast sometimes." He now turned back to look at Paddock. "How'd you lose your friend, son?"

"Trap... trap smashed his hand." Paddock cleared his throat and fought down the lump tugging again at his throat. Maybe, he thought, just maybe if he could tell a little about it, he might be shed of the weight of carrying it with him all this time. "Smashed all the way crossed his hand."

"Sounds like to be the man died of bloods poisonin'," Bass injected. "Somethin' like that can kill a man jest as sure as you'd put a ball into him—only... only it takes

474

longer with poisonin' like that. Man takes a long time to die in such a way—"

"It were all my doin'," Josiah blurted. "I thought he'd know how to be settin' traps. Said he did—watched me too. I shouldn've taken it for true..."

Scratch listened to the younger man's voice trail off, then said, "Go 'head, son. Tell me 'bout it."

"Ain't much to tell when you killed a friend, is there, Scratch?" Paddock responded.

Titus did not reply for several moments. He wanted his young partner to tell him more of the story, not so much to know the details of a man's death as to help Josiah shed the awful weight Bass was certain the young trapper carried—a guilt that would eat at you the rest of your days. However, he finally bit his tongue and decided to let it lie. "You finish your soup," he eventually said softly, beginning to snuggle down into the warmth of his robe. "Then you best pull the charges an' reload our guns for us, son. Then you get you some shuteye. Long 'bout sundown we'll go fetch your traps an' see what beaver you brought up to bait."

Paddock turned to watch the older man disappear beneath his buffalo robe. Gazing back at the fire he finished his broth slowly, lingering over the warmth it began to give to his body. After recharging the weapons in camp, Josiah leaned forward out of his robe to lay more wood onto the embers, then retreated into the warmth of the woolly fur. For a moment he stared out past the edge of the trees at the falling snow in the direction Asa had led his wife. It was strange the things Scratch knew, he thought, without anyone telling him. Like the baby. Just like the baby she was going to have. Josiah tried to imagine how the baby would look. He lay back in the robe and pulled it over his head as he closed his eyes. The thought of playfully tossing a little child into the air and catching it passed through his mind. It was a nice feeling to have inside himself with all the other, darker things. Chuckling softly at a vision of a little baby, its head covered with white hair and beard, and a hook where the right hand should be, Paddock drifted off to sleep.

*　　*　　*

"It be time to move out," Scratch said, bending low over the lump hidden beneath the buffalo robe. Then he put a hand on the lump, found a shoulder, and shook it gently a few times. "Josiah. Wake your ass up, son."

Paddock pushed the robe back from his face and looked up at Bass. He squinted a little and looked about as if disoriented, unsure where he was. Then he felt the cold begin to bite at him and recognized the snow continuing to fall outside their camp shelter. He remembered where he was. Josiah lay back down and pulled the robe over himself.

"Boy!" Scratch's tone was more stern. "Gonna fotch you up side of your head less'n you be movin'—now!" There was not the immediate response from the young trapper that Bass wanted so he slapped the side of the robe, his hand striking the form beneath the hide with a thud.

Josiah's face came shooting out of the robe to glare at the older man. "What'd you go an' do that for?" He pushed the robe down past his chest. "I was comin'. Just gimme time, ol' man!" Now Paddock pulled the robe free from the rest of his body before wrapping the capote closer about himself with a shiver.

"You're to be doin' a job when it's to be done now," Scratch replied, softening his voice somewhat.

"What job you talkin' 'bout now?" Josiah asked.

"Shit! You got more'n half dozen them traps strung out there." Bass swung his arm away from rebuilding the fire to indicate the marsh and the stream. "I ain't one to let you be a lazy nigger what leaves raisin' his traps past the sun gettin' down. You got beaver freezin' up an' snow layin' over your slides an' sets. Don' go playin' the lazy on me, boy. You come up here to this here country to be a child as makes his livin' trappin' the plews. That means there ain't but fewsome rules for the livin'. What there be are for savin' your ha'r an' hide, Josiah. You just foller them rules an' you'll live on till your ripe old age, like me." He had finished laying more pieces of wood on the small fire and now turned to watch Paddock retying the laces for the high-tops of his moccasins. "I don' put much on you. I'm jest askin' that what you do, you do right." Paddock looked up at him. "You go makin' mistakes— maybe takin' the short way round somethin'—ain't gonna make 'er up in these'r hills." Scratch looked above their camp through the branching tendrils of the low trees at

476

the sky. He had always loved the deep, cold blue of early evening after the sun had disappeared from the canopy overhead and just before darkness; time always seemed to hang heavy about him then.

Paddock finished the task of tying his moccasins around his ankles and rubbed his feet thoughtfully for a moment. "My feet are cold," he protested, thinking of the wet and cold into which they would momentarily plunge once again.

"They'll be col't 'til spring green-up, son," Scratch advised, leaning over the fire to absorb more of its warmth. "You'll jest have to be a nigger what's gonna be gettin' use ta that." He heard the young man slowly rustling behind him but did not turn to look in Paddock's direction.

"Let's be goin' to it." Josiah rose from the robe and cradled the rifle across his arms.

"Jest like that?" Bass inquired, looking up at Paddock.

"Just like that," the young trapper replied as he set off through the trees.

Titus scrambled to gather up his pouch and horn, slinging them over his shoulder before taking up his rifle. He looked down at the short-handled tomahawk he had laid out beside his gear for use as a camp ax. Stuffing it in the sash of his capote, Scratch set off a few steps behind Paddock. As they emerged from the trees at the border of the marsh, the air was swirling and dancing with the frigid rhythm of stormy gales. Now and then there were quiet interludes, when the snow glided silently down before it resumed flying in all directions. Both traveled silently, plodding through the mire, each step breaking a crust of ice before it sank into the freezing water that rushed into the hole each footstep made. At the edge of the stream Paddock stopped and momentarily surveyed the watercourse, looking first upstream, then down.

"You 'memberin' your sets?" Titus asked.

"I put my first down round here," Josiah pointed out. "Then went on downstream—just like you told me—from here."

"Find your sign?"

"I'm lookin' for it," the young trapper said, and bent over the ground looking around on the streambank.

"You be wastin' your time, an' mine, lookin' for nary a sign as'll be on the bank." Josiah raised back up and gazed at Bass after his words. "Only sign you got what's worth the lookin' be out there in the water, son. Your stick—that be the way your'n floats." He brought the rifle out of his arms and used it to point into the icy water. Here and there the larger stones dotting the stream's course were covered with white, lacy caps of snow. Among them in the darkening air one could see the tall pole placed in the water at the end of a trap's length of chain. Josiah spotted it and moved off to step from the bank into the stream. "Brung you 'hawk to be chippin' 'way the ice with." Bass patted the head of the weapon that hung from his coat sash. Paddock shook his head and continued into the water holding the loose flaps of his capote together in one hand. He shifted the rifle from right hand to left and made the careful steps it required to cross the rocky bottom of the freezing creek.

"Just pull 'er up?" he whispered back hoarsely to the man on the bank.

"Yep. All that's left save the skinnin'," came the reply.

Paddock raised his right arm into the air to shake down the sleeve of his capote, then dipped the arm beneath the thin crust of ice formed around the pole. His fingers located the ring at the end to pull it free from the rocky bottom. Josiah threw the stick up onto the bank, dancing and bouncing its way over the larger rocks with their shawls of white. He took a deep breath in the bitterly cold air and pulled the chain from the water. He felt the heaviness of the trap as it dragged along the bottom of the water. From the way it felt, he was sure the trap was not where he had placed it upon the shelf dug out of the bank. Instead, he was sure the contraption was coming to him from midstream, from deeper water. All was quiet as Josiah pulled the trap free from the water with a faint crackling of the icy film over the creek. Within the jaws of the trap hung a fat, heavy beaver. The sleek coat glistened with a liquid luster in the dimming light.

"That's one," Scratch commented approvingly. Josiah started toward the bank with his prize held high, suspended from his right hand. He tossed it on the bank and scrambled up behind it as best he could, gripping onto willow branches to give himself help in climbing the slippery, snow-slick grass.

"Whooo!" Paddock hooted triumphantly.

"I'd care to lay you set there be more for the young'un,"

Scratch remarked, "all kinda them critters jest layin' out there a waitin' for Josiah Paddock come pick 'em up out'n the water." He knelt down beside the animal and felt of it with his hand running over the fur. "Big'un', too." Patting the carcass's fat belly twice, he rose again.

"We skin him up now?"

"Yep," was Titus's answer. "You cain't be takin' the critter back to camp for the skinnin'. Too much smell round our diggin's now. Round here—where we are. You do the skinnin' here." He watched Josiah kneel over the animal and pull the big blade from his belt. "Take 'em back to camp to skin out, why, we'll be havin' all crazy, hungry critters for miles round these parts comin' in for the hopin'. Hopin' what blood they's smellin' be what meat they's to be tastin'."

Bass squatted beside the young man and looked all about him from side to side before continuing. "Skin it here an' you don' have to be a nigger what carries the whole thing back to camp, noways. Jest throw the body into the crik an' it'll float on down somewheres. Least-ways, it won' be layin' 'bout givin' sign of you, Josiah." He looked down at the skinning job being done by the young man. "That's right good. Skin it way down there on them legs." He nodded in approval as he watched the rest of the process. When Paddock pulled the hide from the body he began to lift the carcass to toss it into the stream. "Not yet, son," Bass whispered. "There's meat left to the critter what's best to pack with you for the eatin'." He took the knife from Paddock and sliced the flat, scaly tail from the body. After handing the knife back to the young man Bass held the huge appendage in both hands lovingly. "This here be meat fit for the trappin' man. Sweeter'n nibblin' an' chewin' till you're full of happy on some white gal's breasties." He smacked his lips almost unconsciously. "Some right good eatin'."

"Good, eh?" Josiah asked.

"Better'n them breasties—all soft an' mushy on them loverly white-skinned squars back to the settlements."

"When you ever been one to nibble on a white gal's breasties, ol' man?" the younger one inquired, mocking disbelief coloring his words.

"Why, boy, I et me many a time on such flesh as that." Bass then realized he was being made the goat of the question. "C'mon, you smart-assed lil' nigger-hearted

479

polecat. Roll you up your hide an' put it in your coat."
Bass rose and stuffed the beaver tail into the front of his
capote.

"Had you taste to them sinful ladies back to St. Lou,
eh?" Paddock chuckled as he finished rolling the freshly
skinned beaver hide, flesh side in, and put it inside his
sashless coat, stuffing down his leather shirt.

"You're delightin' in devilin' me, boy." Bass reached
out and gave the younger trapper a smart blow where he
sat.

"Whoa!" Josiah wheeled in the fresh snow on the
bank. "Got to you, huh, ol' man?" He danced around,
dodging back and forth in front of Titus.

"Shit," Bass replied. He made a quick move as if to
kick out again at his dodging adversary, then straightened
up. Paddock stopped his playful dancing. "'Tweren't always as ugly as I be now." He looked with a glance in
Paddock's direction. "Man can always get such as them
whore forkers to stick his poker in, plumb center." He
clucked once with his tongue against his cheek. "Any
nigger can blow his whistle in any cache hole what comes
'long. Ain't no special 'bout that." For a moment Bass
looked down at the tops of his moccasins, watching the
wet leather gather a crusting of snow, and standing still in
the short grass dusted with white. Then he turned to
Paddock. "Takes a man, it does, to know the differ'nce."
He looked away, staring at the stream again. He waited
for Josiah to ask him the difference between what and
what, but the question never came. The young man was
silent, intent upon Scratch and his words, standing motionless in the hush of the falling snow. Bass finally
turned to face Josiah, "You b'lieve you're the best happy a
man can be whatever's time you got a gal stuck center. Any
nigger can blow his whistle in a cache hole. It takes a man
what is worth his grit to know the differ'nce. An' a change
it be—layin' with a gal what loves you an' you feel like the
whole damned Rockies is turnin' round on you in layin'
with her." He pursed his lips a moment and dropped his
eyes from Josiah's. "A man comes on such a feelin' maybe
once't in his life—if'n he's a lucky child." He stooped to
push the just emptied trap into the sack containing those
Josiah had not set and rose to move off along the stream.

Paddock followed on his heels, their moccasins making soft crunching sounds against the few inches of freshly fallen dry and fluffy snow.

"You been there, Scratch?" Josiah whispered. Bass stopped and slowly turned around to look at his young companion. Paddock stopped abruptly, his right toes banging into the heavy trap sack Bass dragged behind him. His face grimaced at the smarting pain for only a second, then the hurting was gone in the numbing cold.

"Once't, son," came the simple answer. "Only once't. I was a dumb nigger what had to be movin' on—leavin' all that was good for the first time in my life. Had me squars afore, some as I even been a mule ass to calc'late was my wifes, but I ain't never had me again the feelin's like I had with that gal. White she was—"

"Back east?" Josiah interrupted.

"Don' know me of no white womens out here, does you?" he snorted briefly. "She were the kind that put the twinkle back in a ol' nigger's step, bring the dumb back to palaverin' an' naybobbin' again." He looked away from Paddock for a long moment as if deciding something, then gazed again into the young man's eyes as if the question had been decided. "She were the only thing I figger I ever loved. Awww, I care 'bout some few things, people too—but I mean really loved in all my days, Josiah. It were her. There's been them as've turned my meat to stone an' my innards to grits for a spell—yessirree! But that gal was one to make your innards shine! There's jest a differ'nce, you know? Man can play at bein' happy, jest as many a nigger'll do, but way inside he's gettin et up with the lonelies. Down inside where don' let no other man look, he's bein' chewed away." Scratch now turned back and continued moving through the willows dressing the edge of the stream, dodging back and forth through the bushes that bordered the bank.

"Scratch?" Josiah pushed up close to Titus's left shoulder. "Are you bein' et up inside?" It was Paddock who now waited for an answer that was not quick in coming. Bass continued through the willows, his eyes looking for the next trap set but his mind intent upon the answer he could give the young man.

"I got me near all a man needs, Josiah," he said, finally. "I got me good rifle what shoots true." He hugged the weapon a little tighter to his breast for reassurance.

"Best meat a man could ask of the good Lord brung him by that rifle. I got me good mule what's been a damned purty friend many a time to this here ol' coon—bless Ol' Hannah's heart. Got me whiskey when I needs a wettin'. Got me warm womens in my winter robes too. Out there." He swept the skyline with the muzzle of his rifle. "I got what jest a few of us have—some a best lookin' country the Lord put down for us niggers to gander at. That out there don' belong to no man, Josiah; an' I be one a handful what can live out here to see it. Maybe, jest maybe, it'll always be that way. Meanin', jest a few ever come out to make his stick to float in this country. An' this here nigger's . . . this here nigger's got him a friend or two in the hills: like Hatcher an' you—"

"Hatcher's gone, Scratch," Paddock broke in quietly. Bass stopped suddenly and wheeled on his young partner.

"He may be dead, but he ain't gone!" Titus snapped. Then he shook his head to the side. "Hatcher may be dead, young'un. But the devil be damned if he's gone." He nodded toward the trees across the swamp, at the mountains beyond them cloaked in mantles of white. "Take you a lookee there, my son. Jest stand there an' hear the winter talkin' to you, feel what's bein' said by them hills to you now." He fell silent a couple of minutes. "Now you tell me Ol' Mad Jack's gone, Josiah. You jest try to tell me he's gone. Sure, his bones might'n be buried back to a grave in Pierre's Hole. Dug up by some hungry critter by now, mostlike, but a man's body don' matter a piss much to him after while. You smell that air, Josiah, an' tell me Hatcher ain't with us right now." Scratch sniffled slightly and wiped his nostrils with the wooden sleeve covering his right arm.

"Hatcher's spirit's with us," Josiah commented softly.

"An' his medeecin," Scratch replied. "Yep, young'un, I got me more'n most men jest hanker for all theys life, right here."

"I think I . . . I understand."

"If'n you don' now," Bass began, then paused before he went on, "you will soon, Josiah."

"'Bout the lonelies?" the young trapper inquired.

"'Bout the lonelies, an' a lot more," came the answer. "The lonelies do theys eatin' on you when you're down, son. Man stays busy an' they don' devil you none." He looked back upon the mountains beyond their camp,

"Man jest keep hisse'f busy, listenin' to all what the hills tell 'im, all what Hatcher's spirit tells 'im, he ain't much lonely no more." There was a flicker of a smile at the corner of Bass's lips, hidden somewhat within the mustache and beard, before he moved away downstream.

The two men moved through the slowly darkening hours of dusk to retrieve the traps. Only one had not been a successful set. Scratch continued to chatter cheerfully over Josiah as the young man knelt over carcass after carcass in the skinning process. The conversation, quiet and laced with more tales of Scratch's years in the mountains, seemed to ease the numbing cold biting fiercely at Paddock's fingers. Again and again the hands were dipped into the icy water. Over and over they pulled the jaws of the traps apart to retrieve the furry prize of a successful set. The metal pulled at his flesh time and again, each time Josiah putting his frozen fingers into his mouth and sucking on them until he could feel each one tingling with some returning sensation. Each time it took longer and longer for the flesh to feel rewarmed, but now they had reached the last trap set.

Paddock pulled the beaver to shore and climbed up the bank wearily. It seemed as if his bones throbbed with the deeply aching cold settling within his joints already. As he set about skinning the animal, visions of a warm fire and hot stew played in his head. It helped to ease the pain he was not about to admit to Bass. Finishing by rolling the last plew up and placing it inside his leather shirt, Josiah threw the carcass into the freezing waters. He knelt again to force both hands into the snow, wringing the white stuff between the hands and through his fingers to wash them clean of blood and fat. Suddenly he felt Scratch's hand fasten tightly on his shoulder. Paddock winced a bit as he jerked his head up to look at the older man standing beside him. Titus made no sound, spoke no words. He didn't have to. There was only one finger put to his lips to tell Josiah all the young trapper needed to know. Hearts crawled slowly into throats as blood pounded faster and faster.

Then Bass did an unusual thing. He took his left hand and cupped it securely over his left ear, straining to hear with the right as his head turned slowly through half the points of the compass. Every few seconds of the slow, methodical rotation, he would stop and strain to listen all the more intently. Finishing the half circle, Titus brought his attention to bear on the dark shadows of a willow thicket that ran into a stand of trees to their right downstream. Now he had it spotted and nodded his head in the direction of the trees for Paddock to listen. Bass looked down at his young companion and slowly nodded his head in the affirmative. Josiah strained to hear what the older man had picked up with his ear. It seemed like hours since last he had taken a breath of frozen air. Finally he inhaled, then exhaled, slowly, quietly. He thought he heard something. He was not sure at first; the sound drifting to him across the heavy snowflaked air was faint. Then it became more distinct. It was softly crunching steps—footsteps. He listened intently, looking once up at Bass, whose attention was riveted on the willows that ran from the trappers' location into the trees. Then came a new sound. Soft snorting, like Bass clearing his throat, came to their ears. It was eerie—the way the soft, crunching steps would cease, followed by the gut-wrenching snorts. Strange that both sounds were coming from the same direction. The soft and the harsh. The first making the ears tingle with anticipation for the second, and the last sound ending all anticipation and prompting fear. The fear was more bone-numbing than the cold air wafting across wet, freezing hands.

The raspy sound now had a shadowy form to accompany it. As the shadow broke out of the willow clumps and spotted the trappers it had been smelling, the form stood to full height and came forward on its rear legs shakily. For a flickering moment Josiah's eyes were held open at the sight he had seen only twice before. Those eyes burned with the sting of cold snowflakes drifting against them on the breeze. He could not bring himself to look away or even blink, so fearful was he that the monster would move and he would not be ready.

"Grizz!" It was Bass who broke the spell that had paralyzed both men for endless seconds. Scratch's hand bit into Josiah's shoulder before it was gone, pushing the younger man to the right as Scratch darted to the left. Paddock landed on his right knee, startled. He did not think about what to do. But action came quickly, unexpectedly, instinctively. The mountain rifle was brought to his shoulder, after he pulled the hammer back in the weapon's upward movement. No time taken to aim. Paddock merely felt the sureness of the rifle as his cheek lay along the stock, his eye peering for an instant along the barrel as he touched the trigger. Nothing happened. Powder wet with snow! he thought. His eyes still on the animal approaching the stream-bank, Paddock wrenched his horn around and dropped a few grains into the pan after blowing it clear. Down snapped the frizzen and back to full cock went the hammer. He felt the cold wood against his cheek once more and jerked back on the trigger as his eye stared past the barrel to the animal's chest. A roar followed the spit of smoke from the pan. Josiah swore he had heard the ball thud and tear into the bear's massive chest. The grizzly roared her disapproval and slapped at the right side of her thorax where the lead had struck her. She tore at her side with a paw and roared again, turning to face Paddock. Shaking her head and drawing her lips back to expose yellowed fangs, the female grizzly began her advance on Josiah.

The young trapper rose halfway and stumbled backwards, ripping part of his coat off as he tore at the front of the garment. Inside he reached for the pistol, carrying a small-caliber ball ahead of a heavy charge. Pulling the pistol free from his belt, Josiah heard the roar of Scratch's rifle and jerked to look in the direction of the sound. The bear again turned her attention to Bass, pawing and scratching at the air with one arm as the other scratched at her chest just below the shoulder where Bass's ball had struck her.

"Goddamn!" Scratch hollered. "Bad! Bad medeecin!"

Josiah heard Titus take off through the willows toward the marsh. The bear dropped to all fours and began to prance after the older man. Paddock raised his pistol before the animal raced out of range and fired. She turned just as he pulled the trigger and the ball slapped against her heavy rear end. The grizzly shot forward a couple of steps and turned to look at her rear, then at Josiah, and back at her rear before snorting at the younger man. It was as if she were laughing at him for trying to hurt her.

"Meetin' up with a grizz is the Spirit's way of tellin' a man there's some big doin's in the makin' for him." McAfferty's words broke into the confusion gripping Josiah's mind. Dropping the empty pistol into the snow at his knees, he looked down at his horn to pull it up and poured a quick charge into the palm of his right hand before he heard the sound of footsteps busting through the willows, that sound of labored running as the older trapper slogged his way through the edge of the marsh. Paddock looked up from his loading, and watched Scratch beat his way slowly toward the trees that ran away from the marsh along the stream. Josiah's hand felt a ball and quickly pulled it from the pouch. Dropping it into the first inch of the muzzle he rose and pulled the wiping stick from the thimbles along the underside of the forearm. Into the muzzle it followed the ball and pushed the lead bullet home against the powder charge. The horn was brought to his teeth to pull the plug again and the dusting of powder rapidly spilled across the pan. As if by routine of practice the young trapper brought the frizzen down over the loaded pan as he pulled the hammer back in one motion. Up to his shoulder the huge weapon came and the trigger was pulled. The ball struck the grizzly just as she was turning to follow Bass. Again his shot missed the mark he had aimed for, just below and behind the foreleg. He blew out a quick curse at his repeated failure to bring the monster down. The bear turned toward him. She would attempt to maul the younger adversary who kept throwing lead her way.

"Scratch!" his voice broke through the icy air and echoed from the rim of hills across the marsh. Josiah saw that his partner had stopped and was pulling his stick free of the barrel. The grizzly had Paddock pinned to the stream.

"Get you ass into the water!" Bass screamed at him.

Paddock turned immediately and slid down the bank toward the freezing creek. A foot slipped and gave way, sending him to a sitting position as he continued his descent down the bank. Suddenly the foot caught against a tangle of chokecherry bushes and sent him head first into the water. His rifle flew into the air as he cartwheeled forward; he landed with his knees hitting against the stones dotting the bottom of the stream. Josiah rose to his hands and knees, forgetting the pain, pushing the cold from mind, with only one concern: to locate his weapon.

The grizzly snarled again, more loudly than before, her battle cry reverberating from the hills in the still air as Josiah could hear more noise from the willows as if a herd of ponies was busting through the underbrush. He turned to see first his rifle lying against the bank in the snow, half the barrel submerged in the water, then Bass dashing toward the stream. The bear was right behind Titus.

Paddock exploded off the creek bottom and lunged for his weapon, splashing and falling as he scrambled for the rifle. He remembered he had no charge down his barrel. In desperation he yanked at the powderhorn and turned it bottom up. He had not replaced the cap on the horn. No powder poured from the container. It was soaked from his plunge. In a fiery rage Josiah pushed the horn back to his side and took the rifle in both hands so that he held the weapon like a club. If here he was to make his stand, then he would do his level best to fight off the monster. Raising the rifle over his head in readiness, he watched the old man's dash toward him. The bear brought up the rear, scrambling much faster on all fours now. She lunged forward and took a swipe at Bass from behind, ripping off the bottom of his blanket capote with one huge paw.

The tugging Scratch felt from behind was his cue to whirl around on the bear. There was no longer any use in attempting a foot race with the grizzly. The time had come for a stand. In turning Scratch dipped low and brought his rifle up toward the animal's head. As she plunged forward at the trapper the muzzle of the weapon was shoved into her mouth. If the trigger were to be pulled the ball would enter the roof of her mouth and smash into her brain without the obstruction of thick cranial bones.

In the instant Bass found the trigger the grizzly drew her head back. There was a roar from the rifle and both trapper and grizzly were hidden from Josiah's view behind a curtain of powder smoke. The ball grazed the side of the bear's jaw, sending a portion of the bone and some teeth flying but leaving no mortal wound. She drew back and chomped at the air with her wounded mouth, tasting the acrid powder and salivating around the blood oozing from the small wound. She made a lunge with a paw toward the old trapper as Bass fell backward into the wet snow. Raising the rifle to place it between himself and the animal, Scratch could only think that this was a hell of a way for a trapper to go: a grizzly ripping his guts out while he lay beneath her alive through the agony. He lashed out with the rifle barrel in an attempt to strike the grizzly's sensitive nose. She jerked her head to the side out of the way and batted the weapon from his grasp with

487

a savage swipe of her left paw. The claws came back ready to strike the man, but some rustling of the willows to her left caught the grizzly's momentary attention. Two small cubs broke out from the brush. The flying rifle skittered to the ground and stopped at their feet.

The mother grizzly was now enraged all the more. Not only did she have two humans to contend with, hurting her thick hide with bullets, but she had her children entering the fray against her instructions. She had commanded them to remain behind, out of danger, while she went to investigate the strange scent, that smell of man, the odor of danger. But curiosity had overcome them and they came forth to join in the fun their mother was having.

She drew back from her stance over Bass and leaped at the nearer of the two cubs. With her two paws she delivered blows of punishment against the young animal's head. The cub turned from the beating and scampered away, whimpering as it burst past the second cub. Bass drew his knife and rose to his knees to plunge the blade into the mother's chest. He felt the weapon sink up to the guard, then he dropped back, leaving the knife within the bear. She turned back to look at the man scooting across the snow on his side, then made a swipe at her own flesh to rid her body of the sharp weapon embedded within it. The second cub now decided to cuddle with its mother, and raced to her side, where it attempted to climb aboard the large grizzly for some hugging love. Mother had too much hugging to contend with from the humans. The second cub received the same maternal reception as the first and went its way into the willows, whimpering in pain and confusion.

With only the tomahawk left to him, Bass pulled it from his belt and turned the handle in his palm for ready use. The bear's attention was drawn back to the man now. She attempted to grasp the weapon held at the end of the trapper's arm, trying to rip it from his grip. Titus brought the arm back away from her paw, feeling the searing pain shooting from his right hand into his lower arm. The hand was suddenly warm where it had before been cold, frozen with temperature and fear. Now it was becoming increasingly warm as he brought the arm back, crooked the elbow, and drove the 'hawk forward with all the strength left in the upper part of his body. From his lungs burst a gutteral cry of challenge. "Wa-a-a-a-a-gh-gh-gh-gh!" It was the same battle cry issued before by the grizzly that now exploded from the throat of the old trapper. In defiance of the death he felt sure would be brutal in its arrival, Scratch struck the monster behind the left ear, feeling the 'hawk blade crash through the skull and bury itself within her brain. The bear reeled backward and answered Bass's gutteral cry. She wavered a moment, then fell forward across his legs.

He lay there a moment, trembling with fear. A shudder shot through the grizzly's body and she moved no more. His arms shaky, Titus used them both to claw at the snow and the ground in order to pull himself from under the weight of the fallen animal. Desperately he fought to free himself from the furry prison that held him down. Over and over he snorted with the guttural cry of the battle, struggling to remove himself before the bear rose to finish him off. Clawing and snorting, he battled the wet, dusty snow and frozen grass, fingernails filling with black dirt and pain. Frantic in his fear, Bass attempted to push the animal off his useless legs. He buried his hands within her dark blonde fur and heaved. Then he saw the blood covering his right hand and soaking into the light colors of the dirty capote at the wrist. Staring at the bright blood for only a moment, Scratch snorted repeatedly as he lashed out at the heavy prison, striking, tearing, pushing, and pulling at the monstrous carcass.

"Wa-a-a-a-a-gh-gh-gh-gh!" He was like a man possessed, struggling with his fallen adversary. "Wa-a-a-a-a-gh-gh-gh-gh!" Again and again the terrifying sound bounced back into the valley from the hills. The battle cry surrounded him. His own fear enveloped him. Bending forward, Bass bashed his head over and over against the carcass, repeatedly crying out and sobbing. He could not catch his breath now, but still the loud cry welled up within him, seeking freedom from his bowels. He gasped for air, but still the sound came. He could not now recognize it, for his ears were filled with the hot pounding of his own blood, beating its way to his brain with the drumming of racing footsteps. It was deafening. His lungs struggled for oxygen as he fought against the freezing air. His face stinging from the salty perspiration pouring over his face, Scratch fought to keep his eyes open against the pain. Each time they would voluntarily open flakes of frozen snow struck them and the eyes closed involuntarily. He went back to beating his head against the carcass, crying out in desperation as his whole body pushed and pulled at the weight gripping him.

The sound of footsteps beside him he felt sure was the monster rising. He doubled his efforts and cried out with a voice now hoarse from the agony of harsh, repeated use. Straining to clear his vision from sweat and snow, Scratch thought he imagined a shadow struggling over the carcass. A new sound penetrated his ears.

"Scratch! Scratch!" the sound repeated. "It's gonna be all right!" the voice said. "It's all right now!"

The shadow became hands and arms pulling at the bear's body as Bass pushed. The old trapper felt the weight of the carcass rolling down his legs and finally off his feet. It was as if hell had been lifted from his body, that crushing weight a man feels he might bear for eternity. Scrambling across the grass a few yards, scooting on his side through the snow like a half-crazed animal, Bass whimpered and moaned. Long in catching his breath, he brought his right hand to his face to wipe clear the clouds over his eyes. Deep from within his chest rose the shudders that would not leave him. From his bowels came those paralyzing fears each man attempts to keep locked in some dark, hidden recess. Fears each man attempts to hide from himself.

Josiah was over him now, attempting to grasp the older trapper by the shoulders to calm him, to reassure him. He was having to yell in Scratch's face to make himself heard over the continuing battle cry coming from the older man's throat. Paddock finally took hold of Titus, one hand on either side of his face, and held on as if Bass's life depended upon it. Scratch struggled to free the grip of those hands holding his head. He slashed away at them with his own hands and arms, jerking his head from side to side and snapping at the imprisoning vise with his teeth. His mouth contacted one wrist and he sank his teeth into the leather covering it. Paddock yelled with surprise and yanked the arm away, then sent a clenched hand against Bass's face. He felt his knuckles spread against the old man's cheek in the blow; the head jerk backward, the body toppled into the snow.

He knelt over Scratch for a moment catching his own breath, looking down at the contorted face now twisted in pain and dark fear. Josiah saw the blood across Scratch's cheeks and eyes, the dark red smeared in crazy finger-painted patterns over the face. Scooping some snow into his right hand, Paddock brought it to Bass's face and began gently to wash the blood away. He did not know where the wounds were, hidden by the dried, frozen blood. The cleansing dissolved the blood but located no wound. The cold snow slowly brought Scratch to consciousness.

He jerked as he blinked his eyes, then recognized the shadowy form above him to be his partner. The tension drained from his body like a tingling charge suddenly shut off. He felt the release and plopped his head back into the snow. The cold felt good against his face.

"You're back on my trail now," Paddock soothed. "Just ease off—just ease off some now." Gently he patted the snow against the older man's cheeks and forehead until he could locate no wounds in the flesh. A shudder now and then sputtered through the old trapper's body, but he lay still beneath the nurselike ministrations.

Finally Josiah leaned back from his bathing. Scratch rose to an elbow and looked past his friend to stare at the grizzly. "It be dead? She dead?" he asked.

"Like a stone," Paddock answered.

Bass rose further into a sitting position and started to dust some snow from what was left of the torn capote. Searing hot pain shot through his right hand and up the forearm again. He winced and looked down at the hand. "I'll be god——" His words stopped abruptly as he stared at the wound. Holding the appendage out before him in his lap, Scratch surveyed the damage committed by the grizzly's strike against the 'hawk-holding hand. The little finger was gone completely and all that was left of the finger next to it was a short stub. They had been brutally yanked away from the hand by the sharp claws as the bear swiped and tore at the hand that eventually sent death crashing into her brain. He turned the hand over and over, looking at the back, then at the palm, both sides covered with frozen, coagulated blood. The hard red fluid had stained the wrist of his shirt and was matted on the bottom of the capote sleeve with dirt and fur he had wrenched from the grizzly in his desperate struggle to free himself from beneath the animal's weight.

Paddock stared down at the hand, transfixed and hypnotized. His mind filled with the sight of the bloody appendage staring back at him in the frozen air. There had been a hand like this one once before. Blood and cold. There were only two colors now as he stared at the wound. White and red. Nothing more in his mind except the ill feeling tumbling around inside his stomach and the gusts of wind whipping snowflakes against the side of his face. Bass moved forward to stand, still cradling the wounded hand in his left, and bumped into Josiah as he rose on wobbly legs.

"Does I need to be helpin' you up?" Bass asked as he rose shakily. "I be the one as had near half my hand tored off, young'un." He braced against a gust of wind, then almost lost his balance as the blast of air raced past.

Josiah watched the hand rise, then stood up himself. Scratch bumped against him and Paddock gripped onto the older man's arm to steady him. "Let's be gettin' you back to camp," he suggested to Titus. Still holding onto Bass, Josiah turned to look around on the ground for a moment until he located what he was in search of. After steadying the old trapper Josiah stepped over to the grizzly and pulled the huge piece of Scratch's coat from under the bear's body. Packed with snow, Josiah used the woolen cloth to wrap the wounded hand. He picked up Scratch's rifle and laid it across the older trapper's arms. From there he quickly dumped the pelts he carried into what room was left in the trap sack, picked up his own rifle, and motioned for Bass to head for camp. Paddock stopped for a moment at the side of the fallen grizzly before dropping the heavy sack. He knelt and pulled free the tomahawk from the bear's brain, then noticed the knife buried deep within the animal's chest. With the 'hawk handle stuffed securely in his belt, Josiah pushed aside the bear's foreleg and yanked the knife free. He wiped both sides of the blade clean against the bear's fur and handed the knife up to Bass.

"Didn't wanna leave this here, did you?" he asked as Scratch took the knife to lie in the crook of his left arm beside the rifle.

"Only till she done her job on the devil critter." Bass looked at the weapon. "Only till she bled the b'ar out afore the critter bled me." He coughed and winced a little at the corners of his eyes from the pain. Josiah stood up beside him. "Always leave your sticker in the critter; it'll bleed 'em out in the innards," Bass said. Paddock nodded once and Bass took it as the cue to leave. "C'mon, son. Got me some sewin' to be done." He started off through the willows, then stopped and turned to face Paddock as if in afterthought. "Josiah, you'll..." He paused a moment to glance at the grizzly, then gazed at the young trapper again. "You'll see to it that the critter's skinned proper an' you be bringin' it back to camp? The hide?"

"Yep." He attempted to nudge Scratch in the direction they would take back to their shelter.

"Nawww," Bass shook the nudging arm free from his own. "I mean it true, son. You'll see to it that the critter be skinned proper an' her hide brung back to me?"

"Yeah, yeah," Josiah assured impatiently.

"I mean it. You promise me. You gotta promise me," he stressed. "Tell me true, you'll promise it. That you'll be doin' it for me."

"Aw right, Scratch. I promise." He attempted another nudge against the older man's body.

"Nawww. That ain't good 'nough," he replied adamantly. "Tell me whole thing in words, Josiah. Tell me what you're promisin' this here ol' man."

"Shit, now. You know—"

"Tell me, boy."

He looked down at the grizzly before speaking. "I promise you"—now he looked back at Bass—"I promise you I'll skin the critter out proper, like you say me to, an' bring her hide back to camp, back to you." Looking back at the monster on the ground, Paddock asked, "What in hell you want with the hide for anyway?"

"Said it yourself."

"Huh?"

"I may be a nigger what's needin' that hide in hell—"

"You ain't goin' to hell."

"All kinds a hell for a man, Josiah. All kinds." His words were quiet as he turned and led Paddock into the frozen marsh.

They eventually made it back to camp after a stumbling, staggering battle across the frozen landscape. After pulling the beaver tails from within the front of his shirt, Scratch plopped down beside the fire and took a knife out to poke at the ashes. Here and there live coals were exposed. Paddock dropped the heavy sack near the woodpile and pulled some pieces of timber over to the fire. With them he brought the exposed embers to full life and the growing flames climbed to brighten the darkness now veiling the camp. The shadows were pushed back somewhat by the time he brought forward the kettle and placed the stew over the fire.

"Best be heatin' up some water, fer cleanin' them guns," Bass remarked from his robes.

"Ain't got us 'nother kettle." Paddock rose and looked around.

"Get you one a them cups." Scratch nodded. "Fill 'er up with snow an' set it on the fire. Gonna be a needin' some hot water for cleanin' my paw, too."

After he buried the rolled beaver plews in a pile of drifted snow outside their shelter, Josiah turned back to the fire to do as he had been instructed. Having scooped snow into the cups and set them at the edge of the flames where they would be balanced atop two burning logs, he turned to retrieve the cleaning gear from among their plunder. From time to time during the cleaning and scouring, then reloading of the weapons in camp, Josiah would stir the warming stew in the large kettle. When finally finished with the weapons, he placed another cup of snow over the fire to melt, then leaned forward to stir the kettle once more.

"Leave that be, Josiah," Bass instructed. "Find for me my medeecin plunder." He nodded in the direction of his packs. On hands and knees, Josiah crawled to the baggage and started a search for the one small parfleche. Scratch leaned toward the fire, suddenly very chilled in the rewarming, feeling for the first time now the perspiration frozen in icy rivulets down his back and across the hair of his chest.

"This here it?" Paddock inquired, holding up a small rawhide parfleche, painted in light colors by some nameless Indian artisan.

Bass nodded. "Yep. Bring 'er here to me."

In sliding back over to the fire, Paddock felt the flushes of returned warmth, just enough to remind him how cold he had become. He was now very conscious of the frozen clamminess of his buckskins as they began to soften and thaw. Straining both arms, he tugged at the shirt to keep it from sticking to his body.

"Them skins'll dry jest fine—you leave 'em be," Bass commented. "Lay you out that parfleche for me, so's I can tell you what I'm needin'."

Josiah untied the thongs that held the small rawhide satchel closed. Carefully he pulled the four flaps apart to expose the contents. Within were many small soft leather sacks tied with thongs. Among them were pieces of various plants: roots, stems, and leaves in addition to colorful dried petals which once adorned mountain wild-flowers.

"Need get me some more puffballs," Titus remarked. "Be after next green-up mostlike afore we get down to the prairie."

Tangled in the herbage were several strands of thick animal tendon, sinew for sewing; and stuck securely in a flat piece of soft leather were two large metal needles. Titus took his left hand away from the bundle on his right and pointed out a root to his young partner.

"Take you a chaw of that in your mouth an' start mashin' it up."

Paddock bit off a chunk of the acrid-tasting root and ground into it. A bitter taste exploded in his mouth; he balled up his face to spit it into his hand with a growling sound. "Ugghh!"

"Bite'll be gone jest as soon's you get 'er chewed, son," Scratch coaxed. Josiah brought the hand to his mouth and popped the root back between his cheeks. As he mashed it between his jaws the bitterness faded. Then he swallowed hard, quickly, to rid his tongue of what bitterness remained in the lump on his tongue.

"This good 'nough now?" He brought from his mouth the pulpy root dripping with saliva between his fingers.

"Looks to be," Scratch answered. "Your water ready for me?"

Josiah turned to the cup and noticed it had begun to boil. He dragged the cup across the logs with the end of his coat sleeve and set it in front of the older man. Bass unwrapped the hand, now wet with melted snow and what little blood still oozed from the wounds. Grasping the right wrist in his left palm, he leaned forward and slowly dipped the hand into the tin cup as best he could. The hot water convulsed his whole arm in pain.

"Ah-ahgg! Mother of whores bite down on my ass!" he growled and yanked his hand back out of the water. "Let's you try 'nother way. Take this here piece a my capote." He pushed the scrap across his lap toward Paddock. "Dip 'er in the water there. Then's you can wash my hand down."

Josiah put a corner of the woolen cloth into the water and began to wash the wounds around the missing fingers. It was not a pretty sight, torn and excess flesh having to be pushed this way and that in the simple cleansing. He plopped the root back inside his cheek and laid the wounded hand across his left now to steady it. Again and again he dipped the cloth into the water and brought it dripping to the wounds. The first knuckle of the ring finger could be seen staring back in stark whiteness.

"That's good." Bass drew his hand away from Josiah's grip. "Put the root in the cup to keep it wet—keep it hot." Paddock spit the pulpy mass into the tin cup and looked up at Scratch as if to ask what was to be done next. "Back there, in my plunder—where you dug out my medeecin—you'll find you a small tin, with a cork in the top. Bring 'er to me."

Josiah handed the small tin bottle to Bass, who put the cork between his teeth and pulled it free of the container. Scratch spit the cork into his lap and raised the bottle to his lips. In the firelight the dull sheen of the bottle cast rays of light at Paddock.

"What's that?" he asked, then added jokingly, "Your trader's whiskey?"

The container was brought down from the older man's lips and offered for Josiah to smell only. "Here, take you smell there," offered Bass.

He took a whiff of the tin. "I'll be damned!" he exclaimed quietly. "Had me no idea you brung 'long none of that with you from the Hole." Bass put the tin back to his mouth and gulped repeatedly as if intent on emptying it. "You got you more of that, ol' man?"

"Only one other, like this." He shook the bottle slightly. "All I could keep 'way from them likker-lovin' hounds back to ronnyvoo." He licked his lips and leaned back so that he could rest on his side with the right hand laid out near the light of the fire. "You ain't gettin' you none, if'n that be what you're askin'. Part of my medeecin for mendin' a man up."

"You're gonna be a stingy nigger with your likker, eh?" Paddock leaned in close to Scratch's face, smelling the hot peppers and sweet molasses on the old man's breath. "Well," he moved back, "you just keep 'er to yourself. Don't want me none if that's the way you're gonna be. You're the skinned polecat what's needin' the juicin'. I ain't the one as got chawed an' clawed up by no mama b'ar."

Bass pulled the bottle from his lips. "That were your b'ar, Josiah. One you run onto this here mornin', looks to be." He gulped at the bottle. "Weren't my b'ar."

"Just who you tryin' to make b'lieve that, Scratch?" he asked quietly. "Grizz this mornin' didn' have her no cubs 'long. An' I should know—the critter was standin' over me long 'nough. So, just who you tryin' to make b'lieve that story that it were my b'ar? Me...or you, ol' man?" Bass didn't answer. He looked down at the container of whiskey and brought it thoughtfully to his lips. "Just what was it McAfferty had hisself to say 'bout such things? 'Meetin' up with a grizz is the Great Spirit's...'"

"'Great Spirit's way of lettin' a man—'"

"Yeah. 'Way of lettin' a man know there's some big doin's in the makin' for him.' Big doin's."

"Bad doin's," Bass corrected.

"Like gettin' your hand torn off, eh?" Josiah asked.

"Shit!" he snapped back and pulled another slug of the whiskey from the tin bottle. "Wish't I was young an' stupid like you be, Josiah Paddock. If stupids was beaver dollars, why, I'd be back to St. Louie wearin' fine silks an' smokin' big ceegars, talkin' nasty to them red-dressed ladies right 'longside Ol' Ashley, Lisa, an' Billy Sublette hisse'f. I could cash in your stupids for beaver dollars an' never have to work my ass of 'nother lick ever more. Shit! Boy, ain't you l'arnt you nothin'?" He shook his head slowly, dramatically now. "Wish't I was so stupid as you be, Josiah—to b'lieve that the only bad doin's come from meetin' up with a grizz be a tored hand. Mother of whores, bless me on Sundays! That ain't the half of it, son. That ain't even the *half* of it!" He took another long gulp and swished it around inside his cheeks before swallowing. Offering the bottle to Josiah he said, "Put the cork back to the top. I'm gettin' where you can sew on me now."

Paddock set the corked tin aside and looked at Bass expectantly. "Well?" he finally asked.

"Well?" Bass retorted, looking at Josiah staring back at him motionless.

"Well, what the hell I'm to do now?" Josiah snapped.

"Mother of—" He leaned back his head as if to laugh, then glared at Josiah. "If'n that don' take the circle—this mule-ass does!" He laughed lightly now, then was caught up in a fit of coughing until he had his throat cleared. "You're gonna sew up my hand! You laid out all the proper doin's for it. You're gonna sew up my hand. That's what you're gonna be doin', straightway."

Paddock looked down at the open parfleche, then back to Scratch's face. "With what I'm s'posed to sew you up?"

"Stupid shit! I could be a rich man with your stupids! With the sinew! Good 'nough for the skins you're wearin'. Right? Good 'nough for the skin over my bones, Josiah Paddock. Rip you a lil' thin piece a the stuff from that knot with your teeth, one 'bout like thread it's gotta be." He leaned back to rest his head on the crook of his left elbow and began to hum some off-key notes while Paddock prepared a long thin strand of the animal tendon that was to be the thread in the open-air suturing.

"Now what?"

"Huh?" Bass lifted his head a little, fighting the fuzziness he felt across his face from temple to temple. "Oh, you're not gonna get that sinew through my skin less'n you got a needle on it, boy!" He then set to chuckling some more.

"You want me to sew you up with one a these?" Paddock held up the piece of soft leather that secured the two needles. He looked from them to Scratch's face.

"Ain't got you nothin' better, does you?"

"I'll . . . I'll tear you up with 'em! They too big!"

"They's all I got, Josiah Paddock," he slurred. "Let's jest be hopin' your mama teached you real good 'bout sewin' back to the settlements," he said, giggling and sputtering in his inebriation.

Josiah chose one of the large needles and placed the end of the sinew in his mouth to wet it. He was finally able to get it through the eye of the needle, then scooted forward to pick up the wounded hand so that it could be placed across his lap. "You're feeling all right for me to be doin' this, are you?"

"Feelin' fine, son," Bass lisped a little. "Right pert, an' that's a fact. Ain't no baldface. Ain't no baldface 'tall, boy."

Paddock pulled the flesh over the white knuckle of the ring finger, drawing it up between the thumb and index finger of his left hand and plunged the thick needle into the gathered skin. Bass winced a little but did not move his hand from Josiah's. "Hurtin' you?" Josiah asked.

"Ain't hurtin'. I feel you down there—jest s'prised me is all. Jest you shut up an' keep stitchin' on me. You ain't hurtin' me none."

Paddock pushed the needle and sinew back an' forth through the flesh, drawing the skin tightly over the knuckle. He thought to himself how fortunate this was a jagged, torn wound that had left enough excess skin to complete this suturing process. Again and again he dabbed the finger with the wet cloth, then began his work on the little finger. Carefully he pulled flesh over bone and did the best he could with the torn tissue. After half an hour's work the two fingers and the outside of Bass's right hand were sewn up.

"You done?" Scratch asked after he realized Josiah was finished yanking and pulling on his flesh.

"Best I can do, Scratch."

Bass lifted the hand shakily and stared at it, turning it over and over to inspect the crude sutures. "Looks to be fine, son. Your mama be proud of you, boy, real proud, she'd be." He plopped his head back down on his elbow. "You get your sticker blade hot in the fire there; run 'er over real quick on them places you sewed up. Then put the root down over 'em an' wrap my hand up. Get to it." He closed his eyes, the lids refusing to stay open any longer.

Josiah drew his knife from his belt and placed a few inches of the blade into the coals to heat up. Within a few minutes of waiting for the metal to become hot, he could hear Bass snoring in stuporous sleep. Finally Paddock drew the knife from the embers and cradled the wounded hand in his own left again. Across the remains of the ring finger he pulled the heated metal. Scratch jerked up, pulling the hand away from Josiah. He swore a minute, then lay back down, telling the young trapper to get the job done as quickly as he could. Then he lost consciousness. Over each of the wounds Paddock drew the knife, smelling the seared flesh and hearing the faint crackle as the tissue and sinew burned. Next he took the pulverized root from the tin cup and smeared it over the sutured flesh and finished by tearing some strips from the piece of woolen capote with which he bound up the wounded hand.

Josiah rose to pull Scratch's robe over the sleeping man and sat back down to dip thick stew fron the kettle for himself. He blew on the hot liquid before putting each bite into his mouth, staring out into the dark night as he chewed on the large chunks of boiled meat. The light from the fire danced against the falling snow drifting down around their camp. He ate slowly, making a ceremony of the meal well deserved. He was not sleepy when he finished eating so he lighted a bowl of tobacco and leaned back into his robes.

Later he knocked the ashes from the pipe and sat up, wondering what to do to occupy himself while he could not sleep. Josiah decided to make some coffee. With the water and grounds finally set over the coals to boil, he turned back to retie the parfleche of Scratch's medicines. Taking it and the tin of whiskey back to the old man's packs, Paddock started to stuff them inside the bundles. His cold fingers felt the pages of a book and he pulled the volume free. Scooting back to the light and warmth of the fire, Josiah returned his rifle to its place across his lap and opened the cover. Across the title page was written: *A Collection of Shakespeare's Greatest Tragedies from the Master of the English Stage.* Below was the date, 1824, barely legible from greasy fingerprints; dirty smears obscured the name of the publisher in London.

"Englishers in everythin'," he mused, wondering about the long path the volume had taken from the British publisher to the east coast of America, thence overland to the heart of the Rocky Mountains, where an economic struggle was being waged between the two sovereign states for control of beaver country. What a strange object to be holding in his lap at this time, in this place, Josiah thought. But no more strange, he decided, than the Hudson's Bay dagger McAfferty had held across his lap the night Josiah was given his skins. Slowly he turned through the pages of preface and introduction, reading without purpose for the want of something to do until Bass stirred and awakened.

"You best be sleepin' again now," Josiah suggested quietly.

"Up here next door to Blackfoots country?" he snorted in a whisper.

"You weren't all that damned quiet awhile back."

"It were the likker talkin', son, only the likker," he replied, lifting his head a little to sniff the air.

"Smellin' Blackfoots?"

"Nawww. Jest your stew," Bass answered. "Get me some, will you, Josiah?"

Paddock put the book down beside Bass and rose to dip some of the thick soup for Scratch. "Get this here warm in your belly, you'll be wantin' to rest your bones again."

"Maybe not. Leastways, not right away," was the reply.

Josiah turned around with the bowl of stew and saw Titus leaning over the volume, staring at the pages intently as if to make out the words he should have been able to read. "You'd rather read that book than eat, eh?"

"Nope." He set the book down. "Gonna eat." Bass took the bowl in his left hand and set it on the ground near him. He glanced up for a moment at Josiah and smiled. He took a dripping spoonful to his open mouth, then spoke again around the hot stew. "*You're* gonna read to me, Josiah."

Paddock pulled his robe around his shoulders after taking his place by the fire once more. He was probably just as anxious to do some reading to Bass as Scratch was anxious to have Josiah read to him. It was a diversion on this blustery, freezing night. The wind now and then moaned through the trees like an answering chorus to the howls of the wolves among the hills. Each gust made the flames dance and jig against the pages as the young trapper opened the volume once more.

"*Macbeth*," he began, then looked up at Bass. "You want this first'un? *Macbeth*?"

"Best place as any, startin' with the first'un," Scratch garbled around his hot stew.

"If it suits you." Paddock looked down at the pages. "Act I. Scene 1. Takes place, it does, in a desert area—"

"'Bout like that we cross't jest afore we run onto the buffler? An' Injuns?"

"S'pose so," he answered, a little disconcerted at the interruption but not raising his head to answer the older man's question. "There's a lotta thunder an' lightnin' here

501

now—you gotta picture that in your mind, Scratch. Lotta thunder clappin' an' lightnin' boomin', with the lightnin' shootin' cross't the whole sky, lightin' ever'thin' up ever' now an' then." He cleared his throat as his eyes ran quickly over the first few lines before he began to read them aloud. "Uh, you gotta remember this here story was writ long ago, Scratch. So . . . these here people talk sorta strange . . . diffr'nt we do now. You know."

"Go 'head. Go right 'head." He nodded toward Josiah and motioned with his left hand holding the dripping spoon to have his young partner continue, despite any foreseen difficulties in understanding the language in the drama.

After clearing his throat once more, Paddock began to read aloud. " 'First Witch: When shall we three meet again—in thunder, lightnin', or in rain?

" 'Second Witch: When the hurly-burly's done—' "

" 'Hurly-burly'?" Scratch interrupted with a full mouth of soup. "What's that? What be 'hurly-burly?' "

"Reckon somethin' noisy an' such goin' on," he answered. " 'When the hurly-burly's done, when the battle's lost an' won—that tells it.' Hurly-burly's' be like a battle, with all the noise an' shootin', screamin' an' men runnin' everywhere for their lives. You pick it up?"

"Yup."

" 'Third Witch: That will be ere the set of the sun.' " He looked up at Bass to see if he had another question, but the older man merely nodded for Josiah to continue.

" 'First Witch: Where the place?

" 'Second Witch: Upon the heath.' "

"Where this 'heath'?" Scratch interjected.

"How the hell should I be a nigger what knows what a 'heath' is?" he snapped back. "Prob'ly in England, most like. You want me to read the story to you—or sit here givin' you lessons in everythin' I don' know?"

"You do that ever'day, boy," Bass commented, then snorted with a short chuckle.

Paddock chose to ignore the statement on his ignorance of the ways of mountain men and instead dove back into the reading of the play. " 'Third Witch: There to meet with Macbeth.' "

"He be the one the whole story's named after, ain't he?" Bass looked at Paddock's face just as he asked the question and saw the young man's lips drawn tightly in a straight line across his face. "He a booshway, he some-body? All right. All right. I won' be askin' so damned many questions of you, son. Go 'head. Read to me."

"'First Witch: I come, Graymalkin!

"'All of the Witches: Paddock calls—'"

"That's your name, boy!" Bass interrupted again. "They got your name in that ol' book! You be in that story, too?"

Grim-lipped, Josiah looked up into the older man's face. "I ain't in this here story, you dumb shit-head, mother polecat. An' I don't know what my name doin' in the story. You just shut your goddamned buffler-stinkin' yap an' listen to the readin'. You hear?"

"Anythin' you say. Go on, Josiah," Scratch replied innocently. He dipped the spoon back into his bowl of stew and brought the left hand clumsily to his mouth, dripping the soup on his leggings.

"'All the witches say: Fair is foul, an' foul is fair: hover through the fog an' filthy air...'"

It shook her out of a restless slumber. Opening her eyes, the old woman heard the sound penetrate the lodge again. She sat up slowly, still groggy. The gray, dim light of early dawn barely allowed her to see her exhaled breath that billowed in short bursts before her face.

Her man suddenly jerked upright with the loud voices that mixed with the distant booming. She threw the heavy robe to the side. Her man bolted from his bed across the lodge. From above him he took down his rifle, then quickly discarded it upon his bed. Instead, he quickly chose the bow and cougar-skin quiver of arrows. He rushed from the lodge as she draped a thick blanket about her shoulders.

She plunged across the inches of new, falling snow, feeling its icy sting against her wrinkled face as she pushed toward the low reports of the rifles and the screaming voices. Dogs were yowling as children cried out and women shrieked at one another. The old woman stopped for a long moment, considering just where to go. Most of the women were herding children toward the river. There they would drive the horses before them in crossing the icy waters.

The old woman moved away from the river, and away from the sounds of the battle in an oblique angle toward the rim of hills that stretched to the southeast behind the camp. Slowly, the deafening noise of embattled voices and barking weapons faded behind her to lend only a faint background to the crunch of snow beneath her wet moccasins. The climbing became tougher as she began to battle the deadfall and wind her way through the thick stand of trees that raced up the hillside toward the bald knob above her and to the left. She believed she could make it there before her old, tired lungs gave out. Then, yes, then—she could find safety on the other side of the ridge.

From time to time she tripped and fell to the snow over the hidden deadfall. It was still quite dark here within the great stand of trees through which she fought her way. Her eyes had been growing dim anyway and now she cursed the many winters that made her lungs burn with the cold air she swallowed desperately, her legs burning with the exertion of the climb, her eyes burning with the sting of the falling flakes. She fell again, and decided to catch her breath here on the ground, here on her hands and knees, before she fought to rise again. She was near the bald top on the ridge now, the old woman thought. She raised her eyes to the open spot in the trees at the clearing and her breath caught in her throat.

Three riders sat atop their ponies in the clearing on the ridge top. The three were intent upon the battle below them and had evidently not seen her climb the hill at an angle toward them. Without knowing why, the old woman looked about her quickly. No one else was near. She stayed on her hands and knees in moving to her right to place herself behind a large, downed tree. As she scooted behind the fallen log, the figure in the middle of the trio motioned quickly with his right arm that he took from beneath his robe. The painted warrior on his right took off down the hill into the timber toward the battle. Then the man in the middle began to talk with the warrior to his left.

Should she creep closer? Should she scream out? To bring her people here? This was not like the enemy, to attack with one man leading the course of the attack. Perhaps she could kill the two men left on the knob. Whom was she fooling? She laughed softly to herself. Here she was, an old woman of many winters, thinking of killing these two warriors on the hill. She looked up at the increasing volume of one man's voice and saw the man in the middle slash the air repeatedly with his right arm. There was something strange about that arm, she thought, as she continued to watch him slashing the air in rapid strokes. Then the warrior to the man's left bolted off into the timber toward the battle as the first had done.

The man left behind pulled his robe about him more tightly now. His long, white hair contrasted brightly against the darkness of the robe. The old woman moved slowly, cautiously, more closely through the trees toward the man. Perhaps she could push past him without being discovered. Closer she came to his vantage point until she stopped again. Catching her breath quietly, the old woman stared at the man, to study him, to remember him. After looking back over her shoulder, the old woman knew she would remember this day when the enemy rode down on the village, killing the people. And she would remember this man with the hair of snow on his head and all over his face. She would remember.

But now she must escape to the other side of the hill. Away from what was happening. The old woman rose slowly and was starting off to her right when she tripped and fell against the dry limb of a downed, dead tree. The limb snapped off as her weight crushed against it. Its breaking sounded just like the crack of the rifles below them. Her head jerked up and around toward the top of the hill. The man of white saw her. He put heels to his pony and the animal quickly wheeled toward her.

The old woman rose quickly this time and began to race down the hill over the deadfall and through the dark timber. She could hear him yelling at her. She could hear his pony's hoofs scratching at the hidden limbs and logs. Once she fell and looked behind her through the trees as she rose again. The man of white was getting closer. The timber became thicker just ahead. There was much more deadfall for his pony to fight. She could make it there before her lungs gave out on her.

The sound of hoofs stopped. Perhaps the pony had stumbled. She was afraid to look behind her. She had to look behind her. The old woman stopped momentarily to turn her head. The man of white had drawn his pony to a halt and the buffalo robe had fallen from his shoulders. He had brought his rifle up to his shoulder and was steadying it in her direction. She bolted headlong down the hill toward the heavy timber once more and fell over a large tree that stretched across her path of escape.

The old woman heard first the whine of the ball as it passed over her head in her falling. Then she heard the loud bark of the weapon that had sent the ball on its way. Her body lay still on the snow. She was afraid to catch her breath. He would surely come to see if he had killed her. There was no longer any strength to match her will in continuing the chase. The old limbs refused to move at her heart's command. Her lungs had given up the fight and would not give her breath to rise.

The yelling below her grew louder now. The snow against her cheek grew icy and hard, but she did not move. Someone else was coming up the hill toward her. Toward the man of white. They were yelling at him in the enemy's tongue. He answered the one coming up the hill with a strange twist to his tongue. Then she heard his pony moving away. He must think her dead. Or dead enough not to be worth the trouble.

It was a long time before she lifted her head from the snow. It was the faintness of the screaming, shouting voices, and the booming, barking weapons that gave her courage and strength now to lift the old head. First, she looked down the hill. It seemed as if her people were pushing back toward the village. It seemed as if the enemy was being driven off. Her arms shakily supported her weight as she rose to her feet, then sat down on the large, downed tree.

She took air in, drinking it as though it were a heady mixture of relief and life itself. Finally, the old woman turned to look behind her to the top of the hill. No longer were the riders there. No longer was the man of white directing the others in the attack. No longer was the man of white chasing her. No longer was the man of white aiming his rifle at her back. But she would remember him. She would remember his eyes that filled with surprise, filled with discovery, filled with horror when first seeing her. She would remember this man of white who brought the enemy down on the people.

15

The easy sway of the pony beneath him had set Scratch to letting his thoughts drift from the trail. There was little to worry about now that they had crossed into Crow territory two days back. Fall hunting was over. The streams were freezing up in the north country and the land was settling in for its long winter's sleep.

Bass had finally moved them east toward the land of the Absarokas, anxious as he was to settle in for those short months with his chosen tribe. It was a good feeling, warm and honeylike, that flowed through him these past few days. He felt as if he were going home. There were no other words to express to Josiah how he felt about moving toward winter camp. He had not attempted to express it in any other way. Titus Bass had the rich, full honey glow inside that said all there was to say. He was going home.

The pony under his buttocks had grown used to the old man. It had come to understand the meaning of the swift jabs at its ribs as well as the hand rubbed over the muzzle and between its eyes. He had taken a particular liking to this one pony over the others since the buffalo run. The other Nez Perce animals would be left to carry the baggage of possibles and personal plunder. This one would remain his favorite. They were quite a pair, this young Indian pony and old Hannah. The one eager and strong in its youth, reassuring Titus with its endurance. The other old and set in her ways, taking no guff from the horses or the man named Bass. She was crotchety and peculiar in her aging, and she suited this man to whom she was so attached.

He turned in the saddle to look back at the mule and smiled, slightly curling the edge of one lip at the corner of his beard. Eyes climbing from the animal's sad plodding, Scratch looked behind the mule to the string of ponies snaking their way along his trail. Josiah sat atop his animal, head slightly bowed as if dozing in the welcome warmth of the midmorning sun. The air was brisk and both men felt the gentle caress of the warm glow pouring over them through that high country air. There was a brilliance to the mountains this morning. Everywhere he would look was a shroud of white, dazzling the eyes and filling them with tears to shut out the piercing reflection of light bouncing off the snow.

Scratch blinked at the moisture and turned back around in the saddle. He tugged to the right on the pony's reins and then let them go slack once more, thereby reassuring the pony that they could now descend the ridge into the valley of the stream flowing east to the river.

The boy was dozing but he could not. Scratch had never been able to do that on the trail. There was too much running and catching up to do in his mind. Step by step, as surely as he would stalk game through the forest, Titus Bass had been considering the words of last night's reading of *Macbeth*. Josiah had helped in some way, stopping now and then to run a second time over a passage that remained unclear to Bass. Translating at times, the young trapper had explained what was being said by the faraway characters. Scratch had not asked his partner to explain the meaning of those characters. He knew better. Bass had decided it was up to him alone to figure those things out. For himself. His mind was heavy with it as the pony moved him toward the valley.

What would lead a man to kill another like that? This nigger Macbeth was a friend of the man he intended to kill. What would lead a man to kill a friend? Sure it was, them witches had greeted Macbeth as though he were the king. And he had wondered at it. Duncan was king. Macbeth was only one of them fellers under him. Those old witches had troubled and deviled Macbeth with their hailing of him, sure enough. Maybe only because he had for some time wanted to be king himself. Yessir. That was something he had figured out for himself early in the story. Macbeth had long hankered after the power himself. And now them old hags of the belching smoke and fiery lightning had hailed him as king. That nigger just figured them witches had told the true and he was to be king—no baldface to that.

Macbeth was just gonna nudge things along a bit. Hankering the way he did after being king himself, that nigger was just gonna push things along a bit. Them witches had told him he would be the king; and they ought to know, what with being critters given to the telling of things to come. Was it up to a man to push things along on his own? Or should he wait until things come his way naturally? That nigger Macbeth was an itchy critter—burning like he was to get on with becoming king. Burning so bad he was, setting out to kill a friend, a man he was sworn to, a man who trusted him. He would just have to figure out for himself what the difference was

508

between what he saw and what was real. What was real, though? What was one to figure was real in a world where a man with his wits about him could not tell the difference between good and evil? Was it that Macbeth wasn't to blame after all? How could you be holding it against the nigger when it wasn't the man's fault if he could not tell good from evil in a world turned upside down? Nawww! You just couldn't side with Macbeth on the thing. Not really. Not after he had told Duncan it was his job to do everything in his power to protect Duncan's life and honor. Honor? What was that when the nigger who said it was already planning to rub Duncan out?

Was it only what was natural for Macbeth to consider killing Duncan—no—to plan killing the king, and all the time to come out front with Duncan as if he were the best friend the king ever had? Was it a little sadness he felt now along with anger inside knowing that Macbeth thought he was only doing what was supposed to be done anyway? He'd try to understand, but it was hard to figure how a man could push things, instead of flowing along with them, just drifting along with them.

But it was the nigger's wife doing some pushing too. Women. They could prod and goad a man into doing things he would not think of doing naturally. Women could play the devil with a nigger's mind, they could. Putting things there to grow what had no right to be growing. Them witches and his wife—all women. All of them deviling Macbeth until he didn't know the right sign to be reading. Hold it, hoss. Macbeth had been one already to think about being king. Before them witches hailed him as king. Right? Before his wife started pushing him to do it with her sweet words covering up a black heart. Right? It was Macbeth—yep, Macbeth—who hankered for being king all along and he was only doing what he figured to be the right thing to make it all come to be.

That woman telling the spirits to take from her everything that says she's a woman, just so she can get the murdering done. That ain't natural neither. Ain't natural for anybody, man or woman, to call on the spirits to help in the killing of a man like Duncan. To be sure, a child calls on the spirits to help him raid an enemy's camp. Steal some horses. Make him strong and brave for the battle. He calls on them to choose him over the other nigger. Only natural, that was. But calling on spirits to help murder another man. Calling on the powers that a hoss couldn't understand even when he tries—that wasn't the natural way of things. Spirits weren't around for such doings.

Hoodoos. Hoodoos were for the black, evil things in a man's heart. The dark side of living. Hoodoos were what gave a man a push when he needed one to get on with some black and evil thing. Was it just the thinking of hoodoos that had caused him to shudder just then? Only thing it could have been. Hoodoos to come with the cover of darkness when that woman Macbeth wants them to cover the heaven's light, to block out what she's about to do. She needs their help for both of them, Macbeth and his wife. What a set they were! To side up with hoodoos for the killing. Wagh!

He glanced to his left to look at the ridge above and recognized the two humpback, turtlelike rocks pushed up from the skyline. Bass was close now. Taking up some of the slack in the reins he had given to the pony, he turned the party's movement more sharply toward the creek. When he spotted the small meadow along the opposite bank his eyes searched until they found the small stand of aspen on his side of the creek. Like a cluster of tall, thin sentries, the naked trees stood to mark the spot. Bass led the animals into the stand of trees and turned to address the young trapper.

"Josiah!" he yelled back.

Paddock's head jerked up and looked about him. Surely he would have been confused. "What?" he asked as Scratch slid quietly from his animal.

"Need your help, son."

"Doin' what?"

"Jest c'mon down, now. Tie 'em up."

They quickly strung a length of rope between two trees and attached the pack animals to it. Another length of rope was strung between a pair of trees across the small compound made by the stand of aspen. Here they tied up their riding animals and Hannah. Even here, in this land, Titus Bass was taking some precautions for their protection against having the stock run off and stolen. The thick crust of snow crunched beneath his moccasins as he led Josiah back to the string of pack animals.

"Pull you that small hoe-pick from the animal there." Bass pointed to one of the ponies. Josiah began to loosen the baggage and pulled free the short hickory handle of the pick. "Foller me."

Scratch led Paddock from the stand of trees into the narrow plain formed by the ridge to their left and the creek cutting away at the steep bank to their right. He located the long abandoned beaver lodge in the creek and stepped to the edge of the bank. Immediately he turned his back on the water and began to pace directly toward a patch bare of snow on the ridge.

"One...two...three...," he counted with each step. Paddock followed along, frowning as if none of this made any sense out here. "Seven...eight...nine—"

"What you lookin' for?"

Scratch jerked to a halt, yanking his head around and sputtering, "Ten...or 'leven. Ten or 'leven!" He stomped his foot on the ground once. "Goddammit, boy! You up an' made me loose my count! Damn your hide!" cutting back to the bank. Bass faced away from the creek and began again his measured walk.

"One...two..." He stopped. "Keep your mouth shut, you hear?" Again he paced, "Three...four..." On he went until he reached thirteen. He stopped. "Thirteen," he repeated as he turned around and around on the spot, searching the ground carefully. He knelt and ran the fingers of his left hand in a half circle through the snow to describe a crescent, the horns of which pointed back toward the creek.

"Ask you now what you up to?"

"Now you can know." He rose and looked at the young man. "Cache."

"Ca...cash?" Josiah said, standing now beside his partner to stare at the ground beneath the older man's feet. "Like money?"

"Nawww. *Cache*," he repeated. "Meanin' a hidin' place, mostlike. Parley-voo's word for it, leastways. Lemme see the pick there, son." The tool was placed in his outstretched left hand, and he gripped it near the top of the handle. Slowly, straining with the clumsiness of his seldom-used left arm, he brought the pick over his head and dropped the iron point into the soil. Over and over he rose and straightened, bringing the tool behind his head for another swing as he slowly took one step backward at a time. The half circle finished, Bass knelt back down and swept the whole area off with his good hand, piling the snow beyond the area where he had marked the soil with the crescent some three feet across.

"Need your help now."

"Yeah?"

"Gimme hand pullin' this here lid back."

"What lid?"

"This'un, right here." His bandaged right arm looped back and forth along the line of the half circle in the dusted soil. "Take the dirt off 'n here with the pick. Won' take you but a shake till you got 'er done."

Josiah took the pick handle and stared hard at the old man for a long moment. Finally swinging it over his head, the trapper brought it crashing down into the earth. In pulling it free, Josiah brought up a large piece of earth frozen to the pick.

"Keep at it. 'Long the line, here," Bass instructed.

Again and again the pick bit its way into the earth along the line Bass had scratched across the ground. Occasionally Josiah looked over quickly at the older man staring at the ground, wondering how crazy a man could become to be digging holes out here at the edge of the narrow prairie. And in the middle of nowhere. His arms tore at the pick handle, feeling the resistance of more than dirt. The pick head finally brought up a large branch. Paddock knelt to pull it out of the way.

"Ain't no root," Paddock said, noticing the cut ends.

"Ain't," Bass answered. "Jest 'bout through now."

"Mind you tellin' me what it be then?"

"Keep your swingin' now," Titus said. "Part of the lid, son."

"Lid?" he finally asked.

"What you diggin' up!" Bass was a little frustrated with more questions than work. "Ever' hidin' place gotta have it somethin' to hide under. Here I jest use't the ground itself." He walked away from Josiah along a line of torn earth and knelt to pick up a clod of dirt that he absently tossed toward the stream.

"Man picks hisse'f a place to dig a cache real careful. Then he digs out a circle real careful too, makin' pains to leave the top ground in big pieces. Lays 'em aside, he does. Then he'll spread out a robe, somethin' like that, an' starts his diggin' down through the small hole he's got marked out, puttin' all the extree dirt on the robe. I go down 'bout three feet, then can start widenin' out some as

512

I go down from there. That top part's like the neck of your whiskey bottle."

He tossed another clod toward the stream, watching the dirt fall short of its mark. "Get you that done an' you're ready to cut you some arm-strong tree limbs. Cut 'em to fit down in the lil' cave you made down there." He pointed to the top of the hole that Josiah was beginning to expose. "Shore 'er up round the cave walls like that, makin' sure she won' come slidin' in on you when the ground is beat on from up top, or the rain soaks in down below. Man puts down in there what he want to only then." The pick had made its last ripping journey into the sod and came up with another stout limb.

Bass took the pick from Josiah's hand and nudged him aside. "I'll take 'er from here on." Titus swung the pick wildly with his left arm. Paddock ducked away from the raised tool's crazy arc. Thundering into the earth, the pick slid part way up the handle into the soil.

"Bustin' into a cache lot funner'n makin' a cache a man won' be bustin' into," Scratch snorted. He ripped the pick out and laid it aside. Dropping to his knees, the old trapper clawed at the ground with his good hand, the thin, sinewy arm ripping up limb after limb and throwing each behind him. Some small clods of dirt slid past his hand into the hole he had exposed.

"The neck of your whiskey bottle, Josiah." He looked up quickly at Paddock, then resumed his work. "What you put down for your lid makes the whole cache work. Build up the top with them tree limbs goin' crossfire. Lay your top soil you saved back on. Fill in all the gaps an' that with some dirt from the robe. Then she looks to be like she's finished." He turned up to Josiah. "Well, she ain't finished." Scratch bowed to the earth once more and ripped at the tree branches again. "She ain't. Man as wants his plunder left right here gotta take lotta pains to make certain sure it stays right here after he's gone from these parts. Valley here good for buffler. Feller get him a small herd to run over this here place to tramp down the ground all round the whole country. Take you that robe down to the stream, draggin' it 'long behin't you, an' pour all that extree dirt into the water."

"Why all that trouble?"

Bass jerked to a halt and stared up at Josiah. "Dumb niggers comin' to the hills these days! I got me one to nurse, I do." He lowered his eyes and slowly shook his head. "One a the dumbest niggers they sent out here. They send you out here to devil me with your stupids?"

"Ain't gotta take your shit, ol' man!" Josiah turned on his heel to stomp away.

"Hey! Hey, now, son!" Bass protested. "I only joshin' you a bit now. C'mon over here. Jumpin' Jehoshaphat! Cain't you take you lil' ribbin' for the whole of it?"

"You really think me dumb, don't you?" Paddock spoke as if really wounded.

"Not a bit, boy. C'mon back here." Bass swung his wrapped hand in an arch across the ground to motion the young trapper back to the excavation. "Ain't never seen you a cache afore, have you?"

"Nawww."

"How can I be one to 'spect you to know 'bout 'em then? Eh?" He paused a moment. "That ain't dumb. That's jest ignernce."

"First off you call me dumb! Now you're callin' me ignernt!"

"Hold off there, young'un. Ain't nowhere near the comedown you thinkin' it be. Ignernce is somethin' you don' know 'bout yet. Right? I right!"

Paddock finally nodded his head up and down once.

"Bein' dumb means a nigger forgot what he's found sign of. You only ignernt, Josiah Paddock. Ignernt to ways in the mountains. I'm here to be the child what's teachin' to you. But you ain't dumb. You ain't got you a dumb bone in your body. Sometimes, well, you're slow in the l'arnin', but that ain't bein dumb. Jest slow." The twinkle returned to the corner of his eyes as the deeply engraved crows' feet spread their claws in his smile. "Now, what you think a nigger'd take the extree dirt down an' throw it in the crik for?"

Paddock stared at the ground beneath Scratch's hands, then slowly let his eyes travel to the stream. "Man wants to hide sign of his diggin', right?"

"Yep."

"Well. He cain't let dirt just lay there." Josiah felt as if he had the thing figured out for himself. "Somebody—"

"Or somethin'—"

"Will see it. Throws the dirt in the water to hide the dirt he's taken outta his hidin' place."

"Right, boy!" He slapped his thigh unconsciously

with the wounded hand and winced from the fleeting pain before smiling once more. "See there! You ain't dumb! Give you time to be figgerin' things out for yourself an' you're right smart young feller, ain't you." He saw the glow in Paddock's face so turned his own again to the work at hand. "You run you all that dirt back to the stream there. Run you buffler over the place. Then mayhaps build you a fire right here on the spot. All to hide it from whatever noses be sniffin' round these parts to dig up your cache. White noses an' red, Josiah. There be white niggers up here as'd be lovin' to get into 'nother feller's cache. 'Special if he had put him furs down in the hole—"

"You got you beaver down there?"

"I ain't. But a man could do such. Them big comp'nies does. Make 'em a big cache." He spread his arms wide. "There they hole-up theys furs from the fall catch afore fortin' up for the winter. I ain't one to trust even my cache. Never had me one got into, howsomever. But, still don' trust puttin' my plews down a hole. Like I might never be seein' 'em again. Like havin' 'em 'long with me. Look at 'em. Feel of 'em, too. Knowin' what they'll be buyin' me come ronnyvoo time. Whiskey an' the womens. Umm-mmm! Jest like keepin' my beaver dollars on me, son. No nigger gonna sign my cache, what with all I do to hide it. An' even if he did, wouldn't be gettin' my catch. No way." He fell silent as he pulled the last few limbs away from the hole. The opening to his underground excavation was exposed. Josiah knelt at the side to peer down into the blackness.

"What all you got hidin' down there?"

"Jest keep your breeches on, young'un." Bass started to slide down into the hole. "An' stay right there where I can hand it up to you. You'll see soon 'nough."

His head disappeared into the blackness but his muffled voice could still be heard. The head popped back out of the hole for a quick moment. "You hear me? Keepin' your eyes 'long that ridge, boy? This here hole won' move, but somethin' else might'n be. Keep your eyes movin'." He was gone again.

A hand returned a few minutes later, holding a parfleche. Paddock took it from the hand and put the parfleche beside him on the ground. More of the leather baggage came up through the ground to him, one at a time. Finally the old head appeared, followed by the body as Bass pulled himself from the hole.

Once on the surface Scratch turned around and leaned back into the hole to bury an arm into the darkness. He pulled and slid until a large bundle appeared. Josiah leaned over to help him pull the bundle of heavy hides from the hole. After placing the bundle alongside the small, rawhide parfleches, Bass leaned back and heaved a sigh of finality. The small bundles were painted and some quilled in the same manner as the one in Scratch's pack that contained his medicines. The large one was undecorated, dirty, smoke-burnt, and greasy. It was bound with rope.

"What's in these?" Paddock inquired.

"Gee-gaws, girlews, an' foofaraw."

Josiah formed the words with a silent mouth, letting the impression of them roll past his lips without a sound. He next motioned to the large bundle. "An' that'un?"

"Our lodge. For the winter." Bass put a hand on the hide cover and patted it lovingly. "Not really a lodge, leastways like the Crows make. Jest one I had a squar stitch up for me. More like a half circle. Ain't gotta have you lotta poles to hold it up. Ain't as high as a lodge, neither. Does the trick, though. Not havin' to be draggin' poles round with you to worry 'bout."

"Couldn't a man cut him some poles when he gets ready to settle in for the winter?"

"Nawww. Wouldn't be cured dry by the time. Lodgepoles gotta be dried up to be good an' strong. Holdin' up the weight of the hide cover an' holdin' out the winds." He patted the large bundle one last time. "This here do the snatchin', Josiah. It's home for the winter."

"An' what's these gee-girls an' fow, fow—"

"Foofaraw," Bass finished. "They's pretties make them Crows' eyes shine for my comin' in to winter-up with 'em. Presents, son. Presents a man gives those as'll take him in for the winter. Them there an' what we got us back to ronnyvoo buys us a nestin' place through the nastiest part of the cold moons. Need me some special foofaraw too, what with McAfferty be bringin' in him a Nepercy squar for a winter robe warmer. Don' know me how them Crow take to that, this nigger, don'."

"An' if they don't take to her bein' round for the winter with us?"

"Why, boy, we jest give them Crow more gee-gaws till they ain't got that squar on theys minds. Don' take much, it don'. Never could figger me out why them Injuns bought off so cheap, anyways," he snorted. "I laugh at a red nigger I'm tradin' with, tellin' him he's stupid for givin' me a few plews, maybe even a buffler robe, for a handful of shiny, blue beads. That nigger, you know, Josiah—that nigger goes an' laughs right at me then. Tellin' me I'm the dumb shit in the tradin'. Givin' him some blue beads he can have his squar put on a new pair a mokersons, maybe a war shirt—an' me askin' in trade only them skins. He's laughin' at me for givin' him somethin' what comes all the way from St. Louie, sayin' he's only givin' me what comes right outta these here hills. Furs any man can get, he says, I s'pose we both walk 'way from the tradin' thinkin' the other's a dumb-shit no-mind nigger. S'pose that's what tradin's all 'bout anyways, when you looks at it. Both us happy, thinkin' we got the best of the deal, thinkin' we did the screwin' on the other nigger. You figger?"

Paddock merely nodded his head and turned to look over the ridge. "You wanna be settin' in here for the night?"

"Nawww." Scratch rose on legs wobbly from too long at the sitting. "Put us some more miles behin't us afore we lay robes for the night. Ain't too much more'n we find theys winter camp, I'd care to set. Seein' sign for the past day." He put his arm on Josiah's shoulder. "You help me carry these here bundles a plunder over to the animals an' we'll be gettin' 'em loaded up."

He bent over to heft the shelter cover to his left shoulder, steadying it with the bandaged hand, "Gotta take some things off Hannah an' spread 'em round on the pack ponies. Ol' gal, she always gets to be the one to carry the foofaraw an' lodge. Special, it is, for her. Seems she knows we's goin' in for winter doin's then. See, the ol' gal gets happy twice't a y'ar: come roonyvoo trampin' an' headin' for winter diggin's." He walked with Josiah toward the stand of aspen. "Come to think of it, seems like thems the times a moutain nigger's in the clover too. The prime squeezin's of a man's life! Happiest headin' to winter doin's or ronnyvoo an' a spree. Ever'thin' else jest makes it so a man can have hisse'f a time twice't a y'ar. Mules an' men ain't so goldarned differ'nt sometimes after all. Me an' Hannah jest lovin' the livin'. Not a bit differ'nt we be."

The pouch bobbed and danced under his left arm with the gentle motion of the pony. Now and then a gust of wind would come up to nag at his body where the old, torn capote refused to cover him. From his right fingers he transferred the reins to the left hand that also cradled the rifle. He rose slightly from the saddle and pushed the tattered pieces of the blanket coat beneath his buttocks. It would keep the capote from fluttering with the wind. It would keep him from shivering slightly with the bite in the air that reached its fingers through every gap and fold of his clothing. Was he really getting old? Scratch asked himself. The cold and damp were bothering him all the more of late. Time was when no such thing would have been of concern to him. It was all part of the living. And now the ache in his joints continually reminded him of the years spent splashing in frozen streams, the nights of cold camps and mornings of waking to find snow covering the robe in which he had slept. Reminded him of days of riding in skins that grew chilled in their touch against his body. It had all been part of the living. Then. And now he was scared it was becoming part of the dying.

Bass focused his eyes on the young trapper ahead. He had let Josiah take the lead upon breaking camp, pointing out the general direction they were to travel along the stream leading to the river. Titus had chosen to follow with the pack animals. It was a young man's world, out here. The mountains and this broad sky of iridescent blue belonged to the young man who could claim them. He, like many others, had come here to cling to the richness of his youth, as if those early years were something personal, something private, something to be carefully guarded. How a man could let them slip through his fingers, he decided, it was not for him to figure out. For a moment he looked absently at the bandaged hand, then wondered how he had let his time slip from his grasp. Scratch could not answer the questions.

Where did it say a man had to age before his time? Before he was ready? Just who was making up the rules out here? He shook his head sadly, almost involuntarily. Man growing too old to play anymore is a pitiful creature, for sure. Even worse is the man who admits it and returns east. Been a whole passel of them kind, he smiled. Been a whole passel of them. The smile drained from him. Or was it all the worse for a man to refuse to admit it; to go on fighting it, to grapple with it in the hope—no, in some prayer—of winning, every day offering some supplication that he will lick the thing?

So, which was it? He shook his head again, feeling the braid brush against the side of his cheek. Two fingertips went up to touch the hills and valleys of the crusted hair. Here was youth, he thought. Wearing his hair like this for years—when had he first put it up in this way? Something else he could not remember—what spring he had first taken the Snake gal to his lodge? His eyes squinted with thought. Or was it the fall when he had finally found his furs lost to those three: Silas, Bud, and Billy? He still remembered the names. And the faces. He wasn't totally touched yet. He still remembered.

The waving arm caught his attention. Ahead, Josiah was motioning for him to catch up. He saw Paddock drop from his pony and kneel on the snow-crusted ground, the reins still held loosely in the young man's right hand, the rifle cradled into the notch at his shoulder. Bass did not push his animal. Soon enough. He let the pony continue in its trail pace. He would catch up to the young'un soon enough.

Bass brought the animal to a stop behind the young trapper. Josiah turned from his inspection to glance up at him, then nodded to the short tree branches stuck in the ground to form a circle of stakes some twenty to thirty feet in diameter.

"What's this here?"

"Medeecin."

Again the young eyes found his for a moment, then went back to survey the crude circle of bloodstained branches. Tied to some of the stakes were skin pouches, to others dangling feathers, bouncing in the breeze. A few of the crimsoned markers were topped with locks of long black hair. One held an old trade fusee, its stock broken, the barrel bent around a tree after heating in a fire.

"Whose medicine?" Josiah asked.

"Crow, looks to be."

"Crows?" His fingers took up one of the locks of hair and held it for a moment between his fingers. "For what?"

"They's medeecin," Bass replied.

"You said that—"

"Medeecin over a place they done battle."

Paddock nodded his head once and looked back at the hair across the palm of his hand. "It say who they fought?"

"Yep. It do, that. Blackfoots." Scratch leaned a little to the side of the saddle. "See you them burnt rings round the bottoms there—on the sticks—tells it be Blackfoots. The niggers the Crow got in a tussle with."

"Who come out on the top of it? It say that?"

Bass straightened back atop his saddle, then slowly leaned down over the pommel. "Blackfoots." He spit and let his eyes wander quickly across the sides of the hills.

"Blackfoot, heh. Why the Crows put it up? They ain't proud, are they, bein' beat by no Blackfoot now?"

"Proud ain't got nothin' noway to do with that there. Medeecin it be, Josiah. They put theys medeecin on this place. Mostlike the battle go an' be writ down in the Crows' story 'bout theyselves. Big'un, it looks to been too. You jest don' go off an' leave a man without markin' where he's laid. Well, Crow don' go off an leave a place they lost 'em braves neither—not that they ain't marked the place where Crow blood was spilt on the ground."

Paddock looked at the ground. Only snow. No blood to see. Only snow as far as the eye could reach. The breeze tossed the hank of Indian hair out of his open palm. "'A monument to the dead, huh? Put here by the livin'?"

"That's the medeecin. A monument. They carry theys dead back to the village an' bury 'em up proper. The womens is wailin', cuttin' off theys ha'r an' parts a fingers too. Gashin' theyselves with knives. That be done for the dead. This'r," he said, gesturing across the memorial markers with the bandaged hand, "be done for the livin'.'"

He watched the back of the young man's head. Both of them sat silent a few minutes. Josiah stared across at the circle, not really seeing. His mind conjured visions of other memorials. His mother's resting place out of town on the slope that ran from the north into St. Louis. And one he had never seen, beneath which a man named LeClerc rested for the ages. How would it look? Would a rich piece of marble, carved with name and dates, figures growing out of the relief of its surface, stand guard over the body? It was only fitting for a man's friends and family to give him the best at the last farewell. Only proper. The stone-topped log cairn cleared before his eyes. He remembered it dusted with snow, the white flakes sneaking like worms through the cracks in the logs he had labored to fit together so well. Only fitting. Only proper. It had been the best he could give, and yet now seemed inadequate. Not enough. The man beneath the cairn deserved better, much better, than LeClerc. He saw the trees over the cairn sigh with the breeze and more snow fall from their branches onto the logs.

"Time to go, son."

The vision disappeared in the stinging flurry of tears brought on by the wind. He wiped them and the rivulets from his cheeks with the back of a hand. Promising himself Bass would get better than the simple log and rock cairn, Josiah moved to top his pony. He promised himself. Had he to do it over again, Bass would get something better.

By the middle of the afternoon the warmth had permeated their bodies. Scratch had said they were close now. The two men rode side by side along the edge of the wind-blown ridge. He felt close now too, and Scratch smiled with the thought.

"You figger it that way? Macbeth gonna go 'head an' rub out that Duncan feller?"

"Prob'ly. Leastways, lookin' more an' more to be like he's gonna go through with it," Josiah replied.

"Wagh! Knowed it! I jest knowed it!" Bass made a small jerking motion with his left hand around the reins, forming a tight fist to signify his sureness in it. "Ol' Scratch Bass cain't read none too good, but he sure can figger them doin's out, you give him time to calc'late on it."

Paddock turned briefly to smile in his direction, then looked away. The older man sure had dug into the story with a voracious appetite. And it was good. They had used the reading to take them away from the cold and sometimes hunger on the trail. The book had given them something more than traps and plews and Indians to talk of over night fires and days of creaking, cold saddles.

"We go onto next story, then. Tonight, Josiah. Got this'un figger't out—"

"Whoa!" Paddock turned suddenly to look at the

521

older man. "Now, you just said you figgered Macbeth gonna kill Duncan. That ain't the whole doin's, at all. Ain't but near half the story, Scratch. You ain't heard but half of the readin'. But if'n you're gettin' tired of the tale, we'll—"

"Hold up there, now. You're the one what needs yankin' on the bridle bit, son. We'll be follerin' 'er through to the end. Ain't 'bout to let it go halfway. No sir. See it through to the end. Jest thought maybe that was the tale, what with Macbeth gonna go 'head an' do Duncan in. Wantin' to be king for hisse'f an' all."

"Seems to be just the beginnin'."

"You read it afore?"

"Nope."

"Cain't say as how you'd know if'n the story is over then."

"Jest that I can read an' I knows how many pages is left till the next story starts off."

"You been readin' on 'head of what you been readin' to me?" He squinted the one eye at his young partner.

Josiah shook his head slowly with the humor of it. "You're a trustin' nigger, ain't you, ol' man?" He chuckled quickly. "Just when I s'posed to have me chance to read on 'head of you now? Huh? How am I s'posed to do that?"

"Dunno."

"I read outta the book every night to you, till your ears are tired of hearin' them strange words and the strange way them folks talked. An' every day we ridin' on the trail together. Now, just when an' how am I s'posed to read on in the story 'head of what I'm readin' to you?"

"Said I dunno. I dunno."

"Neither do I."

They fell silent awhile, the plodding of the hoofs over the frozen crust and the swish-swish of the trail-loosened baggage taking up the tempo of a word-silent trail.

"Jest didn' want you gettin' on 'head of me, is all."

"I know, Scratch. I know. I was only fun—"

"Shush!" Bass snapped suddenly, his head turned at a strange angle to listen to the sounds of the forest that had abruptly disappeared. Ahead of them a magpie shot into the air with a rush of its wings and climbed with intent flight.

Josiah turned to look at Scratch. "What the he——"

The words were barely out of his mouth when moving forms appeared at the edge of the trees ahead of them. Then from the sides broke more mounted warriors. Paddock's head jerked at the mere feel of movement around him, uncommon motion that was sensed before seen. From side to side he looked, driven by the impulse that the edges of the forest were closing in on him.

"Hold up, boy." The words were quiet but heavy.

Josiah drew back on the reins and his pony stopped quickly. The pack animals clattered to a stop behind them. His young eyes quickly counted the braves closing in on them at an easy lope, his mind busy calculating the chances of escape. The loose length of his rein dropped across the pommel of his saddle and his right hand slowly pulled the hammer on the rifle back. Just as quickly the left hand opened the free flap of his blanket coat and found the butt of the pistol resting against his tense stomach muscles.

"Best you hold it right there," Bass again whispered. "Had you easy time afore with Bannawks. Ain't gonna be like that now."

Josiah looked at him with a jerk of surprise. Titus had raised his left arm toward the mounted warriors in front of them, holding the arm and hand outstretched halfway between earth and sky.

"Ain't Blackfoot, is they?"

"Crow," the old one answered.

"Fixin' to rob us then?" Paddock asked, his rifle wiggling nervously.

"Tol't you, ease off. Jest loosen up on your tight hitch, boy. These young'uns out to have 'em some fun with some white trappers, is all. Figgerin' what we won' give 'em in presents they'll take anyways. If they take a shine to." The Indians were closing on them now. The pack animals bounced against one another nervously. "Them's jest boys, an' younger'n you, Josiah. Wanna smoke us with theys bluster. Is all."

The braves to their left and right and to the rear had closed up and brought their ponies to a halt, forming a tight ring around the pack animals and trappers. Paddock looked back to the braves coming head on.

"Zat-see saw," one of the larger warriors hollered, telling the trappers not to move.

"Masta sheela," Bass started. He cleared his throat and spoke louder, "Masta sheela. Toshe-bit."

They were completely ringed now, with no chance to break the circle. A few of the braves had dismounted already and were pushing at the pack animals, poking hands at the ropes tying the baggage aboard the ponies and mule. Hannah snorted and brayed, dancing away from the warrior who attempted to touch her.

"Kee-ari shee," said the one beside the largest warrior. Then he spat. It was a slur, telling the trappers they were old women for not having fought.

They would want to play the game to the hilt, all the way, he thought. "Wann kee-ari shee bote," Titus responded.

"Mans koti shari?" the big one asked, inquiring if they were French.

"Wann. Wann." Bass smiled and glanced quickly at Josiah. "Mitsiatki. Mitsiatki."

The big one nodded to those at his sides, then slowly let his pony advance toward Bass. He stopped a short way from the trapper and stared into the white man's face. "Wann kee-ari shee. Pote ani bunet-sa. Pote ani." He smiled and with the words the other warriors stopped their rummaging through the packs and bundles aboard the animals. Josiah turned to see one of the young braves suddenly halt the knife in his hand that had been intended for cutting the rope on one bundle.

"Pote ani," Scratch replied. "My name. Leastways what I go by with these'r Crow. Pote ani, I am to 'em."

The big brave quickly nudged his pony and rode directly to Scratch's side. He stuck out his right hand, fingers open wide. Into it Titus slipped his wrapped hand and each man closed fingers around the other's wrist in a formal greeting. The big one had recognized the old trapper. With the muscle-pumping, teeth-jarring shake over, the Crow warrior used his arm to pull Bass closer to him and encircled the trapper with his left arm, beating him soundly on the back several times before finally releasing his grip on Bass. He sat back straight atop his pony and rubbed the right hand over his left breast.

"Duwa. Duwa-wichi conna-shi."

"Duwa-wichi conna-shi," Scratch replied. "Josiah, he says his heart is glad to see me. His heart is glad when his eyes lay on me."

By now the big one had motioned to the others to

remount their ponies and relax on their weapons. Bass nodded to each one and they returned a youthful smile. He again faced the large man.

In slow, faltering words, Scratch asked of the health of Arapooesh, then smiled broadly when told the chief lived on even now into this winter. He remarked that a chief of greatness would be rewarded with many winters, a warm lodge around him, and a kettle always full of fresh meat. The Indian replied that Arapooesh was expecting him, looking forward to his visit this winter more than others gone before. Bass smiled and asked why. The Crow answered with the peculiar, slurring name for Blackfeet. Quickly the smile disappeared from the trapper's face. He repeated the name for the Crows' inveterate enemy, then asked if they had been troublesome in the past moons since last he had been in Absaroka. The warrior nodded and several others hooted and yelped in answer.

Josiah jerked at the sudden yells and the warriors around him raised their weapons, bows and rifles, into the air to shake while muttering oaths against their age-old enemy.

"Don' care for Blackfoot, seems."

"Not a damn, 'ceptin' to gut an' skelp. They like 'em Blackfoot ponies, howsomever," Bass answered before slipping back into his halting Crow to tell briefly of the battle with the Blackfeet in the valley beyond the three peaks that towered toward the sun.

The copper-skinned man asked many questions as to warriors killed, those escaped, women taken prisoner, and plunder raised by the trappers. He seemed sad that there were no more deaths than Bass recounted for him. He said more scalps should have waved from the muzzles of trapper rifles that day to avenge the white men murdered by the Blackfeet—to avenge the deaths of so many young Crow warriors, friends to those white men.

Bass nodded and looked down at the neck of his pony. He told the Crow brave it was a sad, sad day when so few had the courage to face the challenge and stay to keep the Blackfeet from escaping their hastily built fortress. A sad day when men are concerned more with money and things than with the lives of their friends.

The Crow turned and lifted his head to address the other warriors quickly and several of the braves took hold of the pack animals to lead.

"You gonna let 'em—"

"They doin' it 'cause they honor us. Man carries your plunder for you, says you're good a man as he is." Scratch turned back to the big youth to ask how far it was to their winter village and smiled when he heard it was but a few miles distant. Nudging his pony forward to ride beside the Crow brave, Bass said his heart smiled to think of seeing Arapooesh once more. His heart smiled to feel the welcome of Crow land surround him. His heart smiled to feel at home as never before.

The color of the sky was beginning to darken with the aging of the day when Bass first recognized the familiar ridges that stood sentry along the south bank of the Yellowstone. They would not have far to go for good trapping come next spring, he mused to himself. Close they were, in every direction. Good beaver country, this here.

The big warrior beside him turned to call forward one of the young men who rode alongside Paddock. Kicking his pony into a quick burst of speed, the Indian slowed the animal back to a trot beside Titus and looked past the trapper to the big man for instruction. He told the young one in quick, clipped words to hurry on ahead; to announce the arrival of the white trappers, to tell of the return of Pote ani. After a single gesture of his head the young warrior again put heels to his pony and dashed off, his body leaning forward along the animal's neck, both man and horse stretched out across the crust of snow as if painted with rapid slashes on a canvas. In a few minutes he was gone from sight, having reached the top of a small rise to disappear beyond. The hill was empty as suddenly as the lone rider had covered the margin where the land had risen to meet the sky.

"Where's he goin'?" Josiah hollered to Bass.

"Tell the village we's comin' in," the whisker-wrapped mouth said with a smile.

"Ca-sena benisee?" The words came from the big warrior riding beside him. Bass turned to answer the question of what happened to his right hand, but the warrior asked a second question, "Blackfoot?"

Titus snorted then. "Might jest as well been," he said in English, forgetting himself. With his left hand he made the sign for a huge paw, then remembered the Crow word for the medicine animal.

"Wa wachi?" The warrior asked how the animal was killed.

Bass tapped the head of his tomahawk at his side. The warrior lifted his eyes slowly from the bandaged right hand resting against the weapon and looked carefully into the white man's eyes, measuring them for truth. When he had read what he wanted to in them, his left hand reached out and grasped Scratch's right wrist to raise the trapper's arm aloft.

"Bech toni-seah quanoshum! Bech toni-wua!" the warrior yelled back at the others following, telling them the white man had been injured in a fight with the medicine bear, that he had killed the animal with a hatchet. He waved the right hand for them to see while the young braves whooped their approval.

Slowly the big man let Bass have the right arm back and commented that Pote ani was indeed the powerful friend the Crow had found in the old trapper. Bass smiled broadly but did not reply to the compliment. It was better not to reply. If he agreed, they would think him boasting unduly on his coup. And if he attempted to play down the fight with the grizzly, the Crow warriors might think him less than a brave warrior to denigrate his scrap with the bear. Strange, he thought, how you had to step lightly in what you said around Injuns.

They approached the crest of the small rise over which the single warrior had raced minutes before and the big man raised his hand for the party to stop. He untied the small robe from around his shoulders and grasped it with both hands to wave the hide back and forth over his head.

"C'mon up here, son," Bass told Josiah. The young trapper nudged his pony a few steps forward until he sat beside Scratch so both could look down into the valley where two forks of the Yellowstone tumbled together.

"Ain't that a purty sight for your eyes, Josiah?"

Below the rise the cottonwoods lined the banks of the two water courses. A man's eyes were drawn automatically to the point where the two streams met, and within the V his gaze was greeted with the hints of hide lodges, trails of gray ghosts rising lazily up from their smoke flaps. A few forms could be distinguished along the forks of the river, stooped and huddled forms bent and rising, then bent again in the gathering of firewood.

"Damned near as purty as Billy Sublette's whiskey mules rollin' in after a y'ar's dry!" Titus said quietly but with unashamed excitement. He turned to nod toward the big warrior, who then gave the signal to descend the hill to the village.

As they began to drop toward the river, the movement of men and animals along the bluff was sighted by those forms bent to gather wood. The activity stopped and attention was riveted on the procession coming down the rise. Slowly the big Crow let his pony prance out from the others and took the lead, moving his animal back and forth in a slow, snaking path toward the river. First one, then another, and finally all of the wood gatherers broke back into the trees and disappeared, juggling their clumsy loads of drift timber.

The ponies splashed slowly across the river, protesting the cold rushing water flowing over the shallow ford. Drops of the cold liquid flew into the air and caught each man's leggings as he swayed with his animal's mincing steps across the rock-strewn river bottom. Up onto the wide beach where the wood gatherers had first seen their approach the party climbed and then headed into the trees. Now they could hear the excitement in the voices coming from the village. Now they could see the first light forms of the lodges smudged between the dark cottonwood sentries.

"Absor'kee," Bass mumbled, smiling quietly to himself.

A few young boys appeared ahead of the big warrior and raced alongside the two trappers for a moment, staring up at the white men briefly before darting ahead toward the encampment. Chattering and yelling to their companions, more and more of the young Indians appeared from their play to join in the procession. One youth dashed forward to tap Josiah's leg, then was gone. Another raced forward to touch his arm, then likewise disappeared into the trees. Paddock felt something tap him on the shoulder and turned to see a young boy with a stick in his hand dart away between the pack animals.

"Jest had you coup counted on you, Josiah," Bass snorted. "Young'uns seen you was easy pickin's, they did," chuckled Bass. "L'arn 'em young, that they do!"

The white trappers knew the Crow to be one of the bravest and most war-loving tribes on either side of the mountains, yet they boasted of never having taken a

528

white man's life. Small in numbers, with far fewer warriors than either the Blackfeet or the Sioux, the Crow still clung tenaciously to their ancient holdings against the overwhelming odds sweeping down from the north or pouring out of the east. A proud people, Bass thought. Tough, brave as bufflers in spring, loving their sex and a dirty joke as well as any trapper, these Crow were the best teachers a man could have in the mountains. Proud he was, too, having the village crier proceed them through the village. The old man hobbled slowly before Bass and the big man, carrying a staff he pounded against the ground rhythmically while he wailed at the top of his lungs.

"Walkin' newspaper, that old'un is," Scratch said to Paddock. The tribal crier was a singular position usually filled by an old warrior no longer able to hold council but given this office out of deference to his past deeds. He walked amongst the lodges several times a day to announce tidbits of information, advertising for those articles either lost or found, announcing feasts and councils, hunts or war parties, dances and marriages. And now the shrill old voice rose above the hubbub of the village, commanding all to cease what they were doing and give attention to the arriving party.

On either side of the procession the people began to form ranks. Heads turned to stare at Bass and Paddock, then turned back to chatter with a neighbor before staring once more at the white men. The young boys continued to dart alongside the ponies and mounted riders, while here and there pairs of dark, shy eyes would focus on the younger of the trappers, then drop quickly away before being caught staring too long. Josiah smiled first at this one, then at that one, his eyes busy with all that was to be seen.

"Don' screw your head off jest yet, son!" Bass chuckled as he watched Josiah turning around this way and that to take in all the feminine sights. "Likely to be, them gals'll do the screwin' it off for you afore too long!" He smiled widely as he saw Paddock's toothy grin nod up and down in happy agreement.

One small boy had continued to trot beside Bass, looking up expectantly. Finally Scratch looked down at the child and tapped his pony's rump behind him. The boy's head bobbed up and down excitedly. Leaning slightly to the left, Bass let his left arm down and grasped onto the child's arm as the boy gripped the trapper's forearm with all his strength. With the Indian's foot placed atop Scratch's, the boy swung up behind Scratch and settled himself against the trapper's back, one arm wound tightly against the trapper's side and the other arm busy in waving to his people. He was as proud and happy as could be, now a member of the procession.

Paddock felt the tug at his right ankle and looked down to see another boy, then two, begging to be given a ride with him. He looked over at Bass with a question in his eyes.

"Go 'head, son. They love you for it."

Josiah smiled broadly once again and let his right arm drop. He pulled one boy up to sit in front of him in the saddle. As the first youth straddled the pony Josiah let his arm drop again and grasped onto the second youngster, pulling the boy up to sit behind him on the pony's rump.

"Made you couple friends there, Josiah."

"Looks that way, don't it," he replied, playfully tossing the hair of the young one who sat in front of him. The boy turned and smiled as he looked up at the trapper. "Always like this?" he said to Bass.

"Not jest," he answered, then turned to face Josiah. "Special greetin' this time, for some reason."

The big man finally brought the slow procession to a halt and looked over at Bass. He pointed to the big lodge.

"Arapooesh?" Scratch asked.

The Indian nodded, then called out. Several older boys, in their early teens, stepped from the bordering fringe of onlookers to approach the trappers. Carefully so as not to cause the animals to shy from them, the youngsters grasped the ponies' reins.

"Empty your saddle, young'un," Bass instructed as he helped the boy behind him swing to the ground, then dismounted himself. Josiah felt the Indian behind him slide back off his pony's rump and helped the boy in front leap to the ground. Bringing his right leg over the pommel, Josiah dropped from the saddle. An Indian youth began to lead the pony away.

"Where they takin' 'em?" He looked around to see all their animals being led away by the youngsters, one of the boys having a little trouble with the old, cantankerous mule.

530

"Feed 'em. Water 'em, mostlike," Scratch answered.

"Ain't gonna steal 'em?" Josiah squeaked quietly. "You just let 'em have the ponies?"

"Crow ain't 'bout to steal no ponies what belong to guests of the tribe. Awww, they might see somethin' there they wants to steal some other time, if'n they had 'em the chance't. That'd be fair, you see. But not now. Not when we special to 'em."

Paddock shook his head slightly as he watched the ponies, pack animals, and Hannah being led away through the lodges. Bass understood his confusion, what with Josiah's having heard him say the Crow were the best horse thieves in the mountains. But Indian morality had some mighty strange bends and curves to it, like the twisting course of the Snake River. One thing a man could hold to though: that morality would not be violated, no matter how strong or sweet the temptation.

The big man tapped Paddock on the shoulder and pointed to the tripod that stood beside the lodge door. From the apex formed by the three straight limbs hung the skin of a large white wolf, the hide sewn together to form a medicine bundle. Beside it also hung a mountain lion quiver bulging with arrows. Atop both over the rawhide shield, at the crown of the tripod, dangled a full scalp adorned with the tips of the loser's ears.

"He's showin' you this be Rotten Belly's lodge," Scratch commented.

"Rotten Belly? That him?"

"Nawww. Rotten Belly. Arapooesh. The same."

The rustle at the door flap precluded more explanation. Pushed out of the way, the bear skin covering was parted by a bare arm. The graying head appeared and dipped out of the opening. Before the two white men rose the Crow chief.

He stood for a moment, his aging gray eyes becoming accustomed to the brightness reflected off the snow after the inky darkness of the lodge interior. His lips and the corners of his eyes seemed to smile at the same time as recognition suddenly washed over the chief's face. Bringing his right arm up, Arapooesh placed the palm of his right hand over Scratch's heart. Bass likewise put his hand over the Indian's left breast. They held the position for a long moment, studying one another's face in silence before the Indian removed his hand and placed it over Bass's at his own breast.

Josiah looked on in silence with the rest of those gathered about the two old friends. He studied the manner in which the buffalo robe was thrown over the Indian's left shoulder and under the right arm, the flaps held with the left hand to leave the right arm free for gesture. His gaze dropped from the Indian's eyes and ran past the smooth whisker-plucked cheeks and chin to the bright, dangling ear ornaments. The rim of the ear had been punctured and brass wire passed through the opening. From the wire hung large pink shells and tarnished brass beads.

"Pote ani," he finally spoke, with a voice hardened by the years yet smooth as water-polished pebbles of a stream.

"Arapooesh, my brother." Bass took his left hand and placed it on the Indian's shoulder for a moment.

"It is good for the heart of our people that you have come now, at this time. Our eyes have long grown tired in the waiting for you. But now you have come to join in our winter camp." His eyes wandered to Scratch's right hand against his breast. Slowly he took the bandaged hand into both of his and looked up at Bass. "What is it that has happened to Pote ani? Has the rifle bitten you back?" he asked with a quick smile.

"No, my friend. It was not the rifle. Jest had me a battle with a b'ar."

The gray eyes surveyed Scratch's eyes for a moment. "Then it will be as our dreamers have been told. A white man, a friend to Absaroka, was to come for the medicine dance. To fight alongside our people against the enemy who come out of the north where the Cold Maker lives."

"Wait a minute," Bass stammered. The Crow words had come too fast for him to absorb at one gulp, as the chief knew it might be.

"There will be enough time for this talk later." Arapooesh sought to turn the discussion. He looked beyond Scratch at the young trapper. "Who is the young strong one you bring with you?"

"My . . . my friend. He is young in the ways of the mountains, but he is quick to learn." Bass flashed a smile in Paddock's direction, knowing the young man did not understand the Crow language being shot around him like many arrows. Scratch liked the tongue of this tribe, their words being delicate yet sharp as the edge of a knife, without the guttural, clublike heaviness of so many other tongues.

"You are his chief, then?" Rotten Belly asked, putting his two index fingers together, but with one longer against the other to symbolize a higher status.

"No," Bass answered. "We are together. As one." He put his two fingers together to show them equal in length. "Companyeros," he said in English.

"Coom-paa-yerr-hoss," the chief repeated slowly and smiled. He took a step forward and stood before the young, nervous trapper. Reaching out with the right hand he touched Josiah's breast over the heart, then tapped his own. "We will be friends as Pote ani is my friend. Yes?"

"He's askin' you to be his friend, as we are friends, me an' him," Scratch explained. "Jest nod your head yes, son."

Paddock nodded twice quickly and smiled at the chief, then looked back to Bass to see if more were needed. Scratch smiled at him and then addressed the chief. "We will set up our lodge now, before the sun falls beyond the trees."

"Then you will come eat with Arapooesh. We have much to talk of this night, but it can wait until you have rested from your journey to this place. It can wait until the next sun after you have slept and the trail has drained from your bones." He waved to his side the big Indian who had led the trappers to the encampment. "You will see that our friends raise their lodge where they wish, and will have water and wood for the first night. You will see to this." The big man nodded, then pointed at Bass to have the white man follow him.

The villagers who had gathered to watch the chief's greeting of the new arrivals parted for the three men as the trappers followed the Indian. Most broke off to return to what they had been doing before the procession entered the village, while others turned to chatter with a neighbor.

"Good people," Bass said in Crow.

"Huh?"

"Awww." He realized he had spoken in the foreign tongue. "Said they's good people. You'll be likin' it here for the winter."

He smiled briefly at the young man, then looked ahead at the Indian leading them through the lodges. Grimly he kept the happy pose at the sides of his mouth while inside his mind raced over the words of Rotten Belly. The dreamers' visions had told them of a white man coming to help them fight their enemies. A white man. Was it the bear that had foretold this? Was it the bear? His right hand began again to throb and he gave it his attention.

The small, old woman had built the fire back up after the meal and was excused from her husband's lodge. To Rotten Belly's left sat the two white men while at his right hand were seated four of the older men of the tribe. The only face Scratch recognized in the dancing firelight was that of the big man, the youth who had brought them into camp. He sat by the door as a silent sentry.

From bundles placed at his right hand Arapooesh drew the stem, bowl, and ornaments of his medicine pipe. In the slow, time-honored way, the chief blessed each part before he methodically put the pipe together. Two ancient eagle feathers, their stems wrapped in quills, draped from a porcupine quill-wrapped glove around the wooden stem and it was ready to fill with tobacco. When he laid the pipe across his lap, Rotten Belly opened another, smaller pouch from which he drew tiny pinches of the brown leaf. Carefully, each pinch was introduced into the bowl so that the chief's fingers would not touch the inside of the round hole in the red stone. It was a long process, this ceremony, one which could cause much impatience in many white men not familiar with the ceremony and its sacred significance. Finally it was done and the chief asked to have the bowl lighted for him.

One of the old men leaned forward from his position and took a long dry twig from the embers and held it over the bowl. Scratch looked at the aging, weathered hands that cradled the pipe with love and reverence. Arapooesh drew deeply again and again, until the only sound within the lodge was that of the chief drawing fire into the bowl; the faint crackle now and then as this sliver and that of tobacco caught fire. This too took time for the bowl was big and the stem long. Beside him the young trapper squirmed uneasily, nervously. Scratch put his left arm out slowly and rested it on Josiah's thigh as a father would have done in a church pew to quiet his son's nervous fidget.

The pipe came to Bass as the chief exhaled evenly. The trapper drew the smoke into his lungs and marveled anew at the Crow's tobacco. They grow some of the finest damned honeydew, he thought to himself as the smoke seeped into every corner of his swelling chest. Ain't like that willerbaccy that tastes like last year's moccasins, he mused before handing the pipe to Josiah. Just wish Ol' McAfferty was here to be seeing this. Might just be changing his mind about all them religious notions he's got for himself. It just might do that.

Paddock finished and started to rise to take the pipe over to the big man by the door, but Scratch laid his hand again on the young trapper's thigh, motioning at the same time to return the pipe the way it had come to him. Without words, Bass hoped he had taught the young man that the pipe must not pass the door of a lodge. The pipe traveled from Bass's hands into the chief's to begin its journey in the other direction. Four times it made its pendulum circuit to each of the lodge guests; only the big youth by the door was excepted.

Josiah carefully watched each man smoke, each pulling the smoke he exhaled over his bowed head before passing the pipe on. He watched and wondered why the young man was not allowed to join in the ceremony. Looking at him, Paddock judged the Indian to be not that much younger than he was, perhaps in his late teens. He was big; the firelight, playing off the contours of his well-developed body, revealed a musculature not unlike the valleys and hills of a well-worn watercourse. Why am I to smoke and he cannot? I am a guest, Josiah thought, and with it a brief surge of pride pulsed through him.

With the pipe finally back to Arapooesh after its fourth trip, the chief carefully dumped burnt ash from the bowl and threw the residue into the fire. No unburned tobacco remained. All had been consumed. It was good and the Crow chief smiled. The spirits too had smiled on this gathering.

"The spirits have continued to smile upon you, Pote ani, to bring you from so far to this place," Arapooesh said, turning his head finally to address the white trapper beside him. Bass nodded and somewhat nervously looked quickly at the other old men across the fire from him.

With a gesture of his right arm, the chief swept over his tribesmen. "Our old men have told us of the white man coming. Of the white man coming to us. Of the white man coming to help in our struggle."

Bass cleared his throat, attempting to push down the clawing lump rising in his chest. Arapooesh delicately raised his left hand to silence anything else coming from the trapper so that he might continue.

"It has been foretold for many moons now that the white man would come. There have been those who have laughed at my words that you would be that white man. You, Pote ani. Each man knew you come with the winter's deepest snows, yet they believed this vision told of another white man."

He thought it best that he tell them now of McAfferty's coming, of his Nez Perce wife. Now might be the time. But the chief went on.

"The vision has not been clear to our old men, Pote ani; clear as the mountain streams we would hope the vision to be. Perhaps because it was not to be clear to us until now. Perhaps. In this way we were not to see until more things had come to pass. It has not been clear." Rotten Belly bowed his head and closed his eyes for a moment before continuing. "The pieces have come to us slowly, and yet we are not sure how they are to fit together, as the windpipe fits together; there is but one way given to us. Now, with this dream, we are unsure when we hold all the pieces." With his eyes still closed lightly, the Crow chief raised his face toward the heavens. "The old men speak of one who comes with a hand wrapped in the fur of our brother the beaver."

Unconsciously, Bass placed his left hand over the wrapping on his right. With it cradled in the center of his folded legs, the trapper cleared his dry throat again, forcing against the hot lump coming out of his chest.

"This is the one called on by the spirits to come to us." The chief's eyes slowly opened and descended to look into the fire. "But we are confused. We cannot tell. For there is another man in the dream. A white man too, this second one." He took the pipe into his hands again and held it out before him.

The unsettling queasiness grew stronger within Bass.

Was it McAfferty? Could it be Paddock? Then Rotten Belly continued, "The dreamers know this man has been here before."

Scratch looked at Josiah. No, he thought, no way the boy could have been here before. Surely. The young trapper was watching the chief intently, then turned slowly, having felt the old trapper's eyes upon him. Paddock's eyes smiled with a deep innocence and enjoyment of the unfamiliar ceremony. He does not know what we are saying, Bass thought.

"The dreamers know this man has been here, in this place, before," Arapooesh continued. "But—we know him not."

Bass knew then, and the smell of death invaded his nostrils. It was not the boy. The dreamers would have known him when they rode into camp. They would have known Paddock was the second white man.

Arapooesh rolled his arms back to his chest, and with them came the pipe. Cradling it to his breast for a moment, the chief finally placed it across his lap and sighed. "The second white man—he is not clear to us. We see him coming from the place where the north wind sends his breath down on us. It is cold." A long sigh came from across the lodge. Scratch's attention was drawn for a fleeting moment to its direction, but he could not tell from which of the old men it had come. Titus looked back at Rotten Belly and waited. The old eyes closed and blinked, as if to clear away the mist of nonunderstanding, as if to scatter the mist of sadness gathered there for his people.

"It weighs heavy on our hearts, this dream. The spirits do not tell us well of this thing. We wish to know more but must not be short with the spirits. We will know in time. We will know as we should know."

As the chief turned to look at Bass his dark face seemed to drain of its tension, but the eyes still held their intensity. "When the last moon rose full from the east, our enemy came to this our homeland. They knew where we camped for the winter and rode down on us with a vengeance. Our people fought bravely, but there were many to sing over when the fighting was done. Our enemy knew where we chose to spend this winter. Each new sun now we send out our young men into the cold of the hills." With a sweep of both arms, Rotten Belly encompassed much of a full circle. "There they are to watch

537

as they stalk the game our bellies need. There they are to keep the eye strained for a look at our enemy. With struggle we have moved our winter camp to this place." Both arms descended so that his fingers touched the earthen floor of his lodge. "With pain and heavy hearts we moved through the snow to this place where the two waters meet. Leaving behind many of our brothers, our people, those who fell before the enemy, we left that dark ground behind us and chose this. Now we have the cliffs that rise behind us, while in front of us flow the two rivers." The left hand brushed across the robe on which he sat.

"We will listen to the spirits as they talk to us, for we do not wish to make them angry with the people. There have been too many tears already. You will spend these moons with us in our camp, and we will listen to what the spirits tell us. Sadness holds us in its hand for just so long and now we must be finished with it. We must break free of its hold at our breast as the thongs rip free from our breast in the dance to the Life Giver. Our old friend, Pote ani, has returned. Our words have been said and gone away. These things must not weigh heavy on your heart, our friend. These things are for Crow."

As the chief concluded, Scratch's head hummed with all he had heard. Most of the words he had been able to follow, some he had not. But he had understood enough so that he could grasp the concepts. At times the Crow tongue angered him, the way it was occasionally used by these people. They would dart from thought to thought as one would skip a stone across the water until finally it sank whether one was ready for the next toss or not. So much to absorb. He would have much to think on this night and in the days to come.

Bass turned to Rotten Belly and met the eyes staring into his before he spoke, slowly, falteringly; it had been a year since last he had put so many words together.

"As you say, I am white man. But I come to winter with the Crow, my friends. My brothers, the Crow. When I come, I eat as Crow. I sleep as Crow. I sing and dance as Crow. You give me squaw to sleep with as Crow. And if you need me, I fight as Crow."

He saw Arapooesh nod his head, and across the fire the old men also nodded approval of his slow words. "I am Crow. I am not Crow. My heart is with the Crow. My skin is white." With two fingers he pinched up a fold of wrinkled skin over his cheek. "I am man-in-between, Rotten Belly. I am man many times lost in between. As so many come to your land just for the beaver, I have come in spite of them. When first I came to your land, it was for the beaver alone. Now I return again and again for the land fills my heart. As it will fill the heart of my young friend." He placed a hand on Josiah's right shoulder.

"Here is my strong friend. Here beside me in your land. Together we are Crow for the winter. It is his second cold time in the mountains, this friend. He will spend it here with me so the Crow can teach him what he needs to know. Those things this old man cannot teach him." Scratch put the wrapped hand over his heart and bowed his head slightly. "Those things that are Crow."

Again the heads nodded as they looked from Bass to Paddock, then back to the older man once more. Rotten Belly took the pipe and laid it lightly across his palms. In lifting it he stretched out his arms momentarily, then let his hands rest back in his lap before speaking.

"It is true what you say, Pote ani. To bring the young one to this land to teach him. This is good. For the Crow country is like no other. The Crow country is a good country. Our land is a good land for its people. The Old Man Coyote, Akbatat-dia, has put the Crow people in the right place for them. While a man is in Absaroka he will fare well. Whenever a man shall go out of Absaroka, whatever trail he wishes to travel, he will fare worse.

"If you move on the trail to the south, you must wander and worry over the great flat and barren plains. There the water is always warm and bad for the belly. You will find fever and sickness your companions on the trail to the south of Absaroka.

"If you take the trail where the winds sweep down from the north, you will find it very cold. There the Cold Maker is early in his coming and much late in his going. There he is long and bitter in his bite. There is no grass to the north. And you cannot keep horses where there is no grass. You must travel with dogs. And what is such a country without horses?

"To the west, on the Columbia, which rushes to the Great Salt Water, the people are poor and dirty, and they do not have good clothes. These people push themselves about over the water in canoes and eat fish. Their teeth are worn out, and they grow old too fast for not having proper meat to eat. They are always taking the fish bones out of their teeth. Fish is a very poor food indeed when a man can eat of the deer and elk, bear and goat. The people have poor stomachs to the west.

"Where the sun comes up, the people dwell in villages of earth. They live well, it is said. But they must drink the bad water of the Great River, and it is muddy. A Crow's dog would not drink such water, but yet those people to the east are happy with it. Arapooesh does not understand.

"Where the Great River becomes three rivers in the direction where the sun goes to rest each night, it looks to be fine country. There is good water. There is plenty of grass. And there is buffalo. Much buffalo. In the summer that land is almost as good as Crow country. But when the Winter Man comes it is cold. The grass has gone from the land and the buffalo with it. There is no salt weed for a man's horses. It is fit only for our enemies.

"Here, in Absaroka, Crow country is exactly the right place for our people. We have the mountains with the snow on their peaks, and we have the sunny plains where it is warm. Here all kinds of weather and the best of everything for all seasons.

"When the summer sun burns at the plains and across the prairies, a man can draw up under the snowy peaks of white where he finds the air sweet and cool. There the grass will always be green and fresh. There the many clear streams come tumbling down to meet him from their snowbanks among the mountain peaks. There a man can hunt the elk, the deer, the goat—all animals when their skins are best fit for dressing. There too a man can find the white bears and sheep.

"In the season when the shaking trees turn their leaves to gold and the first breath of cold winds touches your face, when your horses are fat and strong, sleek from the mountain grasses, you come down onto the plains and hunt the buffalo. Or you catch the beaver on the streams as he puts on his winter fur. And when the snows first come, you can take your shelter in the wooded bottoms along the rivers as we do each year. There you will still find plenty buffalo meat for your people and plenty cottonwood bark for your horses. Too, a man can winter in the valley made by the River of the Wind, for there his animals will have all the salt weed they can eat.

"Yes, Pote ani. It is true what you say. Absaroka is the right place. Everything has come to our people from Old Man Coyote. What the white-eyes call the 'Maker of Everything,' our Akbatat-dia, has made good in this country. There is no country like our Absaroka. There is no land like Crow country."

Together the old men murmured their assent to the words of the chief. Many times would he tell white men of what he felt in his heart of Absaroka; many times would he tell them of the love he felt for this place.

"We sit in your hands this winter," Bass finally replied. "We sit in the lap of Absaroka. And we will take no more from its people than we can give." He reached to his left between him and Josiah and pulled forward the large bundle he had carried into the lodge earlier when they had gathered for supper.

With it before him now, all attention was riveted on the gnarled left hand and the clumsy right one as he struggled with the knots securing the package. As the ropes fell away, Scratch carefully peeled back the flaps of heavy buffalo hide to expose the contents. He brought forth streams and waves of brightly colored ribbon and blanket strouding. There were handfuls of hawks bells, which he shook for the Indians. Through his fingers Scratch let pour the brass nails and tacks the warriors would use to decorate their rifle stocks and tomahawk handles. And the beads, of colors to equal a rainbow, he scooped up to pour into the laps of each man. Small packs of vermilion and sugar and coffee he handed to Josiah to deliver across the lodge to each Indian. There were gifts of powder and one-pound bars of lead, spicy grains of pepper and salt, looking glasses and an awl for each man. Finally all that was left was the single tin container within the large hide bundle.

Bass brought it up to set within his lap and took his knife from his belt. With the edge of the blade he carefully began to pry open the lid of the container. After the knife was placed in its rawhide sheath at his side, Scratch took the tin in his hands and rose slightly so that he might scoot up close to Rotten Belly. He held the tin out in offering to the chief.

Arapooesh looked down into the tin, then back to Scratch's face to see the trapper smiling. The Indian bowed forward so that he might smell what was in the tin, then raised his face to look into Bass's again. Scratch nodded, to tell him it was fine, then realized the Indian might not know what was expected of him. He sat the container down before the chief and put his hand into the hole at the top. Bass brought out a small handful of the tiny fruit. Now with the index finger and thumb of his right hand, Scratch picked one of the small pieces and popped it inside his mouth to chew. He then swallowed ceremoniously and smiled.

"There. You try it," he remarked in English, putting the left hand forward to the chief.

Rotten Belly picked one of the fruit from the white man's hand and inspected it closely, then sniffed it. After looking at it for another moment, then at the old men on his right, Arapooesh popped it into his mouth and began to chew. Slowly his lips curved upward at the corners and he nodded once in satisfaction. He swallowed hard as Scratch had done, thinking it was the thing to do with such food.

"Keske-cea?" He wanted to know what the little fruit was called.

"Raisins," Bass answered. "Rai-sins."

"Way-suns," Arapooesh repeated. "Way-suns." Taking another from Bass's hand, the chief held it out for the old men to see, then popped it into his mouth.

"You can eat 'em like that," Scratch said haltingly, mulling over the Crow words he could use, "or like this," and he put the rest of the fruit in his palm up to his lips where he began to chew the whole bunch.

The chief nodded and put his hand into the ten-pound tin. With some to eat for himself, Rotten Belly pushed the tin toward the man on his right. Soon they were all eating the small, dark fruit and repeating to each other, "Way-suns. Way-suns. Ba pono tsi-toma."

Scratch cleared his throat as if in introduction, or interruption, or both. "Rotten Belly is my friend. He is my brother. I bring him gifts for he had the white man winter with his people. I must tell Rotten Belly, my brother, about another man who is coming to winter with the Crow. Another hunter of the beaver. His name is McAfferty." Scratch paused, caught up in the strangeness of the man's

542

name surrounded with the Crow tongue. He repeated the word, "McAfferty," and paused once more, seeing that all eyes had come to rest on him, all attention transferred from the raisins to his words. Some of the old faces about him dropped noticeably as he told of the new white man. Their countenance was not open, not benevolent—only worried.

"McAfferty," he used the word a third time, not knowing why except for emphasis, "he comes to be with Pote ani and the Crow for winter. His squaw is Nez Perce." He saw the almost imperceptible narrowing of Rotten Belly's eyes. "She is the daughter of Nez Perce chief and now McAfferty's woman. She carries his child, this McAfferty's child. He is an old man like Pote ani, old in the ways of the mountains. She is young"—his hand swept low in what he deemed an appropriate gesture— "and is with the child inside her."

Here Bass stopped for a moment and listened to the silence around him, interrupted by only the breathing of the old men. For the first time he really heard the faint wheeze of one of the old ones, each inhalation slightly rattling within the old man's chest.

"Will they be welcome here, as Pote ani and the young brave are welcome?" he finally asked.

Rotten Belly let his eyes rest on Scratch's for a few minutes, then looked down at his hand filled with the raisins. "They could be cause to worry. The vision. But— we have not yet seen this man you tell us of coming here. He is your friend. He may come . . . and we shall all share the dream." As his eyes raised once more to stare into Bass's, they were twinkling again, and there was a grin at his lips as he asked the old trapper, "You do not bring us the raisins to tell us this?"

"No. Raisins are for you anyway. Gifts are for you anyway the Crow decide." He gestured to all of the Indians across the fire from him. "Friends of the Crow cannot be bought. Friends of Pote ani cannot be bought. Pote ani knows this. He does not come to insult you. He does not try to go against the way of the Crow. Pote ani wants to know if they will be welcome. They will be on their way here in the next moon perhaps. What say Rotten Belly and the elders? What say the wise ones:

Buffalo Calf, Moon That Dances on the Hill, Comes from Across, and Plays with His Tongue? Will they be welcome for the winter in the warmth of Absaroka?"

For a few minutes that seemed much longer, Arapooesh studied the silent faces of the old men of the tribe as Bass examined them all. When finally it seemed settled without words from any of the four, Rotten Belly again spoke.

"We have no quarrel with the Nez Perce. And will be honored to warm the daughter of their chief among our lodges. Her time comes and my woman will help with the birth of the little white man with the Nez Perce blood. My woman will help as she does with the women of Absaroka. Your friend, he may come to winter with us. There will be wood and water and game for him too. Pote ani's friends come from far away to winter with him. But with the Crow they can stay, since he too is friend of Pote ani. Those you would welcome into your own lodge, we would welcome too. It is said."

Scratch nodded several times to each of the Indians around the small, dimming fire without saying a word. He reached behind him to pull the empty bundle to his side where he could quickly fold it under his arm.

"The fire becomes low with its light. Pote ani sees it is best for us to leave now. We have been long on the trail coming to this place. Long on the trail coming to this time. We are much honored by the Crow opening their hearts again to this white man. Do not let your hearts be troubled over us for we shall care for ourselves and our own." His face looked through the gray-brown veil covering the smoke hole as he gestured toward the top of the lodge. "The stars grow dim, as do my eyes for want of sleep. We will greet you with the new sun."

Scratch motioned to Josiah to rise with him as both of the white men made their way to the lodge door and slipped past the muscular youth who had remained in his place as sentry. There were few people stirring at the late hour in the village, mostly soldiers who would move through the camp and circle its perimeter until daybreak. Here and there was a lodge still faintly aglow with fire-light, making the hide lodge cover like a dim lantern. Now and then a figure moved within a lodge, but mostly it was the sounds of sleep they heard as they passed.

"Rusty," Bass muttered.

"Huh?" Josiah asked. The suddenness of Scratch's word had caught him off guard in the quiet of the cold night.

"Said I'm rusty," he repeated in a whisper. "Need me a loose tongue to be talkin' so much Crow. Heavy on my mind too. Havin' to put all them words together like that right off. Not been here even a day."

"Yeah," the young one answered as if he understood the difficulty of using a language only rarely put into service. Then he thought Scratch would not really mind him answering in such a way, although he still felt a little sheepish from the long conversation during which he had not understood the words spoken.

"They said it be fit to lettin' McAfferty an' his squar come in to winter here?" Josiah finally asked. The question might make his previous comment sound less absurd.

"Yep," answered the older man. "They puttin' the trust in me. Jest like you, Josiah. They puttin' the trust in me. An' it's a might heavy now. Awful heavy."

"You thinkin' McAfferty cause trouble? Maybe his squaw bein' Nez Percy?"

"Nawww. McAfferty won' be causin' no trouble. Oh, he's a strange critter a' times, that'un, what with them Bible-spoutin' ways. But he minds his manners round the Injuns, he does. No worry there."

"What's so heavy for you?" They stopped beside the low bower shelter thrown up against the cold where they would spend the winter in the Indian village.

"Them dreams 'bout white men, all that," Scratch answered distantly, looking over the top of their shelter at the fog rising off the river. "Them two white men. Arapooesh knows who they be."

"An' you? You know?"

"Got my calc'latin' on that, I do." He threw back the hide flap over the entrance to the shelter.

"You tell me?"

"No sense in a man flappin' his jaws less'n he's sure what he's sayin'."

"So you won't tell me what you're thinkin'?" Josiah queried, following Bass into the shelter and plopping down on the buffalo hides beside the older trapper.

"Nope." Bass unbuckled the belt at his waist and

545

placed it near the spot where his head would lie. Leaning back he let out a long sigh and pulled the heavy robe over his body.

"Ain't sure 'bout it then?" Paddock kept prodding for information.

"'Bout the size of it," was the quiet answer as Josiah slipped into his robe alongside Scratch.

Paddock felt the buffalo fur warm beneath his cheek as he finally closed his eyes and listened to the sounds of the winter night outside. He shuddered a bit and drew further down into the robe to warm another spot for his cheek. Not far off he could hear a coyote calling out among the hills, then it was quiet again with only the faint murmur of the frigid waters of the rivers flowing past them out in the dark, running swiftly toward the Missouri.

He traced it quickly in his mind until he could see the water, now turned muddy and swollen with snags and sandbars, gliding past St. Louis. He wondered if Bass ever had thoughts like this—about St. Louis and things left back there. Drawing his legs up to give the cold less body to touch, Paddock put his hands between his thighs at the groin. It was warm there.

The murmur seemed to come from both sides of him now. Not just from the rivers alone. Then he realized it was the old man beside him mumbling. He listened for a minute to see if he could follow. But the words were too low, too quiet.

"You talkin' in your sleep again," he remarked to Scratch. The mumbling stopped. It was over a minute before anything else was said.

"Ain't talkin' in my sleep, son." Titus finally commented, softly. "Might say I'm givin' my prayers."

"Prayers!" The word seemed incredible. "You! Sayin' your *prayers*?"

"In my own way, Josiah. Prayin' like I been for some time now. Prayin' for this thing to be taken from me. Prayin' 'cause what I was afeared of most looks to be comin' to pass. Man prays when he wants the thing took 'way from him—what he don' wanna have to do." He sighed deeply. "You foller?"

"Nope."

Another long minute passed before Scratch said, "'Night, Josiah."

He waited until he thought he heard the older man's breathing become deeper and more relaxed. "G'night, Scratch."

16

"Somethin' catch your eye, Josiah?" Bass noticed the young trapper studying the group of women at work over a buffalo hide stretched on the ground.

Paddock did not reply so Scratch shook his head slightly and put another piece of wood on their fire. The midmorning sun had just begun to creep over the edge of the shelter they had put up several weeks before upon their arrival in the village, that crude shelter of hides and cottonwood limbs that gave the appearance of a half dome. Where the dome had been cut in half, Bass had finished the winter home by draping the last smoked hide over the front so that it hung to the ground, there to double as a movable wall and an entrance to the small interior. Here he sat this morning with the young man, both tired of the inactivity, at the edge of the fire pit they had dug a few feet from the entrance. The warmth would then radiate within the shelter.

Bass took down his rifle, placed it across his lap, and then dragged to him the leather pouch. After pulling the wiping stick free of the thimbles he began to dig within the pouch for the screw he would put on the end of the ramrod. With it he could pull the lead ball from the barrel. He glanced at Josiah once more and shook his head again, slipping the stick down the barrel with an all too familiar sound.

"You gonna clean that damned thing again?" Josiah asked without even looking at the man sitting beside him.

Bass stopped working the screw into the lead ball. "Got you anythin' better for me to do?"

A gaping silence ensued. Josiah started to look in his direction but did not. Instead he shook his head once and made a quick, slight gesture with his hand. "Nawww. Go 'head with it."

"It bother you?" He began again slowly to pierce the ball.

"Nawww."

Tugging on the ball, Titus assisted its tough retreat from the barrel. "What's . . . what's eatin' on you?"

"Ain't nothin' eatin' on me, Bass."

"Nothin'," he replied. "Nothin' 'cept that the first thing you said to me all mornin' was to ask if'n I was cleanin' my rifle again, when you knowed what I was doin'. Nope. There ain't nothin' botherin' you, noway," Scratch snorted. "You gonna talk 'bout it—get it up an' outta your craw?"

Paddock leaned back on the robes, putting his elbows behind him with his chin pressing against his chest so that he could still watch the young women. Bass looked at the ball he had pulled from the muzzle and tossed it into a tin cup with many others he had pulled in days past. He saw that no answer was forthcoming.

"You got somethin' on your mind. C'mon, out with—"

"Dammit!" Josiah interrupted, suddenly pushing himself forward into a sitting position once more. "All we done since we got here is sit. Sit, eat, an' sleep. Get up from sleepin' to sit an' eat some more. We get so damned tired from the sittin' an' eatin', we go sleep some more. Over an' over an'—"

"All right," Bass interjected. "It's wearin' on you. Wearin' on me too. Man use ta movin' round an' doin' somethin' . . ." He let his voice drop off, not sure of where he wanted his words to go.

Paddock leaned back and rolled onto his side with a crooked arm under the side of his head for support. He began to play with the thick, curly hair of the buffalo robe, picking out the debris of endless trackings back and forth within the small shelter.

"You need you woman to take your mind off'n it all," Bass remarked quietly.

That was just it. A woman. His mind was full of her and he did not feel comfortable with these first tickles of vulnerability. Almost unconsciously, he reached a hand up to envelop the small buckskin pouch that hung from his neck. A woman to take his mind off it all? That was just it. His only problem right now. He could not get her off his mind. He stopped his nervous picking at the buffalo robe and looked at the young squaws again.

"Yep. That might do it. Be worth the try, don't you think?" Josiah said, grinning at the older man. Maybe he could get her off his mind by replacing her with another— if only for a while. And Bass began to grin too, at first fighting the beginnings of a huge smile that developed. "Don' you think it be worth the try?" asked Josiah, and both men began to laugh together, not really sure what they were laughing at, then continuing to laugh harder and louder because they thought it funny that they were finally laughing. Both felt the release in the laughter.

"Shit," Titus snorted. "Somethin' like that always be worth the try, young'un! Always worth the try!"

"Damned sight better'n rollin' over in the middle of the night an' seein' your ugly, hairy yapper layin' next to me!" Josiah chuckled. Then Bass started laughing again. "You feel the same way, don't you? Sometimes—don't you, Scratch?"

"Heh?"

"'Bout . . . 'bout havin' a woman?"

"Oh, yeah," Bass answered absently. "I do, that."

There were times, Bass had to admit to himself, when he did still feel that young hunger, the youthful yearning for the smooth flesh beside him throughout the long night. There were those times when the thoughts of young fingers running over his tired body, massaging, kneading, and teasing all those tight places would weigh heavy on his mind. Yes, Josiah, he thought, I need that sometimes. Sometimes.

What bothered him was that the sometimes were getting farther and farther apart. Was it age? Was it that? Just getting old didn't have to bother that part of a man. Wasn't the age. Nope. Not the age, he convinced himself finally. Maybe a man didn't want to get close with a woman when there's medicine on him. Can't get close. Don't have the hankering neither. Not with the medicine on him. It evened itself out, he thought. Things turn out one way, he'd be finished with the medicine and he could think again of laying with a woman. Things turned out the other way—well, he just wouldn't have to worry then.

"No new snow for 'while," Bass mumbled and gestured with his hand almost imperceptibly while staring at the sky. The pale blue of the canopy was marred only by an occasional high wisp of white cloud. He did not know if Josiah looked at the sky with him or not. Didn't matter, he thought.

"Hunt, gonna be in couple days, Josiah." He kept looking at the sky. There was no answer from the young man beside him as he heard Paddock put another piece of timber on their small fire and scrape through the embers. "We go out with 'em, if'n you'd like."

"That'd suit me."

"Take your mind off'n the gals for 'while, it would, too." He finally glanced at Josiah.

"S'pose it would."

Scratch let out a long sigh and looked again at the small knot of squaws Josiah was intently watching. "Couple of 'em look good 'nough for you," he began. "Couple of 'em even look mean 'nough for me."

"Want you a mean one, eh?"

"Had me all others. S'pose I need me a mean one for a change." He played with the heel of his right foot, digging a shallow trough through the packed snow. He heard Josiah rustling through some of the baggage that surrounded their sleeping robes in the small shelter and fought to ignore the impulse to turn and see what the young trapper was doing. He put his attention on one cloud, watching the white wisps change shape ever so slowly, stretching and parting, becoming two clouds each with its own distinct form, only then to tumble and roll back together to form a new cloud. What beauty in the slow yet ever-constant process of the heavens!

"Meant to thank you," Josiah said later when he had stretched out again beside the older man. "Cain't remember doin' it. But, want you to know I thank you."

"Wha' for?" He rolled his head lazily to the side to see Paddock finally settled beside him.

"The mokersons."

"Ah, the mokersons." Bass looked at Josiah's feet. "Couldn' have you go round much longer with your feet froze up, painin' you." He filled his eyes with the blue canopy overhead. "'Tweren't no trouble."

He thought gently on the boy, how he wanted everything, the best, provided for him. Like the moccasins. Three pairs of winter moccasins. Josiah would continue to wear the Nez Perce pair as the innermost, as the pair cut to fit his foot the best. Over that pair was slipped a pair made by a Crow woman from a hide tanned with the hair on, to turn the cold. The outside pair was made of the tough waterproofed buffalo hide to turn the wet. It could be clumsy, moving about in three pairs of moccasins at first, but a man could learn to walk quietly and move quickly with such an arrangement in little time. A good arrangement it was too, as a man often had to hunt on foot during the winter rather than force his pony through the deep snow and slicing, icy crust.

"When your skins be ready, Scratch?" Josiah inquired.

"Why? You wanna go see 'bout 'em?"

"Yeah. Feel like doin' somethin'. Gotta move round. Maybe get rid of this funny feelin' at my stomach." Josiah moved his arms away from his sides, stretched them, and returned them to wrap around his middle.

"Meatbag botherin' you?"

"Prob'ly just from sittin'—"

"Well, don' jest sit there. C'mon." Bass rose to his feet quickly. "We'll walk off whatever's painin' you."

"Need bring me anythin'?" Paddock asked, getting up.

"Jest your lazy ass." Bass swung an arm around and slapped the young trapper lightly on the rear. "C'mon. Let's tramp."

They stopped for a moment to watch the young women at work over some buffalo hides from a recent hunt. Josiah was interested more in looking over the women than in watching their work. With the squaws on their knees over the hides, fleshing and scraping, he inspected their bottoms, comparing the fat and slim of their anatomies, marveling at the flatness of some and the firm, round tightness of others.

"Really had ass on your mind, didn' you?" Bass teased. "'Tweren't no int'rest to seein' 'bout my skins at all, was it?" He folded his arms across his chest and winked at Paddock. "Got your eye on any one special?"

"Nawww. Not thinkin' 'bout any one special." Josiah knew he was lying. "Just got women on my mind."

"Want you mind now, young'un; this here nigger's been one to lay with a mess a them dark gals. Scratch been one to trap from the likes of the Red River an' the Marias up on the English kentry, clear way down to the Heely, round where the greasers call Taos an' Santy Fe home. Laid me mokerson tracks from the Platte an' Pawnees

551

clear to the water scrape west a the Stonies an' Sweet Lake. That be a heap a kentry what I wored mokerson out on, poured lotta that dirt outta them mokersons too. I read me sign with the best of 'em, an' what I'm readin' on your face ain't the good of it neither. Read it plain as turtle rock sittin' out on the Sweetwater or the three breasties stickin' up 'longside Davey Jackson's Hole. Ain't no coverin' it when a man's got him the womens hunger. An' that can spell a man no good out here, it can. Damn my hide if'n I ain't said to you afore there ain't much sign in a squar's breast, least none lodges there I could ever make out. Had me squars afore, you know, what was call't my wives. An' you ain't seein' me packin' one now, does you?"

Paddock looked from the women at their work to Bass, then went back to watching the fleshing process. He could not erase her from his mind. He could not forget that one night. She had had many men before, he was sure of that. And he had had his share of women. But something there had gone beyond the comforting of his heart and the release of pent-up sexual anxiety. He could not forget her coming to him that night west of the mountains and he still wore the expression that told Titus he wasn't really getting through to the young trapper.

"Best you look sharp now, you hear, young'un? Jumpin Jehoshaphat! You'll be gone beaver afore you leave winter diggin's. That the true. Hola! If'n you ain't got stickin' on your mind, right now, boy! An' a crazy critter it makes a man too."

Bass stepped up beside Josiah and leaned close to the young man so that their shoulders brushed. "Ain't never see'd you what them loverly squars can do to a man if'n he's took pris'ner—done somethin' to piss the whole tribe of 'em off. Why"—he paused briefly to look behind him, more for dramatic effect than to see if there were any listeners to their conversation—"they sees to it such a man gets tied down—flat, he is, on his back. Naked they strip him too. Winter time, makes no differ'nce. Them screamin' squars spit all over him—an' that ain't the worst of it, neither. Some a them harpies an' bangtails sit right down on him an' take the piss or shit, like'n he was no better'n the ground they'd do it on. 'Cause to them, he ain't—no better, I mean."

"Nawww," Josiah protested. "Them?"

"Ain't the half of it, boy. Ain't even the half of it.

Noways." His voice low and rasping, Bass was beginning to enjoy this. "They'll cut lil' pieces off'n yer pizzer, real slowlike. Piece, by piece, by piece, by piece, by—"

"Aw right!"

"Take 'em a sharp stick an' put it to the corner of your eye. Pop the eyeballs outta your head real easy. Slow at that too, if'n they want. Take a knife an' slice round inside your mouth where your teeths are—pull 'em out maybe. Build a fire down between your legs too. Think you been hot down there afore with a squar—jest wait'll they build a fire over your pizzer—"

"You done?" Josiah brushed against Scratch's shoulder as he turned to face the older man.

"Slip a knife or a real sharp stick in the end your tongue—pull it out far as it goes. Then them harpies go to cuttin' it off in real thin slices, like you'd take your meat off'n some hump ribs sittin' by the fire. Throw the pieces, they does, to the dogs. Always got dogs round when they go to workin' over a nigger. All kinds of dogs wantin' that fresh meat, Josiah."

"You done now?" Paddock turned and started off slowly with Bass right by his side.

"One good thing 'bout it all, son. One good thing 'bout the whole consarned doin's." He paused a moment and let Josiah stop walking. Paddock turned to face him.

"Crow don' eat dog. They don'." He strained to keep a straight face. "They jest keep dogs round so them critters can eat the pris'ner!" He laughed now, no longer able to hold it in.

"You think you're funny, don't you, Scratch?" Josiah turned to move off again through the lodges.

"Squars got two sides to 'em, they does. Gotta own up to that right off, Josiah." He walked easily beside the young man, swinging his arms loosely, feeling good in the late-morning sun. Feeling better with himself for the humor and the movement.

"I s'pose I can believe you 'bout all that too, eh?"

"Swear it. I swear it." Bass put his right hand up briefly as if taking an oath. "The gospel on my mother's grave."

Three dogs scampered by and Josiah began to step aside from them, but thought better when Scratch began to snicker.

"True too—the Crow don't eat dog?"

"Yepper." He stopped his chuckle. "One a few peoples what don'. Most tribes does eat dogs. But Crow don'. So if'n you're worried 'bout eatin' dog come time for a feast here 'bouts, don' let it rub your mind. Ain't never gonna eat dog with the Crow, you won'."

They passed the large open area of the village where dances and general councils were held, dodging the children at play in the warm sunlight, stopping momentarily to watch the work of the arrow makers busy with straightening the willow cut to length or shaping the feathers tied at the ends of the shafts.

In the sunlight outside her lodge sat the wife of Holds the Tail. A woman of age, her face showing the wrinkles of wisdom and winters, Comes Running was the Crow squaw chosen by Titus to dress the skins. Her old hands were busy sewing at some moccasins as the white men approached and stopped before her. She did not look up.

"Ictu-a," Bass greeted.

Comes Running continued to slip the awl, needle, and sinew through the leather without acknowledging their presence. For a moment Scratch stood in his place, pondering the situation. Then he leaned close to the woman, his face but a foot from hers now.

"Ictu-a," he repeated, this time louder and slower.

The squaw looked up, startled to see the two men standing over her. Squinting into the light thrown down from the sun as it neared the middle of the sky, Comes Running lifted an old hand slowly to her brow and shaded her eyes. Scratch figured her hearing was beginning to dim with age, and felt the softness in his heart swell for the woman.

"Pote ani," she said, recognizing his face. "Ictu-a," she repeated, and began slowly to rise, bringing her legs under her buttocks and bracing against the side of the lodge. Bass leaned forward to put his hands under one of her arms. For an instant she looked up at him, then took the hand she had used to brace against the lodge and placed it on his wrist. By their combined efforts, she was brought to her feet. She looked at him again and nodded once before moving off to enter the lodge.

"Never wanna get old like that," Josiah commented quietly.

"She's lived many, many winters," Bass replied. "Promise me, son, you'll shoot me when I get where I'm needin' help like that."

"Never be—"

"Promise me, boy," he cut in quickly. "Pains my heart to see such a thing. Be painin' me to think of Titus Bass like that. Promise me, son."

"You sayin' that true?"

"Promise me." He looked squarely at Paddock.

"Sure," he said halfheartedly. "Sure, Scratch."

Bass looked back at the dim hole in the lodge cover and waited, thinking of the labor involved for the old woman in dressing the skins he had brought to her. Rotten Belly had recommended Comes Running as the squaw to tan and smoke the hides, but the trapper wondered now if he should have commissioned another, a younger, squaw to do the work. True, when a woman no longer was able to labor with the chores of camp life, she was no longer deemed a productive member of the community. So many an old squaw kept at the skills she had practiced for many years, even after lesser women would have given up and waited for death.

The back-bending, repetitive tedium of dressing hides could age a woman quickly, prematurely. After soaking the skins for a few days beneath a lye mixture of ashes, water, and buffalo dung, the hides were removed from the solution. At that time the hair would be removed if that was desired. Then the skins were staked out on the ground where the snow was brushed away and secured with strong wooden pins driven through the edges of the hide deep into the earth. The fat and tissue were scraped off with sharp instruments before a mixture of brains and dung of the buffalo or elk was pushed through the pores of the skin, over and over by scraping the mixture across the hide. The bone or rock used in the process was carried over the skin with the full weight of the woman pressing on it. Finally, there was one last scraping to dry and soften the robe.

When this was done, many a hide would then be smoked. The squaw would start a smoldering fire of rotten wood that produced more smoke than flame and heat in a large pit dug in the ground. Standing over the pit was a frame of poles lashed together at their tops, much as a lodge would be. Over this frame the woman placed the hide to be smoked, sewing the edges of the skin together so that no smoke from the smoldering fire could escape. Over the fire the skin was to remain for several days while the smoke seeped into the pores of the hide; that made it capable of being dampened many times while remaining soft, pliable, and in its original shape.

Bass saw her struggling just inside the entrance and knelt to take the skins from the woman. Bass handed one hide to Josiah. "That's your b'ar, an' a purty robe it makes." He looked back into the dim light of the lodge and took the second hide from Comes Running, passing it too on to Paddock. "The wolf you stuck center."

Josiah ran his fingers across and through the thick, dark fur of the second hide, marveling at its softness. He brought it to his cheek just below the eye where there were no whiskers, closed his eyes, and felt the caress of the soft fur. He had not felt anything quite like this before, Josiah thought to himself. Not like this at all.

The woman shooed Bass away from the entrance with a few rapid motions of an old hand. Scratch stood and stepped back from the door to allow her exit from the lodge. Wrapped in a roll under one arm was a hide she carried forth herself, dipping low through the door to stand once more in the winter sunlight.

Comes Running took one arm away from the bundle and began to tug at the worn blue capote Bass had hung over his shoulders. He got the idea, but he was not sure why she wanted him to remove the blanket coat. He took it off and hung it carelessly over his left arm. Chattering at him, Comes Running motioned for him to hand the coat to Josiah. Bass did as he was told and laid the capote over the two hides Paddock held against his chest.

By grasping the side of the bundle beneath her right arm, the squaw shook out the skins for his inspection. It was more than he had expected. Rather than only dressing the two elk hides, Comes Running had tailored them into a crude coat. She held it by the shoulders before him, its bottom dragging the ground in front of the tiny woman. Titus didn't know what to do. Didn't know what to say. The fingers of both hands worked nervously across his palms. He stuttered the words for thanksgiving, thinking those words were not enough to express his appreciation for the gift she had worked long weeks in secret to give him.

Comes Running shook the coat at him, telling Scratch to turn around. Bass obeyed, bending at the knees slightly so that the short woman could put the new coat on the trapper. Through the sleeves he pushed his arms, each hand feeling the softness of the dressed hide. She had fleshed the hides so well that neither was heavy in weight. It would warm him as well as any buffalo robe, yet have the convenience and comfort of a blanket capote.

As the coat slipped over his shoulders and he tugged it into place across his chest, the squaw turned him around to face her. The woman's old hands went to the four thong ties at the flaps of the coat and knotted the thongs. It was good, she nodded to herself. Years of fitting and making clothing for her own man had allowed her to size up any man pretty much on sight alone. Bass nodded in dumfounded satisfaction at the fine fit of the garment, running his left hand down the front of the coat.

She tugged on the coat, making him stoop down toward her face. With both hands she pushed up the wide collar, also of the dressed elk and made from the cape over the bull's shoulders. On this piece of hide she had left the hair, sewing the collar onto the coat so that the fur lay on the outside. In this way, she said, the white man could turn his collar up and have the fur against his cheeks. It was good, he thought. The collar was wide and when turned up would cover his face well above the ears and eyebrows. It was good.

Bass tried to stammer the words of appreciation again and again until she told him to be quiet. "I feel like I gotta pay you more," he said in English, then stumbled through the words in Crow for her understanding.

She shook her head violently and told him she would have no such thing. The gifts he had given her for everything were already enough. More than enough for an old woman. What would an old woman want with anything more, she asked him?

He said he did not know, then added that perhaps she would want to have more gifts to pass on to her children. At his words she looked away from his face at the ground, then back to his face after a moment of thought. She said she no longer had any children, she and her man, Holds the Tail. No longer had any close relatives.

But your two daughters, he protested.

557

The Blackfoot had rubbed them out. With the word "Blackfoot" she spoke with much emphasis, as much as with the words "rubbed out," gesturing one palm brushing over the other.

And your son, Bass remarked, wishing to find some solace for the old woman before him.

Blackfoot too, she answered, again with the gesture to tell of her son's death. He had staked himself out on the sandbar down at a river not far away, a war lance driven through the long sash he wore around his neck, to signify that he would not retreat in battle. He was "Wishing to Die."

And it was better that he had gone over than to have seen the many dead after the battle with the Blackfoot. Again she spat the word out and looked back into Scratch's face once more. No need for more presents, she told him. She had lived long—many winters—and would be ready to go over if it were not for her man, Holds the Tail. He too has many winters past him and talks of dying in battle rather than as an old man, forgotten in his lodge with only his woman to mourn his passing to the other side. Better for him, Holds the Tail had told her, to die in battle so that the whole people would cry at his death.

Bass did not know what to say. Was there anything, he wondered, that would be worth the saying? Speechless, he slipped a hand inside the new coat and drew from his belt one of the butcher knives purchased at rendezvous. Across both palms he presented it to her.

The squaw looked closely at the knife for a moment without touching it. For Holds the Tail, he told her. For her warrior to carry into battle. She glanced up at the white man's eyes for a flicker of a moment and he seemed to catch some hint of a smile behind hers. Comes Running wrapped her old fingers around the knife handle and slid it from Scratch's hands.

It is small enough so that you do not think it is too great a gift, he told her as she ran a finger across the sharp blade. But it is a big enough present to make the white man feel as if he has repaid you for your great gift to him.

Titus put out his right hand and placed it gently on the woman's shoulder, leaving it there but a brief moment while he told her that she would never know the words in his heart that he felt at the fine gift of the coat. It was a great coat that would cut out the winter winds and the wet of snows and rain. His hand slid from her shoulder and suddenly he felt immensely tall, towering over the small woman.

"We will go," he told her, not able to find any more words to say, and motioned Josiah away toward the open area in the center of the camp.

When they were again near the arrow makers, Bass remarked quietly to Paddock, "She has her no young'uns like you. Blackfoot rubbed 'em out. Maybe battle where you found them painted medeecin sticks in the ground, with what ha'r they raised from the Blackfoots on 'em. Likely where she lost her fam'ly."

Paddock nodded, feeling somewhat as if he now understood what the brief conversation in Crow between Bass and Comes Running had meant. He shifted the heavy load of the bear and wolf hides to carry them beneath his right arm, giving Bass the old capote.

"What you figger on usin' these hides for?" he looked over at Titus.

Scratch pursed his lips for a minute, looking briefly at the load under the young man's arm. "Don' rightly know jest yet. Only sure I was that I wasn' 'bout to be leavin' behin't a prime b'ar pelt—that wolf hide neither. Both them good for keepin' a body warm, Josiah. Good robes to keep a man warm, them are."

The sun burst warm across his cheeks, feeling bright in his eyes. They walked on in silence. Bass glanced at the young trapper. "What you thinkin 'bout? Still got the squars on your mind?"

Paddock hesitated, then said, "Nawww. Weren't thinkin' 'bout them." He paused again before continuing. "Strange. Funnylike. What I was just thinkin' 'bout right then when you asked me—well—was..." his voice trailed off. "Ever thought you of lookin' for them fellers that took your furs when you first come to the mountains?"

"Three I tol't you 'bout?" Bass queried, squinting an eye at Paddock.

"Them three: Billy an'..."

"Silas, it were. Bud too," Bass finished. Silence ensued; then Bass said, "You got you some strange notions in your head, don' you, son?"

"Just tell me if you ever thought 'bout lookin' for 'em," Paddock pressed.

"If'n the truth be knowed 'bout it," he paused, "a time or two I thought real hard on it. Then got me thinkin' 'bout other whatnot—"

"Hadn't ever really figgered to—"

"Dammit, boy! Won' you let a man finish up sayin' his piece?" He let his breath out slowly, giving himself time to see to it that Josiah was not going to interrupt him now. "I've thought me 'bout it, I have, on a while. Got me then to thinkin' 'bout other whatnot when it come right down to it. But that ain't to say it ain't been in the back of my head alla time, right there. Thinkin' some day of lookin' them fellers up. Where they'd be, only the devil'd know by now. Been some time, it has, since them low doin's."

"So you really figgered they did get off with your skins?" Josiah asked. "You really figgered they took off with 'em rather'n bein' rubbed out on the upriver, like you told it once?"

"That might be it," he answered. Then squinting at Paddock again, "Why you so all-fired askin' me these 'ere things now, young'un? Jest like a bolt outta the big blue?"

Josiah shrugged his shoulders, thinking he could pass it off as idle curiosity. But he felt the piercing eyes of the older man on him, and glanced over to see Titus staring into his eyes. "You know I might be havin' some fellers come huntin' me."

"Never thought 'bout it like that," Bass said, looking away from the young trapper's face. "But now you make a call on it, 'twouldn't be all that queersome for them parley-voos come lookin' for you." He spat absently. "Jest might be a score you gotta settle up still there."

"Yeah."

"But what that gotta do with me sometimes thinkin' 'bout lookin' for them three niggers?"

"Jest thinkin' 'bout huntin' a man, I s'pose," he replied. "Wonderin' what it'd be like havin' you hunt for me. Wouldn't feel good 'bout it. You huntin' me down, I mean."

Bass chuckled. "You ain't worried 'bout me comin' after you, is you now?"

"Nawww," he laughed.

"Ain't a chance of that."

"Just tryin' to think what it'd be like knowin' a man like you was on my trail."

"That it?" Bass inquired after moments of silence.

"'Cept one other thing," he began.

"An' what's that?"

"Want you to know I'd be for goin' 'long an' helpin' look for them fellers with you—even things up some way. If you was wantin' to put to the trail—"

"You're some now, you are!" Scratch slapped Josiah on the back playfully. "You're really some now!"

Dropping back down to his hands and knees, his breath caught against the lump in his throat once more and he felt like heaving again. He let it come, the rushes of heat and rising jumpiness in his stomach. His head hung loosely between his sagging shoulders as he let it come.

"Go 'head. Right here," he mouthed. "I don't care no more. I don't care."

The stomach lurched and all he could taste was the trickle of stomach acid between his cheek and tongue. Josiah spat, then spat again. Some of the taste was gone from his mouth but the acrid memory of it assaulted his mind.

He wanted to lie down right where he was. On the snow. Here, in the snow and cold and the dark. His arms started to agree with him and began to sag under the weight of the shivering shoulders. Slowly his forehead made contact with the snow. It was cool. So cool. The arms let go and he allowed his head to roll to the side so that his cheek rested against the packed cold whiteness.

He put one hand out and brushed against the hide cover of the small shelter. He was unaware he had gotten back this far after stumbling into the willows down by the river to heave his guts. He would open his eyes just to confirm it, just to make sure he had really made it back this far after the rattling, muscle-wrenching exercise down at the river. The eyes fluttered open and he glimpsed the front of the shelter before the eyes wanted to close again.

Now the cool was turning to cold. And the chills returned. Drawing his legs up close to his abdomen, he began to debate the merits of staying where he was. It didn't matter if he stayed right there, one part of him said.

You'll soon be freezing and that ain't gonna help a thing, what with the way you're feeling, came the rebuttal.

561

Hell with it! Maybe freezing wouldn't be all that bad. Dying might not be all that bad. Feel like I wish I was—dead right now. Have all this over with right now. Right now I'd be dead and wouldn't be wishing I was dead.

You like being warm?

Yeah, I like being warm, he answered the other voice.

Then, you're gonna have to move some more.

I don't wanna move no more.

Just a few feet. A few more feet.

No more!

Just a few more feet—we'll take it a foot at a time. C'mon now.

Making his fingers move against the hide of the shelter, Paddock convinced himself that maybe it was not that far after all. Perhaps it would be better if he pushed himself inside the rest of the way. To the robes. Warmth. Bed. The robes and the warmth. He refused to listen to the jumping stomach. Refused to take no from the aching muscles. He pushed the other part of his mind away and refused to heed those other words. Slowly he pushed with his legs and flailed a minute, but there was nothing for his feet to force themselves against in their struggle.

"The arms gonna have to do it," he thought he said and dug an elbow into the snow. Pushing up on the elbow, he rose, brought himself teetering over the top of the anchor, and fell forward. "That's good. Not far. But good. 'Nough." The fingers ran up to touch the side of the shelter to convince himself he had not landed miles away from it. He rested and caught his breath again.

"One more," he repeated, again and again until the body rose on the elbow a second time. Then he leaned forward so that he could fall another foot or so. The breath caught in his throat and he felt the lightheadedness return.

"Not so fast. Easy. Slow. Go easy."

How far now? He put his hand to touch the front of the shelter, always, always afraid he might have moved a foot away from his goal instead of a foot closer. "It might well be a mile for all I'm—"

"Boy?" The front flap of the shelter opened suddenly and Scratch's voice poured over him, a voice heavy with sleep. "What the hell?"

Josiah felt the man's hands go to his shoulder; then one slipped under the side of his face and raised it gently.

The hand brushed some of the snow from his cheek and he attempted to open his eyes. He wanted to assure himself that it was Bass.

"What you done to yourself?" Titus asked, sliding closer and pushing the entrance cover out of his way. "You hurt yourself?"

"Hurtin'," Josiah agreed. But that did not tell all of it. "Sick—sick—sick—sick . . ." It made him feel worse to tell it. Not better. But worse. Just that word.

"You sick?" Bass asked to confirm it.

Josiah thought he nodded his head slightly in reply, but wasn't sure, wasn't that sure at all. He tried to blink his eyes open so that he could look up at the older man, but they opened to no more than slits. Still dark, he thought, even with his eyes open. It was still dark and he couldn't see.

"Where you hurt? Your belly?" One of his hands ran down Paddock's chest and hovered over the young trapper's stomach. He felt the dampness with his fingertips and brought them to his nose to smell. "You been throwin' your guts!" he exclaimed quietly.

Josiah was sure he nodded then. He felt his head move, and after he had the pounding and heaviness return. Just let it lie here, he thought. Just let my head stay right here.

"We cain't let you lay out here all night." Bass moved a little in preparing to pull Paddock into the shelter. "Get you warm. Down in the robes."

"Sick . . . sick in the belly."

"You're gonna be all right now," Bass chattered as he tugged to bring the young trapper's body under the hide cover. "Coulda laid out there all night. Froze up by the time I found you. Gonna be all right now. Don' know me what made you so sick, son. I had me ever'thin' you've had you to eat . . . laid me down in these here same robes too. Don' know me what it jest might be, Josiah . . ."

By rolling, pulling, and pushing, Titus finally moved Josiah far enough into the small shelter to wrap the young man in a buffalo robe. "You jest lay tight, son. Bass gonna punch the fire a bit. Heat some medeecin for you. It fin'ly got you. Took couple days—but it got hold a you."

Paddock mumbled something unintelligible as Scratch grabbed a small kettle and slid from the shelter. He trotted quickly to the edge of the river in his easy, squat, prairie-

563

chicken gait, dipped the kettle past the cracked ice and loped back to the shelter.

After stirring some of the coals from last night's fire, Bass set some small twigs over the embers and began to blow gently but with a steady intensity on the red glow beneath the new wood. Soon there were small licks of yellow sprouting from the bright red dots of the coals. The yellow brightened, pushed along the dry twigs and grew in size. Adding more and more wood as the fire consumed the smaller material, Scratch eventually had the fire to his liking. Then he put the small kettle over the flames to heat.

Ducking back into the shelter, he rummaged around through the packs of baggage that surrounded their sleeping robes. Unable to locate what he wanted in the dark, he finally leaned toward the front of the shelter and threw open the corner of the hide that served as an entrance cover. The light from the fire aided his search. Titus found the parfleche and slid back to the edge of the fire where he could sit on his robe near the flames' heat.

"Ain't got me much here I can be doin' for you," he muttered as he brought the old parfleche across his lap and began to untie the thongs. "Only do for you what Scratch does for hisse'f when he's tied up in the belly."

Locating the small piece of bear root, Bass tossed it into the kettle. He sat the parfleche far to the side of his own robe and slid back into the interior of the shelter. There he retrieved his powderhorn and pulled it near the light along with one of the tin cups.

"You 'wake?" Bass asked.

Bass heard him mumble something he could barely make out.

"You eat you anythin' more'n what we had us for supper?"

Another soft murmur from the robes.

"Jest what we et here, son?"

And again came the quiet agreement while Paddock rolled over in his robes.

"Cain't figger it." Bass stared into the flames licking the side of the kettle. "S'pose it's jest you ain't got you a mountain belly yet—one what takes to Crow stew. Sure turned it." He dipped a finger into the water to test it, then sat back. "Mind if I smoke?"

There came no answer this time.

564

"Didn' think you did."

Crawling back into the shelter, he located his smoking pouch and returned to the edge of the fire. First pulling the small pipe from the pouch, then adding small pinches of tobacco to the bowl, Bass finally pulled a small twig from the fire and held the bright yellow glow over the top of the bowl. Drawing deeply with several rapid puffs, the tobacco caught and he tossed the twig into the fire beneath the kettle. He leaned back on one elbow and took the stem from his mouth to gaze into the bowl while he blew out the gray smoke, contented with himself.

"Didn' never figger me that Macbeth would ever have the score settled with him the way he did," Bass said, making conversation with the night. "S'prised this child, it did. I jest figgered he'd be gettin' 'way with it, is all. Seemed to there for 'while too."

He drew on the pipe stem again. "Witches tol't him he'd be the king, they did. Jest forgot to tell him 'tweren't gonna be for long. Witches use theys hoodoos to play the tricks on you. Get a man all b'lievin' he's somethin' he ain't. He figgers it all out, but it jest ain't natural. Man as'd count on such things jest as soon spit into the wind an' bet he ain't gonna get his face wet." Scratch chewed on the pipe stem contemplatively for a few minutes.

He was smugly satisfied with himself in those moments, satisfied that everything in the old tale had turned out the way it should. Then the unsettling feeling grew until he admitted that no man came out the winner in such an affair. Although a wrong had seemingly been righted, no good came from the course of events. Each man has his own hell to live, he thought, looking at the bowl of his pipe. The tobacco was burned so he leaned forward and knocked the dark remains from the bowl into the embers. Bass dipped his finger into the water and found it getting warm at last.

"Soon's a man feels like he's safe, that's when the ground starts shakin' under him." He put the pipe back into the tobacco pouch and tossed it toward the rear of the small shelter. "Easiest man for the devil hisse'f to use looks to be a man what thinks he's a man of God. Start off doin' one thing wrong in the name of right—jest gets all the easier each time the devil calls. Black medeecin, that's it." He spat almost unconsciously toward the fire.

"More an' more he's thinkin' he's doin' what's right,

an' he's gettin' deeper an' deeper alla time in the devil's own grip. Devil don' do nothin' to catch a man. The nigger jest catches hisse'f for the ol' red feller; then he ain't got nothin' he can do 'bout it." He let his eyes drop from the dark canopy overhead and gazed into the flames bordering the kettle. As his attention left the sky, a single star shot rapidly across its inky expanse and burned itself out to the west.

Leaning over the kettle Bass saw the water just beginning to roll and took his knife from his belt. With it under the handle he slid the kettle off the embers. "Fix your belly pain up right now." He dipped the tin cup into the steaming kettle, drew it out, and wiped the bottom across his thigh before setting it beside him on the robe. From his powderhorn he poured a small mound of the black grains into his left palm and dumped the powder into the cup. With his knife, Bass began to stir the mixture slowly as he looked over his shoulder at the covered form.

"Josiah. Boy, wake up." He continued to stir as best he could while sliding his butt over toward the sleeping young trapper. "Wake up an' drink this, son." He nudged the slumbering form with an elbow and elicited a low moan from Paddock. "C'mon, now. Drink this up. Then you get back to sleep."

He moaned and rolled toward the older man. Bass held the cup and set his knife aside before pulling the robe away from Paddock's face. "Saw you was in there. Here, now. Drink this, says I."

The eyes fluttered slowly, then opened into slits to stare at the cup. "What's it?" The words rolled across a dry, foul-tasting tongue.

"Medeecin for you. For your belly. Drink up."

One hand finally emerged from beneath the robe to take the handle of the tin cup from Bass. He brought it close to his face and held it for a moment under his nose. "What's in it?"

"Medeecin, Josiah. Drink it. Somethin' for your belly to eat on 'stead of your belly eatin' on itself. Go 'head now." He waved his hand a little impatiently. "Drink it all down."

The thin slits peered up at Bass, then to the cup as it

566

came to his lips. He sipped first, testing the heat of the mixture. "Don' taste all that bad," he murmured over the edge of the tin.

"You 'spect it to?"

"Don't feel like puttin' nothin' down on my belly now—"

"You drink that up. Keeps your innards quiet. Least they won' be chewin' on themselves."

Paddock drew on the steaming mixture again, longer this time, letting the warm fluid run past his tongue and down his throat. It sank to his belly with a warm rush. He shivered a little at the sudden internal heat.

"You ain't gonna be goin' on the hunt with us come mornin', son."

"Don't care to be goin' nowheres."

"I knows it. You jest stay here. Mend yourself. There be other hunts for you to go on. We be comin' back next day. Jest one night out, it looks to be." He saw Josiah nod his head and take another pull from the cup.

Then the young man let his head sag back down into the curly warmth of the buffalo robe. "You all done? Drink it all, did you?" Bass leaned over the cup in Paddock's hand and saw that the broth was gone. "Good." He took the cup and put it near the fire. Bass then pulled the robe back over Paddock's shoulders and tucked it around his neck.

He listened to the sounds of the night for a few minutes and thought it better not to feed the fire any more wood. Sliding into the shelter, Scratch pulled the cover down and brought the edge of his robe over his body. He laid his head down.

"Get you belly full a that medeecin, you'll sleep some through the day. Leastways, be more hunts for you to go on. Know you wanted to get outta camp. But there be more hunts for you to go on."

He listened to Paddock's heavy breathing a moment more, then closed his eyes. Before his mind ran visions of buffalo and elk chasing across the snowdraped hills. And one man, one lone white man was riding an Indian pony after the game. His black braid, flecked with gray, flapped in the air. The fur hat, pulled snugly over his ears, only faintly muffled the sound of the man's voice as he yelled and whooped at the top of his lungs with joy.

17

"Josiah Paddock."

It sounded as if the words were coming to him from across many miles at first, his name traveling slowly back to him from across those many, many miles.

"Josiah Paddock!"

More urgency was in the words now. He tried to remember where he was. Tried to think who would be calling out his name. It was still black. And warm. Where would he be that someone would be calling out to him like that?

"Young Paddock!"

Could it be Bass? Bass already back from the hunt? Yes, it was still black. He could not see. And it was warm. Suffocating. Hard to get his breath. He felt the curly thick fur against his cheeks and lips, against his eyelid as it blinked while trying to open.

Slowly he pushed back the buffalo robe from his face and let the thin gray light creep back into his mind. Rolling his head to the side, he knew where he was. Still in the small shelter. It wasn't bright out. Must be morning. Early morning. Bass was gone. Not beside him in his old robe. Gone. On the hunt, he remembered.

He rolled his head back to lie against the warm spot where his cheek had been when his name was first called. A dream. That's what it must have been. Heard his name called in a dream. He had been sick. It was all part of being sick, he thought. Hearing your name being called from far off. How long had he been sick?

It was then he heard the pony snort close by, heard it paw at the frozen ground near the shelter. Then there were a few footsteps on the hard-packed snow out front and the hide covering the entrance to the small shelter was thrown back. He rolled over in surprise and stared at McAfferty's face looking in at him.

"Mc . . . McAfferty?" Josiah's eyes blinked against the dull light that came seeping in around the small man's form.

"Where's Mr. Bass?" he asked as he settled on his haunches at the entrance to the shelter, the hide cover slung carelessly over his shoulder.

"Gone," was all he could think to say at that moment. He rubbed one eye.

"Aye, that I know. An' gone where, young Josiah?"

"Huntin'. With the Crow."

"When they go?"

That stumped him. He did not know for sure. When did Scratch leave? he asked himself. He rubbed two fingers across his parched lips and felt very thirsty. "Water?"

"Aye. Ye thirsty?" He turned his white head with its light blue fur hat to look over his shoulder. "Some in a kettle here, lad." With that the hide cover slipped from his shoulder and the shelter was dark again. Josiah heard the clink of a tin cup against the inside of the small iron kettle, then the cover was thrown back again to admit the dim light.

"Here it be." He held the cup for Josiah to take. "Doesn't smell like plain water."

Josiah took the cup and brought it to his nose. At least it smelled of something familiar. "Brewed up for me. For my belly," he said, sipping the fluid. Now it was cold. Not the same as when he first drank of it. And it was sweeter, not tasting quite as bitter, like burned powder, as it had before. He sipped again.

" 'They gave me also gall for me meat; an' in me thirst they gave me vinegar to drink.' " Asa settled easily down on the edge of the robes at the entrance so that the hide cover still admitted a small amount of what light remained in the day. "I ask ye again: can ye be tellin' me when they gone on the hunt?"

Paddock looked over the edge of his cup first at the man's face, then past him to the slice of the outside world exposed to him. "It's afternoon?" he asked lamely.

"Aye, but much closer to night now."

"This mornin'. Left this mornin'."

"Ye wasn' to go?" Asa asked.

"Been sick." He sipped the last of what was in the cup and laid his head back down. "Still sick."

" 'For me loins are filled with a loathsome disease; an' there
569

is no soundness in me flesh.' Young Josiah, ye been lyin' with these Crow sluts?"

The question caught him off guard. It came out of nowhere and caught him flatfooted. "No," he answered weakly. "Ain't. No such a thing."

"That's a good lad. No tellin' what ye might be carryin' away from such a bed." Asa looked outside momentarily, then back at Paddock.

For an instant Josiah wished he had been with a woman, wished a young one was with him right now. To warm this chill from his body. To take the fever from his head. But he didn't really think he was much in the mood for courting right then. Not the way he felt. But what about his squaw? McAfferty's woman?

"Where's your wife? Brung her?"

Asa's head nodded once and the smile at the corner of his lips began to disappear before he spoke. "She be where they won' let me see to her. Took her in a lodge on the far side of camp. Feelin' much like ye be feelin', lad. 'Cept she's to be havin' me child. Her time come on us quick. Pushed on last night to get here when we did. Rode all night to get here." He looked outside the shelter again. "Them ol' women took her from me an' shooed me off like I didn' have nothin' to do with me woman at all." He shook his head. "She don' understand them, an' they don' understand her. Be a fine time for gettin' 'em together—"

"She's gonna have your baby then?" he asked weakly. "Now? Your baby's comin' now?"

"Aye!" He turned back to smile at Josiah. *"'A woman when she is in travail hath sorrow, because her hour is come: but as soon as she is delivered of the child, she remembers no more the pain, for joy that a man is born into the world.'"*

"Still talkin' like the Bible, eh?"

"Aye, lad. Been much the source of me strength, lo these long days." He looked outside for a quick inspection of the camp.

"A boy? You hopin' for a boy?"

"Would be a blessin' for this father." Asa looked back at the young man and smiled faintly. "They best be takin' care of that woman, an' me baby—"

"They gonna, Asa. They gonna," Josiah interrupted. "You got her here just on the right side of time."

McAfferty nodded but did not address Paddock's

570

comment. He looked down for a minute before asking, "An' where did Mr. Bass go with the Crow on the hunt?"

"Far as I knows of, they headed down the fork of the river what runs south from here." Josiah gestured weakly with one arm. "South it were to be."

"To come back when? Ye be knowin' that, lad?"

"Scratch said they'd be only one night out. S'pose he meant sometime come tomorrer they'd be comin' back." He sighed deeply. "You ain't worried 'bout Scratch, is you?"

"No, son." Asa smiled a little. "Jest that I be here with a wife that's in the birthin' way. No one understands her. No one knows what I be sayin' either. An' ye be as much good with the tongue as this child is. Mr. Bass knows the tongue, an' the ways, an' might be that I'd be needin' him for that. Of no earthly good on 'nother count. Pick't him a fine time to be runnin' off with them braves—"

"He didn' know."

He nodded again, "It's true. He 'tweren't one to be knowin'. How could he?" McAfferty's eyes skipped over several of the fire-lit lodges before returning to his conversation with the bedridden trapper. "Times there be like this when a man finds himself wishin' for a doctor out here for—"

"A doctor?" Josiah's attention was drawn again to Asa's face. "Where you gonna find you doctors out here, in the middle of these hills?"

With his one hand Asa pushed the fur hat back from his brow to expose the deeply incised furrows across his forehead. "Know me of one," he said, more distantly now. "Chief Factor at Hudson's Bay Vancouver post. The White-Headed Eagle they come to call Dr. McLoughlin—"

"A real doctor—not just callin' hisse'f a doctor?"

"Aye. Still has his surgerin' tools at the post. A man of many mind, fearsome at times: the giant stands wellsome over six feet. An' with his white ha'r hangin' down to his shoulders, an' them piercin' pearls of eyes, the man commands both duty an' respect from all those round him. A strange man, strange man, Josiah. Content to wear his onetime fancy London clothes, what are now patched an' repaired as sets by life in the wilds. He's still a man to hold close to his heart a deep love in things of science—aye, Josiah."

McAfferty played with the fringe along the right arm

while he spoke. "The Lord's set the man down in the wilderness, an' the good Doctor's made himself a haven of safety an' settlement in that same wilderness, all to the credit of his own God-fearin' soul."

Asa fell silent for a moment, and Josiah recalled a frontier post he had known. "Takes a passel a men to be runnin' a fort such a that, what like Council Bluffs," said Josiah.

"That be certain, an' the Doctor has him the men to do the Lord's work for him out there: the Injuns, an' half-breeds, even has him some slaves as've come from some islands out in the great ocean—brung to the fort by ships of the English navy." Asa sighed and was silent a long moment. "There too is the hospital where the good Doctor does what he can to treat the ills of his people in the best of civilized ways in his command. Most men right under the Doctor attached to the fort be Scots like the Eagle himself—all men best suited for bein' wily an' strong of will, them Scots."

"You got you Scot blood in you, don't you?" asked Josiah.

"That is true." Asa turned to glance at Josiah. "Me parents come to this country from Scotland an' I was born in this land. Aye"—he looked away, his mind further west—"that be more'n jest a fur-tradin' post, but truly a community of God-fearin' souls, set in the wilderness of the heathen an' savage. There be a man doin' the Lord's work out here. Aye. There be a man of medicine in these mountains."

"Sounds to be you know the man good," Josiah said.

Cradling the right arm across his left hand and looking down at it, Asa answered, "The good Doctor ministered to me arm while I was out to Vancouver by the big salt. A countryman, he called me—bein' of Scot birth meself. Many night we passed talkin' of many things on his mind." He rubbed the lower arm cradled in his lap. "Offered me, the good Doctor did, a chance at riches to be won in the trade of furs—"

"Be a trapper for him?"

"By the holy heavens above, not as a trapper! What as McAfferty knows the Blackfeets, the Doctor was to send me into that peoples' country to set them on the

572

Crows, even to trackin' the American comp'nies. Those as I couldn't run out with the tribe bin' sorely troublesome, I was to see that the Blackfeets did some steady killin'—"

"You was to see to it that them Blackfoots killed Amer'cans?" The information had been flowing all too fast for Paddock.

"If need be, son, leavin' the English to that rich country alone," McAfferty affirmed. "Get the Blackfeets to trade up with the Hudson's Bay."

With the pain in his head, Josiah could shake it only slowly in response to the story. "That's some. To be carryin' such as that with you . . ."

Asa cleared his throat as the young man's words trailed off and looked outside into the dimming light. "Whilst I been sittin' here sharin' the gab with ye, the light's been fallin' from the sky. Best to puttin' me animals to settle for the night." He started to rise. "I'll be round again recent. Use your fire to make me some supper, if'n ye won' be mindin' me doin' it none?"

"Nope. Not 't all."

The short man got to his knees and brushed his hands off against his thighs. "S'pose all a man's gotta be doin' with himself is wait while his wife's in the labor of birthin' a child. She's such a small thing." He shook his head slightly and was gone beyond the other side of the hide cover. Paddock heard him rise and step away, leading the several ponies toward the river where he supposed McAfferty would have them drink before putting the animals to graze the dry grass for the evening.

Her time had come, he thought. How fast that time had slipped by him in the last few months. It was still a source of wonder to him: life coming from her belly. Scratch should be here for this. He thought again of how the child would look. Closing his eyes and rubbing his cheek against the buffalo fur, Josiah felt the weakness seep back into him. Even the short conversation with McAfferty had drained much strength from him. He was so tired, all over again. The knot remained in his gut. And his head still felt as though it had been repeatedly kicked by the old man's mule. Sleep again, Josiah, he told himself. Sleep.

When Paddock next awakened, the hide that covered the entrance to the small shelter was partially pulled back.

The light from the small fire reflected on the rear of the shelter, creating dancing shadows that entertained Josiah before he turned his head to look outside.

McAfferty was eating supper, his knife busy at his lips. Now and then he leaned over to pick up the small kettle he had refilled with fresh water and to take a drink to wash down his meal of roasted meat. From this view, with his back enveloped by the shadows of the fire before him, Asa looked and acted somewhat like Bass, Josiah thought. He chuckled in spite of himself. The white-headed man turned slowly to look at him, lips and whiskers shimmering with grease.

"You're a fine one, young Josiah," Asa said, wiping the fingertips of one hand over his capote. "Like sneakin' up behind a man to watch him eat."

"Not been watchin' long," he replied weakly.

"An' will ye be wantin' somethin' for that belly of yours?" McAfferty held out the knife on the point of which was speared a piece of elk roast.

Paddock looked at the meat only a moment, then felt his stomach turn again. He clamped his eyes shut. "Nawww." He swallowed hard against the impulse to gag. "I don't want nothin'," he added as sternly as his weakness permitted.

"Ah," Asa replied, as if it were all that could be said, and withdrew the offering. He turned back to the fire and set the meat aside. After wiping his fingers and knife clean of grease, Asa took a last drink of water from the small kettle.

"Tried, I did, to see how the woman was doin'," he informed Paddock. "One ol' squaw, be wife of one of 'em that went with Mr. Bass, she weren't one to let me near the lodge. S'pose it were a good cursin' she give me too for standin' there, listenin' to how it was hurtin' me woman." He looked into the sky for a moment. "I could hear her moans an' screamin' plain as ye'd make it . . ." His voice dropped off for a minute. "Hurts the devil to birth a child. 'Special' to give birth to a child of the Lord, Josiah." McAfferty turned around a little so that he did not directly block the fire's heat from Paddock, shuffling his buttocks so that they would become comfortable once more.

"Would you get me water?" the young trapper asked quietly. "Just a lil' drink?"

"Aye, son." Asa brought the kettle to Paddock, who took it from the whitehair. "It be fresh this time. Filled it meself." He watched Josiah drink slowly and long from the edge of the small vessel, studying the light dancing off the moisture across the young man's brow.

"There be a tale of a young King Josiah in the Good Book, lad. An' I read of it again since't last we parted for me an' mine to head north."

"My mother had told me she give me my name from the Bible," the young man added.

"Aye, she would have, I'd lay sight to that. He was a likely youth, as ye be yourself—at first sure to set what was right with the Lord God: *'For in the eighth y'ar of his reign, whilst he was yet young, he began to seek after the God of David his father; an' in the twelfth y'ar he began to purge Judah an' Jerusalem'*—them bein' the holy lands of old, ye see—*'he began to purge Judah an' Jerusalem from the high places, an' the groves, an' the carved images, an' the molten images.'* Well, now"—Asa sneaked a glance at the young trapper to see that he had Paddock's rapt attention—"This young king of Judah named Josiah was so wantin' of gettin' a name for himself in battle that when some older king of ol' Egypt come to his land to do battle with some other one, this Josiah made him up a plan to trick the older man." He looked into the tiny flames before continuing.

"Ye see, that Egypt king was not wantin' to fight Josiah, but the young king of Judah was itchin' for the fight an' dressed himself up to look jest like the one the Egypt king was wantin' to fight. He come on down into the valley they called Megiddo, then called out for the Egypt king to come out an' fight him, makin' it look like he was some other one. Bad doin's it were, for the Egypt king was never a man to be dealin' fair. When the man he thought to be the king he was wantin' come down in the valley, he jest had his men kill him: *'An' the archers shot at King Josiah; an' the king said to his servants, Have me away, for I am sore wounded.'* 'Twas the way the young king of Judah died in that valley they called Megiddo."

Asa looked closely into the young trapper's eyes for a moment, then moved his gaze so as not to make Josiah uncomfortable. "Jest a story from the book as was the one your mother took your name from." He wondered now whether he should have recounted the biblical tale.

Briefly Asa remembered the days of his youth, when

he had taken up the preaching of the word of the Lord and the saving of souls, only too soon finding himself in the Rocky Mountains.

"Ye've got ye many winters to be spendin' up here in the mountains, lad." He looked toward the patch of sky that hung between the trees and the clouds moving in from the west. "Winters that seem a long time goin' in the countin' when yer a young man." He heard Paddock set the kettle on the ground, but did not look away from the patch of stars. "Seems so long ago, now. So long ago that I too traveled with Mr. Bass. Both of us uneasy at times with the other, but knowin' 'twere good for the both us."

"You broke up," Josiah injected. "Least, you was the one as took off. That's to hear Scratch tell it." He wiped some of the dampness from his forehead.

"Aye. He's not the lyin' devil there." He played with the fire for a minute, putting some more twigs on the coals before he continued. "He's never been one to know where I was off to in the leavin' of him. An' that was to see the Blackfeets, country north of the Three Forks. Spent me some goodly time with them people as it come 'bout. To the close of the winter of '30 an' '31 I said me fare-thee-wells an' pushed on to the south for the spring fur gettin'. Still had me two good hands then." His eyes dropped to the hook where once a right hand had been. "Earned me a claw that spring. 'Bout that ye've heard me speak afore." His eyes moved to Paddock and saw the young man nod in agreement. They were silent a few minutes. McAfferty felt talkative tonight. Strange, he thought, but he felt just like talking to this young white man.

"Why," he cleared his throat finally, "why, why was it you headed for the Blackfoots? By yourself, I mean."

"For y'ars my own ears had heard the talk of them streams up north to the Three Forks, rich they was to be to hear the tale of it." Asa gazed into the fire. "But plews were not the offerin' plate beckonin' to me. For some time afore that, one single verse had been callin' out to me each time I thought meself on the Blackfeets country: *'For, brethren, ye have been called unto liberty; only use not liberty for an occasion to the flesh, but by love serve one 'nother.'* S'pose it was plainly the idea that men were not to be tryin' the Blackfeets country, that it were a place of death for most. I tucked me Bible under one arm with me ol' rifle gun

576

under the other an' pushed north. Freedom's come to mean more to me than bein' safe, lad. *'He hath showed thee. O man, what is good.'* The Lord thy God showed it to me, led me on me way an' watched over me with those people."

"An' they never bothered you, them Blackfoots?" he inquired.

"No. They seemed to take to me for some reason. The Lord had readied them people for me perhaps. Were none of me own doin'. *'For if a man think himself to be somethin', when he is nothin', he deceiveth himself. But let ev'ry man prove his own work, an' then shall he have rejoicin' in himself alone, an' not in another. For ev'ry man shall bear his own burden.'* By me own hook I went to the Blackfeets, an' by me own was I taken in by them people. They seemed to know of me too, from the family tartan." The hook stroked back and forth across the Scottish plaid of the breechclout he wore.

"Hard to b'lieve, what with hearin' the stories 'bout them Blackfoots—"

"An' true many of the tales be. Don' let that slip from ye. Aye, young Josiah. True many of the worst of the tales be. But, *'Blessed is the man that walks not in the counsel of the ungodly, nor stands in the way of sinners, nor sits in the seat of the scornful.'* I was the man to ride smack into that country north of the Three Forks, right into their arms without flinchin'. *'Trust in the Lord with all thine heart; an' lean not unto thine own understandin'.'* It were I, young Josiah, what trusted in the Lord. An' it was He that did the leadin' of me there."

"So you wasn't up to be fightin' 'em back to Pierre's Hole?"

"How ye mean, lad?"

"You wasn't one to wanna fight with the Blackfoots down at Pierre's Hole, 'cause they was good to you. Right?"

He looked briefly at Paddock, then gazed at the fire. He tossed a few more twigs carelessly on the embers. "You're askin' if a man fights with his friends?"

"That's why you shied from the fight," Josiah said.

"The Blackfeets wasn' rightly what ye'd call friends to this man. More like ... allies. Aye. That be closer to the truth of it." He played with one burning twig held in the hook. "We was on the same side. An' we had us the same enemies. 'Twas a contract between us, suited to the both of us. We could do best by joinin' up, it was."

"So"—Josiah felt the dryness in his mouth and throat return—"Why was it you never married up to one a them Blackfoot gals? Got you hitched to Nez Percy, instead?"

"That was last spring—"

"Yes."

"Comin' back from the big fort on the Columbia—Vancouver." He finally tossed the flaming twig out of his hook into the fire. "A present she were, ye might be sayin', from a grateful chief what wanted to hear the word of the Lord spoke to him."

"An' you was in the right place at the right time again."

"In a manner of speakin', ye might be sayin' I was, that." His eyes again climbed to the patch of sky between the trees and the clouds. "Ah, she were a prize too, that'un. Not yet fully eighteen y'ars by her count when she was give to me. An' not like most others, she weren't. Ah, lad. The woman is a strange creature for man to master the understandin' of: *For the lips of a strange woman drip as a honeycomb, an' her mouth is smoother'n oil: but her end is bitter as wormwood, sharp as a two-edged sword.* We married up in a proper Bible weddin', an' that pleased Rain Feather's pappy, as dry as he was for the readin' of the holy word. She were differ'nt, aye."

"Rain Feather. That's her name?"

"Ye wasn' knowin'?"

"No." Josiah's tongue remained dry. "You, you never told me her name—Rain Feather."

McAfferty rose to one knee. "A strong woman. What for her y'ars, she's a strong one. Will make a fine wife to this 'un. A fine mother for the child." He got to his feet and stood between Josiah and the fire. "I best be lookin' on the comin' of the child now. She is without people what understand her, without people what she can understand. She must be feelin' all the more alone now that her time has come."

He let out a long sigh as if in preparation for the trip to the old woman's lodge, as if it were to be a long journey. "I think, young Josiah, that I have fallen in love with her too. I think that I love that gentle, little, frightened woman." He turned before Paddock could respond, stepping around the fire and moving across the snow toward the center of the village, a dark shadow hovering over the pale blue of the night-lit snow.

Sleeps Before the Door was growing weary with the enduring labor of the young Nez Perce woman. But she had continued to derive some of her strength for the long vigil from the frail girl herself, who persisted past much hope of a safe delivery.

Years before the old woman had paid a handsome price to a tribal visionary for the secrets she had used repeatedly in cases such as this. But now her medicine seemed not to be enough, and she grew exhausted from the struggle. Time and again she had rubbed the special mixture of a secret root and a horned toad on the girl's lower back. It had helped little to ease the pain or hasten the delivery. She had repeatedly attempted to give the expectant mother a broth from a special weed she alone knew as batse-kice, so that she could then hold the girl tightly above the abdomen to aid in forcing the child out. Rain Feather had turned away from the soup each time it was offered her, gagging and retching in her refusal to drink. In desperation the old woman had finally made a potion of bice-waruci-se, what the long-ago visionary had called 'buffalo-do-not-eat-it,' a plant that when eaten would put the young woman to sleep so that her labor would be painless.

Kneeling once more beside Rain Feather, the old woman offered the spoon beneath the Nez Perce woman's nose. This time she did not turn away. Sleeps Before the Door asked her to drink of the broth as she cupped the girl's head and brought it up so that she might sip from the spoon. Rain Feather could protest no more. Her strength was waning and her mouth was parched from the panting hours of hard labor.

This broth in the spoon did not smell as the other had. It did not make her think of things dead and dying, pushing her stomach up into her mouth. This was sweet, and the young woman thought of a soup boiled from the flowers that were to bud in the spring. This she would make for the little life in the years to come. And she would tell him of her difficult labor when he was coming to meet her. Rain Feather dipped her head and let the spoon touch her lips, feeling the soup pour over her tongue, moistening the dryness as it flowed back in her throat. The spoon was empty and she asked for more in her language. The old woman understood, and continued to feed her the wet, sweet, thick broth as long as Rain Feather would sip it.

It was good, Sleeps Before the Door thought. Now the woman will have sleep over her eyes while the baby is pushed out. Yet she worried how the young life would ever come, how it would ever make its way out to meet its mother. The baby was still turned to the side and was refusing to move of itself for her. Perhaps, with the young mother with sleep over her eyes, she could push hard on the belly and turn the baby before it was too late in the Nez Perce girl's time. Perhaps.

When Rain Feather wanted no more of the broth, the old woman rose slowly and set the spoon beside the small fire she tended for light. In its flickering illumination, Sleeps Before the Door searched through her bundles of medicines and charms until she located two objects. Hunched now from long hours of bending over the young woman's bed at the rear of the lodge, Sleeps Before the Door took the objects and set them upon the distended abdomen. Next she removed the charm from her own neck and placed the thong on it over the Nez Perce woman's head. The old woman adjusted the baco-ritse, the rock medicine of the Crow, between the young breasts. It was a curious object of sacred charm, to a non-Crow merely a fossil of strange shape and color the woman had found years before, now heavily wrapped with beads of purple, yellow, and red. Perhaps it was now one of the last things the old woman could do for the girl.

She returned to kneel beside the young belly and carefully placed her hands over the two objects she had put upon the abdomen. Her right palm covered the beaded turtle while her left sheltered the beaded lizard. She closed her eyes to shut everything else out, to close herself to the world now as she opened herself to the help of Old Man Coyote. Through him she would bring the baby forth. Through her he would bring relief to the Nez Perce woman.

Sleeps Before the Door let all thoughts slip from her as the words came to her lips. Slowly, she began the ancient song chanted over a mother in labor. This the old Crow woman would sing for the young Nez Perce mother.

Awe raxketa bawasa aciwa
bacua ca daxe tsixere
tset acu tsi cikyata
awaku saat e-rusak
tset acu tsi cikyata
ise ara paei awak o-wate barappe kyata
ciwi-ci kyatawe
micgy iaxba surake opi rake.
Haha huhu haha huhu haha huhu haha huhu haha
huhu.

Her trembling voice grew in its intensity as she sang
the ancient song over and over, rocking to and fro beside
the young woman, her hands continuing to shelter the
medicine charms protecting the belly.

On the hillside I was running,
My knee was skinned.
The wolf mask wearer,
The wolf mask wearer,
On the other side he cannot ease himself.
His face itches; in all seasons he kills.
He gets yellow with fat.
The dogs with their bellies full smoke.
Haha huhu haha huhu haha huhu haha huhu haha
huhu.

Over and over Sleeps Before the Door lighted the
braids of sweetgrass and let the incense smoke pour over
the young mother. Again and again she returned to kneel
beside the big belly and cup her hands over the turtle and
the lizard, there to pray and sing the song old beyond her
many winters.

It had started to snow, only gently though. The fat
flakes spoke of a long-time snow. They were blown by the
winds into the lodge when Sleeps Before the Door went
out to gather more wood for the little fire. The snow was
cool upon her neck but melted quickly when she placed
the twigs on the embers. Slowly the old woman moved,
hunched and drawn, to the young woman's side.

With each passing hour she wanted this girl to have
her baby more and more. Perhaps, she thought, she
wanted it even more than she had wanted her own
children to be strong and straight as the willow-shaft

arrow. Yes! She prayed to Old Man Coyote that this one would be strong and straight for his mother: that she would be proud and filled with the joy that would make her forget this time of travail.

Across the bare belly, stretched and marked with the sign of life within it, Sleeps Before the Door brushed the sprig of sage she had first bathed in the sweetgrass smoke. And she knelt to pray once more to Old Man Coyote, bowing her aged white head over the big belly. Her drawn and hunched shoulders were shaken now with the sobbing that racked her frail body. The old woman moved slightly to peer close to the young face beneath hers, the many tears falling from the aged eyes to splatter across the Nez Perce woman's cheeks and brow. Then she fell to sobbing beside the big belly, both hands still clutched over the beaded charms protecting the mound of life within.

The young woman choked free a sound from her throat. Quiet, like a whimper of the breeze through the willow near the setting of the sun, the low cry moved from the young woman's lips. Sleeps Before the Door slowly brought her face up and blinked through her tears. She saw the young woman's head drop gently to the side as if cradled in its falling. The eyelids were clenched in fierce struggle no more, and the lips were now loosened from their grim determination.

One old hand moved from the belly and hovered above the young woman's nostrils. For minutes that refused to pass, the palm was held over the Nez Perce face. Not a breath of life escaped from the lungs. The old woman moved back to the big belly and knelt so her ear rested across the taut flesh. No longer were there lurchings of the muscles to push the baby out. No longer could she feel the fighting arms and legs of the young life in its struggle to be free.

She sank slowly under the burden of this thing that had happened—sank into a small, tight mass beside the big belly. The old woman shook with the pain of her sobs in every muscle. She cried as she had never cried before.

As he moved quietly from shadow to shadow between the lodges, McAfferty glanced at the position of the moon struggling above the thick layer of pale blue clouds and figured it must not yet be midnight. The village was quiet beneath the falling snow. The few Crow that were stirring he made sure would not see him. Just a precaution, he thought to himself. After all, he was a guest. An unexpected and uninvited guest.

In crossing in the shadows near the great circle he attracted the attention of a large dog. But all the animal came for was a sniff, then passed on without a sound. The one lodge ahead that concerned him shone with a dull glow. The single tripod of poles stood as the only sentry.

Asa stopped in the lodge's shadow and listened a moment. A hush fell with the snow. In and out of his lungs seeped the cold night air of winter. He marveled how easily a sleeping Indian camp could be taken by those unafraid of the cold, and night, and death. He moved quietly out of the shadows to the door of the lodge and knelt briefly before moving to enter.

Inside he heard low sobs broken by a soft whine as the woman sought to catch her breath. McAfferty wondered whether Rain Feather were still in labor after all this time. He agreed that she must be for no one had come for him with the news of the child's birth. It would be the sobs of his wife he was hearing. The iron hook pulled aside the bear hide covering the door and he moved past the opening by feel more than vision.

A step or two inside he stopped and brought himself to full height, there to await the moments it would take to let his eyes grow accustomed to the pale light inside the lodge. Quietly he deeply inhaled, startled at the sweetgrass incense filling the lodge like a cloud. Injun medicine. His eyes softened slowly, gradually, allowing him first to look upon the dull embers of the small fire with its furtive, tiny flames bouncing into the air only briefly before disappearing. Not too warm in here. Then he looked toward the rear of the lodge.

What first he took to be the old Crow woman at work delivering the child he came to understand better as the minutes wore on. Through the heavy veil of incense smoke he began to perceive the scene before him. Still he stood there in some shock that no delivery was taking place; the two women in the lodge were not moving.

His eyes moved along the length of Rain Feather's body until he could see the side of her face, the head in relaxed repose on the buffalo robe. The sobbing came not from her, but from her belly. Asa moved his eyes once more to where the old woman sat crumpled against the huge abdomen. It was the old Crow squaw who cried, McAfferty realized as he began to take those steps that would bring him around the small fire toward the rear of the lodge.

Why is she to cry? Was it not Rain Feather in labor? Was it not his young wife who should be crying out in the pain of birth?

Silently he stopped near the old woman and looked from the white head that shook with each wrenching sob to the bare belly. Rain Feather's big belly, holding within it their child. How strange it looked, distorted and stretched, unnatural for her young body. He looked briefly at the beaded charms, the turtle and the lizard that sat atop the belly. Then he began to understand.

Looking past the folds in the leather dress where it had been brought up above Rain Feather's abdomen so that it might be examined and touched, McAfferty looked at his wife's chest. Between the two soft mounds lay the Crow rock medicine. Another charm. Rain Feather's breast did not pulse and heave from breathtaking. The rock medicine did not tremble with the stealing of each life-giving breath. It was becoming clear now.

Asa knelt quietly beside her shoulders and looked down onto the face. Framing her features was the plastered hair, now dark and dry whereas once it had been lustrous and moist from the exertions of labor. With his left hand he reached out to brush two fingers across the lips that hung loose and cool to his touch. Across her cheek his fingers painted; they could feel the drying crust that had been salty rivulets of tears. The hand trembled as it gently felt the outline of one lid, caressing the orbit and brushing the short hairs of the dark eyebrow. The hand trembled and he did not want the old squaw to see him shaking. The hand convulsed against his will, so he took it from her flesh.

With effort he rose, knowing she had died because of him; died because he had not stayed in the post at Vancouver; died because he had brought the Blackfeet down on the Crow and eventually had had to return for a young woman in labor with their first child. Somewhere along the line he had offended and what was loved most had been taken from him—at the time that was to have held the greatest joy for them both.

Looking from the resting face of the young woman to the hidden sobbing of the wrinkled old one, McAfferty knew. He knew as he slowly, quietly placed a hand on the shoulder of the old woman. The muffled sobs subsided quickly. Then, slowly, the old head began to rise until it finally turned to meet his gaze. The eyes that had haunted him now for so long.

McAfferty was the first to know. But she knew too. The eyes burned back into his with that knowledge. He knew. And McAfferty knew she knew. Her eyes, suddenly clear, widened in frightful recognition. Now they burned with fear, and a fearful hatred long smoldering. McAfferty remembered the white—the snow and her hair. He remembered their eyes as they had locked for a long moment moons before on a hillside near this place. He had charged down the hill and she had fled. Just after she had turned that last time to look back in fear, he had shot. He supposed her dead. Long dead. But, she was here, looking up at him, his hand still resting lightly on her shoulder. He knew she remembered his face, too. He knew. What he must do. He knew.

He reached inside his coat to find the knot on the red blanket sash tied around his waist. He had found it hung against a willow branch in the stream they crossed in leaving Bass and Paddock; Asa had dipped low from his saddle and swept it up. After wringing the wet and most of the cold from it, the whitehead had realized it must be the tie-sash from some man's capote. Then he had knotted it about his own waist as a bright addition to his clothing and forgotten about it. Until now. Except for Asa's hands, the two people were frozen, motionless.

The fingers of the left hand freed the knot in the blanket strip and it was caught up on the hook where once there had been a right hand. He ripped through the dirty, soiled cloth with the hook. With his left hand he took the remaining few inches on one end of the sash and wound it around the base of the hook to secure the strip to his right arm.

Sleeps Before the Door found something inside that could make her move, if only slowly, almost imperceptibly. Her mind fought to control the bitter hatred now welling up within her bowels, hatred that told her to lunge savagely at this enemy. Only a few feet away would be the door. Then she could scream out the alarm to the

585

village. And only a few feet away would be a knife, which she could drive deep within his chest—to even up the grief that had been visited upon her people by this man from the north.

Quickly he ran his left hand down the remaining length of the sash and flipped the cloth over the one hand left to him. Then he pulled it tightly with both arms. Why did she not cry out? She knew him. Why did she not cry out to the Crow? He wondered as his arms began to move toward her with the sash stretched between them.

The old woman now leaped quickly toward the south side of the lodge where she landed among her medicines, scattered by the fire. McAfferty jumped toward her rapidly, looping the sash in midair as it descended over the old woman's head. He snapped the loop shut and began to draw against her weight. Her head jerked back and around, to look at him in surprise, in rage; but no longer was there fear. So it must be for the two of them, she thought. Her breath caught in her throat and she began to gag.

He drew tighter and she began to feel her neck and face gorging with blood as she began to fall back among her scattered medicines. Her old gnarled fingers darted among the objects on the lodge floor until they encircled the handle of a skinning knife. Fighting the heaviness like a great sleep in her eyes, Sleeps Before the Door brought the knife up.

McAfferty saw the glint of steel as it was brought around her side. His right arm loosened the loop about the woman's neck as he struck at the side of her head with the hook. The metal at the end of his arm dug and tore into the flesh across her right cheek. He watched the blood appear, seeping at first, then looked away as it began to gush over the iron tool. Her hand with the weapon dropped helplessly toward the floor as Asa once more tightened the loop. Then he heard the first gurgling sound in her throat.

The knife fell and both hands savagely ripped at the cloth around her neck. They tore at his arms. Again and again she tried to rip through the skin of his coat to tear at the skin on the arms strangling her. In her battle one arm slipped up the right sleeve to expose the full length of the iron hook, embedded deep within its wooden block and lashed to the lower arm.

The old Crow woman ceased her fight and looked

into his face with eyes that were almost serene. He watched the eyes begin to close; the head dropped heavily so that he held the entire weight of her upper body in the sash.

Loosening the grip of his left hand, McAfferty let the small body droop and fall. He bent over the woman and quickly unwrapped the sash from the hook. He would leave it around her neck. Looking into the old eyes, frozen open and staring at him in death, Asa spoke: '*In wrath we take up the sword of Abraham's judgement.*' The eyes would haunt him no more.

Moving swiftly he took two steps and knelt beside Rain Feather's head. For a few minutes he looked again at her face, knowing this would be the last. He bent and lightly brushed her soft forehead with his lips before leaving the lodge.

He stepped into the shadows of the lodge next to the one he had left and waited while his breath caught up with him. He listened. Nothing but the snow. Certain that no one had heard, McAfferty circled behind the lodge and moved into the trees.

He would take a wide circle back to the river, he thought. No dogs to give me away. From his things beside the white men's small shelter he would take only what he needed. From the bundles and parfleches left with the animals, he would choose only what was necessary. And he knew it would not be much.

Then it would be but a small matter to release the five ponies from where he had picketed the animals down by the river. Three he would take: one to ride now and two to follow along to conserve their strength. No, he decided. He would need but one.

Asa looked up to find the moon, to figure out the time it must now be. But the clouds of white falling snow hid the globe's light. He stopped and turned round and round, but nowhere could he find the moon.

All the better, he thought as he hurried on. Make it harder to see me without its light. All the better.

Everything was clear to him now. The webs were gone and he found himself thinking with crystalline clarity. Yes, everything was clear to him now—like the clarity of a mountain pool full of water so pure it was without taste, water so cold it hurt to swallow.

18

Bass pulled the hide entrance cover back slightly to see Josiah still wrapped in his robes. Clucking his tongue inside his cheek, he laid the cover back out of his way and knelt beside the sleeping trapper.

"Boy, you be burnin' daylight now," he said quietly.

A soft groan came from within the cocoon of robes. The body stirred a little, but still there was no attempt at rising.

"You figger on gettin' up for the day, Josiah?" the older man asked, this time nudging the cocoon with a hand. Now the form rolled toward Bass somewhat and a hand appeared to push the hairy hide back from the young face. "Good mornin', there. Was one to be thinkin' you wasn't never gonna make it up an' be part of this fine day. Stopped snowin' an' them clouds look to be burnin' off."

The young hand rubbed over the eyes once; he blinked in the bright light up at the older man. Finally squinting, Paddock looked past Titus to the pony tied in front of the shelter. "What time is it?"

"Don' know me jest what time it be." He looked over his shoulder at the sky. "Looks to be past the midmorn now. How you feelin', Josiah?"

"Ain't too bad," he answered. He had slept in this morning, not really feeling guilty about it. He justified it, after all, on the grounds that there had been a lot of lost sleep the past few nights. And, he had needed the rest, he told himself, what with the sickness he had fought off.

"Thought you might'n still be taken sickly, findin' your carcass in the robes as yet."

"Nawww." Josiah slowly kicked the hides away from his legs and leaned casually on one elbow. "Just catchin' up on what's lost, I s'pose." He watched Titus drop from his kneeling position and sit between him and the fire pit. "You just gettin' back from the hunt?"

"Yepper. That I am." His gaze went to look out over the nearby lodges. "Things be the queersome an' strange, they are.

588

Ain't much the goin' on round here now. Oughtta be more folks up an' to theys chores." He shook his head. "Don' like me the feel of the place right now, I don'." His voice trailed off.

"Ain't it strange you bein' back this time of day? Would figger you'd be huntin' on till there weren't no more light an' come back this night."

"An' that would been the right sure way to be doin' things, too," Bass replied. "Somethin' come up—we come on back early."

"Somebody get himself hurt huntin'?" Josiah rose slowly to a sitting position next to Bass.

"Nawww, weren't that," he answered, still looking over the quiet village, wondering at its cause at this late hour. "Near as I can pick it out, one of them ol' chiefs sent him a rider out to track us down. Sent him word by that boy for Arapooesh to be comin' back. Bring the rest of us, too."

"Got you any idea what it means?"

He shook his head negatively. "Nawww. Don' rightly know. Arapooesh an' his boys sure set the pace comin' back home, they did. Pushin' them ponies through that snow to get here when we did. Just that it be somethin' bad, I'm one to fear, what with them cuttin' into a hunt like they done." He dropped his gaze. "Had to be somethin' a might bad—an' a might queersome—what with stoppin' a big hunt that way."

"You bring you in some meat?"

"Yep, that I did." He pointed to the quarters of elk tossed in the snow beside their shelter.

Josiah leaned forward so that he could see past the older trapper. "You got you bull, eh?"

"An' two cows comin' in later on," he explained. "Arapooesh left him some young braves with the ponies to carry in most of the meat we'd dropped. They was gonna be slow in the travelin' an' he was wantin' to be pushin' back fast as that critter under him could move out. Yep, you an' me got us plenty meat for 'while, Josiah." He started to rise. "You be hungry now? Got your meat bag in tow yet?"

Josiah was suddenly conscious of the pangs within. "You go an' talk 'bout food an' eatin', s'pose I might do me with somethin' to eat. I could."

Bass stretched his shoulders for a moment. "You best be a young'un what's helpin' hisse'f then. You go an' punch life back into that fire. Get them coals up an' cut you some meat from them ribs." He moved toward the pony and packhorse. "Animals some lathered from the ride we

589

give 'em this mornin'. Coverin' the ground we did, they'll be wantin' to lay back an' be chewin' on cotton bark afore anythin' else't." Picking up the pony's rein and the halter rope for the packhorse, Bass stopped in front of Josiah and the fire pit. "I'll put the animals away an' strip 'em. Be back in jest a rooster shake, son."

Josiah nodded without looking up from his huffing and puffing on the coals. With his fingers he had scraped together the gray and black remains into a small pile, then blew the flakes of dead ash and dry snow from what he hoped would be some red embers. As the gray and white disappeared he happily saw the faint red of hidden heat.

From a dry twig he quickly scraped some kindling with a knife, putting the long, thin curls over the embers he had exposed. Now he bent low beside the fire pit and began to blow in earnest, causing the embers to glow more brightly with each puffing breath. Finally the tiny blue from the embers sprang up and caught some of the kindling. He kept blowing, more softly though, until the kindling itself was burning with its own blue flames.

Josiah sat back and put more of the dry curls over the new flames, then set his knife to work again to whittle more. Soon the flames wanted bigger wood. Twigs from a pine branch, then some short pieces of the branch itself, all set in an awkward cone over the tiny flames. Certain of the fire, Josiah rose slowly, feeling the dim remains of the lightheadedness from his sickness.

After a moment the fuzzy feeling across his forehead was gone and he moved slowly over to pick up a front quarter of elk. Dragging it back to the edge of the fire over the new snow, Paddock sat once more and put the knife to work slicing the strips of meat from between the thick ribs. As each wide thong of red meat was freed from the bone, Josiah skewered it to the appolaz roasting sticks that he stuck in the cracks between the rocks ringing the fire. From time to time in his butchering, the young trapper would methodically turn those pieces of meat already roasting before the flames.

Intent over the elk quarter before him, Josiah ignored the faint-sounding footsteps on the snow. Doubtless it was Bass coming back after bedding the animals.

"This be how you're wantin' your meat cooked?" he asked of the older man without looking up. There were more steps across the new layer of white than there should have been. Moving his eyes slowly away from the knife and the elk meat, Josiah saw that the leggings before him did not belong to the other trapper. His eyes followed the legs up until he looked into the face of the big youth who had led him into the Crow encampment.

He stood before Paddock, a rifle laid across the crook of his left arm. Josiah noticed the right hand over the trigger guard and the hammer pulled back to full cock. Quickly his eyes jumped to those other young men standing beside and behind the big youth. They too held rifles in ready. Some were pointed at the fire by Paddock's feet, others at him.

Josiah was caught in the moment, staring down the muzzles of those big-bored rifles. Amazed at their yawning size at this close range, he was still more confused as to why they would be pointed at him. His eyes darted now from warrior to warrior, finally noticing that they had painted their faces hastily. His thoughts dashed back to the quick battle with the Bannocks the fall before; he remembered the rush of ponies toward him across the sage, and the painted faces glaring at him just before he had made his desperate lunge.

The big Indian stepped forward the two paces and was immediately in front of the white trapper. His right hand came away from the trigger guard and was lowered to Paddock. Perhaps they are hungry too, Josiah thought. He leaned forward and took one of the skewered pieces of elk from over the coals and held it up to the big man. Instead of taking the meat, the Crow knocked Paddock's hand to the side, freeing the meat from the trapper's grasp so that it sailed over the flames and skittered across the snow.

Josiah looked down at the empty hand, bewildered by that response. Fear was beginning to rise within him, the fear he had always struggled with; the fear he was afraid would someday make him immobile in the face of danger and challenge.

Looking back up to the Crow's eyes, he saw them narrowed now, no longer open and full of laughter the way they had been when he had first met the Indian when coming to this place. The red paint between the Crow's eyebrows was darkened with the heavy, deep, vertical furrows that seemed to make the eyes all the more piercing. Perhaps he should try to talk with them. Perhaps they could understand. Perhaps then he could understand.

"You don't want my meat," he said slowly, in hopes they would be able to comprehend his English. "Sit by my fire." He gestured quickly to show them seats around the small cooking fire. "Sit by my fire an' tell me what you want."

The big Crow answered him with the same, solitary gesture again. Once more he put out his open hand in front of Josiah. For a moment, Paddock stared at the open palm, then finally looked back into the dark, glaring eyes before returning to stare dumbly at the hand. It moved then, the fingers curling up until only the index finger was left to point at the knife Josiah held in his hand. The white man looked down at the knife he had been cutting meat with and thought he now understood.

"You're wantin' this knife for a present." He was nervous now, but attempted not to show it in his voice. Although he knew they would never understand his words, they would know the sound of fear in a man's voice. They would smell it.

"Didn't get you no presents like them presents from Scratch. The knife make you happy, take it." He held it up toward the Indian's hand. Slowly he opened his hand until the knife handle rocked in the flat palm. The big Crow reached for the blade and took it from the trapper, putting it into his left hand so that he could return the right to the trigger guard. The index finger that had pointed to the knife slipped once more to its place in front of the trigger.

The fear was there. It was impossible to deny it any longer. He felt it tugging at his chest and the hoof-beat thumps that seemed to rock him where he sat. Now the big Crow nodded. Two of the braves came to either side of the trapper and lifted him off the ground, their hands under his armpits.

He thought it best to get to his feet. Besides, he told himself, he couldn't run sitting down. It had all happened too quickly. He was dizzied by it. And if he was to make his break, it had to be now. The two started to move him forward and he used their momentum to shove the warriors away from him. Twisting suddenly he broke free and hurdled the fire. He crashed onto the soft new snow and clawed his way back to his feet to dive around the shelter.

He skidded to a stop, bumping into three more warriors, who had been behind the shelter during the whole thing. They turned him around and pushed him forward, shoving him back toward the others. He jerked away at their hold on him, not wanting to be pinned in with their hands, not wanting to feel their death grips on his arms. The blow to the back of his shoulders made his knees collapse. His legs went out from under him.

Suddenly he found himself on his hands and knees on the snow, feeling dizzy again. Blinking his eyes to fight the blackness creeping over him, Josiah watched the tiny sparks of light shooting across his vision. Hands clawed at him again, gripping him under the arms once more, pulling at him to stand. He would let them. He could not stand on his own, he decided. He was too weak for that. What had hit him? Was it the sudden dash for freedom that had made him dizzy after the days of sickness? He shook that away. It was not what had hit him, Josiah decided. It was who.

Paddock tried to turn his head around to look at the braves behind him as they pulled him up on his wobbly legs. The pain burned at the back of his shoulders and up his neck. A rifle butt, he thought. They hit me with a rifle.

"What the hell?"

Josiah heard Bass's voice. It came from his right somewhere. Over near the fire where he needed to turn the meat over the coals. It would burn if he didn't get back. Only fit for the dogs then. He had to get back. Paddock knew the older trapper had told him to mind his manners with the Crow, so he had offered the meat. Then the knife. Now he was confused. What had he done to anger them? What had he done wrong? But the old man was here now. He would get it all straightened out. He could talk with them.

"Josiah! What the hell's blue-blazes goin' on?"

The voice came through to him again and seemed to crack the thick fog. He turned to see Bass standing near the fire in a half circle of warriors, each one with a rifle trained on the older man. He was taking his knife from the sheath on his belt. It was all happening so slowly now—after things had started off so suddenly, so quickly. They were going to punish Bass, too? For something I've done? I won't stand for it. I can't stand for it, not Bass getting it too.

Josiah tried to shake his arms free and succeeded in pulling one of the warriors off balance so the Indian fell in front of the young trapper. With one arm free he swung around at the Indian on his left. The warrior ducked and smashed Josiah in the face with the small rawhide shield he held on his left forearm. Paddock tumbled forward, falling over the brave he had pushed to the ground. They were on him in an instant, hands and arms, tugging and pulling again. Kicking his shoulders to get him to move, to get him to stand up for them.

"That ain't gonna help!"

He could hear the voice again, breaking through the Crow tongue that surrounded him.

"Goddammit! Fightin' 'em now ain't gonna help!"

They had him to his knees now. Those hands pulling at him from above. Everywhere were buckskins, fringe, and paint. He felt their breath hot against his cheeks as he struggled, felt their hair brush across lips and nose as they fought with him. If he could just get a leg free, stand and kick at them, that would do it. He could come close to killing a man with that kick.

"Don' get you in no deeper, Josiah! Cut your fightin'!"

The young man shot up, not minding the stars and the dizziness crowding his head. He turned to find one of the warriors in front of him and lashed out with the foot. The Indian went sailing to the side as he felt his foot crash against the Crow's chest where a shield was held. Then things went funny again. The pain was back along his shoulders. It crashed to the back of his head and he felt the bottom coming out. He was slipping. Slipping. Past the gray and shooting sparks. Into the black.

"You dumb nigger!" Bass shouted as they hit Paddock again with the rifle. He had no hands binding him and vaulted the fire, sliding to his knees with a crunch to Paddock's side.

The young trapper had landed face down in the snow. The warriors circled the two white men and one reached out his hand to pull Bass to his feet. Scratch knocked the hand away.

"Baci-ri!" he snarled at them.

Behind him, where Bass could not see, the big Crow nodded to say that the warriors were not to attempt touching this white man again.

"Kus-irau. Tsire na-tokum." Scratch told the warriors

he was going no place; there was no place for him to run.
They were to let him look to the young white man they
had beaten.

They let him be. Bass leaned forward and slowly
rolled Josiah over onto his back. Cradling the head in his
lap, Scratch clawed at the top layer of snow and began to
wipe the young man's face with the white cold. Carefully
he pushed the snow over the nose, feeling the cartilage
move easily beneath his fingers. It was broken. Blood
seeped from the left nostril where Bass wiped the snow.
He needed to sop up the blood. He could not have Josiah
look this way. The boy always had a fair-looking face—
nothing to make him particularly handsome—but the broken nose would be enough to mark him. He didn't need
the blood smeared over his face.

Brushing the pink snow out of the mustache and
beard, Scratch clawed more snow into his hands and
massaged some of its cold onto the back of Josiah's neck.
Already a hard knot was rising at the back of the young
trapper's skull. They would have to pack it in snow
tonight, he thought. More snow was brought to the
cheeks again and rubbed over the brow. He saw the eyes
flutter, then slowly open.

"You're a dumb nigger, ain't you now, son," he said
softly, wiping some of the snow out of Paddock's eyebrows. "They had you some five to one right there, and
no chance't to make it to them ponies. You're sure the
dumb nigger, boy, but I still loves you for it."

The eyes continued to stare up at him. Eyes full of
little more than dull light, eyes even without the scared
intensity of an animal you've dropped and now must
shoot with a second bullet to make up for the lack of a
clean kill. They weren't even doe eyes, yet there was a
question in them that bothered Scratch. It nagged at him
as he wiped the excess snow and moisture from the face.
They yearned for an answer, the look in those eyes. And
he had none to give.

The big Crow behind him spoke, telling Bass to help
the young man to his feet now. Both were to come with
them. Both were to attempt no escape. Bass looked about
him for a moment, mentally counting the braves standing
around them, rifles pointing down at the white men in
the hub of the circle, the barrels looking like the spokes of
a wheel on a trader's cart. Just a bad dream, he thought,

as he looked back down, away from the rifles and the warrior who held the trapper's knife. Just a bad dream that would end sooner or later. It would end.

Scratch rose to one knee and pushed Josiah forward out of his lap. He rose slowly, helping the shaky young one get to his feet, letting Paddock lean against him in the rising. Bass pulled Josiah's left arm up and ducked his head beneath it so that he could support the young man in walking wherever they wanted them to go. Wherever they wanted, he thought.

But why? When he asked the big Crow there was no immediate answer. Then the Indian merely replied that the white men no longer belonged in Absaroka. There was now a taking of more than they could give. He finished by saying he could tell no more, motioning to Scratch that he wanted the white men to follow. He started to turn away, then wheeled back suddenly, striding up so close to the older trapper that Bass saw the streaks of red within the warrior's eyes. For a moment, the two men stared into each other's eyes, then the Crow spat out the words, "You have betrayed us, Pote ani. We have been betrayed by this man who says he is our white brother in between." It was then that he turned on his heel and started away.

Gradually Scratch got Josiah to turn and begin hobbling beside him. The several warriors fanned out behind the trappers in a half circle to guard against any attempts at escape. Their low voices were lost in the general commotion growing in the village now. And he could no longer follow their words as the sounds were drowned in the sea of wailing and chanting, curses and prayers, rising and swelling toward them.

From the lodges poured the people of Absaroka, from every direction they flocked to flood the path the white men were taking toward the center of the camp. People who had hailed the white men with smiles and songs of joy when they had arrived. People who now leaned out from the narrow corridor of bodies and buckskin to spit at the white men, to hurl mucous and foul curses. Here and there a woman had fallen to her knees in the snow to wail in mourning. Other women broke from the edge of the narrow path to stand before the trappers and scream, showing Bass their missing fingers, smearing his face and shirt with their blood and spit.

He was glad Josiah was still dazed, barely conscious of it all, his head hanging loosely as he stumbled along beside Titus. There was an immense sense of loss within the old man, knowing that the tribe was venting its rage at him and the boy for whatever had happened. And that was the nagging, troublesome thing now—not knowing the reason. The tribe was in the fiercest of frenzies, lost in the throes of mourning the loss of someone valued and respected by all. And in some way he was part of what had caused it.

The sad procession stumbled forward, pushed and shoved from side to side by the women, the old men, and even the boys who had begged for a ride with them only weeks before. The wailing and the chanting seemed oppressive to him, like the foul breath of torture before death. All that remained was to have the human dung thrown at them. He laughed about it inside, thinking what a relief it would be to have it done; to have it over with and not have to wait for it to come flying from the pushing, shoving, spitting mob.

He shook Josiah as they stumbled along through the pulsating throng, trying to arouse the young trapper. Would it be better for him to face this thing awake? he asked himself. Would it be far better for a man to know what was happening to him? He realized he had no answers. He knew nothing more than that anger was washing around him. At that moment it came hurling from the crowd. Several women stepped forward from the edge of the narrow corridor to heave the dung at the white men. Again and again it struck them.

He knew it was bad then. No longer uncertain, but feeling the release of the waiting drain from him. Quickly wiping his face, Bass knew little of the fecal matter would smear their skin. It was merely the insult these women sought. It was only the chance to heap the greatest of humiliation they could on the two men.

More violently now he shook the young man and saw the head come slowly up to look at him. The eyes blinked themselves clear of the mucous and what little of the human feces hung over his brows in the hair. There was more life to those eyes now, no longer dull. They had the look of the wounded, ready for that second, the final, shot.

"What's it mean?" he asked plaintively.

Bass shook his head. "I cain't say, Josiah. I ain't knowin'—jest yet." He ducked his head as more of the spit came hurling at him, yet he allowed an old woman to wipe her bloody, dripping stubs of fingers over his face.

"They fixin' to kill us? That it? That's it, ain't it?" Josiah's voice rose a bit to make himself heard above the roar of the crowd. "They fixin' to do us in, ain't they?"

Scratch knew not what to answer. The tribe was worked up. Anything was possible now. Their fate hung in the winds, and the winter breezes could blow in any direction. He knew not how to answer the young trapper, except that it must be the truth. Now. He could do nothing less than tell the truth.

"It might be we's to go under, slow," Bass started, his words as slow as the death he imagined was near. "But I ain't knowin' why. You're the one what's knowin', ain't you? You're the one what should have him some pieces to this thing!"

Josiah looked suddenly at the older man. The words had been almost a plea, for an answer from him. But he had asked Bass to explain what it all meant. "Don't get you. Don't know what you're—"

"I'm talking about *you*!" he hollered above the crowd. Everywhere was the Crow tongue he had been trying to follow. Now it did not matter. They would yell in their own language and he would yell in his. Neither one would understand the other. It might be too late for that. "Talkin' 'bout *you* an' McAfferty. That's where the answers is. You both was here. You both knowin' what's goin' on. You tell me, Josiah. You tell me!"

Paddock looked dumfounded at the man who had been helping him along, bewildered at the sudden anger he heard in the words, the sudden tenseness of the older man's body. Impulsively he pushed the old man away and stumbled forward by himself, bouncing off a few of the Indians along the corridor of bodies. Bass reached forward to help him again, but Josiah pushed the hand away.

"Don't need your help!" he spat back at the offer of assistance. He would walk alone, despite the ache along the back of his shoulders, the rising throb at the back of his head, and the pain spreading across his cheeks. He would walk alone with them.

"We's needin' each other's help right now. You dumb nigger. I need you. Cain't you get that through your goddamned thick, mule-ass head? I need you!"

Paddock turned on him, shocked at the words. As soon as he stopped the warrior behind them shoved both of them. Josiah stumbled forward, unsure of his legs and Bass reached out to steady him once more.

"I need you tell me what gone on whilst I was away, Josiah." The words were firm and even now. "There's a lot missin' an' you're the one to be answerin' me." He was up close to Paddock's ear now, stumbling alongside the young man, speaking loudly at the side of Josiah's head. "I know me McAfferty's here, that he come in when I was gone. Some of his ponies down where we put ours."

"Yeah," Josiah replied, "he come in, last night it was." He bowed his head now, things were a little fuzzy still. "We talked some. His squaw was ready to have the baby. Yeah—he brung her in to have the baby. An' he come over to spend some time jawin' with me while she was havin' it. The old women wasn't 'bout to let him be there while his squaw was givin' birth—"

"That's all?" he interrupted. "That's all there be? You ain't seen him since't? He ain't round here?"

"Ain't seen him since late last night. Was still sick. He come round an' we talked some bit. Last thing was he was off to see his squaw—an' the new baby. That was the last time I seen him. Honest. I ain't seen him since!" He looked at Bass, expecting some answer, some comment. But the older man wasn't looking at him. Scratch continued to stare at the pulsing mob about them. The crowd had grown now that they were in the center of the village, in the big, open area reserved for tribal celebrations.

"It be somethin' we may never know, Josiah. May never know—now," Scratch finally remarked as they were brought to a sudden stop by the braves behind them. The big Crow turned and motioned the two men to stay where they stood before folding his arms over the cocked rifle once more. "If'n what you say be true—'bout you bein' asleep most of the time I was gone—it's got somethin' to do with McAfferty. Only way I can figger it. Only way."

"What you sayin'? What McAfferty gotta do with all this?"

"Don' know. Don't know that. 'Cept we gettin' caught in the back flash of this thing. An' the why of it is 'cause
599

we'se white. That's the way I'm figgerin' it. Somethin' to do with McAfferty, what he's done. An' we white, jest like him. Makes no matter I been friends to these'r Crow for y'ars now. Makes no shit to 'em now. I'm jest white again, like McAfferty. You an' me gonna pay 'long with him."

"You think they got him somewhere?" asked Josiah.

"Might'n be. Up to Arapooesh's lodge, might'n be." Bass shook his head and wiped off some more of the spit hurled his way by the mob that continued to press them. "He gone an' pissed 'em off some way—a mighty good job of it, that ol' man did. These folks talkin' like they talk of Blackfoots. Not many times they get so riled—"

Bass stopped abruptly, thinking he should not have said so much about how the tribe was acting, what they might be thinking. It would be well for Josiah to be ignorant of this now. It was good Paddock did not know enough about Injuns to be really scared, he thought. Scared the way he was, but refusing to let it show. It could choke a man, this fear, he thought. Bottle it up inside you and it could choke you if it didn't eat out your insides first. Was good that the young one didn't know enough to be really scared. He would have to battle the fear for both of them, have to control its challenge for both of them.

The waiting was the most oppressive agony. It could hang over a man like a black, broiling cloud. He never knew when it would break and spill on him. All he could do was wait.

"Jest gotta stand here an' take it," he found himself saying, then wondered if he had said it for Josiah, or for himself. Just part of his thoughts, he decided.

"Till they figger on what they gonna do with us?" Josiah said.

Bass turned quickly to look at the young trapper, knowing then that he had spoken out loud, after so much thought. "Till then, son. Don' you figger to be takin' off now; ain't gonna make the river afore you'd have 'em on you. Best we stay here. Right here. Show 'em what stuff we made of. Show 'em we ain't afraid of anythin' they wanna do with us. No sir. We be men good as any others. And they gonna know it now."

The young man did not reply. Too busy in his mind, Scratch thought. Just as well too. If there was to be the killing, he wanted to go first. He knew he could not stand

600

the thought of watching the young one go first. He had to be it, the first one to go. But would that be right? It would mean Josiah would have to watch him die the slow death. He didn't want that. What kind of a thing was that to do to the young'un? He would have to let Josiah be the first after all. He would have to watch his young partner die. It would be hell worse than death itself to witness, but it was far better than knowing Josiah would have to watch him slip from life.

The crowd parted briefly as the big Crow stepped up with Bass's knife in his hand. This would be the start of it, Scratch thought. They are getting things started. The warrior came up to face Titus and took the tail of the trapper's buckskin shirt in his left hand. With the knife he sliced up the front of the shirt, slowly, letting the tip of the knife just graze the white flesh in one long line, just tickling the skin in anticipation. When it was slit open, two other braves came forward and pulled the shirt off his shoulders, ripping it from his arms. It was thrown to the ground at Scratch's feet.

Josiah was next. Told not to struggle by Bass, that it was something minor to be endured, Josiah calmly endured while the shirt was pulled from his body and thrown at his feet. Both men stood naked from the waist up in the cold, sunny light of midday. Their white color starkly contrasted with the earth-brown bodies surrounding them. Scratch looked at Josiah to nod his approval of Paddock's patience; he noticed the white flesh across the chest and shoulders, the brown growing up from the base of the neck and down from the wrists to cover the big hands. And the thin white scar along his belly. He thought he saw Josiah shudder slightly and knew it was the cold. Only the cold.

"They gonna scalp us, Scratch?" he asked, turning to face Bass. "They gonna do that after we killed?"

"They might'n be thinkin' 'bout our skelps be worth somethin'. Yes," he answered. They would not get much with my old hair, Bass mused. Josiah's they would take a real shine to—be something a man could be proud of, hanging from a lodgepole or a bundle. But mine, that would be a surprise for them. They wouldn't know what to make of that medicine. He felt the small curl of a smile at his lips and fought to suppress it. That would be the end to all insults, he thought. To scalp yourself right in front of those who are wanting your scalp! Would be something for him to think on as they killed him, anyway— getting one last laugh on them.

"It be a real sad thing, them only gettin' one good skelp outta the two of us." He turned to glance at Paddock, then winked. The small, grim smile was evident now on his lips.

"How can you be makin' fun now, time like this! Your Absor'kees ready to gut us right here." Josiah, disbelieving of the man beside him, was unable to imagine that a man could smile at death. "You're a strange one, Titus Bass. You be touched by the mountains, that's true." He shook his head sadly for a moment, then turned back to look at Bass. "You're made of some strange medicine, Scratch. Old . . . old man's medicine."

"An' them Injuns might be thinkin' I be big medeecin, too," he replied, putting his left hand up to the back of his head. There he reached beneath the fur hat and worked at the knot on the bandanna. With the tails of the blue cloth loose, Scratch took hold of the bandanna and fur cap with the fingers of his left hand while raising his right arm to join the other at the back of his head.

Josiah watched impassively, knowing what was to take place. Letting his eyes climb slowly from the old man's side where he gazed at the hard, white line of an old wound, past the ugly, pinched, and puckered scar of a bullet hole suffered on the Yampa River years before, Josiah followed up the arm until it disappeared behind the older man's head. The arms were still now as Bass called the big Crow warrior over to him.

"Batawe. Ira-axe barak."

The Crow stepped forward, haughty, a little amused, perhaps sure that the white man was about to beg for his life even though his fate had not yet been decided by the older men of the tribe. But he would enjoy this anyway, the big man thought, watching the white men beg for mercy in the face of death, a death in payment for bringing the wolf-one to Absaroka.

"Di-rupxe-sa." Bass told the crowd he was a brave one. "Di-sake-co aki-sate." He had courage enough to scalp himself. Just then his left hand flew off the top of his head, pulling the fur hat and bandanna with it. Instantly behind it came the right, its fingers holding the long black trophy of years before.

The Crow brave took two faltering steps back and looked away for a moment. A sudden hush fell upon the crowd. All chanting, wailing, and oaths of death ceased. Many of the women and some warriors clamped hands over their mouths in astonishment. When the big Crow looked back, he did so warily, staring at the scalp hung from the trapper's hand. Scratch turned slowly to show them all his patch of bare white skull. The warrior grimly pursed his lips rather than clamp a hand over them. He looked from the hank of hair to the white man's face, then back to the hair, repeatedly. This was hard to believe. The Crow told Bass that he should have waited to be scalped by a warrior of Absaroka—that would have had much honor in it. But scalping one's own head had no honor in the Other-Side-Land. The spirits would only laugh at the white man.

"Bi-i-kya waku," Titus replied, still smiling from the humor of the moment. He told the Indian that he would be the one to watch out for himself. He decided the warrior was only boasting before the others, having suffered this embarrassment by the white man.

"Di-wap-e wima-tsiky," the Crow warrior told him, saying he alone would have the honor of killing the white man, that it rested in his hands and no one else would have that singular honor. The crowd began to howl and wail, their cries filling the air and deafening further conversation between the two antagonists. They were made bold by the words of the one warrior.

Bass looked down at the scalp in his hand, feeling as if the weight of the joke he had planned was now lost on the Indians. He felt angry, more with himself than at the big man or this tribe for its failure. The joke had been good only for the moment. Now it was gone forever—a long forever staring him in the face. Everything had its moment. Everything had its brief time.

"This big nigger's jest finger-itchin' to be guttin' somebody this day," he remarked to Josiah grimly, replacing the dried scalp on his crown. Bass held out the blue bandanna to Paddock, "Here, tie it round my head. Joke's over for this day. Joke's over—an' looks to be on me."

The young trapper stepped behind Bass to tie the cloth around his head while Scratch held the scalp in place. The crowd was back to spitting when they could advance close enough to do so, while back and forth between the Indians' legs crept dogs to peek at what was causing the sensation in camp. Josiah tied the knot. He looked quietly about him, deciding he was not really startled that even the little children were hurling oaths at them. Josiah remembered what Scratch had said in some other context: the Crow learn young. He wiped from the corner of his eyes the mucous that had begun to wend its slimy way down his cheeks, and stepped again to Scratch's side.

A younger brave, perhaps no older than fifteen or sixteen, pushed through the throbbing crowd to hand the big man several strands of rawhide tethers. The big Crow took them from him and shook them for Scratch as the white man had shaken the scalp. He told the white man that he would tie them to the meat-drying racks, saying that it was only fitting, for there they would slowly peel the flesh from their bones, so that death would not be quick and merciful in coming. The dogs would eat the warm flesh from the white trappers' bones—if the dogs did not get sick from eating it and throw the flesh back up. He nodded and several warriors came up from the edge of the crowd to push the white men away.

They were shoved back against the fringe of the crowd that refused to move immediately. There was a lot of yelling again, this time between the warriors and those in the mob as they shoved the trappers back. To and fro they were pushed between the two groups until a woman on the edge of the crowd stepped into view and kicked Bass in the groin. He started to double over, then thought better of showing pain to these people. He fought the sharp pain slashing through his flesh as the growing agony shot into his bowels, robbing him of breath. While struggling to control his pain, he and Josiah were pushed again into the crowd; this time it gave way, but only slightly, to allow them the few steps to the meat preparation rack.

Fighting for air because of the searing between his legs and the nausea in his stomach, Bass was thrown around by one of the braves, his arms taken from his abdomen and wrenched roughly out from his body. A rawhide tether was tightly placed about each wrist. Bass's breath was beginning to come more easily now and the pain seemed to be abating. He looked over at Josiah and found the young man watching him as they were being tied to the meat rack. Their arms were stretched upward to their limits, then bound to the cross-members, where strips of buffalo and elk were normally laid out to dry in the sun after a successful hunt. They stared into each other's eyes for some moments, both wondering if this might be close to the end, close to that time when they would no longer look upon each other.

"Had me hopes for much better things for you, Josiah Paddock," Scratch said, turning his eyes from the younger man, unable now to look him in the face. "Was you to go under—had hoped it'd be . . . some other way'n this. Man's hands tied from him—ain't able to do nothin' 'bout it. Ain't no way for a man to die . . ."

Josiah turned his face from Bass as the older man's words slipped into silence. Pain momentarily seized his wrists as the knots were tied off securely against his flesh. "It gonna be like this, Scratch?" He fought to make the words sound even and flat, void of any emotion. Now he was unsure just how they had sounded to the white man beside him.

Scratch turned to face Josiah, searching for words he could use. His lips moved slightly but nothing came from them. Finally he turned from Paddock, unable any longer to look at him. He nodded a few times, slowly, to indicate yes.

Paddock turned away too, no longer able to look at the nodding head with its gray-flecked braid and fur cap tugged down over the blue cloth. He could not feel anything, and he thought that funny. *Here I am, about to die, and I don't feel nothing.* He searched his mind for emotion. *Somewhere there must be some fear.* But all there was to feel was the dull throb at the back of his head and the spreading rays of pain reaching across his cheeks from the twisted nose. *Just the body,* he thought. *That's all I felt* and looked down the length of his form, past the Nez Perce leggings and the winter moccasins of the Crow. His eyes stared dumbly at the ground between his feet.

"Ain't your fault," he said, looking up to Bass. "Want you know I ain't feelin' it to be your fault for this." He choked back a little against the pain spreading across his face. "Ain't 'nother man I'd choose to be dyin' 'longside, Scratch. Ain't 'nother one 'cept Titus Bass."

Scratch turned at the words, looking at the face with

its nose pushed out of shape, crooked and bleeding still, the red rivulet flowing into the brown-blond hair of the mustache. He ached still, but no longer from the bruised groin. It was an ache he felt for the courageous young man beside him. Above the noisy din of the crowd, over the shrill and strident voices calling for their deaths, Titus Bass looked anew at the man beside him. There was some courage in Josiah Paddock that would bear the old man up.

"Hardest thing—" Bass choked against the sudden catch in his throat, fighting against the interruption it caused. "Hardest thing 'bout dyin' this way—be that Josiah Paddock's the kind to go on to that big belt in the blue." His eyes climbed slowly to the white traces splashed across the soft hue of the sky. Bass watched the clouds moving for a moment. "An' you know where Ol' Scratch be goin', Josiah. I won' be seein' you on the other side. Been some time now I knowed I was goin' to hell in the end. Always thought myself ready, too . . ." He broke off a moment. "Jest gonna miss you, son. Gonna miss you bad. That's the pain in this. A pain—"

The crowd suddenly fell silent. The hush was ominous. Bass turned from Paddock and looked past the big Crow, who also had turned to determine the cause of the silence.

Josiah looked for only a moment more at Bass, then he too watched the crowd swell and move quietly. The Indians parted like water passing over a boulder in the river, closing up behind the man who walked into their midst. From the fringe of the mob stepped Arapooesh, moving slowly forward as the Indians surged back into place after his passing.

The buffalo robe passed over the left shoulder so that the left hand held the flaps closed against his chest. His right arm was crooked at the elbow so that it too lay against the front of his body. In the right hand was suspended a medicine bundle formed from the head of a coyote, its jaws sewn together with sinew, and from the jowls hung a few small locks of hair wrapped in red cloth. From the back of the head was suspended a round loop of willow, wrapped tightly in rawhide, to which was tied a fully stuffed war eagle. Arapooesh stood before the white men, silent, halfway between the trappers and the hushed, unmoving crowd.

Turning to the big Crow, Rotten Belly spoke at last, "Ha-tskite bara cope." He had commanded the Crow to cut the white men free.

The big youth measured the chief for a moment, his eyes the only sign of any objection. In those eyes Arapooesh recognized the youthful rebellion. Finally the chief nodded without another word and asked for the man's knife while he transferred the medicine bundle to the left hand that held the buffalo robe closed. The youth stared down into the chief's empty palm briefly before he brought Bass's knife from his belt and laid it in the old man's hand.

Understanding the words, but unable yet to comprehend the meaning of this turn in events, Bass watched the chief move toward him. Arapooesh brought the big butcher knife slowly up in front of the white man's face and held it there, staring into Scratch's eyes for some time. Then he took the knife away and easily slashed the rawhide tethers that bound the old trapper's arms. He moved without a word to Josiah's side and cut first the right arm, then the left free.

As the trappers let their arms fall and began to rub their wrists where the rawhide had scraped and chafed the flesh, a solitary chant pierced the air. Somewhere in this stilled mob, a single old woman began a Crow death song. Within moments others joined her. First one here, then a few more over there, until many women were howling the high-pitched dirge.

Silently the chief gazed intently at Bass, as if at last determining the rightness of this thing he was going to do. Then his eyes moved to Paddock, measuring the young man whose eyes met his without flinching, as they had when first the two men had met.

Rotten Belly stared at Josiah for a few minutes more, then raised his right arm into the air. Straight toward the sky went the hand holding the trapper's knife. Slowly, like the honks of geese passing overhead on their long journey, the chanting and mourning death wails fell away until silence again prevailed. With no more command given than the raised arm, Arapooesh had stilled the mob. They would grant him this, their respect—recognizing him not merely as tribal chief, but also as the one Crow above all others who had suffered the greatest loss. He had lost his first woman, the first wife he had taken to his

607

lodge, the squaw who had outlived all the subsequent women in his life. His people would grant him this, his choice in mourning her death, for he was chief, he was her man of many winters.

"As Pote ani asked of us, the other white man came to our camp," he began in slow, even words of the Crow tongue. "It was to be. Perhaps. So too was it to be that the other white man was to wear the skin of the black wolf. Perhaps. He was seen by the dreamers, his head wrapped in white ice, cold from the place of the Winter Man." His right arm holding the knife passed across his face once.

"The Nez Perce woman, she was to die with the young one inside her. Perhaps. To pass to the Other-Side-Land without knowing her child in this life. She was to take with her Sleeps Before the Door, my first woman. To help her on her journey to the Spirit Land, she took Sleeps Before the Door. Perhaps."

Bass looked quickly at Josiah and found the young man looking in his direction. Paddock noticed the older man's eyes narrow in receipt of the words spoken by Arapooesh.

"This was all to be, what the dreamers had seen in their visions. We did not know it would be the woman to suffer and die in her childbirth. We did not know it would be my first woman who would die at the hands of the other white man, who wears the skin of the black wolf." Arapooesh brought the point of the trapper's knife to his left breast, pressing the tip of the blade against the buffalo robe. "He has killed again in our camp, the home of the people. He has been here before and we now know who this man is." He raised his eyes slowly to the sky.

"There was little breath left in Sleeps Before the Door when my brother's woman found her in the lodge we shared. Little breath remained for what needed to be said. My woman wanted me to be told of this man. That he had truly been here before." Now his eyes dropped back to look into those of the older trapper. "She had seen him the morning our enemy attacked our camp. This was the man from the north who shot at her to silence my woman from telling of him. This was the man from the north who killed my woman so that she would not tell of the blackness of his heart. But, Pote ani, her words still reached my ears, as surely as if she had been here herself. After the battle, Sleeps Before the Door told me of the man from the north. And with her last breath, my woman told of this same man killing her with both fear and hate in his eyes. Now, Arapooesh must kill to right the loss of one he has loved for many winters." He made a slashing motion with the knife across his left breast and let the arm slip to his side.

"Arapooesh would be one to drive the knife into the black wolf's heart." He finally took his eyes from Scratch and looked down at the blade he held. "But white man must kill white man. It must be this way, even though the thief stole from the lodge of Arapooesh the life of his first woman. It must be this way." He looked back into Bass's eyes once more. "The one who brought the man with hair like ice to us, the one who brought him here among us again, that one must go."

Bass stared back into the intent, light eyes, and nodded when Rotten Belly had finished. But the chief held up his hand to the older trapper, as if to silence anything the white man might say.

"Arapooesh, who stands before you now, he has seen many winters and his hair grows white with flakes of snow from those many cold winters. Pote ani too has seen many cold times. He too grows old with the winters marking his head in their passing. We have both seen many hunts in our times. And Arapooesh has now the young to do his hunting for him, the young ones who are in their time when the grass is coming green. We have passed that time long ago, Pote ani. That time has slipped through our hands as the water of the river slips from our fingers though we wish to hold on to its cold treasure. We have the young to hunt for us—" he nodded toward Paddock but kept his eyes on Scratch—"when the bow and the thunder sticks of the white men grow heavy for us long in winters."

Rotten Belly took a step close to Bass, standing now almost close enough for the trapper to feel the Crow's breath. He continued to look intently into the white man's face for a few moments more without speaking, making Titus feel as if he were looking right through him.

"That is the way of the Crow. The young to hunt for those of us who have seen many winters and many hunts before. That is the way of the Absaroka. It is the wish of

Arapooesh"—he turned from Bass to Josiah—"that the young, scarred one be the white man to do this thing for Arapooesh."

Scratch caught his breath low and held it there. He looked at Paddock and saw the young man's eyes flick for an instant to look at him before returning the chief's intense gaze. He's going to send Josiah after McAfferty; the thought burned in his brain. And the bastard'll kill the boy. His thoughts continued to hum rapidly, attempting to calculate Josiah's chances of finding Asa before McAfferty found Paddock. The odds were nowhere near giving the young trapper a chance in the hunt. Nowhere close to allowing Josiah the chance of even seeing the man he was hunting before a ball came from out there, somewhere, to tear the life from his body. He'd have him a preacher's chance in hell, he thought.

"You tell him, the young one," Rotten Belly said, having turned to look at Bass. "You tell him that he will be the one to go right the death in Arapooesh's lodge, the death of Sleeps Before the Door. You tell him that Arapooesh has him to do it. You tell him that."

Without taking his eyes from Arapooesh, Bass explained in English what had just occurred. "Josiah, seems that McAfferty kill't Rotten Belly's squar. An' he says he's too ol't to hunt now, but he has him the young warriors to hunt for him. But it's gotta be a white man to hunt for a white man, he says. The one as brung McAfferty here gotta be the one to hunt him down. But he says I'm too ol't, like he is. We got us the young'uns to do our huntin' for us. Rotten Belly"—he paused, moving his eyes from the chief to the younger trapper—"Rotten Belly is havin' you go hunt McAfferty down." He waited a moment to see if something stirred behind the eyes staring back at his. There was no hint, no betrayal of what was behind them. "But... but, Josiah, I'll tell him you want me to do it. You want me to go 'stead of you. I tell him—"

"You tell him," Paddock interrupted, looking at the chief's face as he spoke to Bass, "tell him I'll go. Tell him I'll bring McAfferty's scalp with me when I come back here to the Crows."

Bass swallowed hard, choosing his words in the Indian tongue, selecting them as carefully as his burning mind would allow. "The young one says to Arapooesh he will go for the chief of the Crow. To do this thing for Arapooesh,

He says for me to tell you he will not return without the white man's scalp—"

The big Crow youth came forward suddenly to Rotten Belly's side and protested. "The white man will not return with the scalp Arapooesh needs. The white man will not return to Absaroka. You cannot put your trust in this one! You have not known him but this winter's moons. He will go the way of the other white man, gone—from Absaroka to disappear beyond the mountains!"

"Bu-aka!" Arapooesh commanded the young man to silence without looking in his direction. A few murmurs rose from the crowd.

"It is this one you must have to go for you." The big brave pointed to his own breast, and refused to be quiet in spite of the chief's sharp command. "It was I who first met the white-haired one winters ago, when his hand was cut off. I was the one who cut the hand from his arm to save his life. Now I will be the one to cut his heart out to take his life. It was this one" he again touched his chest with a single finger—"who first knew the white-haired man when we had stolen trappers' ponies. They came to take them back and we had not chosen our camp well. We were all young and hungry for honors. The white-haired man was with us and did not know we had been raiding for ponies from a trappers' camp. A white man's bullet cut away the white-hair's hand. Arapooesh, it is this one who will go to cut away the scalp for you." He had almost, almost begged.

The chief shook his head. "The white man, the young one will go." He nodded then to Scratch to affirm it. "Crow do not hunt white men to kill them. We will not turn from a fight when one is brought to us, even when our enemy's skin is light. But Crow do not hunt white men. The young, strong one with Pote ani will go."

The big Crow stepped suddenly between Rotten Belly and Josiah, "Arapooesh must know he is a man without relatives!" The supreme verbal insult was delivered, and several of the other warriors on the fringe of the crowd, along with many of the women, clamped their hands over their mouths. "The young white one is without honor. For he has no relatives!"

"That one—what's he sayin'?" Josiah snapped at Bass.

"Young'uns itchin' for the fight. If'n it cain't be me or you, it's gonna be McAfferty. Says he was with Asa when

611

he got his hand blowed off. Then Arapooesh tol't him you're still gonna go. The big'uns jest tried to cut you down a few whacks, sayin' you had you no honor, Josiah. Said you had you no relatives to cry an' wail over your death."

"He's all that sure McAfferty's gonna kill me, eh?"

"Not that rightly. Jest what he said 'bout you was the worst thing one nigger can say 'bout 'nother."

Josiah turned his eyes from Scratch to glare at the young Crow. Arapooesh had watched it all and read what was flashing between the two men. It must not go any further. "Is not Arapooesh the chief of this band?" The big Crow nodded finally while still returning Paddock's glare. "Will not my people mourn if the young white man dies—as Arapooesh will mourn?"

The young Crow turned then to look at Rotten Belly, disbelieving what he had heard the chief say. "Then the young one will die, for he has no spirit helper!" He then spat on the ground at Josiah's feet. "No man can hope to return to his people from a battle without a spirit helper." The young warriors about the man whooped their agreement, waving their weapons in the air. "No man can be brave without the spirit helper. No man can do for Arapooesh what Arapooesh wants done without—"

"I will be his spirit helper." Bass stepped forward so that he too could stand between Rotten Belly and Josiah. "I will go with him since there has been no vision seeking and the spirits have not spoken to the young one. I will be his spirit helper."

Slowly Arapooesh turned to look into Scratch's eyes. The hooting braves fell silent. The chief held out the right hand and slowly opened his fingers that clutched the trapper's knife. Bass took it from Rotten Belly's hand. "Pote ani will be the young one's spirit helper," said the chief. "If the young one is to die in this thing"—his eyes seemed aflame—"then his spirit helper is to die too!"

Scratch nodded once in answer to the chief's words, knowing full well that if Paddock was killed by McAfferty, he could no more return to Arapooesh and these people. He knew then there would only be days of wandering, always uncertain of those who would be following on his trail to make things finally right for Arapooesh. Ironically, he was now to help Josiah on a manhunt, and only two days before Josiah had offered to go with Bass to hunt for three old faces, three old friends.

"Pote ani does not fear this thing, Arapooesh believes," the chief continued. "He knows there is no use in lingering in this life when one's time has gone. Why should a man linger, like the wildflower in spring holding onto hope of passing the heat of the summer and the cold of the coming winter? Only the earth and the sky are everlasting. It is men that must die. Our old age is a curse." His eyes fell from the blue expanse overhead and looked again at Bass. "And death in battle is a blessing for those who have seen our many winters."

The chief turned to face Paddock and shifted the medicine bundle from his left hand to his right. Holding it before him to present it to Josiah, Arapooesh spoke: "It is as I had hoped, this thing. The young one will go, and he will travel on the journey with his spirit helper as it should be. He will not be without a medicine bundle to give him strength and courage for the time ahead, to bind him with the spirits who will carry his life in their mouths." He gave the coyote's head to the young white man.

"And he will have a medicine song for him in preparing for battle. It is Crow. It is the wish of Arapooesh." The chief began to chant the high-pitched words of the medicine song:

When I come from behind,
I will carry two songs with me.
I will have my medicine here upon my chest.
You I am hunting—you are poor now.
Look to me!
Beyond the hills I have stayed,
From there I have come here now.
Long time will I be the eagle.
Long time have I been coming here.
I shall ride after the wolf in the mountains.

When he had finished it a fourth time, Rotten Belly asked Bass if he had planted the words in his mind so that he could teach them to the young white man while they were on the trail. Bass answered that he would remember, saying that such things were always to be remembered well.

Arapooesh slipped his right hand inside the robe and pulled a thong from around his neck. As it came over the chief's head, Bass recognized its significance. The hunter on a journey of revenge would be marked by the tribe. It was the old way, dating back winters without count, to the time when ponies first came to the Crow.

"You will tell the young one what I am to do," Rotten Belly admonished.

"Josiah," he started, turning to look at the young man so that he could meet Paddock's eyes, "Arapooesh gonna take some of your flesh—off your arms." He saw Josiah look quickly at the chief. "They gonna scar you, with the mark of the pony. Prints on your arms, for the hunter. It's the way, son. An' Arapooesh be watchin' how you take it."

The Crow chief stepped up to Josiah's left arm, the one close to the heart. He took the wrist in his left hand as he brought the eagle foot up before Paddock's face. "You look at me, Josiah. No use in watchin' what gonna happen. Jest ease off an' it won' hurt you much," Bass instructed.

Titus watched the young eyes turn to him, still with some question in them. In a moment Scratch could read the pain as the skin was first punctured; he saw Josiah's eyes flinch momentarily, then half close in response to the tearing at his flesh.

Rotten Belly slowly cut the skin on the outside of the arm, just below the shoulder, with one of the sharp eagle claws. He drew his line with care; the blood oozed freely from the wound. Soon completed was the graphic figure of a pony's hoof print, the bottom of which pointed down the arm. Then the chief cut another, below it, just above the elbow. He moved to the right arm and twice marked it also with the pony hoofs.

Scooping some snow with his left hand, Arapooesh washed the cold, white moisture over the wounds of the right arm. The cold helped momentarily to ease the bleeding and a little of the pain. He looked once at Bass and nodded, knowing the old trapper would certainly understand his approval of the courage shown by the young white one.

"He's gonna take some skin off you now—just a lil'—like graining a hide," Scratch explained, trying to console at the same time.

The eagle claw bit under one of the ends of the upper print on the right arm. Back and forth he began to cut. He worked the claw in a scraping, slicing motion until he had removed a long strip of skin from the arm. Into Scratch's hand he placed it. The second, third, and fourth prints were marked by skin removal and their flesh was also put into Scratch's hand.

When Arapooesh finally wiped snow over the four wounds to bathe them, Bass spoke. "It's done. No more, Josiah." He stepped closer to the young man. "You done jest fine. Did me proud of you." He smiled despite pursed lips and moist eyes.

The chief finished bathing his hands in the snow and washed the blood from the eagle claws. He rose and held out a hand, into which Bass put the four strips of flesh. The chief nodded to Josiah in final approval, then turned back to Scratch.

"You tell the young one, this night, what will be done with his flesh," he told the old trapper. "You tell him one piece of his flesh will be burned each coming of the stars for the next four nights by our medicine seekers. They will say prayers for him as his flesh is sacrificed to the spirits. Tell him he will carry the scars of the flying pony for all his days as a blessing of those spirits. And you say to the young one that the smoke from his burning flesh, with its ashes—when it is finished, all is scattered on the wind so that our prayers will journey with him. You tell him this, when the stars come this night."

Arapooesh turned briefly as if to address the crowd, then returned his eyes to the two trappers. "Do these men not have shirts to cover their shoulders? Does the Crow steal from those we send out from us as our warriors?" His voice was clear, ringing, and solemn.

One of the young braves came forward with the shirts that had been cut from the trappers' bodies. He held them out for the white men, then stepped back into the fringe of the crowd. The chief touched Josiah's and called out for a woman to come forward. "She will sew the shirts so that the wind will not cut through to your flesh on the journey." Taking the garments from the men, Arapooesh handed them to the woman, who moved back into the crowd and disappeared. "She will have them ready when you are to go."

"We want to go before the sun falls more from the

615

sky," Bass replied. "We will need little and will do without much."

"The two white men will have their pick of the finest ponies Absaroka has to offer them."

"Pote ani and the young one thank Arapooesh. Our hearts are filled with the ponies and the honor," Bass replied. "But, we will go on our journey with ponies that are ours."

"The spotted-rump ones, from the Nez Perce beyond the mountains?"

"Yes," Scratch answered. "They will be the ones for our journey, for this hunt. They will carry us well on our way. We wish to take no more from Absaroka. The white man has already taken more from Arapooesh than he can ever return. We will ride the Nez Perce ponies."

"It is said," Arapooesh responded. "Let all the people now move to prepare for the burying of Sleeps Before the Door." His voice was still steady and strong. "She will rest near the place where the two waters come together. It should be so. Go now, and make her body ready for the journey to the Other-Side-Land, and we will take her from the rear of the lodge. Beside her will rest the young woman with the baby still in her belly. Their time at dying grew like the meeting of these two waters. Their last journey will be together. Go now, and prepare the women—and the Nez Perce as you would our own. The white men have their trail to travel and we have our songs to sing over those who take their final journey from us." Arapooesh raised the right arm again and with it the crowd began to move away, each person toward a family lodge to prepare for the burial ceremonies.

Bass watched the Indians disperse for a few minutes, then turned to speak to Rotten Belly. "Arapooesh has done much for Pote ani, much for the young one who comes with me to winter with the Crow. Our lives have been truly in your hands, just as we have been in the lap of Absaroka."

"There is no need for these words," the chief replied. "It is only as the dreamers have told it from their vision. Pote ani is the coyote to hunt the wolf with the young one. To be the young white man's spirit helper. Pote ani was the one to step forward toward the other white man in the vision. That is what has been told to us, and we have seen that this much will come to pass."

He paused briefly to look into Scratch's eyes for one last time. "All that remains is to see which man will die. This the spirits have not shown us. This must still be for us to decide. It is all that remains for us to find out on this journey you take. The spirits talk to men on mysterious winds and not often do we on this earth have the chance to decide. Pote ani is to hunt and follow and catch this wind that has passed over Absaroka. You will see that the young one fares well in his search. That much a spirit helper must do."

He turned abruptly and walked slowly from the two white men, who were now alone, only minutes after they had been amidst a hooting mob closing in from all sides. And now they were to go on their way, while the Crow were to see the two women on their journey into eternity.

"You go an' roll them robes up," Bass instructed when they had returned to their small shelter, "an' Scratch'll pick plunder." Motioning with an arm, he sent Josiah inside their winter home. "Best to get yourself that capote on, too." Scratch picked up the elk-hide coat to put over his shoulders. "Smear you some of that bear grease on them medeecin cuts. Wrap 'em up good too. Won' be healin' up for some time, but the grease'll see to it they don' get 'em et up with the poison. You do it, first off." He saw Josiah nod affirmatively and reach for the small bundle that contained the rawhide pouches stuffed with the animal lard.

"You wanna take some grease for patchin'?" Paddock asked.

He thought a moment, then answered, "Nawww, son. That medeecin bear give us good patchin', true. But not for this here weather. The cold does it some strange things to a rifle barrel, an' the ball you loads up too. That grease has it the mind to be freezin' up on you in the cold. Nawww, we'll jest be stayin' with a spit patch, Josiah. 'Sides, I'm takin' other plunder, only what we'll surely be needin' one way or 'nother. Travel light is the way a nigger travels fast."

He looked away from the young man, off into the distance, as if discovering some faraway thing of importance. "Minds me too, best to have me a lookee to McAfferty's plunder. This child'll get him some mind of what that nigger's taken. Jest might come in handy, knowin' what he's left him behin't." He nodded in agreement with himself as the elk-hide coat slipped over the second arm.

After continuing to stare off at the river, Bass spoke again, "Josiah, you jest get me one buffler robe."

"Just one? You sure?"

"Be 'nough, what with them others I'm gonna take 'long with me: the bear an' wolf skins. You roll 'em up in the buffler robe."

Paddock had smeared the hard thick lard over the wounds where the strips of flesh had been removed from his arms until it softened, then pulled the blanket capote over his shoulders. "You wanna cut some elk up for the travelin'?"

Bass shook his head. "You jest get you that pemmeekin. That's the trail food. We ain't gonna be worryin' none over a fire an' fresh meat. No fire for warmin' us. You jest roll up them three robes for each us. An' no fire for cookin'; you're to plunder up that pemmeekin." He knelt down into the shelter and crawled back where the bundles were stored. "I'll put you some balls an' powder, what I'm thinkin' you'll need. You take you your sticker an' that fancy parley-voo pistol of your'n. Make sure to that. The sticker an' the pistol."

"Never did get me a taste for that pemmeekin," Josiah commented as he pulled the rawhide pouches out of a canvas bundle and tossed them one at a time near the two rolls of buffalo robes.

"You jest gotta eat it. Ain't gotta like it none," Bass replied. "Way to my figgerin', we ain't gotta be eatin' trail vittles that long anyways. As I lay my sights to it, McAfferty's only got him lil' more'n half day on us. We cut into that real quicklike soon's we get on outta here. We ain't gonna be needin' to eat trail vittles for long." He went back to digging through various parcels of personal belongings to extract those few items he threw into a trap sack already emptied for the journey.

"You wantin' Hatcher's pistols?"

"Nope. Leave 'em here."

"Looks to be it, then," Josiah remarked with finality.

"Get you that ol' wool blanket capote of mine, son. Roll it up an' tie it to them robes."

"We got us robes, don't we? An' you got you your new coat?" He sounded doubtful of the need of taking along the remains of the torn capote Bass had requested.

"Wool for short leggin's. Make us some mittens too. Figger we might stop sometime an' cut that blanket coat up. Then move on some more."

Paddock retrieved the worn blue coat and began to roll it into a small tube. "You ain't figgerin' to stop afore night falls, like you always done?"

"Be the purely waste of good time, that would. An' that's what we ain't got us—time. Way I figger it, McAfferty's movin' east or west only. Nigger goes east, he know this man named Bass don' like him them Sioux. An'"—he paused a moment to finish wiping down the barrel of Josiah's rifle with grease—"he goes west, nigger's countin' on makin' it to Blackfoot country. You see, we gotta be movin' all the time he's movin'. An' we gotta keep on movin' after he's stopped. It's a hard trail you gone an' picked yourself, Josiah. A hard, cold trail starin' you down now." He clucked his tongue once and handed the rifle to Josiah. "Here you now. Got me Scratch's medeecins?"

"Nope. Didn't think me—"

"Titus Bass ain't movin' less'n he's got him his medeecins. No tellin' but what them cuts on your arms need 'em some mendin' up 'long the way. Or my hand still." He stared at the tight, tender flesh that had knitted itself over the missing fingers and down the outside of the right hand. "You best be grabbin' my medeecin parfleche . . . an' that prayer bag of your'n."

Josiah tugged the otter-fur cap won at rendezvous over his head and scooted out of the shelter to stand. Both men bent to pick up a load of robes and bundles before skirting the lodges to head down to the area where the horses were picketed. Hannah snorted as she caught wind of the old man.

Bass dropped his load of gear beside their ponies and went over to nuzzle the old mule. "Sorry, you sweet ol' lady. Ain't goin' on this'un. You'll be stayin' here, you will." He rubbed her gently between the ears. She seemed to understand the man all too well, seemed to comprehend that she was to sit out this journey. Her eyes concentrated on his.

"Now, Hannah. I done said it real plain. You ain't goin'. Jest gotta pick me one of these here ponies to be packin' plunder for us, the boy and me." She threw her head to the side, away from his caresses. "You're jest like a woman, ain't you, ol' gal? Not gonna get your way, so you go an' play the hurt on me." He attempted to reach for her head again but the mule stepped away, moving a little distance around her picket.

"She ain't gonna stand for you leavin' her behind," Josiah said as he threw the saddle on his pony.

"Lookin' that way," Bass responded. "But I ain't yet met me a woman what I wasn' able to get to thinkin' my way." He moved slowly toward the mule. "You ain't gonna be no whore 'bout this, is you, gal? Nawww. You'll understan't, won' you?" He continued to coo while the mule moved slowly away from him around her picket pin.

"I've met up with some stubborn women in my life," Josiah said, drawing the saddle's cinch tight and flipping down the stirrup. "Some as I'd say be as stubborn as a mule. But Hannah do take the prize." He chuckled a little and moved toward Scratch.

"You jest leave me be a few minutes, son," Bass replied. "Go get you the last of that gear. Bring them rifles. I'll be ready to go when you get back. An' Josiah . . . clean yourself up, son—"

"What?"

"Your face, I mean. It all right? It ain't hurtin' much now?"

"Nawww."

"You do look the sight—"

"Said it don't hurt much," he protested, a little too strongly. "I'm fine. Just fine. I'll carry it all right. You don't worry none."

Bass reached once more for the waltzing mule and Hannah again evaded his caress. "You're both stubborn, you know, Josiah? Both you. Well, you jest go get them rifles. I'll be ready when you show up. I'll be ready."

Paddock moved off without another word and headed back to the shelter. He did not have to speak. Bass could hear him snickering as he wound his way out of sight through the cottonwoods back toward the village.

Titus Bass was ready when Josiah appeared again and stopped as soon as he saw the old man. He stared for a few moments without speaking, looking at Bass just finishing the saddling of a fresh pony, the buffalo runner. He dropped the stirrup and turned around to see the young man standing behind him. Josiah stepped forward and tossed him his rifle, then handed him the shooting pouch and powderhorn. Bass hung the strap over the pommel of his saddle and took the shirt from Paddock.

"Get your'n?" he asked, taking off the elk-hide coat so he could put on the shirt.

"Yep." He opened his capote to show that his shirt too had been sewn up the front where it had been cut.

"All right. I'm jest hopin' the sinew don' go an' rub me raw here." He pressed his fingers along the new vertical seam before he put his arms into the sleeves of the coat and laid the elk fur collar down over his shoulders.

"You ready?" Paddock inquired.

"Yep."

"Got a pony saddled up for the packin'?" Josiah asked knowingly.

"Hannah's goin'." He turned as the eyes dropped from Josiah's.

"I see me that." Josiah stifled a chuckle. "Ol' gal wouldn't be takin' no for an answer, eh?"

"Titus Bass jest figgered him we'd be needin' a pack animal anyways. An' Hannah's best here what is broke for packin'. So"—he turned to take up the lead rope strung out from the mule—"I'm takin' her." Bass put a foot in the stirrup and climbed into the Spanish saddle, his knees tucked high. "Sides. Don' have me many friends, an' you don' go pissin' them off what you got."

Paddock mounted his pony and nudged his animal forward so that he could stand beside the older man. He looked over at Bass without saying a word, although Scratch could easily read what was on Josiah's face and in his eyes.

"What's so goddamned funny, boy?" he protested.

"You know, Titus Bass," Josiah began, trying to stifle a chuckle. "You're just a ol' fake, you are."

"What you mean by that?" he snapped.

"You come off like you're the meanest thing on two legs—and four legs, for that matter. An' inside, all the time, you ain't nothin' but a lil' calf. Soft you are, inside. Got you feelin's what you don't wanna show—let others see 'em." He watched Bass turn away and stare down at the pommel of his saddle. "Ain't nothin' to be ashamed of—"

"I ain't 'shamed of nothin'."

"You're some, Titus Bass. An' this child's proud he's got him you for his pardner." He reached over to lay his hand on the older man's shoulder. "Proud I be to have you for my spirit helper. 'Sides, that's what you been to me all 'long anyways, ain't it?" He patted the shoulder once and recradled the rifle across his left arm, feeling the pinch at the drying of the raw flesh. "Let's be ridin'. McAfferty's had him 'nough time to get a lead on us. Which way we s'posed to go lookin' for him?"

Bass looked at the young man, now that the sentimental talk was over. He gazed briefly into the young eyes, then stared across the river. "We'll be tryin' west," he said, stretching himself slightly as if in preparation for the long ride ahead. "Cross the river an' we'll be knowin' better. New snow last night gonna be medeecin for us. Trackin's good sight now. Jest have to dust the new stuff off the hard an' we got his trail. Why, son, we'll even know us right where he was when the snow quit, an' I can calc'late how big a set he's got on us. I'm jest figgerin' that we lay our sights to him headin' toward Blackfoot country. Take us a few miles afore we get free of snow what the Crow tromped round in, then I'll know for the certain."

"How you gonna be so sure?" Josiah asked, nudging his pony forward as Bass put heels to the other animal and gave a slight tug on Hannah's rope.

"Asa's pony be cow-hocked—"

"An' how you know so much 'bout that pony?"

"You jest be thinkin' 'bout it now. We spent us some time trappin' with the nigger, comin' up from roonyvoo with him. Don' you think this child be knowin' what tracks his pony makes?"

"If he took him that pony," Josiah remarked.

"He did."

"Never thought me to have a look for such things." Josiah replied as they headed down the snow-covered beach onto the shallow ford.

"Never thought me I'd have to be huntin' the man—follerin' him an' them cow-hocked prints someday." Scratch knew it was a lie as soon as it came out of his mouth. Titus Bass had known he would be here, doing this, for some time now.

The animals splashed across the ford, carefully picking their way through the cold water that swirled against their bellies and over the men's feet. Hannah snorted once, and Bass tugged on her rope to show that if she was not to be left behind, then she was to be quiet about the hardships. He hoped the young man was prepared for the hard times ahead too. If he was to lie anymore, he would have to make sure it was all for the boy's benefit. Like that lie about someday having to follow the cracked hoof. That was for the boy, he told himself. Don't hurt nothing, a little lie like that.

By the time they had traveled less than four miles on the north side of the river, Bass brought Josiah to a halt and handed the young trapper Hannah's rope. He slid from the saddle and knelt beside the pony. Past the new snow into the hard crust his fingers probed, tracing the outline of the hoof print. Stepping forward a few paces with the reins still in his hand, he knelt again and traced another print, feeling for the small scar within the print that had stamped the soft, new snow.

He raised his head and looked to the west, glancing briefly at the position of the sun as it began its fall from mid-sky. Scratch stared into the west along the river for a few minutes more, lost in his thoughts. He finally said, "McAfferty's heading west," nodding forward. "Gonna try to make it up to them Blackfoots. Might be planning on staying with the river till she ducks south into the land of the Spirit Smokes. Strike out from there over to the Three Forks. Trail ain't hard to foller now, Josiah." He rose slowly and came back to stand beside the pony.

"He ain't got him that much a lead on us. It be jest a chase now," Bass said, looking up at Paddock. "Jest a chase. Less'n it up an' snows." Bass glanced at the western sky. "That's when this here nigger's work is cut for him. It snows—ain't jest a chase no more. Then it come to be a hunt. Then it come on to be the real beaver, son."

Paddock turned from Scratch to gaze at the sky. He gave the pony heels and they moved off at a walk, the tracks he and Bass were following between their animals. They were quiet for a while. Scratch finally broke the silence.

"You really figgerin' you got me all sized up, huh?" Josiah looked at him. "What you mean?"

"'Bout me jest coverin' somethin' up inside—what you was sayin' when we left camp."

"For bein' so damned smart 'bout some things, you sure can be dumb 'bout others!" Paddock laughed then, thinking of what he had just said. "You hear that? Now

623

I'm gettin' to call you the dumb one! You get that, ol' man? I got away with callin' you the dumb one!"

"Never said me I knowed ever'thin'," Bass protested faintly. "Jest 'member you that when it's time you go thinkin' you got a nigger figgered out—that be when he up an' s'prises you. Josiah, you jest 'member that, you young jackass."

He watched Paddock snort at him and not reply. But the words stuck with Bass. Words he was one to know were all too true. Just when a man thought he had someone figured out, all the pieces seeming to fit, that's when the bottom broke from the barrel and it all poured out. That's when you lost what you had just paid for.

Scratch laid the buffalo robe down, fur up, where he planned to sleep briefly before he would again force the march. Next he laid the wolf hide, then the bear robe over the others, also hair-side up. Onto them he settled his body, bringing all three hides across him as he rolled up in their warmth. Settled at last, the older man let out a long sigh and pulled his head partially into the warmth of the cocoon he had made for himself.

Josiah stepped over from the animals burdened under the heavy robes and let them drop to the ground beside the buffalo cocoon. "Why you ain't wantin' even a lil' fire?"

"Don' need us no fire." The words were somewhat muffled inside the robes. "Jest light to bring niggers in on us—"

"McAfferty?"

"Nope. We ain't that close behin't him yet. Might'n be some brownskins out havin' look-see where the Crow got 'em a winter camp. 'Sides"—he shifted his position a little so that he faced where Josiah was unfurling his bedding—

"Fire jest takes a man time to start, gettin' the wood an' strikin' a light—all that. You use time now an' get some sleep."

"If I can," he replied, slipping down on the snow beside the old trapper. "Man can't get him much sleep when he's froze up."

"Won' be here that long, son. You jest shut your eyes an' it'll be no time 'tall till I'm pushin' you upriver."

Paddock settled in, snuggling the otter cap down further on his head. He moved his hips about in a small circle, trying to make a depression in the new snow for his comfort. It was no use. He wiped his nose on the blanket capote sleeve. "We be huntin' any other fellas you think of—best to make it come summer, maybe early fall." He waited for an answer from the old man. "Scratch? You hear me? Last hunt we make in the cold, this'un."

The words had such an air of finality that Bass had to snort a chuckle. "Just 'nother time of the year a man's gotta live out here. Jest make hisse'f a home wherever he is, best way he knows how. Injuns do it, Josiah. Do them fine. These'r doin's all rustled up by the Cold Maker, what the Crow call him. Know him too as the Winter Man. Talk of him bein' white as the snow you're sleepin' on—comes ridin' outta the north lands in the smack-dab of a real winter white-out. Shakes his ol' buffler robe an' the sky fills with snow. A real blazin'-blue norther. Ridin' over the mountains on his white pony, snortin' the snow—"

"That how he get it to blow then?"

"Nawww, that's the wind, son." Bass paused as he moved in the robes a bit, finding a cold place for his cheek. "An' that be a whole differ'nt thing from the Winter Man. You see, Injuns claim to it that they seen the Winter Man on his pony, seen him like I see you. But the wind—that's some differ'nt now. You cain't see it. Yep. That a man can only feel in his bones. Crow back there look at it like'n the wind is Old Man Coyote's messenger, bringin' his words to his people. Sometimes usin' the wind to take people to him, too."

No reply came from the young trapper for a few minutes. He heard Josiah roll over in his robes and knew that he was still awake. "Jest think 'bout them things till you get asleep," Bass said. Still no reply. It perplexed Scratch not to be answered. "Josiah? What you thinkin' 'bout?"

"McAfferty."

"What about the nigger?"

"He gonna be hungry, maybe thirsty, while we on his trail? Just thinkin' an' wond'rin' 'bout things like that."

"You don' go troublin' your mind with things like that now, son. Ain't no use to it. 'Cause the man we chasin' ain't gonna be worryin' 'bout no food an' water. None of that. He'll not have to be thinkin' 'bout bringin'

625

down game, neither. No sir. All his ol' bones'll need is water. An' Asa won' have him no trouble with that; won' be gettin' thirsty a bit, not with snow layin' ever'where you care to look. Man eats him snow to satisfy a thirst-cravin'. Nawww, Josiah, no need to be thinkin' Asa's gonna go without him a thing in this hunt. He ain't."

Paddock was silent. And chilled. Was Asa cold too? Josiah was also hungry. He had not taken much of the pemmican that Scratch had offered back on the trail as they rode into the dark hours. And the cold was making the pain across his face and shoulders ache the more intensely. Was Asa as miserable as he was? Would he be unable to sleep, like me? Josiah wondered. Maybe he wants to talk, to make the cold hours of darkness more bearable in some small way.

"We catch up to McAfferty," Josiah began, "we gonna scalp him. Mean, am I really to go an' scalp McAfferty?"

"What you think this whole thing's 'bout, Josiah?" The words had an edge to them as he pulled the hide back from his old face a bit to address the younger man. "You thinkin' we jest gonna go off ridin' round these hills till the nigger gives hisse'f up to us? You think we ain't gonna have to kill him? Huh? You think that man out there ain't gonna try an' kill you afore we get the chance't to gut him? Awww, Josiah. Them Crow back there'll want that white hair from you, to show 'em you done it proper. An' you tol't ol' Rotten Belly yourself you was gonna be bringin' him back the nigger's ha'r. That's your word you give Arapooesh—your word on it. He coulda gone an' sent him out twenty braves to get the man, but this here's medeecin. Big medeecin. Pickin' one white man to go after 'nother white man what kil't one of the tribe. You gotta be bringin' that skelp back for Rotten Belly. That be all he wants from you now—that skelp. When you go an' lay it in his ol' hands, then he knows someways the soul of his woman'll rest a lot easier in the Other-Side-Land. You know? 'Cause you brung him a skelp from the man as kil't her, an' that'll make the spirits happy. Make 'em feel better 'bout lettin' that woman come over to the Other-Side-Land. No sir, This ain't no winter funnin'. You best make your mark to that now, Josiah. This here's medeecin of the prime grade. You don' come through with it an' the whole Crow nation be down on our asses. This be the strongest of Injun doin's. Medeecin."

It was quiet for a few moments while Paddock seemed to be contemplating the old man's words, measuring them, hefting them about in his own mind, trying out their bulk and surprised at the sudden weight of this thing. Had he really known what he had agreed to back there? He wondered now. Had he really known what was required of him by Arapooesh? It was a duel, he decided. Just like a duel. Between him and LeClerc. Nothing more. At least that's what he had thought until now. But the last one was a duel he had had to run away from when it was over. And, now, this was a duel he had to go through with so that he did not have to run. There was a difference. There was the importance. That was the medicine.

"Scratch?"

"Yep?"

"If this here thing's all the big medicine it s'posed to be," Josiah asked, "then do I get to look into that medicine bundle the chief give me?"

"Nope." He answered stiffly. "Man makes his own bundle, he knows what he's put in it. These doin's—you got your bundle from a chief. That be like it's come from the whole tribe. An' you hurt your medeecin you go lookin' in the bundle. You read my sign, Josiah? You don' go hurtin' your medeecin by tearin' into that bundle."

"Bad to do—"

"Dang'rous. Jest playin' with them spirits, is all. You want 'em on your side now. Jest you don' go playin' with 'em."

"Just wanted to know."

"Now you know." He rolled away from the young trapper. "Lemme get some sleep now. You'll be wishin' you had you yours afore too long."

"Night, Scratch." There was no answer from Bass.

Paddock lay in his furry roll listening to the sounds of the night and to the muffled snoring of the old man. His toes ached a little and he was without any hope of warming them by a fire. Somewhere deep within he ached for her too. And hope was dimming that he would ever warm himself with her intimate gift. Only the coals of memories remained to him.

Josiah sat up and tucked the end of the robe beneath his feet in hopes of warming them. He lay back and pulled the hide over his head again. He recalled Scratch's admonition some time back when he had complained about his cold feet to the old trapper: "They be cold till spring green-up, son. You'll jest have to be a nigger what's gonna be gettin' use to that."

Much he would have to be getting used to. Cold feet. No fire. Food that choked him and caught against the gag in his throat. Eating snow for water. Riding into the night until the moon reached the top of its climb in the sky. And taking another scalp. The hair of a man he had known. A lot to be getting accustomed to all at once. A lot for him to stomach in one bite.

He closed his eyes and felt the draining on his muscles. He had watched a man he knew die in the snow. And another in the swamp beyond the three peaks. Now he had to kill a man he knew. A lot for him to stomach.

Paddock heard the rustling sounds beside him. The soft noise penetrated his half sleep. He would listen a minute or two before looking to be sure. Gently he pulled the buffalo robes away from his eyes. Over the edge of the robes he could see only darkness stretching above him and the bright pins of light that looked like stars, reminding him of the sparks of brightness he had seen before blacking out when his nose was broken. It was the same. The brilliant fragments of light thrown up against the dark background—but these lights were not moving, spraying from his eyes as the others had.

Sky, he told himself and rolled his head to the side so that he could see the inkiness of the trees splashed against the light blue of the snow in the moonlight. Still night, he thought. And colder. Where was the moon? He turned his head to search for it.

"Roll out," Scratch whispered to him, hearing the young man moving within the furry cocoon.

"Ain't even playin' at dawn yet," he protested, a little angered at having to move from the robes now that he enjoyed their security from the night breeze brushing his face.

"We gonna be miles from here when it starts playin' with bein' light." Bass knelt to gather the buffalo-wrapped bundle into his arms and hefted it to his shoulder. "You c'mon now." He moved toward the animals.

He listened to the man move across the snow, the crunch hard yet quiet as the old man stepped through the white dust. Cold fingers tugged the hat down on his head and he unwrapped himself. The cold would not bite at him right away. His body was still warm. For a while. Telling himself he had better keep moving, Josiah hastened to roll the robes and knot them into a bundle, which he took to Scratch.

"I'm seein' you didn' take your rifle into your robes," Bass nodded to the tree where stood Josiah's rifle.

"Had me the pistol," he answered, not really acknowledging the criticism.

"You keep both them with you from here on out. You go into the trees take you a piss, shit—if you got anythin' in your stomach—you keep 'em both with you. We'll be eatin' a goodly piece into McAfferty's lead this day. From here on out."

Josiah helped Scratch lift the robes to Hannah's side where the older man began to lash the bundle to the crude pack frame cinched to her back. "You're used to this, ain't you?" Josiah asked.

"What's that?" He kept busy with the knotting.

"Ridin' till you're ready to drop. Sleepin' just a few hours, if that. Gettin' up afore it's light to ride some more. Used to that, ain't you?"

"Much as a man can get used to such a thing, I s'pose," Scratch answered. "Have had me times when I jest up an' made myself keep movin' through the whole night—no sleep 'tall, Josiah. Don' seem that long ago now. Bad deal on a deck, bad show of cards for this nigger, why I might be ridin' for two, maybe three, days or more. Sit on a pony that long, one day jest runs right into 'nother after 'while. Maybe I'm havin' to run after some 'Paches. Or gettin' chased myself by some 'Siniboines or Rees. You might'n be sayin' a feller can get used to such a thing. But he jest keeps thinkin' 'bout one thing after 'while: gettin' him some sleep. That one thing keeps him goin', it does. 'Cause when he can finally lay in the robes for a few hours, he's ready for the ridin' all over again. Seal-fat an' sleek again, a nigger feels then. Losin' sleep ain't no special thing." He yanked on the short end of the rope. "There," he patted Hannah's shoulders. "We'll be strippin' bark for the animules this evenin'. Give 'em somethin' to keep goin' on too."

Bass slid his hand along the mule's lead rope and

loosened the knot over the low branch. He trailed it behind him as he stepped to the pony and started to put a foot in the big wooden stirrup.

"Scratch," the young man said as he settled down on his saddle. "Been meanin' to ask you somethin' ever since we started out yesterday."

"An' what that be?" Bass did not push himself from the ground.

"McAfferty got him a good eye?"

"What you mean, son?"

"Is the man a good shot?" He sounded a wee impatient with the older man's nonunderstanding. "Is McAfferty a good shot?"

"Far as I 'member." Scratch finally pushed himself slowly up onto the cold saddle in the dim moonlight. "A damned good shot." Stuffing the tail of the elk-hide coat beneath his buttocks, he pulled on the reins to guide the pony down the side of the slope. "To think 'bout it now, he was always better'n me."

19

The cold did not help the ache that came from being long in the saddle, but Josiah felt he was getting accustomed to it. Maybe he was only numb from the cold by now, asleep from the buttocks down. Scratch had kept them moving throughout the day, stopping only occasionally for a few minutes to scoop up some snow to eat. Around noon they had found some dry grass, blown clear of its snow, and there had halted to let the animals feed and to cut the blue woolen capote into pieces. Long rectangles of the old coat were wrapped around their legs from knees to ankles and bound with cut fringe. Then Bass had crudely cut tracings of their hands from the blanket and sewn them with sinew to make something similar to mittens from the wool blanket.

This brief pause in the chase would not matter as long as the weather held up. As long as they could follow McAfferty's tracks as easily as trailing a buffalo herd returning home. Scratch had kept his eye on the sky to the west throughout the day, especially when he found that Asa had crossed to the south bank of the Yellowstone to follow a small river out of the flats and into the hills toward the upreared peaks on the southern horizon.

He had dropped from the pony and felt the hoof prints to be sure before starting south along that small river's course. Bass had wondered then what Asa was thinking. McAfferty was leaving the flats along the river, leaving the rolling hills where he had easy going, and was heading into the river valley where travel would be more difficult, going would be slower.

Scratch had stared for a few minutes to the south where the river ran, looking toward the distant mountains, those peaks that threw up a northern border to Johnny Colter's private hell, the place where the Indians said the Thunder Spirits roared and smoked.

Until that moment Titus Bass had thought he had Asa figured out. Until that moment when the trail turned south from the Yellowstone, Scratch had figured McAfferty to be hightailing it west to the Three Forks and Blackfoot country. He tried the rest of the afternoon to piece it together in his mind, but it kept coming up like a torn patchwork quilt.

They had found where McAfferty had spent the night, beside a fire. That was not like a man trying to stay ahead of his pursuers. Not at all like a man who wanted to evade those who hunted him. And the ashes of the fire were not that cold when Scratch had checked them. McAfferty had spent an easy night, it appeared, not at all like a man looking over his shoulder, worried about those following him. It did not set right—and now the man turning south, away from the Yellowstone, away from his trail toward the Blackfoot country. Strange for a man running from the death he had to know was following.

Scratch had led them up the ridge that formed the sharp western wall of the river valley. He wanted to ride the rimrock rather than be caught in the valley by eyes watching from above. Better to ride the ridge. Always better to ride the ridge.

It would not be long until darkness overtook them, he decided, and they would have to descend to the valley floor. There they would again cross McAfferty's trail so that it could be followed slowly, carefully, in the dark hours to come. Besides, with the sun having gone down and the light beginning to disappear from the sky, it was all the colder here on the ridge, where the wind could batter a man. Before long he would have to start looking for a place where they could drop into the valley.

McAfferty and Macbeth. Both of them. One of the two had killed and lost control from there on out, he thought now. The other had killed and finally gotten control of things. Yes, he decided, they were the same in many ways. But now more and more differences separated the two men who shared a common heritage.

He had to give Asa credit. No matter what he thought now, he had never known McAfferty to be crazy. He had always kept his head about him, never doing anything stupid. Never had been one to go off half cocked. Frightening it was at times, the certitude of this hunted man. Especially when Bass put his own uncertainty up alongside McAfferty's sureness now. He glanced back at Josiah, as if he thought the younger man could hear his thoughts, then looked into the valley again.

It made him uneasy to consider that Asa was the one really in control of this thing. Asa under control and exercising his will. He was choosing where he would be followed and how by those who hunted him. And that made Bass uneasy. Very uneasy.

Josiah had looked up about the same time Scratch had turned to glance in his direction, then turned away to gaze westward at the disappearing border of light on the mountains a little north of west from them. He felt the pony under him lose a step on the icy snow and catch itself before stumbling. But the following steps were unsure and unsteady.

Paddock felt the bottom peel suddenly out from under him as the pony slid away, sending its rider sailing with it. He thought he cried out as it happened, but perhaps it was only the sound pushed from his lungs as he hit the rock and tumbled down the steep slope. He rolled and rolled, not knowing how or when he would stop. It was motion for itself, and no escape from it.

Scratch jerked around at the short cry and watched as Josiah pitched over the edge of the rimrock behind the pony. Paddock's rifle skittered to the edge and stopped, all that was left of the young trapper. He reined his pony to a halt and pushed himself from the saddle. Bass scrambled across the ice that threatened his footing back to the edge of the cliff.

In the dim light below him Bass saw the two forms. Man and animal. One was moving. Scratch decided it was the pony trying to stand. Beyond it was the man, thrown against a snowbank that had broken his fall. That form was without movement.

Titus pushed the rifle back from the edge and sat down to ease himself over the rocks. He half slid, half stumbled his way to the pony, which attempted to stand on a broad shelf where its fall had ended. From the way it strained to rise, Bass knew at least one of its legs was broken. He pushed on down, however, sliding to a stop at the deep snowbank where Josiah, dazed, was shaking his head slowly.

"Easy now. Jest real easy, son." Bass came up to his side. "Don' be movin' right yet, now. Look you over for broke bones afore you go usin' 'em." He laid his rifle in the snow beside Paddock, then felt over the young man's arms and legs. "You move ever'thin'?"

Josiah clenched both hands a few times and wiggled his toes, "Yeah."

"Hurt anywhere?"

"Just my face." Josiah moved a hand up to his nose, but Scratch held it from touching the distorted flesh.

"Don' go doin' that," he said, letting go of Paddock's hand. "Looks to be you might'n busted it real good this time. She were crooked afore, an' she's really bent over to the west now. Jest leave 'er be—be the best. Here, lemme help you up." He put an arm behind Paddock to help him rise. Together they made the slow, steady climb back up to the shelf where the pony neighed its pain and frustration.

Scratch took his arm from Paddock and knelt beside the animal, feeling along its right foreleg that continued to collapse beneath the pony when it attempted to rise. Broken, he thought. Then he heard the wheeze of the animal's breathing.

"Broke leg, son." He turned to Josiah. "Got it some busted ribs, too. Busted in the fall. Bad ribs. Crushed its lights purty good in takin' the spill over them rocks," Bass said, looking up at the edge of the rimrock. "She ain't no earthly good to you now. Cain't be movin', lamed up the way she is."

"Have to put 'er outta her pain, then," Paddock said.

He reached into the loose flaps of the capote and brought his pistol out. He looked down at the pan to check the load and brought the hammer back while inching toward the animal.

With the sound of the pistol lock, Bass turned to see Josiah readying to shoot the animal. He put out his hand and knocked the pistol arm aside. "Nawww," he whispered sharply. "Cain't go shootin' out here. That blast'll bounce round down in the valley. We gettin' close in on McAfferty now an' we don' want that nigger knowin' where we is. You cain't be shootin' that pistol."

"How you gonna—"

"Cut its goddamned throat," Bass snapped. "You go on up the top an' pull my robes offa Hannah. Tie 'em up behin't my saddle. Pull one of your'n off an' lay it over the pack saddle on her back. I'll be up in jest a shake, now. Go on." He watched Josiah turn and make his snail's crawl to the top of the ridge, rocks breaking loose and falling away below him as he made his steady climb through the snow. When the young trapper finally clambered over the edge and disappeared from sight, Bass turned back to the pony.

Setting his rifle in the snow above the horse, he untied the bottom thong of his coat and reached inside to pull out a knife from the back of his belt. Quickly he stepped over the animal's neck and grabbed its bottom jaw in his left hand. The pony attempted to break free of his hold and the trapper had to struggle a bit before leaning forward against the back of the animal's head to lock it into the curve of his shoulder. The knife slashed quickly, deeply, its work over in one stroke. Scratch felt the warming blood hasten across his bare wrist. He remembered a time past when he had felt the warm fluid wash over the cold flesh of that right hand.

The pony snorted a few times. Bass could hear the wheezing of its severed windpipe. He stood back to watch the darkness spread over the snow beneath the animal's head. As the pony's last breath was taken, Bass bent forward and wiped the bare wrist clean of most of the blood across the mane, then patted the animal on the head one last time. "You done Josiah good. Brung him this far." He looked south, up the valley, in the half light. "Hannah have to get the boy the rest of the way."

Bass turned and retrieved his rifle, then cleaned his

knife in the snow before plunging it back into the sheath. He felt for the handle in the other sheath at his belt as he started his climb, thinking it was always good to have at least two stickers with him when he went wading into a fight. Always good for the backup. He turned and stopped, then slid back to the animal, a little angered with himself. With some difficulty he loosened the cinch of the saddle but could not get the wide strap entirely free. He tried to move the animal, but the dead weight of the carcass, plus his inability to get a firm footing in the new snow, proved it was senseless. They would just have to do without.

Paddock turned as Titus crawled over the rim and got to his feet. "You wanna carry this trap sack with your pemmeekin in it?"

Scratch took it from him and slung the sack from the pommel of his saddle. "Couldn' get your saddle out from under the pony," he said, winded from the climb. "You wanna take mine to use on Hannah?" He slapped the saddle with his left hand.

"Nawwww," Josiah answered. "Just use this robe over the pack saddle. Lead rope for reins. Be fine." He wiped the mucous and a small amount of blood that still trickled uncontrollably from his nostrils onto his capote sleeve. "Let's just get down off this here ridge afore one of us gets killed." He swung himself onto Hannah's broad back in front of the roll of buffalo robes.

"We find us a place to do jest that," Scratch said, and climbed into the saddle.

By the time they reached the edge of the small river hugging the eastern border of the narrowing valley, the pale light of the sun's falling had disappeared, to be replaced by the moonlight reflecting off the snow. In a stand of young cottonwoods Bass finally brought his pony to a halt and slid to the ground. Josiah pushed clumsily from Hannah's back, then put the robe back in place over her spine. They tied the two weary animals to a willow and went in search of cottonwood to peel.

Armloads of it were brought back to where the animals were tethered. Both men set to peeling the juicy bark from the short firewood-size pieces they had cut. It was a slow, cold process, as the men had to sit in the snow at their labors. A piece of the wood was placed between their knees and the knife pulled toward them in a shaving motion. As handfuls of the vegetation appeared between the men, one of the trappers would stand to work the cold kinks out of his bones by taking the bark over to the pony and mule.

"Here," Bass remarked as he dropped a load of the shavings. "Want you should watch this, Josiah." He bent over and picked up one of the small limbs, then laid it in front of Hannah.

The mule seemingly knew what to do for Scratch, which was to help herself. She put one front hoof on the middle of the limb and bent her head down to work her teeth into the bark. In pulling her head back slightly, the mule was able to peel short lengths of bark from the limb.

"I'll be damned," Josiah exclaimed quietly, watching the mule serve herself.

"She be a smart ol' lady," Bass replied as he came back to sit with Paddock again. "Leastways, she knows to be gettin' her own vittles while the gettin's good, I s'pose." He put his knife back to work, "L'arnt her that herse'f some time back. All I gotta do is set some cottonwood chunks afore the ol' gal, she does the rest. Less'n she gets to peelin' 'em slower'n her belly wants it; then she lets me know I've gotta peel some too." He turned to glance at the old mule, seeing her gnaw at the limb as a dog would take after a bone, pulling the bark from it.

"Scratch, you don't mind me askin' you 'bout the dead, do you?"

He cleared his throat thoughtfully before answering. "What kinda things you wanna know from me?"

"Just," he began, then thought a moment, "just 'bout what they do with them bodies back there. Them women— McAfferty's squaw an' Rotten Belly's woman. What they was fixin' to do when we left camp. 'Bout buryin' an' all. That's what I'm askin'."

"Well, now," Bass began, somewhat relieved that the question was different from what he had feared, "they do 'em differ'nt for men an' the womens. Man dies in a lodge like them squars did, that lodge wouldn' be lived in' again, 'tall. No sir. Man's squar give 'way ever'thin of his they don' go an' bury with him, an' then the other squars cut the lodge to pieces."

"What she do? The man's squaw then?"

"She last till winter, maybe. An' she dies. Got no one to feed 'er. No one to take 'er in. She's like you—ain't got her no relations, no kin when her man dies."

"So she gives ever'thin' up?"

"What ain't buried with him."

"An' what 'bout a squaw dyin'? How's that differ'nt?"

"They won' cut a lodge up an' use it to wrap the body if'n it's a squar what died. Arapooesh still be one to live in that lodge." He stopped his knife a moment. "All the mem'ries live with him in it, too." He went back to peeling the bark from the limbs. "Where the squars died, they take 'em outta the lodge right there. Lift up the lodge cover an' bring 'em out that way when they got the bodies all the ready for buryin'."

"Why they go to all that trouble—not just takin' the squaws out the door?"

"Bad way for pleasin' the spirits, it'd be. Some other'll likely die in the lodge then, if'n they did that: takin' the bodies out the door. No sir. Cain't do that. Jest wrap the body up in her best skins—ones what are saved for special times—paint 'er up an' put 'er in the yeller part of the ol' lodge cover, what they call 'em the *acde-cire*. Wrap it round an' round with buffler sinew. Then they take it out the side of the lodge."

"Crow put 'em in the ground, dig a hole?" asked Josiah.

"When they can, maybe," Bass answered. "Man they might'n be puttin' up 'bove the ground even if it weren't froze up like it be in the winter. Round this time of y'ar, they'll be puttin' them squars in a tree—keep the wolves from the bodies, you see. Right proper tree buryin', it is."

" 'Cause Arapooesh is a chief, eh?"

" 'Cause it shows respect for the one what's died. Shows respect. Not jest 'cause it be his woman. Done to show respect to the one what's dead. Help 'em on the way to the Other-Side-Land. Last thing the livin' can do for the dead, that is. A proper tree buryin'."

Josiah set his knife aside and scooped up the peeled cottonwood, taking it over to lay before the two animals. He returned and sat again by the older trapper, "This Rotten Belly, he 'bout the biggest chief them Crow ever had 'em?"

Scratch stopped his knife a minute and contemplated. "Not as I can rightly say. He's some, now, he is. But bein' the biggest they ever had 'em? Hmmm," he said thoughtfully. "Seems where I heerd tell of a chief of them Crows some time back, way back, as I rec'llect now. Yep, seems it was some time afore we'd been here in the mountains, it'd been, too. Afore white men. He was said to be some big medeecin, that'un was. Heerd it tol't that one time they was havin' 'em a good scuffle with the Snakes down in the valley of the Windy River. An' them Crows gettin' the worst of it too. They tell of this chief goin' an' tellin' the sun an' moon to be standin' still for two days an' nights, whil'st they rubbed them Snakes out—what with the Snakes so skairt with the sky standin' still like that. Whipped them Injuns' asses, them Crow, it's tol't—all on 'count of that chief stoppin' the sun an' moon from movin' in the sky."

"Sounds like you're feedin' me roonyvoo horseshit again. Them big tales fit only for a greenhorn. An' I ain't no greenhorn no more," he protested.

"Nawww, now wait jest a pinch there. This be no baldface, son. It's what them Crow tell 'bout the tribe. Story 'bout the people. There were such a chief, certain. Had me some Crow braves even show me a place where this same chief changed him a whole prairie of sagebrushes into goats—anteelope—one time. The tribe was near onto starvin' an' didn' have 'em no luck bringin' in game. Down south on the Windy River he done that: makin' meat for the whole camp outta sagebrushes." Bass nodded in agreement with himself.

"Shit," Josiah commented.

"An' up on the west bank of the Big Horn," Scratch kept right on, "them Crow tell 'bout a spring what they say was bitter an' bad tastin'—bad for your belly, like the water you likes to drink so much, Josiah. They tell it that this chief gone an' waved his ol' medeecin staff over that spring an' turned it to sweet-tastin' water. Flowin' right there outta the side of the hill, it were."

"You're full a shit believin' them tales, Titus Bass. Even more full a shit thinkin' I'm gonna believe 'em, too." He shook his head from side to side. "How come you like them Crow so goddamned much. Knew so much 'bout 'em, an' you ain't never took you a wife, a Crow squaw?"

"Never had me to," he answered simply. "Man takes him a squar to pack round with him—Crow squar, that is—he ain't get much to say 'bout most ever'thin' then. She runs the lodge, she runs him jest 'bout, them Crow.

Give a squar so much say over a man—why, you might'n jest as well give them womens the right to take a pee standin' up! Like we does!"

He and Josiah laughed softly for a few moments before Scratch continued. "Ain't got me no use for womens now, 'ceptin' they make a man a good robe-warmer. Damned sight better'n them bangtailed whores back to St. Louie what want your money an' a good time to boot! Squars good for the lovin' in the robes, them Crow womens is. My, my." He smacked his lips as if pondering past pleasures.

A bangtailed whore. Most likely that's what she was. He dimly recalled the night of release and comfort in that small room. Her whiskey-sweet breath and musky body scent. A trickle of sweat between those large, soft breasts. She hadn't said much to him, and he recalled missing that now. Just a few words, that's all. Just to let him know she had known what he needed most then. Maybe just a whore. But was the Flathead woman any different? Hadn't she had many men before? He wasn't sure now. And he did not like the discomfort the thought caused him.

"Asa's squaw was a fine-lookin' woman, she were," Paddock commented quietly. "Sad thing, her dyin' in givin' birth to McAfferty's baby."

"She were punkins, that'un were. Certain sure a loss now," Bass agreed.

"Talkin' of McAfferty, you did look over his plunder for what he left? See what you was lookin' for?"

"What wasn' left behin't were what I was lookin' for, Josiah," he answered. "Jest to see what the man took 'long with him."

"An' you see?"

"Travelin lean, Josiah. Real lean. Like a nigger what ain't gonna be on the trail long—to think of it. 'Bout as lean as a coon wishes to get, headin' off in the winter hills like he is." Bass looked out past the trees toward the river. "He ain't fixin' to be by hisse'f for long out here. That" —he paused a moment—"that, or he got hisse'f somethin' else in mind." For a few seconds Scratch continued to stare in the direction of the icy river, then looked at the pile of cottonwood peelings they had between them. He rose slowly and put his knife into its sheath.

"You done?" Paddock asked.

"Got 'em 'nough to eat." He knelt to pick up some of

639

the bark. "Might's well get us lil' sleep right here since't we stopped. Let them animules eat 'while. Sleep some, then be pushin' on."

He dropped the peelings between the two animals along with two more limbs for Hannah to work over on her own. Bass loosened the knots tying his robes behind the pony's saddle and let the hides fall to the ground.

"When you're ready to get into the robes, tie up the pony's rein to your waist belt."

"He ain't gonna run off from us tied up to that bush," Josiah replied.

"True, that might be. Jest that havin' the pony tied to you hisse'f, anythin' what makes a fuss with him gonna wake you up first whack." He looked out beyond the growth of cottonwoods across the narrow valley. "Any critter—any nigger—comin' in, animal smell him first off an' get squampshus 'bout it. He'll wake you right up, smart." Looking back at Josiah, he nodded. "You jest do it, son. Won' keep you from sleepin' much, it won'. Ain't too much sleepin', leastways, afore we push on upriver. You been singin' your medeecin, ain't you, son? If not out loud for me, in your head?"

"Ever' day—lotta times. Thinkin' I got it down good, now," he answered.

Bass had thrown his robes down and crawled inside them, looping Hannah's long lead rope to his belt while Josiah finished peeling the last of the limbs before him. Paddock carried the last of the bark to the pony and dropped his robes to the ground. A few feet away the old man, moving into slumber quickly, snored easily in his sleep, weary from the second long day on the trail.

Paddock did not feel especially sleepy himself and turned back to the pony, wondering if he should take the saddle from its back for the older man. His own body was sore and stiff from his recent slide down the icy ledge. He stepped to the pony, brushed against the medicine bundle, and stopped.

Josiah stared at it for a moment, then turned to look at the hide-covered form asleep on the ground a few yards away. He watched Bass for several minutes, then quietly slipped the bundle's rawhide loop from the pommel of the saddle, taking it over the buffalo-hide trap sack. Stepping away so that the two animals hid him from the older man, Paddock knelt on the snow in a spot where the moonlight sneaked through the cottonwood branches. He took the knife from its sheath and carefully cut the thick sinew that bound the bundle together at the back of the coyote's head.

Into his mind leaped the song given to him by Arapooesh and he jerked nervously to stare at Bass. The old man was still sleeping, still snoring. His head was playing tricks on him, Josiah decided. He would just go ahead and let the song hum through his mind.

When I come from behind,
I will carry two songs with me.

The Crow words were slowly becoming familiar to him and he was growing more comfortable with them. During the past two days he had stammered and stumbled over a few of the phrases in the foreign tongue, but his mind seemed to sing them to him perfectly tonight. His mind sang them perfectly.

I will have my medicine here upon my chest.
You I am hunting—you are poor now.
Look to me!

Slipping his hand into the back of the coyote's head, Paddock glanced up at the moon as if to give thanks for the pale light. There would be enough to inspect the bundle's contents, enough rays of the moon to show him what the coyote head held in mystery.

Beyong the hills I have stayed,
From there I have come here now.

He remembered the chief's voice climbing high on that last part, the wail of the foreign words reaching into the peaks with its call. He thought too of his own voice cracking when he tried to master those high, thin-air notes for Bass, and laughed a little at himself. Takes a high-flying bird to sing up that high, he thought.

Long time will I be the eagle.
Long time have I been coming here.
I shall ride after the wolf in the mountains.

As his hand disappeared into the back of the coyote's head, Josiah mused that he had been a long time in coming to this place, a long time in getting to this time. Many miles and moons. Now, in this valley, beside an unfamiliar river, he was Josiah pursuing a man he had met as a friend only a few months before. Josiah recalled his meeting up with Titus Bass, the rendezvous, the scrap with the Indians back beyond the three peaks, the chance to run buffalo. He remembered his chance to run from the Bannocks. He'd lifted some hair then. Black hair. Not white. McAfferty's would be white. Pure white.

Paddock's fingers touched something of coarse cloth and pulled it from the back of the bundle. It was something long as it stretched from the coyote's head. When he had it all in both hands, Josiah turned the wide piece of cloth over and over, inspecting it. Then he realized what was familiar about it. Resting the piece of cloth against his coat, Josiah knew it was the sash to his blanket capote, the one he had worn since Charles Keemle had given it to him in St. Louis. The day he had begun to move toward this place, toward this time.

When had he first missed the sash? Where had he dropped it? Back in the Crow village? No. He could remember tearing fringe from Scratch's leggings and attaching them to the capote, and that was before they had run onto the Crow warriors. Must have been before. But when?

Josiah flipped the sash around his waist, ran it through the two small leather loops on either side of the coat, and tied it off in a knot at the front. Smoothing it out with his bare fingers, he thought it was good to have it back, after all this time, however it had come to him across the miles and moons since he had lost it.

He remembered. It had been the day Bass killed the medicine bear. Yep. That day, near as he could recall after all this time. Last time he remembered having it, out with the traps in the cold and the freezing wet. Josiah shuddered involuntarily to recall it and put his hand back into the bundle.

What he touched next had feathers and he brought it out. It was a small stuffed swallow, a mountain swallow. Looking at it only briefly, Paddock set it on his lap and put his hand in for something else. He felt something hard and pulled it out. Just a piece of bone. But in looking more closely at the object some eight inches long, he found it was not merely a bone. Holes had been painstakingly drilled at each end; the middle was wrapped in porcupine quills. He ran his fingers back and forth over their rough pattern before setting it in his lap with the stuffed swallow.

Something sharp nicked his fingers when next he plunged into the bundle. He pulled the object out—a large bird's foot, with a short length of the shriveled leg still attached. Josiah pressed a finger pad against each of the long claws, testing their sharpness, then set it in his lap. Another search uncovered the final treasure of the bundle. It felt soft to his touch as he brought it into the light, and emitted a strange odor. Wrinkling his nose, he took the small buckskin pouch to his nostrils in spite of the rancid odor emanating from it. Like something dead, he thought, and put it back into the bundle without further examination. Each object in his lap followed until the task was completed.

Not such a mystery now, Paddock decided. Except for knowing what each object meant, and why those particular things had been included in this bundle, especially that small, smelly pouch. He wrinkled his nose at the thought of it. Like rotting meat it had seemed. Crow were strange people, believing in all that. Scratch too. Telling him not to open the bundle up and have him a look inside. Nothing there to hurt a man, make him scared to look inside it.

Paddock rose slowly, tugging on the pieces of cut sinew. He decided he could tie them back together. Eleven knots and it was as good as new. Almost. He put his mitten back on and moved to the pony, then slipped the rawhide thong over the pommel. Looking back up at the sky, he concluded that nothing bad was to happen for the secret inspection of the bundle—after all, he hadn't been struck dead by a bolt of lightning. Nothing like that. He patted the dried coyote head once and knelt to pick up his bundle of robes.

The moon's reflection on the snow lighted his way as he stepped over beside the sleeping man and set the hides down quietly. When they were untied Josiah quickly wrapped himself in them and dropped his head back into the fur. He remembered the song so much a favorite of Hatcher.

I'm just a poor, wayfaring stranger,
Traveling through this world of woe.
Yet, there's no sickness, toil, no danger
In that bright land to which I go.

I know dark clouds'll gather round me,
I know my way is rough and steep.
Yet beautiful fields lie just before me,
Where God's redeemed their vigils keep.

I'm going there to see my brothers,
Who've gone before me by one.
I'm just going over Jordan.
I'm only going over home.

He lay on his back for a few minutes and let the song
have free course in his mind. He watched the sky and
sang Hatcher's favorite song.

A clear, frosty night, and his feet weren't cold anymore. Not that cold. A little chilled, but not frozen
as they had been before the Crow woman made him
winter moccasins. Damn! The hurt of those thoughts
returned. Think about women and one woman will
invade your mind. His loneliness for her was growing
and soon his control of that loneliness would reach its
limits.

He wiggled his toes and turned over on his belly. He
pushed the knot in the sash to the side so that it would
not stick into his ribs. Like a rock, such a thing could be.
Sleeping on a rock. But then a man could get used to
many things. He decided he was living proof of that. Out
here a man could get used to many things.

Bass was shaking him. Josiah pushed the robes from
his face and looked out at the darkness of another black,
early-morning getup. The moon was still riding its high
path above them. Scratch stepped away from him without
a word. The young trapper, deciding he might as well get
it over with, tore the robes from his legs. Might as well
get back to the cold now. Scooting from the robes onto the
snow, Paddock stayed on his knees while rolling the hides
into a tight bundle and rewrapping the cords around it.
He stood and moved to the mule's side.

"See you didn' tie the pony off to your belt." Scratch

jerked at the knots that would secure the buffalo robes behind the saddle with the bear and wolf hides. He sounded edgy in the cold.

"Forgot," Josiah answered, only then remembering.

"Be glad you got you my help on this ride, Josiah Paddock." The older man turned and stepped over to the young trapper.

"I am, that," he replied quietly. "Forget me things at times." He looked up to see Bass staring at his waist. Josiah looked down, then continued to tie the robes to Hannah's back.

"Where you find your sash-belt?" Bass asked, nodding at Josiah's waist.

"Had it round." Josiah was feeling sheepish now. Stupid and sheepish.

"Had it with your plunder, then, eh? Didn' have it when we come on this tramp." Scratch moved around to the other side of the young man so that he could look at Josiah's face in the pale light. "You ain't wored it for some time now. We even made you up some tie whangs for the front of your capote." Suddenly he pushed his face close to Paddock's. "Where'd you get the sash belt?" His voice was at once sharp, demanding, accusing.

Josiah turned to look at him. "Said, I had it round."

"Where?"

"Just . . . round, somewhere—"

"Ain't good 'nough, boy! Where'd you come on it? Is that your'n?" He began to move to the other side of Josiah again. "Or you come on it by stealin'?"

Still glaring at Paddock, Titus backed away slowly, heading for the pony. "Huh? Where'd you steal it?"

"Didn't steal it, Scratch!" he lashed back. Funny how Bass always had a feeling for these things, he thought. Always knew how to get to the heart of things, scrape away the distortion and unearth the truth. "It's mine," he said quietly, looking down once more. "Been mine . . ."

"You lost it long time back, an' I'd like to know where you found it!"

"Why you so all-fired burned up 'bout a lil' sash belt of mine, Scratch? What differ'nce it make to you, or anybody? What differ'nce a lil' sash belt make at all?" He shouldn't have, he knew now; those impulses get a man into trouble. He wished he had not.

Bass sighed deeply as he stopped by the pony. "Jest a

might strange, ain't it, son, it showin' up at a time like this? Ain't it?"

"S'pose—"

"Real goddamned, ever-lovin', whore-buckin' strange!" He seemed to tremble slightly as he glared back at Josiah. "Somethin' jest showin' up like that, right outta the big blue," Bass said, throwing his right arm into the air. "An' you, not tellin' me where you come by it. Don' you think that all a lil' queersome? Jest a might strange, boy?"

"Said I s'pose so—"

Scratch suddenly turned and reached for the medicine bundle, twisting its loop on the pommel as he jerked a mitten off the right hand. His fingers felt along the back of the coyote's head, telling him of the knots tied there, confirming the bundle had been broken into.

"Awww, you young, stupid nigger!" He jerked around to look at Paddock.

"Wasn't thinkin' it would be hurtin'—"

"Wasn' thinkin's is right!" he snapped back, then lowered his head and shook it slowly from side to side. "Goddamn!" he said quietly, finally raising his eyes to stare at the sky. "Goddamn. Goddamn! *GODDAMN YOU, JOSIAH PADDOCK!*" he shouted.

"Wha-a-a . . . what's this all 'bout?" He took a step toward Scratch and stopped. "Why the hell you so riled up?"

"Oh, you done it to both us now, Josiah. Both us. You done it real good!"

"Why the devil—"

"The bundle! This goddamned bundle!" He slapped the coyote head so that it swung from side to side.

"The sash belt is mine, Scratch!"

"It's what the nigger kil't with! What McAfferty used to kill him Rotten Belly's woman! Cain't you see! Cain't you see what you've gone an' done?" He turned to the pony and bent his head against the saddle.

Paddock's fingers ran along the woolen sash. "How you know that? How you so goddamned all-fired sure of that?"

"He told me hisse'f, Arapooesh did," he said, hanging his head between his arms over the saddle. "Took it from her neck hisse'f." His words were quieter now, more remorseful.

"You know that for a fact?" Josiah asked, staring at the sash around his waist.

"Rotten Belly come down where I was packin' Hannah, whilst you was getting something back to camp—must've been . . . goddamn, I don' remember." He turned suddenly to face the younger man. "But what matters is you've gone an' broke into that bundle! The medeecin's out now, you let it slip out! Gone!" Bass hung his head again and let it swing from side to side. Almost under his breath he sighed and added, "Rotten Belly put him his own flesh in there, Josiah. His own flesh to add to your medeecin."

"Now you ain't one—"

"Hoodoos, Josiah!" He stomped over and picked up his rifle. "Your strong medeecin's gone an' there's hoodoos lookin' down on this whole thing now!"

"You're scared, ain't you?"

"Goddamned right, I'm skairt!"

"Of McAfferty?" Josiah started to snicker.

"To hell with that nigger!" Bass came back to the pony. "Ain't skairt of him. It ain't him a man outta be skairt of." Bass looked all about him as if suspecting something to be coming out of the cottonwoods or the willows for him. "And you'd be a smart one to be skairt too. Now you gone an' done this thing to both us."

"Done what?"

"Gone an' spoil't the medeecin you had—the medeecin we both had us." He looked to the pan to check the priming.

Josiah moved the few steps that took him to Bass's side. He went to put a hand on the older trapper's shoulder, but just as it landed Titus jerked away. "Scratch?" He looked at the man's back. "I don't want you down on me." There was no answer, no movement from Bass to tell him that the old man had heard. "What I done, I'm sorry for. Don't know what come over me, go lookin' in the bundle the way I done. But I don't want you down on me, Scratch. You gotta believe me. I don't want my only friend down on me."

Titus slowly faced Paddock and grabbed the young man's neck with his right hand, pulling Josiah into him. "You're a dumb shit. You are that." He let go gradually so that he could again look into Paddock's eyes. "Maybe now you listen-up to the ol' man? Heh? You listen what the ol' man tells you?"

647

Josiah nodded and looked down, away from the other man's eyes and their intense gaze. "I'll be one to listen to you, from here on. Swear it." He glanced back up. "Just ain't wantin' you down on me like that ever again. Had you funnin' me afore, callin' me all sorts of things, but just now, that was somethin' differ'nt, Scratch. You was really mad at me."

"I was."

"No more?"

"S'pose not. Leastways, it don' help nothin'."

"Swear I'll listen—whatever you say, here on out. All right?"

"All right, Josiah," Bass said, after a pause. "You check your primin' an' load up. We...we gotta see this thing through to the end." Bass turned to look at the mule. "You sure you wanna ride Hannah?" He thought of the broken bundle. "You can ride the pony an' I'll take the mule," Scratch said, starting toward Hannah.

Josiah waved him back, "I'll ride her. You stay with the pony, up front. Hannah an' me gettin' along just fine now, the two of us. I'll be just fine on the old gal." He retrieved his rifle from the tree. "Don't you worry none 'bout me now Scratch."

"Cain't help it," he replied softly. "This is the day we come on McAfferty. Best you do ever'thin' I tell you from here on. Got that?"

"Yeah—"

" 'Cause from here on, Josiah—we ain't got your medeecin bundle watchin' over this thing." He pushed up into the saddle and took the rein into his left hand so that his right could caress the trigger guard. "Nigger ain't far 'head an' we ain't got your medeecin workin' for us. None of your medeecin. We on our own now, son."

The false dawn, that first faint paling of the sky, bent over the hills to the east when Scratch stopped his pony and sniffed the cold air. He turned his head and listened for a while to something Josiah could not hear. The only sound reaching his young ears was that of the animals quietly snorting in the frigid air, the steaming breath misting from their nostrils. Bass finally slipped from the pony and handed the rein up to Josiah. He put one finger to his lips and motioned for Paddock to stay put. Then he stepped off into the trees.

In a few minutes he was back at the edge of the cottonwoods and willow where Josiah could see him. Scratch motioned for the young man to follow him. Paddock nudged Hannah forward and pulled on the pony's rein, leading the animals into the timber where Bass disappeared. When they came on him again the old trapper was crouched in an area where the snow had been tramped down by man and horse.

"He camp here recent?" Josiah whispered.

Scratch looked up from what he was intently studying and rose, dusting his hand off on the front of the elk-hide coat. "Real recent, son." He turned to look at Josiah. "Last night."

"We close then."

"Real close. Ashes ain't a bit col't. You could be roastin' the nigger's guts on 'em with a little work. Figger we ain't got far to go till we see."

"How long?" Josiah's whisper cracked the cold air.

Bass looked to his left for a minute and studied the eastern sky. He wiped his hand across the front of his coat and moved toward the pony. Taking the rein back from Paddock, he put a foot into the stirrup and rose off the ground with the heavy rifle in his hand. "By the sun, if'n I don't miss my guess on it." He settled down on the saddle and adjusted the bottom of his coat. "We got us less'n two hour maybe, afore we come up on him."

He nudged the pony forward into a slow walk this time, moving out of the stand of trees along McAfferty's path in the snow. Things would be moving more slowly from here on. He could smell it now and turned to glance back at the young trapper atop Hannah. Yep, he looked ahead again, he could smell it now.

The breeze out of the northwest brushed gently along his whiskers, bouncing the braid against his cheek. The cottonwoods up to this point had not grown close enough to allow a man any cover for an ambush. But now they suddenly stood thicker, their bases matted in a wild tangle of willow.

Scratch again brought his pony to a halt and took a whiff of the breeze. It wasn't coming from the right direction. The wind wasn't right for him. He decided he would have to move closer to the thicket to let his nose work. Best to do that on foot now.

Handing the horse's rein once more to Paddock he slid quietly to the new snow and moved south in a wide arc toward the river. He did not want to be following directly in McAfferty's tracks as he pushed into the undergrowth, but he kept the tramped snow ever in sight. The tracks led him to the edge of the river and disappeared. Bass stopped to listen, trying to absorb every sound carried to him on the breezes rustling the air at dawn. Remaining crouched for a few minutes until he was satisfied, he moved off slowly toward the bank, keeping low in his zigzag journey toward the water.

Near the edge he stopped again. Bending low over his rifle with his face still up in the breeze, Scratch brought his rifle up close to his body and pulled the hammer back slowly to full cock, slowly until he could feel the muffled engaging of the lock. Dropping to his knees he took one considered step after another through the willows until he was finally at the water's edge and slid down on his belly. He set the rifle in front of him, the stock under the long barrel resting on top of his left arm, the muzzle still hidden with him in the undergrowth. The remaining fingers of the right hand played lightly along the trigger guard.

From here he could see the tracked snow on the bank to his left as the prints disappeared into the water. Near as Titus could tell, McAfferty had not left his pony's back in crossing the small river. His eyes searched the opposite bank until he found where Asa had pushed onto the snow once more. It was to his right, up a way, and he nodded silently to himself in agreement. McAfferty had not moved directly across the river to the opposite side. Instead, the hunted had moved upriver some thirty or forty yards before emerging from the icy water.

Careful, he had been, but with the snow on the ground Bass was certain McAfferty really did not expect to lose those who followed. Still, he was taking a few precautions. Just making a show of it. More and more he became convinced of the feeling. Asa was just making a pretense of eluding his hunters.

He remained in the snow watching the opposite bank for some time before he let his eyes move up the hills across the river. Asa had gone through the water, then the tracks headed east along a small creek into the hills. He imagined the creek becoming lost in the mountains that reared their gray heads where the sun would soon break overhead. Probably figuring to get up into those mountains and bust over toward the Windy River. Head south, maybe toward the Green. It was certain McAfferty wasn't heading west to Blackfoot country anymore. That was clear when the trail cut south from the Yellowstone into this valley. Maybe head on down to Touse. And senoreetas. And lightning and pass brandy. Funny it was now. He thought he had McAfferty all figured out for heading on a fast, straight course to the Three Forks.

A hawk circled the valley to the south, calling out once and disappearing over the western rim after gliding on the warming air currents. Bass watched the big bird drift in its slow, lazy circles until the hawk was gone from view. Yep. Just as fast and straight as the hawk would move. That's what he had figured. But now things were different and he must reevaluate his earlier calculations as to Asa's intent and motives. A hawk would hunt in the open, hoping to spot his small prey skittering across the grassy flats and bare hills. But a wolf—now that hunter would just as soon stalk his prey from the cover of timbered, snow-draped slopes and ridges. The wolf would use the terrain to his advantage.

He bent his head forward and licked at the new whiteness before him. It was cold and good on his tongue. Bass brushed his mustache and beard against the furry collar of the coat and sniffed the air. Nothing to smell now, even in this clean, lung-searing air.

Gradually he scooted quietly back from his place on the bank behind the willows and rose to a low crouch so that he could stay hidden as he skittered back to Josiah and the animals. He would have to think about these new things, Bass told himself. Important as it was to keep his mind empty and receptive to the mutest sound, the slightest change in the air, he knew this was important too. He would have to consider just what the hunted was intending to do.

Moving quickly around the pony so that he stood between it and Josiah, Scratch began to loosen the tight bundle of fur he had slung from his pommel. "Crossin's clear, son," he whispered without looking up at Paddock. He felt Paddock's questioning eyes on his back. He dropped the trap sack to the ground and freed the rawhide knots that secured the eight pieces of buffalo hide in the sack. "C'mon down here, son," he requested. He drew one of the knives from the back of his belt while Josiah slid to the ground beside him.

"We gonna go on over?" Josiah whispered.

"Yep," he answered, "jest soon's we wrap these 'critters' feets." The knife was put to work slicing fringe from the legging seams. Bass handed Josiah some of the strips. "Here, you tie four of 'em up together into one long'un. We need us eight of 'em."

Paddock began to knot the long fringes together until there were eight of the whangs on the snow beside him. Scratch picked one of them up and slid to one of Hannah's forelegs, then looked quickly back to Paddock, "You keep your eye peel't, Josiah. I'll do this myself."

Josiah rose and slid his rifle part way over the saddle so that he could look along the bordering growth that traced the river's path. Now and then he would glance at Scratch working quietly around the two animals. Bass raised one hoof at a time and put the large piece of buffalo hide under it, then let the mule put her foot down again. He gathered up the edges of the skin and encircled the ankle with the leather whang, finally knotting it tightly. One leg at a time until both mule and pony wore their crude winter moccasins.

"The critters' feet look bad?" Paddock asked, thinking the hide would serve as protection for the unshod hooves.

"Not so much that, Josiah." He kept at his work on the pony's last legging that refused to remain tight. "Will keep 'em lil' more quiet now. Icy snow can cut the critters' legs up—split a hoof too, for that matter. But we settin' by somethin' else now. These'll make 'em walk more quietlike in the snow. Jest like a coyote's got him furry pads in the winter. For stalkin' quiet in the snow, you see." He rose and took his rifle back in hand from where he had leaned it against the mule's side. "Got you any more of that old capote we cut up for mittens?" Bass asked, pulling his pair back over the cold hands.

"Yep."

"Get it," he said, then put his eyes to work inspecting the nearby river bank.

Josiah moved quietly to his side with the remains of the blue woolen blanket. Picking his knife up from the snow, Bass helped the young man unfurl what was left of the cloth. He sliced two long pieces, laying them one at a

652

time over Josiah's forearm, then returned his knife to its sheath.

"I best do this myself too." He gave Paddock his rifle to hold and took the two strips of cloth from his arm. He threw one over his shoulder and moved to stand beside Hannah's head. Sliding it carefully across her forehead above the eyes, Scratch brought it slowly down until the mule was blinded. He tied the strip off at the back of the jaw where it would not slip down when the animal opened her mouth. She did not fight or protest the loss of sight. Bass took the other strip from his shoulder and did likewise with the Indian pony. Like the mule, it did not protest. "Maybe so it's been blinded up afore," he commented as he turned back to Josiah for his rifle. "Or the critter more blind anyway'n I thought afore."

"What them for anyway?"

Scratch picked up the pony's rein from the snow and put a foot in the wide wooden stirrup before answering. "We make 'em blind now, 'cause we close. Critters don' need 'em to see from here on. We'll lead the way." Bass swung into the saddle. "Them critters don' see, they stay more quietlike from here on out." He nudged the Indian pony along the path he had taken to the river bank.

Josiah followed as the older man took the new path rather than trace the tracks in the snow where McAfferty had left the bank. The animals stepped quietly into the slow, cold water. The men let the mule and the pony move at their own pace across the river. One step at a time it was, while Bass continued to scan the opposite bank and the hills rising up from the water.

"Where you get them pieces of hide from?" Josiah whispered as they neared the bank.

"McAfferty's robes."

"You just cut 'em up?"

"He weren't gonna be cuttin' 'em up for me now, was he?" Bass replied quietly, speaking out of the side of his mouth. "An' the nigger ain't gonna be usin' 'em anymore, is he? Not now, he ain't."

"Be usin' his plunder—"

"Least the nigger can be doin' for me," he snapped back, to silence his partner at his side. "Don' know what you thinkin' 'bout, son. We gonna kill that man, less'n he kills us first. An' you're all so goddamned worried 'bout cuttin' his robes up."

653

Before they reached the opposite bank, Bass pushed them north, downstream. After covering more than a hundred yards, Bass reined the pony to the right and let the animal claw its way up the snowy bank. Just another precaution to be taking along with all the others. Asa had moved south, upstream, before he had touched the snow again. And they would move away from the whitehair while they were exposed midriver. Bass watched Josiah point the blinded Hannah up the bank. He then steered his pony right, to move along the eastern side of the river toward the creek running into the mountains.

"This be all too easy, ol' man," Josiah commented a few minutes later as they pushed up the small watercourse. "Trackin' a man in this new snow, what with you knowin' the tracks his pony makes anyway. It's all too easy."

Scratch nodded without looking in his direction, his eyes continuing to sweep from side to side and climbing every now and then to the tops of the hills at their left and right. "Too easy," he answered after a minute.

"You ever track a man on foot—mean, him an' you both on foot?"

"I have that, Josiah." Bass coughed against his mitten as quietly as he could, feeling the tightness in his chest testing him. The sun was just beginning to rear its bright head over the peaks now. That would help to warm the cold fist he felt beneath his ribs. Might do a lot to help.

"How you gonna do that, you knowin' only what prints McAfferty's pony makes?"

"We come on that time, it'll be all too easy, the same." He nodded quickly down at Josiah's leg. "Asa ain't one to wear him winter mokersons, he ain't. Never been, to think of it."

"What that gotta do with it?"

"Well, you jest gotta look how a man's mokersons is cut to know how to track him. All them southern tribes—Shians, Comanches, 'Rapahoes, too—theys mokersons cut with the inside edges straightlike. The toes of 'em cut so's to look like the man as wears 'em is walkin' with his feet all pointed in. Tell a Pawnee mok right off—it bein' like what we put on the critters' feets. Jest sets his foot down on a piece a leather, like we did the hoofs, brung it up round his leg to tie it off. You can see them wrinkles plain as your face in the trackin'. Them Crow make 'em goodly, smooth mokersons, with none of them wrinkles an' sewin' seams you see on t'others. Mine, Josiah, mine be like them 'Rapaho kind, 'cause, you see, I walk kinda funny what with my—"

"What all that gotta do with trackin' McAfferty on foot?"

"If'n you'd hush your mouth, I'd be l'arnin' you on it now," he answered, after a moment's pause. "You tell me who made them mokersons for McAfferty?"

"His squaw."

"An' who made your'n?"

"Crow squaw. Don't know her—"

"Nawww, you jackass. Your first'uns. The ones as McAfferty be wearin' as he's never took to winter mokersons. Who made you your first'uns?"

"Nez Percy squaw."

"Yep. See you anthin' in that, son?" He turned briefly to look at the young trapper.

Paddock thought a moment, then it finally hit him. "Same woman made the mokersons, didn't she?"

"You're bright, now. Real bright." He flicked his eyes quickly again. "Mokersons made by the same squar gonna make 'em the same tracks, ain't they? All you gotta ever see is what tracks your inside pair makes, an' you'll know what the nigger's gonna look like."

They pushed up the side of the hill that put them above the stream. They moved along through the low brush until Bass could find cover in the aspen dotting the landscape in large stands. He reached the first and stopped again to lean forward over the pony's neck. His neck followed the broken snow down at the edge of the stream, and traced the prints until he could no longer see them along the climb. Bass moved his gaze forward to study the side of the hill before them, inspecting those places where a man could hide and double back on his pursuers to escape, inspecting those places that offered the greatest danger to him and Josiah. Scratch nodded and put the pony into motion again, guiding the animal between the pale trees to climb a little higher along the hill.

"You ain't follerin' his tracks," Josiah said.

"Ain't 'tendin' to," Scratch replied.

"How you know you ain't follerin' a elk, deer maybe?"

"I know, boy. You best b'lieve me. I know."

655

"Purty damned sure, ain't you?" he asked. "Maybe too sure?"

"If'n I wanted to know me any better, I'd go have me a close look down there. But I don' need to," he remarked. "Even take me a sniff of them prints, too."

"Smell 'em? You're bullshitting me again!"

"Nope. I ain't in the least, son." He jerked his head backward a little in gesture. "Fire back there we come on—McAfferty's?"

"Yeah?"

"Tells the tale of it. Well, the nigger's gone an' burnt him some sage over the fire—"

"An' you smell that?"

"I did. McAfferty's gone an' smoked his skins in the sage smoke he burnt last night. Prob'ly smoked ever'thin' he's got on him now, too."

"Medicine?"

"Nope. Nigger ain't one for Injun medeecin. Not that'un, he ain't. Nope, Josiah. That's to be gettin' rid of his smell—the smell of a man."

"An' that's what you'd go sniffin' for—on his tracks?"

"In a manner of speakin'. Injuns'll do it too. You watch 'em. Out huntin', an' they come up on a trail, them red niggers tell how old the trail is jest by lookin' at it. Them coons'll get down on hands an' knees crawlin' over the ground on that trail; go sniffin' at the pony tracks, man tracks too, if'n they got 'em to sniff on."

"You let your nose foller the man, eh?"

"The looks of it, s——"

Up the canyon beyond the first ring of hills there rang the low blast of a rifle. Bass jerked almost uncontrollably with the sound, at once certain they were not being shot at, yet still caught completely off his guard by the shot. He sat motionless as the pony snorted quietly, listening until the echo had disappeared from his ears, dissipating among the encompassing hills.

"Asa?"

"Yep. Seems the likes of it."

"We found him all right." His hoarse whisper was excited. "Just like you said, we found him now."

"Won' wash, Josiah. That don' wash now." Scratch shook his head slowly for a moment and turned to look at Paddock. "No, son. McAfferty's found us."

The older man wheeled in a tight circle that put him

656

facing Josiah and reached over to untie the blanket blind-fold from Hannah's head. Then he did the same with his own pony. He stuck both within the belt tied around the elkhide coat, drawing the ends of the blanket strips down into his crotch.

"Don' be needin' these now." He wheeled back around and moved the pony forward again, faster now that he knew they could ride over the first ridge before they would be anywhere close to danger from the hunted man.

He pushed on now, more certain in a simple way. But he didn't like it, not one bit. Slowly, almost reluctantly, Scratch began to inspect the pieces of it in his mind. First there was the matter of the plunder McAfferty left back in the Crow camp—too much left behind. It had nagged at him only slightly until later, when he finally began seriously to consider just what Asa had on his mind. Too much left behind. Too little taken with him on this long journey.

But he remembered justifying it, thinking Asa was going to travel lean, going to move fast. He was on his way to the Three Forks and beyond, he had thought then. Straight into the home of the Blackfoot. Back to friendly people. Then that got twisted and didn't figure anywhere close to being right anymore. McAfferty suddenly turned south from the Yellowstone. He wasn't heading over the mountains to the Three Forks any longer. He had turned south to head up this river valley.

And the pony with the cracked hoof had been moving quickly at first, through the first day or so, he remembered. Scratch had been able to tell about McAfferty's speed by looking at the animal's gait, how far it was between strides. He could tell at a glance the distance between hoof prints. Then he had noticed they were closer together last night under the moon. Not just because it was dark and harder to travel in the dim light. No. McAfferty's a better pony man than that. No, he had deliberately slowed up, no longer trying to outrun his hunters. He was letting them catch up. The nagging finally began to burn in his mind then.

By the time they had come upon the fire just before dawn, Scratch had grown all the more uneasy about it. The fire. Taking time to build one, for whatever reason—even smoking his clothes so Bass couldn't smell him. It was another rotten chunk he hated to see laid in place.

Not liking the shape the puzzle was taking. The ashes still warm in his bare hand as he ground them into his palm in anger, desperation, fear—something.

Why had he been so slow in realizing it? Why had it taken this long? He shook his head, hoping to clear it of the cobwebs.

Cobwebs—like gray hair. That was a laugh. Man starts getting gray hair, might as well have cobwebs for brains. You're old, Titus Bass. Be facing up to that, now. Now. An old man refusing to own up to it; out here still trying to play the young game. The whispers of age had been deviling him for some time now. But they were only whispers and he had shut them up well enough. But that was before. Things rang louder now, torturing his ears. Rustling like an ill wind through the cobwebs. You're old, Titus Bass. Quit now, while you still got you the chance.

He clamped his eyes shut, making himself as blind as the pony had been before he removed its blindfold, hoping to shut off the voice up there—out there—all around him. It was gone, and he slowly opened his eyes again, relieved to see only the snow and hills, green and white and blue. Oh, Lord, but he didn't want it this way. Not the end, not this way. No. No end. He wanted no end to it. But time had slipped by him, stealing away each night as he slept. Another day stolen from him. Time he had wasted. And during the day while he knelt hunched and bent over the traps and the streams, it had crept up behind him to steal away from his grasp. Through his fingers. The years might as well have been water one picked up in a bucket with the bottom rusted out. Right through the hands. So fast. Staying so briefly. Time gone now, and never to hold again.

Bass believed there was only one more part of the puzzle to go now. Then he would be sure of it. Positive of what he had been blind to all along the trail getting here. Just one more piece and he'd know. The shot told him, but he wanted to be sure.

Could be a lot of things, he decided. A lot of things. Nigger ran into a bear. Something like that, maybe. Just maybe. Or, his pony slipped and the rifle went off as he fell. Perhaps. The last possibility he did not even wish to consider and pushed it out of his mind. Asa wouldn't shoot himself because we're getting close, so close now. No, he wouldn't be one for that. That didn't fit with all the other pieces. Nope. Not just because we're breathing on him now.

Some of them had already gone back. Lot more will be going back, too. Getting out of the mountains. Didn't belong here in the first place anyway. Go on back east! Go on back to them people settlements. Get out of my mountains!

My mountains. The sound of it rang good to him. Being up here, now, that was all there was to him, after all was said and done. Being free up here, in his mountains—far, far better than being back there where you were always safe. Safe and sane, maybe. Go on back east! Damn all you coming out here and trapping up these streams! Go back to scratch your fields until the day you drop behind some plow you've gone and hitched yourself to. Corncrackers! You don't belong out here anyway! These mountains belong to the likes of me! The likes of us—McAfferty and me.

At the bottom of the draw they found the carcass. Scratch slipped silently to the snow and looked at it quickly, then scanned the wooded hillside leading away from the carcass. There the tracks went. Over that hill.

McAfferty hadn't even taken the saddle. Hell. What was he thinking about. No use to Asa now. Some Injun would love finding that. He knelt by the carcass of the dead pony and shuddered involuntarily. Just the cold, he told himself. That's all. He sighed deeply and put a finger out to touch the hole in the animal's head. Blood already frozen in the cold. Wish the sun would get on up there. Warm things up for me.

The pony's eyes were taking on that death glaze. The head lay at a weird angle on the flat whiteness at the bottom of the draw. Right where it had dropped. Never to move again. And the footprints of the hunted, circling the carcass one time, pulling something from behind the saddle, then hurrying up the hill. Did not even take him a robe. Everything left here. Everything left behind.

The cough grabbed at his chest again, racking against his ribs as he fought to suppress the noise of it. He could not. It was out of control. Too late for that. It was out of control. The whole thing was beyond his control now. When a man finally chose his spot and was waiting for you to come to him, you had lost. The man had finally got control over his own time and had picked the place. He awaited the hunter. He had wrenched from this thing the last vestige of power he could. The time and the place.

All too often a man had it sneak up on him. From behind. Out of the dark. Death usually came that way. For very few men death was chosen after the time and the place had been settled. Death was no longer an enemy then. It could be your partner. And you still got to call some of the shots for it. Your partner then, and not the enemy that came stealing up behind you in the dark when you weren't ready, weren't looking. No longer would the man's time slip through his fingers or pour out of the bottom of that rusty bucket. He had taken the power to himself.

That was the meat of this whole thing, wasn't it? The bloody red lean of it. He had taken control of the time and the place, and you had come running along behind him. Eyes closed. Thinking you were chasing him all the way. That was the meat of it—who was the hunter and who was the hunted in the end?

"Scratch?"

The old man jerked a little when the boy's whisper pierced his thoughts. He did not turn to look back at Josiah. He did not look up at his partner on the mule. Bass kept his eyes on the marks across the snow that disappeared over the hill.

"We got him now, Scratch." There was still no reply or movement of recognition from the old man. "It's real now. Before it was like, like . . . we was chasin' a ghost. Somethin' like that. Follerin' his tracks, comin' on his fires after he'd gone. But now it's real. An' he's shot his pony. He's on foot an' we can catch him afore you know it—"

"Shut up!" he suddenly yelled, jerking his head to look up at Josiah. "Close you goddamned mouth an' listen to yourself! Jest listen." He rose slowly and looked back at the trail up the hill. "That all gonna be a waste now. Worryin' 'bout catchin' up to a man on foot—it's all a goddamned waste of time thinkin' 'bout that now!"

He coughed. The sharpness below his ribs was growing. "McAfferty's gonna find us! It's his game now." Bass finally slipped a foot in the stirrup and climbed into the saddle as if every bone in his body were in revolt. He eased the hammer back from half-cock and pushed the pony into McAfferty's tracks.

Paddock had been silenced. Scratch's words had done the trick. Suddenly, viciously, he had seen the old man turn on him. But now they were close to the hunted man and he didn't need Bass along any longer. He could take it from here on out. From here on out.

"I can do this thing on my own, Scratch," he said. "Do it alone. You stay here an' wait for me. I can go on from here by myself."

Scratch jerked back savagely on the pony's reins and whipped the animal around until he was right beside the young man, skidding to a stop in a white cloud of new snow. "Shit!" He shook his head from side to side. "Ain't you the fool now for thinkin' such things. Goddamn! Why, boy, I'm the best thing for you since't your mama's milk! An' you're goin' through it with me right here!"

Again he yanked on the rein and jerked the pony's head to the side in pushing back up the hill. Boy'ad been dead one before now, he thought. Maybe that wouldn't have been so bad, letting him go by himself. He could have waited back with the Crows. No! He couldn't let himself think that. He didn't believe it anyway.

The next draw was rocky. Boulders were strewn up and down the sides of the hills. But none of them was really big enough for a man to hide behind. Bass measured them and let the pony move down the slope through the trees, picking his way carefully as they dropped out of the sun's light once more. Maybe they should move back into the trees even more. Maybe follow him on foot from here. At least take some of the load off the pony and Hannah the rest of the way.

"Scratch?" he whispered suddenly.

"Don' bother me!" he snapped in a raspy, fluid bark. It surprised him, the sound of his own voice now. The heaviness in his chest was growing like a huge weight suspended inside of him.

"Scratch, dammit!"

"Said not to bother me." His nose peaked into the air and he sniffed as best his lungs would let him draw in the long breath. Another, shorter breath though. And a third quick sniff. He pushed on toward the edge of the trees that reached out near the bottom of the hill. They would stop there, on the other side, and unload the animals, he thought.

At the bottom of the draw he cut quickly up toward

the stand of aspen. Not much cover, but there were many of them. Pine on up ahead too. They could drop the baggage in the aspens and go on up the hill where the tracks led. Stop there in the green trees.

"Scratch! Dammit! Will you lis——"

The blast roared through the narrow draw, echoing off the ridges above them, bouncing back at him from the trees he had wanted to reach. So close. They had been so close. And now it was as if he was jerked around to look behind him at something he did not want to see. Slowly he watched the old mule pitch forward, throwing her rider over her neck and into the open just below the small white cloud above them on the hill.

"Hannah!" Bass screamed, the voice cracking against the raw throat. Bass wheeled his pony around to look for some movement in the trees above them. "Hannah!" he found himself yelling again as he viciously kicked his heels into the pony's ribs. The animal shot forward, kicking up the dry, white powder as it bounded toward the young trapper.

"Ba-a-a-ass!" Josiah came up to his knees and scooped his rifle out of the snow.

Scratch shifted the rein to his right hand, stuffing it in what fingers remained, clutching it tightly alongside the rifle. He jerked back on the pony's head as he passed above the young man, wheeling the animal around in a tight circle so that he would be between Josiah and the next shot. He had a few more seconds before he could expect Asa to have reloaded. A few more thumps of the heart battering against his ribs.

"C'mon, boy!" he brought the pony up on the struggling trapper so that Josiah stood on Scratch's left. He put his empty hand down and grabbed for Josiah's left wrist. Pulling up, he swung the younger man behind him as well as he could while the pony dashed through the snow toward the trees.

Paddock clung with his left hand clutching the old man's free arm, his left foot stuck in the left stirrup Bass had emptied for him. He struggled to get his right leg kicked over the pony's rump but the hides strapped behind the saddle prevented it. Josiah's rifle bounced precariously beneath his armpit as that right arm clung to the back of the saddle. The right leg was useless, repeatedly being kicked out of the way as the pony clawed across the flying powder, the animal's flared nostrils snorting blossoms of white mist from them.

They were near now. The trees. Just get into the trees. Another blast rent the air. Bass felt something move the pony downhill. He heard it thud against the animal but the pony kept moving headlong where the old man directed. He's been hit and he's still moving for me, Bass thought. Still moving for me. Damn! What an animal!

Once into the dim light of the stand of aspen Bass let go of Josiah's arm and felt the young man slip to the ground and heard him skidding across the snow. Bass vaulted off the pony and reached out with his left hand to keep a grip on the long rein. He jerked the animal around so that he could look at the pony's right side. Lord, why were his eyes misting now? Because of the pony. What a damned fine animal! Hit and it kept moving under him! Kpet moving for him!

No blood yet. He kept looking while the pony snorted. Then he found the hole. The bullet had hit the saddle just behind his right thigh, where the frame was thickest and the rawhide binding the wood together of many thick layers. He stuck his hand under the saddle and felt no wet, no blood. The fingers ran along the inside of the frame and he found no exit hole. His left hand came out and he poked the little finger into the hole and felt the flattened, lead ball. Bass smiled and stroked the animal's withers momentarily before he slapped the pony on the rump, sending it down the draw away from them, away from McAfferty. The animal darted off through the trees, clattering quietly down into the narrow vee as Scratch turned around.

Paddock had crawled up behind two aspens where a boulder had long ago rolled against the trees. Bass skittered over to him and went to his knees. He looked out across the open they had crossed to get to these trees and found the carcass a little below them. She lay motionless, still carrying her pack frame and baggage, her head pointing downhill. The mule had wheeled and dropped as the bullet entered her head. Death had been merciful. At least that.

"Dammit, Scratch! If you'd only listened to me!" he rasped breathlessly. "I was tryin' to tell you!"

"Tell me what, boy?" He turned to look at Josiah.

"You never listen, never will listen to me."

"Tell me what, Josiah!" He was more insistent now.

"Goddammit, ol' man! I saw him! I saw him movin' up there on the hill just—"

"You saw McAfferty?"

"Weren't him, not rightly, Just saw a . . . somethin' movin' up there—tryin' to tell you. You never listen to me. I'm just the boy to you. I tried to say somethin', an' the nigger almost got me!"

Bass sighed a little. His eyes returned to the lifeless carcass across the slope on the snow. "If he'd wanted you, son, you'd be down there right where Hannah's lyin' now."

Paddock looked past the old trapper down at the carcass of the mule. "He weren't aimin' for me then?"

"No way. The nigger wanted Hannah. Not you." The thought suddenly clutched in his chest with all its heavy tightness. Hannah. She was gone now. Suddenly ripped from him by the thing up the hill. What the hell was it for? What purpose did it serve, shooting the old gal? Except that McAfferty knew what the mule meant to him. After all these years—to see her lying there in the snow. No longer could he whistle to the mule and watch her ears twitch as she trotted over to him. No more to watch her snort when he laid a piece of cottonwood before her to chew. Asa had cut off his last chance of escape when he had sacrificed the pony back there. And now he was chipping away at Bass's too.

"I'm sorry . . . sorry, Scratch."

He turned and looked again at the young trapper beside him in the snow. "After you cut into that medeecin bundle, I thought me better 'bout you ridin' on Hannah." He choked on the words a little, then thought it better not to go into that now. It was water already past them. "Ain't your fault, son." He tried to console himself with the same words.

"Just wanted to tell you. Afore it's too late. I'm sorry—'bout the medicine bundle. 'n' Hannah. 'Specially 'bout Hannah, Scratch." He looked down at his rifle. "Just wanted you to know—"

"I know," he interrupted. "I know. It don' help now. Don' help. Ol' gal's dead"—he looked down the hill at the carcass—"an' my heart is small, Josiah. My heart is small an' it's on the ground." What a waste, Bass thought, McAfferty shooting his own pony. And now killing Hannah

664

this way. He didn't have to do it. What a goddamned waste! But the thing up the hill wasn't leaving any rough edges now, no loose ends dangling in the winds. McAfferty was sure with it; he was cutting himself off from everything. Like friends, old friends of another day. And he was cutting Bass off too. Closer and closer it was getting to the point where there was no sense in either of them trying anymore. No sense in going on with the living. Piece by piece, each had fallen into place for him; he had been blind not to see it before. Soon there would be no way out for either of them.

"This be where we part comp'ny, son." He started to rise on one knee.

"Wha-a-a?"

"You're stayin' here, Josiah. Stayin' behin't from here on." He started to move off on his knees but Josiah jerked him back.

"Now wait just a goddamned minute here! You just wait! I was the one as them Crow told to come after him—"

"An' I was the one he knew would." He started off again on his knees.

"You sure that's the way you want it to be then?" Josiah asked.

Scratch turned his head a little to look back at the young man. "Yep," he answered. "That's the way it's to be." Titus looked up the hill to where he had read McAfferty's last shot, then studied the trees above their position and pushed off around the boulder.

He heard it more than felt it at the first instant. It was a dull clunk, the sound in his head. For that flash of a moment left to him, he imagined it might have been a ball hitting a tree. Made the same sound. Then he knew what it was as the sparks shot from his eyes and the black poured over him like a dark, liquid curtain, pushing him down into the snow.

Paddock knelt over the old man and reached out to touch him with his left hand. "Sorry 'bout doin' that, Scratch. Real sorry. I done 'nough 'gainst you already— with Hannah. You got me here, brung me all the way." He looked up the hill toward the pines he would make a dash for. "But this 'un is mine from here on. You ain't gonna take it from me, Scratch. You cain't take it from me, not now. The nigger's mine, you see. Mine alone. An' the scalp'll be yours, yours an' Rotten Belly's. For his woman an' . . . an' for Hannah. I tried to tell you, but you wouldn't listen to me. Never listened to me, did you, Scratch?"

Scooting to the side of the boulder Josiah knelt motionless for a few minutes, lightly touching the small, buckskin pouch against his chest, listening intently to the sounds in the forest. How he wished he weren't so alone. His fingers ran along the tattered ribbon wrapped around the top of the pouch. This was for him to do alone. Josiah tried to concentrate on listening. Any sound from the hill. He waited to be told, but it was up to him alone now. No one was going to tell him what to do. Quickly he looked at the old man lying in the snow, then pushed himself away from the boulder into a crouched run.

His feet slipped a little, biting at the dusting of new snow, but he moved forward with the help of his left hand, clawing his way up toward the trees. Make it to the trees and he would be as far up as McAfferty had been when Hannah was shot. Almost there. His breath seared at his lungs in the climb, the air burned in his throat. Just a few more feet . . .

He heard the plunk of the ball about the same time he recognized the blast of the rifle from the trees beyond him. Without thinking, he fell forward onto the snow, then belly-crawled the last few yards into the pines where the low-hanging branches would give him cover.

You missed, Asa. You missed me. S'posed to be such a damned good shot! He smiled and looked back down the hill in hopes of seeing the tree where the ball had struck just in front of him. You led me too far, McAfferty. Wasn't moving that fast, you see. So you went and led me too far. He was glad that his foot had slipped and he had lost ground at the right moment. Small things like that were important. Things like stumbling.

Bass heard the rifle boom through the thick, liquid blackness. It seemed to jar him loose from the dark hold on his mind. Slowly he opened his eyes and felt the scorching pain in the back of his head. He was dazed, confused. What had happened? Why was he lying there in the snow?

Suddenly he jerked up on an elbow and his head bit at him again, hammers beating against the back of his eyes. Mustn't do that anymore, he told himself. No more. It hit him. As sure as the boy had hit him. Josiah was gone. He started to twist his head to look, then moved more slowly as he remembered. Slow and easy there. He saw the tracks in the snow leading from where he lay up the hill to the pines. And the boom in his ears. He remembered that too.

Bringing himself up on the elbow, Scratch inched forward across the snow to the edge of the boulder. Now he could see the patches of buckskin between the pine boughs up the slope. He watched for a few moments and saw the light patches move within the dark green sea. Boy made it up the hill all right. Good boy! Good! Then Bass remembered the blow coming from behind. He brought his legs up under his body to sit at the edge of the rock.

"Josiah!" he yelled. The buckskin patches moved toward him a little. "You're a damned fool, boy!"

"This be mine now, Scratch."

"No it ain't." He scooted a little forward. "It's 'tween him an' me! Ain't none of your'n, son! Got nothin' to do with you!" He watched the buckskin patches spread out as the young man moved slowly to the edge of the thick pine boughs.

"You stay back!" hollered Josiah.

"Ain't none of your'n—"

"You just stay back now! You get back in—"

Bass saw it happen. It seemed unreal at first. The body jerked violently around with the force of the blast. Spinning. Spinning. The young man disappeared into the thick green boughs.

Bass twisted on reflex to look to his right above the place where Paddock had dropped from sight. From the pines he watched the mist of white smoke blossom and curl toward the sky until it grew long fingers and hung within the branches. The rifle's roar was still loud in his ears as he jerked back to search again for the buckskin patches. The smoke was drifting downhill to the tree where he had last seen the young trapper. But no buckskin patches remained among the dark green.

How bad was he hit? Scratch flipped up the frizzen and blew the old priming out. He had often seen the familiar twisting jerk caused by the ball wrenching Paddock around. Bass yanked the stopper from his priming horn with his teeth and spilled the fine grains into the pan. He let the stopper hang from its thong attached to the horn and brushed the excess powder away before snapping the frizzen down. The boy was hit. And he needed to know how bad.

"Josiah!" he hollered at the peak of his voice.

The sound of the word bounced back at him from the hills, growing faint each time it rocked over him until it barely nudged his ears with its memory. Bass ran his index finger over the edge of the flint in the hammer.

"Josiah!" he screamed. Again the only answer was the echo dying slowly as it wasted itself across the canyon.

He could be dazed, just dazed, he thought. That's all. You can wing a man, just crease his skull a might, and it will knock him flat. Just a flesh wound. Still knock you flat. And out. He can't hear me because he's knocked out. Bass had to be sure.

Ripping loose the knots on the top two thongs holding the coat closed, Titus tore it from his arms and flung it behind the boulder. He took the rifle in his right hand as his left sought out the two knives along the back of his belt. Set. As set as I'll ever be. Glancing out from behind the boulder for an instant, he turned back around and wondered how he might make it up to the pines where Josiah was knocked out. He looked around him for something, anything. He saw it. Scooting on his buttocks back along the boulder, he reached for the elk-hide coat and dragged it toward him across the snow.

Make him waste a shot, he decided. Give me a few seconds to make it up the hill to where Josiah is. Where Josiah is needing me. Grasping onto the collar with his left hand he dragged it behind him to the edge of the rock. Bass checked the frizzen's position over the pan again and brought the left arm violently forward, flinging the coat into the air right in front of the boulder.

He was off across the snow as he heard the lead slam into the rock behind him. He scrambled up the side of the slope. The seconds ticked off inside his mind, the seconds McAfferty would use to reload. He was sweating already. Not even halfway yet. Move, you old man, move! He fell to his knees and clawed to get back to his feet. Move, goddammit! Move your old ass!

"Josiah!"

He heard the word crash around him again, heard it bounce back and forth over him as it had before, not knowing where it had come from as he fell again.

"I'm comin' for you!"

Then he realized he was yelling. It was his voice he heard all around him, coming back again and again and again from the hills and canyon walls. It was his lungs that ached from the exertion, his throat that was raw from the strain of his promise.

"Jo-si-ah! I'm comin' for you! I'm comin' for you, boy!"

He slid through the snow the last few yards as he started to stumble again, and crashed through the low branches of the pine. The rifle in his hand was held high and caught on the snow-capped limbs; Bass was twisted around before he came to a stop within the cover of the trees.

"Aw——" The rest caught in his throat.

The young man had been thrown several feet from where Bass finally landed. Face down in the snow, the rifle lay across the back of Paddock's head where it had come to rest after its spinning, twisting journey.

Quickly Titus began sliding toward the body, pushing himself across the soft powder with his legs and left arm. Dragging himself to the boy, he started to touch the young trapper, but stopped and pulled back his hand. Instead, he knocked the rifle away into the white powder with his left arm; the weapon bounced against the overhanging limbs so that some of the snow on the branches fell across Bass and the body. He dusted it off.

"Aww, boy," he whispered.

Scratch grabbed the wide collar of the capote and tugged Paddock over, rolling him on his back. He stared down into the young face for a moment, then dusted the snow from Josiah's brow and beard. The head hung limp. The eyelids were lightly closed. No look of pain marked the face with its twisted nose. No agony from the wound twisted the lips. Bass ripped open the front of the blanket coat and pulled the loose sash down so that he could expose the chest.

His hand felt the wetness before he saw it. Bass brought his hand up and stared at the fingers, studying the faint red film on his palm. He pulled the right side of the coat back more and saw it. The hole in the right breast, just above and outside the nipple. A dark brown was spreading around it. Seeping slowly. Like years slipping through his fingers. The stain against Paddock's buckskin shirt was growing, slowly discoloring the leath-

669

er. Like slow-motion ripples in a still pool, the blood seeped from the wound.

He suddenly brought his head down to the chest and listened briefly. He could not hear the heart. Bass pulled a knife from his belt and sliced down the new seam in the front of Josiah's shirt as best he could. Yanking the cut sinew apart, Titus again put his head to the chest. It did not move for him. His cheek felt no rustle of breathtaking. His ear heard no heartbeat. He brought his head up with a jerk to stare at the face again, the head lying on its side in the snow.

His eyes dropped slowly to the wound, which oozed bubbly, frothy blood. Gradually he began to pull the shirt back together over the bare skin. Then the coat. Scratch straightened it as well as he could and patted the chest with the left hand.

"You come . . . come so far," he whispered, turning so that he might sit by the body. He stared past the pine boughs across the slope where he thought McAfferty might be. "So far, Josiah."

Bass continued to study the side of the hill while his mind began to wander. Glancing down at the body stretched beside him, the old trapper struggled to pull the arms free so they could be folded across Paddock's chest. Finally the weight of the body was no longer on the arms and it was done.

"Better," he whispered. "That's better."

He saw the small red stain on the snow that had been covered by the right arm. Small, so small—like the wound. Man gets hit in the lights, however . . . well, he wouldn't think any more about it.

"Long way, Josiah." Scratch gazed back along the hill. "Them squeaky boots of your'n an' that belt you had cinched up an' pinchin' round a empty belly." He started to laugh but found himself starting to cry. "Come a long way, son. Long way with me."

It finally clutched him tightly enough that he could no longer fight it. Slowly the tears came at first, stinging until they broke loose to pour down the wrinkled cheeks. The sobbing was low, quiet. He tried to confine the noise of it within his wheezing chest and coughed against the lump rising at the base of his throat. The boy's gone. Ain't gonna . . . ain't gonna be with me . . . and Hannah too. He blinked away some of the moisture and glanced down the hill to the mule's carcass across the snow. Hannah too. She were old, anyway. Maybe better to go under like this—not growing old so she cain't see, maybe cain't hear me when I call.

He shook with the sobs as they returned, looking back at the young trapper's body beside him. He wiped his nostrils along the sleeve of the shirt and sucked some of the mucous back into his nose. Your nose ain't hurting you now, is it, son? Least now you won't have it hurting you none. Not now.

Bass reached up and gently touched the twisted nose, seeing the small trickle of red at the corner of Josiah's lips. He went to wipe it away but it stuck to the flesh and the whiskers. Frozen.

"I was comin' for you," he hoarsely whispered against the sobs. "You jest had to hol't on lil' longer, Josiah. Jest a lil' longer. I was comin' for you." He brushed some of the long brown hair back from the cheek. "Tol't you I was comin' for you. It were a damned-fool thing you done to yourself. I was comin'—"

"Mr. Bass!"

The sharp voice cracked the air to interrupt him. Scratch jerked his head and brought the rifle up. He waited as the sob and his breath caught against his ribs.

"Mr. Bass!"

It had moved away a little. The voice. Back along the hill away from them. Away from him and Josiah. A good cry. That's what he'd had himself. He had gone ahead and let it all out. Just busted out bawling like a lost buffalo calf. And he felt better for it.

"Mr. Bass!"

McAfferty's words echoed farther away now. He's moving away from us, Josiah. Don't have to worry none. I've had me my cry and my heart is stronger for it. I've had me my cry. You don't have to worry about me, friend. Don't have to worry—

" 'Thou hast also given me the necks of me enemies; that I might destroy them that hate me!' "

Scratch parted the folds of the red blanket coat and felt along the belt until his fingers touched the pistol. He brought it out and held it in his left palm, gazing at the shiny brass, the delicate engraving and inlays. Flipping the frizzen back and looking at the charge, he pulled it back against the flint. He slipped it into his belt and slung the pouch over it. Fancy damned thing. St. Louis parley-voo pistol. Weren't much good, anyway. He patted it, then glanced at Josiah as if to say thank you.

"The Lord thy God, *'He teacheth me hands to war, so that a bow of steel is broken by my arms!'*"

He looked back across the snow as McAfferty's words faded against the hills. Wiping his nose a last time, Bass took a deep breath and let it out slowly. He wasn't really angry with himself for having the cry. It had been a long time coming. It had done him some good. Now he felt the emptiness inside him ready for McAfferty. The tears were gone. He was ready.

Bass turned to gaze at the body. He readjusted the young trapper's arms so that they lay neatly across the lower chest, and straightened the big collar of the red blanket coat. For a moment Scratch touched Josiah's brow, then slowly let his fingers descend down the cheek. He removed his hand, rose to his knees, and crawled out to the edge of the pine branches.

"*'The wicked plotteth against the just, an' gnasheth upon him with his teeth!'*"

Asa was moving on, farther up the hill. Climbing through the snow, past the thick stands of pine and brush along the canyon wall, Bass decided he would move straight up the hill with McAfferty. Not right behind him. Over here though. He turned and whispered, "You was worth the trouble you meant me, Josiah Paddock. Knowin' you . . . it were well worth the trouble." Scratch left the overhanging limbs and began his crawl up the hill.

He could see the split patches of light blue between the pines above him. Close to the top now. The sun was up. Would be awhile yet getting to where it would warm his bones. But then he would feel better. Long time coming until the bright, yellow fingers would touch Josiah's body. Just as well, perhaps. Perhaps. Stay back in the dark under that tree. Critters won't get the body that way. Drag it away. Unless they smell the boy. Not that soon, he decided. Won't smell that soon in this cold. But he would just have to see that the body was put up in a tree before he headed back. Before he left.

Bass stopped a moment just below the top of the rise. Was he going to leave the young trapper's body behind? Would that be what he would do? He was confused and shook his head. Not thinking too clear, are you, old man?

Mind is giving way on you. What you was afraid of too. It slipping away on you. Along with your time.

Asa's still got the power over this thing. He's got control over his time. Calling all the shots, he is. You'd better start thinking about that. Push the other things behind you for now. Like getting the boy buried proper. That would have to wait. Take things slow and easy, one at a time. One at a time.

He saw the movement then. Just something out of the corner of his eye. Up along the top. To his right. Bass held his breath for a few moments, squinting as he studied the place where he had seen it move. He would wait for the nigger to move again. Then he saw McAfferty. It was not so much the man he saw as the flashes of movement behind the pine branches.

Scratch heard him too. The soft, padding steps as the man trotted through the timber toward the top of the hill. To where there were no trees to give him cover. Bass moved up against the side of the large pine and leaned against it. He brought the rifle up and laid it against the trunk, looking down the barrel with the muzzle pointed where he was figuring Asa would leave the trees to race across the open patch in trying to reach the other side.

As the whitehair emerged from cover, he seemed to explode from the pines as he moved across the powder. Scratch studied him for an instant along the barrel of the rifle as the front blade moved with the target. Ain't got him a coat on neither. He's stripped himself for the fight. Then the finger twitched before he was ready, and he watched McAfferty dive down the opposite side of the hill before the smoke from the muzzle billowed out to obscure his line of sight on the target.

When the air was clear he blinked his eyes at the top of the hill. It was empty. He wasn't sure if he had hit McAfferty. The way the man had dropped right out of sight. He could be lying on the other side. Dead. Maybe with a hole in him. Maybe only waiting for me to come see. Better move, he thought, glancing into the green boughs to notice the gray-white smoke hanging delicately within the pines. Better move. He put his hand into the pouch at his side and brought out three lead balls. Popping them into his mouth, Titus rose to a low crouch and skittered to his right toward the top. Slow. He did not want to go directly to the top. He would circle around a little. And wait.

By the time he had crossed over Asa's trail to the crest of the hill, Bass was wheezing. The fingers were tightening on his chest, squeezing between his ribs as he fought against them for air. Too old for this anymore. He slid down against the trunk of a large tree and listened awhile. Must have got him, he considered. Must have blown him over the top.

Gradually the breathing came easier and he noticed the patch of sunlight on the snow near his feet. It's getting there. The sun. I can be in it soon. Get warm again. Shake this thing on my chest. Shake it loose from me. Scratch started wheezing again a little and coughed to force the fist from his body. It helped a little.

" 'For the wrath of man worketh not the righteousness of God.' "

He jerked around and lay flat on his belly. The words had come from over the hill. He knew then he had not killed McAfferty. Knew that Asa had waited for him to come check. But he had tired of waiting. Felt like flapping his jaws some more. Got tired of waiting. Just like he got tired of the chase, too. Moved south down here instead of running to the Blackfoots. But then, Asa was ready to die. He had decided somewhere back there—wherever a man argued with himself over something like that. And he had decided.

More than he could say for himself. He hadn't thought about it that much. Just figured with Hannah and the boy taken from him, might as well be his time too. Might as well.

"Damn! Wish't I were a better shot." He cursed himself. "Wish't I—"

" 'By thee have I been holden up from the womb: thou are he that took me out of my mother's bowels.' "

The voice had drifted over the opposite side some more. Farther away. He's going to let me follow until he's ready. For me or him. Then he'll decide that. All I know is that it don't matter no more. Not now.

Bass had finished reloading and leaned back against the trunk with a sigh. He closed his eyes a minute, feeling the air moving in and out of his lungs. Boy wasn't moving air when I touched him. Heart wasn't ticking neither. He opened his eyes again to find himself staring at the growing patch of sunlight on the snow. It gave the powder a faint, delicate yellow cast, not as dark as when a man would urinate on it. Scratch studied it more and more until he knew for sure what he felt like doing.

Rising slowly with his left hand against the trunk to help push himself up, he stepped out into the patch of bright light and faced the east. So warm on his face. He closed his eyes as he faced the sun. So warm, pouring over him like a hot-spring bath by the Stinking Water. His arms came up from his sides until they were held straight out from his shoulders. He breathed deeply the air into his lungs. The air was warmer here.

"Bia tsimbic da-sasua," he said quietly the first time. Almost like a prayer at first, it seemed to him. He said it louder now: "It is a good day to die." He sucked in a big breath and yelled, "Bia tsim——"

" 'The heathen are sunk down in the pit that they made: in the net which they hid is their own foot taken.' "

Bia tsimbic da-sa——"

"Mr. Bass!"

"... da-sasua!"

"Mr. Bass!" The whitehair's voice cut the air again. "There's little time for that now!"

Little time? Shit! You're the fine one to be talking about time, McAfferty. "Bia tsimbic da-sasua!" he yelled once more. You're the fine one. When you've gone and picked this place and this time. You've picked it.

"Titus Bass! There be little time left! 'Whatsoever thy hand findeth to do, do it with thy might; for there is no work, no device, no knowledge, no wisdom in the grave, wither thou goest!' "

Scratch opened his eyes slowly and nodded toward the sun above. It was better now. Then he moved to the top of the hill where McAfferty had dashed across the bare spot in the snow.

"McAfferty!" he sang out. "McAfferty! McAfferty! McAfferty!" Bass hollered to the tops of the pines as he dashed across the open spot and started down the slope on the other side.

The blast roared below him and he saw the white puff of smoke sprout out of the trees just as he slipped to his side and rolled down the hill. Scratch twisted and turned in the snow, feeling the snow skidding up his sleeves, dusting the inside of his leggings and breechclout. He finally came to a stop against some bushes and slid behind them so that he would be on the uphill side of the thick brush.

"Damn you, Bass!" McAfferty yelled out. " *'Deliver me not over to the will of mine enemies! Deliver me from blood-guiltiness, O God, thou God of me salvation.'* "

"I come to take you, McAfferty!"

He dashed away from the bush and skittered across the dry snow to a stand of pine. Sure now, he was, the man had only one gun. Below him, beyond where he calculated Asa stood, the narrow gorge grew into a box. The walls would rise as they descended, towering over them both now. Has him only one gun. Bass wanted to stay in the sunlight. Better than the darkness for his bones, for his lights.

"I'm comin' for you, McAfferty!"

The canyon boxed itself in, and the two of them with it. Bass would use it, as McAfferty must be thinking too. He would work the side of the hill to stay above the nigger. Work down on him. Work him into the end of the small rock-rimmed bowl.

" *'O wretched man that I am! Who shall deliver me from the body of this death?'* " Asa's voice was not quite as sharp now, not quite as loud, as it bounded from wall to wall within the bowl. "Was hopin' they'd be sendin' 'em some braves after me, Mr. Bass." He paused a few moments. "Mr. Bass?"

"I hear you, McAfferty!" His voice was louder than he thought it would be.

"Said, I was hopin' they'd be sendin' 'em some braves after me—them Crow." He paused. "S'pose I knew it'd be you that'd come."

"An' Josiah?" He stopped behind a tree to listen.

"The boy? Didn' mean to kill him. Truly didn', Mr. Bass. An' afore, I took me a bead on Hannah, thinkin' it was you as was ridin' her."

"Kilt her too, McAfferty—her too!"

"Had to be, Mr. Bass. Had to be," he replied. " *'My wounds stink an' are rotten 'cause of me foolishness!'* Had to be. I had me somethin' took from me. The mule was . . . jest to even up the score. Don' you see, Mr. Bass? Don' you see it now?"

He could hear Asa moving farther down into the

676

bowl, and toward the northeast where the walls grew higher, and narrowed in to tower above the men. Bass moved to his left to stay above the whitehair, cautiously skittering from tree to tree. He followed the words as they were spoken; followed the other sounds when he could hear them. He watched McAfferty when he could see the man, able to catch only fleeting glimpses of the buckskins against the dark background of the trees. Like a ghost flitting from parapet to parapet along ancient castle walls.

"No," he finally answered. "I don' see it, McAfferty. Don' see why you kilt Hannah!" He looked behind him at the edge of the sunlight along the western edge of the bowl. It was back there now. He had left the sunlight. Left it behind.

"'Wash me thoroughly from me iniquity, an' cleanse me from me sin; me sin is ever afore me.' I wasn't worthy, Mr. Bass. I'd sinned against the Lord an' had somethin' great in me heart took from me. The squaw... the squaw was took from me. 'Against thee, thee only, have I sinned, an' done this evil thing in thy sight.'"

He had watched Asa stop. At least he could not see or hear any more movement. "You took from me 'cause your God took from you, McAfferty? That it? That the meat of it?"

"Man gets old, Mr. Bass," he replied. "Man gets old an' finds him a woman what loves him—a woman what he can love back, fin'ly. Man were ready to stay on the path of the Lord for her—an' she were took from him. With the baby. That man's baby!"

Scratch dropped a few yards down the slope along the run of trees growing beside a small erosion cut. He could get closer, closer still. Keep the man talking. Just keep the man talking and work his way up on McAfferty.

"It fin'ly come down to jest you an' me, Mr. Bass?"

It sounded close to Titus now, the voice. But then Scratch heard the padding of moccasins across the snow and knew Asa was moving up the side of the bowl across from him. To get to McAfferty now would mean having to go all the way back, all the way around the side of the bowl to stay above him. That, or drop on down into the bottom.

"Jest you an' me now, McAfferty," he yelled back, then looked over his shoulder at the side of the hill above him. There the sun splashed its light on the snow and through the trees. It would be warm back there, if he went the long way around. Bass gazed down at the bottom of the bowl where the debris of deadfall and hundreds of boulders were strewn in the snow. Might make it through the bottom, with them rocks for cover. Might. It was cool down there. He decided he really did not need the warmth of the sun any longer. He realized he was sweating.

"For the woman. Mr. Bass. This is for the woman!"

Scratch moved off within the trees until he was near the bottom of the small bowl where the pines stopped, where the boulders and snow and deadfall took their places. Deadfall. Hurdles and obstacles he would have to dodge and climb over on his way. He looked back up at the sunlight once again, then decided he had made his choice. He would cross the bottom.

Vaulting out from the pines Titus scurried across the snow in a half-crouch, zigzagging back and forth in the new powder as he dashed toward the first boulder that would give him some cover. He leaped over the trunk of a dead tree and heard the clunk of the ball land in the wood. It hit right beside the spot where his left hand had pushed him over the obstacle before he heard the muffled blast of his opponent's weapon. He rolled to the side of the boulder on his belly. Tucking the rifle butt against his shoulder and bringing the muzzle down on the movement back in the trees, Bass squeezed the trigger.

Bass now rolled to his left behind the boulder, flipped over twice, and stuck his head out from behind the rock to check on the shot he had made. He heard the crashing as McAfferty ran through the trees and brush above him. Damn! Still moving. To the left. *Damn!*

Scratch rolled behind the boulder again and sat up with his back against it. He yanked the powderhorn to his chest and shoved the butt of the rifle away from him in the snow. Pulling the stopper from the horn, Scratch put it against the muzzle, then thought better of it. Shit! He poured the powder down the muzzle. No pieces of burning patch in the barrel. Wasn't using patches now anyway. He let the horn fall back against his side. He pulled the muzzle to his lips and spit one of the balls into the end of the barrel, then yanked the wiping stick from its thimbles on the underside of the stock. He rammed the ball home against the powder and brought the stick out. One more ball against his cheek, caressing it with the tongue. Slipping the ramrod into his left hand with the rifle so that he would have it ready for the next load, Bass poured the priming powder into the pan and snapped down the frizzen.

Scooting to his right once more to follow what his ears picked up, Scratch saw the man moving slowly up the side of the hill. Getting a climb on me to get out of range. Try to make the top. Titus stretched out on his belly, then took the wiping stick and jammed it into the snow. He wiggled it quickly back and forth to test its steadiness as he glanced for an instant at the figure moving slowly up the steep slope. Fighting the snow too, ain't you, McAfferty. Not just me.

Bass bought the bottom of the fullstock down on the top of the wiping stick so that he could grip the top of the ramrod while the fingers of that left hand steadied the weapon on it. Easing his shoulder against the buttplate, Bass took a deep breath and moved the front blade up across the snow. Right on the small, dim figure. He brought the hammer back, let out his breath slowly, and pulled.

His shoulder felt strange from the imperceptible shock against it as the rifle roared. Bass thought it was the load. He hadn't measured it. Too much powder. Man gets to know his rifle, his own loads too. Knows when something ain't right. Like an old friend you know too well, a rifle could be.

The smoke hung over him. He let the rifle drop off the wiping stick and set his chin down in the snow so that he could study the side of the hill below the gray-white cloud. He watched McAfferty slip and lose the hold on his rifle. Strange, he thought, how he liked watching the man sliding backward down the slope, slowly rolling over on his back. Slipping in the snow behind his rifle. Down through the white like a dark tiny bug he could not see clearly.

He watched until Asa disappeared into the brush near the bottom. Might have winged him. He then rolled behind his boulder to reload. Last ball in his mouth. When the powder was poured down the muzzle and that ball spit into the barrel, he remembered the wiping stick at the side of the rock. After reflecting a moment, Bass lay out on the snow and stuck his leg around the edge, kicking at the ramrod. No good. He would have to try with a hand. Bit by bit his arm crawled across the white until his shoulders slipped past the edge of the boulder. Made a good target now. His fingers finally touched it and he shot back behind his cover. His gun primed, and hammer drawn back, Bass tucked the ramrod down along the barrel in his left hand and rose to his knees. He listened for a few minutes and heard McAfferty moving through the brush above him again. Back toward the top.

Angered that he had missed such an easy shot at that black bug on the snow, Bass stood suddenly and ran from the boulder. He dodged rocks and crawled over the dead-fall between him and the side of the slope. He came to a stop behind the boulder before the hill rose away from him. Rest. Just a minute. Let his breath catch up with him. He waited and closed his eyes, listening to those faint sounds that came every now and then to his ears— Asa moving away from him up the hill. Never had him a clear eye on the man. Either he was a ghost moving the trees across the hill, or he was a small, dim spot against the snow. Never had seen McAfferty that well.

Old man's eyes giving out on him. Going dim at the end of his day, end of his time. Use them while you have them. For as long as you have them left to you. He wasn't sure what made him do it, even when he realized what he had done. But Titus stood up and moved around the side of the large granite boulder. He could hear Asa all the better here, standing out in the open as he was. And making a good target of himself to boot. McAfferty could pick him off if he wanted to. But he remained right where he stood, outlined against the white powder background, beside the gray granite symbol of security.

After a few minutes he could hear nothing more of the whitehair. No more noise of a man moving through the brush along the side of the hill, no more the evidence of his slipping and fighting along in the snow. Bass had been a long time in the open too, daring Asa to take a shot at him. A long time. And he hadn't shot back.

Pushing away from the side of the boulder, Bass stepped to the slope and climbed toward the spot where he had last seen the whitehair fall. He stopped a few times to catch his breath, bending at his waist and letting the air come into his body in large doses. He even stepped from the cover of the trees to look up the side of the hill. Give him a good target again. But still McAfferty hadn't taken advantage of the frequent opportunities.

A little to his left he saw the path of disturbed snow where Asa had slid down the hill and moved quickly over to it. No tracks, just the marks of the slide. He dropped down along the path until he saw it. McAfferty's rifle. the nigger run off and left his rifle. Scratch looked slowly up the slope to follow the moccasin prints as they climbed through the trees to disappear above him. Now he shook his head from side to side. Nigger's really wanting to die. Wanting to die bad. Leaving his rifle behind like this.

Stooping to pick up the whitehair's weapon, Bass knelt to his knees and laid his own rifle against a thigh. He pulled the frizzen back and found the pan still had powder in it, though it had been dusted with snow. Wet. Bass pulled back on the hammer to play with it.

"Shit!" he whispered under his breath and glanced up the hill. "Lock's broke. Jest left it here. Took off an' left a busted gun behin't." Scratch rose and took the barrel of his own weapon in the fingers of the right hand. He let the whitehair's rifle slip from his grasp with the left. It fell silently into the powder near his feet. There was a quick, faint whistle in the air; he felt something bite into his thigh just below the hip.

He staggered and fell backward, and began to roll down the slope. Just like McAfferty. Over and over he tumbled across the snow toward the bottom of the bowl. Didn't hear him shoot me. Man never carried a pistol, what he knew of. The burning in the meat of his right thigh bit at him again and again as he whirled down the hill. He did not try to stop his fall. He was confused. Just a whistle, he thought. Just a little whistle cutting through the air before it bit the leg.

"The bow!" he yelled.

He had forgotten the bow. He rolled over to claw vainly at the soft powder. Furiously he now slashed at the snow beneath him as he slipped down, down, farther down. The bow! He had forgotten McAfferty had the bow with him. Stupid nigger he was. He hadn't even noticed it when he examined McAfferty's plunder. Hadn't even seen it was gone. How was he to know? From the carcass of the pony, behind the saddle, those footprints now loomed in his mind. One time to circle the dead pony and head up the hill. How was he to know? He hadn't been looking for something like that. The bow! And the nigger's good with the goddamned thing.

He came to a crashing halt against the boulder he had left minutes before. The leg burned. Breathing hard, hurting everywhere, he put his mind to feel. The leg dominated his thoughts as he lay crumpled against the boulder. Nigger's got me dead to rights now. He slowly moved his left hand around to feel for his rifle. Back up the hill.

He would have to look. Finally he moved his eyes to gaze down at the leg. Just below the bottom of the hunting shirt he saw the dark ring beginning to bubble and grow, slowly enlarging across the leather legging. In the center of the dark stain was the ragged stub of the arrow shaft that had broken off during his downhill tumble. He ran the right index finger over the splinters of the broken shaft, wiggling it a little.

The sparks shot into his eyes, blinding him, and he felt the claw wrench at his stomach. It robbed him of breath, just as he had begun to get it back. He decided against shaking the shaft anymore. He stared at the few splinters of wood peeking out of the hole in the leg. The stain continued to grow like petals radiating from the blossom.

Looking back up the hill where he had left the rifle as he fell, Bass did not think he could make the climb again. He puffed more slowly now as breathing became regular once more. He looked back at the leg. Gotta do something with it.

He took a knife from his belt and began methodically to slice fringe from those remaining on his leggings. He laid them neatly across his lap as they were released from the seam. Quickly he wove them into a long thick whang to tie around the leg, then slipped it beneath the thigh a few inches above the splinters. Bass put a knot in it and pulled the whang tight against the pain that chewed through him. Both hands struggled against the end of the cord.

Scratch grabbed the knife again and cut a small slice in the legging, moving up, then down, from the hole. Not good enough. The whang by itself wasn't good enough. At least the blood wasn't pumping out of the hole. At least that. But still it continued to ooze from the hole. From his pouch he took the small knife he used to cut patches and set it on the top of the first knot in the whang. Both cold hands put another knot over the knife, then a third to secure it. Moving the handle around and around in a circle, Scratch watched the bleeding from the wound slow. Then it stopped.

He held the patch knife down with his wrist and wrapped the ends of the whang around the loop that had first circled the leg, finishing with several knots so that the knife would stay in place to control the red ooze. He wiggled his toes. They weren't numb from the loss of blood or circulation. Then he knew he would have to move, for he heard a faint rustle in the trees above him.

"'One generation passeth away, an' 'nother generation cometh: but the earth abideth forever.'"

He had to move. Scooting back, Scratch bumped against the rock and turned quickly. Gotta get up. His fingers tried to bite into the granite as he pushed himself up on the left leg, holding the right one out from the hip. Gasping, the old man hobbled around the side of the boulder just as another whistle passed by his arm. He collapsed behind the boulder, struggling to fight the gray mist crawling into his mind.

"'The sun also riseth, an' the sun goeth down, an' hastens to his place where he arose.'"

Not only the words now, but also the footsteps. He heard them coming down the slope. Bass knew he had to move again. Even before he had caught his breath. He shoved himself away from the boulder and stumbled onto the bottom of the bowl. He hopped on the one good leg and swung the right one out, letting it touch the ground to steady him in his bouncing march through the snow.

"'The wind goeth toward the south, an' turneth about unto the north; it whirleth about continually, an' the wind returneth again accordin' to his circuits.'"

The sun was just reaching the flat, open bottom of the bowl. It was coming to him. All he had to do was reach out for it. He could make it. He had to. McAfferty's voice was close behind him. Probably just on the other side of the boulder. He'll see the blood and know I'm a critter set for the skinning. He'll know for sure now.

Just gotta make it to the sun. Just make it to the warm. Be all right then. Everything be all right then.

"'The wind goeth toward the south, an' turneth about unto the north.'"

Closer he's coming. Behind me. I feel him. Gotta look behind me now. Bass turned and looked over his shoulder. Can't see him. Like a ghost you can't see. You just feel him.

" 'It whirleth about continually.' "

Just to the edge of the yellow light. Just to the sun and he would be all right. The large, dead tree blocked his way. He slid to a stop and looked to the left. Then to the right. The sun and warmth and yellow were straight ahead. Right over the deadfall.

The pain pierced him. Can't stop. It'll catch up with you. The hurting. It'll catch you. Move, old man. Move. Scratch fell forward against the dead tree, his tired arms crawling to pull himself over on his left side. Into the warm. Into the sun. Feeling the yellow pour over him. Feeling the pain against his ribs.

Bass wondered if he had broken any ribs in the fall. Like Josiah's pony. Asa was coming to put him out of his misery now. Just shoot me. Don't slit my throat. Go ahead and shoot me. He had to get off the ribs if they were broken. He couldn't breathe like this. He was in the warm yellow now and should be breathing better. Bass decided he would have to move off the pain in his right side.

Slowly rolling onto his left side, he brought the remaining fingers of the right hand up to the rib cage near his shoulder and started down. One at a time he counted the bones, feeling them carefully to check for the broken ones. His fingers hit the butt of the pistol and stopped. Didn't remember the thing. Fancy thing. He thought he had lost it somewhere. Back up the hill. From where McAfferty was coming—coming for him.

One at a time the two fingers left on the hand and the thumb clumsily encircled the pistol butt and pulled the weapon from his belt. His thumb reached up and pulled the hammer back. Only thing left me now. He ain't gonna cut my throat. Just shoot—shoot myself before that. He brought his chin off the snow and looked at the edge of the yellow moving past him, down his body slowly, brushing him with the warm light in wide, bold strokes. Just lay here on your belly and let it wash over you. Let it warm your bones, old man.

"Mr. Bass."

The voice was close. Scratch twisted his neck so that he could look over his left shoulder. Asa stood on the dead tree right behind him. The whitehair moved a little to his left along the top of the fallen pine and stopped. He stared down at Bass, his eyes narrow. The bowstring was taut as the iron hook pulled back on the arrow. Can't let him cut my goddamned throat! Gonna have to do it, do it myself. Shoot.

"'He hath bent his bow an' made it ready.'" McAfferty was not smiling within the white hair on his face. "An' the Lord's seen to it I had me one last arrow for what was needin' done. My last." He waved the weapon a little, the single shaft stretching the bowstring.

Bass could not take his eyes off the man standing over him. Always he had looked down upon the short whitehair. Always. And now McAfferty towered over him like the canyon walls. Titus watched the pale yellow light pushing the shadows back, pushing them up the dead tree to where Asa stood, moving toward the whitehair's feet. Don't want my throat cut. Shoot, shoot myself first.

"Didn't mean to kill the boy," he began. "Want you to know that now, Mr. Bass. S'pose I always knew you'd be the one comin' after me, always knew it'd be you. An' when I seen the thing move in the trees, I had me no choice but what to shoot. I'd thought it was you, Mr. Bass. Didn't mean to kill me the boy, though. But this was to be somethin' 'tween the two of us. Aye, Mr. Bass. Jest you an' me. So it evened itself out, I s'pose, killin' young Josiah. Evened things up, like killin' Hannah for you."

Scratch watched the yellow climbing up the dead tree, moving across the gray wood, splintered and split in places. The light was reaching for McAfferty's feet. Bass moved his eyes back and forth, up and down: from Asa's lips, to the arrow pointed at him, to the rising light stretching for the whitehair's moccasins.

"It may be that it were a prophecy from the Lord," McAfferty continued. "The night in the Crow village I talked with young Josiah. Tol' him of the Bible tale of one he was named for. Aye, a young king Josiah, what ruled all of ol' Judah. Tol't the boy 'bout how the king was wantin' to fight so bad he went out dressed up as 'nother man. An' got himself kilt. The word, Mr. Bass. The word tol't 'bout it then. An' it's come to pass. The good Lord tol't it to be. You see? All this. An' now I'm headin' west, toward the big salt once't more. Wind's blowin' me that way, It brung the two of us here, an' I'll be the one what walks from this place."

The light had crawled to the wood just below the moccasins. Bass swallowed hard and saw the bowstring stretch back, tighter as the hooked arm pulled away from him.

"I'll be the one what the Lord's chose to carry the wind—"

Scratch rolled onto his right side and pulled the trigger. The pistol was close to his ear, deafening the trapper for a moment with its blast. He had not worried about the load. And not about the priming. Funny, the things a man thinks about after he's fired. The boom returned again and again to his head, bouncing back and forth across the bowl.

He watched McAfferty's mouth open wider. It started to move up and down slowly, forming no words, making no sounds. Gradually the hooked arm moved forward, slowly, until the string was taut no more. The bow sagged and pointed at the ground, releasing the arrow into the snow. Scratch looked at the eyes, wide and dark against the white hair. Two black pebbles set in the snow. His mouth moved but nothing came out. The hook climbed across the chest to the wound. McAfferty weaved a bit and pitched forward, straight toward Bass. The bow tumbled from his grasp.

Asa's body fell across him, knocking the wind from his lungs. He felt the pain at the side of his head, high up on the cheek. It ran from the corner of his eye into his whiskers along the left side of his face. The light was gone from him. It was dark again. And he could not breathe. He tried, but felt smothered by the darkness that reeked of sage. He wanted to escape the crushing weight of the thing on him. His chest heaved, yet he could swallow no air.

Its spirit had returned for him. The bear had landed on him!

Bass began to claw and push at the darkness of the weight over him. No trembling now as there had been before—the last time. No frozen, immobilizing fear now. In desperation, Scratch struggled with the darkness smothering him. He fought to free his head, to suck at the glorious, clean air, to yank it into his lungs. He had to have it to fight the thing pinning him to the ground.

He had to be free of it before it rose at last to claw and rake his face again. He would not think of the pain along his cheek. It was small compared to the size of his heart, Scratch thought. Push it from me. Get it off me.

"Wa-a-a-a-a-gh-gh-gh-gh-gh-gh-gh!"

The sound leaped from his throat as he pushed against the dark prison about him. Now one arm was free. His right. The two remaining fingers and the thumb clutched the pistol tightly as the arm flailed at the darkness suffocating him. Savagely he battered at it. He was fighting for his life. He must beat the thing away.

"Wa-a-a-a-a-gh-gh-gh-gh-gh-gh-gh!"

Whipping his head back and forth, Scratch tugged and pulled at the ground to move away from it. Just get out from beneath it.

"Wa-a-a-a-a-gh-gh-gh-gh-gh-gh-gh!"

The battle cry did not echo from the hills. It was stifled by the dark weight over him. It was smothered at his lips. The thing could not hear his challenge this way. It would not know he had the medicine on him. He whipped his head back and forth, trying to free his face from the deep odor of sage smoke, the thick suffocating cloud swelling over him. He had to let it know he had medicine.

"Wa-a-a-a-a-gh-gh-gh-gh-gh-gh-gh-gh-! Wa-a-a-a-gh-gh-gh—" He moved the thing and his left hand felt the belt. The medicine animal had no—

He tugged on the strap of leather and felt it moving again. Bass stopped and waited. Seconds ran together into a beaded thong of time. He knew he was moving the thing from him. It was not beating with a life of its own. He was moving it.

He lifted the thing from his body, pushed it aside into the trampled snow. As the ugly darkness moved from his face, warm light streamed over him again. And air. Pure, sweet, glorious air. He pulled it into his lungs, starving for the feel of it filling his chest. He sucked at the cool flow. Never had anything tasted so good. Never had he been so starved for its nourishment.

The sinister weight gone, Bass rolled to his side. On

his elbows and one knee, he dragged the right leg, clawing himself inches away from it. Bass let his forehead collapse slowly against the snow. The touch was cool. Good. He waited until the flow of air into his hungry chest came easier; it tasted honey-sweet along his tongue, like heaven in his mind.

The pain at the left side of his eye nagged. Scratch reached out to scoop some of the white cold into his left hand and lightly touched it to his cheek. It burned with the eye. Slowly he brought the snow from his flesh and looked at the hand. The white was stained with the red of paint, war paint. The color of revenge for the Crow.

He threw it away and scooped more into his hand, bringing it to the burning rivulet along the side of his face. He felt the snow melting and brought the hand from his flesh. More red. He needed more white now. White for the fire in his face. Over and over he scooped the snow with his hand and lightly brushed it across the corner of his left eye and over his cheek. His hand was now flecked with red paint. Like splattered blood when a man smashes a tomahawk into a skull.

Gradually he turned to look back across the snow at the dark thing that had smothered him. The old man recognized the body stretched over the white. It was a man. McAfferty. He had won, and remembered. The moving mouth with no sound slipping from it. The wide, disbelieving eyes. The bow slipping from the hand as the whitehair tumbled toward him. He remembered, and crawled to the body.

Reaching out to roll the man over, Bass blinked. The pain shot back into his eyes, searing the side of his face with torment. Scratch looked down the arm and let a finger touch the iron hook, covered with the red paint of revenge, a small strip of flesh still clinging to the cold metal. The blood was frozen as he wiped the finger over the hook. The claw. The medicine bear had scraped his flesh again, to mark him once more. The wolf claw had taken the sacrifice of flesh, and in revenge, let the blood flow as freely as red paint.

The dark stain on the buckskins below the hook spoke mutely of the life that had seeped from the hole in the chest. He knew the bullet had smashed bone, sending splinters and fragments shooting through the lungs with it, the shards of death tearing through the body to rob it of life. A hole like the boy's. A dark splash against the flesh with the blood rippling out around it. A dark pool that sucked life from the body.

Slipping his knife from the belt, his hand passed over the second sheath, an empty one. Two knives always needed on the trail. One remained behind where he had stopped the flow of blood from his body. He pulled the whitehair toward him so that the body rolled onto its stomach, and took the fur cap from the lifeless form. Quickly gathering the white hair into his hand before he might decide not to go through with it, Scratch twisted the long locks into a tight strand and pricked the flesh with the point of the blade. The knife circled the skull quickly. Placing his left knee on the back of the neck, Bass yanked at the hair until it began to rip free from the bone. Not just the topknot. The whole scalp he must take. It involved time, and patience beyond what he thought he would now have. Finally the white hair and pink-red flesh hung loosely in his left hand, wafting easily on the breeze that lightly tugged at the scalp.

Bass rose and held it up to the sun climbing out of the east. He turned toward the warm, yellow light. Then he raised the right hand with the knife toward the bright orb, its warmth pervading him.

"For you, this is done," he spoke in Crow. "For you it is over now. No more. It is over now." He closed his eyes, letting the heavy lids slide down slowly against the intense light, feeling the warmth caress his cheeks.

"Arapooesh!" he yelled at the top of his lungs. "McAfferty!" His arms were outstretched in an offering to the sun. "Josiah! Josiah! Josiah!" He felt the warmth running over him in waves, felt the warmth flowing from his eyes to his cheeks.

"Bass! Bass! Bass! Bass! BASS!"

The echoes rolled over the lone man in liquid waves accompanied by the sun's warm rays. Over and over he answered the hills as they called back to him. Again and again he yelled out to let them know who this man was who stood in their heart.

"BASS! BASS! BASS!"

20

When Bass reached the pine tree once more, the bright sun had reached the middle of the path it relentlessly traveled each day.

The shaft had finally been pushed through the flesh as he had lain beside the boulder. The lean red meat had then been wrapped in a wool legging until the flow had frozen on its own. The long struggle up the slope, dragging the weight behind him, was over. The weight stretched across the snow would catch no longer at the grabbing scrub growth to make him stop. No more would he have to halt and catch his breath until the waves of faintness passed from him, the while leaning on his big rifle as on a crutch. He had brought the heavy weight up the hill, then down the other side to the bare trees near the bottom of the draw. Only then had his bleeding stopped, and he had felt the warm liquid flow no more. By then it had become cold.

Having found the pony, he had gone to the other animal's side. Bass had knelt by Hannah then, touched the hard, cold flesh so like his own. When his sobbing finally ceased, Scratch had taken the knife out again. Selecting the small forelock between the long ears, he had cut it. Part of Hannah would remain with him the rest of his days. The cold memento had been dropped inside his shirt before he had taken the heavy load from her back and carried it to the pine tree.

As he crawled under the green boughs toward the body, Bass knew only one thing remained to do. He looked down at the arms crossed over the lower chest where he had laid them and took the empty pistol from his belt. Slowly he pulled the flaps of the red blanket coat apart and slid the muzzle of the weapon into the young trapper's belt.

"Cold." The word was quiet.

Scratch pushed the muzzle past the leather band against the stained buckskin shirt.

"So cold," came the pleading whisper again.

He touched the blanket coat but stared at the beautiful pattern of the Damascus steel one last time before letting his fingers slowly pull the flaps over the weapon.

"So cold . . . Scratch," begged the whisper, tugging at his heart.

He continued to stare at the red wool that buried the pistol. "I know, son, I know."

"Keep . . . me warm, Scratch. Please keep me—" The whisper was interrupted by a faint racking sound filled with fluid.

Scratch blinked slowly against the wide ribbon of pain along the side of his face before he let his eyes move from where he had buried the French pistol under the coat, past those thongs he had put on the coat after the sash was lost. "I cain't warm you no more, son. No more, now . . ."

"Please, Scratch. Please."

"Cain't now, J——"

"I . . . I'm sorry I done this to . . . please help. Warm—"

"Cain't help you, now, Josiah." His eyes moved on their slow climb. He would have to, but not yet. Not just yet. Couldn't look at the young face yet. The voice was enough to tear his heart out—tugging in a whisper at his ears, clawing inside his mind.

He closed his eyes, letting the heavy lids droop once more. "Tired. So tired," Bass whispered back at the voice. So much life wrenched from him this day. Bass put his left hand up to straighten the red collar on the boy's coat and saw the thin lines of dried blood where his old flesh had been scratched by the thorns and brambles. He patted the wool collar and finally let his eyes touch the young trapper's face.

The boy's eyes were almost open. Dull, half closed—but looking back at him. Bass could not take that. Not letting the boy look at him like this. Even in death. He could never think of those eyes looking back at his again. He would have to forget them, forget their pleading.

"Keep me warm, Scratch."

"I cain't now. You know I c——"

He had heard the words in his mind again. And now he had watched the lips part slightly in speaking them.

"Please..."

The lips moved again. The words were not in his mind. They were in the boy's mouth. In his throat. Talking to him. Medicine.

"Josiah?" He bent low over the face, putting his cheek lightly over the lips.

"Please," was the raspy whisper he heard. Bass felt the word from the lips against the pain along his cheek.

He brought his head slowly up and stared at the face again. He began to fumble with the top thong on the red coat, his eyes faintly misting.

"Please, Scratch..."

His fingers were cold and would not work as he struggled with the leather thongs. In desperation he took his knife out and cut the top two thongs. He pulled the flaps of the red coat apart just slightly so that he would not have to look at that wound again.

"Keep me warm...all...keep me warm now..."

Scratch bent his head to the chest and held it there for only a moment as he had before. Nothing. He jerked up and gazed at the lips.

"Warm..."

They moved. He dropped his head back to the chest, letting his ear and the ribbon of pain rest against the flesh over the ribs. "Tell me, Josiah," he whispered. "Tell me now, son. You want me to keep you warm? Tell me. Tell me now, Josiah!" He was beginning to sob.

"Now...yes. Warm..."

The faint whisper tugged at his mind again. But this time he felt it stronger. The movement in the chest with the words. That vibration high on the middle of the ribs as the words came to him, near the small sweet-smelling pouch of the Flathead girl. Not long enough, he thought. He hadn't waited long enough before. The breath had been so light before, so light without the pleading words. He slid his ear quickly over the left side of the chest, past the buckskin pouch, and pressed his head against the flesh. There. There it was. Faintly, the ticking of the boy's heart. He could hear it. Now that he waited, and listened with all his mind. He could hear it, the soft murmur of the organ pulsing lightly, quickly, to balance out the flow of blood from the body. Like a delicate watch, it ticked so quietly. But it beat. It beat! No more did blood flow from the body. The wound was frozen. The cold let life seep from the hole no longer.

"Josiah!" he yelled as he picked his head up from the chest, feeling the wet warmth streaming down his cheeks against the side of his nose. "Josiah!"

"Warm ... yes—" A cough rattled his words; a gurgle came from the back of the throat.

Bass felt the streaming now and did not fight it. He felt the juices welling within him and he would not stop them. Raising his head toward the fragment of light penetrating the green tendrils, he stared at the sky.

"Josiah! *Josiah!* JOSIAH!"

It was late afternoon, and he had made Paddock warm in the buffalo robes. The sun was slipping on its journey to the hills in the west as he had finished the crude litter slung behind the Indian pony. Bass had lashed his one buffalo robe across two lodgepole pines, then tied the poles to the saddle atop the one animal left to them.

Now he moved slowly with the burden in his arms toward the pony. The animal waited patiently for the old man to step slowly, carefully across the soft snow, moving with his burden toward the travois. He braced himself against the pain of the empty hole in his leg and gently lowered the burden into the buffalo-hide bed. Bass then wrapped the boy up with the three remaining robes. He bent low over the young trapper's face, near the ear to speak.

"Gonna cover your head, son. Warmer. Keep you warm."

"No," whispered the trembling lips. "No. Wanna see the sun. Watch it go down. See it on the mountains. Please. Watch the sun on the mountains, Scratch."

"Yes. All right, Josiah." He stepped away from the travois to loosen the knot in the pony's rein and pulled it from the tree limb. "We'll go home now, son."

Home? Could he just go where it was warm? Anywhere. So long as it was warm. He wanted to feel their flesh against his. Their soft fingers tending to his wounds. Josiah slowly raised his left arm beneath the weight of the robes to touch the small pouch once more. He needed her warmth now, more than ever, maybe even to live. Then he heard the crunch of the hard snow somewhere near him, and he realized warmth and comfort could come now from only one person. And he was comforted in knowing Bass was with him.

Scratch took the rein into his left hand and pushed the rifle into his right armpit as he gently tugged the Indian pony forward across the side of the hill, its snow now scarred by the movement of men and animals—across the slope below the wooded hills and high granite peaks that looked down on them in the waning light. Slowly he stepped through the snow, not feeling the cold that billowed up around his feet and ankles as the powder broke before him. He led the pony across the small creek toward the river that would take them back to the Yellowstone, to follow the wide water as it tumbled east to the place where the two waters met. Where the old man waited for them to return with the hair.

He heard the young man call and turned to look back at the litter. Then he stopped the pony and hobbled back to Paddock's side, still clutching the long rein.

"Josiah?" he asked, without going straight to the boy's side, not really sure he had heard his name called.

"What's that?" he asked faintly. "In the tree?" He wanted to point for Scratch but weakness restrained him.

Bass understood. He knew without having it pointed out to him. He looked at the bare cottonwood.

"McAfferty," he answered quietly. "Buried proper. Proper, Josiah."

"Thank you, Scratch," he replied after a few minutes. "Thank you for doin' it that way."

The old man turned back to urge the pony into a walk once more. Behind Josiah stood the bare, lonely tree where the body lay lashed across its limbs. Sharp thorns and brambles lay about the base of the trunk having been pulled there so that no dark thief of the forest would steal the cold flesh that was to remain forever in this place. Beneath the man lay the dark hide of the wolf. And wrapped over the lifeless form was the hide of the medicine animal, the great bear.

Beneath the warm robes Paddock held the scalp in both hands. He took the long white tendrils into his fingers and clutched them tightly. Rocking gently in the travois, he watched the tree drop farther and farther behind him, then closed his eyes to sleep.

ABOUT THE AUTHOR

Terry Johnston lives in Broomfield, Colorado. Born in 1947, he has led a varied life as roustabout, school teacher, printer, paramedic, dog catcher and car salesman while immersing himself in the history of the American fur trade of the early West. He has written extensively for magazines on the history of the opening of the West. This is his first novel, one of three that will span the period from 1831-1840.

ALLAN ECKERT'S NARRATIVES OF AMERICA

Allan Eckert's Narratives of America are true sagas of the brave men and courageous women who won our land. Every character and event in this sweeping series is drawn from actual history and woven into the vast and powerful epic that was America's westward expansion.